Sketching Mr. Darcy

LORY LILIAN

SKETCHING MR. DARCY

ISBN: 978-1-5151-4059-7

Graphic design by Ellen Pickels

Special thanks to Margaret Fransen and Ellen Pickels for their support and assistance in publishing this book.

Prologue

Brighton 1801

A bright August day enhanced the beauty of Brighton beach, caressed by small waves breaking tentatively against the shore.

The warmth was gently cooled by a soft breeze, and the water was so blue that it seemed to be one with the serene sky. Large parties of visitors walked and talked animatedly while admiring the beauty of the sea.

One young couple made a distinct impression as they seemed more courageous than the others, stepping closer to the water, arm in arm, smiling tenderly and glancing frequently at each other. The lady gently held the hand of a girl whose beauty was impossible to miss though she was no more than twelve. In front of them, a younger girl whose brown hair had escaped her carelessly tied bonnet and danced in heavy locks on her nape ran back and forth towards the waves, holding closely in her arms an English setter puppy.

The small group stepped nearer the water until several waves touched their feet, which greatly amused the younger girl—who laughed cheerfully, stepping into the water with little concern for her shoes and petticoat—and scared the older one, who took a few steps backwards.

The gentleman and the lady smiled warmly at the girls' singular reactions. A moment later, however, they called for the brown-haired girl to return immediately, as she was standing where the water was nearly to her knees.

"Uncle, I have never been so happy in my life! There is nothing as beautiful as the sea! And I cannot thank you enough for the most precious gift I have ever received. I am so glad that I am finally ten and can have a dog!" The girl caressed the puppy, her dark eyes sparkling with delight.

"Lizzy, I am glad you are happy, dearest, but please be careful. The waves can be quite dangerous. What should I tell your father if anything happens to you?"

"Do not worry. Nothing will happen to me. I am a very good swimmer," the girl said, throwing down her bonnet, and her uncle, as well as the lady on his arm, could barely hide their laughter. The girl's energy and happiness were quite contagious.

"Please be careful, Lizzy," the blonde-haired girl said gently.

"I am fine, Jane. Look, the puppy loves the water too. He is so brave. I love him so much."

"Lizzy, you will become ill from the sun if you keep taking your bonnet off, missy." The lady tried to sound severe. "If your mother knew that we allow you so much liberty..."

"Oh, please do not tell her, Aunt. You are the best aunt that ever existed! And do not worry, I never fall ill. I am very strong. You may ask Papa."

She ran towards the water again while her companions could hardly restrain their laughter, following her with their eyes. The girl jumped against the breaking waves, together with the puppy, careless that her dress was wet and sandy. She asked Jane to join her but with no success.

A few minutes later, her attention was unexpectedly drawn elsewhere. With the dog in her arms, she hurried to a little girl who was tightly holding the hand of an exceptionally beautiful, elegant lady. They were followed by two other women and a man who appeared to be the lady's servants.

Lizzy greeted the lady then knelt with little ceremony and put the puppy in front of the girl.

"Georgiana, I am so glad to see you again. Look, he missed you too, you see? Don't be afraid. He is wet because he fought with the waves." She laughed while the younger girl shyly attempted to touch the dog, glancing at her mother for approval and receiving a warm smile of encouragement.

With an alarmed look to his wife, Mr. Gardiner hurried to his niece.

"Lizzy, come here this instant, child. I beg your forgiveness for troubling you, madam." Mr. Gardiner bowed to the lady, his embarrassment impossible to conceal. However, the lady replied kindly.

"There is no need to apologise, sir. Lizzy is an old acquaintance of ours. Oh, and so is Jane," she continued, glancing at the other girl, who curtseyed properly, still holding her aunt's hand. "We first met a week ago, when they were at the beach with their governess, and have encountered each other nearly every day since. They are such lovely girls, and Lizzy is a true delight. She was so generous to show her little puppy to my daughter, who is sadly afraid of dogs," the lady continued while her daughter timidly began to pet the puppy.

Suddenly, the lady glanced behind Mr. Gardiner, and a surprised smile brightened her eyes.

"Madeleine? What are you doing in Brighton? What a lovely surprise!"

"Lady Anne!" Madeleine Gardiner was all astonishment, curtseying properly. "What an extraordinary surprise, indeed. Lady Anne Darcy, please allow me to introduce to you my husband, Mr. Edward Gardiner. We married two months ago. Lizzy and Jane are his nieces."

"Oh yes, I remember. Mrs. Reynolds wrote to me. How lovely! I have been in Brighton since May. It seems the air is beneficial to me and to Georgiana, the doctor said. Please allow me to congratulate you both on such a happy event. Mr.

Gardiner, I hope you know how fortunate you are in your choice of a wife, sir. There are few young women as remarkable as Madeleine," she said warmly.

Mrs. Gardiner blushed while Mr. Gardiner bowed again with gratitude and respect. They spoke a few more minutes. The ladies shared a keen interest in various subjects, and the manner of their conversation astonished Mr. Gardiner exceedingly. Though he deeply loved his wife and knew quite well her worthiness, he also heard that Lady Anne Darcy was the mistress of a large and beautiful estate that was only a few miles from the town of Lambton where Madeleine's father had owned a shop. He could hardly believe that a lady of such stature could treat the daughter of a shop owner with such warm amiability.

It was almost noon, and the beach was becoming less crowded. The three girls and the puppy seemed to enjoy playing together so much that they showed interest in nothing else.

"I have had a most pleasant time, but I am afraid we must return home now," Lady Anne said kindly. "Thank you for coming to greet us, Lizzy." She smiled as she caressed Lizzy's red cheeks. "You have such beautiful eyes, Lizzy—so full of life and joy. Never allow that to change, my dear," she added then wished them a good day, and walked slowly to their carriage, which was waiting nearby.

"Good day, Lady Anne! Will you come again tomorrow? Jane and I like to play with Georgiana. We will wait for you," Lizzy said energetically. No answer came, but from the small window of the carriage, the lady and her daughter sent back warm smiles and gentle waves of their delicate hands.

"That was Lady Anne Darcy of Pemberley? She is very beautiful," said Mr. Gardiner.

"Indeed, she is the most wonderful lady that has ever been. She is so kind, so generous—her father was an earl, you know—and her husband, Mr. Darcy, is said to be the best master and the best landlord. I was happy to see her again, but it saddens me so to know she is unwell. Did you notice how pale she is? She has been ill for more than five years now... We all hope and pray that she will recover soon, but I truly fear for her," Mrs. Gardiner whispered, careful not to be heard by the girls.

"That is sad, indeed," Mr. Gardiner said, calling his nieces as they walked to the carriage.

They arrived at the small cottage they had rented for their stay in Brighton, and the girls told Mrs. Johnson—the owner of the house, who also assumed the role of governess—about the beautiful lady and the girl with the most blue eyes ever who had come to the beach again and played with them.

For an entire week, Lizzy and Jane went to play on the beach every morning and every afternoon, either in the company of their aunt and uncle or of Mrs. Johnson. They met Lady Anne Darcy and Georgiana twice more, but during the last days, the beautiful lady and her daughter did not appear.

By the end of the week, the weather turned colder and cloudy. Saturday morning it even rained a little—a short summer rain. In the afternoon, Mr. and Mrs. Gardiner went to call on some friends, and the girls remained inside, under the strict supervision of Mrs. Johnson. Two hours later, however, the sun tentatively appeared from behind the clouds.

Lizzy played with her dog in the back yard then begged Mrs. Johnson to take them to the beach. Jane did not dare support her sister's insistent request, but Lizzy's smile, her pleading eyes, and her words of wisdom about how beneficial the sea air was made Mrs. Johnson laugh and comply.

The beach was lonelier than usual. Only a few visitors found delight in walking on the wet sand. The wind was blowing vigorously, and the sound of the waves crashing against the shore competed with their voices. Lizzy hastily put down the puppy, which started to run back and forth while she chased it, completely careless of the state of her gown and shoes.

Mrs. Johnson walked at a slow pace with Jane, occasionally stopping to speak with old acquaintances. Suddenly, Jane pulled loose her hand and ran away, screaming. Disconcerted, Mrs. Johnson ran towards Jane, who continued to cry. Immediately, people gathered on the shore, and then Mrs. Johnson observed with horror that Lizzy had disappeared. From Jane's cries and screams, Mrs. Johnson spotted Lizzy, struggling against the waves. She ran in despair, crying the girl's name. Lizzy struggled to respond from afar, while her small body was defeated by the swirling water.

Suddenly, a man was seen to throw himself into the water, and a few terrifying moments later, Lizzy appeared in his arms. He seemed tall, as the water barely reached his chest despite the angry waves. With apparent ease, he stepped holding the girl in his arms. Mrs. Johnson and Jane ran to them. Lizzy was crying as if she were badly hurt. However, it was soon obvious that she was crying for the puppy lying still in her arms. The young man put her down, and Mrs. Johnson and Jane hurried to her, but she continued to call to the dog as she knelt on the wet sand.

The young man knelt near her then took the puppy from her small hands, warmed him in his palms, and then rubbed his belly with gentle, insistent strokes. Seemingly endless moments later, the puppy's small cries made everybody gasp in surprise, and Lizzy stretched her hands to take it, her tears mixed with the laughter of happiness. The young man held the puppy in his hands a little longer as it wriggled to right itself, a little dizzy. He caressed the puppy gently, and it licked his hands then stretched and licked his wet face. He smiled and gently placed the puppy in the girl's outstretched hands. She placed a soft kiss on its small nose, and the puppy instantly returned her kiss. Then she lifted her eyes to the man kneeling in front of her and said reverently:

"Thank you so much, sir, for saving my puppy. You are a true hero. I never met anyone as brave as you, not even in the millions of books that I read. I shall never forget you!"

He smiled, obviously amused, while Mrs. Johnson, pale and tearful, struggled to thank him.

"Sir, there are no words to express our gratitude for saving Lizzy's life. Please let us know with whom we have the honour of speaking, I am certain Lizzy's uncle will wish to—"

"There is no need to trouble yourself, ma'am…and surely no reason to speak of gratitude. I am glad I was here and that I could be of some use to the young, imprudent miss—and to her puppy," he interrupted the lady decidedly while glancing briefly at the girl.

"But there must be some way to thank you, sir."

"There is. I would wish Miss Lizzy to forever remember that water can be dangerous. She must promise me she will take care of herself and of her dog…a very lucky dog indeed."

"I promise you," she said, and he smiled again while quickly walking away, followed closely by another young man who seemed to be his companion. Drops of rain forced them to leave the beach immediately, so Mrs. Johnson had no choice but to hurry home with the girls.

The extraordinary event was much discussed during dinner. A doctor was fetched, and his examination brought relief to the adults and to young, tearful Jane, while Lizzy could not understand why the others did not realise that she was perfectly well.

For days, Mr. Gardiner tried to discover the young man's identity, but to no avail. They had no indication of his name or age, and neither Lizzy nor Mrs. Johnson remembered his face well enough. All they knew was that he was young—Mrs. Johnson estimated he must have been more of a grown-up boy—most likely not yet twenty. With so few details and after a long and unsuccessful search, they concluded that he must have only passed through Brighton, never to be seen again. All they could do was remember him fondly and express their gratitude to him, wherever he might be.

As for Lizzy, though his features were blurred in her recollection, she vividly remembered him over the years. In her young mind, she knew without a doubt that he was the most courageous man who ever existed, so like the heroes from the books she loved to read.

She wrote about him on the first pages of the red velvet-covered diary given to her as a present by her Aunt Gardiner and even attempted to sketch his portrait several times—as witnessed in the following pages of her journal—but the face of her saviour remained lost.

However, she did not forget her promise to him—and she named her dog *Lucky.*

Chapter 1

Longbourn, 27 November 1811

Elizabeth listened to her cousin Mr. Collins confess, with equal ardour and self-confidence, his reason for coming into Hertfordshire with the design of selecting a wife. His words left no doubt about the identity of the woman who was fortunate enough to be selected by him.

Mr. Collins's proclamation, offered with such solemn composure, made Elizabeth so near laughing that she could not use the short pause he allowed for an attempt to stop him further, so he continued to list his reasons for marrying—insisting upon the fact that Lady Catherine herself advised him to do so—and also the motives that drove him to choose as a wife one of Mr. Bennet's daughters. He declared he was perfectly indifferent to her lack of fortune, and then he started to speak about the violence of his affection. At that moment, Elizabeth understood it was absolutely necessary to interrupt him.

However, a quarter of an hour later, after a long, contradictory discussion during which she struggled to make him understand that she had no intention of accepting his marriage proposal, Mr. Collins seemed still unmoved in his decision to secure a positive response. To such perseverance in wilful self-deception, Elizabeth ceased to make any other.

She opened the door and, with quick steps, moved to the staircase then entered the breakfast room. A moment later she heard her mother's shocked voice and Mr. Collins's affected response. She easily understood that they were coming to talk to her again, so she seized her bonnet, coat, and gloves and left the house. She could not endure a confrontation with both Mr. Collins and her mother without becoming truly uncivil..

She angrily paced along the yard and through the gate until an obstacle forced her to stop. She laughed and petted the dog, who was rubbing against her feet.

"Lucky, you should stay home. It is very cold, and you are not quite so young anymore, boy."

But the dog—a splendid English setter, spotted black and white—seemed determined to contradict her words and impetuously ran through the gate then waited for her to follow him. She laughed and ran after the dog, suddenly light-hearted. For more than ten years, Lucky's effect on her mood had been immediate and beneficial.

Pacing in a hurry, she admitted to herself that neither Mr. Collins's proposal nor the manner of his address had been a surprise to her. For more than a week, she had noticed not only his special attentions to her but also her mother's encouragement. Could she have done aught to deter Mr. Collins's decision and make him see reality before the awkward moment occurred? Had a woman any means to avoid such unpleasant moments in her life?

Likely not. Mr. Collins appeared to be a master of seeing and understanding only what he wished. Consequently, it happened at the ball that, when he unceremoniously introduced himself to Mr. Darcy, Elizabeth vividly remembered that gentleman's stern countenance, unpleasant surprise, and complete disapproval and disdain at being approached by the parson. Yet, Mr. Collins had declared himself to be content with Mr. Darcy's reception.

In truth, the entire ball had been a continuous source of mortification. Mr. Wickham's absence, the first set with Mr. Collins, Mary's unworthy performance at the piano forte, her mother's incautious statements about Jane and Mr. Bingley, Lydia and Kitty's improper flirtations with the officers, her father's careless tolerance of every faulty behaviour, and on top of everything, Mrs. Hurst and Miss Bingley's disdainful glances and Mr. Darcy's contemptuous looks. Not to mention his unexpected request for a set—it had been an equal surprise for her as well as for those in attendance. What could he mean by dancing with her? Merely to make her uncomfortable? That was not unlikely, coming from him.

Elizabeth walked until Longbourn was left far behind. She stopped to catch her breath, and suddenly she shivered with cold. It was the twenty-seventh of November, and winter already seemed to demand its due.

Lucky had slowed his pace too. The ground was muddy and slippery on the narrow footpath that took her through the grove up towards Oakham Mount. She found a wooden stump and rested on it a moment with Lucky rubbing against her feet. She petted the dog and allowed the fresh air to calm her before returning home. It would be a long, tedious day.

She eventually gathered herself together enough to return at a steady pace. Through the trees, she spotted the pond where she spent time fishing with her father and uncle and playing with her dog when she was a child. Lucky recognised the surroundings and ran towards the pond, and Elizabeth impulsively followed him.

When she was near the edge of the pond, her shoe slipped and she slid down the steep bank into the dirty, cold water.

She cried from the shock of the frigid water that covered her instantly, and she scrambled to stand. The water was only a little above her waist, but she felt her feet sinking into the mud. She tried to walk towards the bank and climb out, but the ground was soft, and it was difficult to move her feet. She stood still for a moment, shivering and laughing nervously at the absurdity of the situation: there she was—stuck in the mud. A fair punishment for rejecting Mr. Collins, her mother would have said.

She looked around to find a spot where the pond's edge might be easier to climb, and with great effort, she finally clambered out. She needed a few moments to regain her breath, then attempted to rise—which seemed more difficult than ever, as her shoes were muddy.

Elizabeth walked reluctantly towards the main path, the dog following her closely. Cold, shivering, and barely feeling her feet, her hands, or her face, she continued to walk as quickly as her frozen feet allowed.

Suddenly, Lucky scampered off in a great hurry, barking loudly and oblivious to her calling him back. She recognised the sound of a rider approaching, and her heart skipped a beat. Her first thought was to hide and avoid being seen in such a dreadful state. Immediately, she thought better of it: she clearly needed help to reach her home.

After five years of friendship, Darcy still could not understand how Bingley was never ready on time despite having so many servants around. They had planned to leave for London early that morning. Yet at noon, Bingley was not at all prepared for the journey.

With all his belongings waiting in the main hall, Darcy decided to take a final ride around the neighbourhood. He was certain that he would never see those grounds again nor those who lived there. It was time for them to return to their lives—which had little to do with Netherfield, Meryton, or Longbourn. Charles was determined to return in a week's time, but Darcy was confident that his friend would finally see how unreasonable were any plans regarding Netherfield—or the Bennet family.

If Darcy had any remaining doubts about the validity of his judgment, all disappeared before the preposterous lack of decorum displayed during the ball by almost every member of the Longbourn family—except Jane Bennet. And *her*.

If he were to be honest and fair, her behaviour was not beyond reproach either. The conversation during their dance was just at the edge of rudeness, and he did not miss her allusions regarding Wickham. She seemed—for some reason—upset with him, and if he were forced to stay in that county longer, he knew he would be tempted to discover the reason. Fortunately, fate was good to him, and he would be gone soon with no chance of meeting Elizabeth Bennet again.

He spurred the horse, growing angry at his own weakness. How was it possible that he was counting on fate to decide for him? How could he dismiss the unreasonable attraction he felt for a young country girl with nothing to recommend her but a pair of fine eyes, a witty mind, and a sharp tongue? He had known—in a most private way—many women who could easily surpass Elizabeth Bennet in many respects. Yet, not for a single moment had he ever had difficulty keeping his senses and his reason under good regulation. He never needed to make any effort to master his self-control—as he had never lost it before.

What on earth is happening to me? How is it possible to be so ridiculous as to dream about her, to fantasise about her, to seek her company, to stare at her while she speaks or dances with others, to chat and flirt with her in such an adolescent manner...? That was precisely the kind of behaviour for which he used to scold Bingley so many times, and no one—himself included—would imagine that he, Fitzwilliam Darcy, could act in such a way. Yet he did so each time he was in her company—either during the day when fate ensured their meeting or at night in the darkness of his room when her image, her laughter, her teasing voice, her sharp glances, and her sparkling eyes troubled his sleep and tormented his mind and his body. He had not been himself since almost the first day he arrived in Hertfordshire and could only be content and relieved that everything would end soon.

He was abruptly wakened from his reverie by the loud barking of a dog, and his horse reared, almost throwing him from the saddle. He cursed and yelled at the dog, but the animal continued to bark, dashing back and forth.

Darcy dismounted and tried to touch the dog, but he growled then ran and returned again. Darcy followed him. Only then did he hear a woman's voice. Not far away, he noticed a silhouette that was walking hesitantly, as though injured.

"Ma'am, are you hurt? There, let me help you," he said, grabbing her arm as she turned to him and almost fell again.

A moment later he froze, staring into the eyes that opened in surprise. "Miss Bennet?!"

"Mr. Darcy!" Her lips were blue and trembling as she forced a smile.

"What are you doing here? What happened? Are you hurt?"

"No, I am not hurt. Only my pride is." She attempted a joke, her lips trembling. "You are very kind to help me, sir, but I would not wish to ruin your coat. I think I can walk by myself."

Darcy stared at her, astonished and lost. The only familiar thing was her eyes, still bright and lively; otherwise, her appearance was entirely altered. Aside from her dirty clothes, she was completely frozen, struggling to overcome the trembling of her lips and hands.

"Miss Bennet, are you alone? Forgive me—what are you doing here?"

"Oh, I just came for a walk, and I had a small accident. It is nothing, really. I shall go now."

Elizabeth hurried to depart from him. Surely, it must be some sort of punishment to have Mr. Darcy, of all the people in the world, encounter her in such a disastrous situation. His eyes searched hers in earnest, and she was certain she could read a severe disapproval of her looks, as happened when she appeared at Netherfield on foot.

He withdrew his hand, which was holding her arm, and called for his horse. She hoped he would leave. There was nothing worse than his silent deprecation. But he removed his coat in a great hurry and put it around her shoulders, wrapping her in the thick fabric.

"This should help you a little. You must be frozen. You look truly ill," he said severely, and her cheeks blushed with equal shame and growing anger. She imagined she looked truly ill, but was it so difficult for a gentleman not to point that out? She was prepared to refuse his help as sharply as he deserved. It was more difficult to bear his rudeness than the cold.

"I am afraid you are in a dangerous state. You must return home at once." His voice turned unexpectedly friendly, and she stared at him disconcerted.

"Thank you, sir," she heard herself replying hesitantly. "Yes, I must return home…"

His hands were still resting on her shoulders as he wrapped his coat about her. She felt suddenly uneasy and called her dog to avoid Darcy's eyes then started walking.

The dog growled in warning, uncertain what the man was doing to his mistress. Elizabeth forced a smile. "He is not friendly with strangers, and he is very protective of me."

"Yes, he seemed very protective, which is a good thing. Miss Bennet, you cannot walk back home. It will take you forever. Please use my horse. I will send someone to fetch it later."

She glanced at him, barely giving credit to what she heard. Was he willing to remain on foot, dressed only in his frock coat so far from his residence? Mr. Darcy, of all men?

"I thank you for your care, sir, but it is not very far from here…besides, I am a too poor a rider to venture taking your horse. But I greatly appreciate your offer. Oh, I am afraid I have ruined your coat completely—such a shame…" Her voice sounded incoherent even to her as her chin trembled and her feet grew heavy. His gaze became more insistent.

"You must realise it will take you hours to return home in such a state. I have started to became cold myself, and I am not wet at all," he said. "I see only one way for both of us to avoid catching a dangerous cold. Perhaps it is not the most proper method, but it is certainly the fastest. We shall ride together to Longbourn."

She looked at him in shock. "Sir, please do not think me ungrateful, but you must see how unreasonable *that* sounds. We cannot possibly ride together! It is not… How could we?"

"I understand your concern, and I am perfectly aware of the impropriety. However, for the moment, I am more concerned about our health than our reputations." He attempted a smile then continued in earnest. "Had my sister been in a similar circumstance, I would consider her safety and well-being more important than anything else."

She watched him in silence. He seemed to be right: her immaculate reputation would be of little use if she were to die from cold, as her father would certainly say. She looked around a few times to delay a decision then reluctantly nodded in agreement, wondering again how she could have stumbled into such a horrible situation, and with none other than Mr. Darcy.

He immediately lifted her into the saddle then mounted behind her. His arms supported her as he took the reins, and the horse's pace soon increased. Elizabeth's hands clenched his arm, and she closed her eyes, trembling—from the cold as well as the distressing ride.

"Are you well?" he inquired, and she nodded while her hands tightened on his arm. She tried to look after Lucky, but her uncomfortable position offered little freedom to move.

"Your dog is following us, do not worry. Surely, he would not allow you to be abducted by a strange man," Darcy joked, and she had no reply. He appeared utterly unlike his usual self!

"He is a beautiful dog, though not very young," he added. "How old is he?" She noticed his effort to lighten their awkward situation and finally replied, meeting his eyes for a moment.

"He was ten last summer. He has been with me since he was a puppy. Your dog is beautiful too though he is much larger than Lucky." She paused, feeling herself warming with each moment and suddenly aware of his presence too close to her. She laughed nervously then continued. "If I were to believe Miss Bingley, everything about you seems large: your dog, your horse, your estate, your house, your library..."

She heard herself talking, and instantly her own words seemed wrong and highly improper. Her poor attempt at teasing him sounded ridiculous, even rude, to her own ears. But he suddenly laughed—openly and with no restraint, as she had never heard him before.

"I never thought of that, but you might be correct. However, you should not give complete credit to everything Miss Bingley says."

She watched him laughing and could not hide a smile at how different he looked.

"What about Mr. Bingley?" she asked after a short hesitation. "Should we give credit to what *he* says? Oh, has Mr. Bingley left for London?"

A few moments of silence followed, and his countenance become stern.

"We have finally arrived," he eventually replied and rapidly dismounted, opening the gate and taking the horse by the reins, his actions watched closely by Elizabeth. His disposition had changed in an instant for no apparent reason. *What a distressing man,* she thought.

In the back garden, the horse stopped, and Darcy helped her down without a word.

She could barely move, wrapped as she was in his long, thick coat. She felt her wet hair about her temples in great disorder, and her lips trembled. He put an arm around her shoulders, and they walked to the main entrance with Lucky pacing between them. Only a few steps and she would be in the warmth of her home and away from the stressful presence of Mr. Darcy. She was thankful for his help, though. She could not imagine reaching home without him.

She started to express her gratitude and apologise again for ruining his coat, when the main door opened, and a din of voices broke the silence. Elizabeth startled and turned quickly. Her feet slid, and she would have fallen had he not been alert enough to catch her.

"But depend upon it, Mr. Collins," Mrs. Bennet was saying with complete self-confidence as she followed the parson outdoors. "Despite Mr. Bennet's lack of involvement, Lizzy shall be brought to reason. She is a very headstrong, foolish girl and does not know her own interest, but I will make her know it, and she will surely accept you—have no doubt."

"Pardon me, madam, but if she is headstrong and foolish, I know not whether she would be a desirable wife to a man in my situation who looks for happiness in the marriage state. If she persists in rejecting my suit, perhaps it were better not to force her into accepting me because, if liable to such defects of temper, she could not contribute much to my felicity."

"But sir, you misunderstand me. Lizzy is not—"

"Mrs. Bennet, I am grateful for your support, but I need time to ponder this in peace. I shall gladly accept Miss Lucas's invitation for dinner, and we shall discuss this again tomorrow. Miss Lucas, Miss Maria, let us hurry. I cannot be—"

He suddenly stopped, hardly able to bear the shock: a few steps away was Miss Elizabeth, wet and dirty, in the arms of Mr. Darcy and wearing the gentleman's coat. Mr. Collins's stupefaction was matched by Mrs. Bennet's cry, which immediately attracted from the house the other Bennet sisters, as well as Mr. Bennet himself.

"Lizzy, where have you been? We have been looking for you all over the place! I have never seen you look so dreadful! And precisely in front of Mr. Darcy! Just when he found you tolerable enough to dance with you! Oh, Mr. Collins, I assure you she is not always—"

By the time she turned to lessen the damage to Mr. Collins's impression, the gentleman was already departing at a quick pace, followed by Charlotte and Maria Lucas. Charlotte looked at her friend, worrying whether she was hurt or not. Jane embraced her sister while Mr. Bennet decidedly sent his younger daughters and his wife inside.

"Lizzy dear, are you well? What happened to you?" he inquired with deep concern.

"Oh, I am perfectly well, Papa. Forgive me for worrying you. I stupidly fell into the pond near Oakham Mount, that is all. It was fortunate that Mr. Darcy happened to be in the vicinity. He truly saved my life. I doubt I would have been able to return home by myself."

Mr. Bennet looked at the gentleman—to whom he had barely spoken a few words since they first met—standing near his daughter who was dressed in his coat. His jacket and trousers were wet and dirty.

"Mr. Darcy, I am not certain how this all happened, but please allow me to thank you. And please enter. You both look very cold—"

"Sir, I believe Miss Elizabeth should immediately be taken care of. I am afraid she is in great danger of falling ill. She has spent quite some time in this cold weather. Perhaps a doctor should be fetched." He addressed Jane, who had removed his coat from Elizabeth's shoulders and taken her sister's trembling hands.

"Yes, we shall do that…thank you, sir," Jane whispered.

As she was pushed forward by her worried sister, Elizabeth barely managed to thank Mr. Darcy, who bowed silently. Climbing the stairs, she turned her head and briefly met his stern gaze. He looked no different from the man she had known the last two months.

With all the ladies departed, the gentlemen remained in the main hall, facing each other, equally uncomfortable with the disturbing situation. Finally, Mr. Bennet spoke.

"Mr. Darcy, I shall send my servant to Netherfield at once to fetch you dry clothes. In the meantime, I can offer you a warm robe and a glass of my brandy. It is the least I can do since you do not wish to accept my gratitude for your generous assistance to my daughter."

Darcy hesitated a moment, glancing at the door through which Elizabeth had disappeared. He considered that he had never visited Longbourn before, nor had he ever wished to until that day. Perhaps he could delay a few minutes.

"That seems a good arrangement, sir. And a glass of brandy would be just fine, thank you," he finally accepted.

His host gave instructions to a servant, then Darcy followed him into another room where Mr. Bennet filled two glasses.

"You have a handsome library here, Mr. Bennet," Darcy said approvingly.

"It is a small room and there are not as many volumes as I would wish to have. But the library is my favourite place in the house," Mr. Bennet answered.

"Mine too." Mr. Darcy looked around, his eyes perusing each book.

"I imagine your library is much larger, though." To his surprise, Mr. Bennet noticed a smile twisting Darcy's lips.

"It is larger, but when we speak of libraries, it is not the size of the room but the quality of the books that makes the difference. I recognise a few exceptional volumes on your shelves."

"You have an excellent eye, sir. I confess to being very proud of each of them. More brandy?" Mr. Bennet offered and filled his guest's glass again.

"I dare presume that Miss Elizabeth inherited her passion for books from you," Darcy said.

"She has, and that makes me exceedingly happy. Although—may I dare ask—when did you notice Lizzy's passion for books? I am only curious as I know you and Lizzy are not particular friends," Mr. Bennet inquired in jest, and his guest's countenance changed.

"I had the pleasure of spending time in Miss Elizabeth's company when she stayed at Netherfield…I hope Miss Bennet has sent for the doctor?"

"I am sure she has. Mr. Jones—the apothecary—should be here any moment now. I thank you for your concern and for everything you have done for my Lizzy today."

"It was a fortunate coincidence which took me to that path—and in truth, it was Lucky who drew my attention. Unfortunately, by the time I met her, she had already stood quite a while in the freezing weather. That is why I insisted she ride back to Longbourn."

"Lizzy rode? That is astonishing. I know she is not fond of riding."

"No, not quite… I offered her my horse, but she refused, so we rode together. I apologise—I admit that was not the best nor the most proper solution, but I was afraid any delay might affect Miss Elizabeth's health."

"Sir, you are surely not apologising! Can you imagine that I care about propriety when my daughter's life is involved? I believe your decision was the correct one."

Their conversation was interrupted by the sound of Mrs. Bennet's voice in another room, and Mr. Bennet smiled, emptied his second glass of brandy, and filled it again.

"I should apologise for exposing you to the madness of our house—which is today even worse than usual. Mr. Collins proposed to Lizzy earlier today. She must have been very distressed to allow such an accident to occur. I do not remember her ever falling before."

Darcy stiffened and frowned. "Miss Elizabeth will marry Mr. Collins?"

"Marry him? No indeed!" Mr. Bennet laughed. "Poor Mr. Collins, he is not unkind in his judgment. As he will inherit Longbourn after my death, he thought it his duty to propose to one of my daughters. First I thought he would propose to Jane, but I guess he noticed that her attention was otherwise engaged, so he proposed to Lizzy—what a joke!"

"So…Miss Elizabeth refused him?" Darcy inquired then suddenly realised the impropriety of his question and apologised. However, the brandy, as well as the relief of having his daughter back home, had made Mr. Bennet more inclined than ever to make fun.

"Of course, she refused him! That is precisely why my wife is so troubled. She still believes she can convince Lizzy to accept, and she expected me to force her. As if I were the kind of man to force my daughters to do anything… I cannot even force Mary to stop singing, as you saw last night. Besides, I doubt anyone could force my Lizzy to do anything against her will. I was concerned that she might consider sacrificing herself for the family's safety as my wife insisted. But fortunately, my daughter is as bright as I expected her to be."

"Indeed, Miss Elizabeth seems to be a very bright and decided lady," Darcy said seriously, glancing through the window. The last hour seemed unreal. He was prepared for a peaceful day spent on the road to London, and things had turned out utterly different. If only Bingley had been ready on time. That thought, however, made him shiver. If he had gone early as he planned, what would have happened to her? She would have walked back home eventually, but at what cost?

"Should I call for some refreshment, Mr. Darcy? You must be hungry."

"Not at all, sir. In fact, I will leave as soon as your servant arrives. Bingley must be waiting for me. We shall leave for London today. I only took a short ride before our departure."

"Truly? Then it was an extraordinarily fortunate coincidence that you happened upon Lizzy—a coincidence for which we must be even more grateful. And will you return to Hertfordshire? Mr. Bingley told me last night that he planned to stay in Town only briefly."

"I could not say for sure… There are several aspects that must be taken under consideration. Besides, I am not certain of my own plans yet."

"I see… I hope to have the pleasure of meeting you again soon, Mr. Darcy."

The servant finally arrived from Netherfield, and Darcy hurried to change in the guest room. He felt torn between his eagerness to finally leave Longbourn and his worry at not knowing whether Elizabeth was well. However, he had not much time to consider as the servant informed him that Mr. Bingley was ready to leave and only awaited his arrival.

He returned to the library to take his farewell. Despite everything, he had truly enjoyed the short conversation with Mr. Bennet, and he slightly regretted that he had not attempted to deepen his acquaintance with the gentleman during his stay in Hertfordshire.

In the main hall, the apothecary greeted them with an exuberance that disconcerted Darcy.

"Sir, what a story I have heard! So you saved poor Miss Lizzy—what a sweet girl! I have known her since she was an infant. I must go and see her. I hope to give you a favourable report. She must be truly ill since you had to carry her in your arms, I was told."

"Mr. Jones, I would expect you to examine the patient before speculating about her illness," Darcy answered severely. "Gossip and time-wasting are not useful in situations like this."

Mr. Jones frowned and babbled an excuse, hurrying upstairs followed by Jane. A moment before he left the house, Mr. Darcy turned to his host.

"Mr. Bennet, if you have time, I would appreciate it if you would send me a letter to let me know that Miss Elizabeth is well. If necessary, I can easily arrange for my doctor to examine her. London is only a few hours away, and my carriage could bring him in no time."

"It will be my pleasure to write you, sir. And I shall remember your generous offer, though I truly hope it will not be needed. Have a safe ride home…to London, I mean. And please convey my best wishes to Mr. Bingley."

"I will. Good day, Mr. Bennet."

Chapter 2

On his way to Netherfield, Darcy's mind was spinning from all that had occurred in a short time. His anger grew, clasping him in its icy grip.

That clergyman considers himself worthy of Elizabeth? He embarrassed her just by dancing with her! The effrontery of the man! Did he truly expect that she would accept? And he had the impertinence to ask Mr. Bennet to force Elizabeth into a marriage?

On the other hand—why not? Can a country girl like Elizabeth Bennet, without fortune or connections, hope for anything more than a clergyman—especially one who is expected to inherit their estate eventually? It is an all too common arrangement.

The mere thought of Collins touching Elizabeth—kissing Elizabeth—made him sick. Fortunately, that would never happen, but it did not mean that another man would not do the same. Yes, without question, he was losing his mind! It was truly madness. It could not be! Fortunately, he would leave the county and never have to bear her company again.

But of course, that did not mean he was not worried for her. He could do nothing more for the present. However, he would keep the promise he made to Mr. Bennet: he would inquire after her state and, if necessary, make sure she had the best medical care possible.

In truth, Mr. Bennet proved to be—in the short time they had spent together—a pleasant gentleman. If he had more time, he would wish to know him better. But there would be no time to know anyone better as he would likely never return to Netherfield again.

Late in the afternoon, Darcy and Bingley were finally ready to depart for London. Bingley was in a great hurry to *leave* as he was in a great hurry to *return*. He spoke enthusiastically about his satisfaction with the previous night's ball and his plans to host another as soon as possible. He also expressed his concern about Miss Elizabeth and his hope that he would find her fully recovered on his return.

Darcy listened to his friend's animated chatter for some time, and he was tempted to interfere, but he had neither the will nor the energy to begin a debate. He would see what was to be done in a few days once they were settled quietly in Town.

Mr. Jones left Longbourn, and his report, though surprisingly good, did not put Jane's mind at ease. Elizabeth was not well: her cheeks were red, her eyes sparkling, and she was covered in two thick blankets that did little to prevent her shivering.

For the next few hours, Jane did not leave Elizabeth's room, watching her sleep disturbed by coughing and trembling. Mrs. Hill, the housekeeper, came from time to time, bringing medicine and tea. Mr. Bennet came once to ask about his favourite daughter while the youngest sisters entered the room so often and loudly that Jane kindly asked them to cease their visits.

Eventually, Elizabeth awoke and took a large cup of tea, laughing at her worried sister.

"Jane, there is no reason for concern, I am very well indeed. This situation is similar to those days at Netherfield when you were ill and I took care of you. Except that there is no Miss Bingley or Mrs. Hurst around—a pleasant change—and no handsome gentleman to worry about me, which is not so pleasant a change," Elizabeth said smiling.

"I noticed Mr. Darcy was quite concerned about your state, Lizzy. I confess I never expected it from him, and I felt ashamed for misjudging his good nature."

"I would not necessarily assume that Mr. Darcy has a good nature just because he was worried for me. I do appreciate his help, and I know I have every reason to be grateful for his presence. I cannot stop wondering about the intent of his unusual kindness, though. I would rather say that it is *not* in his nature."

"Lizzy, try to sleep. I think you are being unkind and unfair," Jane scolded her in jest.

"Well my dear, you are always kind and fair, so I must compensate for it somehow," Elizabeth concluded while her sister wrapped the blankets more tightly.

The hours passed, but Jane's alarm did not. She had no reason to mistrust Mr. Jones, but his optimism seemed contrary to Elizabeth's state. Late in the afternoon, Jane visited her father in the library and confessed her concerns while he listened with increasing worry.

"Papa, if Lizzy feels worse tomorrow morning, I would suggest you fetch a doctor."

"Yes, we should do that. Mr. Darcy asked me to keep him informed about Lizzy's condition. He said he would send his doctor if necessary. Do you think we should write him?"

"Let us hope we have no reason to disturb Mr. Darcy and his doctor. Lizzy has always been strong and healthy. I hope she will be fine. But Mr. Darcy's offer is truly generous..."

"Yes it is... He is a strange fellow, is he not, Jane? He did not just bring Elizabeth home, but he seemed truly preoccupied with her well-being. That was such a surprise after everything you told me about him. And you know, I only spent half an hour with him, but he seemed a very pleasant kind of man. I am sorry that my opinion contradicts yours so completely."

"I believe you are correct. I have always felt that he is not as bad as we were tempted to judge him. Mr. Bingley values his opinions and his character very much."

"Oh, then there is no doubt left. Mr. Bingley could not possibly be wrong!" Mr. Bennet teased his daughter with a lighter tone while Jane blushed violently and left the library.

During dinner, there were few other subjects to be discussed besides Elizabeth's fall. Mrs. Bennet was certain that it was a proper punishment for her reckless refusal of Mr. Collins, and she did not cease expressing her opinion until Mr. Bennet intervened and asked his younger daughters about their walk to Meryton.

"Oh, we had so much fun, Papa," Lydia finally burst out. "Mr. Collins talked constantly, but I barely listened to him. And Charlotte is so strange. She seemed to approve of him and asked him more questions, as if he had anything interesting to say. We met Wickham and Denny. They could not believe what we told them about Lizzy. They laughed about Mr. Darcy giving his coat to Lizzy. Wickham said that Darcy is very fond of his clothes, and he would be very upset if Lizzy ruined it and… Oh, it was so amusing. We all agree on that. And—"

"May I ask what was so amusing about Lizzy's accident? Do you believe it to be a joke to share with everyone around Meryton? Did it cross your silly mind that your sister might have died? And those two idiots officers—did they have nothing else to entertain them?"

All the ladies frowned and paled at Mr. Bennet's violent outburst. In twenty years, he had never spoken in such a manner nor been so furious. He abandoned his place and demanded his dinner be sent to the library—another thing that had never happened before.

Once he left, Lydia spoke again. "Surely, he cannot forbid us to laugh at Mr. Darcy just because he brought Lizzy home! Everybody dislikes Mr. Darcy, you know that, Mama!"

"I do know, but let us not trouble your father on that subject for the time being. If there is anyone to be blamed for this unhappy situation, it is Lizzy herself. Had she accepted Mr. Collins's offer, we would all have been happy and joyful now instead of arguing."

"Mama!" Jane's voice, determined and reproachful, silenced Mrs. Bennet and the girls, who looked at her in disbelief. "It is very unfair to blame Lizzy or fail to acknowledge the debt we owe Mr. Darcy. We all should think seriously about what happened today and pray to the Lord that all will be well in the end. Now forgive me. I shall go and see how Lizzy fares."

Jane's reaction was at least as surprising as was Mr. Bennet's, and the youngest sisters, together with their mother, needed more than two hours to discuss their strange behaviour. When they finally finished their dinner, they had reached no conclusion, except that, had Lizzy married Mr. Collins, their vexation about being turned out of the house when Mr. Bennet died would have disappeared, and that would have made them all very happy.

London, 27 November

AFTER DINNER, GEORGIANA RETIRED TO HER ROOM, TELLING HER BROTHER ONCE more how happy she was to have him home. Darcy moved to his library, allowing himself to rest in the large armchair. What a day it had been!

During the journey, Bingley never ceased chatting. He was eager to return to Netherfield—poor fellow. Darcy must have a talk with him to make him understand the risk attached to such a plan. Or perhaps he would be charmed by another beautiful face in a couple of days—as had happened so many times before—and everything would be settled.

Alone in his library, a feeling of peace surrounded him. He was finally safe from his weakness with so many miles between them. It was very likely that he would never see her again, but he could not stop thinking and worrying about her. She was fortunate that her father was not the kind who forced his daughters to seek an advantageous marriage, or else she would have been in a dreadful position.

Mr. Bennet did not seem to be wealthy. His daughter marrying his cousin would have solved all their problems, and yet, he did not even take that into consideration.

That was not his concern any longer. He had no right to think of whom she would or would not marry. His only worry was her health. The apothecary did not seem prepared to handle a difficult situation, and Darcy could not possibly trust him with Elizabeth's health. Though he had no wish to ever see her again, he needed to know she was taken care of properly. He should talk to Dr. Taylor tomorrow morning and ascertain his advice.

Tired, distressed, and dizzy from the fine brandy he had enjoyed, Darcy glanced at the stack of papers on his desk, demanding his attention.

But his mind was engaged with images of Elizabeth. Only last night he had danced with her at the ball, and he still remembered—quite vividly—the sensation of her hands, her gloved fingers tentatively resting in his, her sharp glances during their conversation, the smile resting on her red lips, her figure moving gracefully to the rhythm of the music.

Then, her shocking appearance in the woods, alone, trying to keep up her spirits and fighting her own weakness—cold, wet, shivering in his coat, her trembling lips as she tried to thank him for bringing her home and her last glance just before she retired to her room...

He forced his reason to see the excellence of his decision to leave Hertfordshire, putting a safe distance between him and the haunting eyes of Miss Elizabeth Bennet. However, neither his strength nor his customary self-control could save him from the burgeoning feeling that she was not yet safe and he should have done more for her.

London, 28 November

Darcy woke more tired than he was the previous evening. Georgiana greeted his appearance at the breakfast table, and Mrs. Annesley, his sister's companion, expressed her delight in seeing him. He tried to be pleasant company but felt relieved when the meal ended. He approved his sister's plans for visiting her aunt Lady Matlock—and then he closed the library door behind him.

He went to the window, staring at the cloudy autumn weather and wondering how *she* spent the night. He briefly considered whether he should send an express to Mr. Bennet. Could he do such a thing? Might his gesture be considered improper?

He was embarrassed by his unreasonable behaviour and remembered his reproaches of Bingley's concern for Miss Bennet's illness at Netherfield. At the time, he considered Bingley unreasonably anxious for a mere cold, and now he was no better. If Miss Bennet recovered in only a few days, Miss Elizabeth—who seemed stronger and better accustomed to outdoor activities—would surely do the same. The sharp claw that had gripped his chest since the previous day was just a foolish reaction, as were all his reactions regarding *her*.

He startled, brought back from his thoughts, when the door opened impromptu and his cousin Colonel Robert Fitzwilliam barged into the room. He took a comfortable seat and inquired about the trip from Hertfordshire and about Bingley. Darcy had little disposition for small talk, but he could not reject his cousin. The colonel gave Darcy information about his family and the latest news in London. Finally, he looked at his host intently then rose from his chair, walked around the room, and sat again.

"We have been friends since we could barely walk, so I shall ask directly: Darcy, did you know that Annabelle is in Town? She is asking about you."

"I did not know," Darcy replied sternly after a brief hesitation. Silence fell on the room again, each man holding the other's gaze.

"She made her appearance about a week ago, and she is asking about you."

"Yes, you just told me. Is there anything else?"

"It seems her husband died a couple of months ago—her second husband, Lord Stafford."

"I see..." Another long moment of silence, then Darcy poured himself a glass of brandy.

"You seem preoccupied... Are you...have you met her at all these past few years?"

"I do not see why you would question my private business since I never question yours, Robert. But be it as you want since *you* seem strangely preoccupied with this subject. No, I have not seen her for four years. Is there anything else you want to ask me, Robert? Are you curious about the last time I saw others of our acquaintance, or is this the only case?"

"You may mock me, Darcy, but you know that I have reason for concern. So you have not seen her in four years. What about now? How does this affect you? And let me tell you something else. She has been seen in the company of James!

What do you think of that?"

"My cousin James?"

"Yes, your cousin James Darcy, the son of your other uncle."

"I fail to understand your meaning. Why is it so extraordinary to have seen my cousin in the company of a lady? He is frequently in a woman's company..."

"So he is—in the company of women, drink, cards and trouble. God knows whom he resembles. His late father, your uncle, was an excellent man—but that is not the issue here as you very well know. How is it he knows Annabelle? I had no idea they ever met."

Darcy released a short laugh, looking at his cousin with mocking puzzlement.

"I am quite surprised to see you are so well informed about Lady Stafford's acquaintances."

"Annabelle and James mean trouble separately. I tremble to imagine the harm they could do together. We should speak to James. I heard he has gambling debts again. I will ask my father to invite him to dinner one evening. What about Annabelle or Lady Stafford or whatever? She is asking about you," the colonel repeated. "Will you meet her?"

"Robert, I have no interest in continuing this conversation. I just realised that I must speak to Dr. Taylor about a matter of great importance. Will you meet me at the club later? Then I plan to visit your parents. I have not seen them in quite some time."

"Why do you need Dr. Taylor? Are you unwell?"

"I appreciate your concern, but though I am five years your junior, I am not your youthful companion any longer, and I am perfectly able to take care of myself." Darcy smiled.

"I know that too well. There is no one more able to take care of himself—nor more stubborn and aloof. So you just dismiss me? Do you have nothing else to say to me?"

"I did not dismiss you, quite the contrary. But I do have urgent business now. Please forgive me. As for the subject of your obvious interest: the lady's presence in town is not my concern, whether she is a friend of my cousin or not."

Longbourn, 28 November

ELIZABETH ATTEMPTED A SMILE WHEN SHE MET HER SISTER'S WORRIED LOOK.

"Jane, I am fine. Please do not worry," she said lightly.

"You may be fine, but you are not well, Lizzy. Even Lucky can see that. Poor thing did not leave your bed, nor has he eaten anything since yesterday. Please be honest with us. We shall fetch a doctor if needed. Even Mr. Darcy offered to—"

"Please do not speak of another offer from Mr. Darcy. I am in his debt already, and I do not wish to trouble him further—with anything."

"I understand, dear, and I do not suggest anything of the kind. I meant that he easily recognised the seriousness of your state and wisely insisted on a doctor."

"You know I have never been seriously ill before. However, I shall not oppose anything you decide. After all, there is nobody wiser than you. And please ask Hill to bring me some soup—and a little meat for Lucky. We will eat together."

As much as she tried to keep up her spirits for her sisters' sake, Elizabeth could not deny that she had never felt so ill. The pain in her throat was like a sharp knife, and her head hurt so that she hardly kept her eyes open.

Lying in her bed, closely watched by Lucky, Elizabeth worried less about her state than about the extraordinary meeting and the astonishing change of behaviour in Mr. Darcy. It was not surprising that he had helped her. Such a gentleman, by his nature or perhaps his education, would have helped any person in her situation. However, it was more than that: he was caring, friendly, worried, and even gentle. Jane said that he insisted a doctor be fetched and asked Mr. Bennet to inform him of her progress. What had induced him to behave in such a way?

What had changed in the short hours since the Netherfield ball where he had been as cold and aloof as ever? It was true, he had asked her to dance, but the set they shared was scarcely pleasant. Yet, the very next morning, Mr. Darcy appeared a completely different person, one to whom she felt deeply grateful. Finally, she thought she had the answer: Mr. Darcy must have seen her as the sister of Mr. Bingley's future wife, and it was only natural that his behaviour towards her would improve so strikingly. Yes, that must be the simple yet reasonable explanation. *Dearest Jane, she will be so happy—as happy as she deserves!*

Elizabeth's state steadily became worse. Mr. Jones's remedies seemed of little use, but there was nothing else to do, so they followed his measures strictly. In the afternoon, her sleep became more peaceful. Her fever dropped, and her coughing ceased. Finally, Jane could breathe in relief, and she went downstairs for the first time since the accident to give her family the good news. With no little surprise, she heard different voices speaking animatedly in the living room. She entered hesitantly and found her younger sisters and her mother speaking cheerily with Mr. Wickham and Mr. Denny. They all appeared to be in excellent spirits and did not restrain their amusement when Jane greeted them politely.

"Jane, what do you say of this surprise? Look who has come to ask about Lizzy!" Lydia said.

"Miss Bennet, is Miss Elizabeth feeling better, I hope? We were shocked to learn of her accident and could have no peace before coming to discover more details about her health."

"She is a little better, thank you, Mr. Wickham. She will be pleased to hear about your visit."

"I hope so. Please send her my regards," he said with a large smile and a friendly gaze. Jane's countenance remained unmoved, so he continued with a meaningful change of voice.

"And please tell Miss Elizabeth that I am sorry for my absence at the ball. I promised that I would attend, but as the time drew near, I found that I had better not meet Mr. Darcy—that to be in the same room, the same party with him for so many hours together, might be more than I could bear, and that scenes might arise unpleasant to more than myself."

"Is that so? I am curious that you would presume such a thing," Mr. Bennet said from the doorway, casting an inquiring gaze at the cheerful group. "For now, though, I am content to see that you are all in an excellent mood. It is good that you have nothing to worry about." His expression was stern and his displeasure obvious. However, his wife and two youngest daughters chose to remain focused on their guests.

"Papa, don't you know how cruelly Mr. Darcy treated poor Mr. Wickham in the past?"

"No I do not know, Lydia, and I am surprised that you are so acquainted with Mr. Wickham's past," Mr. Bennet replied sharply.

Mrs. Bennet intervened. "Well, truth to be told, we are not surprised to discover that Mr. Darcy is a cruel man. I knew that from the evening he refused to dance with Lizzy. It was cruel and very ungentlemanlike. And you must know that everybody missed you at the party, Mr. Wickham. I am sure all my daughters would have enjoyed dancing with you."

"Speaking of dancing, I was so shocked that Mr. Darcy invited Lizzy to dance. What a strange man—to dance with Lizzy and no one else." Lydia chuckled with Kitty.

Mr. Wickham looked surprised. "That is strange indeed. I have rarely seen Darcy dance unless the lady was a close acquaintance. But, of course, I could be wrong. I have not been in Darcy's company at a ball in the last five years or so—just before my godfather, the elder Mr. Darcy, passed away. He was an excellent man and very fond of me—"

"Mr. Wickham, you are so kind to entertain us with stories from your past, but I would suggest you postpone such sparkling conversation for another time when, hopefully, my daughter feels better. Now if you will excuse me, I will return to my library. If my cousin Mr. Collins happens to return from the Lucases, ask him to keep you company. He has enchanting stories about Mr. Darcy's aunt, so it will be like a family reunion."

THE BENNET FAMILY GATHERED FOR DINNER, AND CONVERSATION TURNED FROM Elizabeth's fever to the officers' visits and then to the news that Mr. Bingley's sisters had left Netherfield for London that same day. Mr. Collins did not keep them company as he was flattered to receive another invitation to dine at Lucas Lodge. His regrets were more eloquently expressed than the others wished to hear.

When the second course was served, the servant informed them of a visitor. A gentleman of Mr. Bennet's age with impressive posture and a severe countenance entered decidedly.

"Please forgive my intrusion at this improper time. I am here to see Miss

Elizabeth Bennet. Mr. Darcy believed I might be of some use to her. Here is his letter for Mr. Bennet." The gentleman addressed the man whom he believed to be the master of the house.

Six pairs of eyes around the table stared at the stranger in disbelief until Mr. Bennet finally rose and, with great difficulty, greeted the unexpected guest.

"I am Mr. Bennet, Elizabeth's father. Please come in, sir," he said, taking Darcy's letter and opening it impatiently.

"Oh, you came from London directly?" Mrs. Bennet loudly intervened. You must be tired after such a journey! Would you like something to eat? Please take a seat, sir."

"I thank you, ma'am, but first I wish to see Miss Elizabeth. I will gratefully accept your invitation afterwards," the doctor replied with cold politeness. Barely gathering herself and incredulous but relieved for such unexpected help, Jane asked the doctor to follow her.

In the dining room, the rest of the Bennet family noisily expressed their surprise at such an extraordinary event while Mr. Bennet continued to read his letter.

"Oh, I am sure that must be Mr. Bingley's doing. I am certain he convinced Mr. Darcy to send a doctor for Lizzy because he knew how distressed poor Jane must be. Oh, he is such a nice, handsome gentleman—so considerate! And five thousand a year—what a fortune for dear Jane!" Mrs. Bennet said with no little enthusiasm.

Mr. Bennet glanced severely at his wife, but he found neither strength nor desire to contradict her. In the letter, Mr. Darcy apologised for his daring assumption in sending Dr. Taylor without Mr. Bennet's approval, and he expressed his hope that, by that time, Miss Elizabeth was already fully recovered. In such a case, he said, Dr. Taylor would immediately return to London without disturbing them further.

Mr. Bennet was intrigued before such a generous, unusual gesture from a man who was almost a stranger to their family. He had not written to Mr. Darcy yet, as he promised, since he believed the gentleman to be more polite than worried when he asked to be informed about Lizzy's condition. Now he was proved completely wrong. *What can be the meaning of this?* In any other case, Mr. Bennet would presume that the gentleman's gesture was a sign of deep admiration for his daughter. But this was Mr. Darcy—who once did not find Lizzy tolerable enough even to dance with her! *Why would he care for her health?*

Then it crossed his mind that, at the Netherfield ball, Mr. Darcy seemed to have changed his opinion of Lizzy since she was the only woman he asked to dance. His thoughts were not clear due to his fatigue and worry, so he put the letter down and decided to consider the matter again in the next days—as soon as Lizzy was fully recovered.

Half an hour later, Dr. Taylor and Jane entered the library, silent and obviously concerned. The report was cautious and restrained.

"I do not wish to worry you unnecessarily. Generally, I would not be concerned for a cold when it comes to a young lady with Miss Elizabeth's spirit and strength. What worries me is that her lungs might be affected. She spent quite some time walking in freezing weather with wet clothes. We should also be very concerned about fever. As Miss Bennet told me, it went up and down rapidly several times a day. This can cause serious, long-lasting problems, but let us pray and hope that will not be the situation here."

"We are very grateful for your care, sir. What shall we do now? Should we fetch the apothecary to instruct him about what is to be done after your departure?" Jane asked.

Dr. Taylor sketched a smile. "Unless you wish me to, I shall not return to London until Miss Elizabeth shows improvement. I have taken a room at the Inn in Meryton."

This extraordinary news increased Mr. Bennet's shock to such an extent that he required an immediate glass of brandy. He looked at his older daughter, who was left wordless.

"Sir, I…we have no words to thank you enough… I cannot believe that—"

"Mr. Bennet, please do not make yourself uneasy. My partner can take care of my business in London, and I relish the prospect of a few days in the country. I shall come and visit Miss Elizabeth three times a day, but you may send for me at any time."

"Sir, we insist that you stay at Longbourn. I dare say you will find our guest chamber more comfortable than the inn. I will send my servant to inform them of your change in plans."

Mr. Bennet's insistence, together with Jane's delicate intervention had the desired effect, and Dr. Taylor was comfortably installed in the guest room within minutes.

The family and their unexpected guest reunited in the dining room to finish their dinner. Countless questions could be read in the ladies' glances, but none dared to express them. Mrs. Bennet briefly inquired about Mr. Bingley, but Dr. Taylor declared he had not seen him for a few months—an answer that deepened the ladies' puzzlement. Towards the end of the meal, which lasted considerably longer than usual, Mr. Collins returned.

At the knowledge that Dr. Taylor was Mr. Darcy's doctor from London, Mr. Collins's countenance changed. With great excitement, he asked the doctor whether he happened to know Lady Catherine de Bourgh. At the doctor's positive answer, Mr. Collins hurried to assure him that her ladyship was in perfect health a few days ago. He then continued to give unnecessarily detailed news about the lady until Dr. Taylor returned to his patient.

It was almost midnight, and Jane had lain in bed next to her sister, touching her forehead from time to time to check her fever. However, Elizabeth's head was spinning and painful, not from illness but from the incredible event that Mr. Darcy—at his own discretion—had sent his doctor from London to take care of her.

The sisters continued to talk for some time upon the subject, but neither of them could find a satisfactory explanation for such a generous gesture. Elizabeth attempted to suggest that most likely Mr. Bingley was behind it all, but Jane—though flustered and delighted with the praise of that gentleman—told Elizabeth that the doctor had not seen Mr. Bingley in months. Eventually, Jane concluded—and Elizabeth had no choice but to agree—that Mr. Darcy had done everything for no other reason than his generous, kind nature, one that Mr. Bingley often praised but Elizabeth failed to acknowledge. It was difficult for Jane's loving heart to admit that her sister had been wrong in this, but she was relieved and happy to know that Mr. Darcy's true character finally had been discerned.

Jane was now more certain than ever that the history between Mr. Darcy and Mr. Wickham must have been a great misunderstanding, one that surely would be clarified someday.

Later in the night, Elizabeth fell asleep, and Jane looked at her with tearful eyes. She glanced at Lucky who, having been banished from their chamber during Dr. Taylor's examination, was now watching them curiously from his corner. Jane stretched her hand towards him, and instantly the dog came to the bed and licked her hand.

She smiled and caressed him while whispering, "We have no reason to fear, Lucky. I know all will be well now." For the first time in the last few days, she truly believed her own words, relieved and confident of her beloved sister's complete recovery now that Dr. Taylor was there. She closed her eyes for a moment, and sleep claimed her—while Lucky remained alert next to the bed, guarding them.

Longbourn, 4 December

Dr. Taylor stayed at Longbourn for five days and decided to leave only when Elizabeth's recovery was beyond doubt.

At first, the doctor's presence troubled Elizabeth exceedingly. The knowledge that, for some strange reason, Mr. Darcy had sent a doctor from London to assist her was distressing.

So much trouble for her silly, imprudent behaviour made her deeply ashamed. She insisted that there was no need for the doctor to waste his valuable time taking care of her. After all, as her own mother had said when Jane was ill, nobody dies from "trifling colds."

Fortunately, Dr. Taylor appeared to enjoy Mr. Bennet's company and declared more than once that he had a delightful time in Hertfordshire.

The news of the London doctor's visit quickly spread from the day of his arrival. Mr. Jones came to make his acquaintance and spent more hours at Longbourn than etiquette would require. Also, Lady Lucas and Mrs. Long called on Mrs. Bennet to see for themselves what a London doctor looked like. They agreed that he was worthy of much admiration. The information—proudly shared by Mrs. Bennet—that the doctor was none other than Mr. Darcy's own physician astonished the visitors exceedingly.

With each passing day, Elizabeth's state improved remarkably. Dr. Taylor showed his admiration for the fact that "the illness has not defeated her spirit" and seemed impressed by her knowledge and passion for books, so he challenged her opinion on more than one subject.

From their enjoyable conversations, Elizabeth discovered that the doctor had been attending the Darcy family for more than twenty years. He spoke little about that subject, but he seemed very fond of the family and did not hesitate to praise highly the late Mr. Darcy and Lady Anne and to express his admiration for the present Mr. Darcy.

For some reason, he seemed to believe that Mr. Darcy was closely acquainted with Elizabeth's family, and she found no way to contradict him, nor did she wish to. Whatever faults Mr. Darcy might have and however unkindly and haughtily he might have treated everybody during his stay in Hertfordshire, the generosity he showed to her and her family left her with gentle feelings of gratitude. If he ever returned to Netherfield with Mr. Bingley, she would not lose a single moment before thanking him properly.

On the sixth day, precisely when a long letter of thanks from Mr. Collins arrived, Dr. Taylor left, and life at Longbourn was ready to return to its usual routine.

With God's will, everything was fine again, so Mr. Bennet returned to his former habit of secluding himself in the library for most of the day while Mrs. Bennet found the strength to remember that nothing would have happened had Elizabeth accepted Mr. Collins's generous proposal.

Chapter 3

Elizabeth was spending the first morning since her illness in the living room, when extraordinary news shattered the peace of Mrs. Bennet and the entire household.

Lady Lucas called with Charlotte and informed them that, just before he left the county, Mr. Collins had proposed to Charlotte and she had happily accepted him. He was expected to return soon and settle everything for the wedding.

The knowledge of this arrangement was almost too much for Mrs. Bennet's nerves, and she lost not a single moment in making her disbelief universally known. Surely, it must have been some sort of mistake as Mr. Collins was most desirous to marry Lizzy!

While their younger sisters could barely restrain their amusement, Jane and Elizabeth tried to form a proper, though not very convincing, congratulation.

Elizabeth saw that Charlotte recognised her censure and disappointment. Yet neither of them said anything upon the subject, and when Charlotte took her farewell, Elizabeth found the strength to embrace her friend and wish her felicity in her marriage.

Once the guests departed, Mrs. Bennet continued to cry and complain, requiring Hill to help her to her room as she felt too weak to stand and face their dreadful future.

Mr. Bennet's emotions were more tranquil on the occasion. As he later confessed to his eldest daughters, it gratified him to discover that Charlotte Lucas, whom he had been used to think tolerably sensible, was as foolish as his wife and more foolish than his daughter!

The next day, Charlotte returned with only her sister, Maria, and while the younger girls amused themselves, Charlotte required a private moment with Elizabeth. After a cup of tea, Charlotte finally spoke decidedly.

"I could go no further without discussing this with you, Lizzy, as you are as dear to me as a sister and I value no one's opinion as much as yours."

"The feeling is mutual, Charlotte, you know that."

"I know. That is why we must be honest with each other. I did not fail to see your disapproval about my marital arrangements. I felt that you were horrified and disdained me."

"Oh, Charlotte, please do not believe that—"

"Do not attempt to deny it, Lizzy. We know each other too well. You did not hesitate to reject Mr. Collins when he proposed to you, and you could not imagine or accept my acceptance of him. But Lizzy, do not hurry to judge me harshly. Not all of us have the courage or the will to reject an honourable gentleman with a good situation in life or to refuse a comfortable future just because the gentleman is not particularly handsome or witty or able to satisfy our romantic dreams and hopes to be married only for the deepest love," Charlotte said bitterly.

"I do not judge you, Charlotte, but you are my best friend, and I know you are such a wonderful woman! You could find a much better husband than Mr. Collins—I am sure."

"What do you mean a *better* man, Lizzy? He has a satisfactory income and good connections. He is kind and seems to have good intentions. What could be better than that? And why should I hope for a 'better' one? What do I have to tempt a 'better' man? No dowry, no connections… And to be honest—though you are younger and more beautiful and witty and charming than me—what else do *you*, Lizzy, have to offer a man in your hopes to attract a 'better' one? Why such arrogant hopes?"

Elizabeth knew Charlotte well enough to recognise that she was angry and hurt, and her friend's sharp inquiry left her silent and disconcerted for a moment.

"I do not want to fight with you, Charlotte. From that point of view, you are right of course. I have nothing in my favour to entertain my 'arrogant hopes' as you named them. I made my decision, and I will have to accept it, just as you made yours. But dearest Charlotte, it is not about being handsome or witty or about romantic hopes. Could you truly believe that Mr. Collins has had time to know you and to develop real affection for you as you deserve since he proposed to you only three days after he proposed to me? That is my main worry. You deserve nothing less than to be appreciated and cared for."

"Mr. Collins might not have had time to develop true affection for me, nor I for him. But, as I have no reason to think ill of him, to doubt his character or his intentions, I feel confident enough to take my chances, trust my luck, and wait for affection to come later."

"What if it does not come? What if you are not able to respect your husband? How will you bear the marriage? How will you bear the regret that you might have been happy if—"

"I will compensate with a good household, with the hope of children, with a comfortable home, and with the chance of helping my family if they ever need it. Lizzy, you are lovely and have a sharp mind that has always impressed me and made me admire you. But you are also a hasty judge of people's characters—and a little vain. Only consider your opinion of Mr. Darcy and Mr. Wickham. You like Mr.

Wickham, but for what positive reasons? Do you know him to be generous, kind, loyal? Or do you declare him to be your friend only because he has a handsome appearance, pleasant manners, and favoured you from the beginning? On the other hand, Mr. Darcy refused to dance with you, and I know your vanity was hurt by his rejection though you did not admit it. Consequently, you declared him as possessing the worst qualities and retaliated by being rude to him. What if Mr. Darcy had danced with you that first night at the Meryton assembly and declared his admiration for you? Would you have been so disposed to disapprove of him?"

"Charlotte, this is not about Mr. Wickham or Mr. Darcy—"

"No, it is not. It is about my future husband, Mr. Collins, but the situation is similar. He is neither the handsomest nor the wittiest man alive, so you believe him incapable of having any good qualities such as politeness or consideration or industriousness. You rejected him in a moment, but did you take time to consider whether you were wise in doing that? Forgive me, but considering your position, are you aware that you might not receive another proposal from anyone with as good a situation?"

"I am aware, Charlotte… In fact, I am resigned to my fate, and I shall remain an old maid and help Jane care for her children." Elizabeth attempted to joke.

"What if Jane does not receive a proposal either? What if Mr. Bingley does not marry her?"

"Oh, I am sure he will. If not, another gentleman will surely meet and fall in love with her."

"Perhaps or perhaps not, Lizzy. Do you realise that you place the entire burden on Jane's shoulders? And let me remind you: had Mr. Bingley not leased Netherfield and never met Jane, Mr. Collins likely would have proposed to her. Do you believe that she would have dared to refuse him, oppose your mother's will, and put the entire family at risk?"

"I…do not know…"

"You may laugh at Mr. Collins now, but have you considered what will occur if something happens to Mr. Bennet and none of you has made a favourable marriage? Where will you all go, Lizzy? Who will keep you? Let us hope Mr. Bingley does marry Jane because one of you needs a very wealthy husband to take care of you all. Otherwise, you, Jane, or any of your sisters will gladly accept any offer, even from someone with more faults than Mr. Collins has. And would you then not regret that you so hastily rejected him?"

The two dear friends looked into each other's eyes, trying to read the other's mind and heart. Neither of them moved nor spoke, and they barely breathed. Eventually, Charlotte moved closer, took Elizabeth's hands, and spoke, her eyes tearful.

"Forgive me for being so harsh, Lizzy. I want you to understand me and not despise me for my choice. I could not bear to lose your love and respect. All I want is a comfortable home, a good husband, and a life without fears for my future. And I know my choice has made my family happy too. These things are more important than any of Mr. Collins's faults."

"It is I who should apologise, Charlotte. I was only concerned about your happiness. I love you as dearly as I do my sister, and I would say the same to Jane. But if Mr. Collins has the good fortune of gaining your affections, he will be a very happy man, and I will be very happy for you. If this is your wish, I offer you my sincerest congratulations."

"It is, Lizzy. Oh—and you should be grateful that I will marry Mr. Collins as you know that you and your family will be always welcome in my home. But I do expect Mr. Bennet to be healthy and sound for at least another twenty years, so no rush on that." Charlotte laughed, and they embraced each other tightly, holding the embrace for some time.

"Charlotte—I would happily sleep in the woods to know you happy," Elizabeth whispered.

"I know you would, dear Lizzy. But let us hope that will not be the case. You have had enough excitement in the woods for a while!

THE NIGHT AFTER CHARLOTTE'S VISIT, ELIZABETH FOUND LITTLE REST AS HER friend's words troubled her more than she realised. She still could not approve Charlotte's decision and shivered at the mere thought of having her friend sharing the marriage bed with a man long before they shared affection, respect, and tenderness. Nevertheless, it was Charlotte's choice, and she was neither a simpleton nor a reckless young girl who did not know her mind. So all Elizabeth could do was to respect her friend's decision and put aside her own opinion.

However, Elizabeth could not cease thinking of everything Charlotte had said about her being hasty and vain—and misjudging Mr. Wickham and Mr. Darcy based on her wounded or flattered feelings. She also thought about Jane and knew that Charlotte was right. Jane would not hesitate to put her family's safety above her own feelings, and Elizabeth felt the guilt for placing the entire burden of a safe marriage on her sister's shoulders. She hoped that Mr. Bingley would return soon and everything would be resolved perfectly.

As for Mr. Darcy and Mr. Wickham, though Elizabeth had no reason to change her opinion about the latter, she had already suffered a change of mind regarding the former. At least she admitted that she failed to recognise certain good qualities that he undoubtedly possessed. Even before her talk with Charlotte, Elizabeth had decided to make amends for her behaviour towards Mr. Darcy as soon as they met again.

As the days passed, Elizabeth's concerns moved entirely towards her elder sister. Jane had looked pale and distressed for some time, but it was easy to understand the cause: she had sacrificed her sleep and rest to watch over Elizabeth. However, when the second Miss Bennet improved and recovered completely, the eldest looked even worse than she had during Elizabeth's illness. Elizabeth feared that her sister might feel ill herself, but Jane assured her that was not the case. Worried and sensing something was troubling her dear sister, Elizabeth insisted with repeated inquiries until Jane ceased her resistance and confessed the reason for her distress.

"It is nothing to worry about, Lizzy. I just received a letter from Caroline yesterday—did I mention that I wrote her a few days ago? She informed me that they are all settled in town for the winter. So there are no hopes for Mr. Bingley to return to Netherfield anytime soon."

London, 13 December

Darcy had been in London more than a fortnight when he received Lady Matlock's third invitation for dinner—and he found no reason to refuse or delay it again.

He dearly loved the Matlocks as they were his closest remaining family, but his mind was too engaged with his own troubled thoughts to bear family dinner chat.

He had been reluctant to send Dr. Taylor to Longbourn before asking Mr. Bennet's consent. Though his intentions were good, it was presumptuous of him to make a decision about a lady to whom he was in no way connected. Mr. Bennet's only concern, however, was that his daughter was well and sound, and he proved it through a letter of gratitude that Darcy received after Dr. Taylor's arrival at Longbourn. He had been correct in worrying about Elizabeth's state. God knows what might have happened had she been left in the care of the apothecary. Fortunately, she had fully recovered, so he no longer had reason for concern.

Bingley was another troublesome case for Darcy, as Bingley's spirits had fallen so that he barely looked like his usual self. Darcy had had a long talk with his friend, expressing his doubts about Miss Bennet's true feelings, that she might be pushed to accept his suit in order to assure her family's security. Somehow, his own words seemed unconvincing even to himself, so it was no wonder that Bingley had left him in the middle of the room and had refused to see him since then.

His uncle Lord Matlock announced that he wished to speak about an important problem affecting the entire family, and Darcy could easily guess what that problem was. Annabelle's presence in Town at that precise moment was dreadful. He truly could not set his mind to think of it nor had he the strength or will to do anything about it.

Darcy happened to meet her on the street one day, and he briefly greeted her as both were in company. After that, he received three notes from her, asking him to call on her—which he wisely ignored. He expected the situation to become more complicated as gossip would surely arise and spread all over London. The Matlocks would be affected by the rumours, and he owed them at least the assurance that, as always, he would do the right thing.

As for himself, he could not care less about the rumours surrounding Lady Annabelle Stafford. He planned to leave for Pemberley with Georgiana as soon as possible.

At Pemberley, he could be alone with his thoughts: regrets, sorrows, struggles, memories, and the image of the only woman who had ever captured his heart—and from whom he could not possibly free himself—Miss Elizabeth Bennet.

DARCY WAS NOT SURPRISED WHEN, ARRIVING AT THE MATLOCK RESIDENCE FOR a family dinner, he found there, besides the earl's sons and daughter-in-law, his cousin James Darcy—the only son of his father's younger brother. James greeted them so loudly that he embarrassed Georgiana. It was clear that he had already enjoyed several drinks.

Despite a long succession of disagreements, Darcy held great affection for the only cousin on his father's side and was pleased to see him, but James's presence there was an unmistakable sign that dinner would be anything but peaceful.

However, between light conversation and exquisite courses, dinner passed pleasantly for both Georgiana and Darcy. He congratulated himself on accepting Lady Matlock's invitation since lately he had been such poor company for his sister.

Afterwards, the earl invited the gentlemen—his two sons, Darcy, and James—to enjoy a drink in the library while Lady Matlock, her daughter-in-law, and Georgiana remained to amuse themselves. As Darcy was thinking he might have unfairly presumed his younger cousin would be a troublesome companion, James approached with a glass of brandy.

"So, Cousin Darcy, how are you these days? What interesting news do you have?"

"I am fine, thank you, James. Nothing interesting, I am afraid."

"Really? That is not what I heard." He laughed, finished his brandy, and poured himself another.

"I do not understand your meaning, James, but that is not unusual. I rarely understand your jokes. I suggest you find another means to amuse yourself since my life is so dull."

"Oh, you are being too modest. I was told by a friend who resided in the neighbourhood that you had quite an exciting time in Hertfordshire."

"You will end this trifling conversation immediately, James. I suspect which friend gave you such information, and as always, everything that person says is not only untrue but offensive."

Lord Matlock joined them. "What are you talking about, James? Is this more of your nonsense?"

"No nonsense, Uncle. I heard there was an incident involving Darcy and a certain young lady in Hertfordshire. It sounded quite strange and somewhat amusing, considering it was Darcy whom we were discussing. I am interested to hear *his* side of the story."

"It is nonsense, James, and it pains me to see that age makes you no more wise or proper. I demand you have the decency to change the subject immediately and never repeat it. You may amuse yourself, but your reckless behaviour might also jeopardise the reputation of a most honourable young lady."

"What are you both talking of, Darcy? What incident? What young lady? And

James—no more brandy for you this evening."

"It seems that Darcy was lost in the woods with a young lady. They returned home after some time, and it was reported that their appearance was far from proper. I heard the lady became ill afterwards. It is not clear whether it was from the cold or from some other cause."

He laughed and gulped another brandy, and to everyone's shock, Darcy grabbed him by the coat and pushed him violently against the wall. James Darcy froze in shock and dropped his glass as he stared at Darcy's sharp, furious expression.

"You never know when to stop, you idiot," Darcy said, his jaws clenched.

"Darcy, for heaven's sake, calm yourself! What is wrong with you?" Lord Matlock intervened. "Darcy, please!" he repeated as he tried to free James from Darcy's grasp.

Darcy reluctantly pushed his younger cousin away then stepped to the window, glaring outside as he struggled to regain his breathing as well as his countenance.

"Darcy, please sit down. Have another glass and let us try to speak calmly."

"Uncle, Georgiana and I must leave now. Thank you for a most delightful dinner."

"You want to leave? So unexpectedly? Come, Darcy, you cannot possibly be upset with James. You know how he is."

"I am not upset. It is time to leave, and I must fetch Georgiana." He turned to his cousin and said in a low voice, "Do not dare repeat that story. Do not dare spread malicious gossip to amuse yourself at the expense of an innocent young lady, or you will bear the consequences. And be sure you tell the same to the idiot who came to you with this foul tale. He will ruin you, James, and today you convinced me you no longer deserve my assistance."

"Oh come, Darcy, why so serious and resentful? I was only joking! Tell him, Robert—is it not true that all men make such jokes? Do not be angry. I meant no harm," he said, hurrying to stop Darcy but with little success.

"James, be quiet," said the earl. "And Darcy, please do not leave in such haste. You will only frighten Georgiana. Let us not start a fight in the family, despite James's usual stupid jokes. We all understand this is a matter of great importance to you, Darcy, and I trust James will have enough wisdom to be careful what he says about such a delicate subject. Will you share the story with us?"

Darcy emptied his glass in two gulps then took a few deep breaths before he felt confident enough to conclude the awkward situation. He was equally angry with his cousin and with himself for losing his temper so easily, but he recognised that his uncle's advice was sound.

"There is not much to say, Uncle. I will relate the incident so you realise that James's report is devoid of substance. During our stay in Hertfordshire, we became acquainted with a family who owns an estate three miles from Bingley. Bingley and his sisters visited the family several times and invited the eldest Miss Bennet to Netherfield on several occasions. The day we left, I took a ride while Bingley prepared himself to leave. Unexpectedly, I met Miss Elizabeth Bennet—the second daughter of the family—walking through the woods after falling into a pond—a minor but potentially dangerous accident. You can imagine: the freezing water, the wind, the cold… She was unwell and could not return home alone, so I offered my help and brought her to her house safely. That was all."

The earl watched him in shock. "Then why did James suggest…? And how did he know…? Forgive me for insisting, but you must see my puzzlement."

"Yes, James, do explain it to our uncle. How did you gain your intelligence, and why do you suggest that something improper occurred?"

The younger man laughed nervously and attempted a joke as he tried to produce a reasonable explanation, but Darcy interrupted him coldly.

"During our stay in Hertfordshire, I was unpleasantly surprised to find Wickham in the neighbourhood. He had joined the militia quartered in Meryton. Strange, is it not? And I believe he was also on friendly terms with the Bennet family, so naturally, he heard the news and lost no time in spreading his malicious opinion until it reached our idiot cousin."

"Darcy, I did not—"

"Silence, James," shouted the earl. "That explains everything—that miserable, ungrateful scoundrel. Nothing good ever came from him. And you, James, never cease to amaze me. Despite countless mistakes and failings in your past, you have learnt nothing. This will bring you to ruin, mark my words, boy."

"Precisely," Darcy intervened. "Now, James, speaking of your friend Wickham, here is what I would like to know. Since he pretends to be a friend of the Bennet family, I wonder what Mr. Bennet will say when I inform him of the tale Wickham is spreading. I wonder how Wickham will be received by honourable Hertfordshire families in the future."

"Darcy, surely you cannot do such a thing. You would not… We were only joking."

"I can and I will. I have long ceased to show any favour or understanding of Wickham's vile behaviour. I will not hesitate to expose him completely to everyone I know should he dare bother me again. And this applies to you, too, James. I warn you here in the presence of our uncle and cousins. This conversation is over. Now forgive me. It is time for me to leave."

He left the library, followed by the earl, while the colonel and James remained behind.

"I cannot believe your path keeps crossing Wickham's—what a misfortune! I am truly sorry that James ruined this evening for you, Darcy."

"Please do not feel uneasy, Uncle. It is I who should apologise for reacting so violently. But I would not wish for Miss Elizabeth Bennet's good name and reputation to be jeopardised because of Wickham's desire to attack me—or James's reckless behaviour. She is truly a remarkable young lady, and she became very ill after this incident. Dr. Taylor said that her life was in danger and she bore the illness with great courage and strength."

"Dr. Taylor? Does he know Miss Bennet and her family?"

"No, he… I was afraid that Miss Elizabeth's state might take a turn for the worse without proper care, and the apothecary did not seem trustworthy. So I asked Dr. Taylor to visit her and offer his help if needed, and it was. He spent almost a week helping her recover."

The earl was astonished. "I see… It was indeed fortunate that Dr. Taylor was there to take care of the young lady. Well, Nephew, thank you for joining us at dinner. It has been quite an evening. I wish you and Georgiana a good night, and please be kind enough to save me a few hours tomorrow. I will call on you after breakfast. I believe we have matters to discuss.

"Very well, Uncle—I shall wait for you."

London, 14 December

The morning after the dinner with the Matlocks found Darcy distressed and tired. His anger against his younger cousin had not abated after he left. He refused breakfast and retired to his library, sitting at his desk stacked with papers. He knew very well that he would not touch them that day either. He could hardly remember a time in the past five years when he had been less diligent about business.

So it was that his cousin Colonel Fitzwilliam found him an hour later when he entered without knocking—as usual. "Good morning, Darcy."

"Good morning, Robert, nice to see you. I was expecting Uncle to call."

"Oh yes, Father said he would come around noon. He has something to attend to first," the Colonel said and paced the room several times before he sat. "I hope you are not still upset about James. We were sorry that we invited him the same evening as you and Georgiana. We thought he would enjoy a nice family dinner, but—"

"I am sure he enjoyed dinner, maybe too much. I am not upset that you invited him. There are other things that bother me, I shall not deny it, but it is not your fault."

"I imagine there are. Let me know if I may help in any way."

Darcy glanced at the colonel. "You look like someone who could *use* some help, Robert."

"No, not really… It is just that… Darcy, I know you might get angry with me, but I cannot help asking you. The lady in Hertfordshire James talked about—this Miss Elizabeth Bennet—is she the young lady of whom Bingley spoke so warmly? The one you said was not a proper match for him because of her family situation. Her name was Bennet, right?"

"It was her surname; you are correct. But the lady Bingley spoke of is Miss Jane Bennet—Miss Elizabeth's eldest sister. Why do you ask?"

"Nothing, really. I just thought that Bingley has not looked like himself lately. I know you congratulate yourself on saving him from a delicate situation, but he seems quite unhappy."

"Bingley is easily charmed and easily unhappy when it comes to a lady's beauty. I have seen him in similar states of mind and heart more times than I can remember."

"I hope your estimation is correct. *I* would not dare interfere in such delicate matters."

Darcy laughed. "Then how is it you interfere in *my* delicate affairs all the time?"

"That is different. I never imply that I know what is best for you, Darcy."

"Of course you do—all the time." Darcy laughed again.

"I see you are decided to mock me. Be it as you wish. I am certain that you had the best intentions in mind, but as I said, I hope you are not wrong about Miss Jane Bennet and Bingley, and I hope Miss Elizabeth Bennet will not be exposed to any nasty rumours that might affect her reputation and her life. I imagine it must be hard for you to bear that the Bennets' fate has been affected in such a tragic way because of you."

"What on earth do you mean? I have no doubt that I have been correct in my estimation of Miss Bennet's feelings for Bingley. He will thank me for that one day. As for Miss Elizabeth—I have done nothing more than was necessary to protect her life. How can I be blamed for that or for any nasty rumours that might arise? Should I have left her alone in the woods, risking her life—just to protect her from harmful gossip?"

"I know you are angry with me now, but if you think on the entire situation in a reasonable way, you will see that I am right. The eldest Bennet sister has lost a most advantageous marriage because of your intervention, and you cannot be certain that Bingley ever finds a better wife. And now Wickham and James are spreading malicious rumours involving Miss Elizabeth, and for that she might never receive an advantageous marriage offer—only because of you, because Wickham wished to harm your reputation."

"Miss Elizabeth Bennet seemed quite charmed by Wickham, so she should well bear the outcome of any gossip spread by her favourite."

"That sounds bitter and sharp and quite inelegant, Darcy. Very unlike you—"

"Robert, it was delightful talking to you, but I have matters to finish before my uncle arrives. May I help you further? If not, you must excuse me now."

"I will leave; do not worry. I am just sorry to find that Miss Elizabeth had a preference for Wickham. From your previous description, she seemed a worthy young lady. Could she be such a poor judge of character? And if so, should you not have warned her about the man?"

"Robert, you have crossed many lines today. You should leave now, and for the future, I recommend that you find better subjects of conversation than those involving ladies."

"I shall go to see Georgiana. Good bye and I wish you a better day than it has been so far. And don't be upset. You know I have the best of intentions for you, as you do for Bingley."

THOUGH DARCY WAITED FOR HIS UNCLE'S CALL, NOON CAME AND WENT, AND Lord Matlock made no appearance. Since he had little interest in his papers, he decided to spend a few minutes listening to Georgiana, who was practicing at the pianoforte. His presence in the music room was received with great delight by Miss Darcy and her companion, who discreetly retired, allowing the siblings to talk in privacy.

"Do you have a preference for what should I play, Brother?"

"No, dearest—anything would be a delight."

Georgiana started to play then turned to her brother. "I had a lovely time at dinner yesterday."

"I am glad. I see you are amiable with your new cousin Maryanne. I believe Thomas has made a good choice of a wife."

"Oh yes, she is lovely, and she is almost as silent as I am." Georgiana let out a small peal of laughter. "But Thomas is also quiet and reserved, so they seem well suited to each other."

"Based on that reasoning, I should take a wife who never speaks, never dances, and never goes out unless to the theatre or opera," he attempted to joke.

"Oh, I hope you will not do that," she replied then suddenly blushed and apologised. "Forgive me, Brother. I only hope you will find a wife to make you happy. That is all that matters to me."

"Do not worry about being honest, dearest. Quite the contrary—let us presume you have the chance to find me a wife. How would you like her to be?"

Georgiana stopped playing, staring at her brother. "Are you in earnest?"

"Yes, I would truly like to know your opinion on the matter."

"Oh, I never thought of that… What I would like most is that she appreciates your character and generous nature. I would like her to be bright enough to understand how smart you are, to enjoy reading so she can admire the books you cherish, and to enjoy spending time outdoors so she can love Pemberley's grounds. Oh yes—and to play the piano so we could have duets when you are away on business, to laugh and talk more than we do so the house should not be so silent, and to know how to dance so she could teach me someday."

Darcy laughed wholeheartedly.

"So many requirements, dearest! I thought I was too demanding, but if we are to consider your list, I am afraid I will never marry. What about her family or her wealth or her beauty—nothing about these matters?"

"Well, I imagine she must be beautiful enough for you to admire her and must be an honourable person for you to choose her. As for her wealth—I am not very familiar with that… I do not believe we should worry about it. I only wish to see you happy, Brother."

"Dearest, why do you keep saying that? I am quite happy with you and with our family."

"I know you are, but…I want to see you happy in other ways. I know how much you have on your shoulders with all the business affairs, with so many tenants and with our family demands, and with Aunt Catherine insisting you marry Anne, and with James making so much trouble, and the way I disappointed you…" she continued tearfully.

"Georgiana, you could never disappoint me! You do not know how proud I am of you and how delighted I am that you care and worry so for me." He embraced her tenderly. "And that you are smart enough to understand that I do not intend to marry Anne, despite the fact that I really care for her," he ended with a smile in his voice.

She laughed through her tears and looked at him. "I am not a child anymore, William."

"I know you are not, dearest, and that truly frightens me. But I am happy that we can speak so honestly. Please know that I always love to hear your opinions on any matter."

"Thank you, Brother," she said then turned to start playing again, her heart light and joyful.

Two hours later, Lord Matlock finally was announced. He fondly greeted his niece and asked his nephew to speak privately. His haste foretold the gravity of their discourse.

Darcy filled two glasses with wine. "I trust you are well, Uncle? I expected you earlier."

"Yes, I had something to attend to. Catherine wrote and asked me to take care of some problems, but I am well, thank you. What about you, Darcy? You are not upset, I hope?"

"No, do not worry. How is Aunt Catherine? And Anne?"

"They are both fine, as usual," the earl said, emptying his glass. "Catherine inquired about you quite insistently. You must realise that she is very hopeful about a certain event. She mentioned that Anne is the perfect age for marriage."

"Uncle, please let us not renew that subject. We have discussed it since I was twenty, and despite my deep affection for Anne, my decision was made long ago."

"I do not want to make you uncomfortable. You have grown up to be a very wise man, Darcy, and I am as proud of you as I am of my own sons. I trust your judgment more than I trust theirs—in most matters. Therefore, I hope the things that made you refuse to marry Anne when you were twenty will not have equal influence on you now, eight years later."

Darcy paled slightly. "There were no *things* that made me refuse to marry Anne, Uncle, only the nature of my feelings for her. My parents understood and accepted my decision. I would hope that you and Aunt Catherine would do the same."

"I *do* accept your decision—more to the point, it is not for me to accept it or not! You are your own master, and no one can force you to do anything. However, I will tell you what I told my sons: in matters of marriage, you must allow your mind to speak louder than your heart. Feelings are important, but your sense must be stronger. But you do not seem to have the sort of feelings to induce you into a marriage with anyone, though almost any young lady from the *ton* would be delighted by your preference! Or am I wrong? Is there anyone whom you consider worthy to be your wife?"

A brief hesitation did not escape the earl. Darcy averted his eyes for a moment then replied, "You are not wrong, Uncle… Still…"

"Then—I apologise for insisting, but why is Anne not as good as anyone else? You are at an age when you must consider marriage most seriously. I am sure you do not forget that you owe at least one heir—a male heir—to your family."

Darcy released a nervous laugh. "No, I have not forgotten that most of my properties are entailed to the male line, Uncle. But I am not quite old enough to worry about that. Besides, if things go wrong, I will always have Pemberley to support Georgiana and me."

"I am glad this subject amuses you, but I would not want to see the fortune you and your father have struggled to acquire wasted by James on games of chance. And you must admit my point: since you do not have a certain preference, Anne could be the best choice. She would be happy to become your wife any time. It could be a perfect match for both of you. She would have a husband to care and provide for her, while you would have a wife who would cherish you and be a good mother for your children. And she would never give you much trouble. You would always be free to do what you please outside your marriage—"

"That is not much of an incentive. I would not use Anne merely to provide an heir. And when I marry, I surely do not plan to choose a wife who will not give me much 'trouble,' as I do not intend to do what I please 'outside' my marriage. I would rather have a less obedient wife who would give me a little trouble," he replied in a lower voice and averted his eyes again. The earl noticed his reaction and frowned.

"But, Uncle, you said you wished to talk to me about an important matter. *This* was it?"

"No…no," said the earl as if searching for the right words. "There is something else entirely…" he said, pouring some brandy. "I wanted to speak about your cousin James."

"About James? He is what you wish to talk to me about? What else has he done?"

"Nothing more than he usually does, as you saw last night. But there is something more worrying. Did you know James to be on friendly terms with Lady Stafford, the former Annabelle Weston?"

Darcy's countenance changed instantly, and he knew his uncle saw it. He breathed once more to regain his countenance before replying.

"Robert told me a few days ago. But it was not a surprise. Each of them is entitled to be friendly with whomever they like. May I ask why you are concerned?"

"I am concerned about this Lady Stafford…"

"So, now we come to the real subject of our discussion," Darcy said sternly.

"I am sorry if I offend you, but previous experience shows us what might come from her. We cannot take these things lightly. And the present situation is even worse. Unlike in the past, she now has all the fortune and means she needs to accomplish her goals."

"I thank you for your concern, but I am certain her goals are different from what you suspect. Time changes many things, and I believe all of us have gained in age and wisdom."

The earl glanced at his nephew, filled his glass again, and spoke severely.

"Lady Matlock met her at the modiste a few days ago. She did not hesitate to inquire after you and to publicly inform Lady Matlock that she plans to call on you. She said, and I quote, that she is happy you 'have not married yet,' and she intends 'to renew and deepen' her acquaintance with you. Your aunt was shocked. That woman is even more impertinent than she was years ago! And I believe she will call on you—or perhaps she already has?"

Darcy stared at his uncle in disbelief. "I do not know what to say… I cannot imagine what came over Annabelle to address Lady Matlock in such a way…"

"And now she seems to be friendly with James. I hope you understand my worry and my insistence on talking to you. We cannot afford to show weakness and tolerance towards such behaviour. I cannot impose upon your private life or upon your preferences, but I shall do everything to protect my wife—and my niece Georgiana."

Darcy remained silent. He would not normally allow anyone to speak to him in such a tone, but he admitted that the earl's anger was not without justification.

"Uncle, my preferences would never go in the direction of harming my family. As for Lady Stafford calling on me, I would never allow such a display of impropriety near my sister."

The earl breathed deeply and paced the room for some time. "What worries me is that moment of weakness that often affects men's judgment, especially when a beautiful woman is involved. And when the woman is Annabelle Weston, or whatever she calls herself now, no man is strong enough. I could not blame you for it."

"I assure you that I am in no danger of allowing any weakness to affect my judgment. Any preference I might have had eight years ago has long passed. I have not spoken to her in four years, and even then you must remember how things were settled."

"Yes, I most certainly remember…and I am certain that she remembers, too. Circumstances are completely different now—and in her favour."

"I believe this is much ado about nothing, truly. No matter the circumstance, there is nothing to worry about in regard to myself, I assure you. I shall never allow our family to be exposed to ridicule. Besides, I plan to leave for Pemberley with Georgiana after Christmas."

"Yes, that might be a good plan for now." Darcy filled his glass again, and the earl continued to speak, his tone completely changed. "I hope you do not mind—I just happened to meet Dr. Taylor this morning. We had a pleasant time at the club, talking over a few drinks."

Darcy gazed at his uncle sharply. "You just happened to meet Dr. Taylor? How astonishing."

"Yes… And, among other things, we discussed his errand in Hertfordshire. To be honest, I was quite surprised that he spoke so highly of the young lady he treated there."

"Uncle, I did not expect you to take James's gossip seriously and to make inquiries about a story I already related to you. And I am displeased that Dr. Taylor spoke of it."

"Forgive me for upsetting you. I confess my curiosity was aroused but not by James's report. As for Dr. Taylor—did you request his secrecy?"

"I did not."

"So, there is no reason to blame him. He has committed no fault. I told him that I already knew the story from you—which was true—and I only asked how he liked Hertfordshire."

"I see… Now that your curiosity has been satisfied, may we move on from this incident?"

"Indeed we may. So—will you and Georgiana come to us for Christmas dinner?"

"Yes, we shall—as always."

"Excellent." After several comments about the weather, the earl left.

Darcy leant back in his armchair, his eyes closed, attempting to regain his countenance. He had a strong feeling that things were out of his power and he could do nothing to regain control.

Several hours later, Lord Matlock prepared himself for the night, watched closely by his curious wife. He spoke of his sister Catherine's insistence that Darcy marry Anne, and he confessed to Lady Matlock his discussion with Darcy about the delicate subject of Annabelle Weston, Lady Stafford, and sharing his worries.

"Darcy has never disappointed us before, despite his young age. I have often admired his wisdom and the strength of his character. However, I am afraid he still has a weakness about that woman. He denied it, but I sensed that he hesitated… and he avoided my gaze as if attempting to hide his true feelings, especially when I asked him about marrying Anne."

"Do you believe him capable of marrying that woman?!"

"I do not think him to be so unwise. My fear is that she might force her presence on him in some way. I imagine she would do anything to have his child. We can do little but pray and trust his excellent judgment. Thank God, he will leave for Pemberley soon. Besides…"

"Is there anything else you wish to tell me, husband? Is there more to this?"

"No there is not…not really… It is just that…there is no real trouble, only some strange happenstance that roused my curiosity as it is so unlike Darcy…"

"Darcy? What do you mean? Surely, you cannot expect me to go to sleep in such a state! I could not possibly find rest unless I know all the details."

With some hesitation but undone by another glass of brandy, Lord Matlock related the particulars of the story he had heard the evening before, starting with James's report, then Darcy's explanation, and finally, Dr. Taylor's detailed narrative.

Lady Matlock listened in silence, her surprise and curiosity impossible to conceal. She disapproved her husband's indelicate interference in Darcy's private affairs and expressed herself to be against Lord Matlock's decision to extract more details from Dr. Taylor through a doubtful strategy. Consequently, Lord Matlock did not dare tell her of his equally improper attempt to gather information about the Gardiners. He might tell her when he had some results—and only if future events required it.

Chapter 4

London, 16 December, evening

Some time after dinner, Darcy was told that he had an urgent call. Puzzled, he entered the main hall and frowned. There was Annabelle Weston, alone, waiting, a daring, challenging expression in her eyes.

He hesitantly moved forward and considered how he could escort her out with as little disturbance as possible when she spoke with animation. "Mr. Darcy, what a delightful surprise. I have waited so long to see you. I hope you missed me as much as I missed you."

"Lady Stafford—this is a surprise indeed. Has something happened of a tragic nature? If not, I would suggest you postpone our conversation. This is not the time for a call."

"Something tragic has indeed happened, but I cannot tell you here. Shall we speak somewhere more privately? In your room, perhaps?" she whispered, and he took a step forward, gazing at her. He breathed deeply, attempting to maintain his temper.

"Let us go to the library. Stevens, allow us ten minutes then please come and show Lady Stafford out," he addressed his servant, who nodded in agreement.

Darcy took her arm and conducted her to the library, closing the door.

"Lady Stafford, why are you here at this time of day? In fact, why are you here at all?"

"I have missed you. I have not seen you in four years. What could be more tragic than that? I sent you notes, asking you to visit me. They must have been lost, so I had to come myself. You have been in town for more than two weeks, and I have not caught a glimpse of you."

"Your notes were not lost, but I saw no reason to call on you. I understood you to have met several of my relatives lately, and they all confirmed you to be fine."

"I cannot be fine without you. I have not been fine for eight years. I missed you so much…"

"Annabelle, do not start. I ask you politely to be reasonable and wise. I thank you for your visit, but it is time for you to leave."

"I will not leave before you look me in the eye and tell me that you did not miss me at all."

"I did not miss you, Annabelle. Please, do not force me to be rude, and please do not allow this obsession to expose you to ridicule. You did not truly miss me. You are only stubborn and unable to accept disappointment. You always strove to reach your goals by any possible means. And you always enjoyed being theatrical."

"I do not deserve such harsh treatment. Why do you reject me so severely? Why do you not even allow me to speak with you? I have wealth and fortune and name and means. I want nothing from you but your company!"

"Annabelle, you have known the nature of my feelings for many years. I never attempted to deceive you or to pretend to be what I was not—unlike yourself. Your wealth and your name make no difference to me! I wish you all the best, Annabelle, but I have no desire to see you again, and that is my final word. Be wise enough to stop offending my family, or I shall be forced to take measures."

"'Measures' you say? I dare you to do it! What kind of 'measures' could you possibly take against me? I shall do whatever I want, whenever I want! You can neither silence me nor keep me away nor instruct me about what to say or to whom."

"This call has come to an end, Lady Stafford. I will ask Stevens to see you out."

"You may still have Stevens, but everything else has changed. You have become a cold-hearted, haughty, unpleasant man, whom nobody likes. You are only tolerated because of your connections and wealth—a horrible man who compromises silly country girls in the woods—is that how you amuse yourself now? Is that what satisfies your pride—young, innocent girls? Are you at least aware that you have made a fool of yourself, pursuing a country nobody who favours the son of your father's steward over you?" Her eyes were arrows of fire, her lips narrowed in a grimace, and her voice louder with each word.

Darcy stared at her in silence and shock, his jaw clenched in anger. He felt the blood leaving his face and found it difficult to breathe without losing his temper completely.

"Lady Stafford—you shall leave now," he said with restrained severity. He took her arm and carefully but decidedly led her from the library. Stevens glanced at them but stepped forward while Darcy accompanied her to the carriage. Her face's beautiful features were distorted by fury, and when he tried to close the door, she grabbed his hand.

"Please forgive me. I did not mean to offend you. Please do not be upset. Will you come and speak to me tomorrow? I shall wait for you all day. Will you come?"

"Good night, Lady Stafford," he said sternly, and the carriage rapidly departed.

Darcy stood several minutes in front of the house, oblivious to the freezing, sharp wind. His head reeled painfully, seeming to suppress his reason and his sanity. What had just happened? *That idiot James told Annabelle about Elizabeth? And how is it he knows so many details? Is Wickham also in Town?* What could he do to stop the danger that seemed to grow so carelessly and jeopardise Elizabeth?

How had things come to such a horrid outcome? Did he truly save Elizabeth's life only to ruin her happiness forever as Robert said?

He recollected the discussion with his uncle and the tormenting events that led to it, starting eight years before.

Yes, his uncle had reason for concern. His short conversation with Annabelle was proof of that. She was unreasonable and seemed determined—in a ridiculous, stubborn manner—to have him back. She had never been prudent in her behaviour, and it looked as though time had brought little improvement. He must have another discussion with her. Things could not remain as they were, especially as she seemed to direct her anger towards the person least involved and most innocent in the matter—Elizabeth. He could not allow Annabelle to draw their family—or Elizabeth's—into a scandal.

His thoughts were still ensnared by recollections of Elizabeth's eyes, her smile, her laughter, her teasing, her wet lips twisted in mischievous smiles, her complexion… Her love of books, her enjoyment of outdoor walking, and her elegance in dancing were just as Georgiana said earlier. Yes, he was certain that Georgiana would have liked Elizabeth very much if he had chosen her—but he had not!

He felt guilty for lying to his uncle when he asked whether he had any preference for a wife. He did have a preference. He was certain that Elizabeth would have been the perfect wife for him. But he had not lied when he said that he did not consider her as a choice.

He only imagined what the earl would say if he introduced Mrs. Bennet to him—or the youngest Bennet sisters. He laughed bitterly as he decided finally to return to the house. Yes, she would have been the perfect wife for him, and he would never need to "do what he pleased" outside his marriage. He knew that she was what he had wished and waited for all those years, but he could not possibly choose her. He would likely never see her again. Maybe the earl was right after all: Anne would be as good a wife as anyone else.

If he could only protect Elizabeth from the dangerous gossip that seemed to be spread about maliciously. He must think of something to stop what he had started.

Longbourn, 16 December

At Longbourn, life had returned to its usual routine. Elizabeth's recovery was complete and her accident soon forgotten as other unfortunate events captured the family's interest.

Mr. Collins left Hertfordshire, and he shortly sent Mr. Bennet a letter of thanks, written with solemnity and gratitude. He informed them, with many rapturous expressions, that Lady Catherine heartily approved his marriage to Miss Lucas and wished it to take place as soon as possible, which he trusted would be an unanswerable argument with his amiable Charlotte to name an early date for making him the happiest of men.

On receiving the letter and sharing it with the family, Mr. Bennet was the only one amused. The ladies of Longbourn had more important reasons to be preoccupied.

Jane had sent Caroline an early answer to her letter, and she was counting the days till she might reasonably hope to hear from her again. When Miss Bingley's letter arrived, it put an end to all doubt. The first sentence conveyed the assurance of their all being settled in London for the winter and concluded with her brother's regret at not having had time to pay his respects to his friends in Hertfordshire before he left the country. Praise of Miss Darcy occupied the chief of the letter. Her many attractions were again dwelt on, and Caroline boasted joyfully of their increasing intimacy and ventured to predict the accomplishment of the wishes disclosed in her former letter. She wrote also with great pleasure of her brother's being an inmate of Mr. Darcy's house and mentioned with raptures some plans of the latter with regard to new furniture.

Elizabeth, to whom Jane soon communicated most of this, heard it in silent indignation. Her heart was divided between concern for her sister, resentment against all the others, and complete astonishment at this news that contradicted her previous assumptions.

She had been certain that Mr. Darcy's generous treatment of her and their family was entirely due to the prospect of a future alliance between Mr. Bingley and Jane. However, only a fortnight later, it seemed that neither Mr. Bingley nor Mr. Darcy had any intention of returning to Hertfordshire.

Elizabeth was certain of his sisters' participation in this change of Mr. Bingley's plans. But how was Mr. Darcy involved? It was a subject on which reflection would be long indulged, but for the moment, she could think of little else except Jane's wounded peace.

Mrs. Bennet's deep and endless irritation about Netherfield and its master, which started the moment Jane shared the news with the family, made the situation worse and increased Jane's sadness. She confessed it to Elizabeth in a moment of solitude.

"Oh, my dear mother has no idea of the pain she gives me by her continual reflections on him. But it cannot last long. He will be forgotten, and we shall all be as we were before. He may live in my memory as the most amiable man of my acquaintance, but that is all. I have this comfort at least: that it has not been more than an error of fancy on my side, nor has it done harm to anyone but me. I shall certainly try to improve my spirits."

"My dear Jane, you are too good. Your sweetness and disinterestedness are really angelic. I do not know what to say to you. I feel as if I had never done you justice or loved you as you deserve. And I feel that I had bestowed my appreciation on a man who does not deserve you and has proven unworthy of our admiration."

"Dear Lizzy, do not pain me by thinking Mr. Bingley is to blame and saying your opinion of him is sunk. We must not be so ready to fancy ourselves intentionally injured. We must not expect a lively young man to be always so guarded and circumspect. It is very often nothing but our own vanity that deceives us.

Women fancy admiration means more than it does."

"You cannot stop me from judging him, because your happiness is more precious to me than my own. A man should not allow himself to be so easily persuaded against his heart."

"You persist, then, in supposing his sisters influence him. But why should they try to influence him? They can only wish his happiness, and if he is attached to me, no other woman can secure it."

"Your position is false. They may wish many things besides his happiness. They may wish his increase of wealth and consequence. They may wish him to marry into a family that will bring more advantages to them than to him. I do not doubt Miss Darcy's merits, but I am certain they cannot be better than yours. She cannot be better than you in any way."

"Beyond a doubt, they do wish him to choose Miss Darcy," replied Jane, "but this may be from better feelings than you are supposing, and she may well be better than I am in many ways. They have known her much longer than they have known me. No wonder if they love her better. Lizzy, please let us not speak of this any further. My present pain is nothing in comparison of what I should feel in thinking ill of him or his sisters. Let me take it in the best light—in the light in which it may be understood."

Elizabeth could not oppose such a wish, as she could not bear to see her sister's suffering increased by her words, and from that time, Mr. Bingley's name was scarcely ever mentioned between them.

"Lizzy," Mr. Bennet said he one day, "your sister is crossed in love I find. I congratulate her. Next to being married, a girl likes to be crossed in love a little now and then. When is your turn to come? Here are officers enough at Meryton to disappoint all the young ladies in the country. Let Wickham be your man. He is a pleasant looking fellow, and he possesses such a great talent of sharing tragic stories from his past and blaming the whole world for his misfortune. He should jilt you creditably."

"Thank you, sir, but a less agreeable man would satisfy me. And I believe we should not be so eager to make fun of Mr. Wickham's past misfortunes, Papa."

"Perhaps not, my dear, but then he should be less eager to narrate them to anyone who is willing to listen," said Mr. Bennet.

Elizabeth could not deny that her father's opinion of Mr. Wickham was possibly correct. They saw him often, and to his usual amiable manners was now added a general unreserve. His claims on Mr. Darcy and all that he had suffered from him were openly acknowledged and publicly canvassed. Everybody was pleased to think how much they had always disliked Mr. Darcy before they had known anything of the matter.

Everyone seemed to forget Mr. Darcy's involvement in saving Elizabeth and the help he offered by sending his doctor—except Mr. Bennet, Jane, and Elizabeth herself. Hearing Mr. Wickham's assertions made Elizabeth uneasy. She remembered that Mr. Wickham declared he would *never* say a word against Mr. Darcy in public. How quickly that changed once Mr. Darcy left Hertfordshire!

She did not blame or disbelieve Mr. Wickham, but she could not remain insensible to the evidence of Mr. Darcy's kindness and generosity, which proved his good nature.

From time to time, it crossed Elizabeth's mind that Mr. Darcy himself could have had an influence on Mr. Bingley's decision to stay in London for the winter. If there was indeed a connection between Mr. Bingley and Miss Darcy, it was only natural—though deeply unfair—that he do everything in his power to separate Mr. Bingley from Jane. Such ungenerous interference—if real—did not speak highly of Mr. Darcy's character, but Elizabeth did not hesitate to split the burden of guilt between him and Mr. Bingley himself. What kind of man allows himself to be convinced by his friend against his own feelings?

Four days before Christmas, the entire house was preparing for receiving Mrs. Bennet's brother and his wife at Longbourn. Mr. Gardiner was a sensible, gentlemanlike man, greatly superior to his sister by nature as well as education. The Netherfield ladies would have had difficulty in believing that a man who lived by trade within view of his own warehouses could have been so well bred and agreeable. Mrs. Gardiner was an amiable, intelligent, elegant woman and a great favourite with all her Longbourn nieces. Between the two eldest and herself especially, there subsisted a very particular regard, and both Jane and Elizabeth were eagerly awaiting their dearest aunt's visit.

Mr. Wickham and Mr. Denny called on Longbourn that day, and the former was received with joy by the ladies as he had been away for several days. Mr. Wickham cheerfully related that he had been in London, visiting some old friends, and he amused the ladies with lovely details about the Season in Town. Mr. Bennet did not leave his library.

London, 18 December

LADY AND LORD MATLOCK WERE ENJOYING REFRESHMENTS AND CONVERSATION when they received their daughter-in-law's unexpected visit, her manners far from her usual calm.

"Mother, I had a terrible morning! I met *that* woman at Madame Claudette's, and it was the most horrible meeting I have ever had! I could hardly bear the shame while Louise finished my measurements. I must find another modiste. I cannot risk meeting that woman again."

"Woman? Of whom are you talking, Maryanne?"

"Of that Lady Stafford! Darcy's old acquaintance! I did not know her, but we met three days ago at the theatre when we went with Darcy and Georgiana. I had no idea who she was—Thomas told me afterwards—as I was shocked by her manners even then. She was with James and a few others in her box, and during the interval she approached Darcy, right in front of Georgiana. He put an end to the conversation immediately, but even when the play started, she kept looking towards us and speaking quite loudly with her companions. And this morning, while I was trying on my new ball gowns, she just entered and inquired after Darcy! She suggested that… She mentioned that she hoped Darcy was well, as when she last saw him at his house, he seemed pale and tired!"

The ladies stared at each other, their faces changing from flushed to pale, while the earl was stunned into silence. With great difficulty, the ladies continued the conversation in a calmer manner. An hour later Lady Maryanne left, and the Matlocks discussed the matter themselves.

"The situation is growing worse with every day that passes, and there are rumours around Town that cannot be stopped. I believe you should talk to Darcy again, husband. He might be upset, but he will understand our concern eventually."

"But what should I say to him? Surely, I cannot ask him if he met that woman again!"

"No indeed, but you can warn him about the increasing rumours and their influence on our family—especially Georgiana. You know that nothing is more important to Darcy."

"What truly astonishes me is this woman's behaviour. If she is determined to have Darcy, how can she imagine that she might convince him by offending his family? She should know that such actions only push him away. Women in her situation are usually more discreet. She is either impertinent or desperate. In either case, she should be treated with caution."

"Women in her situation are often not in the possession of such name and fortune. And yes, she should be treated with great caution, husband. Darcy should know how to do that."

"Darcy has not been himself since he returned to Town. Have you noticed? That worries me too. He has spent little time either with us or with Georgiana, as if he tries to avoid us. Something has happened to him, and I am afraid to discover what. I am afraid this woman may continue to pursue him and catch him in a moment of weakness. Just imagine what would happen if she were to carry his child. I do not believe she will rest until Darcy either leaves Town or marries or something—and maybe not even then…"

"I noticed the same, husband. I feel sorry for him. He has had so much on his mind and now that… And that tale about the girl in Hertfordshire… Did you hear about that?"

"No, let us hope that at least that has come and gone. Darcy seemed to be very worried that the rumours started by James and Wickham might affect that young lady's reputation. You know, I spoke to Dr. Taylor… His report about that Miss Elizabeth Bennet was quite impressive. He found her to be a courageous, spirited, bright young woman. And he was also impressed by the eldest Miss Bennet—who seemed to be a true beauty."

"Yes, you told me, husband. You also told me that you investigated the girl's relatives in Town—Mr. Gardiner, I believe? I wondered why you did that."

"When I heard all those rumours, and I found that Darcy sent Dr. Taylor from London to Longbourn, I felt that there must be more behind it. The references about Mr. Gardiner and his wife were exceedingly good. He is a well-respected tradesman and quite wealthy. But Darcy has not said anything more since then, so I believe I worried for no reason."

Moments of silence followed. Lord Matlock filled a glass with brandy while his wife enjoyed a cup of tea. Finally, he spoke hesitantly, glancing at his wife.

"You know, you may disagree with me, but…I almost regret that the stories about Miss Elizabeth Bennet were not more malicious. Darcy will surely never marry Anne, but he might do his duty towards a beautiful, spirited, bright young woman he admires—though she is the daughter of a country gentleman—who had been compromised by the gossip arising from his own behaviour…What better protection could there be against the mischievous schemes of a woman like Lady Stafford, who uses her charms to deceive men, than the presence of a beautiful wife with strength and dignity, who will likely require little time to give him a child? And what better way for our family to regain peace and comfort? That Miss Elizabeth might have been the best weapon to put an end to this war."

"Lord Matlock, what are you saying? You cannot use a young girl to protect our comfort! And surely you cannot have Darcy marry a woman who is so far beneath him when he could easily have any young heiress in Town! The situation with this Annabelle woman has come, and it will go. We cannot change our lives because of it! I truly believe you should have no more brandy, husband!"

DARCY PUT ASIDE HIS PAPER AND GLANCED TOWARDS THE WINDOW. IT WAS SNOWing gently. Bingley had left the previous day to visit his friend Mr. Bertram and spend the Christmas with him and Darcy hoped he had arrived at his destination safely.

HE REMAINED LOCKED IN HIS LIBRARY, AS EARLIER THAT DAY MISS BINGLEY AND Mrs. Hurst called on Georgiana, and he had no inclination to meet them. To his sister he had barely spoken since they met Annabelle at the theatre three days earlier. Darcy could not remember another time when he had been so embarrassed: Annabelle impertinently flirted with him in front of his sister and his cousins. The memories of the times when he had been smitten by Annabelle's beauty and charms were not enough to temper his anger and disgust at the changes in her behaviour and character. It could also be true that she had always been so, but he lacked the wisdom to see it, and she lacked sufficient money to display it.

Darcy startled when the door opened and his cousin Robert appeared in the doorway.

"In my regiment, the officers speak of you and Miss Elizabeth Bennet," the colonel said angrily. "In a very nasty manner! There are rumours accusing you of merely pretending to be an honourable man all these years—that you are dividing your attention between Miss Bennet and Lady Stafford. And that in the end you will marry Anne de Bourgh. Now, can you imagine who would say such things?"

"Robert, how is it you spoke of such matters with your officers?" Darcy asked sternly. He found it hard to breathe, so he opened the window.

"I was told because, fortunately, I have the respect of my men. So you have to choose whom you want to kill—James or Wickham? I will take the one left."

"Be serious, Robert. Thank you for your concern, but you do not have to kill anyone for me. I beg you to not repeat this to anyone, including your parents. I must find a way to put an end to these rumours immediately."

"Very well, but—"

"Please do not be upset, but I must ask you to leave now, Robert. I need to think."

The colonel attempted to say more, but he found himself unable to reply properly. From the door, he turned to Darcy once more, but he was staring out the window, his shoulders straight, his arms crossed, oblivious to his presence. The colonel closed the door slowly.

21 December

Lord and Lady Matlock, together with the colonel, were having a peaceful dinner when the servant announced their nephew Darcy. Their surprise quickly turned to worry, which increased when he refused to sit.

He briefly paced the room then said coldly, "I considered it my duty to inform you of my intentions, as you have been as close to me as my own parents. Tomorrow at dawn, I travel to Hertfordshire to ask for Miss Elizabeth Bennet's hand in marriage. I imagine you will be angry and will oppose my decision, but nothing can change my mind. I know that, for you, the prospect of connection with a family so beneath our own is a great shock, and I expect you to put distance between us. I only hope that, in time, you will be able to forgive me and allow my future wife to be part of the family."

Silence followed, all three Fitzwilliams unable to speak. Darcy bowed briefly and turned to the door, but the earl rose from his chair and held his arm.

"Darcy, please, take a seat, son, and let us speak calmly. Nobody will distance themselves from you, and we are surely not angry with you. But we *are* deeply shocked."

"But what happened?" Lady Matlock inquired. "I believed the gossiping had ended and—"

"It has not ended," the colonel said. "Not at all…"

"Aunt, believe me that I have thought of little else for the last two weeks. At first, the mere idea of this resolution was impossible for me to consider. But the more I think of it, the more I am convinced that it is best for everyone—though I imagine it is hard for you to admit it at the moment."

"It is surely the best solution for Miss Elizabeth and for her family. But how will it be for you? And for Georgiana? Being Mrs. Darcy will not be an easy task for a country girl," said Lady Matlock, and Darcy tried to reply, though he felt bewildered by his relatives' attitudes. Was it possible that they were accepting of the entire situation?

"Miss Bennet is an exceptionally smart young woman. I have no doubt that everything she does not know, she will learn quickly. She is also a kind and generous person. I feel confident that she will be an affectionate sister for Georgiana."

"What about you? How will this marriage be for you, Darcy? Are you certain about it?"

"It will be as good as can be expected under these circumstances. And yes, I am certain."

"So you seem to have made up your mind. Have you announced your arrival to the Bennets? Are they expecting you?"

"No, I only decided this afternoon myself. I plan to speak to Mr. Bennet when I arrive there. I have great hopes that he will approve my resolution to this difficult situation and that he will help me have a private meeting with Miss Elizabeth to present my proposal to her."

"It seems you have thought of everything. Please bring us news as soon as possible."

"I will leave at dawn, and I plan to return the day after tomorrow. I will call on you then."

"Do you want me to come with you?" the colonel asked. "I can be spared from the regiment for a couple of days if you believe my presence may be helpful."

"Thank you, I appreciate your offer, Robert. Your presence at Longbourn might be very useful indeed. I want to keep the matter private from Mrs. Bennet and the other daughters until Miss Elizabeth decides. And that will not be an easy task, as you will discover."

"Very well, come and collect me at dawn," the colonel said.

The sun had not yet risen, and Darcy and the colonel had been on the road for hours.

After sleepless weeks, once he made the final decision, Darcy felt an enormous relief. He would do it: he would propose to her, and she would be his wife. It had been so ridiculous to fight against the obvious and against fate, as there could be no one better for him.

Mile after mile and hour after hour, his heart became lighter, and his concern turned into joy. He wondered what she would say when he proposed. Surely, she could not expect such a thing. Marrying him was certainly never considered by her or her family. *Nor my family nor me*, he laughed to himself. He remembered her smiling at him, teasing him, glancing at him. Now all those things would happen in the solitude of his home—of *their* home.

They finally reached Meryton and stopped at the inn. He asked for the best rooms, food, and drink, and for a servant to be sent to Longbourn immediately.

He was less than two miles away from her.

Longbourn, 22 December 1811

At Longbourn, two days before Christmas Eve, there was constant commotion. In addition, the Gardiners were expected late in the afternoon. Around eleven o'clock, Mr. Bennet left the library to give the ladies some most unexpected news.

"I just received a note from Mr. Darcy. He has some business in the neighbourhood, and he wishes to call on us. He is staying at the Meryton Inn for the night. He is travelling with his cousin Colonel Fitzwilliam, Lord Matlock's younger son. I will send John to tell Mr. Darcy that we will be honoured by his visit."

Jane turned pale in a moment, and Elizabeth felt her cheeks colouring for no reason. Mrs. Bennet stared at her husband in shock for a long moment then finally burst out.

"Mr. Darcy? And the son of an earl—in my house? And he is a colonel? Oh Lord, what is happening? Jane, Lizzy, Hill! What time will they arrive? Mr. Bennet! You cannot bring such news and then leave! Oh, just imagine what Lady Lucas will say. Charlotte marrying Mr. Collins is nothing to this! Oh, they are staying at the inn? Girl, go and change your clothes. you look nothing like you should in the presence of an earl's son!"

The din became insupportable, and Elizabeth and Jane moved to a corner of the room. Mr. Darcy's visit three days before Christmas was the most shocking event. Surely, it must be related in some way to Mr. Bingley. Otherwise, why would he stop at the inn and come to visit them? Was it possible that he was announcing the wedding of his sister to his friend? Such news would certainly be intolerable for poor Jane. But why would he come to inform them personally? Something was strange and certainly not in a good way.

An hour past noon, the guests arrived. The gentlemen were received in the drawing room, and Mr. Darcy performed the introductions.

More shocking than the visit was the revelation that the colonel was completely opposite in temper and manners from his cousin. Colonel Fitzwilliam's voluble amiability conquered the ladies in moments.

Mr. Darcy behaved as his usual self. He took a seat in a corner, close to Mr. Bennet, and intruded rarely in the conversation. Several times, Elizabeth met his glance and attempted to smile in a friendly manner, but his countenance remained serious.

"So, Mr. Darcy, is Mr. Bingley in good health? He will not return to Netherfield soon, I understand," Mrs. Bennet inquired bluntly, and Elizabeth saw Jane turn as pale as the wall.

"Yes, he is in good health," Mr. Darcy replied. "Unfortunately, we have not seen him much lately as we both have been very busy. I am not certain of any of his future plans—"

"Oh well, he may do as he likes. Please tell him that the entire neighbourhood awaits his return soon—maybe for the summer?"

"I will tell him as soon as I see him, ma'am," Mr. Darcy said.

Elizabeth was relieved: once again, Miss Bingley's words were nothing but mischievous deceptions. Mr. Bingley seemed not to have been *engaged* with Mr. Darcy and his sister at all. And had he been in a sort of understanding with Miss Darcy, he would surely not leave to spend Christmas with other friends. Jane's face turned from pale to crimson, and for the next minutes, she suddenly became more animated and involved in the conversation.

Mr. Bennet declared that he and Mr. Darcy would retire to the library as they had some business to discuss. Their departure brought little discomfort to the ladies as neither gentleman participated much in the conversation. Elizabeth was the only one who wondered about the nature of her father's private business with Mr. Darcy, but she found no satisfactory answer. Her curiosity turned to astonishment when Hill returned some minutes later and whispered in great secrecy that her father was waiting for her in the library. Glancing around with puzzlement, she met the colonel's look for an instant. Then he averted his eyes. She had no time to wonder further, so she silently rose from her seat and left the room while the others remained captivated by the colonel's entertaining tales.

Chapter 5

Once in the library, Elizabeth was invited by her father to sit. Darcy was standing in front of the window, watching her with an impenetrable look.

"Lizzy, I asked you to come here because there is a matter of a great importance that we need to discuss with you. In fact, it is the matter that brought Mr. Darcy here today."

"What is it, Papa? Is someone ill? You look so grave. You give me a fright." She attempted a joke, but her father did not return her smile.

"Mr. Darcy will tell you everything, my child. No, nobody is ill, but it is quite grave, I might say. Lizzy, I will be next door in my study, as I want you to speak to Mr. Darcy alone. Please listen to him with patience and composure. I so understand and agree with Mr. Darcy's point of view, but your decision is all that matters. I shall never force you against your will."

"Papa, now you truly frighten me. Force me to do what? Please, tell me what is happening."

"In a moment, dearest," Mr. Bennet said and kissed his daughter's forehead before leaving. Elizabeth looked after him in disbelief. She had never seen her father in such a state before.

She turned towards Darcy, hoping to see something in his face but with little success. Suddenly, she knew what to say first to break the tension.

"Mr. Darcy, I am at a loss to understand my father's words, and I confess the reason of your visit is a little frightening. But I am happy to see you nevertheless, sir, as I have long been desirous to thank you for your generous involvement in saving my life. My gratitude—"

"Miss Bennet, please do not speak of gratitude. I am afraid you will not think so highly of my intervention once I tell you the reason for my present visit. This unfortunately is due to a situation that might rather be called unpleasant at the very least."

"I am very sorry to hear that, sir, though I doubt anything might change my opinion in this matter. What has happened, sir? Is it about Mr. Bingley? Has anything happened to him?"

"Mr. Bingley? No, no...he is reasonably well. He is spending the month with some friends in the country as I already told Mrs. Bennet."

"Oh, yes, you did mention that, and it is quite surprising. Miss Bingley informed my sister that Mr. Bingley— Forgive me sir, I distracted myself. You were speaking of an unpleasant situation… Is your family in good health? Miss Darcy…?"

"Georgiana is very well, thank you. She is in Town, spending most of her time with her companion and with Lady Matlock, our aunt. She enjoys Christmastime very much."

Elizabeth looked at him with a smile as she briefly considered how easily Miss Bingley's mischievous lies had been exposed. Mr. Darcy seemed worried and embarrassed, and Elizabeth wondered at the reason for this extraordinary visit that troubled her father so. In what possible way might she help him alleviate an *unpleasant situation*? He spoke further.

"I cannot apologise enough for my lack of wisdom, which is wholly responsible for these unfortunate developments. Had I been able to anticipate the associated risks—with what at the time appeared to be a simple situation to be taken care of immediately—I would not have been so hasty in making a reckless decision. I can only apologise, and I hope that…"

"Forgive me for interrupting you, but you seem to be apologising to me, and for the life of me, I cannot understand why. You must allow me to thank you for your kindness and generosity for not only bringing me home but also sending Dr. Taylor all the way from London. I truly believe that, without your intervention, I might have been in great danger."

"Dr. Taylor is an excellent physician, and I am glad his presence helped you, but please do not make yourself uneasy. He is a doctor, so that is what he should do."

"Only if you asked him to," she said, smiling with genuine gratitude. "You cannot deny that you have done it, nor can you stop me from thanking you."

"No, I cannot deny it, and I this was an even greater mistake, but at the time I believed that your safety was more important than other considerations."

Elizabeth paled. "What do you mean *a mistake*, sir?"

"I am ashamed that I have to relate such things, but I have been informed of some malicious rumours caused by your accident and by Dr. Taylor's presence at Longbourn. Reports of a disturbing nature, which have already reached Town, seem likely to soon harm our reputations, and our peace. I was shocked when I heard of it. I do not recall our family ever having been subject to such rumours before."

She paled, and her hands shook as cold shivers travelled along her spine and embarrassment combined with shame drained the blood from her face.

"Mr. Darcy, I… I never heard anything about such rumours. How is that possible?"

A moment later, she was silenced by a horrible realization. "Sir, I have no words to apologise. I know my younger sisters are not the image of discretion or decorum, nor are my mother and my Aunt Philips. But I am certain they never meant anything harmful. Please allow me to speak to my father and see what can be done. I am deeply ashamed and pained that your generosity brought distress to your family, and I feel guilty that your kindness harmed your reputation and your tranquillity rather than being rewarded by general acknowledgement."

"I do not believe your family is to blame for the rumours—at least not for those I heard. The tale was started and spread by someone familiar with your family but also with connections and some influence in London. And it is not just the reputation and peace of my family that I worry about, but also of yours."

"Oh..." she whispered. They looked at each other for several moments. His countenance was stern, and she felt her cheeks burning. "Do not fear for my family. We are rarely in Town, and even when we are, so few people know us that our reputation cannot be affected. As for here in Meryton, everyone knows the truth. But do you have anyone in mind, sir? I cannot imagine that someone who was a familiar presence in Hertfordshire and also in London would want to harm *your* reputation," she said with Miss Bingley's image clearly in mind. *Who else could it have been?*

"I do have someone in mind, but it is difficult to put the blame on someone without clear proofs. Besides, the harm is already done, and I see only one way to repair the damage I created. I have spoken to Mr. Bennet, and he agreed with me, but he warned me that he has no intention of forcing your will in any way."

She looked puzzled. "Yes, he just said that. Forcing my will, sir? In what way?"

"Miss Bennet, I am certain this is not the way you imagined such a situation to occur, and please believe me that it is an equally great shock to me that I am doing this, but I have given it much consideration. I see no other way of solving the problem, and I cannot allow it to persist. I cannot expose my sister and myself to the gossip of the town. And of course, I cannot allow it to affect your reputation and your future, considering that you have done nothing wrong. We must find a way to protect our families through an arrangement that, in the end, might turn out to be to the advantage of both. Miss Bennet, would you do me the honour of marrying me—of becoming my wife?"

She stared at him in complete shock, seeking some sign of amusement, while she stopped breathing and her heart skipped several beats. Surely, he was joking.

"Marry you, sir? Do you not believe that would be too much punishment for Miss Bingley if she is the source of these rumours? She might die from the shock!" She laughed, but his countenance became sterner, and the colour left his face.

"Forgive me, Miss Bennet, but I fail to understand your amusement in this situation..."

"I am deeply sorry, sir, but I could not imagine that you truly intend to marry me because of a few rumours. Surely, you must see that such a thing would harm both of us much more than some idle reports and affect our futures in even more dramatic ways."

"And may I ask in what way becoming my wife would harm you? How would a marriage with me affect your family more dramatically than the prospect of having your reputations ruined? Is your opinion of me so poor that you can see nothing worse than marrying me?"

He spoke in haste, watching her with obvious disbelief, which proved that he had not expected her answer. She could not remember exactly what she had just said, but she was certain that her answer was the only reasonable one.

What is he thinking? So he heard some rumours that affected his family and decided that the only way of putting an end to them was to marry me, to protect his pride and his good name. What kind of rumour might it be to induce him to endure all of my and my family's faults and marry me? What on earth can be behind all this? And what kind of marriage does he imagine it will lead to? But does that really matter, after all?

She breathed deeply and took time to reply. There was Mr. Darcy, proposing to her, waiting for her answer. Here was the opportunity to marry a man who would be able to support her family in times of need, the opportunity to join one of the most illustrious families in the country, the opportunity to place Jane in Mr. Bingley's path again in the future and save her sister from the danger of accepting a marriage proposal from a man who would make her unhappy, just to save their family. And all these good things just by accepting that she enter into the most astonishing arrangement ever. This man was the opposite of Mr. Collins: well educated, well read, and as handsome as he was smart—yet, a man who never said a kind word to her while he was at Netherfield, always looked at her to find fault, obviously disapproved of her family, most likely had had some influence in taking Mr. Bingley from Jane, and did not hesitate to put his own will above his father's in rejecting the living for Mr. Wickham. A man worth ten thousand a year—who had saved her life.

Slowly, she raised her eyes and started to speak, clasping her hands in her lap.

"Forgive me, sir. That is not what I meant. I am just saying that things could not possibly be so bad that they compel you to make such a gesture. I thank you for your honourable proposal. I know it was not easy, and I appreciate that you are thinking of me and my reputation in addition to your own. But I am sure everything will soon be forgotten."

"Am I correct in assuming that you reject my proposal, Miss Bennet? That you do not wish to marry me? To be honest, I am quite shocked. I was certain that you would appreciate the fairness of my gesture. I had no idea that you think so ill of me that you would jeopardise your family and your future rather than marry me."

"Mr. Darcy, I beg you, please, let us sit and discuss this reasonably. Please."

He looked at her intensely then sat. Then he rose, paced the room, and sat again.

"Sir, I would be lying if I said that I do not see the advantage of such a marriage for me. And my opinion of you is not ill, sir. In fact, I am not oblivious to your qualities. I admire your knowledge, your strength, your education, the brightness of your mind. Any woman would be happy to marry you, I believe."

"And yet…? I sense there is a 'but' following here," he said sharply. "Forgive me for being so blunt, but I will not deny that I am disappointed by your response."

"There is a 'but,' sir. Surely, you remember that we were not even friends when you were in Hertfordshire. You always had something to reproach me for—and likely you had good reasons, I admit. You cannot deny that you disapprove of my family's behaviour and never attempt to conceal it. You hardly spoke a word to my father before my accident. And you disapproved of and discouraged Mr. Bingley's attachment to Jane. I will honestly confess that I was astonished by your kindness when you found me in the wood. It is not that I believed you to lack compassion, but I would have expected you to send a servant to take me home than to do it yourself, and it was even more surprising that you thought of my health enough to send Dr. Taylor. I will always be grateful to you, but I cannot possibly marry you only because of some gossip."

She added, her eyes holding his: "Had I less respect for you, sir, I would accept your proposal without a thought. We both know that such a marriage would be a gift for my family. But I cannot allow you to marry a woman you dislike merely for the maintenance of your reputation. How can you even consider that? It might have been any woman in my place that day. It was *not* your choice whom to help then, but it *is* your choice whether to marry someone who happened to be in your path. Gossiping tongues will soon stop wagging, but the marriage would remain, along with my family and your poor opinion of them. You will come to regret your decision and to hate and despise my family and me even more, and both our lives will be ruined. I cannot do that to you precisely because I *do* respect you—nor can I do it to myself. I believe I am entitled at least to a marriage of affection, respect, and mutual understanding."

The emotions and tension made her eyes tearful. Her hands trembled, and she entwined her fingers together tightly. She felt his eyes staring at her, and then he suddenly whispered:

"Miss Bennet, please have a glass of water. Forgive me for being so harsh. It was not my intention to hurt you further." She took the glass from his hands and drank greedily from it while he continued in a warm but determined voice, his countenance lighter.

"I understand your surprise, and now that I am thinking more clearly, I understand your reasoning. You are indeed fair, and your words prove your character. Will you… May I continue to speak more on this subject?"

"Please do, sir," she said, but he needed a few long moments to find the words.

"Thank you. To be honest, I do not even know how to better word my reasoning…how to express my thoughts so you will better understand me…"

"Mr. Darcy, since we find ourselves in this awkward situation for which neither of us is guilty, dare I suggest that complete honesty would be the best way to reach a solution? Rather than searching for proper words, sir, just speak openly."

"Very well…" He took a seat in her relative proximity so they could face each other.

"Before going any further, I must clarify some of your observations. It is true that, on occasions, I disapproved of some of the behaviours displayed by your younger sisters, and that I put little effort into speaking with your parents. If my attitude was offensive, I apologise. Whatever my feelings might be, it is surely not for me to be the judge of others' manners. However, I never saw anything at fault in your and Miss Bennet's behaviour, and I believe no one could find anything to blame in either of you. It is not the time to speak of my approval or disapproval of Bingley's affection towards Miss Bennet. I did form an opinion based on my own observation, and I confess I did share it with Bingley, but I trust he has the wisdom and strength to make his own decisions eventually."

He averted his eyes a moment then continued.

"As for you and me not being friends, I am astonished that you consider that to be so, but I take the blame entirely, and please be certain that my reasons had nothing to do with you as a person. Since we are speaking honestly, I cannot deny that I have, for some time, admired your love of books, your wit, and your brightness of mind, and I found great pleasure in talking to you whenever I had a chance, which I know was not often."

He stopped, gazing at her, while she listened in disbelief.

"Having been in each other's company rather often, I considered you a close acquaintance, despite my outward manner, and so did not hesitate to make sure you arrived home safely when we met in the wood. Afterwards, I sent Dr. Taylor, as I feared that your life might be in danger without proper care. And that is where I might have been wrong. I should have, perhaps, written Mr. Bennet and asked him to keep secret the connection between Dr. Taylor and me. That way, most of the rumours might have been avoided."

"You have done everything with genuine care, and only someone with a horrible lack of honour might blame you. I most certain do not, nor my family."

"I thank you. You said that I would have done the same thing for any woman I found in such a precarious situation, but I must contradict you. I probably would have lent her my coat to protect her from cold and fetched someone, but no more. And you may be certain, Miss Bennet, that I would never make an offer of marriage to a woman whom I did not consider worthy to be part of my family—as my wife and as Georgiana's sister. I might sound proud and arrogant, but I do know what is required to be Mrs. Darcy, and I would not risk having someone unworthy occupy that place, despite her unfortunate situation."

She smiled. "I may speculate that there are several women who would like that place very much and likely would perform better than I."

He did not smile back. "Likely there are others who would *wish* that place but allow me to doubt they would perform better than you."

"I thank you for your generous praise, and I appreciate your effort. But may I dare ask, sir, what you have to gain from such an arrangement, assuming we reach an agreement?"

"I must have your word, your commitment that you will be the Mrs. Darcy that my family and everyone in my care deserve—which is difficult and will require much work. You will first have to bear me, which will not be an easy task. Even more, I will not deny that, in order to be absolutely certain, should we come to an agreement, I have a few conditions—most reasonable I may say—that I want from you as the future Mrs. Darcy."

"I understand that. Mr. Darcy, you said that you would not have made this marriage offer to just anyone, despite any situation that may have arisen—and I am flattered that you said you admired me—but I must ask you something else. Had this situation not occurred, would you ever have considered making me a marriage offer?"

He hesitated a moment, holding her gaze in silence. "I confess I would not have," he finally said, and she forced a smile.

"That is precisely my point, sir, and though I now understand your reasoning better, it also applies to me. In truth, had someone asked me, I would easily answer that you were the last man in the world whom I might consider marrying because I was certainly the last woman to whom you would propose."

"Perhaps…but I have not the smallest doubt that I could never hate you, Miss Bennet. Quite the contrary, I make you this offer with the hope that, in time, our marriage will became a reasonably good one and give neither of us cause to repent it. And, as I said, I believe it will be to the advantage of both of us and our families."

"Then you have more trust than I have. However, I shall not reject your words, sir, not after this conversation, which was truly helpful. I believe it has helped us to know each other better and surely helped me to sketch your character better. If we had more time, perhaps such decisions would be easier for us to make—the decision to marry, I mean. If we agree upon it, how soon should the wedding take place?"

"As soon as I can obtain a special license. Miss Bennet, I understand your restraint. In a normal situation, even in the case of an arranged marriage, a time of engagement would make it easier to become accustomed to each other. Sadly, this cannot be the case. This would be a marriage arranged in particular circumstances. The causes that generated this situation are of a difficult and hasty nature. Postponing things will not put an end to them.

"Is the gossip truly so malicious? Would you please tell me what is said? I cannot imagine. Really, I cannot," she dared say, her cheeks coloured with embarrassment.

"It is very malicious. It is said that we had been involved in a secret attachment and that we intentionally met in the wood…that we were seen in a compromising position…and that I left you and sent a doctor because the reasons for your illness were of a different nature…"

With each word, Elizabeth became increasingly pale from the pain gripping her chest. She felt herself trembling, and her eyes burned with tears, unable to hold his gaze.

"How could anyone say such things? And why, for what purpose? Does your family know about it? I will never be able to face them… Oh, dear Lord…"

"My aunt, uncle, and cousins do know—Georgiana does not—but you must not worry. They do not believe it in the slightest, as the colonel's presence proves."

"I cannot comprehend… Why would anyone spread such dreadful information? What can be the purpose of doing it? What would anyone have to gain?" she repeated as she fought back tears, her turmoil increasing.

"I do not believe it was intended in such a way. But someone spoke carelessly, other persons took the words and twisted them further, and so on. And the gossip prevailed because I have always been careful not to expose myself to any kind of compromising rumours. I believe that excites some people. You must see now why I feel guilty and why I insist on a marriage proposal. It is my responsibility. Since I did nothing to prevent the gossip, I must shelter you from its effects."

"But will a hasty marriage not confirm the gossip?"

"It may or may not. But marriage will certainly give them no other option than to accept it, and at least your family will be protected from harmful consequences."

"I must confess I am shocked and cannot think properly. However, I can see you are correct. And...may I ask—you said you have conditions and requirements and... Can you tell me what they are? I believe I must know them before I give you a definite answer."

"Do not worry. We can speak of the details tomorrow before we leave. There is no need to trouble you further today. There are still details of the arrangement that I need to establish with Mr. Bennet and that will be added by my lawyers to the final settlement. As for the requirements of you personally, they will not be difficult to accomplish. I asked Georgiana what qualities she would like to see in a woman who is to be my wife. And she said—I can quote quite precisely—'I would like her to be bright and to enjoy reading and spending time outdoors and to play the piano.' I believe that is a rather accurate portrait of yourself."

She released a nervous laugh. "Thank you, sir, you are very kind. Though I am afraid Miss Darcy will be vastly disappointed by my skill at the pianoforte."

"I dare contradict you, Miss Bennet. But, on a more serious note, there will be many things you will probably need to learn to fulfil your position, as I am certain you understand not only the advantages but also the responsibilities that come with marrying me. However, the most important is that I need your commitment that you wish this marriage to become genuine. I need a true family, a mistress of my estates, a sister for Georgiana, and a mother for my children. I need to know that, despite the unfortunate circumstances that forced this marriage, my wife and I will share respect and trust and confidence at the very least."

She daringly held his eyes while she spoke decidedly, her voice slightly trembling. "Mr. Darcy, rest assured that, if I decide to enter into this marriage, I will do it with good will and commitment. I too wish to have a true family, sir."

"I am glad to hear that. And now I have to ask—forgive my preposterous assumptions, but I must know—besides the objections you have raised, are there other impediments that might prevent your accepting my proposal, impediments of a more personal nature?"

He was uneasy in the asking, but she replied without hesitation. "No, there are not."

"Thank you for your honesty, Miss Bennet, and please allow me to put you at ease about a delicate matter. As I said, there is no time for a period of courtship or engagement in this situation, but I am not insensitive to your concerns. Even if we are to marry in a few days, I do not expect to…I mean…I agree that we will need time to become accustomed to each other, and I am willing to allow you all the time you need. The marriage will be made in haste, in fact, but will not be hastened in spirit, if you understand my meaning…"

"Thank you, sir," she said, blushing and averting her eyes. *Does he really mean what I imagine he does?*

"I believe we should speak to Mr. Bennet now. That is, if you are decided…Are you?"

"Yes, I believe we should," she whispered. "I am decided… I doubt there are many choices, considering the nature of the gossip and the other arguments… I think it is the only thing to do…" she whispered as she left to inform her father.

Elizabeth entered Mr. Bennet's small office, which was connected to the library, and met her father's eyes—and she finally ceased her fighting, allowing tears to run over her pale cheeks. Mr. Bennet embraced her, puzzled about what to do next. He had never seen his beloved daughter in such a state.

"Forgive me, Papa," she said with trembling voice. "All is well. Do not worry. Mr. Darcy and I agreed to marry as soon as he procures a special license. He said he will return tomorrow to establish all the details. Now I beg you and Mr. Darcy to excuse me. I shall retire to my room. Please tell the others that I have a terrible headache and need to sleep a little.

The gentlemen's visit at Longbourn lasted more than three hours, and Mrs. Bennet could not have been more thrilled. She insistently invited them to return for dinner, declaring that a meal at the inn was not what they deserved. But Darcy rejected the invitation with decided politeness, promising to call again the next day before their return to London. Mrs. Bennet dared not argue with Mr. Darcy. As soon as the gentlemen retired, Mr. Bennet returned to his library, and Jane hurried to see how Elizabeth was feeling. Only then, did Mrs. Bennet notice that her second daughter was absent and wonder how she could be so rude as to abandon such important guests as Mr. Darcy and Colonel Fitzwilliam.

Inside the carriage, the colonel declared he had been entertained and highly enchanted by the Miss Bennets—each charming in her own way

"So, how did it go? And why on earth did you refuse Mrs. Bennet's dinner invitation? Surely, the food and company would have been ten times better than at the inn!"

"You may go if you wish, but I must give Miss Elizabeth a little time to recover. I need time to recover myself. She rejected my proposal, Robert. Miss Elizabeth Bennet refused me, and I had to plead for her acceptance. Can you imagine that?"

Elizabeth spied the gentlemen's departure from her window, and while she followed them with her eyes, her mind still could not comprehend what had happened. Her eyes burned and her head was so painful that she needed to press her fingers against her temples, but with little relief. She lay on the bed and buried her head in the pillows.

Chapter 6

An hour later, the fact that Mr. Darcy had asked her to marry him seemed still a dream from which she had yet to awaken. Who could have spread such horrible falsehoods about her and Mr. Darcy, and to what purpose? She found no fault in Mr. Darcy's behaviour towards her. He seemed to be an honourable gentleman—of that, she had no doubt. But marry him?"

Alone in her room, Elizabeth's head ached while her anger grew towards Mr. Bingley and his sisters—and with everyone she felt to be guilty in the situation. Then she started to cry. She fell asleep and woke to the din of voices and slammed doors, a sign that the Gardiners had arrived. It was dark outside, as dark as the thoughts and meditations that continued to trouble her mind and extinguish the joy of seeing her relatives. A knock on the door and Mrs. Gardiner's appearance forced Elizabeth to leave her bed and embrace her aunt.

"Lizzy, my love, I hope you do not mind. My brother Bennet told me what happened. I know you want to keep it secret for the present, but the need of speaking to someone—"

"I do not mind, Aunt. In fact, I am relieved that you already know. I do need to speak to someone, but I did not feel strong enough to tell Jane. I am so happy you are here."

"As am I, dearest. Now—about this extraordinary situation that just occurred—I heard you spent quite some time talking to Mr. Darcy, so I imagine things did not go smoothly. You look sad and exhausted," Mrs. Gardiner said gently, caressing her niece's face.

"I was so astonished; I still am. It never crossed my mind that Mr. Darcy… I was shocked when he helped me to get back home and then sent me his doctor…and now he asks me to marry him in a few days. I still cannot believe this is happening."

"From what you wrote me, you and Mr. Darcy had never been friends. It must be hard to consider being married to a man you hardly know."

"I feel so helpless. My life has been decided outside my will because of some mischievous tales. Everybody in the neighbourhood knew that Mr. Darcy and I disliked each other. Who could possibly start such horrible rumours, implying that he and I… Oh, Aunt, if you knew the things they said… I begged Mr. Darcy to tell me, and then I felt so ashamed."

"My dear, I am sure you will discover the truth eventually though it is of little importance now. Let us talk instead about what is happening now. Your father said he will not force you to do anything against your will. So, Lizzy—what is your will?"

"Aunt, I know my father will not force me, but what choices do I truly have? With our lack of dowry, there is little to recommend us. And with such gossip burdening our reputation, what little we had will be gone forever. With my marrying Mr. Darcy, my family will be sheltered, and all my sisters will have a chance to find happiness. Perhaps, if Jane crosses Mr. Bingley's path again…"

"Yes, Mr. Bingley seemed to have been a desirable match for Jane, and it is sad that it did not happen, but what worries me even more are the feelings with which you accepted Mr. Darcy's proposal. It is not your will but rather the burden you agreed to carry, the sacrifice you agreed to make for your family. You seem angry and bitter, so I must ask: Are you angry with Mr. Darcy because there is another man whom you had hoped to marry?"

"Not at all, Aunt. I might be angry and bitter, but it does not have to do with Mr. Darcy himself. We had the chance to speak today more than we did during his entire stay at Netherfield. I have little with which to reproach him regarding his behaviour towards me. "

"Very well—I am relieved to hear that. I was afraid that… You mentioned Mr. Wickham quite often in your letters, and I thought you might—"

"Oh, Mr. Wickham is not… I mean—he is, beyond all comparison, the most agreeable man I ever saw, but he is certainly not the reason for my concern regarding this marriage."

"Very well… Now—may I ask what you told Mr. Darcy when he proposed to you?"

"I was so shocked that I laughed and I refused him because I believed it to be dangerous and ridiculous to marry over idle reports. I could not imagine that he would enter into such a marriage willingly. I knew how much he disapproved of me and my family, and I also suspected that he had influence on Mr. Bingley's decision to leave Netherfield."

"Oh, dear Lord…and what did he say?"

"He was shocked, too, by my refusal…and angry. But then we talked, and he understood my reasoning. He was persistent, however, and he came up with some logical arguments of his own…and I finally understood that he was right. This is what should be done."

"I see…Lizzy, you know that I grew up in Lambton—a small town only five miles from the Darcys' estate, Pemberley. I knew Lady Anne Darcy quite well. She was the most wonderful lady that ever existed."

"Yes, you told me that. You seemed quite charmed by everything related to

Pemberley."

"You may laugh, but you do not understand what it means to be part of that family. You do not know the extent of their name and their fortune. I would never imagine that someone from my family could one day become a Darcy, and I cannot help wondering why Mr. Darcy would want to marry you! Yes, you are beautiful, smart, witty, kind, and generous, and I love you dearly. But I imagine there are many other young ladies equally beautiful and smart with impressive fortunes and connections who would be happy to marry him."

"I asked myself, and I asked him the same. He said the gossip was his fault, and it was his duty to propose to me and protect both our families from the rumours. I felt he was forced by his honour and by his concern for his family to propose, and that is unfair to both of us."

"Yes, I understand that—partially. I mean—he heard the reports, and he came to propose to you, though he could have pretended to be oblivious and waited for the rumours to disappear in time. But once you refused him, he could have left. Yet, he persisted and tried to persuade you to accept him. Why? Forgive me for being insensitive to your feelings, but you and your family have everything to gain from this marriage while he wins nothing."

"I asked him that too. He said that he wanted to put an end to the gossip as soon as possible to protect his family. And he said he was certain that I would be suited for the position of his wife. He said he would not have proposed to me, all gossip aside, had he not been certain that I would be a proper Mrs. Darcy," Elizabeth replied, her emotions growing.

"He said that? Truly? It is equally astonishing from someone who—according to your own words—always disapproved of you and refused to speak more than two words with you."

"It is astonishing. He even said that he always admired me during his stay in Hertfordshire! I find it hard to believe, but why would he lie to me? Oh, he is so difficult to understand…"

"He seems a very sensible and wise man, capable of recognising and appreciating your qualities, Lizzy. And, if he considers you suited to be the future Mrs. Darcy, he has made you an extraordinary compliment. I hope *you* are wise and sensible enough to recognise that."

"Do you not believe me capable of accomplishing the duties required of being Mrs. Darcy? Do you doubt I am suited for the role?"

"I believe you capable of accomplishing anything you want, Lizzy. The question is: Do you want to do this? Are you willing to go through the circumstances that forced this alliance and to really become Mrs. Darcy? I am sure Mr. Darcy is not an easy man to live with, and the fact that you do not really know each other—nor will you have time to do so before the marriage—will only make things more difficult. You will need patience, wisdom, and strength. As Mrs. Darcy, you will have a duty to raise this marriage to the level of your predecessors. I am sure Mr.

Darcy will expect and demand a lot from you, and so will everyone else. It is not something to be taken lightly."

"I know that, Aunt. There are many things I need to think of before tomorrow. Besides, Mr. Darcy already told me that he has some requirements. I shall see if I can—or want to—accept them. Both he and I have time to change our minds. Nothing is decided yet."

"You should search both your heart and your mind before making the final decision, Lizzy. Search deeply and earnestly. This is a decision for your entire life, a decision that will affect many people besides you and Mr. Darcy, starting tomorrow."

"I know that, Aunt. If I could only make 'tomorrow' wait a little longer."

At the Meryton Inn, Darcy and the colonel had a quiet dinner—too quiet, especially compared to the din of voices outside. The colonel declared he would take a stroll to visit the small town, and Darcy encouraged him to do so. He was in no mood for conversation.

Alone in his room, with only the company of a glass of wine, Darcy's thoughts flew to Longbourn. *What is she doing? Has she said anything to her family?* Likely not as she surely did not need additional pressure on her shoulders. It was clear to him that the prospect of such a marriage was nothing but a burden from which she still hoped to escape.

How was it possible? He had left Hertfordshire less than a month before in order to escape the dangerous attraction he felt for the daughter of a country gentleman. He gave her more attention than he had to any other young lady. Every day he sought an opportunity to catch a glimpse of her or speak a few words with her, and every sleepless night at Netherfield, he blamed himself for his obsession and his weakness. His heart pounded wildly, his eyes sought any sign of recognition, and he shivered every time she was close to him—ridiculous in a man of his age and experience. Never had his mind and body responded in such a powerful and disturbing way to a woman's presence, and that weakness shamed him.

He was convinced that she understood his feelings, and was waiting for his attentions. Every time she spoke to him, there was a mixture of sweetness and archness in her response. He never knew whether he should feel offended or admire her for wit. Her soft lips were always twitching in a most tempting way, her eyes sparkling, and her eyebrow deliciously rising in challenge. However, he knew that Elizabeth Bennet could not be more than a pleasant memory to him—one he would remember his entire life. Her family, her connections, her situation in life forbade any further plans of a serious nature. Therefore, not wanting to trifle with her or her feelings, he had decided to avoid further attentions to her that could raise expectations impossible for him to fulfil. And in the end, he left.

But her memory did not leave him for a moment, and the sleepless nights at Netherfield continued when he returned to London—together with the guilt he felt for Bingley's poor state of mind and heart. More than once, he questioned his judgment of Miss Bennet's feelings. Did he advise Bingley to leave the neighbourhood in an honest desire to protect his friend, or was it polluted by his selfish need to stay away from Miss Elizabeth?

Fate had decided for him, placing them both in circumstances that allowed few choices. He had run from Elizabeth Bennet, and he was now forced to return. No—not forced. Fate only gave him an excuse to ignore old convictions and the demands of duty that had trapped him for so long. He made the decision to propose to her, but with great shame, he now admitted to himself that he weakly hid his own desires behind a mask of honourable intentions.

He began the journey to Longbourn with an easy heart and high expectations, even more so when he found that the Matlocks were ready to accept this marriage. It was one less fight on her behalf. He was convinced that Georgiana would love Elizabeth in an instant, so it seemed everything was in his favour. With God's will, before the year ended, Elizabeth would be his wife. And he was certain that, once he put aside the consideration of her family's behaviour or her lack of connections, Elizabeth herself, with her character and her spirit and her brightness, together with her generous, friendly nature, would be the perfect choice for him, for his family, and for everyone in his care.

He had expected her to be surprised for a moment and then to show joy and happiness in her sparkling eyes. He had been prepared to tell her that he planned to stay in London for only a little time after the wedding and then leave for Pemberley. He had been certain—still was certain—she would love Pemberley.

Then he had arrived at Longbourn to confront the first shock as he talked to Mr. Bennet. That gentleman with five daughters and very little dowry for them, and with his estate entailed to his cousin—was not pleased at all that a man of his fortune had asked for his daughter's hand in marriage. He was polite and considerate, and he appreciated Darcy's concern, but he was rather incredulous and cautious in responding to Darcy's request. He declared that the only one who could decide was Elizabeth, and again Darcy was certain that he could anticipate her answer. And he was wrong again.

Miss Elizabeth Bennet had refused his marriage proposal, and even worse, she seemed convinced that they had never been friends, that he always disapproved of her and her family, and she could not believe his intention to marry her. She seemed more inclined to confront the damage of the rumours than to marry him.

Could he accept that? He had no doubts that, once she gave her word to him, she would surely be a wonderful sister for Georgiana and a perfect mistress for his estates. But what about him? Could he bear to know that she would accept marital intimacy out of duty? Should he marry her, knowing she had no affection for him, or live far away from her, yearning for her in the years to come?

He filled another glass of brandy and paced the room, staring out the window. The streets were still animated, and he spotted a few officers, wondering whether Wickham was among them. For a moment, he considered searching for Wickham and confronting him—but to what purpose. He would surely deny any involvement like the coward he was, and besides, the damage was done. Darcy was sure that Wickham never intended the tale to grow to such an extent, nor was he the one implying that Darcy and Miss Elizabeth had been involved in anything improper. Wickham would likely attempt to make fun at Darcy's expense and speak of it to James who recklessly repeated it—two idiots making sport during drunken card games. Even killing both, as Robert suggested, would not change the situation—were he certain that he actually wished to change it.

Darcy remembered Elizabeth's answer when he asked her whether she had any personal reason to refuse the marriage. At least he had no fears that she might feel affection for that scoundrel. He knew she had been honest as she had been honest in everything she said to him—honest and rational. All her arguments were correct—even her mention that, had she respected him less, she would have accepted his proposal without delay. She was right. In truth, she reacted exactly as a woman of sense, education, and character would react when she received a proposal from a man whom she believed to be indifferent to her and for whom she felt little affection beyond gratitude and consideration.

The problem was that he was not at all indifferent to her, and her gratitude and consideration were far less than he desired from her.

Around midnight, the colonel returned and knocked on his door, asking whether he was awake. Darcy was tempted not to respond, but then he admitted that the bottle of brandy would be easier for *two* people to finish, so he invited his cousin to enter.

"Are you still upset about Miss Elizabeth's answer? Did you finish half of that bottle alone?"

"I am not upset. I want to sleep. I am quite tired."

"Darcy, I know you well enough to guess your feelings. I never saw you so affected by a woman as you are now, and I should be worried about this situation had I not trusted your judgment. If you came to admire Miss Elizabeth and wish to marry her, there must be something special about her. You will find a way to accomplish it—you always do."

"Robert, I do not wish to speak about this."

"Forgive me. I will not insist. It is just that… To be honest, I believe her refusal speaks highly of her character—and of her courage. I wonder whether any other woman in her position—or even in a much better one—would consider refusing you."

"Robert!"

"Very well, I will speak no more, but I have to ask: How is it possible that you were so certain of her acceptance? I mean—you already admitted that you had long admired her, and I can easily understand why. And I was under the impression that she was aware of your admiration and welcomed it. If that is so, why would she reject you?"

"Apparently, she was not aware of my admiration—quite the contrary. She believed I disproved of her and only looked at her to find a blemish. It seems that my manners were not as eloquent as I thought."

"Your manners? Really? Have you ever thought your manners eloquent?"

"I am glad you are amused, Cousin."

"Yes, I am. It might be the brandy. Darcy, even you must realise that there is much room for improvement in your manners. I can easily imagine a young woman being frightened by the prospect of marrying you. Even I am startled by your manners sometimes, and I have known you since the day you were born."

"You should go to bed. It is very late," Darcy said coldly, and the colonel laughed again.

"My point exactly," he said, gulping the rest of the brandy. "Now, I do not want to trouble you further, but spending two hours with the younger Miss Bennets and their mother can be quite enlightening. Is it true that, the first time you met Miss Elizabeth, you refused to dance with her and called her 'tolerable and not handsome enough to tempt you'? And that you never spoke more than a few words with anybody, including the Bennets, during your two months' stay at Netherfield? And when you did speak two words, one was an offense to someone nearby? The entire family seemed shocked that you danced with Miss Elizabeth once and that you escorted her home when she fell in the pond. How on earth could you believe that she was aware of your admiration and would welcome your proposal?"

The colonel's amusement increased while Darcy turned white—too stunned to even be angry with his cousin. Did all of Hertfordshire know that he offended Elizabeth at the Meryton assembly? Had she heard him and known all that time? And what did they mean that he offended everyone? Surely, that was another exaggeration of Mrs. Bennet.

"Well, at least you can be sure that the gossip was not started by the Bennets. They would never imply that you and Miss Elizabeth were involved in an improper relationship. Good Lord, they would laugh themselves to death if they were told such a thing."

"The younger Miss Bennets and their mother speak too much nonsense. They will never learn decorum. You can take none of their remarks seriously."

"That may be so, but if half of what they said is true, you have many things to repair, Darcy. Upon my word, your wealth and the threat of a scandal might not be enough for Miss Elizabeth to accept you if she is anything like you described. Your only chance is to win Mrs. Bennet to your side. She would surely force her daughter to have you."

"Robert, are you finally going to sleep?" Darcy inquired sternly, gazing at the fire.

"I might… Or I may go and ask for another bottle of brandy. It is your choice, Cousin."

"Well, the night is still young…and yes, I did call Elizabeth 'tolerable,' but it was Bingley's fault. He is so annoying sometimes that I will say anything to silence him."

"I can surely sympathise with that, but he is nothing compared to his sisters. Wait just a moment. I will bring the brandy, and you may tell me the whole story. By the way, did I mention that I spotted Wickham? My offer to kill him is still open if you change your mind."

They passed the chief of the night talking and enjoying the brandy until the colonel declared himself defeated and barely found the way to his room.

Hours later, alone in his room, Darcy stared at the fire, considering whether he should add another log, but he did not. As the night progressed, silence fell upon the small town, and the darkness seemed even blacker. It was a painfully long time until morning and even longer until he would be able to call at Longbourn. His patience had never been tried as sorely, and the brandy was no help until it plunged him at last into a deep sleep.

Although she slept but little the entire night, Elizabeth felt rested the next morning. Her aunt helped her to see the entire perspective of their difficult situation. If she and Mr. Darcy decided to enter into this marriage and she made her vow to him in church, she would do it with an open heart and commitment. She would not allow anger and bitterness to poison her marriage, no matter how painful or awkward the circumstances that had led to it.

She thought ceaselessly of the implications of marriage. Her cheeks coloured with shame as her mind briefly considered that her main duty would be towards her husband. He seemed a demanding man, accustomed to having his way. What would he demand of her? He said he would allow her time to become accustomed to their marriage. What would that mean? She had read enough to know of men's lack of patience in such situations. Could he be different? Could he be patient with her because he had no interest in intimacy? He said he admired her wit and her brightness and that he considered her suited to fill the role of Mrs. Darcy. He only mentioned that he expected to have children someday. He acted quickly to end the gossip through their marriage, but showed no interest or eagerness beyond that.

To pass the time more pleasantly, Elizabeth went out into the yard with Lucky. Nothing could make her feel better than frolicking with her dog in the fresh air and sunshine.

An hour later, Lucky suddenly abandoned her and ran to the gate, barking. A large carriage stopped, and Mr. Darcy, together with Colonel Fitzwilliam, joined her in the yard. Lucky jumped to greet Darcy, and he was rewarded with a pat on his head. His muddy paws left visible traces on the gentleman's coat, and Elizabeth called the dog in embarrassment.

"Mr. Darcy, I heartily apologise for Lucky. I do not know what came over him. He is usually very restrained with strangers and avoids anyone outside the family. It appears he is suddenly so friendly that he has ruined your coat. Please allow me to take it in to—"

"Miss Bennet, please do not make yourself uneasy. My coat will be fine. As for

Lucky—he might be restrained with strangers, but we have met several times, so we are practically friends now." Darcy smiled, his light voice leaving Elizabeth speechless.

She suddenly realised that her hair and clothes must be in great disorder from her spirited play. She felt her cheeks blushing as she answered the colonel's polite inquiry about her family. Elizabeth guided them to the living room where the family was waiting then excused herself and ran upstairs to change into something more proper, wondering why she felt in such high spirits.

Several minutes later, when she returned to the parlour, Elizabeth was surprised to see Mr. Darcy speaking amiably with her aunt and uncle. He glanced to her, and she responded with a polite smile, but he quickly returned his attention to his companions. While the colonel was surrounded by Lydia, Kitty, Mrs. Bennet, Mary and even Jane, and enjoyed the ladies' attention, Mr. Darcy seemed to have a more quiet but no less pleasant time in the company of Mr. and Mrs. Gardiner. Mr. Bennet stood in a corner, watching in silence.

Drinks and refreshments were served, and Mrs. Gardiner asked Elizabeth to join them.

"Lizzy, I was just talking to Mr. Darcy about Derbyshire. There is no more beautiful place in England, and no more beautiful place than Pemberley in the whole of Derbyshire."

"I will not attempt to contradict you, ma'am. It is such a wonderful surprise to discover that we have been practically neighbours for so many years," Darcy said with warm politeness.

Elizabeth stared at him, wondering whether he was aware that these were her relatives from Cheapside, of whom Miss Bingley commented with so little civility.

"You know, sir, I remember your coming into my father's shop with Lady Anne. You were about nine or ten years old. You were riding a tall, dark horse, and I recollect our surprise that you could master such a strong, large stallion."

"That was Black Knight. I still have him at Pemberley," Darcy replied, and a smile warmed his countenance. "He was strong and impressive but very gentle. He was easy to ride."

Elizabeth watched her relatives' interaction with Darcy, mesmerised, as if she were seeing each of them for the first time. She never saw him so friendly before, nor had she seen him smile so frequently. She briefly considered that smiling suited him very well.

She was obliged to depart from their group when her mother called her. A few minutes later, she noticed her father and Darcy walking outside the room. Her heart skipped a beat.

Another half an hour passed before Elizabeth saw Hill in the doorway and noticed the small sign meant only for her. She slowly left her seat, glancing at her aunt, and exited the room as the colonel was asking Mrs. Bennet how frequently balls were held in Meryton.

When Elizabeth entered the library, she was not surprised to meet only Mr. Darcy.

"Miss Bennet, Mr. Bennet will join us shortly to conclude our discussion. But before going any further, I need to ask whether you have made a final decision. Have you changed your mind since yesterday?" he inquired, and their eyes held briefly.

"No...I have not changed my mind if we can agree upon the requirements you spoke of."

"Ah, the requirements... Most of them were expressed yesterday. There is nothing more important to me than my family, and I expect my wife to feel the same. Other than that, I do wish and hope to have children someday. You are fond of children? I hope we could..."

He seemed deeply embarrassed, and she decided to help him, her cheeks burning.

"I am very fond of children, and I hope to have children of my own...someday..."

"Excellent...I am glad to hear that. Is there any particular requirement that *you* have?"

"No, not a requirement, but there is something I must ask you, and I hope you will answer me with the same honesty as yesterday. Sir, what do you expect from me regarding my family? You said your family is the most important thing for you. What about mine?"

He looked at her in puzzlement. "I am afraid I do not understand your meaning."

"We both know your opinion of my family—of my sisters' and my mother's behaviour. I do not expect them to change dramatically, but I love them dearly. So my question is: How will our marriage alter my relationship with them? How often will I be allowed to see them? Will I have your permission to visit them—or to invite them ever to visit me?"

Her voice carried a trace of her emotions, and her heart now became heavy. She startled when she felt his fingers taking hold of her hands, and both withdrew them.

"Miss Bennet, I am so sorry that my previous behaviour led you to such painful concerns. Please allow me to express myself clearly. I expect my wife to be dedicated to my family but not to the exclusion of her own. How often you will be allowed to see your family—that will be your decision entirely. Naturally, if we speak of your leaving our home and visiting your family, I would wish to be informed of such plans. As for inviting your family to visit you—such a decision is entirely yours."

"Thank you, sir. That is all I needed to know."

"But Miss Bennet—forgive me for inquiring—what made you believe that I would forbid you to see your family? Was my behaviour so ill as to make you believe me a cruel man?"

"No—it is just that... Forgive me if I offended you. It was not my intention."

"Do not trouble yourself. You did not offend me. Please know that I will always prefer you to ask me directly and to tell me of anything that worries you."

"Thank you—you are very kind."

"If there is nothing else, we should ask Mr. Bennet to join us. I wrote down my offering for the settlement, and I wish you both to read it before—"

"Mr. Darcy, I really do not believe that is necessary," Elizabeth said, but Darcy had gone to invite Mr. Bennet who was waiting in his study. He entered and sat near his daughter while Darcy hastened to read the settlement.

Elizabeth heard Mr. Darcy's words, but she barely comprehended his meaning, as she was more preoccupied in watching his face than in hearing the arrangements he was offering.

"I thank you, Mr. Darcy," she heard her father saying. "I believe this is a more than generous arrangement. I see nothing that needs to be added to it."

"Very well, sir. I will ask my attorney to put everything in an official form. Also, I will try to obtain a license as soon as possible, but it will likely be after Christmas—I mean, if that is acceptable to you, Miss Bennet. Would you rather wed here or in London?" As he spoke, his countenance changed continuously, proving that he was at least as uncomfortable as she was in discussing these necessary practical arrangements for their future lives.

"I believe it would be better here at Longbourn. My mother and my sisters would like to participate. The time is very short. I hope I can manage—"

"If there is anything I may do to help you..."

"No, I believe I will be fine, but there is something very important that I wish to ask you. In fact, I have a special request." Both gentlemen looked at her in surprise, waiting for her to continue. "I imagine this requirement might appear unreasonable, and you will probably refuse it, but it is truly important to me..."

"Please do not worry, Miss Bennet. If it is possible, I shall not refuse it."

"I would like to take Lucky with me. I have had him since he was born, and he has rarely been away from me. I cannot abandon him..." Darcy looked at her in surprise, blinking repeatedly, his mouth half open in disbelief.

"That is your request? Forgive me. I did not expect it. I thought you wanted... but of course... Surely, you cannot believe that I would refuse it. Of course you may take Lucky."

"Thank you, sir. I truly appreciate it. Now, if you will excuse me, I shall return to the others. I trust you will both decide on the best course of action from now on."

She gave them a forced smile and quickly exited the library. In the hall, she leant against the wall and attempted to regain her breathing and subdue the headache that threatened once again. It was all settled—her future life was settled. She would marry Mr. Darcy, and she did not even know his given name.

Inside the library, Darcy remained still, gazing at the closed door.

Mr. Bennet broke the silence. "You seem surprised by Lizzy's request."

"I confess I am..."

"Mr. Darcy, you clearly do not know my Lizzy, but I hope you will endeavour to remedy this. I know I might appear arrogant to you, considering the differences in our families and the advantages we will receive from this marriage, but I do not hesitate to say that you could not find a better wife than Lizzy if you will get to know her and allow her to better know you in exchange. I supported you in this arrangement, but I am not at peace with it, and as time passes, I am more worried that I might have made a mistake. I allowed myself to be convinced by my hasty impression that you could be a good husband for Lizzy. If I was wrong, I will never forgive myself, and I will do everything in my power to repair my error."

"Mr. Bennet, I understand your concern, and I thank you for your trust. You may have no doubt that I shall do everything in my power to be a good husband to Miss Elizabeth and give her as happy a marriage as possible. That was my goal when I proposed to her, and I have discussed this with Miss Elizabeth. Please be assured that I am entirely aware of her qualities, and I truly value them. I know I could not find a better wife."

"I am glad to hear that, sir. I have to warn you, though. If Lizzy becomes unhappy and wants to return home, I will always open my arms to her. I was not a good father by way of providing my daughters with tempting dowries, but I did make sure that each of them was as happy as possible—and I will continue to do that for as long as I live."

"I understand. I am confident that sooner rather than later your worries will be dispelled. And for that, you will always be welcome to visit your daughter whenever you desire without announcement or invitation."

"That is good to know. I might be tempted to take advantage of your words when the weather improves. Now let us return to the others. Everything is settled for now."

Mr. Darcy and Colonel Fitzwilliam remained at Longbourn for another hour. They enjoyed drinks and refreshments, and Mr. Darcy even engaged himself in conversation, mostly with Mr. and Mrs. Gardiner. Quite often, his gaze travelled towards Elizabeth and met hers. Once or twice, they even smiled at each other. Mr. Bennet was more restrained and silent, but nobody noticed except Elizabeth—who asked him several times whether he wished something to drink—and Darcy, who glanced at him almost as often as at Elizabeth.

When the time for departure arrived, Mrs. Bennet asked Mr. Darcy—twice—to convey to Mr. Bingley her best regards and wishes to see him again soon then complimented him on his large and most elegant carriage. When they were almost outside, Lucky demanded attention, and Darcy leant down to pet him. He was surprised when he heard Elizabeth whispering to him.

"There is something else I forgot to ask you, sir. I do not even know your given name..."

He answered with a smile twisting his lips and a low voice so no one else could hear him. "It is Fitzwilliam. Fitzwilliam Darcy. And yes, I know it is a little strange, but it is a family custom. My sister calls me William."

Elizabeth had no time to answer but returned his smile. Soon the carriage disappeared from their sight, and Mrs. Bennet, as well as her younger daughters, could not find enough words to express their excitement about the unexpected visit. Mrs.

Gardiner and Jane said little, and Mr. Gardiner joined Mr. Bennet in the library.

Elizabeth ran back to her room then threw herself on the bed, closing her eyes without allowing her mind to think of anything. She did not know how much time passed before she rose from the bed and slowly opened the drawer of her small cabinet. She found the diary she received as a gift when she was ten years old and in which she only wrote once—about the day she almost drowned in the sea and a young man saved her life. She caressed the diary's cover, opened it slowly, then turned the first pages and put down a few words:

"Today is the day which changed my life forever. Today I accepted the offer of marriage from Mr. Fitzwilliam Darcy—my future husband."

Chapter 7

London, 23 December

Darcy arrived home long after dinnertime, exhausted from the torment of the last several days—and very hungry. He had last eaten at Longbourn, and he was forced to admit that Mrs. Bennet could honestly be proud of her choice of victuals.

A cold shiver travelled along his spine as he remembered Elizabeth's coming towards him and asking his given name. That small, intimate exchange, right there with her family, meant more to him than everything they previously discussed. She was not in the least curious about the settlement, she asked no other favour from him than to take her dog with her and to be allowed to visit her family, and she showed no interest in any material aspect of the arrangements—but she was interested in learning his name. And she smiled at him—that little smile that usually twisted her lips and lit the sparkle in her eyes. A mere question and a simple smile aroused more sensations than the attention bestowed upon him by every young woman he had ever met. It left him wishing for more—yearning for more. *Less than a week and she will be here...*

He startled when Georgiana entered the library and greeted him warmly, her look carrying obvious curiosity but—as always—not daring to ask.

"Dearest, I am glad you are still awake as I have something of great importance to tell you. I am sure it will be quite a shock, but I will say it directly. I was in Hertfordshire to ask Miss Elizabeth Bennet to marry me, and she consented. The wedding will take place shortly."

His words had a more extraordinary effect on Georgiana than Darcy expected. She first stared at him in disbelief then sat and turned pale. He took her hands gently. "Forgive me for not telling you earlier, but I was not certain how things would end. I know it is late to ask your opinion, but I would love to know what you think."

"You know best, Brother. If you believe she is a good choice, I have little to say. It is just that I never suspected such a thing. You never mentioned your intention to... And so soon?"

"I know it seems rushed, but I am sure we will both manage to accommodate it."

"But what should I do? Will I have to move to my own house? It is Christmas..."

"Do? Move? Dearest, what questions are these?" He gently kissed her forehead and tightly clasped her trembling hands. "There is nothing you need do except welcome her to our family. I hope that you will grow very close. Do you remember when I asked you a few days ago what you expected from my future wife? I assure you that Miss Elizabeth is everything you desire. I have no doubts that you will like her very much."

"I am sure I will if you speak of her so warmly. I also hope she will like me. But, forgive me for inquiring, why so soon? Please do not be upset with me..."

"I will do my best to explain it, but the situation is not easy to share with my little sister. I told you earlier that Miss Elizabeth had an accident when I happened to be there. She became very ill afterwards, and I sent Dr. Taylor to help her recover. Everything seemed to end satisfactorily. Then, to my horrified surprise, I heard vile reports about Miss Elizabeth and me that had spread all the way to Town—reports as far from the truth as they are malicious and painful. Our Matlock relatives heard them too. So, after due consideration, I decided that, to put an end to the vile tales before they could harm our family's reputation and good name, the best solution would be to marry Miss Elizabeth Bennet."

"So you are forced to marry so soon. You were trapped into all this. But do you know who started the gossip? What if... Forgive me. I do not mean to be rude, but..."

He gently caressed her hair. "Do not worry about asking. You fear that the Bennet family might have invented the tale in order to trap me, do you not?"

"I do. It is just that...even Robert jokes about young ladies trying to trap you all the time."

"I am certain the Bennets were not involved in spreading the gossip because I know who is responsible, and one of them is our cousin James."

"Oh... I am so sorry."

"And speaking of being trapped, Miss Elizabeth rejected my proposal. In fact, she tried to convince me to wait and allow the gossip to run its course."

Georgiana gasped in surprise and stared at her brother, who was strangely calm while confessing such astonishing events. "She rejected you? Why? I thought you admired her!"

"I asked her the same. It appears that my manners and my behaviour while at Netherfield led her to believe that I completely disapproved of her and her family. She was as shocked at my proposal as you were. I needed all my powers of persuasion to convince her."

"But, William, I do not understand. Why would you...? May I ask why you insisted...?"

Darcy's smile paled for a moment, and he found no words to explain. He was certain his sister did not miss his hesitancy. Georgiana was not a young girl any longer.

"I did it because, as I told you in my letters, Miss Elizabeth Bennet is truly a remarkable lady. And, aside from her family situation, she has all the qualities that I want and hope for in my future wife and your future sister. Her rejection only proved her worthiness once more. There are few young ladies with the courage to refuse an advantageous marriage. Though I was at first upset, I am now actually pleased to know that she is not a fortune hunter and has strong beliefs and values to which she is loyal. I have not the smallest doubt that she is truly the best choice I could make. Please trust me in this."

"I trust you all the time, Brother. And I agree that Miss Elizabeth showed courage and strength. I will grant her that. But I will need to be convinced that she is worthy of your admiration—that she reciprocates it. I do not question her qualities, and I will gladly welcome her to our family, but I will only love her as a sister when I am sure she loves you."

"Very well, my dear sister, that is fair enough. Please keep this secret for now. Tomorrow I will procure a special license. I do not want to make it public before everything is settled, and I certainly do not want anyone else to ever find out the reasons for this marriage."

"Of course. William, you said Aunt and Uncle Fitzwilliam know about this. What about Aunt Catherine?"

"As I said—only after everything is settled. Now let us rest. Tomorrow will be a busy day."

The Matlock residence was still animated at a late hour, and Robert was received with equal joy and eagerness. He gave his parents the news according to what he previously agreed with Darcy.

"I spent little time in Miss Elizabeth's company, but I can say with certainty that she is beautiful and bright. Her father is a very interesting gentleman—quite attached to his books. He and Darcy seemed to have a good understanding of each other, which is helpful. Mrs. Bennet is a very...animated lady. I imagine she was a remarkable beauty in her youth. She still has pleasant features. And she has five daughters who all inherited her beauty. Fortunately, the eldest two also inherited their father's intelligence." The colonel laughed.

"I imagine they were all beside themselves with happiness when Darcy proposed to Miss Elizabeth. In truth, no matter how beautiful the girls might be, I doubt they could ever aspire to such an alliance."

"Yes, well...I would describe their reaction with more tempered words, Mother. I can say with surety that neither Mr. Bennet nor Miss Elizabeth is a fortune hunter. Miss Elizabeth is a decided young lady with strong opinions and personal values, and Darcy's wealth carried little weight in the conversation. Fortunately, he possessed superior persuasive skills as well as a powerful argument. In the end, everything turned out as Darcy wished."

"Surely, you do not imply that a country girl from Hertfordshire refused to marry Darcy?"

"Father, please ask Darcy for further details. I just wanted to dispel any worry you might have regarding Miss Elizabeth's character and to assure you there is a good chance this marriage will turn out to be exactly what Darcy needs."

"Very well, son, I believe this will do for now," Lady Matlock said kindly. "I shall wait for Darcy to come with more details about the wedding date. Then I must make arrangements about a ball to introduce the new Mrs. Darcy. Oh, I have quite a good feeling about all this. What a strange development..."

"Yes, but," Lord Matlock interrupted, puzzled and vexed, "a country girl from Hertfordshire refused Darcy? How can that be? Why would she do that?"

"Husband, you should be less concerned about that and more concerned about your sister Catherine's reaction. *That* is something worth worrying about!"

LONGBOURN WAS AS ANIMATED AS EVERY YEAR AT CHRISTMAS TIME. EXCEPT FOR the Gardiners and Mr. Bennet, Elizabeth's secret remained unknown. She wanted to speak to Jane, but she did not feel confident enough to decide what to tell her, so she delayed the confession until she knew all the details. More than ever before, Mrs. Gardiner's presence was a blessing for Elizabeth, as she had someone to share her concerns, to understand, and to advise her.

"Dearest, I must say that, from the little time we spent with Mr. Darcy, I have nothing to reproach him for, and your uncle agreed with me entirely," said Mrs. Gardiner. "He is perfectly well behaved and polite, and if there is something a little stately in him, it is confined to his air and is not unbecoming. You told me so many things about how proud and disagreeable he is, but I have seen nothing of it."

"I was never more surprised by his behaviour yesterday. I suspected he would be civil with my family since we were discussing the prospect of a future marriage, and I had already reproached him for his previous lack of politeness. But with you and uncle, I might say he was more than civil. He seemed really attentive."

"He was! And he invited your uncle to visit Pemberley and go fishing with him. I still cannot believe it—me, visiting Pemberley and my husband fishing with Mr. Darcy! You must see that this is a compliment to you, Lizzy, and another proof that he is endeavouring to gain your good opinion. Surely you must appreciate that."

"I do understand and appreciate that, Aunt. I am not insensitive to Mr. Darcy's efforts. But have you not visited Pemberley? You seemed well acquainted with the estate."

"I am well acquainted with the estate from the outside. I never entered the house. My family was not on intimate terms with the Darcys. But do you not remember that you yourself met Lady Anne?"

"I? How is that possible? When? I have never been to Lambton."

"Not in Lambton but in Brighton. Do you remember when your uncle and I married? You were ten years old, and that year we took you and Jane with us."

"It was the year you gave Lucky to me as a present and he almost drowned in the sea."

"Yes—and you with him. I will never forgot how scared I was when I heard… but anyway, you used to play with Lucky on the beach, and you met Lady Anne who was there with her daughter—Georgiana, I believe was her name. She was about five or six years younger than you. Apparently, you became quite friendly with both Lady Anne and her daughter even before I became aware of your acquaintance. What a strange coincidence, indeed!"

"I met Lady Anne and Georgiana? How astonishing! I do not remember either of them at all, and I would wish to, so very much! Please tell me more: How was the late Mr. Darcy?"

"It was said that he was a fair master and all his tenants had the comfort of a good income. I also heard that he was very devoted to Lady Anne. He passed away only a few years after her death. He was quite an impressive man—much like the young one. Mr. Darcy—your Mr. Darcy—seems very much like him."

"He is not *my* Mr. Darcy," Elizabeth said, blushing.

"Perhaps not yet. But he is very generous with you, from what I heard about the settlement—and very, very handsome."

"Aunt!" Elizabeth blushed once again.

"Lizzy, that is nothing to be ashamed of. This may be a shock to you, but no man is really kind, gentle, patient, and amiable all the time, and a woman must compensate for this if she wants to keep a happy marriage. God knows that I married your uncle for the deepest love, and my affection has not diminished in the slightest, but sometimes he drives me out of my mind—more than four children together. I imagine the best of men are the same. In cases like this, it is very helpful if the man is handsome. You will surely bear his faults easier."

"I never heard you talk like this before!" Elizabeth said in disbelief.

"Well, dearest, you have never been almost married before," the lady replied. "Now, will you join me in the kitchen to see what Maria is cooking? I will make my special apple pie. Did I mention that I got the recipe from my great-aunt Teresa? She was a cook at Pemberley even before Mr. Darcy wed Lady Anne. When she was too old to work, Lady Anne used to ask her to make her pies for special occasions at Pemberley. I believe Aunt Teresa made a dowry for her granddaughter just from what Lady Anne paid for the pies." Mrs. Gardiner continued to laugh, and Elizabeth could not but wonder at her aunt's levity.

Around noon, they were surprised by the visit of Mr. Wickham and Mr. Denny. Elizabeth politely introduced them to her uncle and aunt, and, as expected, mere minutes passed before the previous day's visit of Mr. Darcy and Colonel Fitzwilliam was mentioned.

"I was shocked to hear that Darcy and the colonel were in Meryton—and stayed at the inn," Mr. Wickham said. "I cannot imagine what business they could have in the neighbourhood as Mr. Bingley is no longer at Netherfield. Darcy had no other acquaintances in the county."

"Well, as you claim to having rarely seen Mr. Darcy in the last years, I venture to assume that he might have made new acquaintances about whom you have no knowledge," replied Mr. Bennet.

Mrs. Bennet ignored her husband's sarcasm. "Oh, I do not know what business they have. Mr. Bennet might know as he spent quite a lot of time with Mr. Darcy. But they were very polite, and they seemed to enjoy Longbourn exceedingly as they stayed several hours, two days in a row. Surely, it was a sign of respect towards our family. And the colonel is so handsome and so pleasant! We all liked him extremely well."

"Yes, the colonel is very amiable, very gentlemanlike. Very different from his cousin."

"Yes, very different. But I think Mr. Darcy improves on acquaintance," Elizabeth intervened.

"Indeed! I am surprised at your changed opinion of Darcy, Miss Elizabeth. Is it in address that he improves? Has he deigned to add aught of civility to his ordinary style?"

"I could not say for certain why my opinion is changed. It is more that, from knowing him better, I better understand his disposition. Besides, it cannot and should not be forgotten that Mr. Darcy saved my life."

For a moment, he was silent. Then he said in the gentlest of accents, "You, Miss Elizabeth, who so well know my feelings, will readily comprehend how sincerely I must rejoice that he generously took care of you and that he is wise enough to assume even the appearance of what is right. His pride in that direction may be of service—if not to himself then to many others—for it must deter him from such foul misconduct by which I have suffered."

"Oh yes, Aunt," cried Lydia, "Mr. Darcy was so cruel to poor Wickham. He refused to give him what was rightfully his by the late Mr. Darcy's will. I am sure he did that because he was jealous of Wickham."

"Really? That is almost unbelievable. I will write my cousin Mary Ann for all the details she knows about Mr. Darcy. You know, Mr. Wickham, I grew up in Lambton, and my cousin still lives there. She is very well informed about events in the neighbourhood."

Surprised by her aunt's statement, Elizabeth glanced from her to Wickham and did not miss the sudden alarm that appeared in his heightened complexion and agitated look.

"Mrs. Gardiner, I would be grateful if you inquired no further. I mean—as I told Miss Elizabeth previously, it pains me to speak badly of a Darcy or to hear anyone do so. I would rather keep the entire matter private if you would be so kind."

"As you wish, sir. I can easily understand your desire for privacy, but I was misled by your sharing the story with my nieces. Anyone wanting to keep a secret should think twice before doing so. But we had better change the subject as this one seems uncomfortable for all of us," Mrs. Gardiner said with a polite smile.

"How do you like Meryton?"

That brief exchange made a strong impression on Elizabeth. She understood her aunt's little scheme in suggesting that she would ask for more details of the story, as well as Mr. Wickham's panic and insistence on her not doing so. It was enough for her to realise that she had been hasty in giving such full credit to a man whom she barely knew.

That night—as well as the night before—Elizabeth slept poorly, thinking of Mr. Darcy and the various contradictory things she knew about him. Strangely, her mind returned to their brief exchange just before he left when he told her his name. That memory seemed to trouble her, and his warm expression would not leave her thoughts. *What sort of man is he?* She remembered their discussion at the Netherfield ball, and yes, she had not managed to sketch his character, but she would have plenty of time for that—a lifetime.

On Christmas Eve, Mr. Bennet was informed of a visitor. He requested the gentleman be sent to his library, and a minute later, the servant called Elizabeth too.

"Lizzy, I received a letter from Mr. Darcy. He sent me the settlement written by his attorney and informed me that he will receive the license on the twenty-sixth so the wedding can take place on the twenty-seventh. If this is acceptable to you, I will send him the answer straight away. He also said that he will arrive in Meryton on the twenty-sixth in the afternoon. He suggests that you both leave for London after the wedding breakfast."

Her words tumbled out nervously. "Yes, that matches our tentative plans. On the twenty-sixth? That is quite soon. We should proceed as we discussed. We have so many things to do. When should we tell Mama and my sisters?"

"Lizzy dearest, please breathe deeply and try to calm yourself. Do not worry. We will talk tomorrow about what and when we will tell the family. Mr. Darcy says an announcement will appear in *The Times* on your wedding day as we planned. All will be well."

"Yes, I know, Papa... Do not worry. I shall be fine. All will be well. I know that..."

Elizabeth returned to the others a few minutes later and Mr. Bennet not long after her. The rest of the dinner was animated, full of joy and happiness for everyone—save Elizabeth and her father who barely said a word.

When the dinner was over, Elizabeth went to her chamber and spent several minutes looking at every piece of furniture in the room where she had lived twenty years and where she was allowed to remain only three more nights. It was all settled, and it was time to speak to Jane then to her entire family. But she would wait until after Christmas. She wished for one more normal Christmas at Longbourn as it would be her last.

On Christmas morning, long before anyone else was awake, Elizabeth was impatient to acquaint Jane with all the particulars. With long-prepared calmness and carefully chosen words, she told her beloved sister the important parts of the discussion between Mr. Darcy and herself. As Elizabeth explained the circumstances of her engagement, Jane's complexion turned pallid and tearful.

"Dearest, what a nightmare you endured all alone. Why did you not tell me sooner? How is it possible for someone to turn a generous gesture by Mr. Darcy into something horrible? And why would someone want to compromise either of you? It is just unbelievable!"

"Yes, it is, but what is done is done. You understand now why we decided that the best solution was to marry as soon as possible. I hope you do not blame me for this."

"Blame you? No! But are you sure you can enter into a marriage without love?"

Elizabeth fought her tears. "Well, all I have to do now is to make sure I fall in love with Mr. Darcy, and all will be well. Aunt Gardiner says that his being handsome will make his faults easier to bear. I am just not sure whether he will ever find me tolerable enough to love!"

"Oh, Lizzy, how can you joke so easily? I am so sorry you have to go through this turmoil!"

"I have hopes that everything might be well in the end as Mr. Darcy said. Please hope and pray with me. By the way, Jane, Aunt Gardiner told me that we met Lady Anne Darcy and Georgiana ten years ago. Do you remember when we went to Brighton?"

The sisters talked for another hour, troubled by the prospect of separating and astonished by the extraordinary coincidence. They also discussed the possibility of meeting again quite soon as Jane had been invited by Mrs. Gardiner to stay in London with them for a month or two. Although neither dared to speak of it, both secretly wondered whether occasions might arise for Jane to meet Mr. Bingley too.

On Christmas Day, during a time of shared joy at the dinner table, Mr. Bennet suddenly demanded the family's attention. Elizabeth turned pale while her mother was only faintly aware of her husband speaking. She was not accustomed to listening to him during dinner conversations. Mr. Bennet gulped a little wine then a smile lit his face.

"Mrs. Bennet, I know that, for a whole month now, you have been upset with Lizzy for refusing Mr. Collins's proposal and even more upset with Charlotte Lucas for accepting it."

"Oh, Mr. Bennet, it is cruel of you to remind me of such terrible things on Christmas Day!"

"My dear, I trust this reminder will make you all the happier with my news. Also, I fancy that Lizzy may soon become your favourite daughter. Now, as to the news: three days ago, Mr. Darcy proposed to Lizzy, and she accepted him. He also asked my consent, which I granted. So, briefly, they will marry on December 27 in Meryton with a special license."

For several minutes, nobody breathed. Finally, Mrs. Bennet commenced to gulp and blink repeatedly. Then she turned pale and leant back heavily in her chair. Elizabeth and Jane hurried to her while Mr. Bennet sent Kitty to fetch Hill's salts.

Shortly, Mrs. Bennet began to recover, to fidget about in her chair, get up, sit down again, wonder, and bless herself.

"Good gracious! Lord bless me! Only think! Mr. Darcy! Who would have thought it! And is it really true? Oh, my sweetest Lizzy! How rich and how great you will be! What pin money, what jewels, what carriages you will have! I am so pleased—so happy. Such a charming man—so handsome, so tall! Oh, my dear Lizzy! Pray forgive me for being so upset with you before. I hope you will overlook it. Dear, dear Lizzy. A house in town! Everything that is charming! Ten thousand a year! Oh, Lord! What will become of me? I shall go distracted."

She needed a pause to breathe, then she instantly turned pale, and everyone was afraid she might faint again. "But my dearest child, what nonsense is this to marry in two days? We have no time to prepare you properly! You need new gowns. We all need new gowns—and to prepare the wedding breakfast and—"

"Mama, I discussed these things with Mr. Darcy, and we agreed to leave for London immediately after the wedding. Considering the bad weather, his relatives will not be able to attend except Colonel Fitzwilliam. So there will be no need for special preparations."

"No need? My child, what are you talking of? All of Meryton will be there even if you leave for London immediately. I will not sleep a moment until the wedding. Oh, just imagine: you will be married long before Charlotte Lucas—a real miracle. Oh, Lizzy, you were so smart to refuse Mr. Collins—such a disagreeable man and not at all handsome! Oh, wait until Lady Lucas and Sir William hear about this! Ten thousand a year and very likely more! 'Tis as good as a Lord! And a special license. Oh, and of course his relatives cannot attend. Who could imagine an earl staying at the inn? It is not to be borne! But my dearest love, tell me what dish Mr. Darcy is particularly fond of, that I may have it when he arrives."

Nothing else was discussed that evening except the unbelievable news, and Elizabeth felt deeply grateful and relieved when it was time to retire. Mrs. Bennet made quick plans to visit her sister Philips the next morning, and she also proposed to call briefly on Lady Lucas. Elizabeth cringed at hearing such plans, but there was nothing to be done for it.

Fortunately, it started snowing that night, and by the morning, everything was covered in white. After breakfast, the weather warmed, and the snow became a dense, cold rain. Mrs. Bennet was devastated that her visits had to be postponed, but she could not control the weather. She had to content herself with staying at home near the fire and discussing future balls and the grand opportunities that would arise for her other daughters.

Mr. Bennet sent his footman with a note for the parish clergyman with all the details of the wedding, and he smiled to himself imagining the man's shock at the news. Afterwards, he retired with his brother Gardiner to the library and demanded they not be disturbed.

Elizabeth spent the time searching her closet carefully to decide which gowns deserved to be taken with her to London and, more importantly, which gown she should wear on her wedding day. Mrs. Bennet complained about the tragedy of not having time to order new clothes more suitable to her new position, but Elizabeth was content that everything was settled. However, her peace and tranquillity were still absent. Strangely, she felt no fatigue. Her mind and her body did not desire nor require rest.

London, 25 December

DARCY RELAXED IN HIS ARMCHAIR WITH A GLASS OF WINE, GLANCING FROM THE fire to the window and back again. The next morning he would leave for Meryton, and Lord Matlock and Thomas had surprised him with their decision to attend the wedding with Robert. Darcy appreciated the importance of such a gesture, and felt gratitude for his relatives. Without their support, it would be a formidable task for Elizabeth to adapt to her new role. Either way, she would have to contend with London gossip. He was well aware of that.

Everything was arranged for Elizabeth's arrival. The household, as well as Mrs. Annesley, had been informed. He had given specific orders regarding their return from Hertfordshire, including the preparation of a special dinner. With the help of Mrs. Annesley and Mrs. Thomason—the housekeeper—Darcy chose a young maid, Molly, to serve Mrs. Darcy.

Darcy rose, opened the connecting door, and entered his wife's apartment. In two days—two nights—she would be there, and he was still unable to believe it. Night after night, he had dreamt about her more times than he cared to admit. Her image had tormented his mind for so many weeks that the reality of her presence only steps away from him was difficult to accept. He knew that she would be there as a result of unpleasant circumstances and only partly of her own free will, but she had also indicated a willingness to make this marriage work—and he trusted her words.

He had promised her that he would not force her to consummate their marriage before she was ready, and he intended to keep his promise. Even more, since he discovered that she was not aware of his admiration and scarcely returned it, his pride had been wounded and his self-confidence shattered. In all his reveries, she was smiling at him with sweetness and desire, gently caressing him, abandoning herself to him, and opening her soul and body to him. Such were his wishes and dreams, and the idea of her mere acceptance to avert the negative consequences of malicious tales, was appalling and heartbreaking. If they had to marry in such haste, it was his duty—more than hers—to be certain that they would truly become husband and wife.

Darcy fell asleep long after midnight with Elizabeth's image in his mind, wondering how she would look with her hair loose about her shoulders.

Longbourn, 26 December 1811

LATE IN THE AFTERNOON, MRS. PHILIPS CAME TO HELP HER SISTER, WHO WAS barely able to breathe from the turmoil of her emotions. Somehow, Mrs. Philips felt blessed by association to the extraordinary fortune that had befallen her sister's family.

When Hill announced visitors, the family was shocked to see Mr. Darcy in the doorway with not one but three gentlemen companions.

Elizabeth's eyes briefly met and held Darcy's, and she felt her cheeks colouring as she looked towards others. She politely smiled at the colonel, and while the presentations were made, Mrs. Bennet and Mrs. Philips, as well as the youngest Miss Bennets, fell into silence. The gentlemen took their seats and began enjoying refreshments while carrying on a light conversation with Mr. Bennet and the Gardiners. Mrs. Bennet and Mrs. Philips were still unable to speak coherently while Lydia, Kitty and Mary excused themselves. Eventually, Mrs. Philips left, and her sister took no notice of her departure.

Elizabeth glanced at Darcy whenever she had a chance. She could hardly believe that such illustrious personages were visiting her and that they were so polite and amiable with her family. In fact, they would soon be *her* family!

At one point, Lord Matlock himself asked Elizabeth to sit by him, and he gently conveyed Lady Matlock's regrets that she could not attend the wedding and her wish to meet for dinner as soon as Elizabeth was settled. She was stunned.

After a long struggle, Mrs. Bennet regained her voice enough to ask the gentlemen to stay for dinner, and when they accepted, she went so pale that Elizabeth feared she would faint again. Fortunately, the matron's excitement overcame her nervousness, and she disappeared towards the kitchen to make sure the prepared dishes would rise to the expectation of an earl, a future earl, and her future son-in-law with ten thousand a year.

Darcy finally approached Elizabeth. He offered her his arm and she hesitantly took it.

"Please forgive me for not telling you in advance of my uncle and cousin's intention to accompany me."

"I beg you, do not apologise. It was quite a lovely surprise. I truly appreciate their presence and their effort in coming. Besides, they are very pleasant company."

"Yes they are—unlike me," he said seriously, but she could feel a smile in his voice.

"Surely, you are not fishing for a compliment, sir." She smiled, glancing up at him.

"Not at all—I only speak the truth. It will be your duty to help me improve my manners."

"I am sure—and you proved me right—that your manners are perfectly charming whenever you are willing to display them, sir. You do not need improvement in manners but in your desire to please."

"Then you shall help me in this," he added, their gazes fixed for a moment. They arrived at the dinner table, and since the seating had not been previously specified, he hesitated a moment then sat beside her. Jane was across from Elizabeth with the colonel beside her. The earl and the viscount were seated near Mr. Bennet and Mr.

Gardiner. Mrs. Gardiner strategically sat near Mrs. Bennet and the younger sisters.

"Is Miss Darcy well?" Elizabeth inquired in a low voice.

"Yes, thank you. She looks forward to meeting you, as does Mrs. Annesley, her companion."

That was all they said to each other that evening, but each was aware of the other's presence. He was attentive to her, filling her water glass and handing her what she needed from the table. She occasionally glanced at him while talking politely to his relatives.

The entire dinner went better than either had expected, and the guests complimented Mrs. Bennet for a pleasant and delicious meal. When the four gentlemen left Longbourn, it was almost midnight. After their departure, Mrs. Bennet needed another hour to express her delight in receiving such a visit and her admiration towards the gentlemen's politeness and handsome appearance. Mrs. Gardiner was the only one who sacrificed herself to listen.

Elizabeth retired to her room, overwhelmed by the day's events. She appreciated Lord Matlock's presence as powerful proof that his family supported the marriage, and she was grateful for their guests' kind behaviour towards her family. As for Mr. Darcy—her future husband—he was unchanged except for friendly glances and smiles, slightly improved manners towards her family, and gentle teasing when they spoke privately to each other.

Her fears of and reluctance to the marriage had diminished considerably since the day of the proposal, but the thought of leaving her home and family forever on the morrow clutched at her heart and took her breath away. She knew that, after the wedding, she would be entirely subject to her husband's will and power. She hoped and prayed that he truly was a good man. Besides her own observations, she relied on what her aunt knew of the Darcys. Surely, a wonderful lady like Lady Anne and a fair, honest man like the late Mr. Darcy could not but raise a good man with good principles. However, despite all her self-assurances, it was nearly dawn when she fell asleep.

Longbourn, 27 December

THE WEDDING MORNING STARTED WITH A DIN THAT MR. BENNET PERCEIVED AS madness. He asked for a few private minutes with his daughter, and he embraced her tightly, which he had not done since she was a child. When they looked at each other, they were both tearful.

"My dear girl, please do not cry. At least one of us should be strong. I feel guilty enough for insisting upon this marriage, and I need to hope that all will be well. Are you frightened?"

"Papa, I am not frightened, and you are in no way culpable! You have been nothing but fair and supportive to me. Any other father would have forced me to marry someone with Mr. Darcy's situation, but you did not. This marriage is entirely my and Mr. Darcy's decision. I am only sad that I will not see you every day as I am used to. I will dearly miss you!"

"You will be deeply missed, Lizzy, but I have good feelings about your marriage from what I have seen these past days. Darcy invited me to visit you any time I want without any previous announcement, which I believe is proof of his genuine good intentions. He also invited us all to visit Pemberley in the summer, but I think such insanity will pass, and he will withdraw the invitation. In truth, I am impressed by how well he and his relatives bore your mother and sisters. They seemed men with remarkable self-restraint and mastery of their patience," he concluded, and Elizabeth laughed heartily.

"In earnest, Lizzy, I believe that Mr. Darcy is a man who, in disposition and talents, will most suit you. His understanding and temper, though unlike yours, will answer your wishes if only you will make the effort to know him. I feel, my child, that this union will be to the advantage of you both. By your ease and liveliness, his attitudes will be softened, his manners improved, and from his judgment, information, and knowledge of the world, you will receive benefit of greater importance. And he already admitted that he understands and values your qualities and is confident of a happy future for this marriage."

"I shall do everything in my power to contribute my share. I promise, Papa."

"I know you do, my dear. Now let us go. Your mother cannot bear her nerves any longer."

They embraced again, more closely, then left the house together. It was settled. Everything was packed and ready to be loaded into the carriage, including Lucky, who had been highly agitated for days as he felt something extraordinary was about to happen. Despite other reasons for worry, Mrs. Bennet could not conceive that Lizzy intended to carry a dog to Mr. Darcy's sophisticated townhouse. But since he agreed, she feared to contradict him. She was still incredulous that such a man was determined to marry Lizzy, who was not as beautiful as Jane nor as joyful as Lydia and who also possessed a peculiar preference for roaming outside with her dog.

Curiosity and the shock of the extraordinary news brought most of Meryton to the church, and nothing could have been more rewarding for Mrs. Bennet's ego than the expression on the faces of Sir William and Lady Lucas when they extended their good wishes.

The ceremony was beautiful, Mrs. Bennet believed, but immediately afterwards it began to snow again. The guests returned to Longbourn for a brief breakfast. After Elizabeth's luggage was loaded and a very emotional farewell taken, the party headed towards London.

Darcy, Elizabeth, and an excited Lucky took one carriage, while the earl and his sons travelled in another. Mrs. Bennet remained outside, staring in their direction long after the carriages disappeared from her sight, still wondering at the miracle that had just happened. Then she quickly sent a servant to invite her sister Philips, Lady Lucas, Sir William, and Charlotte—as well as five other families—to visit. She had an excess of special dishes and comments to share with them all.

Chapter 8

The carriage was the largest she had ever seen, but it still felt close inside as she was inches from—and alone with—a man. Elizabeth sat face to face with Mr. Darcy, glancing out the window and watching the Hertfordshire estates disappearing one by one.

"Would you like another blanket? It is quite cold," he said gently.

"No, thank you, I am fine." She forced a smile.

"I was in a hurry to leave while the roads are still passable. If it continues snowing this way, it might become difficult to reach London."

"I understand that. I think it a wise decision."

"We shall stop in the middle of our journey to change horses and have some tea. We should be home by late afternoon."

Her "home" was miles away at Longbourn. "Very well," she answered.

Lucky attempted to find a place to rest, but the carriage floor was cold and hard. Darcy called him, and the dog hesitated a moment then jumped up and settled down on the warm, soft blanket. Darcy petted him briefly then met Elizabeth's gaze.

"Thank you," she said. "If he bothers you, I can have him by me."

"Not at all. This is the gentlemen's bench," he said, and she smiled openly.

Another period of silent staring out the window followed. Elizabeth's eyes were drawn to him from time to time, but he seemed preoccupied with admiring the passing scene.

"I believe we should speak a little, you know. It would look odd to be entirely silent for half a day together," she said suddenly, and he smiled, remembering her words from the ball.

"Very well—as I told you before, everything you wish me to say will be said."

"Oh, come, sir. That is not fair. We cannot possibly have the same conversation again. I would hope by now that you have discovered an interesting subject."

He laughed openly. "Very well, let me try. I know you are fond of books but not so fond of talking about them. So, shall I attempt the theatre? Or the opera? The season is open, and we shall have many opportunities to enjoy the performances if you like."

"Oh, yes, I would like that very much. Jane and I…" She paused and looked at him in earnest. "My Aunt Gardner has invited Jane to stay with her in London."

"Then you should consult with Miss Bennet and Georgiana about what plays you would like to see. I shall happily keep you company."

Elizabeth stared at him in disbelief. He held her gaze for a moment, and his countenance softened when her eyes sparkled with joy and her lips opened in a warm, heartfelt smile.

"Thank you. You are very kind. As for the subject of our conversation, anything would do."

"Then we may start by your not calling me 'sir' or 'Mr. Darcy' and my not calling you 'Miss Bennet.' It sounds awkward since we just married. Would you not approve, Elizabeth?"

Strangely, she felt a cold tingle down her spine when he spoke her name, and she tried to sound light and easy as she replied, but her voice was more a hesitant whisper.

"I do approve it, William—very much indeed."

"Good… Before going any further, there is a very serious matter we need to clarify at the beginning of our marriage. When we first met at the Meryton Assembly, my behaviour was highly improper. I cannot apologise enough for it. I recently discovered that you heard me speak to Bingley, decline to dance with you—and call you 'tolerable.' I am sorely ashamed of that, and I deeply regret my words. In fact, I regretted them almost immediately."

Elizabeth scarcely believed her eyes and ears. She could not decide whether she should answer seriously or impertinently. He seemed resolute, so she replied in the same manner.

"I cannot deny that I heard you and was a little offended…and yes, your manners were not the best that evening. I accept your apology, and please believe that I forgave you long ago."

"I thank you—you are most generous."

"Not at all—I confess I said many severe words about you in the days after that assembly."

"I am sure all of them were well deserved. But then, I did invite you to dance three more times, and you accepted only once."

"Three times? When do you mean? Surely, you were not serious on the first two occasions."

"Quite serious, truth to tell. But I took the rejections graciously. You must grant me that."

"Indeed." She felt warmer and more at ease with each word they shared.

As the time passed, she inquired further about his family and about looking forward to meeting them. He spoke warmly of his sister and of the Matlocks. Then, in a more grave tone, he told her about his Aunt Catherine, her desire for a marriage between him and his cousin Anne, and the expected opposition from his aunt. He had sent a detailed letter informing her about the marriage, but he entertained no hope that Lady Catherine would be sanguine about the news.

"Unfortunately, I expect her to be disagreeable when we first meet, but you must not worry. I will protect you from her anger. She can be very...unkind."

"You are very thoughtful, but there is no need to worry about me. I am quite able to protect myself when necessary. What truly worries me is your cousin Anne. Did she also hope for a marriage with you?"

"You are as considerate as I imagined you to be, Elizabeth. No, Anne and I discussed it long ago, and she did not wish such a marriage any more than I, so there is no need for concern. And I know you can protect yourself. I have seen you answer Caroline Bingley's mischief."

His tone turned lighter, and when she responded with a smile, he continued. "I am afraid I am the one to blame for Caroline's rudeness too. The day you refused my first invitation to dance at Sir William's, I confessed to her that I admired your fine eyes, and I believe she was not happy about that."

"You told her you admired my eyes at Lucas Lodge? But that was almost at the beginning of our acquaintance—before we came to stay at Netherfield!"

"Yes indeed..." he admitted, and their eyes locked again.

"Oh..." she said, feeling suddenly warm and not understanding why. She forced a laugh as she continued, "But do not blame yourself. I am sure Miss Bingley would have been rude even without your confession. She seemed quite proficient."

They openly smiled at each other with a meaningful gaze, and as the snow increased, she suddenly turned the subject to the weather. He asked her again whether she was warm enough; she was. Eventually, the carriage stopped as they had reached their resting place. Darcy helped her out, and she leant on his arm, stretching her legs and enjoying the fresh, chilled air. They walked together into the inn with Lucky closely following.

The reunion with the Matlocks was pleasant. Elizabeth had several cups of warm tea while the gentlemen preferred spirits to fight the cold. They ordered food, and Elizabeth, more at ease than before, enjoyed conversing openly with the earl and his sons. An hour later, they resumed the journey. Inside the carriage, Lucky immediately jumped on the seat beside Darcy and curled up. Elizabeth laughed.

"I am amazed to see how quickly he has attached himself to you. He has never done that before, not even with my parents and sisters. I cannot imagine what has happened to him. I am grateful that you allowed me to bring him."

"I could not possibly refuse such a lovely requirement," he said then smiled again. "I have a confession to make: when you told me you had a special requirement, I thought you wished to ask me about something quite different—your pin money, the jewels not stipulated in the settlement, or something similar."

She looked at him with wide eyes, and he continued. "As your father said, I still do not know you well enough, but I will be delighted to discover more of your true character every day, Elizabeth."

"As will I, William," she replied through a small, gentle smile.

There was silence again for some time, and then she suddenly said, "I, too, have something extraordinary to tell you. My Aunt Gardiner reminded me that I met Lady Anne and Georgiana ten years ago. Is that not astonishing?"

"When did that happen? Have you been in Derbyshire?"

"No, not in Derbyshire. The year my aunt and uncle married, they invited Jane and me to travel with them to Brighton. We were there almost a month. Jane and I used to go to the beach with a chaperone—Mrs. Johnson—every day, and apparently we became quite friendly with your mother and sister. My aunt was well acquainted with Lady Anne, and she was amazed one day when we all met. Unfortunately, I do not remember any details as I was very young. But my aunt knew Lady Anne, and she spoke with the warmest affection and admiration of her. She said she was truly the most beautiful, kind, and generous lady who ever existed. I am so sad that I do not remember her more vividly."

"Yes, she was. That is quite an astonishing story," he said briefly then suddenly leant back in his seat and turned his head to stare out the window. It was not difficult for Elizabeth to understand the sadness on his face. To lose a wonderful mother at such a young age was surely heartbreaking—and to have your father follow her several years later must have been a burden almost too difficult to bear for a young man with a younger sister in his care.

"I am sorry that my story saddened you," she said gently, and he turned to her.

"It is not your fault. I should apologise for being such poor company on our wedding journey. I was quite touched by the strange coincidence, and I believe Georgiana will be surprised and happy, too."

They returned to watching the road, and Darcy absently petted the dog. Elizabeth smiled, pleased that she finally found something to say to lift their spirits.

"You know, the same year we went to Brighton, I got Lucky as a gift for my tenth birthday. I remember him to be the most beautiful puppy I had ever seen. That memory is quite vivid. And I was devastated that I almost lost him. One day, we went to play on the beach. I still remember its being a rainy, windy day, and I was with only Jane and Mrs. Johnson. Lucky ran towards the water, and I hurried to catch him. Then I do not know what happened, but Mrs. Johnson said a wave took Lucky and me, and it seems both of us almost drowned. We were fortunate that a young man entered the water and saved us." She paused a moment then laughed, slightly embarrassed. "I am sure you must think I developed a habit of falling into water at an early age."

She expected him to share her amusement, but his countenance remained stern. "You were both fortunate indeed," he finally said in earnest. "Do you know who the young man was?"

"No, regrettably. Mrs. Johnson said he was young, but neither of us remembered his features. I still recall how he brought us out of the water, and the puppy seemed dead. I remember crying. Then he did something, and Lucky recovered miraculously. I named my dog 'Lucky' because our saviour said he was a very lucky dog—which was true. Uncle Gardiner attempted to discover the young man's identity and even searched for him in the town for several days but with no success. We believe he was only travelling through Brighton, and his presence was our good fortune. We never forgot him, and we never shall. So now you know, sir—forgive me—William. If you ever hear me speak about the hero of my life, it is about that young man," she concluded with an open smile, still puzzled by his reaction. The kind, amiable gentleman from the first part of their journey seemed gone, and the severe Mr. Darcy returned. Elizabeth had no hint of what she had done wrong.

"Thank you for sharing the story with me. We shall be home in less than half an hour."

"Very well. But did I say something wrong? I can see that you are upset and—"

"I am not upset, but I thank you for your concern. Here, we have just entered London."

Elizabeth was certain she was correct in her observation, but she respected his desire not to discuss it further. Soon, the carriage stopped in front of a large, impressive house, and Darcy stepped outside then offered her his arm and helped her out. She breathed deeply and looked closely at the tall building barely visible through the curtain of heavy snow. This is his home—our home, she said to herself.

He put her hand on his arm and smiled. Lucky, on his leash, was spinning at their feet.

"He is as nervous as I am," she said, forcing a laugh.

"Neither of you have reason for any anxiety, I assure you. Let us enter. It is very cold."

The door opened, and a large hall widened in front of her, revealing a butler, a maid, and an older woman waiting in line. Darcy greeted them and made the introductions: they were Stevens, Molly, and Mrs. Thomason, the housekeeper.

"I will show Mrs. Darcy to her apartment, and we will call for Molly shortly," he said. Elizabeth could feel the servants' stares following them with curiosity and wonder.

She had no time to worry about them as he stopped in front of another door and opened it slowly, waiting for her. She moved a few steps, then stopped and gasped as she looked around, barely able to breathe from the beauty around her.

"This is your apartment. Here is the main bedroom, there is a small office, and here is another smaller room, which is used for bathing. The maid will explain everything to you. The footmen will bring all your belongings immediately." His voice was calm and composed, but she found no words to answer. She glanced at the walls, the furniture, and the carpets, amazed by the elegant, harmonious arrangements.

"These rooms belonged to my mother. I moved into the main suite when my father passed away, but these chambers remained untouched. You may change anything you wish."

"It is perfect," she whispered, glancing at him then around the room again. "Just perfect…"

"I am glad you approve of it. And here is my apartment. Do you want to see it?" he asked tentatively and opened the adjoining door. She glanced inside his chamber. It was similar to hers, only the furniture was of a darker colour and with more severe lines.

"I asked Molly to arrange a place for Lucky in the corner of your bedchamber. I believe he should sleep in your room for a few days until he becomes accustomed to the place. Then he may be moved into your small office." Elizabeth looked at him in silence then placed her hand on his arm, her eyes holding his.

"You are very kind and considerate. I am astonished at how you thought of everything."

Darcy placed his hand over hers, returning the smile. "I will call for Molly to help you arrange your things and prepare for dinner. Would an hour be enough time? You must be hungry. I know I am. Georgiana and Mrs. Annesley will dine with us if you do not mind."

"Mind? I look forward to meeting them both. I shall be ready within an hour."

He withdrew his hand and moved towards his room. Then he stopped in the doorway. "Would you prefer to lock the doors? It is entirely your decision—however you would feel more comfortable."

The question took Elizabeth by surprise and she hesitated, her cheeks burning. "I believe we should close the door, so that Lucky won't trouble you. But I see no reason to lock it." He nodded in silent agreement, but she did not miss the light in his eyes.

A few minutes later, the maid arrived, and Elizabeth could not say which of them was more nervous. Elizabeth needed a few minutes to calm herself and to calm Molly before she decided what to ask her, how to arrange her clothes, and what to wear for dinner.

Before the hour ended, Elizabeth was ready. She gazed at her image in the mirror, reasonably content with her appearance. She dismissed Molly, and when the maid exited, Darcy entered, not from his room but from the hallway. Elizabeth smiled at him. Then she looked silently at the young girl who seemed to hide behind him.

"Elizabeth, allow me to introduce my sister, Georgiana. I believed it would be easier for you two to meet before dinner. Georgiana, this is Elizabeth."

"I am very happy to meet you, Miss Darcy. I have heard many wonderful things about you."

"And I about you, Miss Bennet… Oh, forgive me, Mrs. Darcy." Georgiana turned pale, and Elizabeth noticed her hands were trembling. She needed but a moment to understand that Miss Darcy was exceedingly shy and uncomfortable about their meeting.

"Please do not worry. I still think of myself as Miss Bennet." Elizabeth smiled.

"Yes, I believe we will all need a bit of time to adapt to our present situation.

Let us sit for a moment," Darcy invited them both. "Elizabeth, I was just telling Georgiana about the extraordinary coincidence of your meeting her and our mother ten years ago."

While they spoke, Lucky approached tentatively, watching the new guest. Darcy called him, and the dog stepped closer to his feet then moved to sniff Georgiana. Elizabeth was afraid the animal might reject Georgiana, but he continued to move around her. Georgiana stretched her hand and Lucky sniffed it then sat beside her. She gently petted his head.

"Unfortunately, I do not remember much about that meeting, but I am very happy to make your acquaintance again. And it seems my dog remembers you." Elizabeth laughed.

"I do not remember either… I was five or six years old then," Miss Darcy whispered.

"Elizabeth, I told Georgiana about your enjoyment of theatre and opera. I believe you will have many things in common."

"I understand you are very fond of music and play exquisitely at the piano forte."

"Not really—but I am fond of music. My brother says he enjoyed your playing very much."

"I am afraid Mr. Darcy was too generous with his praise. Someone as proficient as you are will surely find my playing quite wanting, but I hope my technique will improve by association with you," Elizabeth replied with a large, genuine smile, and Darcy laughed, observing that they were both being too modest.

"Elizabeth, would you like a short tour of the house before dinner?"

"I would love to see the house if you and Miss Darcy would be so kind as to show me…"

Darcy was impressed by Elizabeth's elegant gesture of including Georgiana in their plan. He offered an arm to each of them, congratulating himself on performing the introduction in an intimate environment. Things appeared to go even better than he hoped. He could easily see that his sister was already partial to Elizabeth.

They started with the first floor, and Elizabeth was shown the drawing room, the dining room, the music room, and finally the library. Next, they moved to the gallery, and Elizabeth was immediately drawn to a large painting representing the master of the house, wearing a striking resemblance to Mr. Darcy, with such a smile over his face as she remembered to have sometimes seen when he looked at her. She briefly glanced at him and saw that smile again. She felt her cheeks blushing.

"This is a beautiful portrait of William from when he was three and twenty. There is a similar one at Pemberley. Our father ordered them," Georgiana said with no little emotion.

"And here is one of our mother and Georgiana. It was painted nine years ago, the year she…" He paused, watching Elizabeth who stepped in front of the painting as if mesmerised. She moved closer, took a few steps backward then closer again, and gently brushed her fingers against it in a caress.

"I do remember her," Elizabeth whispered with a trembling voice. "I remember her very well. Jane and I believed we had never seen such a beautiful lady. I remember her soft voice, her gentle smile… How could I have ever thought that I forgot her? And I remember the girl with the blue eyes too." She then turned around, watching them with tearful eyes, her lips slightly trembling. "I remember you, Georgiana."

Georgiana glanced at her brother, then her blue eyes danced with tears, and she stretched her hands towards Elizabeth, who took them briefly then gently embraced the girl. Darcy watched them, not daring to interfere. Yes, fate had a strange way of playing with their minds and souls.

After a time, Elizabeth and Georgiana broke their embrace, sharing embarrassed smiles. Elizabeth dared to glance at Darcy, wondering what he would say of her presumption, but she could read nothing in his countenance. Georgiana suddenly remembered that Mrs. Annesley awaited her, so she left them with the promise of meeting at dinner in a few minutes. Elizabeth and Darcy looked at each other in silence before Lady Anne's portrait.

"Forgive me. I do not know what came over me. I could not control my emotion. That has never happened to me before. I hope I did not disturb Miss Darcy."

He moved a step closer and gently took her hands in his. She did not oppose him but waited quietly. Without a word, he gently lifted her hands to his chest. She did not dare move as the touch of his fingers strangely burned her bare skin, imparting a sensation she had never felt before. Holding her eyes and searching for a sign of opposition, he bowed his head and gently touched the backs of her hands with his lips. She shivered, but she did not withdraw her hands. He gently brushed her fingers with his then smiled.

"Welcome to the family, Mrs. Darcy. Now let us dine. I believe we are expected."

Dinner was a warm family gathering: Mr. Darcy smiled more than ever before, Miss Darcy tried to overcome her shyness, and Mrs. Annesley possessed perfect manners and a gift for conversation. Elizabeth felt almost her usual self, barely able to believe the kindness of her new family. She briefly remembered how ill Mr. Wickham spoke of Miss Darcy, and she grew angry with him for his ungenerous description. Surely, no one could believe Miss Darcy to be proud and cold.

The dinner smoothly came to an end, and they retired early. Darcy escorted Elizabeth upstairs, neither of them looking at the other. She wondered what would happen next as they had not spoken about this moment of their marriage since the day of his proposal. What would he do? What did he expect of her? She did not dare to ask herself what she wished him to do next, so she waited in silence.

Darcy opened the door to their apartments and entered her bedchamber.

"Dinner was lovely—thank you," she said.

"I am glad you enjoyed it. Molly prepared your bath, and she will help you to get ready for the night. I shall come to see you later if that is convenient."

She stood still, staring at him, not knowing how to reply. She shivered when his fingers removed a lock of hair from her forehead. What will he do next?

"Elizabeth…" His low, warm voice rushed at her heart as he took her hands in his and spoke further. "I have not forgotten what I promised you, nor shall I break my word. I could not wish for a better first day of our marriage, and I only hope your feelings are the same."

"Yes, they are… And I heartily thank you for your kind consideration, Mr.— William. I know it is your right to…that it is my duty to…"

He smiled again and kissed her hand once more. "As I said, you should enjoy your bath and prepare for the night. I shall come to say goodnight later but only for a moment."

He left through the adjoining door, and she glanced after him then startled when she heard Molly's voice. The maid informed her that Lucky had been fed and her bath was ready. Elizabeth was content to enter the tub and wrap herself in the soft care of the hot water, her eyes closed, left only to herself and her thoughts.

Darcy's last words, reassuring her that he intended to give her time to accustom herself to her new position, had been the only thing missing for that day to be perfect. She could not imagine a more considerate, generous, and kind man than her husband proved to be this first day of their marriage. With every new moment in his company and every opportunity of knowing him and understanding him better, she realised how little she had known him before and how unfair had been her judgment of his character.

He surely was not an easy man to live with, and he was still a puzzle to her. She could not forget his strange changes of disposition during their journey or the moments he looked at her with an expression she could not read—just as she could not forget his severe, haughty manners when they first met in Hertfordshire. All these were parts of Mr. Darcy—her husband—a man who had described himself as being resentful and having enough faults, and a man who wished to share his life with her and even insisted on doing so.

Her body became heavier as her mind and her heart grew lighter. She recollected the emotional moment as she recognised Lady Anne Darcy in the portrait, still wondering about the force of her reaction. Surely, she was too tired, missed her family too much, and was too worried about her future. But he was so kind, so gentle. She shivered again, remembering the touch of his fingers on her skin, the softness of his lips on her hand…

"Mrs. Darcy, are you well? Forgive me—I want to help you out as the water is almost cold."

Molly's voice and worried look brought Elizabeth back from her thoughts, and she smiled at the maid. Only then did she feel the coolness of the water and hurry out. A few minutes later, she was dressed in her nightgown and robe. She thanked Molly, dismissed her for the night, and was greatly amused when she heard the maid's sigh of relief. The poor girl was truly nervous. She needed to talk to her tomorrow to calm her.

Her own nerves were tried when a knock on the door startled her. She invited Darcy to come in and remained motionless in surprise when he entered wearing only a robe and nightshirt. The first thing she noticed was his bare neck. She gulped several times then managed to look up at him. He seemed as surprised as she was, staring at her in silence, and she suddenly worried whether her hair, left loose on her shoulders, looked all right.

"I just came to ask if all is well and to wish you good night."

"Yes, everything is fine, thank you."

"Good—good… Is there… Is there anything you wish to do tomorrow? Oh, but we can better talk about that tomorrow. I imagine you must be very tired."

"No, I am not. In fact, I believe I am tired, as I confess I hardly slept more than a few hours during these last nights since… I hope I sleep better tonight."

"Yes, I hope that too. Well then—good night." He took a few steps then turned hesitantly.

"Would you like to have a glass of wine with me? I mean, if you do not…"

"Yes, I would like that very much," she heard herself answering, and he immediately disappeared into his room and returned with two bottles of wine and two glasses. He arranged them on a small table near the window and invited her to sit in an armchair. It was snowing again, and the streets were empty, covered with a brightly shining carpet. With surprise, she watched him take a small blanket and cover her with it. She did not even attempt to object.

"Two bottles of wine? You really believe one is not enough?" She laughed to hide her nervousness.

He laughed back in obvious good spirits. "I believe this wine will be more to your liking. Lady Matlock—my aunt—and Lady Maryanne, Thomas's wife, are very fond of it."

He poured her glass half full and toasted her. Then she moistened her lips in it, took a sip, and sighed. "Oh, this is very good indeed. I rarely drink wine, but this tastes wonderful."

"I am glad you enjoy it. A little wine will help you sleep better."

"I hope so. Oh, how beautifully it is snowing. I love when it is snowing. Winter is so beautiful at Longbourn."

"I like snow too, but I would rather be home to enjoy it in peace. I am glad we arrived here in time. This weather can be dangerous on a long journey. That is why we do not go to Pemberley for Christmas unless we have decided to stay there at least three months. Pemberley is beautiful in winter, too."

"Yes, my aunt told me that. May I please have a little more wine?" He was surprised to see that she had already emptied her glass. He filled it again and smiled.

"I am pleased you enjoy it, but you should be careful. Its taste is pleasant, but its effect is strong."

"Oh, do not worry. I shall be fine. When will we go to Pemberley?"

"I am not certain. If for me alone, I would leave as soon as possible, but I imagine you will enjoy staying in Town for the season—and my aunt Matlock has planned some balls and dinners for us to attend in order to introduce you to London society, she says. She will better explain that to you directly."

"I imagine many people will hate me. Do Caroline and Louisa know about the wedding?"

"They surely found out today as the announcement appeared in the newspaper."

"Is the house secure, do you think? It is good that Lucky is sleeping with me for protection."

He laughed heartily. "I am here to protect you too. But I hope you have no reason to fear."

"Oh, I would not count on that. And I would like a little more wine. This armchair is so comfortable, and the blanket is so soft. Look how lovely it is snowing. I will only stay up a moment longer..." Her voice became weaker, and she dropped her head as her eyelids drifted closed. He smiled, and his heart melted as he saw her so young, so fragile, curled in the armchair, covered in the blanket, and falling asleep. The fatigue and the two quick glasses of wine had overcome her completely.

He gently took her in his arms and placed her in the bed then covered her with a blanket. She sighed and sought a better position. He again wrapped the blanket around her then tried to rise from the bed and leave. She suddenly opened her eyes and took his hand. Her eyes were sparkling from the wine, and she could barely keep them open.

"You are a good man, Fitzwilliam Darcy. You are not as frightening as I believed you to be."

"You believed me to be frightening?" He was half amused and half embarrassed at taking advantage of her situation and attempted to leave, but her hold on his hand prevented it.

"Yes! Well, to be honest, the first time I saw you, I believed you were very handsome. That is—before you started to speak and offended everyone around you. And you refused to dance with me..."

"Will you ever forgive me?" he asked in jest, a large smile on his face, but she answered very seriously.

"I am sure I will, eventually. You are even more handsome when you smile. You should smile more."

"Very well, your wish is my command. Now, we should go to sleep. You are very tired."

"Oh, I am not tired at all..." She barely spoke, her eyes closed.

"Yes, I know you are not tired, but it is almost dawn."

"I am a little warm. I need to take my robe off." She rose to sit.

"Here, let me help you." He gently opened her robe and removed it from her shoulders. Then he laid her against the pillows.

"Thank you," she whispered. "You know, Mr. Darcy, we are actually spending the wedding night together, are we not?" She was barely coherent, and finally released his hand.

"Yes, we actually are." He smiled. "Good night, Elizabeth."

"Good night, Mr. Darcy…William," she managed to reply in a low voice. Then her breathing became regular as sleep took her completely.

Darcy remained still, watching her closely. Her face was serene, her eyes resting behind long, dark lashes, her lips slightly parted as she breathed steadily. Her beauty was astonishing and nearly stole his breath away. Her hair was spread out on the white skin of her shoulders, and the smooth fabric of her nightdress was moving with every breath, gently caressing her skin. She gently sighed in her sleep, smiling at a dream known only to her. He removed a lock of hair from her temple. She sighed.

What was it about this young woman that bewitched him so completely? What was so different about her that his control was so easily lost? How was it possible that he needed to struggle so to keep his own promise to her—that he was so tempted and eager to taste the softness of her lips? How would he be able to keep his own promise, and for how long? And what was fate doing to him? Why was it playing with his mind? How was it possible that, of all the girls in the world, she was the one who needed to be saved by him—twice?

He gently touched her hair again, smiling. He had no doubt that she was the young girl he had saved from the sea ten years earlier—strange, frightening, extraordinary coincidence but real nevertheless. He had been in Brighton with Robert, visiting his mother, whose state of health was failing.

He vividly remembered the day Dr. Taylor told him her health was declining with every passing day and there was nothing he could do. He ran out to walk on the beach, alone with his fear of losing his beloved mother, when he saw the little girl and the puppy taken by the waves. He had entered the water without hesitation and taken the girl and the puppy to shore. He did not remember the girl's features. He barely remembered looking at her face at all. But he did remember her brave, small voice, thanking him—not for saving her but her puppy. And he clearly remembered telling her that her puppy was truly lucky.

That the little girl proved to be Elizabeth and that she remembered the situation so clearly were equally amazing and disconcerting. Yes, fate was laughing at him.

He leant and gently caressed her hair again, watching her beautiful, serene face. "I am your hero from ten years ago, Elizabeth. But I cannot possibly tell you that—not now. I cannot use the past to make you accept me, but I shall be your hero again one day!"

Chapter 9

London, 28 December

Nestled in bed, Elizabeth looked around. It was full daylight though the curtains were still closed. She spotted Lucky in a corner, sleeping soundly. Only then, did the revelation strike her: she was in her new apartment in her new home.

She tried to recollect which of her memories was real. Her meeting with Georgiana, the paintings in the gallery, and her remembrance of Lady Anne, the dinner…then he came with a bottle of wine, and she remembered them talking and drinking—and nothing else.

"We are actually spending the wedding night together, are we not?" she had asked him, and the meaning of her words coloured her cheeks and put a knot in her stomach. How did she dare say such a thing? She could only hope that he would blame the wine she had drunk—which was equally outrageous for a lady. Indeed, what would he think of her?

She rang for Molly. The maid helped her dress and told her that Mr. Darcy had been in the library for at least two hours. Miss Darcy and Mrs. Annesley were in the music room. No, they had not breakfasted yet. Yes, Molly had taken Lucky out and walked him briefly.

Elizabeth left her rooms in search of the others with Lucky trotting at her feet. She glanced around to remember where the main rooms were situated. She finally found the library, briefly hesitated, and then knocked and opened the door after she heard his inviting voice.

She saw Darcy at the desk and tried to read his expression. He greeted her and encouraged her to come forward. At his side, however, was his dog, Titan, a Great Dane with spots similar to Lucky's but of a much more impressive size. Titan showed his displeasure towards the newly arrived animal. Both dogs seemed ready to fight, but Darcy's strong voice calmed Titan and made him retire to the fireplace. Lucky was still fixed on his opponent.

"They need to learn to accept each other. I will ask Stevens to take them together on a long walk every morning. Titan has been accustomed to master the house."

"We appeared unexpectedly. It is no easier for the dog to accept our intrusion than it is for the rest of your family," she said, attempting a smile while he helped her to sit. "I overslept. I am sorry. I usually wake up very early."

"You are part of my family now," he said in earnest. "I am glad you rested longer. I believe you were very tired." A small smile appeared on his lips.

"Yes, I was." She paused a moment then continued, daringly. "I know I had one too many glasses of wine last night. That has never happened to me before. How did I get to my bed?"

"Easily…with a little help." His smile grew. "Yes, it was obvious you were not accustomed to the wine. I hope you are well?"

"Yes, perfectly well, thank you," she replied, trying to hide her embarrassment.

"Excellent. Then allow me to inform you about our daily plans. I need to work several hours after breakfast. Georgiana studies every day around noon, and Mrs. Annesley watches her. You could join them if you want, or you may find a book to read if you prefer. Lady Matlock sent a card. She wants to visit if it is convenient for you. She will host a small party on New Year's Eve. I believe she plans to introduce you to some of her friends. This might be a daunting task, but I am afraid it must be done." He paused briefly, allowing her time to answer, but Elizabeth only nodded, a tentative smile frozen on her lips.

"I took the liberty last week, after we agreed upon our marriage, to order you some new gowns. Lady Maryanne helped me. You will need them for the Season and for the Twelfth Night Ball. A modiste will come later to take your measurements for the final fitting. Please feel free to tell her anything you wish to change. I ordered five gowns. You may add as many as you think necessary."

Elizabeth watched him in silence, as she wondered how he could change so frequently in such a short time. He spoke, with no smile to warm his countenance—just a business arrangement. No detail escaped his attention and nothing remained outside his control. She knew he was doing it for her benefit, but she missed the previous night's short encounter when he seemed so open and at ease in his casual clothes as he invited her to have a glass of wine with him and carefully covered her with the blanket.

Which of his many faces truly belongs to him—to my husband, she found herself wondering as she spoke up with a calmness that surprised her.

"Thank you, I believe five new dresses will be more than enough."

"Then shall we go to breakfast? Georgiana and Mrs. Annesley must be waiting for us."

He politely directed her to the breakfast room while he continued to speak of the next days' events. Elizabeth listened and approved in silence.

They all gathered at the breakfast table, and Georgiana, as well as Mrs. Annesley, greeted her with obvious pleasure. To Elizabeth's astonishment, Lucky hurried towards Georgiana, and she welcomed him with a smile and a caress.

Mrs. Annesley informed Elizabeth that she had Mr. Darcy's permission to visit her expectant daughter in Scarborough for three months, beginning at the end of February, and she asked whether Elizabeth had any objection to that arrangement. Elizabeth had none.

Soon after breakfast, Darcy returned to his business, and to Elizabeth's disbelief, Lucky joined him, abandoning his mistress with only a brief glance. Despite the revelation of their previous encounter, neither Georgiana nor Elizabeth found much to say to each other, and a sudden awkwardness fell upon the chamber. Mrs. Annesley inquired about the Bennet family, and Elizabeth answered warmly. Then she mentioned her relatives in town and that she expected her sister Jane to arrive soon with her uncle and aunt.

Later, events followed precisely as Mr. Darcy had said. The modiste came to take her measurements, informing her that two gowns would be delivered on December 31 and asking whether she could possibly come to the shop for the final fitting of the Twelfth Night ball gown. Elizabeth accepted it, spoke little, and thanked her.

As the modiste left, Elizabeth felt burdened by the complete silence of the house and recollected that time of the year at Longbourn: much laughter, many fights and arguments, and voices raised in joy and happiness. Nothing at Longbourn could compare with the splendour of her husband's house, yet it seemed so still, lifeless, and cold in its perfection. She wondered whether anyone ever spoke or laughed loudly in that impressive edifice.

She glanced through a window. It was still snowing steadily, and she missed the smell of freezing air. Perhaps tomorrow she would take a stroll around the house. Yet, it was not likely, as she was expecting Lady Matlock's call—a visit that brought Elizabeth equal curiosity and concern. What should she expect from such an illustrious lady who was aware that she only married because of unfortunate events and malicious gossip?

Elizabeth ceased her thoughts, and after a brief hesitation, she returned to the library door and knocked reluctantly. Darcy's voice invited her to enter.

"Is everything well? Were you pleased with the modiste?"

"Yes, all is well, thank you. I only wish to borrow a book if you do not mind. Oh, and I should take Lucky. He can be troublesome at times."

"Please choose any book you prefer. Shall I help you? Do not worry about Lucky. He is quite well behaved," he replied with a warm smile, and she felt herself suddenly blushing.

Elizabeth stepped around the impressive library, overwhelmed by the richness of the book collection. She looked at each item, but she felt herself growing warmer as her husband's gaze burned her back. He was staring at her—she was certain of that—and she imagined he was impatient with her indecision. In haste, she grabbed a volume of Shakespeare.

"I believe this is it. I will return to my room to read now."

"As you wish. Will you not join Georgiana in the music room? She is with Mrs. Annesley."

"I do not want to interrupt her in the middle of her practice. I hope to meet them later."

She left the room in a hurry and noticed that he continued to stare at her. He still made her uncomfortable, something their marriage had not changed in the slightest.

Darcy gazed at the closed door. He had been tempted to ask her to stay and read on the couch near him, but somehow he had felt ill at ease doing that, which was quite ridiculous. After all, she was his wife.

He was unaccustomed to the idea of Elizabeth being in his house. Thinking of her had kept him awake so many nights that it seemed unreal to have her so close. Yet, she was quite real. And she still kept him awake—which was proved the previous night when, unlike her, he had barely slept at all.

He had found their little interlude the previous night quite charming, but once he was alone in his room, sleep would not come. Her presence in the next room troubled him until dawn: her image, her scent, her smiles, her teasing words, her eyes glancing at him through her eyelashes, the softness of her skin when he removed her robe, her hair falling heavily on her bare shoulders, her warm body undisguised through the thin fabric of her nightgown.

He regretted his promise not to consummate their marriage for the present. He knew he could help her enjoy their marriage bed, and it probably would strengthen their bond. A moment later, however, he rejected such thoughts, which he knew to be only the result of his weakness, selfish desire, and strange lack of control where Elizabeth was concerned.

Unable to determine the proper way to behave around her, Darcy adopted the same strategy as he had when she stayed at Netherfield in the autumn: he put a little distance between them. Accordingly, he addressed her with more propriety and less warmth than the previous night, and he pretended to be very busy as a reason not to invite her to join him in the library. He felt it was safer that way.

He must find a way to keep his weaknesses under good regulation and to respect his promise. He would not impose on her until he was certain that she welcomed his attentions. He could think of nothing more horrible than her surrendering to him only because it was her duty to do so. He might be able to make her body enjoy his attentions, but that was not enough.

Lucky and Titan barked at the same time when Stevens entered the library, apologising repeatedly, and handed Darcy a letter. Darcy opened it and easily recognised Annabelle Stafford's handwriting. He put it on his desk then took it up again and glanced at it. She had obviously discovered the news of his marriage, and her anger was clearly expressed. He threw the letter in the fire, wondering when he would receive a similar letter from Lady Catherine so the party would be complete. Fortunately, he knew that Caroline Bingley would never dare to write him directly, so he had one less thing to worry about.

On the way to her room, a sudden thought changed Elizabeth's mind, and she turned towards the gallery. For some time she admired the portrait of Darcy then the one of Lady Anne and Georgiana. She also dedicated many moments to looking at a painting of the entire family, noting her husband's resemblance to his parents. She was determined to understand his true character, but the task was proving difficult.

She remembered his asking her whether she wished to lock the doors between their rooms. At that time, she answered without much thought. She truly had no reason to distrust him, and he was obviously content with her reaction. Besides, of what use would it be to lock the doors. He promised that he would not impose on her. If he wished it, she would be forced to accept his will anyway, doors locked or not.

Elizabeth was surprised that she enjoyed their time together before falling asleep the previous night. She remembered that he carried her to the bed and helped her to remove her night robe, and she could not fight her embarrassment and the revelation that his closeness was not at all unpleasant. If she only knew what he was thinking and why his smiles appeared and vanished so easily.

She knew she needed to be patient. It was only the second day of their marriage. She would dearly love to speak to Jane about all this, but Jane was far away—as was her previous life.

Leaving the gallery, Elizabeth met Mrs. Thomason in the hallway.

"Mrs. Darcy, is anything wrong? May I help you in any way, ma'am?" she said worriedly.

"Everything is fine, Mrs. Thomason. However, tomorrow I would like to speak to you about the household and to better know the staff. I barely met them for a few moments."

The housekeeper's disconcerted expression did not escape Elizabeth, but the answer came with perfect politeness. "To know the staff better? Certainly, Mrs. Darcy, as you please. May I dare ask…is there anything special that you require from them? Shall I prepare them…?"

"No, nothing special. I simply want to speak to them a little and, as I said, to find out more about running this house. You seem to do an excellent job."

"Speak to them all? There are twenty-two and… Of course, as you wish, Mrs. Darcy."

"Tomorrow we might begin by talking, just the two of us, and in the next days we shall find a way for me to speak to each of them without detaining them from their jobs."

"Very well, ma'am. I shall wait for you to ring for me anytime you please, Mrs. Darcy." The housekeeper still seemed troubled. Elizabeth attempted to re-assure her once more that there was no reason for concern, but Mrs. Thomason excused herself and left.

Elizabeth was neither oblivious nor insensitive towards Mrs. Thomason's feelings.

The sudden appearance of a new mistress was surely an event that brought much distress and worry below stairs. In truth, becoming the mistress of Darcy's household so suddenly brought much distress to herself too.

Elizabeth finally returned to her room and put the book on the bed. Then she took her diary and wrote hurriedly, wishing to make as vivid as possible the first impressions of her new family—especially of the man with whom she would spend the rest of her life.

"Since yesterday, Mr. Fitzwilliam Darcy has been my husband, and although I still cannot believe that this marriage is real—it seems so far from what I had dreamt of—my husband was nothing but kind and considerate during the first day and night of our marriage. And yet I know little more of him than I did a week ago except that he can smile when he wishes to…and that he is the son of the most remarkable lady I have ever known…and that Lucky seems more attached to him every day."

She closed the diary then glared outside. If she were at Longbourn—or even in London with her own relatives—she would run out to feel the snowflakes on her face. Surely, Lydia and Kitty—and perhaps even Jane, together with their young cousins—were doing so. They would likely prepare for the ball on the last day of the year. The Meryton assembly would be fully crowded. Most of Meryton loved the balls, especially the last one of the year, except her father—whose tastes seemed strangely similar to Mr. Darcy's.

She wondered for a moment whether her husband or Miss Darcy would be interested in a walk, but she shortly abandoned the idea. She felt the silence fall heavier with each passing moment. Only the burning fire was lively.

She startled when she heard her husband's voice. He was standing near the door as Lucky sneaked between his legs and hurried to her.

"Forgive me for the intrusion. I wanted to see whether you approve dinner in an hour."

"No intrusion at all—please come in. I was just looking outside. It is snowing so beautifully," she said, slightly embarrassed. "Yes, one hour would be perfect."

Darcy stepped closer and spoke with warmth and concern. "Are you well? You seem troubled. Is there anything I can do for you?"

"It is nothing. I was thinking of my family. Such days are always lively at Longbourn, and snow is one of our favourite things. We used to play outside in a quite unladylike manner."

He smiled and, to her utter surprise, took her hands in his. Her fingers remained still, and she suddenly felt very warm as he spoke in a low voice.

"I imagine you miss your family. I am afraid our company is far from entertaining."

"I do miss my family, but it is not the fault of your company. It is just that everything has changed so quickly, but I am sure tomorrow will be much better."

"I spoke with Georgiana. She said she would like to spend more time with you and to play together at the piano, but she did not dare to trouble you."

"Truly? I would love to practice with her too. Perhaps we can do so tomorrow. I am a little ashamed of my lack of proficiency. Fortunately, she seems kind enough not to laugh at me."

"No one could find any reason to laugh at you. I look forward to the pleasure of hearing both of you play if you would indulge me."

Her fingers moved slightly, and his touch tightened gently. "I should prepare for dinner," she said, and he released her hands, his fingers lingering for an instant.

"I shall fetch you in an hour." Elizabeth's eyes remained fixed upon the doors then glanced at her hands as though she could see the marks of his touch. She felt cold shivers along her arms as she remembered the warmth and softness of his fingers.

Elizabeth changed her gown in a hurry and found herself anxiously awaiting his return. He was right: his company was less than entertaining, but it was not at all unpleasant.

Darcy returned, and Elizabeth noticed that his neck cloth, of a dark green colour, suited him nicely. She blushed and averted her eyes. He offered his arm, and she took it without hesitation, then he covered her hand with his palm. She smiled, but he took no notice.

DINNER WAS AS PLEASANT AS IT WAS THE PREVIOUS EVENING AND EVEN MORE SO, as all three of them grew more at ease with every passing moment.

"Oh, I will surely miss this beefsteak when I leave," Mrs. Annesley declared. "I should ask the cook to give me the recipe."

"It is my favourite too," Darcy said. "It is delicious, although our cook at Pemberley used to make it somewhat differently. I truly miss the former taste of dishes at Pemberley."

"As do I," Miss Darcy agreed. "I vividly remember an apple pie that was always my favourite. I was just thinking that I have not eaten that particular pie in many years."

"I remember it too," Darcy added as he gently caressed his sister's hand. "We used to enjoy it quite often when my mother was still with us. It was the favourite of us all. I believe it is why we think it tasted so differently than other apple pies."

"Yes, I am sure you are right," Miss Darcy whispered. "Perhaps I just missed the taste of childhood." She averted her eyes and forced a smile while she turned to Elizabeth and apologised for her improper reaction during dinner. Before Elizabeth found the words to reply, Darcy continued warmly, glancing at them both.

"My dear, we are all family here and must not apologise for what we feel, nor must we hide our emotions. Besides, I am sure Elizabeth misses the dishes from Longbourn too."

"Oh, I do," she replied animatedly, attempting to dissipate the emotions. "Our cook, Mrs. West, is very skilled too. And usually, this time of the year, my aunt Gardiner spoils us with some exquisite recipes stolen from her aunt in Lambton."

"Did I understand correctly that Miss Bennet will come to London after the

New Year with Mr. and Mrs. Gardiner?" Darcy inquired.

"Yes. My aunt invited Jane to spend a month in London with them."

"I was thinking—perhaps we can invite them to dine with us the day after their arrival…if it is convenient for you and they have no other fixed engagements." A tentative smile lit his countenance, his dark eyes resting upon Elizabeth's surprised expression.

"I…I would like that very much, thank you. Oh, I am sure they will be happy to accept the invitation, and I will be so happy to have them all here!"

Darcy turned to his sister. "Georgiana, I am sure you will like Miss Bennet, as well as Mrs. and Mr. Gardiner, very much. They are delightful company."

"I will be very happy to meet them," Miss Darcy declared.

"And they will be happy to meet you too," Elizabeth said. "My aunt admired your mother. She always said that such an exceptional lady could rarely be found."

"Unfortunately, I do not remember her very well," Miss Darcy whispered. "Most of what I know is from what my brother told me. Perhaps Mrs. Gardiner could tell me more."

"I am sure she can! You resemble Lady Anne very closely. My aunt will be impressed."

"Thank you," Miss Darcy replied, her emotion obvious.

They enjoyed dinner in silence for some time. As soon as the meal was over, Mrs. Annesley and Georgiana retired, the girl apologising to Elizabeth for being such poor company.

Darcy invited Elizabeth to the settee, and she had a cup of tea while he enjoyed his brandy.

"As I told you, we are not a joyful company," he said.

"I hope my remarks did not upset Georgiana. She seemed a little sad…"

"Do not worry. It was not your fault. She is often sad when we speak of our parents. We feel their loss most painfully, even after all these years."

"I cannot imagine how it would be to lose both parents at such a young age. You seem very close to each other."

"We are—at least I hope so. I believe that, for some time, she considered me more a father than a brother. I am very fond of her. She is my only close family. Forgive me—she was my only close family. Now you are here too."

More than his words, his voice stunned her, and her eyes remained locked with his in complete silence. Then she suddenly said, wondering about her own words as she spoke:

"I am very happy to be here."

Darcy stared at her, his surprise obvious and his gaze so intense that she bore it only a moment before averting her eyes. He took hold of her hands, raised her right one, and placed a warm kiss on the back of it, his lips lingering. Shivers shattered her skin, and her cheeks burned. He did not release her hands, and she did not attempt to withdraw them.

"Thank you for suggesting my relatives come to dinner," Elizabeth finally spoke.

"There is no need to thank me. Their company gives me pleasure. Besides, I imagine you are anxious to meet your sister as soon as possible," he replied, releasing her hands.

"Yes, very anxious… I shall write to Jane immediately to tell her about the invitation."

"Then I would suggest we retire so you will have time to write the letter."

Once inside their apartments, both remained still in the middle of the room, gazing at each other, uncertain how to proceed. Lucky walked around their legs for a short while then lay at his place in the corner for a well-deserved sleep.

"So Lucky was given to you by Mr. and Mrs. Gardiner the same year you were in Brighton?" Darcy inquired, and Elizabeth felt relieved that he provided a subject of conversation.

"Yes—can you imagine a better uncle? To take his nieces on their first journey with his new wife and give me a dog for my tenth birthday. Truly astonishing!"

"Quite astonishing. But I am sure neither you nor Miss Bennet gave them much trouble. I am sure you were proper and well-behaved young girls."

"Oh, I am embarrassed to say you are wrong." Elizabeth laughed. "Jane was always perfectly well behaved, even from a young age. As for me, I am afraid I still do not excel in that area—as you have witnessed with disapproval several times."

"I rarely disapproved of anything in you," he replied in earnest, and her smile vanished while their gazes held. "However, I confess you surprised me several times with your habits, especially walking across fields in bad weather. That can be very dangerous."

"I am not sure 'surprised' sounds better than 'disapproved,'" she joked.

"Surprise surely does not mean disapproval. You cannot argue with that although you seem decided to contradict me, Mrs. Darcy," he replied in jest.

"Oh, I must have given you the wrong impression. I would not dare to contradict my husband, Mr. Darcy," she teased him. His countenance became more serious.

"Elizabeth, I do hope you will continue to contradict me anytime you wish. I have always admired your spirit, your courage, and your determination in expressing your ideas. I do not want you to feel that you need to change because we have married."

His words surprised her once more, and she needed a few moments before she was confident to reply properly. "Thank you for telling me that. And you may count on my impertinence in the coming years too if that is your wish, Mr. Darcy."

He laughed openly, and she joined him while their hands entwined. They looked at each other for a few long moments, then he slowly withdrew.

"I had better go to my room. You must be tired. It is quite late."

"Oh, I am not tired. I have done so little today that I cannot be tired. And staying inside all day long is not very helpful for my sleep either."

"Yes, I imagine. Tomorrow my aunt will call, and that might take some time.

And in the morning, I have some business to attend to, even before breakfast. But the day after tomorrow we shall take a long walk in Hyde Park. The snow is beautiful indeed."

"I would really like that very much! I look forward to it."

"As do I. Now I shall leave you…that is, if there is nothing else you need. You should ring for Molly to help you for the night."

"Yes, thank you, I do not want to detain you longer. Good night then…"

Darcy placed a chaste kiss on her hand and walked towards his rooms. From the adjoining door, he glanced at her. She was looking at him too. He wished nothing more than to stay longer and enjoy her company, and he could easily see that she was not opposed to it. He had held her hands several times that day, and the feel of her warm, soft fingers moving shyly in his palm still affected him. He wished to stay longer. He wished to stay for the entire night, but he left and closed the doors, forcing himself not to return. After a few minutes, he heard Molly's voice, and his mind filled with images of Elizabeth writing her letter on the small table, dressed in her nightgown, barefoot, her long hair falling loose…

That night, however, his mind was more at peace, and sleep finally took him. He had every reason to be content with the slow development of their relationship, and he had no doubt that, this time, he did not misunderstand her willingness to be around him.

In her room, Elizabeth postponed the letter for the next morning, but she filled two more pages in her diary, wondering why her husband, who declared his admiration for her several times, did not even ask her to have a glass of wine before they went to sleep. Only a small glass would suffice—enough to talk more about the walk he had promised her.

Chapter 10

London, 29 December

Dawn had barely broken when Elizabeth awoke. She guessed it was around seven o'clock. There was no sound from her husband's chambers. It was so early that Lucky glanced at his mistress then returned to a peaceful sleep. She moved towards the windows. It was no longer snowing, but she could hear the wind blowing briskly.

She dressed by herself, quickly arranged her hair, and began another letter to Jane, which turned into a lengthy three full pages. She knew her sister was worried about their sudden marriage and hasty departure, and she wished to assure Jane—and her father—that her new life was tolerably better than she expected. Elizabeth also dedicated a full page to express her joy and excitement at having them all as guests for dinner as soon as they arrived in London and making the arrangements for the opera and theatre.

Once the letter was finished, she could still detect no movement from her husband's room. She even considered knocking, but she immediately stepped back, her cheeks burning. She dared not enter his room at such an hour. He was likely to be improperly attired.

With a quick glance in the mirror, Elizabeth left her chamber and silently descended to the lowest level of the house. She looked around—the space was significantly larger than she was accustomed to at Longbourn—and stopped at the doorway of a large kitchen filled with people chatting and having their tea. On the stove were pots where the cook—a lady in her forties with pleasant features—had undoubtedly started to prepare the day's food.

The first to observe Elizabeth's presence was a maid. Her face instantly paled, and she almost dropped her cup. The others immediately stood and bowed, alarmed expressions altering their faces. Molly stepped forward, pale and slightly panicked. Elizabeth smiled.

"Please forgive me for bothering you so early. I woke some time ago, and as the others are still asleep, I wondered whether I could have a cup of tea before breakfast." Her voice was light and friendly, but the servants seemed to become more uneasy, avoiding her gaze. Molly was the first to recover.

"Of course, Mrs. Darcy, please forgive me. I did not hear your ring. I am very sorry. I will bring you the tea and something to eat at once."

"I did not ring, Molly. I came directly. I thought this would give me the opportunity to meet all of you again. And no food is necessary. A cup of tea would be perfect." To everyone's disbelief, Elizabeth sat in a chair near the table. The servants gaped at her, speechless.

The cook approached with a kettle and a fresh cup, served her, and asked her preference for sugar or milk. Elizabeth's gentle thanks, and her invitation for the others to resume their places were a signal for the staff to start breathing again—although not very steadily.

Elizabeth expressed her satisfaction with the tea, then she mentioned her delight at all the food she had enjoyed in the last two days. Less than half an hour later, as she finished her tea, Elizabeth engaged Mrs. Carlton in a discussion of beefsteak and the secrets of its taste.

Suddenly, the room became silent, and Elizabeth noticed the housekeeper, Mrs. Thomason, in the doorway—apparently in shock.

"Mrs. Darcy…" the housekeeper barely managed to whisper. "Is something wrong, ma'am?"

"Not at all, Mrs. Thomason. I woke very early, so I came down for a cup of tea. I had the chance to re-acquaint myself with this wonderful staff that you manage so efficiently."

Mrs. Thomason's astonishment increased. "But you may just ring anytime you want, and we will be happy to serve you. There is no need for you to come below stairs."

"It was a genuine pleasure, and I hope to repeat it soon. I thank you all for your company and for the excellent tea," she ended with a smile. As she departed, Elizabeth was not surprised when she saw Mrs. Thomason trotting after her.

"Mrs. Darcy, is everything well, ma'am? Is there anything that displeased you?" Elizabeth stopped and turned to her with the same broad smile on her face.

"Mrs. Thomason, I appreciate your concern, but truly, there is nothing wrong—quite the contrary. My good opinion of the household only increased on knowing them better."

"Thank you, Mrs. Darcy, you are very kind. I am glad everything is fine. If you will allow me, I would like to suggest that you not trouble yourself below stairs in the future. We are all at your disposal, and nothing would make us happier than to serve you if—"

"I believe we are making too much of this. I was pleased to meet the people who work in the same house with me, and I assure you that I will do so again should the opportunity arise," Elizabeth said calmly. She returned to her chamber to end the discussion while Mrs. Thomason remained behind. Elizabeth could feel the housekeeper's stare on her nape.

Her rooms were empty. Surely, Lucky had been taken outside by one of the servants. The doors to her husband's apartment were open, and she glanced inside. It, too, was empty.

"The master is in his study." Molly answered the unspoken question, and Elizabeth startled and turned to her maid who had entered unnoticed.

"He was there very early," the maid continued. "Breakfast will be ready in half an hour."

"Molly, I would like to send this letter to my sister. And after breakfast, I will need some help to prepare myself for Lady Matlock's visit."

"Of course, ma'am." Molly was about to exit then turned to Elizabeth. "Forgive me for being so bold, ma'am, but I must tell you that the entire staff was very pleased with your visit. They never… No one from the family has ever come down and had tea with them."

Elizabeth laughed. "Thank you, Molly, but I am sure they were more shocked than happy."

"We first were afraid that we had done something terribly wrong and you were displeased or upset. But then again, in such a case, you would not have come such a long way to the kitchen only to tell us that," Molly concluded, her eyes down, her voice slightly trembling.

Elizabeth dismissed the maid, barely containing her amusement. At Longbourn—or even at the Gardiners' house—friendly talks with the servants were so frequent that no notice was taken of them. But then again, the number of servants was much smaller—as was the number of stairs to reach them.

DARCY HAD WOKEN EARLY, AND HE TRIED TO ATTEND TO HIS DUTIES. THE HOWL of the wind was the only sound in the room. Titan was asleep near the fireplace, and Darcy briefly wondered what Lucky was doing: surely, sleeping soundly in her room, near her bed.

He had been married for three days and two nights, and he still could not sleep as before. He clearly remembered when restful sleep had ceased. It was the same night Sir William Lucas insisted he dance with Elizabeth. He asked, and she refused him. At that moment, her sparkling eyes and teasing smiles began to haunt his nights and his dreams. Since then, she had refused him twice more: once at Netherfield and then at Longbourn, when he proposed to her. He hoped that he had become wise enough to stop asking things she would refuse.

"Sir, breakfast will be ready soon," Stevens informed him while handing him a note. "And the servant who brought this is waiting outside for your answer."

Darcy opened the note. Annabelle was asking for a short, urgent meeting that very evening. He felt irritated and needed a moment to form the proper tone to reply.

"Please inform the servant there is no answer. Should I have one later, it will be delivered personally." Darcy rose from his seat and moved to the fireplace then back to the window to calm himself. Such impudence was incomprehensible and irritating!

He heard a knock at the door, and Mrs. Thomason stepped tentatively towards his desk and lowered her eyes with apparent uneasiness.

"Yes, Mrs. Thomason, may I help you with something? Is there a problem?"

"No, not really, sir. I just wanted to inform you… I thought you should know… Mrs. Darcy was below stairs earlier this morning."

"Really? Below stairs? What did she need?"

"Indeed, sir, I asked the same thing. Apparently, Mrs. Darcy only wished to speak with the staff. She…Mrs. Darcy had tea with the servants in the kitchen."

Darcy could not hide his surprise sufficiently to conceal it from the housekeeper. However, he managed to hide the smile he felt on his lips before continuing.

"Yes, and…?"

"I hope I keep the staff under good regulation… If Mrs. Darcy is displeased in any way…"

"Did Mrs. Darcy say she was displeased with the staff?"

"No, sir, quite the contrary. She congratulated me for the way the household was run."

"Then I cannot understand the reason for this discussion. Is there anything else?"

"No… Yes… I have been working here for ten years now, and no one from the family has ever had tea with the staff in the kitchen. Servants should know their place, and the mistress having tea with them might give the wrong impression, especially if repeated."

"So, in other words, you disapprove of Mrs. Darcy's gesture and suggest it not happen again. Is that correct?"

"Yes," the housekeeper answered in some haste. Darcy watched her sternly, and she immediately changed her voice. "I mean, no, sir! I could not possibly disapprove Mrs. Darcy's decision. It is not for me to judge what the mistress does. I only wished to—"

"Well, I am glad we agree on that. Mrs. Darcy is the mistress of this house, and the entire household is under her supervision, so she may do and go as she pleases." His voice was harsh, and he noticed the housekeeper's pale countenance, so he changed his approach.

"Mrs. Thomason, I understand it is difficult for everyone to adjust to the recent changes in our family. I am pleased with the way this house has run for more than ten years, and I am sure Mrs. Darcy was honest when she congratulated you. I know things were done in a certain way for the last decade, but Mrs. Darcy has her particular way of doing things that might be beneficial for all of us. We—and I include myself—will all have to adjust to that. I assure you that one could not find a better or kinder mistress than Mrs. Darcy."

"Yes, sir…" The housekeeper's distress was obvious, and she was unwilling to move.

Darcy felt his patience waning. He had always appreciated Mrs. Thomason and never had reason to complain about her, but she had suddenly become irritating.

"Is there still more, Mrs. Thomason," he inquired, forcing himself to be calm.

"I just wanted to let you know that Mrs. Darcy suggested the cook add some ingredients to the steak for dinner. I hope you will like it. She also asked that the cheesecake be replaced with an apple pie. Mrs. Darcy insisted on a recipe she said she had from her aunt. I hope you and Miss Darcy will enjoy it. The cook obeyed Mrs. Darcy's request."

Darcy did not hide either his surprise or his smile.

"I see—you are afraid that we might not like the new dishes and wish to be certain that I will not blame you or the cook," Darcy said lightly, and the housekeeper's distress grew as she attempted to defend herself. "Please do not worry, Mrs. Thomason. Anything that Mrs. Darcy suggests I shall accept gracefully. I believe that is one of the main duties of a married man. Now you will excuse me. I have some work to finish." His obvious good humour barely managed to dissipate the housekeeper's distress.

Darcy relaxed in the armchair, and a wide smile lit his face. Surely, the servants were shocked to see the mistress asking for tea in the kitchen. No one except Elizabeth would have done that! And poor Mrs. Thomason—after being in complete charge of the household for ten years, she must find it hard to accept such novelty in a few days.

He found himself exceedingly pleased by all the trouble Elizabeth had taken—and most of all for her suggesting a change in the meat course and a specially made apple pie. He was eager to taste it, and dinnertime seemed far away. She truly took to heart the commitment to her new position, and she seemed to adapt quite well to the family.

Half an hour later, breakfast was ready. The ladies were already at the table, chatting in a friendly manner. He enjoyed Elizabeth's happy countenance and warm greeting.

"We were talking about the weather, Brother. It is so cold and windy."

"Well, it should be cold and windy in December." He smiled and felt Elizabeth's gaze. Their eyes held for a moment, but neither spoke. The conversation turned to Lady Matlock's visit—expected in about two hours—and again to the weather.

After breakfast, Elizabeth went to change for the visit. Shortly after she entered her room, a knock on the door announced her husband, and she invited him in with an open smile.

He approached, took her right hand, then kissed it briefly. She blushed and thought it rather warm in the room.

"Did you have a restful night?" he asked, and she held his gaze while replying.

"Yes, very restful, thank you. I woke up quite early, and I thought you were still sleeping, but I found that you went to your study even earlier." She attempted to smile and speak lightly while she barely moved her fingers in his.

"It is true: I did not sleep much and thought I may as well work."

"I am sorry to hear that. You are well, I hope?"

"Yes, very well, thank you. I heard you had tea in special company today."

"Yes—very pleasant company. I imagine Mrs. Thomason informed you?"

"She did. She was a bit worried since it was something she had never seen before."

"Do you disapprove of it?" His smiling gaze was answer enough, but she had to inquire.

"I cannot disapprove of anything you wish to do. As I told Mrs. Thomason, you are the mistress and may do whatever you please. You may even come and have tea with me in the study before breakfast." He took her other hand in his. She blushed and returned the smile.

"I shall remember that. I have also done something else. I hope you will enjoy it at dinner."

"I am sure I will."

They remained standing in the middle of the room, holding hands, and Elizabeth briefly noticed that his eyes seemed even darker at such an intimate distance. Her hands in his seemed suddenly very warm—too warm—while she felt cold shivers along her arms. The feeling was so new and strange that it embarrassed her, but she did not withdraw her hands until he finally released them.

"You look lovely," he said. "This dress is very becoming to you."

"Thank you. I hope to make a favourable first impression on your aunt." She was slightly uneasy and wondered why she felt nervous receiving a compliment from her husband.

"I am sure you will. And I hope that you will approve of my aunt. Besides Georgiana, the Matlocks are my closest family, and I am very fond of them."

"You know I approve of Lord Matlock and Colonel Fitzwilliam, so I eagerly look forward with pleasure to meeting Lady Matlock and Lady Maryanne."

"Excellent," he concluded, and shortly thereafter, they returned to the drawing room where they met with Georgiana. Elizabeth had but a little time to compose herself before she was to face the long-awaited call of Lady Matlock and her daughter-in-law.

The introduction to their ladyships proceeded smoothly. Both visitors congratulated them on their wedding and expressed their hope that Elizabeth would adjust to her new position. The ladies also said that their husbands had been pleased with their stay in Hertfordshire and asked Elizabeth whether she missed her family.

"Elizabeth, I am very pleased to meet you prior to the private ball on New Year's Eve. Your presence is eagerly anticipated as everyone is wondering about you." Elizabeth blushed, Georgiana looked frightened, and Darcy had a disapproving countenance.

"Aunt, you said this would be a small family dinner. You said the same thing last year, and there were thirty people. How many will there be this year?"

"Darcy, you are always opposed to these gatherings! And I am afraid Georgiana has taken her cue from you. I was happy to hear from Robert that you are more desirous of society, Elizabeth. I have heard you are an excellent dancer too."

"Oh, I would not want to disappoint your ladyship. But I do like to dance." Elizabeth smiled.

"Speaking of the party, I hope you approve of your gown's fabric," said Lady Maryanne.

"I most certainly do. It is wonderful. I thank you, Lady Maryanne."

"Please call me by my given name. Your husband made most of the choices. He specifically asked that two dresses be delivered before the party, and I doubt anyone would dare disobey him." The lady laughed, and Elizabeth thought she was equally beautiful and friendly. And she was teasing Darcy, which Elizabeth found especially amusing.

"I shall thank my husband too." Elizabeth smiled, her cheeks suddenly crimson.

The conversation continued in a pleasant way as Lady Matlock asked about Elizabeth's younger sisters and her relatives in Town.

"My uncle and aunt have a lovely house in Gracechurch Street. My sister Jane will come to stay with them for a month. My uncle is in trade." Elizabeth waited to see an expression of contempt on the ladies' faces and was determined to stand up for her relatives.

"And very successful, from what I hear," came Lady Matlock's surprising answer, which left Elizabeth speechless for a moment.

"Yes, he is, thank you…" she finally managed to reply.

"Lord Matlock enjoyed your uncle and father's company very much," her ladyship said.

"Lord Matlock is very kind." Elizabeth smiled.

"No, he is not!" Lady Matlock laughed. "He never says anything out of pure kindness—very much like Darcy—except that he likes to dance more."

Drinks and refreshments were served, and the visit lasted another hour in animated conversation. The ladies left in good humour, expressing their wish to see them all soon.

Elizabeth could not have been more pleased or more surprised by their first meeting. The ladies did not for a second make her feel unwanted or unwelcome in their family. She was content and relieved that her aunt and uncle, as well as her sisters, would be in no danger of impolite treatment by her husband's relatives. So, when Darcy asked her opinion of the visit, she honestly and warmly declared that she had a delightful time.

During the afternoon, Mr. Darcy returned to his study, and Elizabeth joined Georgiana in the music room. In a corner, lying on a thick carpet, Lucky rested near the fire. After a while, Darcy entered to inform them that he was going out and would return in an hour or so. Elizabeth was curious about his departure, but she dared not inquire about it.

An hour later, they were surprised and pleased to receive Colonel Fitzwilliam's visit. When he heard that Darcy was out, declared he was fortunate to enjoy the ladies' company alone.

Inside the music room, the colonel was offered drinks and refreshments. He implored Georgiana to play certain music for him, and she readily agreed. While he enjoyed her performance, the colonel engaged Elizabeth in conversation. He approached the subject of the private dinner and ball.

"I believe these situations to be very stressful for Darcy, but he bears them graciously, and fortunately, they seldom occur—compared to the occasions when he succeeds in having his own way. He has great pleasure in the power of choice and always chooses as he pleases." The colonel laughed.

"William always does what is right, not what he pleases," Georgiana intervened decidedly. "And you should not make fun of him when he is absent, Robert."

"You are correct, of course, dearest. Darcy always does what is right," the colonel admitted in jest. He then turned towards Elizabeth and asked her how she had been since she arrived in town and whether she enjoyed London.

"I have always enjoyed London but have had little time to see it since we arrived. In truth, I have not left the house for the last three days. How is the weather, Colonel? Is it very cold?"

"Not at all—the snow has stopped and the weather is rather mild for the season."

"I love when it snows. Back home at Longbourn, I could hardly wait to walk in the snow, and Lucky enjoyed playing in it. I remember returning home, both of us almost frozen."

"Well, this is wonderful weather for a walk. Would you all like a stroll in the park? We may take Lucky too if you wish."

"That would be a lovely idea, Colonel," Mrs. Annesley approved. "I believe a short walk in the park would be beneficial for all of us."

"Oh yes, a wonderful idea, indeed," said Georgiana.

Elizabeth was also happy with the prospect. A mere glance out the window affirmed sunny, inviting weather. As the Colonel hurried them to make ready, a sudden thought stopped her, and as "Mrs. Darcy," she did what "Lizzy Bennet" never would have done.

"I believe it is a wonderful idea too, Colonel. However, I suggest we wait for Mr. Darcy. He will be home soon. Perhaps, he would like to join us."

"Oh, do not worry. The park is quite close to the house. Should he wonder where we are, he will see us from the window," the colonel replied with little ceremony.

"Still, I would like another cup of tea before we go. May we bring you something, Colonel?"

"I, too, would like another cup of tea." Mrs. Annesley took a seat near Elizabeth. "And I believe Mrs. Darcy is right. We should wait for Mr. Darcy."

"I shall have a glass of wine, then," the colonel acquiesced. "So, shall we have a little more music before we leave?"

"And where do you plan to go, if I may ask?" Darcy's voice drove all eyes to the door. He stepped in, a light expression on his face. "What a surprise to find you here, Cousin."

"I was in the neighbourhood, and I thought I might have a drink with you. You were out, so I proposed to accompany the ladies on a walk in the park as the weather is so lovely. But Mrs. Darcy suggested we wait for your return. Now that you are here, would you join us?"

Darcy held Elizabeth's gaze a few moments. "The weather is lovely, indeed. A walk in the park would be very beneficial. I apologise to the ladies that I did not think of it myself."

"Well, I am always more diligent in knowing what ladies like," said the colonel, and Georgiana chuckled as Darcy threw him a quick, disapproving look.

"It was snowing and windy earlier, so a walk was not sensible," said Elizabeth, smiling. "I shall go and prepare myself. I would like to take Lucky too."

Not waiting for a reply, she hurried upstairs with Lucky at her heels, followed at a more sedate pace by Georgiana and Mrs. Annesley. Darcy smiled as his wife left the room.

"Elizabeth is apparently happy with a walk. She must have felt trapped, staying in the house for so many days in a row. And should I dare ask where you have been?" the colonel asked.

"I had something to settle with my solicitors regarding the northern property. It still gives me trouble. And I took a final look through the settlements for Elizabeth. I will have them ready tomorrow and will send them to Mr. Bennet for his approval."

"I somehow doubt that the Bennets will find anything objectionable in the settlements. But your wife might complain that you had more important business than walking with her."

"Stop talking nonsense, Robert, and do not assume that you know what my wife may complain about. Have another glass, and tell me what you are doing in the neighbourhood."

The ladies returned rather quickly. Darcy asked his butler to join the excursion and take care of Titan and Lucky. He wished to comply with Elizabeth's desire but was not certain of the dogs' behaviour, and he was in no disposition to chase after them.

Their small group exited the house, and he smiled as he saw Elizabeth stop briefly, close her eyes, and deeply breathe the fresh air. It was getting dark, the streets lamps glimmered, and the moon shone in an unclouded sky. For a moment, Darcy thought that he, indeed, had been thoughtless with Elizabeth as Robert implied. He gently took her hand and put it under his arm. She glanced at him then tightened her grip, grateful for the support.

"I appreciate your help to prevent my falling. Surely, you have just cause, considering my history. It must be a relief that there are no swamps around here," she said with a large smile. Her cheeks quickly turned rosy from the cold, and her eyes sparkled.

He let out a laugh and said courteously, "It is my pleasure to have you on my arm."

The colonel had offered his arms to both Georgiana and Mrs. Annesley while Stevens followed with Lucky and Titan on their leashes.

The park, which they reached within minutes, was empty. As it had snowed for several days in a row, the bright powder rested on the paths and clung to the tree branches—fresh, clean, and untouched. Elizabeth released her husband's arm and slowly stepped along the path through its white coat of snow.

Lucky, set free, played happily, running back and forth to his mistress while Titan waited obediently near his master.

Georgiana tentatively followed Elizabeth, stepping in her tracks. Darcy finally encouraged Titan to play, and the dog—tall and impressive—ran joyfully along the path and quickly chased after Lucky. Elizabeth laughed and called both dogs to her, petted them caringly, then threw fresh snow at them. The dogs barked and tried to catch the flakes.

They resumed their slow progress along the path. Elizabeth took Darcy's arm again, holding tightly for support, as the ground was slippery. The colonel supported the other two ladies, and they maintained a steady pace for almost half an hour in friendly conversation before the colonel mentioned his parents' dinner and ball.

"So, Elizabeth, would you do me the honour of securing me a set—perhaps even two?"

"Thank you, Colonel. I will gladly secure you any dance not claimed by my husband. Although I did not imagine this would be a regular ball."

"My mother's notion of a dinner party is quite peculiar. And do not worry about Darcy. He does not enjoy dancing. Besides, it is not fashionable to dance with your wife."

"Be so kind as to allow me to decide what I enjoy," Darcy said. "And I surely will not have a debate about what is or is not fashionable. I intend to dance a few sets with my wife."

"Several sets? Truly? You are suddenly fond of dancing? Quite a shocking change!"

"One can easily change after marriage, you should not be surprised," Darcy responded in earnest, and the colonel laughed. Elizabeth blushed and smiled back, slightly embarrassed. She wondered whether her husband was joking, considering his serious mien.

After the dogs frolicked around Elizabeth for some time, their interest turned to Darcy. Titan found a long, thick branch half-frozen on the ground and brought it to his master. Lucky attempted to take the branch with little success. The dogs' playing amused all of them, and Elizabeth moved towards Georgiana to allow Darcy the space to discipline the dogs—who cared for little else except their play. Lucky jumped on Darcy to be petted, and immediately, Titan did the same—except that his impressive stature pushed his master backwards. His feet almost slipping, Darcy reached for support and stumbled against a tree. His abrupt contact shook the snow from its branches with a predictable result.

He glanced at the others, who laughed shamelessly, and then at the bewildered dogs. He attempted to maintain a serious countenance as he brushed off the snow. He felt melting snow dripping on his temples, his cheeks, and his neck, and he removed his hat to clean it, precisely as he heard both Elizabeth and Georgiana cry, "No!"

A moment later, a small avalanche fell on his head, and he closed his eyes before he shook his head and tried to dust the snow off with a gloved hand. As all the others laughed, Darcy began to feel uncomfortable. Then Elizabeth suddenly stepped up to him, took off her gloves, and gave them to him, saying, "Here, let me..."

He helpfully leant his head towards her, and she gently cleaned the snow from his hair then moved slowly to his temples, his face, and his neck, covered by its cloth and now full of snow. Her fingers were soft and gentle, and they warmed his chilled flesh. He closed his eyes, allowing himself a moment to be spoiled by her unintentional caress.

When she stopped, he opened his eyes and met her sparkling gaze and red cheeks. Her lips wore a smile as she asked, "Is that better?"

"Much better. But your hands must be cold and wet. You cannot put them in the gloves."

He took off his own gloves and held her hands in his. Elizabeth admitted that he was right: her hands were damp and frozen while his were warm and comforting. She could hardly take her eyes from him as she vividly recollected the astonishing sensation of touching his hair and his face, wondering why she was affected by such a small gesture.

Her knees became weak when he closed his palm tightly. Sheltering her hands, he lowered his lips and blew hot air on them. She felt his lips touching her fingers, and she was unable to move. Even as her hands warmed, cold shivers unsettled her.

"Are you cold, Elizabeth?" he asked in a low voice, and she replied with a weak, "No."

"Now, let me help you with your gloves," he said, after which he donned his own and then offered her his arm and continued their walk as if nothing had happened. The others in the party seemed oblivious to their interactions, except that the colonel teased Darcy several times about being more mindful of the shrubbery.

The walk lasted more than an hour, and they returned home, delighted, chilled, and eagerly awaiting dinner. The colonel declined an invitation and hurried to his house while all three ladies went to their rooms to change. Lucky ran past Elizabeth's feet and did not stop until he reached his place by the fire in her chamber, falling asleep immediately.

WHEN THEY SHORTLY REUNITED IN THE DINING ROOM, IT WAS PAST THEIR USUAL hour for dinner. Miss Darcy's cheeks were still red, and even Mrs. Annesley expressed her delight with the walk. Elizabeth and Darcy faced each other at the dinner table, exchanging glances occasionally.

The first courses were served, and they all paid undivided attention to their plates. Then the beefsteak was brought in, and as they enjoyed it, Mrs. Annesley said, "How is it possible that this dish improves day by day."

"I agree, but I believe it must be that the walk increased our appetite," Miss Darcy agreed with good humour.

"The reason for your greater enjoyment of the steak might also be that Elizabeth suggested the addition of some new ingredients," Darcy intervened with a sip from his glass of wine.

"Or perhaps Georgiana is right—it is the result of our walking so long in the wintry weather. That also does wonders for the appetite," Elizabeth replied with a slightly embarrassed laugh. "I also agree with Mrs. Annesley: all the food is excellent in this house."

At the end of the meal, dessert was presented on an elegant tray. Miss Darcy looked at it and smiled. "Oh, it seems Mrs. Carlton has decided to surprise us. I expected cheesecake, but she made apple pie. Quite delightful, I am sure."

Elizabeth glanced meaningfully at Darcy, and he smiled and said nothing. He then asked for a large slice of pie and began to eat it when, only few moments later, he stopped and gazed at Elizabeth, surprise in his expression.

"This pie is exceedingly delicious," Mrs. Annesley said.

"Indeed it is," said Georgiana. "And it is different from the pie Mrs. Carlton made last week. I would not say that last week's was less delicious, but this has a special taste that seems familiar, but I cannot recollect from where. I will have another slice, please."

"The pie is truly different," Darcy said with surprising seriousness. "It seems similar to the apple pie we used to eat at Pemberley a few years ago."

"Oh, that is so true! What an extraordinary surprise! I was just saying yesterday that I miss that pie. This is such a wonderful coincidence! How did Mrs. Carlton know?"

"Elizabeth asked Mrs. Carlton to bake this pie. She gave her a special recipe, and I must ask you, Elizabeth, where you obtained it. How did you know?" His gaze rested on Elizabeth. His countenance was unreadable, and Elizabeth forced a nervous laugh.

"Oh, it is nothing of consequence. As you know, my Aunt Gardiner lived in Lambton in her youth. She had a great aunt who seemed to have been a cook with the magic touch. Aunt Gardiner said this aunt also worked for Lady Anne a few years. My aunt enjoys cooking whenever she has time, using the recipes from her late great aunt, and I often stayed with her and helped out. So when I heard you speaking of the pie, I thought I might give it a try. I am very happy you like it, but the merits for the execution are entirely Mrs. Carlton's."

"Auntie Teresa was Mrs. Gardiner's aunt?" asked Darcy. "We all remember her! Everybody at Pemberley used to call her Auntie Teresa, and she was indeed the best cook I have ever known. This is quite shocking." He stared at Elizabeth, his countenance troubled and slightly pale. "Is such a coincidence possible?"

"Indeed it is, just as I made Lady Anne's acquaintance ten years ago. Fate is so astonishing!"

"Elizabeth, thank you so much. That was so thoughtful of you," Georgiana said with obvious emotion. "A wonderful surprise, indeed."

"You are most welcome." Elizabeth smiled at Miss Darcy and Mrs. Annesley, but she felt her husband's intense gaze. She turned to meet his eyes a few times, but she could read little in his preoccupied expression.

Dinner ended quite late, and Georgiana declared she would retire to her room as she was quite tired. Mrs. Annesley wondered that she had resisted so long as she was exhausted, and so their lovely evening came to an end.

Elizabeth returned to her apartment on her husband's arm. When they reached her rooms, Darcy opened the door for her and followed her inside. In the middle of the chamber, he stopped and took her hands in his, a warm smile on his face, his look bright with delight.

"I must thank you for everything that happened today, Elizabeth. In truth, I cannot remember when I last had such a wonderful time."

"There is nothing to thank me for. I confess I had a lovely time, too."

"Yes, but it is more than that. Besides having a pleasant time together, you proved once again that your presence is valuable to all of us. You spared time to talk with the servants, and then you took the trouble to surprise my sister—and me—preparing something for us that we remembered from our childhood. I cannot say how grateful I am."

He was still holding her hands, and his thumbs gently caressed her fingers. She allowed herself to enjoy the special sensation, her cheeks crimson and a smile curving her lips.

"I only did what I felt was right, and please believe me that both tasks gave me pleasure, although in a different way."

"You are very thoughtful and generous with the other's feelings."

"That is not true, I am afraid," she said laughing, her voice slightly nervous. "But I think it is one of the greatest advantages of marriage: there is at least one gentleman—your husband—who has vowed to always speak favourably of you and compliment you."

"I truly hope you will find other advantages to marriage," he replied in earnest, his fingers caressing hers as they gazed at each other. "I know I already have… And for this I have to thank you again. Do not think me oblivious to the difficulty of the last two weeks for you, Elizabeth. To have to enter so unexpectedly into a hasty marriage, to leave your parents and your sisters and all the places you love and move into a new home with people you do not know, far from your relatives—I can only imagine what you have been through. And yet, here you are, behaving graciously, bearing my relatives' questions, and adjusting to the plans made by others after you spent so many years with the freedom to do what you liked. I do not know whether any other woman would bear all these things in such a remarkable way. I was right that I could not possibly find a better wife, and not for a moment do I regret that I insisted this marriage take place."

He was solemn, his dark gaze deepened, and she felt her cheeks and neck flush. She attempted to laugh with little success as she answered: "It is no surprise that you are right, Mr. Darcy; you always are. We all know that." She then turned more serious. "I shall not deny that I had a very difficult fortnight, and I do miss my family very much. I am anxious to see them, and I count the days until they arrive in town. I am not oblivious to your efforts in this marriage either, William. And I must say that, at this moment, I do not regret that I accepted your proposal, and I have great hopes that things will become even better."

For some moments there was complete silence, disturbed only by the sound of the fire burning forcefully and the wind outside while they remained still in the middle of the chamber, their hands and eyes held in silent communion.

"I shall leave you to sleep now," he eventually said without moving. He hesitated an instant, then his eyes narrowed, and the shade of a smile played on his lips.

"Elizabeth, would you mind if I kissed you?"

His words took her so completely by surprise that her heart nearly stopped, only to start racing wildly afterwards.

"I… No… I mean—I do not mind." She managed to hold his gaze for only a moment longer, enough to see a warm smile light his face as he leant slowly towards her. She averted her eyes then closed them and waited, breathless. She could feel his warmth move closer, and his lips burned her skin long before they actually touched her. Slowly, as gently as a caress barely felt, his lips touched her left cheek near the corner of her lips. She stopped breathing, and her heart beat so strongly that she was certain he could hear it. His lips were soft and delicate, lingering on her skin a little while before they tenderly moved to her other cheek. It was a sensation she had not felt before, and she waited eagerly, wondering whether there was more. But he withdrew a little, smiling at her, and kissed the back of her hands.

"Good night, Elizabeth. Have a restful sleep," he said warmly then left the room and slowly closed the connecting doors after him.

Alone in the middle of her room, Elizabeth looked at the closed door then touched the places on her skin where his lips had rested. Sometime later, lying in her bed with the blanket wrapped tightly around her, just before she fell soundly asleep, Elizabeth wondered whether she had wished her husband a good night.

Chapter 11

London, 30 December

A sense of excitement she could not explain woke Elizabeth several times during the night. She thought of the past day's events with equal joy and wonder. She was surprised to discover new things about the man she had married and to see him in a new light, much more favourable than she expected. Blushing, she admitted that this *new light* illuminated other qualities: he seemed even more handsome.

It was still early when she rang for the maid. Tired after the previous day's frolic in the snow, Lucky had slept the entire night, and he woke full of energy, sniffing at the door to Darcy's apartment. She scolded the dog and asked Molly to take him from the room.

Elizabeth inched closer to the same door, attempting to catch any sign of movement. She felt ridiculous and, instead, concentrated on a new letter to Jane to occupy herself. Half an hour later, Molly told Elizabeth that the dog remained with the master in the library. So *he* was awake, too. Uncertain how to proceed but too impatient to remain still, Elizabeth left her room. It was half past eight—too early for either Georgiana or Mrs. Annesley to be downstairs—so she knocked at the heavy library door, and entered only when she heard her husband's invitation.

THE PREVIOUS DAY WAS SO DELIGHTFUL THAT DARCY COULD NOT STOP THINKING of it. He vividly felt the touch of her fingers while she cleaned the snow from his face. She was unaccustomed to such an intimate gesture with a man; her fingers were timid and her touches bashful but so sweet and gentle. The sensations aroused in him when he warmed her hands in his were unfamiliar and kept him awake for the longest part of the night. He briefly wondered how long he would manage to keep his sanity since he had barely slept a single restful night in the last two months—and even less in the last few days. However, the lack of sleep equalled his delight in her behaviour and obvious inclination towards him.

His gratification increased when she appeared at the library door so early in the morning.

"Forgive me… I do not want to disturb you. I would just like a new book to read… "

"You do not disturb me—quite the opposite. Please come in. I was looking at some letters I received. Did you sleep well? Would you like a cup of tea or coffee before breakfast?"

Elizabeth laughed at him. "Yes, I slept very well, thank you. And I would love a cup of tea."

Darcy rang for tea and coffee then sat in his usual armchair.

"I see that Lucky favours you over me." She smiled. "He seems to enjoy male company."

"I am pleased that he and Titan are at peace. Titan accepted Lucky rather easily."

"I believe it happened because he obeys his master and does everything you ask of him."

Darcy looked at her, unsure how to take her words. The smile on her face was the same he had witnessed several times in the past.

"Is it good or bad that Titan obeys me?" he inquired further, and she gulped some tea, hiding her lips behind the cup before she replied.

"It depends. Discipline is good if there is enough freedom that it does not feel like a cage."

Darcy looked at her in earnest, searching her expression as he asked in low voice, "Do *you* feel caged, Elizabeth? In this marriage, I mean…"

She stared at him for a moment and then averted her eyes before returning her gaze to him again. "I do not—not now. It is nice that you asked me, though." She smiled nervously.

"I might not always be mindful on your adjustment to life here. Georgiana and I have our routines, and we might appear thoughtless at times. I hope you know that you may do whatever you wish and ask whatever you like."

"I know that—and no, I do not think either Georgiana or you are thoughtless."

"Good. After breakfast. I need to attend to some business, and I shall obtain your settlement from my solicitor. You will be able to read it tonight, and then I shall mail it to Mr. Bennet."

"Settlement?" She seemed puzzled, and he smiled with contentment. "That is the last thing on my mind. I am sure all is well in that respect."

"I thank you for your trust. There is another important thing I forgot. I must give you the jewels that belong to you now. Would tonight or tomorrow morning be convenient?"

"Of course, anytime you wish." He was puzzled by the lack of interest in her expression regarding two subjects that would surely animate any woman. A moment later, her eyes were shining, and another smile touched her lips.

"If it is not too much trouble, could we take another walk before dinner?"

"I was about to ask you the same thing. A walk before dinner does wonders." He smiled back, surprised by the joy on her face—greater than any discussion of jewels or pin money could produce.

Breakfast was announced, and Darcy offered Elizabeth his arm, which she took without hesitation. Soon after, Darcy took his farewell, declaring he would return in the afternoon. He left with a glance at his wife and hoped that he saw slight disappointment on her face.

TOGETHER WITH MRS. ANNESLEY, ELIZABETH SAT ON THE SOFA, ENCHANTED BY Georgiana's amazing skills at the pianoforte. Georgiana was living through the music, and her talent pervaded the music room. Elizabeth remembered a conversation she had at Netherfield. Miss Bingley declared that Miss Darcy was a truly *accomplished* young lady. For once, Miss Bingley was correct in her description: Georgiana was truly accomplished, and her manners, the way she spoke, her posture, her smiles—not to mention her musical talent—all confirmed a quality education and a praiseworthy character.

In the middle of Georgiana's performance, a servant entered tentatively, glancing from Elizabeth to Georgiana as she was uncertain how to proceed.

"What is it, Janey?" Elizabeth asked in a friendly voice.

"Ma'am, there are two ladies asking for Miss Darcy: Miss Bingley and Mrs. Hurst."

Elizabeth wondered about the propriety of such a visit—without previous notice—and uncertain how to proceed. Georgiana seemed troubled—she was pale and silent.

"I believe we should ask them to return when William is home. I cannot imagine why they would come without giving notice," Georgiana eventually said.

"Dear Georgiana, we cannot do that since they called on *you*. And they are your family's friends, not complete strangers. Etiquette can suffer a little when it comes to friends." Mrs. Annesley's calm voice was not enough to put Georgiana at ease, but she said nothing more.

Elizabeth smiled as she stepped towards the door and took Georgiana's arm gently. "I have a strong feeling that this visit is related to the news of my marrying your brother."

"Oh..." said Georgiana while they walked to the room where her guests waited.

"Dearest Georgiana, how I longed to see you," Miss Bingley cried in delight for a moment before she stopped in complete shock.

"Caroline—what a lovely surprise," she answered in a small voice. However, the guests' eyes were locked on Elizabeth.

"Miss Eliza—I can hardly believe that I find you here! How is it possible? I read the news of Mr. Darcy's shocking wedding, but I was certain it must be a bad joke. Is it a joke?"

"Miss Bingley, Mrs. Hurst, what a surprise indeed. Neither Georgiana nor I expected any calls since Lady Matlock and Lady Maryanne visited us yesterday. I imagine you happened to be in the neighbourhood and stopped by for a cup of tea. Please have a seat."

Astonishment and concealed anger left both visitors speechless. They seemed uncertain whether to stay or leave. Finally, curiosity overcame other feelings, and they sat on the sofa, continuing to stare at Elizabeth and ignoring Georgiana and Mrs. Annesley.

With perfect manners, Elizabeth rang for tea and refreshments.

"So it is not a jest?" Miss Bingley inquired impatiently.

"If you refer to the wedding news, Mr. Darcy and I married three days ago."

"But how is that possible? It cannot be! What do you mean you are married?" The irritation in Miss Bingley's voice was so piercing that Mrs. Hurst added in a more proper manner.

"We heard the news of Mr. Darcy's marriage, and you surely understand our disbelief, Miss Eliza. We first believed someone was attempting to laugh at Mr. Darcy. I would never have expected such a shocking alliance to happen. I mean… we just left Netherfield a month ago…all of us… We never imagined Mr. Darcy would return to Hertfordshire, let alone to—"

"I imagine it was a shock for you, Miss Bingley, Mrs. Hurst." Elizabeth answered with calmness and, seeing Georgiana's discomfort, tried to change the tone of their discussion.

"Is Mr. Bingley in good health? Shall we see him soon, too?"

"No…I mean yes, he is in excellent health. He is spending some time at a friend's estate, twenty miles from London. I doubt he will return soon to Town," Mrs. Hurst said.

"I am glad to hear he is well. I will be very pleased to meet him again whenever he returns."

"But this marriage— Indeed it was a shock," Miss Bingley continued, ignoring the last words. "I never suspected Mr. Darcy could make such a step. This must be a mistake. We never suspected such an inclination—to lead to such a union!"

"Mr. Darcy is not an easy man to read. He does not express his inclinations openly," Elizabeth replied, thinking that rarely were more true words said.

"Being his intimate friends for such a long time, we already know that," Miss Bingley interrupted abruptly. "However, he never hid his opinions from us—quite the contrary. We also knew when he approved or disapproved of something."

"Then our situation must be an exception." Elizabeth began to feel quite cheerful and did not fail to notice Miss Bingley's growing anger.

"Perhaps…but I also know that your *own preference* lay elsewhere, Miss Bennet. I would rather say that you disliked Mr. Darcy. You displayed it quite obviously several times."

"I congratulate you on your keen observation of others' preferences, Miss Bingley. It is only one of your many accomplishments."

"Well, one does not need to be a keen observer to notice your inclination. I am sure there were very few people in Meryton who were not aware of your preference. By the way, how did Mr. Wickham take the news? You were very good friends. I am sure he was quite surprised. Although I am certain now that, being in a position so above everything you were accustomed to, you will hardly keep your old friendships and old *preferences*."

Elizabeth noticed Georgiana's pallor as she stared at Miss Bingley. She imagined that Miss Darcy was shocked by her being friends with the son of Mr. Darcy's steward. She must loathe the mere mention of someone whom her brother despised so. Elizabeth was so annoyed that she wondered how she would be able to remain calm should Miss Darcy make a disapproving remark about her friendship with Mr. Wickham.

"In this you are mistaken, Miss Bingley. I shall not change my preferences or my affection just because this marriage gives me a privileged position. Perhaps, you are not such a keen observer of my character after all, Miss Bingley, or privy to my likes and dislikes."

"Well, I dare say one can hardly tell now how another will or will not change their habits in the future. You are obviously not aware of what being a part of the *ton* involves. And it truly makes me wonder once more about the peculiarity of this alliance."

"Miss Bingley, I am sorry our situation makes you wonder so. I would not want you to bother yourself exceedingly. If you have further questions, perhaps you should ask Mr. Darcy himself. You should call again sometime, perhaps when Mr. Bingley visits. By the way, my sister Jane will be in town soon. I believe she wrote you about her arrival."

"Indeed, I have not received such a letter from dear Jane. She is well, I hope?"

"Very well, indeed. She will be pleased to see you both. As I said, you should call again, together with your brother, at a time when my husband is home."

"My brother will not be home soon. He seems to be very comfortable at his friend's estate. The location is splendid, and I understand there are several young ladies who hold his interest. He wished to relax after he left Netherfield, and Mr. Darcy encouraged him to do so. Mr. Darcy always takes good care of Charles and only wishes the best for him. That is why Charles followed his advice to leave Netherfield and remain in town for the winter. In truth, without Mr. Darcy's insistence, perhaps Charles would be in Hertfordshire now. We were fortunate that Mr. Darcy wisely observed the inconvenience of Charles staying in that area. I cannot but wonder why he did not use that wisdom in his own case."

As Miss Bingley's voice became stronger and more animated, Elizabeth felt the blood drain from her face and cold shivers tremble along her arms and spine. She stared at Caroline Bingley, whose self-sufficient smile cut her to the quick. If Miss Bingley hoped for a victory, that was surely her reward. Nothing could hurt Elizabeth more.

Elizabeth remembered Jane's suffering when she learnt that Mr. Bingley had gone with no intention of returning. She could not believe what she heard, yet her judgment told her it must have been true. It was her husband, who convinced

Bingley to leave Netherfield—and Jane. It was her husband who made her sister suffer! Now Jane was alone, Elizabeth was trapped with the man who had caused it, and Mr. Bingley was unlikely to return soon.

She felt all the eyes in the room on her, and she struggled to gather herself together. She could not possibly allow the Bingley sisters to see how angry and hurt she was.

The visit lasted another half hour, and Elizabeth was forced to witness their insincere praise of Georgiana and their mischievous remarks about the Bennet family. She was too exhausted from quelling her anger and disappointment to respond as they deserved, so she mostly listened in silence, fighting the headache that overwhelmed her.

As soon as they left, Elizabeth excused herself from Georgiana and ran to her room. She knew Miss Darcy was not at fault, but she could not bear to speak to her either.

She paced the room in anger with no cordial feelings for either the master of the house or his sister, so she startled when she heard the latter's small voice from the door.

"Elizabeth, please excuse me for bothering you. I knocked, but I am afraid you did not hear me. I just wanted to see whether you are well. May I bring you anything?"

Miss Darcy's voice was so warm that Elizabeth found no reason to reject her, and a trace of shame softened her voice. Miss Darcy reminded her precisely of Jane's sweet temper.

"I am fine. Forgive me. I just have a terrible headache."

"I need to apologise for Miss Bingley. She was truly rude to you."

"Please do not apologise and do not worry about Miss Bingley. I became accustomed to her rudeness after being in close company with her for more than two months."

"Then I shall leave you to rest. Elizabeth, I just want to ask you—forgive me for being so bold—Miss Bingley said you were friendly with Mr. Wickham? Does he happen to be in Hertfordshire? Were you closely acquainted?"

Well, there, so that was the reason for Miss Darcy's kindness. She wanted more details to report to her brother. Elizabeth's voice sharpened. "Yes, Mr. Wickham was in Meryton. He had joined the Militia. Did you not know? And I am glad to call him a close friend although I know that Mr. Darcy disapproves of him."

"I am very pleased to hear that. I have not seen him in a few months, and I hoped he was well. It is good that he found a commission in the Militia and had the fortune to have you as a friend. I imagine William was displeased to find that..."

Miss Darcy's voice was shy and hesitant, and Elizabeth's curiosity grew beyond her concern for her own sister. Considering Mr. Wickham's statements about Miss Darcy, Elizabeth would never suspect such a warm concern of her new sister-in-law about the named gentleman.

"Mr. Wickham told me a little about his connection to your family. I know he grew up at Pemberley. I understood Mr. Darcy was a most excellent man and very fond of him."

"Yes, that is true. My parents...we were all very fond of Mr. Wickham."

"Except your brother, I would imagine."

"Oh, it is not... William was not... He just... William is the best brother and the best gentleman. He is always faultless, and he expects everyone to be the same."

"Yes, I suspected as much." Elizabeth's voice was sharp. Of course, Mr. Darcy was a man without faults. Even Miss Bingley said so, and she was not to be contradicted!

"I understood you have not seen Mr. Wickham for quite some time," she continued, and Miss Darcy turned absolutely white then crimson and lowered her eyes.

"No, not in the last six months. That is why I was pleased to hear he is well. I shall leave you to rest now, Elizabeth. Thank you and..." She took a few steps then returned, her voice low, unable to hold Elizabeth's gaze. "I am sorry to ask you such a horrible thing... I do not want to upset you, but if I am not asking too much, could you please not tell William about our discussion? About Mr. Wickham, I mean? I would not wish to upset him."

"You must not worry about that, I promise you." Elizabeth took her hands as her anger increased. How was it possible that Miss Darcy was afraid to mention an old friend's name in front of her brother? Was she not allowed to decide whom she liked or disliked? Was she not allowed to have her own feelings and make her own decisions? Was this how "the best brother" who was "always faultless" behaved?

After Georgiana left, Elizabeth found no rest. She moved from the bed to the windows, attempted to read with no success, tried to write Jane—but what was to be said?—then took her diary and filled a couple of pages. An hour later, her fingers aching from nervous writing, she moved to the windows again. It was getting dark.

A large carriage stopped in front of the house, and she recognised her husband's figure. She breathed deeply to calm her nerves, wondering whether she should confront him. Could she say nothing and only hope that Jane would meet Mr. Bingley again and they would be reunited? At least that much good should come from her forced marriage.

Elizabeth's attention was suddenly drawn outside. Mr. Darcy stepped to the gate, then he returned and faced a young woman—a servant most likely. A few words seemed to be exchanged, and Mr. Darcy hesitated, looked around, and then turned and walked towards another carriage that was stopped farther down the street. Elizabeth changed her position so she could see better. He looked inside the carriage, and a moment later, he entered it.

Elizabeth became intrigued, but she could not see who was in the other carriage. Shortly, her husband appeared again, and entered the yard then the main door. The strange carriage drove by slowly, and Elizabeth saw a shadow within, looking towards the house, but no distinctive figure.

She returned to the middle of the room, wondering about the strange incident.

Who would wait for him outside in the cold and refuse to enter? They were obviously important for him since he moved towards them. Was this considered genteel behaviour among the *ton*—to have a clandestine discussion on the street in the middle of winter?

While she struggled to read something, she heard knocking at the door that separated their rooms. She put the book down and, without knowing why, rose to her feet.

"Good evening, Elizabeth. I just returned home and came to bring you the settlement so you could read it. It is quite windy outside. I believe we should postpone our walk. Instead, I could show you the jewels if this is a good time for you."

"I thank you, but I have a terrible headache. I am not inclined to walk or to read—or to dine. I believe I shall retire very early tonight."

"Is anything wrong? Are you unwell?" His voice turned serious and he moved slightly towards her. She took a step back.

"Nothing is wrong. There is no need for you to worry. I am just not hungry. I had enough tea and refreshments earlier with Mr. Bingley's sisters." She became aware that her voice had turned cold, but she could not restrain herself. His gaze fixed upon her face.

"Elizabeth, you are obviously upset. One glance is enough to see it. I would guess their visit was not to your liking."

"You should not hurry to judge what you see from a glance, sir. The visit was no different from other occasions in Miss Bingley and Mrs. Hurst's company, except perhaps more revealing and less entertaining. Now if you do not mind, I would like to rest."

She turned her back to him, and she thought he left; however, the fact pleased her far less than she expected. She startled when his fingers touched her shoulder.

"I know you well enough to see that you are upset and angry with me. We have promised honesty to each other, so I expect you to tell me what the problem is and allow me to make amends if necessary."

"You surely do not know me well enough, Mr. Darcy. That would not be possible since we barely spoke a dozen times before our wedding and not much more after we wed. I find it dangerous to speak of honesty at this time, and I am afraid I might not be able to choose my words properly if I speak further. So I would rather allow you to enjoy your dinner."

"I have been honest with you since we first talked at Longbourn, so I am not afraid to speak of honesty. I insist on the same civility and inquire of what you accuse me."

She breathed deeply and paused. Yes, he might have been honest since they discussed the possibility of marriage. She had no proofs to debate that. But before?

"Since you insist, I shall tell you, sir, but I cannot promise to be civil. Yes, I am upset and angry since I discovered the reason for my sister's present unhappiness and the person responsible for convincing Mr. Bingley to leave Hertfordshire, perhaps even against his heart. Can you deny that this is the result of your involvement? And can you blame me for being upset and angry at the man who cruelly threw my sister—one of the sweetest and most kind persons in the world—and perhaps his friend, too, into misery and despair?

While she spoke, her eyes watched his face closely, and to her shock, she noticed he seemed too little affected by her words, even slightly relieved.

With assumed tranquillity, he replied, "I have no intention of deceiving you or denying my part in separating Bingley from your sister, but I understand why you are upset and angry."

"But you seem quite calm and untouched. It is clear you have neither remorse nor shame!" She moved along the room, unable to bear his gaze. The room seemed small and cramped, and she felt trapped.

"I did what I considered to be just at that moment. I have no reason to be ashamed of trying to act to the benefit of my friend. Everything I did was for his well-being."

"And may I ask why my sister was the opposite of Mr. Bingley's well-being? What is it that you held against Jane? What faults so horrible did you find in her?"

"Elizabeth, we should sit and talk calmly. In truth, I find no fault in Miss Bennet. Even from the beginning of our acquaintance, I have admired her beauty and her manners. But there were other aspects that formed my opinion at that time and convinced me that it would be best for Bingley's future—"

"And who are you to decide what is best for everybody? Why not leave Mr. Bingley to judge what is best for his present and future. Who gives you the right to decide the fate of people around you in an imaginary act of friendship? What does that say about your character?"

"I find it unfair and impolite to speak of my character only because I tried to advise my friend in a way that I found best for him at the time. And why do you accuse me of deciding for people around me?" His temper betrayed him, and his voiced became hard.

"You know that very well to be true! You find great delight in imposing your will on your friends, your relatives, your wife, your sister, my sister, and your long-time acquaintance to whom you denied his rightful legacy and jeopardised his life, causing poverty and misery. You believe yourself the owner of everyone's will and fate, sir, and I am sure you are not!"

"You should not speak of things about which you do not know, Elizabeth, and not take the side of those you know only by their appearance!" said Darcy with heightened colour, his tone severe and cold. "And pray tell me why you mentioned my sister in your account?"

Elizabeth quickly collected herself and avoided his eyes. He seemed troubled, and she finally rejoiced in her success. At least she succeeded in affecting him, too.

"I spoke of Georgiana for no particular reason. You know quite well that even the colonel mentioned your tendency to control everyone!"

"Robert speaks much and not always wisely!"

"He might—as we all do from time to time—because we cannot be as perfect as you are, sir!" she answered sharply. "And if you do not wish me to speak of things about which I do not know, perhaps you should have the politeness to inform me before I discover the facts from others. I did not expect you to honour me with your civility at the beginning of our acquaintance, but I foolishly hoped things would change once we married!"

"Surely, you do not accuse me of a lack of civility towards you! I have done everything in my power to see to your comfort, and I have offered everything in this marriage! I did answer every question you asked me, both before and after our wedding!"

"I shall not deny that you answered all the questions I asked you, and I have no complaint about your behaviour towards me! But that does not blind me to the ungenerous way in which you interfered in others' lives or reduce the gravity of your plotting with your *intimate* friend Miss Bingley to separate Mr. Bingley from Jane! I would rather have you mistreat me than ruin the happiness of my beloved sister!"

"I shall remember that, Mrs. Darcy. Perhaps, I should expend less effort in pleasing you, after all, as it seems a useless endeavour!"

He exited the room, pulling the door after him so forcefully that Lucky ran and barked at it. Elizabeth called the dog back and sent him to the corner, wiping the tears from her cheeks.

She was barely able to breathe from anger, her fists clenched, biting her lips to stop her tears. How dare he? Offending her when he was the one to blame? Yelling at her? And not the smallest attempt to apologise, no sign of remorse for what he did? He decided it was best for Mr. Bingley to leave Jane, yet he insisted on marrying her! What can be the explanation except that he was used to having his own way in everything? And poor Georgiana, no wonder she was afraid to express her support of Mr. Wickham, considering how angry he became at the mere mention of that gentleman's situation.

What was she to do? How could she bear living with such a difficult man? She surely would not agree to abandon her friends, her opinions, and her will only to please him!

And what ungentlemanlike behaviour—to declare that he would not make efforts to please her! Was that not the duty of a husband? She had no reason to complain about him so far, but surely that was because the marriage was at his insistence, and he had his way!

Only a day before, he walked with her, and she had such a nice time. She started to enjoy his company and foolishly hoped she could have a good marriage after all! What a simpleton she had been! If not for Miss Bingley and Louisa Hurst's visit...

She paced the room, her anger increasing. Did she need Caroline's confession to remind her of her husband's character? And she allowed her to see her anger when she heard of Mr. Darcy's involvement! How was it possible to be such a fool as to indulge Caroline Bingley?

Some long moments of struggle and poor attempts at self-control followed, and nervous tears rolled down her pale cheeks. With growing restlessness, she continued to pace the room, increasingly frustrated by her situation.

Poor, dear Jane...her sadness was mostly due to the intervention of Mr. Darcy, who considered Jane a menace to Mr. Bingley! There was nothing more ridiculous! And for what? He admitted that he had no reproach against Jane, so obviously, it was something related to their family. Even if he might be right in that aspect, surely Mr. Bingley's family was far from perfection! If she were to be mean, she could easily state that, while her father was a gentleman, Mr. Bingley's fortune came from trade! And Mr. Bingley's sisters or brother-in-law could hardly be considered models of decorum!

She tried to sit then moved around the room again. *She* had not been a model of decorum either in that discussion with her husband! She could have confronted him about the entire situation in a different manner. Dearest Jane would surely be saddened by such a display of anger. She briefly wondered whether any servant heard their argument. It was very likely, considering that both of them had raised their voices. Yes, she upheld her beliefs and her sister, and he could not blame her for that as he himself told her more than once that he wished her to continue to do so. She felt proud of that but not her manner of doing it.

She leant back in the armchair, her fists still clenched, and gazed outside. It was snowing steadily again just like the previous evening before they walked in the park. That seemed such a long time ago. Suddenly, as her mind went blank, every other thought vanished except one: who was in the carriage that had stopped in front of the house earlier?

She could not say whether an hour or a few minutes had passed before knocks on the door startled her. She regained her composure enough to realise that it was the inside door, so she rose to her feet and straightened her posture as though preparing for battle before she asked her husband to enter. It was not over yet.

THE DISCUSSION THAT TURNED INTO A FIGHT TOOK DARCY COMPLETELY BY SURprise, and by the time he left Elizabeth's room in anger, he still could not entirely recollect what occurred. He had returned home from the club in excellent spirits, content to finally have the settlement finished and hoping that both Elizabeth and Mr. Bennet would be pleased with it. He looked forward to arriving home and spending some pleasant moments with Elizabeth before dinner, perhaps showing her the jewels and choosing the set she would wear the next day.

The previous evening's walk was still vivid in his mind, and he could not remember when he last felt so pleased to spend time in someone's company. Elizabeth was as charming, witty, and friendly as he could hope.

The moment he stopped in front of the house, he was shocked to be approached by Annabelle's maid and even more shocked to discover she was waiting in her carriage only a few feet away, insisting she speak to him. That was completely nonsensical, and at first, he was tempted to censure the servant most severely. But then he realised it was not wise to start a fight with Annabelle in full view of everyone. So he entered her carriage briefly and demanded that she stop making a fool of herself. Annabelle insisted she needed to speak to him in private as she had some difficult problems for which she needed his advice, and she seemed serious and troubled enough. So, in a hurry to leave the compromising situation and slightly preoccupied that she might have been in some real trouble, he promised he would call on her in the next two days.

He then entered the house and was surprised to find neither Georgiana nor Elizabeth nor Mrs. Annesley in the music room. The doorman informed him that Miss Bingley and Mrs. Hurst had called, and Darcy was certain that such a visit was a daunting task for both his sister and his wife. He was also certain that Elizabeth's strength and intelligence were good weapons to contend with Caroline Bingley, and when he entered his wife's chamber, he anticipated an amusing description of the visit and teasing comments about Miss Bingley's admiration for him.

Instead, he found Elizabeth in a state of anger that disconcerted him. First, he thought that she might have seen him entering Annabelle's carriage, and he wondered why she was so upset about a situation she knew nothing about. Shortly after he discovered the real reason, he was equally relieved and troubled. So, Caroline Bingley lost not a moment in informing Elizabeth of his part in Bingley's departure.

Although he felt no qualms about his decision at the time—and was convinced that he did what was best for his friend—he was not indifferent to Elizabeth's distress. And he had to bear the embarrassment of *plotting* with Bingley's sisters and explain that to Elizabeth.

In retrospect—and better knowing both Jane and Mr. Bennet—Darcy often wondered whether he had been mistaken in his judgment. Yes, he should have spoken with Elizabeth about these things, and perhaps that was the perfect moment to do so. Yes, she was upset, but she would surely understand his point of view.

However, in an instant, their conversation took a turn that Darcy failed to understand. She accused him of being uncivil and insensitive and of imposing his will upon everybody! She mentioned even Georgiana. What could she possibly know? She was so harsh towards him—and deeply unfair. And of course, she did not miss the chance to insinuate that he took away the "rightful legacy" from an old "acquaintance." He easily recognised Wickham's words, and from that moment, he lost any mastery of his reactions. Anger overcame his reason, and he little remembered what was said—except that Elizabeth would rather have him mistreat her than ruin Jane's happiness. At that, he answered something, but he did not remember the exact words. The only vivid memory was her pale, troubled expression, the shadow in her eyes, and the door slammed behind him.

Darcy's anger grew with every moment. Nothing had changed: she was as unreasonable as ever and as ready to believe the worst in him. How could she take Caroline's words to heart and not give him a chance to defend himself? Was that the proper behaviour of a wife?

Even if he had been wrong about Bingley, was he not the one who encouraged her to invite Jane to visit them? Could she not see that his intentions were for the best? Could she not appreciate his attempt to please her? Surely, he did more than any other man would have done in his position. After all, she was the one who had all the advantages in this marriage, and she was still ungrateful!

And Wickham—her interest in that poor excuse for a man seemed as vigorous as ever. Her remarks now were similar to those at the Netherfield ball. He wondered whether she spoke to Wickham in the days before their marriage; likely, she did. Elizabeth accused him of not *informing* her, but how could he tell her about *that*? It was too soon for such a disclosure although Wickham had not restrained himself from exposing his part in the matter weeks ago. She seemed eager to believe a man without honour and never questioned his account.

Darcy poured himself a glass of brandy as he moved from one chair to another, paced the room, then sat again. With a second glass of brandy in hand, he approached the window. It was snowing just like the evening before. It would have been suitable weather for another short walk after dinner, if only they had not fought so violently before and if he had not declared that he would no longer try to please her. Although, he had to admit that walking together alone in the park was for his pleasure as much as hers. And, if he was to think more clearly, he had also acquired some advantages from this marriage. Her bare fingers wiping the snow from his face and her eyes sparkling under the moonlight might have been some of them…

He glanced at the closed door and slowly approached it. Then he returned to the table and filled a third glass of brandy. A moment later, he threw it into the fire, exciting the flames. He returned to the door again and listened, but the heavy wood did not allow him to hear much. So, without giving himself time to think and properly decide—or knowing what he would do next—he knocked.

"ELIZABETH, MAY I COME IN? I WOULD LIKE TO SPEAK TO YOU AGAIN."

You may do whatever you want. It is your house, and you are the master, she was tempted to say aloud, but she regained her composure enough to reply shortly, "Of course."

She stood still, watching him. He held her gaze for a short while then lowered his eyes, took a few steps, and started to speak.

"I had not been long in Hertfordshire before I saw, in common with others, that Bingley preferred your eldest sister to any other young woman in the country. While I do not wish to diminish your sister's merits, I had often seen Bingley in love before, so I did not take his preference seriously. During that ball, I discovered that Bingley's attentions to your sister had given rise to a general expectation of their marriage. From that moment, I observed my friend's behaviour attentively, and I could then perceive that his partiality for Miss Bennet was beyond what I had ever witnessed in him. Your sister I also watched. Her look and manners were open and cheerful as ever but with no symptom of peculiar regard, and I remained convinced that, though she received his attentions with pleasure, she did not invite them by any participation of sentiment."

"You were mistaken, sir!" Elizabeth interrupted with haste. "Jane is not the kind of person to openly display her feelings, yet this does not make them any less ardent. I assure you that Mr. Bingley's attachment was closely mirrored by Jane's affection."

"If you are not mistaken, I must have been in error, which I shall not even attempt to deny with the superior information that I have gathered in the meantime. But a month ago, the serenity of your sister's countenance and air was such as might have given the most acute observer a conviction that her heart was not likely to be easily touched. I had also noticed a great insistence that this marriage shall take place, coming especially from your mother and shared by all your neighbours and friends. Consequently, I found my young friend in danger of entering into an unequal marriage, into a family who—please forgive me for paining you, but that was my opinion at the time—was beneath him, bonding his life to a woman he admired and fancied to be in love with and who only accepted him to please her family and to secure their future. It was my genuine conviction that such a marriage would ruin his life. Everything that passed that evening at the ball confirmed my opinion and urged me to save my friend from what I deemed to be a most unhappy connection. I briefly spoke to his sisters during the ball, and our coincidence of feeling was soon discovered, and, alike sensible that no time was to be lost in detaching their brother, we shortly resolved that I should go with him the next day and they would follow us shortly."

"It is strange to hear you speaking of your 'coincidence of feeling' with Mr. Bingley's sisters," Elizabeth interrupted him sharply. He did not reply to her comment but continued.

"We accordingly went—the only exception being the delay due to your accident. His sisters joined him the next day, and as soon as they arrived home, they pointed out to Bingley the certain evils of entering into an alliance with your sister and bringing as the strongest reasoning my opinion. He came to me and inquired what I thought of the situation and especially of your sister's feelings. I shall mention that some of the things I held against the union had diminished after the short time I spent at Longbourn in your father's company. I found that Mr. Bennet was a gentleman who put his daughters' happiness beyond any advantageous marriage and would never force any of you into an alliance against your will. Therefore, I was unable to advise my friend against your family—except for connections in society and the lack of decorum of your mother and younger sisters."

There was another glance and a short pause before he spoke further.

"I again apologise for offending you, but I wish to speak honestly. My opinion of your sister's feelings for him and my suspicion that she was willing to marry him for mercenary reasons did not vanish, and I presented them to Bingley. After that night, I barely saw him at all. He avoided my company and left London for another friend's estate. His change of spirits was obvious, and it made me believe that I might have been wrong in my judgement that it was a mere infatuation. I planned to speak to him again, but all the events that ended with our marriage, as well as his departure, put a barrier to my resolution. I am willing to condemn the reasons that governed me to interfere and to make amends. And I hope you believe me that, if I have wounded your sister's feelings and yours, I deeply regret it."

They were facing each other, their countenances severe, their faces shadowed by distress.

"And I must apologise for my ungentlemanly manner in handling our earlier conversation and for the preposterous things I said. I know they cannot be forgotten or forgiven, either by you or by myself."

"I must apologise, too. My manners were hardly what they should have been. And I do believe you. I cannot imagine your hurting Jane or Mr. Bingley on purpose, but you did, I am afraid. *That* cannot be easily forgotten or forgiven."

She wondered whether she should speak further. She heard her voice, harsh and distant, but she could not change that; it mirrored her feelings. It was time for the truth.

"Miss Bingley implied to Jane that Mr. Bingley is expected to enter into an engagement with Georgiana. She implied that it was an event already arranged and soon to happen."

He looked at her in disbelief. "Surely, you are joking..."

"I am not, but now I know that to be another lie from Miss Bingley."

"Although I would be content were she someday to bestow her affection on someone as worthy as Bingley, such an arrangement never crossed my mind," he said, troubled.

"Mr. Bingley is a worthy gentleman, but that is more than I can say about his determination."

"Please do not blame Bingley. The fault is entirely mine. I thank you for listening to me. I shall leave you to rest now. Dinner must be ready. Molly will bring you something to eat."

She stared at the fire a moment as a battle raged between Lizzy Bennet and Elizabeth Darcy. The former wished to leave the house and wander around the park in the snow, alone with her dog and her thoughts and angry with all those who hurt her sister. The latter straightened her back and replied decidedly.

"That will not be necessary. I shall be ready and join you for dinner shortly."

His face lit slightly. "I am glad to hear it. We will be happy to have your company."

When Darcy left the room, Elizabeth felt a heavy burden lift from her chest and shoulders; she could breathe again. She knew she made the right—no, the *proper*—decision.

He had come to apologise, and they spoke in a civil manner. He told her the details of his involvement, even those that embarrassed him. He admitted his fault and his errors and declared he was ready to make amends. She could not forgive him, nor could she ignore this new insight in her attempt to understand his true character. However, the fact that such a proud man saw his wrongs and came to apologise immediately was solid proof that he was neither selfish nor insensitive.

Besides that, she clearly remembered that even Charlotte—who had known Jane for a lifetime—suggested she should show her feelings more openly. If Charlotte had doubts about Jane's feelings for Mr. Bingley, how could a stranger see beyond Jane's serenity? *In such cases, the man should not have the presumption to interfere,* she replied to herself, growing angry again. *Surely, he can resist giving his opinion just once in his life.*

Elizabeth had little time to think further on what occurred. That was a task for later. For the time being, she was expected downstairs, and she hurried to join the others.

Dinner proceeded more solemnly than on the previous evenings. Elizabeth's attention turned from her husband to her sister-in-law. Once her anger and distress about Jane diminished, the conversation with Georgiana increasingly occupied her mind. Elizabeth also recollected her husband's anger when he scolded her not to speak of "things about which you do not know"—a remark that surely referred to Mr. Wickham.

She remembered that Wickham described Miss Darcy as a proud and unpleasant sort of girl, and he let her believe that there were no recent connections between them. And yet, Georgiana specifically mentioned that she had seen him a few months ago and she was worried about his well-being. During their brief talk, Elizabeth was first tempted to believe that Miss Darcy had tender feelings for Mr. Wickham and her brother strongly opposed them. But not a single word, gesture, or sign from Mr. Wickham suggested that he held Miss Darcy in special regard—quite the contrary.

Elizabeth was inclined to accuse her husband of being unfair to Mr. Wickham, and she was certain their mutual dislike was due to disagreements and perhaps faults on Mr. Wickham's part that Mr. Darcy had treated more severely than he should. After all, he did say that he might be called resentful and his good opinion, once lost, was lost forever. As her uncle Gardiner once said, when two men fight, the truth is never on one side.

However, when it came to Georgiana, Elizabeth could never imagine any misunderstanding. Who could possibly judge her proud and unpleasant? And who could fail to see her kind and affectionate nature? Was Mr. Wickham such a poor judge of character? Or was there something more? Was it possible that Mr. Wickham intentionally and meanly spoke ill of Georgiana only because she was the sister of his enemy? If so, what did that say about Mr. Wickham's character? And what did it say about her own wisdom since she believed him entirely from the first?

It was the fourth day of her marriage, and her world became increasingly puzzling. And she dared not ask the questions for which she wanted answers. Though her husband told her the detailed story of his involvement with Jane and Mr. Bingley, he said not a word about Mr. Wickham. And she had no strength to inquire—at least not yet. Also, approaching Georgiana directly seemed impossible to consider for the present.

After dinner, at Mr. Darcy's kind request, they moved to the music room. Georgiana searched for a piece to play when she suddenly displayed a timid smile.

"Elizabeth, would you like to play and sing with me?" The girl's request took Elizabeth so much by surprise that she looked around and knew not what to say. Mrs. Annesley warmly supported Georgiana's suggestion, and Mr. Darcy only watched her in silence.

"I would like that very much, thank you, although I am afraid you will regret your invitation as you might be quickly appalled by my poor skill."

"I am sure that is not true. William has told me how much he admires your talent."

"I cannot imagine why he would say such a thing," Elizabeth answered lightly as she walked to the piano, glancing at her husband who hid a smile behind his glass.

They chose a piece, and Elizabeth sang while Georgiana played. Elizabeth knew her performance was not very good, and she felt her husband's gaze on her quite acutely. Their fight still affected her—and likely him as well. There were still things weighing heavily between them, and she found herself restrained and slightly embarrassed during her song. But she lowered her eyes and saw Georgiana's friendly face and warm smile.

Gradually, she relaxed, and when she finished the song, both Georgiana and Mrs. Annesley expressed their admiration. Elizabeth looked at her husband—who sat silently, his face wearing a slight smile. Then she joined Georgiana in her enthusiasm and kept her company for another hour.

Elizabeth had decided to join the family for dinner as a gesture of truce and civility towards her husband and agreed to play with Georgiana to ease her obvious distress. However, she returned to her apartment at the end of the evening with an easy heart and high spirits. She congratulated herself for not remaining isolated in her chamber. After all, she was the mistress of the house, and she had to consider her duties over her personal feelings.

She knew husband was also pleased with the progress of the evening. He thanked them both for the lovely music and expressed his hope that such evenings would be oft repeated. When the ladies retired, he declared he still had some work in the library. He embraced his sister then bestowed a proper kiss upon Elizabeth's hand, and held it a moment longer.

"Good night, Mrs. Darcy, and thank you," he said in a low voice, holding her gaze.

"Good night, Mr. Darcy."

Once Elizabeth snuggled within the softness of her bed, thoughts invaded her again. She recalled the conversation with her husband and with Georgiana, and along with her earlier concerns, something else began to trouble her. Darcy had diligently pointed out to her all his reasons against an alliance between Jane and Bingley: her family's improper manners, their poor situation in life, her mother's unyielding resolve to find good matches for her daughters. He also insisted that he believed Jane not to return Mr. Bingley's feelings, and he said he could not allow his friend to be trapped and unhappy in a loveless marriage.

But all of those reasons were equally valid in her situation. Why would her family's faults not weigh more heavily with regard to him than Mr. Bingley? And, if he doubted Jane's feelings for Mr. Bingley, he surely must know that her feelings were not at all favourable towards him, and yet he proposed to her, ignoring every barrier. Regardless of their commitment to eventually make a good marriage, he did allow himself to be trapped—in fact, he had built the trap himself—and she could not understand why.

She eventually fell asleep, but her mind, filled with all sorts of dreams, allowed her little rest. As dawn broke, she found herself wondering how many sets her husband would dance with her at the dinner party. She might have asked him directly had she known that, in the next room, he slept not a moment longer than she did. The only difference was that, when morning came, she slept soundly while he woke, dressed, and silently went to his library.

Chapter 12

London, 31 December

Around ten o'clock, Elizabeth noticed Molly slowly enter the room and take Lucky out. The maid returned a minute later and helped Elizabeth dress while informing her that the others were already downstairs for breakfast.

"And ma'am, a little earlier someone brought a large package for you…an apprentice from the shop… she said there are two of your new gowns. I shall fetch the package at once."

"Very well, thank you," Elizabeth said and hurried to the dining room. She noticed that her husband looked rather tired and wondered how difficult the previous night was for him. Strangely, she felt content that he seemed preoccupied with their fight. It was the best proof that his remorse was sincere.

Breakfast passed mostly in silence. Towards the end, Mrs. Annesley began a conversation about the upcoming party and asked Elizabeth whether she was pleased with her gowns.

"I have had no chance to see them, but I will do so immediately. Would you both like to come with me and help me try them on?"

The ladies' response was as animated as expected, and while they left together, Elizabeth felt her husband's gaze on her. She did not turn her eyes towards him, though.

"Elizabeth, if it is convenient for you, I would like to see you in the library for a few minutes. There is something I need to give you, and there has been no chance as yet."

"Of course, I shall meet you after I try on the gowns," she answered briefly.

The unpacking and trying on of clothes brought her more joy than she expected, encouraged by the enthusiasm of her companions. The garments fitted her perfectly, and while Mrs. Annesley admired the skills of the modiste, a thought suddenly crossed Elizabeth's mind and made her blush violently: her husband ordered the gowns and seemed to know her measurements perfectly.

Both gowns were splendid, but all three agreed that, for Elizabeth's first London ball, the perfect choice was the cream with golden threads at the neckline, shoulders, waist, and hem. It was impressive in an elegant way with no ostentation, and Mrs. Annesley said it perfectly complemented Elizabeth's hair and complexion.

Half an hour later, she went to speak to her husband, and her anxiety increased. She knocked and waited. He was in the doorway, stretching out his hand to her.

"Are you pleased with the gowns? Do they fit properly?" he asked while she took the same place as the day before.

"Yes, very pleased—they are beautiful and they fit perfectly. I must say, your taste in ladies' gowns is exquisite; Mrs. Annesley said so," she teased him, and a smile appeared on his lips.

"I am very glad you like them. I shall only detain you a little, as perhaps you should rest before the ball. I wondered—did you have time to read the settlement? If you approve of it, I would like to mail it to Mr. Bennet tomorrow."

"I confess I have not read it. My mind was occupied with other things, and I could not concentrate on it. But as I said, I do not have the smallest worry, so please mail it to my father. I can read it anytime. I have no concerns in this respect."

"Very well, as you wish." He opened a drawer, brought out three large jewels boxes, and put them on the desk. One by one, he opened the boxes, exposing the pieces to her curious eyes. She gasped in surprise, her palm covering her lips as her eyes opened widely.

"These are splendid," she whispered. "Truly beautiful..." She gently brushed her fingers over the jewels, which were arranged in sets of earrings, necklaces, bracelets, and rings of the same stones and colours.

"I have not opened these boxes since my mother passed away," he said in a low voice. "There are several others at Pemberley. Hopefully, you will see those too very soon."

She glanced at him, overwhelmed by the beauty in front of her, which took her breath away—not so much because of their obvious value but because of their beauty and by what they meant: the legacy of Lady Anne for the new Mrs. Darcy. Did she truly deserve that title, acquired through an arranged marriage? Surely, Lady Anne never imagined such a possibility. Otherwise, she would have made a codicil regarding what a mock "Mrs. Darcy" should receive. And yet, her husband had been insisting for the last two days on giving her the jewels when he could have postponed the gesture or never done it.

"William, I do not think you should give me these jewels. I should not wear them."

His face darkened, and he frowned. "Why would you say that?"

"Lady Anne prepared these jewels for your wife, but I doubt she considered you might enter into a forced marriage. I am not sure that, at this time, I am the 'Mrs. Darcy' for whom these jewels were meant. I feel I am claiming something that is not rightfully mine."

"Your concerns honour you, Elizabeth, but aside from the peculiar circumstances of our marriage, I am certain these boxes belong to you—in every possible way. I trust you will care for and cherish them as the person who offered them deserves."

Elizabeth struggled to smile and prevent her threatening tears. He took her hands in his, and she allowed her fingers to rest in his palms while they gazed at each other.

"Then I shall wear the delicate set of garnet and diamonds tonight—and the tiara. I believe they will match perfectly the cream and golden gown."

"A perfect choice," he whispered, mirroring her tentative smile. "I still remember how lovely the silk flowers and small pearls shone in your dark hair at the Netherfield ball."

She stared at him in complete surprise and released a nervous laugh as her face turned red.

"Your attention to detail is impressive, Mr. Darcy."

"It seems that is not always true, but this is another matter," he said more lightly, releasing her hands and taking a sealed letter from his desk. "I wrote to Bingley to inform him of our marriage, and I asked him for the favour of a private talk when he returns to London. I shall mail the letter express, and hopefully, he will receive it by tomorrow."

"It is lovely that you send him news," she said as composedly as she could. "But I believe it is Mr. Bingley's turn to decide whether his future happiness is truly related to Jane and to act accordingly. He cannot allow anyone to tell him what to do. Forgive me if I seem harsh, but I am convinced that your blame for involving yourself in Mr. Bingley's life is equalled by his ease in allowing others to decide his fate."

"I understand your disapproval of both my and Bingley's behaviour, but I beg your forbearance in his case. I believe his greatest fault is his modesty and lack of confidence in his own discernment. The blame for that situation was entirely mine."

She said nothing, but her expression showed her disagreement.

"I also wrote to my Aunt Catherine two days ago, but I am afraid I have no doubt about the way she will receive the news. Unfortunately, we can shortly expect a very angry letter. I must tell you that I asked the servants to inform me about any letter or note sent directly to you unless it is from your family. I hope you don't mind."

She laughed. "Not at all. I will inform you directly should I receive anything dangerous by mail. It is lovely that you want to protect me from the written revenge of your disappointed relatives. It is easily balanced by the amiability of the rest of your family."

"I surely hope so. Now I believe you and Georgiana should rest a little before the party. I expect it might be a difficult evening. Shall I help you to take the boxes to your room?"

"No, thank you, I am fine. I shall see you later." She took the boxes, and he kept her company towards the door where they separated with polite smiles.

About an hour later, Darcy found that his work suffered from lack of attention and decided to rest as well. On the way to his apartment, he took a turn down the picture gallery out of a strong sense of longing. He wondered what his parents would say of Elizabeth. Even more—would he have ever met her if his parents were still alive?

As he moved along the hall, he frowned. In front of the portraits—so deep in thought that she failed to notice his approach—was Elizabeth. A tight knot gripped his stomach and made him stop. He silently admired her, mere inches away, for a few moments before he finally whispered her name so as not to startle her. She turned to him, and he easily perceived the emotion on her face and the tears glistening in her eyes.

"I felt the need to see Lady Anne again," she explained, slightly uncomfortable.

"I, too...and I am most pleasantly surprised to find you here."

"I remembered something that I must have forgotten over the years. When we met in Brighton ten years ago, Lady Anne told me one day that my eyes were full of life and joy, and she told me never to allow that to change. At that moment, I did not know what she meant, but her voice went deep into my heart. I believe it was the last time we saw her..."

Elizabeth turned towards the image again, and she felt her husband's hands gently resting on her shoulders. She did not move or say anything, allowing the moments to pass in silence. She observed that Lady Anne had the same blue eyes as Georgiana, but there was something in her gaze that resembled Darcy. Next to her in the large painting, the late Mr. Darcy looked tall, handsome, strong, and quite severe, and Elizabeth wondered how the delicate Lady Anne accustomed herself to a husband who seemed so different.

"What do you think your father and Lady Anne would say of this marriage? Would they approve of me?" she heard herself asking. She felt his hesitation and the tension in his hands, which still lingered on her shoulders.

"I believe they would have been displeased with the idea of our marriage at first—for all the reasons we have discussed. It was their expectation—as well as mine—to marry someone from our circle. But I have no doubt that they would have completely approved of you. I believe my mother certainly would have come to love you."

"Thank you for being honest with me, William."

"I admire your intelligence too much to ever attempt to deceive you, Elizabeth. Come, let us go to our rooms now. We both need some peaceful rest before the party."

Elizabeth glanced at her image in the mirror and smiled. The garnet and diamond jewels were glowing on her skin, beautifully completing the creamy, golden gown. She was ready. From his apartment, her husband appeared, dressed as impeccably as always. He stopped a few feet away, gazing at her until she felt her cheeks colouring.

"You look beautiful, Mrs. Darcy. Truly beautiful."

"Thank you, Mr. Darcy, you look quite dashing yourself. But I confess I am overwhelmed by the beauty of these jewels. I find myself somehow clumsy in wearing them."

He took her hands, inspecting the bracelet resting over her delicate silk gloves then gently moving a lock of her hair to expose the earrings. Elizabeth stopped breathing the moment his fingers brushed her ear. Then, as gently as a breeze, he caressed the necklace shining on her skin. Although his touch was as brief and subtle as a heartbeat, she shuddered and blushed, wondering at the strange sensations she struggled with in his presence.

"The jewels are beautiful, but no doubt their brightness is increased by the person who wears them. I see no clumsiness, only your eyes shining like the diamonds. And no, I am not just complimenting you. I have noticed almost from the beginning of our acquaintance that your eyes have a special brightness, both when you are very upset or very happy."

Elizabeth felt her cheeks and neck burning. She appreciated his kind attempt to dissipate her worries with an elegant compliment—a proper gesture for a gentleman—but his voice and eyes were so serious that she could only say, "Thank you."

He offered his arm, and they went downstairs where Mrs. Annesley and Georgiana awaited them. Compliments were exchanged among the ladies, and Darcy helped all three to the carriage. It was snowing, and the chilly air cut Elizabeth's breath, but she stood a few seconds to admire the white-covered street, hoping the snowflakes would cool her florid face and conceal her constant embarrassment.

Matlock Manor was nearby, so they arrived within minutes. The building was as splendid as the Darcy townhouse, Elizabeth thought, gazing at the impressive facade.

The colonel greeted them and escorted Georgiana and Mrs. Annesley into the house while Elizabeth walked with Darcy. They arrived before the other guests, and Lord and Lady Matlock with the viscount and Lady Maryanne welcomed them warmly. The house was beautifully decorated. In the large ballroom, a few musicians prepared their instruments.

Lady Matlock expressed her approval of both Elizabeth and Georgiana and congratulated Elizabeth on her choice of jewellery.

"So, I understand this is more a private ball than a family dinner party," Darcy observed.

"Oh, do not look so displeased, Darcy," said Lady Matlock. "And it *is* a family party as all the guests are our relatives."

Darcy rolled his eyes. "I am sure they are, Aunt, but we all know how generous you are in defining 'family.' Also, we know you enjoy hosting large parties, and everyone admires your proficiency in making everything perfect. Anyway, we are all very pleased to be here."

"It is my pleasure to have you. It will be so interesting to introduce Mrs. Darcy to the guests. I can only imagine how shocked they all were by the announcement.

Oh, do not take that the wrong way, Elizabeth, but everyone is shocked that Darcy married. There were so many young ladies who—" Lady Matlock suddenly stopped with obvious uneasiness.

The colonel laughed. "Yes, it will certainly be an interesting evening. At least nobody will have reason to disapprove of Elizabeth. You look truly stunning. By the way, Mrs. Darcy, before things go completely wild, which sets did you reserve for me? Has your husband decided which one he is compelled to dance?"

"He has," Darcy intervened seriously, and the colonel laughed louder. "I believe it would be fair to have the first and last sets with Elizabeth. You may have the supper set if you like."

"Oh, how generous you are, Cousin," the colonel replied. "It will be the greatest pleasure to have Mrs. Darcy's company during the dance and at dinner."

"So, Darcy," the colonel continued, "I hope you are aware that, if you dance with your wife, you must join in the other dances, too. I am sure many young ladies would be pleased to solace their disappointment in your marriage by enjoying your company for at least a set."

"I am pleased to add to your amusement, Cousin," Darcy concluded, thinking the opposite.

"Oh come, Darcy—let us have a glass of brandy. Hopefully, it will loosen your haughtiness a little. I am sure the ladies will do just fine by themselves for now." Both moved towards the library with Lord Matlock and the viscount.

With delight, Elizabeth noted the entrance of a gentleman she truly admired and looked forward to meeting again: Dr. Taylor. He immediately spotted their little group and stepped towards them. The greetings took place with warmth and pleasure. After he expressed his delight in seeing Georgiana and Mrs. Annesley again, he bowed politely to Elizabeth.

"It is a pleasure to see you again, Miss Bennet. Forgive me, I mean 'Mrs. Darcy'! What a lovely surprise! And what a happy, swift development of our story!"

"I am very happy to see you again, Dr. Taylor, and to have the chance to thank you for—"

"Nonsense, Mrs. Darcy! I am glad to see you looking beautiful, indeed," the doctor repeated, and Elizabeth laughed and invited him to sit with them. He accepted the invitation and spent some minutes asking Georgiana how she took the news of her brother's marriage, and Mrs. Annesley about when her daughter was due and how she was feeling.

During the next half hour, more than fifty guests filled the house as Lady Matlock introduced everyone to Elizabeth. She easily lost track of the names and titles, but she did not miss the curiosity in their eyes or the wonder and disapproval of several raised eyebrows. As Lady Matlock said, they all seemed to be relatives, and shortly, animated murmurs flowed throughout the ballroom. Elizabeth returned to Georgiana, and she felt slightly uneasy. Every pair of eyes seemed to be fixed on her. There was no doubt about whom the assembled guests were conversing.

Lady Matlock and Lady Maryanne joined their group again while a gentleman with agreeable features and a charming smile approached them and bowed properly.

"Lady Matlock, allow me to express my gratitude for the invitation. Your party is as delightful as I expected. Georgiana, dearest, you seem prettier with every passing day. Allow me to hug you, my dear. Lady Maryanne, your appearance is a joy, as always."

"Stop flattering us, you rascal. Elizabeth, this is James Darcy, your husband's cousin on his father's side. James, this is Mrs. Darcy," Lady Matlock spoke lightly.

"Mrs. Darcy—what a lovely surprise! Allow me to welcome you to our family and to express my admiration for your beauty. Your marriage to Darcy was the greatest surprise of the *ton* this month, and I hoped I would have the pleasure to meet you tonight."

"Mr. Darcy—it is a pleasure to meet you, sir." Elizabeth curtseyed graciously while considering the resemblance between her husband and his cousin.

"The pleasure is all mine, I assure you, and I shall take advantage of this moment to ask you to secure me a set. I am sure your card will be full soon. And perhaps we will have the chance to speak more and know each other better as we dance."

"You are too kind, sir. I will be delighted to speak more with you," Elizabeth said, trying to sound as friendly as possible to her husband's cousin.

In truth, Elizabeth was pleasantly surprised by Mr. James Darcy—who seemed to be an amiable gentleman, much like the colonel. She glanced towards the corner where she knew her husband stood, and she met his stare. Strangely, his countenance was dark and preoccupied, completely opposite to what she expected, and Elizabeth felt disconcerted. Was something wrong? Would she never learn what pleased or displeased him?

As if responding to her thoughts, her husband approached them, followed by the colonel, while Lady Matlock and Lady Maryanne left to attend to other guests.

James Darcy greeted the gentlemen animatedly, and Darcy responded rather sternly. He moved near Elizabeth and Georgiana, and James laughed.

"Oh, you must not worry. I do not mean to steal your wife. I only asked her for a set. However, I can understand your being completely charmed and hurrying to marry within days. Not even the patience for a proper engagement—how strange of you!"

"As always, your jokes are rather improper, James. You are correct about my being completely charmed by my wife, though. With every passing moment, I congratulate myself for insisting that Elizabeth accept our sudden marriage. As for the engagement—I try to compensate for its absence. I can only hope my wife does not regret it," Darcy said and placed her hand on his arm. Elizabeth looked at him for a brief moment, and her cheeks coloured. She was not certain what to believe about such a display or about his daring and barely proper comment.

"Well, most people believe that Mrs. Darcy is the one who trapped *you* into this marriage and wonder how she did it," James continued, and Elizabeth paled at this offensive remark.

"Then you may inform them that they could not be further from the truth. I had to use all my powers of persuasion to convince Elizabeth to accept me, and I happily succeeded."

"Good, now that we are all clear on that subject, I shall leave you," the colonel said. "Lady Constance is looking at me quite insistently. James, I think Lord Matlock is waiting for you."

Darcy looked at Elizabeth with concern. "Are you well? You must forgive James. He never knows when to stop before crossing the line from joke to offense."

"Yes, I am well; do not worry. There is nothing for which to forgive Mr. Darcy. He seemed quite pleasant and friendly. I must agree, however, that his remarks were rather improper."

"Yes, he possesses the gift of charming people and making friends rather quickly, but he loses them as easily," Darcy said, and Elizabeth remembered similar remarks about Wickham at the Netherfield ball. She glanced at Mr. James Darcy then back at her husband and wondered what his cousin did that deserved Mr. Darcy's disapproval.

"I thank you for protecting me against the rumours and accusations that I have trapped you," she whispered, and despite her uneasiness, she forced a smile.

"I said nothing but the truth. I shall do what is necessary to protect you. As for rumours—do not worry. James will spread my words around the room and around Town very quickly," he concluded, and Elizabeth covered her mouth with her gloved hand to hide a laugh, her other hand still resting on his arm.

"So there was a strategy involved. However, were you not too harsh with your cousin?"

"Not at all, I assure you. I have known him since he was born, and I have great affection for him, but his behaviour in the last years deserves to be met with severity. But enough of that. I want you to enjoy this evening. I know you are fond of balls and parties." He smiled.

"I do like to dance. And speaking of that, be assured that your effort to dance with me, despite disliking the activity, is not unappreciated," she teased him.

"It is no effort. As I said, one might change one's likes and dislikes after marriage," he whispered, leaning slightly towards her, and Elizabeth struggled to regain her composure as she again noticed many pairs of eyes on them.

Darcy looked around then continued in the same quiet voice. "My Aunt's New Year's dinners were always large gatherings, but not quite like this one. I think she extended the list of guests precisely to introduce you to London society. I should apologise. I am afraid you will not have an easy evening despite your enjoyment of parties."

"Oh, there is surely no need to apologise—not after you promised to dance 'several sets' with me," Elizabeth replied in the same teasing manner. "And I feel I owe Lady Matlock my gratitude. It is a relief to be 'introduced' to London society in her house. However, I surely hope that not all of London society is here tonight."

"Fortunately, many people have left London and will only return for the Season. And I am very pleased to see that you are amused by the situation. I was concerned that you might find the entire dinner party a bit overwhelming. I know I do."

"I doubt that anything might truly overwhelm you under any circumstances," she said, her voice a mix of teasing and gravity. He responded with another smile.

Elizabeth's spirits rose with each passing moment. The short conversation with her husband helped her to relax, and she quite enjoyed their brief, playful exchange.

They danced together but spoke very little. Most of the time, their eyes were on each other, and each time the steps required it, their hands met, and Elizabeth felt his fingers linger over hers a beat longer than necessary. She blushed, but she entered quickly into the little game and began to enjoy it. Sharing a small gesture with her husband in a room full of people who examined her with harsh curiosity was pleasant in a strange way. Darcy complimented Elizabeth's appearance and her elegant dancing, and she reminded him how much Sir William had admired his dancing skills even in Hertfordshire.

"Both then and now, my dancing skills are highly improved by the performance of my partner. Even Sir William agreed on that," he said, continuing their teasing banter.

"Indeed, sir, your pleasant conversation and sense of humour are excellent and valuable additions to your ten thousand a year. If Meryton society had benefitted more from your talents, I am sure their admiration would be boundless."

He struggled not to laugh, but when the dancing steps allowed it, he leant towards her only a little to say in a low voice, "Now your eyes are truly sparkling, as I told you earlier. And if you speak of my qualities, madam, please do not neglect my being tall and handsome, as Mrs. Bennet generously pointed out several times."

Her smiling eyes and her lips, tightly concealing her laughter, offered the only reply such a statement deserved. Every minute of the dance found Elizabeth more at ease and more delighted with the company of her husband, and the chance of just gazing at him allowed her to discover many expressions, small gestures, frowns, and smiles that she had missed earlier. At the same time, she found herself in the midst of a strange tumult of feelings that made her warm and flushed or cold and shivering from one moment to the next. A deep sense of regret overwhelmed her when the music stopped.

DARCY HELD ELIZABETH'S HAND AND CONDUCTED HER TO GEORGIANA. THE ladies remained by themselves while Darcy joined the colonel and a few other gentlemen.

"Elizabeth is truly a remarkable woman," the colonel said, handing him a glass of brandy. Darcy said nothing, and his cousin continued. "You looked like a real, normal newlywed couple—and quite affectionate with each other, I might say."

"We *are* a real, normal newlywed couple, Cousin," Darcy replied in earnest.

"I am glad to hear it. Am I to understand, then, that all is well? As you expected?"

"Very well." He finished his brandy then suddenly looked towards Elizabeth as the music started again. "Lord Clayton just asked Elizabeth to dance?!"

"Is that a statement or a question?" said the colonel, laughing. "Well, they have moved to the dance floor, so you have your answer. Do not tell me you are jealous."

"You are quite annoying sometimes," Darcy interrupted hastily. A few moments later, he attempted to join a conversation with Lord Matlock, struggling not to glance towards the dance floor too often, until Lady Matlock approached their group and demanded from the young gentlemen whether any unmarried lady was lacking a partner and to perform their duties accordingly. Thus, Darcy, the colonel, and the viscount obeyed, and each invited a young lady to dance. None of them looked as burdened by the task as Darcy.

Trying to pay attention to his dance partner, Darcy met Elizabeth's laughing eyes, and he had no choice but to allow a smile to light his countenance. Then, he finally turned to his partner, Lady Clarisse, the eldest daughter of Lord ______, and inquired whether she was enjoying the party.

That set came to an end and the next began, which brought Elizabeth and James Darcy together. Elizabeth had only a few minutes to exchange brief words with her husband before he withdrew to a corner when the music started.

From the first steps, Elizabeth noticed that her partner was a skilful and elegant dancer. He did not wait a moment before he expressed his pleasure in her company.

"I am very happy to meet you at last, Mrs. Darcy. I heard wonderful things about you."

"Truly, sir? I am very surprised. May I will ask from whom you heard these 'wonderful things'? I know my husband to be guarded in sharing his opinions."

"Oh, not from Darcy, that is certain. In fact, he was so slick that he did not even tell us about your marriage. We had to learn of it from a newspaper. But we do have a mutual friend who seemed to enjoy expressing his admiration of you quite openly."

Elizabeth watched him with puzzlement, so he continued, his smile even larger. "I am speaking of Mr. Wickham. I can see you are surprised. He and I have known each other since we were children, and both of us spent much time at Pemberley. He—"

"That is quite surprising indeed. I would not have guessed it."

"Well, you may imagine, then, how surprised I was to hear of your marriage. I never heard Darcy reveal any such intention. Even more so, I knew your preferences lay elsewhere. However, it is understandable that a young woman might prefer a man of means and the situation in life that Darcy can provide, even if his manners are not always faultless. These qualities are more desirable than amiability and charm."

"Mr. Darcy, I am at a loss to understand your meaning. Surely, you do not imply that I had some hidden purpose for entering into this marriage. And you certainly know nothing about my preferences!"

"Oh, I did not… That is not what I meant. I just know that you and Mr. Wickham were good friends and…we were both surprised that you decided to marry on such short notice."

"Mr. Wickham is indeed a friend of my family. But that does not diminish my appreciation for Mr. Darcy and surely does not give anyone reason to presume that I would tolerate vicious comments about my husband. Besides, knowing Mr. Darcy for a lifetime, you more than anyone must know his true worthiness—besides his wealth that you slyly mentioned."

"Of course…I am sorry if I upset you, Mrs. Darcy. I apologise if my jokes offended you. That was surely not my intention, and you are right—I know very well Darcy's good qualities."

"If it was a joke, you have no reason to apologise, sir. I appreciate a good joke, and I am glad we clarified the situation. As you are my husband's only relative on his father's side, I would not want to begin our acquaintance with a misunderstanding."

"I thank you. You are very generous."

The rest of the dance proceeded with little conversation, but Elizabeth could not escape the feeling that something was wrong, and that made her uncomfortable. It was not so much what James Darcy said but his voice, the hidden meanings of his words—as if they were sharing a secret against her husband. And Mr. Wickham—why did his name appear again under questionable circumstances? What could he possibly have told Mr. James Darcy about her? She and Wickham had not been such close acquaintances as to be mentioned to strange parties. And how was it possible that a member of Darcy's family was on such friendly—rather intimate—terms with Mr. Wickham? So, they had time and opportunity to discuss her and her marriage, and somehow Mr. Wickham declared that her preference lay on his side? Although it was not untrue—and she could not overcome the blame she felt for behaving so carelessly in that respect—would a gentleman say such a thing?

Despite Mr. James Darcy's dancing skills and his charming smile, Elizabeth felt relieved when the set came to an end. She observed her husband approaching, and she managed to put a smile on her face as James Darcy thanked her for the privilege of her company. Again, his smile and flattering words made her rather uncomfortable.

Darcy rarely took his eyes from his wife while she danced with his cousin. He knew her well enough to recognise an amused expression, but he also recognised her forced smiles, and he worried about what James might have told her. He noticed her eyes searching for him several times, and that pleased him. He was content to see that, in difficult moments, she unconsciously looked to him for protection. As soon as the music stopped, he went to offer her his arm, which she took without hesitation, and helped her sit near Georgiana.

Elizabeth stood up with Colonel Fitzwilliam during the supper set and joined him at the table as well. At her other side was Georgiana, and by her, Mrs. Annesley.

Her husband was directly across from her with a young lady at each side, and he was a little more animated than she had seen him in Hertfordshire. As for herself, she quickly adjusted to the colonel's charming manners, and his friendly behaviour succeeded in putting her, as well as Georgiana, at ease.

Lady Matlock's private ball ended right after Mr. Fitzwilliam Darcy danced the last set with his wife—a happenstance as strange and unfashionable as their dancing the first together. Many of the guests had been certain that Mr. Darcy was somehow trapped into marriage by that country girl, but the gentleman's behaviour towards his wife left them puzzled and shocked. What caused this unexpected change in Mr. Darcy's behaviour, and what arts and allurements did the new Mrs. Darcy possess to succeed where so many had failed?

It was snowing steadily when the Darcys left Matlock Manor. Georgiana and Mrs. Annesley hurried inside as soon as they arrived home, but Elizabeth—on her husband's arm—seemed unwilling to enter.

She looked around at the snow shining under the streetlights then closed her eyes, allowing the snowflakes to caress her face. She waited, silent and breathless, until his lips, warm and gentle, kissed the water drops from her cheeks then tentatively rested upon her lips and tenderly tasted them for a moment. Only for a moment.

Elizabeth was still holding her eyes closed when her husband placed one arm around her shoulders. "It is very cold and very late. We should go in now, Mrs. Darcy."

Chapter 13

London, 1 January 1812

Around ten o'clock, long past his usual morning hour, Darcy woke, still wearing a smile of contentment. He enjoyed the ball more than he expected, but he remembered little beyond Elizabeth's smiles, her glances, and her face caressed by falling snowflakes and lit by a streetlight, her eyelashes covering her sparkling eyes when he bent to touch her lips.

He shivered at the memory and became amused at his own childish reaction. He had come to admire Elizabeth during the last months, and he admitted his growing attraction for her in the week since she became his wife, but his feelings had changed and grown with a haste that almost troubled him. He knew that he was deeply in love with his wife, and he was not certain whether that was a good or a dangerous thing; regardless, he could not fight it.

He had never experienced such feelings before. He had felt attraction at times, and he had enjoyed the pleasure of being in the intimate company of beautiful women. Yet, the joy and delight of tasting Elizabeth's lips for a moment or touching her warm, silky skin under her sparkling jewels aroused in him senses he did not recognise. As he briefly closed his eyes, he indulged himself and imagined her in utter abandon to his impatient and greedy kisses, her lips releasing a moan of delight as his hands caressed her softness and—

Darcy startled at the sound of a strong, demanding bark. He smiled and opened the door. Elizabeth was scolding Lucky, but his appearance drove the dog towards him immediately.

"I am so sorry. Lucky seemed to feel your every move, and he is such a beggar for your attention!"

He was delighted to meet her warm smile and flushed cheeks. He petted the dog and smiled then moved closer and took her hands, looking into her eyes.

"Good morning, Elizabeth. Did you sleep well, I hope?"

"Yes, very well… I was a little tired, but I truly enjoyed the evening. I just finished writing my 'thank you' note to Lady Matlock."

"Ah, yes, the note—I forgot about it. Well, there is no wonder you were tired.

You danced every set. But I imagine that usually happens to you."

"Well, not quite… There have been occasions when gentlemen were scarce, and I happened to remain without a partner." She held his gaze daringly, their hands still entwined, and her right brow rose in challenge while a teasing smile twisted her lips.

He laughed. "You cannot still be upset with me for that unfortunate evening. Rest assured that I have blamed myself many times since that rude comment. Surely, my regrets have washed away my faults! Pray, tell me: What may I do to gain your forgiveness?"

"Well, your breaking the rules by dancing with your own wife twice in one evening was an excellent start! I can safely say that you are very close to the redemption point, Mr. Darcy."

She laughed too, and he suddenly released her left hand, slowly removed a lock of brown hair from her temple, and then caressed her face gently. "Your eyes are sparkling again, Elizabeth…" he said, and her laughter vanished as she averted her eyes from his heavy, dark gaze. But her right hand remained in his.

His voice turned lighter as he continued, pointing outside the window. "Georgiana and Mrs. Annesley are still asleep, and I imagine breakfast will be quite late. Would you like to join me for a short stroll in the park? The weather is beautiful."

"Yes, I would like that very much." She replied with such haste that it brought another smile to his lips. "I shall be ready in a moment."

"Excellent! I suggest leaving Titan and Lucky at home. They can play in the back garden."

Elizabeth hurried to dress. *He wishes to walk alone with me. Not even the dogs will join us.* She was not certain whether the prospect troubled or pleased her, but she admitted to herself that she was eager to be ready, and her heart began to race.

A few minutes later, Darcy offered her his arm while he instructed Stevens to take care of the dogs and to tell the others that they would return shortly.

Elizabeth felt equally lighthearted and uneasy as she tightened her grip on his arm. Since the previous evening, she could not put aside the sensation of his lips on hers. She had never imagined that a man's hands or a mere kiss could arouse such feelings inside her. His small gestures—holding her hands, touching her skin while caressing the jewels, his stares, smiles, teasing or compliments—threw her into a tumult of sensations and questions difficult to answer. They had been married for six days. She had slowly adjusted to her new life and new home. She had become closely acquainted with Georgiana and even with him. He had been kind and considerate, and they both had put effort into making the marriage work. But it was much more than that: he often behaved as if he were…courting her… in a way she had not been courted before.

She had never kissed another man, nor held another man's bare hand. But Charlotte had been kissed twice by two gentlemen—one, two years ago and another, last year—and she told both her and Jane that it was not remarkable, not different from pressing one's own hand upon one's own lips. Elizabeth cast a glance out of the corner of her eye. Her husband had barely kissed her. She was not even certain it was a real kiss, but it surely did not feel like pressing her hand to her lips—not at all.

"Elizabeth, is anything wrong?" She realised that he asked her something and she missed it.

"No, forgive me…everything is fine. The weather is beautiful indeed—"

"I asked whether you have news from your sister. When do they arrive in Town?"

"I only received one letter from Jane three days ago. They should leave Longbourn today or tomorrow, as far as I know. To be honest, I am a little worried, but I know my uncle and aunt are there, and I trust them completely. Nothing can go wrong with them."

"I am sure there is no cause for concern. The weather has been quite bad lately, and the mail sometimes has great difficulties."

"You are probably right. This view is just wonderful," she said, looking around. "I always loved the trees covered in white fresh snow when I was home—I mean at Longbourn."

He covered the hand resting on his arm with his other hand. "I trust you will love Pemberley, too."

"Oh, I am sure I will, and I confess I look forward to seeing it. My aunt said it is truly the most wonderful place she has ever seen. I suspect she insisted on my marrying you only to be able to see the interiors of Pemberley." She laughed then felt his grip tightening and turned to face him. He looked concerned, but she smiled daringly and held his gaze.

"You already knew my aunt insisted on my accepting your proposal…but now I am very glad she did."

His face lit a little, and his lips twisted in a hidden smile. With horror at her wanton thoughts, she found herself wondering how it would feel for those lips to press harder and longer on hers, and she knew she turned crimson. But he replied lightly, "Mrs. Gardiner is a wise lady—very wise indeed. I would be delighted to have her as a guest at Pemberley."

"You are very kind. My aunt would be honoured by your words." She paused a moment then continued in excellent spirits. "With that, you are completely forgiven for calling me barely 'tolerable' and refusing to dance with me, Mr. Darcy."

"You are generous indeed, Mrs. Darcy," he replied, equally amused.

They walked in silence for a while then he spoke in a serious tone. "My mother always wanted to have a school in Lambton for all the girls in the neighbourhood. She said that learning the basics of reading, calculating, music, cooking, and sewing would help the girls support themselves and perhaps be wiser in choosing their husbands. She thought it was unfair that girls after childhood had no other interests than to find a man to support them, which was why they often fell for some unworthy man who treated them horribly."

Elizabeth watched him, so surprised that she had nothing to say. That Lady Anne would have such concerns for the girls in the county and that he—the master of Pemberley—seemed to give sincere thought to that idea, was truly astonishing.

"Unfortunately, my mother was not strong enough to finish what she planned. During her last years, she spent as much time as possible with Georgiana. She suffered deeply knowing she would soon leave her daughter at such a young age. My father and I joined them as much as we could when she was in Brighton. The sea was beneficial to her health for a while. Cold winters from the north kept her mostly inside, but she loved Pemberley very much and could not stay away long. I remember playing with Georgiana in the snow—she was four or five years old—and mother watching from the window..."

In the empty park, with few visitors occupying the frozen pathways, Mr. Darcy—the most severe man she had ever met—spoke to her about his mother, his voice heavy with emotion. She felt her eyes stinging with tears as she entwined her fingers with his.

"I look forward to seeing Pemberley," she whispered.

"And I look forward to showing it to you," he replied, and her heart began to race again. "As soon as the weather improves, we may discuss leaving town. I do know you wish to spend time with your sister and relatives. And the Season will open in March and—"

"Oh, we should not worry much about the Season. I would just like to see what might happen...with Jane and..." She stopped, but it was clear to both that she referred to her sister and a certain gentleman who was momentarily out of town.

"Well, Pemberley is a very large estate. It can easily accommodate many guests, and I am sure your family would enjoy it, too. I know Bingley and his sisters always have."

"I am sure they would—thank you. I hope you know how much I appreciate your generous invitation. Although my father was certain you would withdraw it once you thought better of the prospect." She laughed, and he joined her, declaring Mr. Bennet was wrong this time.

They slowly turned towards the house. Darcy complained he was starving and hoped breakfast would be heartier than usual. She replied that she did not remember having been so hungry in a long time, and he concluded that they finally felt the same way about something. She blushed and said nothing more.

Only a few moments walk from their home, they saw a carriage stop in front of them, and a mirthful voice erupted along with the unexpected appearance of its owner.

"Darcy, Mrs. Darcy, what a surprise!" James Darcy jumped from the carriage and bowed to her. She smiled politely, noticing her husband's arm tense.

"Walking in the park in such cold weather? Quite singular, I might say."

"Not as singular as your being awake this early after a night of partying," Darcy replied. Elizabeth felt the tension increase in his body. His countenance was dark, and he frowned, his lips narrowing in anger.

"True." James laughed. "But I had a promise to keep, and I could not break it."

"That is also quite singular," Darcy replied sharply, and Elizabeth could not understand her husband's resentful reaction towards his close relative. Her attention was soon attracted to the carriage where a woman of remarkable beauty appeared and James helped her down.

"Well, at least Mr. James Darcy is a gentleman who keeps his promises," the lady said with a charming smile. "Now, would anyone be so kind as to perform the introductions since we are freezing here? Either Mr. Darcy will do as we have known each other for years."

James happily obliged. "Mrs. Darcy, may I introduce Annabelle Harwood, Lady Stafford—an old friend of ours. Annabelle, this is Mrs. Darcy."

While she tried to curtsey with politeness and conceal her curiosity, Elizabeth startled as she heard her husband's severe voice.

"This is hardly the place to perform introductions, and we surely do not intend to make you freeze; therefore, please excuse us. My wife and I must leave now."

"Well, I would rather have had this conversation at Lady Matlock's ball, but it seemed my invitation was somehow lost. I am pleased to finally meet Mrs. Darcy. All of London society was curious and puzzled about your marriage and your wife's secret identity."

Elizabeth heard herself speaking with a sharpness she had not intended. "I hope that London society has better ways to employ its time, Lady Stafford. If not, I am sure everyone who attended the ball last night realised there was no cause for curiosity or puzzlement. It is unfortunate that your invitation was lost. I understand Lady Matlock strives for perfection, and I cannot imagine how such a thing might have occurred." Her stomach tightened in a cold grip, and a sense of worry enveloped her as she watched Lady Stafford's twisted smile and her gaze upon the Mr. Darcy whose arm Elizabeth was holding.

"Oh, you must not believe everything you hear about Lady Matlock—or about others in the family, Mrs. Darcy. Take my word: you will have to face quite a lot of surprises. And in order to carry on a proper conversation, I would gladly accept a cup of tea at either your house or mine," Lady Stafford concluded with a confident smile. Elizabeth was stunned. Did this woman actually invite herself to their house? And how dare she look in such an impertinent way at her husband while she was holding his arm?

"Unfortunately, neither proposal is acceptable," Elizabeth said quickly. "We already have fixed engagements with our family, and we are expected at home immediately."

Elizabeth saw an expression of displeasure on Lady Stafford's face, and she was certain the lady would reply in an equally harsh manner. However, it was James Darcy who spoke first.

"Well, I am part of the family too, Mrs. Darcy. I hope you remember that."

"We do remember that, James," Darcy replied with severe politeness. "You are welcome to join us without further invitation as soon as you conclude your present engagement with Lady Stafford. Now, please excuse us; we are in quite a hurry."

They slowly resumed their walk, and Elizabeth took a last glance at Lady Stafford, whose displeasure had turned to anger. Darcy's hand gripped hers more tightly. She did not need to look at him to feel his distress increasing. They were only a few steps away when Lady Stafford called him. "Mr. Darcy, please remember that there is something of great importance we need to discuss. Any time or place would be agreeable to me."

Elizabeth instantly looked at him while his gaze was fixed on the lady's face. He wore an unreadable expression, one she had never seen before. "Good day, Lady Stafford," was all he said, and his step quickened, his hand never releasing hers.

They arrived home in minutes. Georgiana appeared in the doorway, asking where they had been and insisting they hurry to the breakfast table, which they did.

Overwhelmed by a distress she could barely control, Elizabeth forced herself not to look at her husband, whose gaze on her was unrelenting. The more she thought about the strange incident, the more certain she became that the meeting was not accidental. A revelation struck Elizabeth and took her breath away: Lady Stafford's carriage was the one she had seen days earlier, waiting in front of the house—the one into which her husband had entered and stayed a few minutes. And they still had "something of great importance" to discuss. They seemed to be old acquaintances, and considering the lady's daring address to them and especially to him, their connection must have been a very *particular* one.

She was suddenly thirsty and drank some cold water, staring at her plate as she felt the strange sensation of her fingers trembling. *What on earth is happening to me? Why am I being so foolish? How can I be so troubled by someone who seems to know my husband?*

She reminded herself that the lady was no different from Miss Bingley, who claimed to be his intimate friend. Then how was it possible that she was so displeased with that little exchange in the park and could think of nothing else? The circumstances of their marriage were unusual, and she knew little about his acquaintances, be they women or men. But she did know that most gentlemen had several *special ladies* among their acquaintances. She felt her cheeks burning, and she grew furious with herself. Why would she care?

"The food was excellent," she suddenly said, smiling at Georgiana. "Now, if you do not mind, I shall go and rest a little. I think I did not sleep enough. I feel very tired."

Darcy hurried to open the door for her then closed it behind them. They looked at each other briefly, and she forced a smile. "Are you well?" he inquired, searching her eyes.

"Yes, perfectly..."

"Would you like to... I would like to explain to you what happened...the meeting, I mean."

"There is no need for explanation. I only hope you did not mind that I refused Lady Stafford's invitation. I am afraid my manners were a little harsh."

"I assure you that there was nothing wrong with *your* manners, Elizabeth. In fact, I found your answer to be perfect. I must apologise that you had to stay so long in the cold to speak with James and...I can see that you are bothered by it. I know I am, and—"

"Oh, you must not apologise. You did all you could to shorten the conversation. And I am quite well. I am just tired. Perhaps, the long walk in the cold was too much after a night of dancing." She smiled but averted her eyes.

"Then it would be better to rest. I confess I enjoyed our walk very much, Elizabeth."

"As did I..."

"Shall I see you later? I shall be out for an hour or so, but I will return soon."

"Very well," she said in some haste and left the room while she wondered where he might go and where he had gone every day since they married.

Her reason scolded her for her foolishness, and she knew she should be ashamed for such thoughts, but she could not free herself from them. Her head was spinning, and she felt as though knives were attacking her temples. He offered to explain about the meeting, and curiosity almost overwhelmed her. She refused out of embarrassment and distress. What was to be explained? His own anxiety mixed with anger spoke volumes. Would he dare to explain the particulars of his acquaintance with Lady Stafford? Probably not. And even if he did, would she dare listen to such a thing? It was better to pretend she was not interested.

She threw herself onto her large bed while Lucky looked at her curiously. A few minutes later, she rose and paced the room. The exchange with Lady Stafford, though short, reminded her of the discussion with Bingley's sisters days before. All of them were impertinent and offensive. They treated her with a superiority she could no longer ignore. And what was that remark that all of society was curious about her "secret identity"? Was she not worth knowing before she became Mrs. Darcy?

Elizabeth felt a slight gratification that her own replies were not kind, and she was relieved that her husband called her impertinent answer "perfect." No matter the nature of their relationship, he was displeased with the meeting and with Lady Stafford's attitude. He was even harsher when he told James that he might visit after he finished his business with the lady. And yet, shockingly, instead of leaving their *impolite* company, Lady Stafford insisted that she still had important things to discuss with him. Who could this woman be? If only her aunt would return sooner, she might help her understand! But Jane and Mrs. Gardiner were far away, and her only companion was her diary, so she turned to it as to her closest friend and filled three long pages before her mind began to ease and rest.

Eventually, she rang for Molly to ask for some tea. Surprisingly, the maid did not appear, so Elizabeth rang again. Two more attempts were required before Molly finally arrived, and Elizabeth wondered whether everyone in the house had made a pact to upset her that day. She was about to ask Molly about the delay but the maid's red, swollen eyes and her torment, poorly hidden behind a proper smile, turned Elizabeth's discontent to worry.

"I beg your forgiveness for being late, Mrs. Darcy. I did not hear the bell. I am so sorry."

"Please do not trouble yourself so, Molly. What is the matter? You seem very ill, truly!"

"Oh, I am fine, ma'am. Thank you for your concern… I am well… What is your wish?"

"My wish, Molly, is for you to sit down and tell me what is wrong. You are obviously not fine, but apparently, you do not trust me enough to tell me about your problem."

"Oh, please do not say that, ma'am! And please do not ask me to sit in your presence. I could not possibly do that. I am truly well, it is just that…"

"Yes? If you are well, is anyone else *not* well? Is that it?"

"Mrs. Darcy, I do not know how to say it… It is Janey— I do not think you remember her…"

"Of course I remember Janey. What happened to her? Molly?"

"It is just… Janey has worked in this house for almost four years now. She has three children, and her husband left them a month ago. Her younger daughter, Cathy—she is four, and she is very ill. She has been ill for some time now, and Janey is so sad and worried, she barely sleeps at all at night. She is tired, and that is why she broke the vase…and Mrs. Thomason was upset. She said the vase cost more than Janey's pay for a whole year…but Janey will pay for it, and we will help her… Mrs. Thomason said Janey broke two plates last week, and she overlooked that, but the vase cannot be concealed and—"

"Molly, wait, wait! Please speak slower. I cannot follow you! Janey's daughter is four, and she is very ill. Who takes care of her when Janey is not at home?"

"Oh, her daughter and son—they are eight and nine, I think—such good children…"

"Very well. So, Janey broke two plates last week and now a vase?"

"Yes, a very expensive one. Mrs. Thomason said the vase belonged to the family for many years… And Janey should pay for it but it will take some time…and Mrs. Thomason said she cannot say what will happen to Janey but she is such a hard working girl and she…"

"Molly, does Mr. Darcy know that Janey's daughter is ill?"

The maid looked at Elizabeth in complete shock as if she did not comprehend the question.

"Mr. Darcy? The master? I do not believe he knows. Why would he?"

"Why? Because he might help! Does Janey have a doctor who treats her daughter?

Does she have money for that?"

"Oh, Janey could not possibly trouble the master with her problems. None of us who work in the house have children, only Janey. She started working after Cathy was born...but she promised from the beginning that the children would not affect her work here."

"What about Miss Darcy? I imagine she does not know, either. But Mrs. Thomason knows. And she decided to have Janey pay for the vase. Am I correct?"

"Yes ma'am—Mrs. Thomason has been very good to Janey. Most housekeepers would not accept a servant with small children...but now she said she is not certain what will happen."

"Molly, please tell Mrs. Thomason that I want to speak to her. I shall wait for her here." Elizabeth struggled to keep her temper while the maid hurried to obey her request.

Mrs. Thomason was another one who treated her with superiority, even from the beginning of their acquaintance, and now she dared to make such serious decisions without even informing the mistress of the house! Surely, the housekeeper did not take her seriously enough to report to her what was happening.

Well, this has to end immediately! She would not pretend to be amused and untouched by other people's rudeness any longer. She had to respond appropriately to her position. And helping a servant who had been working for the family for more than four years and was suffering for her ill child was a way to start. How was it possible that nobody in the family knew about it? When Hill's husband caught a bad cold, everyone at Longbourn—including Mr. Bennet—worried about him until he got well. But Mrs. Thomason knew, and she made all the decisions about the staff—so what else was possibly needed?

Elizabeth needed all her strength to maintain her composure when the housekeeper entered. She seemed troubled and avoided looking at Elizabeth.

"Mrs. Thomason, a situation regarding a broken vase has come to my attention, and I would like to know the details." Elizabeth forced herself to sound calm.

The housekeeper stared at her in obvious surprise, disturbed and pale.

"It was entirely my fault, Mrs. Darcy. I broke the vase, and I am willing to take full responsibility for it! I cannot express how deeply I regret it, and I leave it to you to decide how I should pay for my mistake."

It was Elizabeth's turn to stare at the housekeeper, her lips parted but unable to speak. She rose from the sofa and paced the room, attempting to recover, then stopped in front of the woman, narrowing her eyes while searching her face.

"Mrs. Thomason, I know it was not you who broke the vase."

"Indeed, it is all my fault, Mrs. Darcy, and nobody else is to blame. I assure you that—"

Elizabeth put her hand on the housekeeper's arm and forced a smile of comfort.

"Mrs. Thomason, let us talk of Janey and her daughter. We will worry about the vase later."

Mrs. Thomason's amazement was such that her legs weakened, and she sat in the nearest chair, looking at Elizabeth in disbelief. She covered her mouth with trembling fingers and needed some time before she was able to speak clearly.

As Mrs. Thomason revealed the entire story to her, guilt overwhelmed Elizabeth. She blamed herself for judging the housekeeper hastily and thinking her rude, cruel, and self-important. She came close to censuring Mrs. Thomason when, in truth, she did nothing but try to help in the best way she knew.

"Mrs. Thomason, I was wondering: Why did you not tell Mr. Darcy about this situation? Does Janey have a good doctor to take care of her little girl? Does she have enough money to take care of her? It must be a terribly difficult situation for a single woman."

"Ma'am, there are twenty-two servants in this house, all well paid and treated better than in other places. That is enough help from the master. There are so many people depending on him here, at Pemberley, and on all the other estates he runs that it would not be possible for him to take on the burden of individual problems. Most households do not accept servants with small children because that always causes trouble at work. Janey was recommended by one of our loyal servants. I liked her, so the master agreed to hire her. At that time, Janey's mother was still alive, and they were all living in her house. Her husband was always a rascal and did not help her at all. Thank God he left…pardon me, ma'am!"

Mrs. Thomason's arguments were sound, and Elizabeth felt guilty again. The housekeeper saw things more clearly than she did. Mr. Darcy could do only so much—which was more than other masters did. It was time for Mrs. Darcy to do the rest.

"You are right, of course. I shall speak to Mr. Darcy, to decide how to proceed. Please do not worry about the vase. I know Lady Anne would value the well-being of a child more than any vase, and Mr. Darcy could not think differently."

"Mrs. Darcy, I do not know what to say. Thank you, ma'am… I do not want to upset either you or the master with the situation of a servant. We will find a way to—"

"Mrs. Thomason." Elizabeth interrupted the woman as warmly and calmly as she could. "It is my duty as the mistress of this house to be troubled with everything regarding those who live here—servants or family. Let us speak again later. You may go now."

The housekeeper left the room, and Elizabeth sat on the bed, deeply troubled. The entire story affected her so that her previous worries seemed insignificant, and she felt ashamed for giving them so much consideration. Not only Mr. Darcy but also she—as Mrs. Darcy—had many people depending on her and many responsibilities. Why should she care about some Miss Bingley or Lady Somebody?

She rang for Molly again and sent her to inquire whether the Master had returned home. Molly answered without delay: he had been in his library for more than an hour.

She quickly changed her gown, arranged her hair, then left the room in a hurry. It was time for Mrs. Darcy to have a long and difficult discussion with Mr. Darcy.

AS SOON AS ELIZABETH DEPARTED AFTER BREAKFAST, DARCY RETIRED TO HIS library and emptied a glass of brandy. He then threw the glass into the fire. Anger took complete control, and he still could not believe that Annabelle dared to follow him, to approach him when he was with Elizabeth, and to speak to her so impertinently.

He could see Elizabeth was surprised, troubled, and even angry—only minutes after she gratified him with her smiles, her teasing, and her compassion during their walk. The day had been perfect, and everything changed acutely with the appearance of Annabelle. He felt a strong urge to go to her house and confront her, but he restrained the temptation. Surely, Annabelle would take that as a personal triumph, and he had no patience to argue with her unreasonable demands.

Darcy went to talk to Robert, but his cousin was out, so he stayed only a few minutes to have a drink with his uncle then returned home. He was eager to speak to Elizabeth, and he thought to go to her several times, but he was afraid he might disturb her rest, so he waited impatiently and considered what was to be done.

While in the library, he received the mail. Among the papers, he spotted Lady Catherine's handwriting and reluctantly opened her letter. After reading a couple of lines, he put it aside. He expected strong opposition to his marriage from his aunt, but the words she wrote about Elizabeth were difficult to read. His first impulse was to write her back and demand she temper her behaviour; otherwise, he would end all interactions with her. However, as in Annabelle's case, he allowed a little time to calm himself before taking action. It was surely one of the most disturbing and infuriating days he could remember.

A knock on the door and the unexpected appearance of Elizabeth brought him equal relief and curiosity. She declared she needed to speak to him about a matter of great importance.

"I wish to talk to you about something very delicate regarding Janey. Do you remember her?" He stared at her, completely disconcerted, wondering whether he heard her correctly.

"Janey? I know she has three small children. Mrs. Thomason was in some doubt when she hired her, but I know she has no reason to complain about her work."

"I am glad you remember. The thing is...I feel I must do something for her. Janey's husband left them a month ago, and the children are all alone at home. Her younger daughter is only four and seems to be very ill. You can imagine that poor Janey does not sleep at all at night, and she must be terribly worried all day..."

"But Elizabeth, I do not understand—what is precisely the matter? Does she need some extra money to pay for the doctor, or...?"

"I asked the same, but I think it is more than that. Can you imagine a mother knowing her three small children are alone all day long, one of them being ill?

How do the children manage by themselves? It is winter and cold and their father left them… I am sorry for being so incoherent. I do not know why this affects me so. I feel I should do something."

"How did this situation come to your attention?"

She paused and looked at him. He was preoccupied, but he seemed interested and willing to listen. She wondered how he would react, so she carefully chose her words.

"Because she is so troubled, Janey broke a vase—an expensive one. She and Molly and Mrs. Thomason are deeply distressed, and I believe they are worried that you will dismiss her. She promised to pay for the vase, but I do not see how she can do that."

His expression darkened. He searched her eyes for some time, and she held her breath. He was the master, and any decision was his. He suddenly rose and moved to the window, looking outside a few minutes, then returned and resumed his seat in front of her.

"And what do you intend to do, Elizabeth?"

"I am not certain. I would like to allow Janey to stay home with her daughter until she is better. If you agree, I will pay her salary from my pin money during that time. And I would also pay for the vase."

"If you wish…" She felt his gaze warming her face. She could not read his expression nor guess whether he approved her suggestion.

Elizabeth became troubled by the long silence before her husband finally spoke.

"And how long do you plan to keep Janey at home?" he inquired calmly.

"I cannot decide now…until her daughter is better."

"Very well…but what if her daughter—or one of her other children—becomes ill again?"

The question took Elizabeth by surprise, and she stared at him, not knowing how to reply. She suspected he spoke in jest, but he seemed serious and his calm began to trouble her.

"I did not think that far ahead. Let us hope it will not happen."

"Well, it is very likely to happen. Three small children alone in the middle of the winter will surely risk at least a dangerous cold. Now about the vase—I understand your wish to pay for Janey. However, here is my question: what if one of the other servants—or four of them—break more objects and they excuse themselves for being tired because of problems at home? Who will pay for those items? And what if half of the servants ask to be allowed to stay home to take care of someone in their family?"

Elizabeth went from crimson to pale in an instant, her distress quickly turning to anger.

"You mock me, sir, and I dare say this is hardly the proper time!"

Darcy smiled at her and gently touched her hands, tightly clasped in her lap.

"Not at all, Elizabeth. But we have more than two and twenty servants, and I imagine most of them have difficulties—perhaps not as urgent as Janey's, but for each of us, our own problems assume great importance. I have said before and I repeat: you are the mistress of the house, and you are entitled to do whatever you want. You may dismiss the entire staff tonight and hire a new one tomorrow, and nobody may question your decision. But if you wish to be a fair mistress—as I am certain you will be—you must have the same rules, good or bad, for everybody. Otherwise, there will be gossip about your favouring some of them, and—even worse—they will sabotage those who are suspected of being your favourites."

With every word, Elizabeth's spirits flagged. She let her eyes get lost in his gaze while she clenched her hands to stop their trembling. She bit her lip and barely managed to speak.

"So you say I should do nothing for Janey?"

"No, not at all. I say you should find a way to help her for the long term, not just for a few days, and in a way that is fair to the other servants."

"She glanced at the fire, then to the window, then turned to meet his eyes again. "Would you please tell me how to do that? It seems I cannot find the proper solution by myself..."

Darcy took her hands in his and quickly pressed his lips to her fingers. "You cannot find the solution because there are some particular things about the household you do not know yet. I am sorry for not taking the time to explain all the details to you. Some of the servants live in the house, but I am quite certain there are rooms below stairs that are not occupied. I was thinking—if this is acceptable to you—to suggest that Janey move here with her children. That way she will be able to perform her duties without wondering whether her children are safe. Further, she will save the expense of food and firewood, and she will be able to pay a few pennies a month for the vase. It is not about the price but the fact that we have many valuable objects in this house, and I expect all servants to be careful with them and to take responsibility if something is broken. What would you say?"

Elizabeth watched him, unable to conceal her surprise, each of his words a revelation. He seemed to take each detail into consideration and to think about all the implications of every decision. She could not say whether she was more astonished and admiring of his wisdom, or embarrassed at her own emotional and irrational suggestions.

"I believe that would be a perfect solution—if Janey agrees. It seems fair and just and also very convenient. I do not know what to say. I am... You seem to be always right, William. And no, this time I am not speaking in jest. You always think of everything,"

"No, I am not always right, as you well know." He smiled. "I have made a lot of mistakes over the years, and I have had to learn to think of everything because it takes more time and effort to solve a problem than to prevent it. So I try to take everything into consideration before I make a decision—and I still miss some."

"I find it difficult to believe that you miss anything, Mr. Darcy." She smiled back. "Now if you will excuse me, I shall fetch Mrs. Thomason, and we will talk to Janey together."

"Very well—let me know the result. I suggest they move as soon as possible—even today. We shall send for Dr. Taylor to check on the girl, and we shall ask him to stay for dinner."

"Move in today—and Dr. Taylor. Excellent indeed… See? You always think of everything."

He laughed, and to his utter surprise, she raised herself on her toes and placed a quick kiss on his cheek, whispering, "Thank you," as she ran out of the library.

Darcy brushed his fingers over the spot where her lips rested. Elizabeth's smiles, her glances, her teasing, and her serious admission of his carefulness—and the small kiss of gratitude—were proofs that she had moved past the unpleasant incident in the park and that she took her duties seriously. He felt proud of her involvement and her generous willingness to give up a significant amount of pin money to help a servant in need. And he felt equally satisfied with her wisdom in coming to discuss it with him and in accepting his suggestions. He knew her to have a sharp mind and to be as proud as she was smart, yet her fairness and good judgment exceeded other emotions.

He poured himself a glass of brandy and laughed to himself. She was so serious when she declared that he seemed to always think before making a decision. He recalled a time that he did not think of the consequences of his actions—not for an instant—and it had changed his life forever. Yes, the effort in dealing with the outcome was greater than it would have been to prevent it—but what a worthy, rewarding effort it was!

Janey trembled, her eyes down and her hands clasped in front of her, listening to Elizabeth.

"Janey, I know you are very worried, so I shall not prolong this conversation unnecessarily. Mrs. Thomason and Molly told me of your problems. I have discussed with Mr. Darcy what is best to be done under these circumstances, and—"

"Oh, I am so sorry." Janey spoke in a barely audible tone, and completely white faced.

"What would you say to moving into the staff wing of the house with your children? There are two adjoining rooms with two beds each that I believe would suit you all. And you will spend less time walking to and from work. Your children will be safer here and…"

Janey blinked repeatedly as tears fell down her cheeks. She shook her head in disbelief. Mrs. Thomason and Molly hurried to put her in a chair, but she only stayed a moment before quickly rising.

"Mrs. Darcy… Move here? But I thought… Will you not fire me? Oh, and what the master said—is he angry with me? I will work hard to pay for the vase and… How can I possibly move here? Oh, I cannot occupy two rooms. One would be more than enough, and—"

"Janey, please calm down or else we will never be able to understand each other. If my proposal is acceptable, Mrs. Thomason will send two men with you to pack your things and move here tonight—no need for further delay. Dr. Taylor will examine your daughter later. As for the vase—we will talk again in a few days about the best way to compensate for it."

The maid's emotion was so intense that Elizabeth felt overwhelmed herself. She could not imagine what was in the young woman's heart and found little strength to oppose her when Janey knelt before her and kissed her hand. Shocked, fighting her own tears, Elizabeth leant down and forced Janey to rise while the maid continued to thank her.

"Janey—make haste. It will be dark soon. And wipe your tears. Your children will be frightened to see you so troubled. I shall come and visit you once you are settled."

A few minutes later, Elizabeth was alone in her room, looking at her hands still wet with the woman's tears. She lay on the bed and closed her eyes, defeated by emotion, slowly realising the power and the burden of their "ten thousand a year." She did not hear the door open or her husband enter the chamber. She felt a gentle touch on her shoulder and turned to face him. They looked at each other a long moment, then he carefully pulled her to his chest. His arms around her took her breath away, and his warm lips, tenderly kissing her temples, washed away the weight from her shoulders and from her heart.

"William, please forgive me for being so emotional. This situation has affected me greatly, and I somehow feel a little sad though I should be happy for Janey."

"Please do not apologise for being kind and compassionate. I am glad that we could solve this matter and that we managed to work on it together." He paused a moment then smiled, looking at her intently. "You know, last night at the ball, my cousin was surprised that we looked like a 'real, normal newlywed couple' in his words."

Her face and neck coloured slightly. "I believe we are…almost…" she attempted to joke.

"Robert does not know *all* the details of our marriage, so I told him that we *are* a real, normal, newlywed couple," he replied, and she blushed even more but kept her smile.

"I feel that today I learnt a valuable lesson, and I have you to thank for that, William. In truth, every day since I came to London, I have learnt a valuable lesson."

"We have each learnt something daily in this last week. We learn from each other to the benefit of both."

"Very true… But William, we forgot to talk to Georgiana before deciding to allow Janey to move into the house with her children. After all, this is Georgiana's home, too."

"You are right, of course. I shall speak to her immediately although I am sure she will be very pleased. In fact, I am certain she would have made the same decision if she knew about the situation. It is just that, since she is so young, we have not directly involved her in household concerns yet, even more so as she had a quite difficult time this last year…"

Elizabeth did not miss the last part of his statement, but he changed the subject before she had time to inquire further.

They all reunited later for dinner and Georgiana, together with Mrs. Annesley and Dr. Taylor, congratulated Elizabeth for what they called "an extraordinary proof of mastering the household." Elizabeth received their words reluctantly and pointed out her husband's merits, but he refused to accept any recognition of his involvement and stated that, if not for Elizabeth's kindness, no one would have dared to bring the story to his knowledge.

Around eight in the evening, Janey and her children were settled in their rooms. Dr. Taylor interrupted his meal to examine the little patient and returned rather soon with the report that the child suffered from a very bad cold and a dangerous weakness that could have put her life in danger. He wrote a long note to one of his younger partners and sent a servant to deliver it at once and to return with the medicines he requested. Elizabeth and Georgiana met the children and spent a few minutes with them. The elder ones—Peter and Libby—thanked them for being allowed to move into the house. They seemed quite intimidated, and the ladies' kind smiles were not enough to put them at ease. Cathy—the youngest—was already asleep, so she was not disturbed.

The ladies wished them all good night and returned to the dinner table where they were delighted to find Colonel Fitzwilliam, who had come to see Darcy. The colonel's curiosity in being told the latest news was scarcely satisfied, and he decided to join them for the evening, even more so as he had something to discuss with Darcy. Half an hour later, one of Dr. Taylor's partners, Dr. Philips, arrived with the required medicines and herbs.

The day's disruption finally came to an end, and the family enjoyed their meal in harmony. The colonel was in his usual good spirits. He complimented the ladies and teased Darcy about the previous night's party, where his dancing skills were much admired.

"Elizabeth, it is hardly necessary to say that every gentleman at the ball admired you."

"Thank you for the praise, Colonel, but I doubt you have canvassed every gentleman at the party." She laughed. "However exaggerated your compliment might be, I confess I enjoy it, and I am glad you did not mention the ladies' opinion on the matter."

"Well, it would be an extraordinary event for the ladies to approve of another woman's beauty. I dare say ladies treat their own kind with much more severity than men do."

Immediately, all three ladies at once contradicted the colonel's harsh comment, but he refused to change his opinion and asked for the other gentlemen's support.

"I second my cousin's statement that everybody admired Elizabeth last night. As for the second one, I cannot pretend to be as knowledgeable as he is in such matters."

Elizabeth blushed at her husband's compliment, wondering why she was more sensitive to what he said than to the colonel's words. She then spoke in jest:

"Well, we have few chances to contradict a gentleman who seems to be a true connoisseur of ladies' characters. But I insist that I always recognise and admire a beautiful lady—even if I happen not to like her or I consider her a rival."

"Yes, so do I," replied Georgiana, supporting Elizabeth, and the colonel laughed again.

"Dearest, this is certainly true in your case because you never see a woman as your rival, nor do you ever dislike anyone, but you are an exception. I am willing to believe Elizabeth, too, since I have no proof with which to contradict her—yet. But I shall remind you of this conversation when you face another lady who competes with you in something."

"Well, enough of this. I believe we should find another topic, less heated," Darcy said, glancing at Elizabeth. He recollected the meeting with Annabelle and James earlier that day in the park and Elizabeth's sudden change of spirit and sharp conversation with them.

Dinner continued with dessert, a discussion of future events in town, and the arrival of Elizabeth's relatives. Later, Elizabeth and Georgiana played for the gentlemen for more than half an hour before the ladies retired, while the gentlemen remained in the library to continue their conversation.

Chapter 14

After the departure of Dr. Taylor and Dr. Philips, Darcy shared with his cousin the disturbing meeting in the park. Their close friendship allowed Darcy the freedom of speaking uncensored about Annabelle Stafford's impertinence and James Darcy's stupidity.

"She surely trapped James by offering monetary support. There is no other explanation."

"Yes, I imagine that, but I wonder what she hopes to gain. What on Earth is in her mind?"

"Well, it seems she is determined to gain *you*."

"That is nonsense. She cannot think to gain me by behaving like a lunatic. Besides, when we met last time, I told her that there was no chance to renew the *old acquaintance*."

"She thought she still has some power over you and will continue to use it. I know this kind of woman quite well. I have had my fair share of this sort of behaviour. Fortunately, I am not as desirable a man as you are, so the reactions were less strong," the colonel laughed.

"I never promised Annabelle anything that I was not ready to offer, and I expressed my opinion very clearly many years ago. She seemed much more reasonable back then, and this is a true mystery to me. She now has a name and means to live her life as she desires. She is a beautiful woman; she might easily find a husband. Why would she persist in an endearment with no success? If things go on in the same manner, I shall be forced to take measures. The idea of being harsh and rude to a woman that once was a close acquaintance pains me. Yet, something will need to be done…"

"And what did Elizabeth say?"

"Elizabeth is a very smart woman. I am sure she guessed there was something peculiar behind that awkward conversation. She was quite harsh in her answers to Annabelle."

"Perhaps you should tell her the truth…to avoid further uncomfortable meetings, I mean."

"Elizabeth and I have a very fragile understanding at this point. We have just started to accommodate to each other. How could I possibly say to her, 'Do you remember the woman we met in the park? We had a private relationship about eight years ago, and now she is chasing me around town, trying to insinuate herself back in my bed. And I suspect she hates you, so try to avoid her if you happen to meet again.' Is that what you had in mind, Robert?"

Darcy's voice grew more animated and angry as he paced around the library with the glass in his hand. The colonel laughed harder, and Darcy finally gave up his serious tone.

He dropped the glass when he suddenly discovered Elizabeth, standing still a few steps from the door, dressed in her nightclothes, her hair down, and holding a candle, which she dropped when he called her name. He hurried to press his boot on the burning candle then turned to her with wonder and worry.

"Elizabeth, is anything wrong? Do you need something?"

"No—forgive me, please, I did not want to disturb you. I could not sleep, and I wanted to find a book. I thought everybody was already asleep. I shall leave you now; good night."

Darcy had no time to reply before she hurried out—and he did not intend to, as he could easily understand her embarrassment at being seen by the colonel in such informal attire.

He filled their glasses and silently resumed his place in the armchair.

"Mrs. Darcy is a beautiful woman. You might turn out to be a very fortunate man, despite the forced start of your marriage," the colonel said, and Darcy held his gaze.

"She is indeed… And it is true: I am quite fortunate."

"I am glad. I was just wondering: if this is the case, why is it that you are here with me in the middle of the night while your wife does not know whether you are asleep or not?"

Darcy narrowed his eyes with displeasure. "What kind of question is that?"

"A right question. I do not want to pry; forgive me. I am just worried."

"You have no reason to worry, I assure you. And your question is right, after all. Let us retire for the night. I did enjoy spending some time with you, though."

"I forgot to ask: Will you come to the opera the day after tomorrow? It is supposed to be quite a spectacle, and Thomas and Maryanne planned to attend, so I am forced to keep them company. Maryanne invited Lady Isabella too, and I do not want to be alone with them. I hate raising unrealistic expectations."

"So you wish us to come as a shield to protect you from Isabella Simmons. I wonder why. She is beautiful and witty and possesses a large fortune, I hear."

"You seem to approve of her, yet you did not marry her," the colonel replied sternly.

"True…but then again, she always favoured you over everyone else. I believe you avoid her because she is too smart for your taste, Robert."

"Nice remark—and very amusing, indeed. This must be your payback for my earlier indiscreet question. I guess I deserve it. So, will you come?"

"I shall ask Elizabeth, but most likely we will join you. If Miss Bennet and the Gardiners arrive in Town by then, Elizabeth will probably want to invite them, too."

"Perfect—the more, the better. Good night for now."

The colonel left the house in an excellent disposition, and Darcy returned to his apartment, wondering about Elizabeth. She surely must have heard something, but how much and how strong an effect it had on her he could not even speculate.

He knocked and entered at her invitation. She was sitting in the bed, reading, and the first thing that crossed his mind was how beautiful she looked. The second was the colonel's openly expressed admiration and his very improper—but true—question.

Elizabeth stared at her husband, holding the book from which she had not read a single line. She could think of little else but the words related to *Annabelle Stafford* that she heard in the library. That was why she dared to approach them in such an impertinent manner. "Back in his bed…" That meant that she had already been there.

Her cheeks were burning with shame for her listening to the conversation and anger for her own silly reaction. What was her business in this, after all? Surely, there were more ladies whom he had visited before. He was a man of the world, after all. But—was he still visiting someone? Perhaps Lady Stafford? Elizabeth knew for sure that he entered her ladyship's carriage a couple of days ago, but was he entering her house too? Oh, for Heaven's sake, why was she so silly and irrational? Why did she even care about that?

And now, he was standing in the middle of the bedchamber, smiling at her.

"I just came to tell you good night. Are you well, Elizabeth?"

"Quite well, thank you." She averted her eyes and was surprised to see him sit on the bed. Lucky came to sniff his hand, received a gentle pat on his head, and returned to his sleep.

"There is something I would like to discuss with you," he said, and she startled. "Would you like to attend the opera the day after tomorrow? It is a special performance of *Artaxerxes.*"

"I would love that! I heard a great deal about it from my aunt!"

"We will go with my cousins, Maryanne, and a friend of hers, Lady Isabella Simmons."

"Oh, another lady," she replied sharply then turned pale, horrified by her reaction.

He seemed rather amused. "Yes, another lady, but one you will like, I dare say."

She noticed that he assumed she did not like the *other* lady. Well, we cannot both like her, she thought as she struggled to keep her countenance.

"If your relatives arrive in Town by then, we will be happy to invite them, too."

"I just received a letter from Jane sent two days ago. They delayed their return because it snowed heavily and the roads are bad."

"It is a wise decision. I am glad to know, and you have no reason for concern."

"Yes, I too…"

There was silence a little while, and he continued to smile then gently caressed her hair.

"I shall allow you to sleep now. I just want to tell you that… You are very beautiful, and I feel very fortunate to be your husband. Good night, Mrs. Darcy."

She stared at him, unable to find a proper answer, and he departed without waiting for her reply. Her head was spinning, and her heart pounded. Why did he say that to her? And why did mere words matter so much? More importantly—why was she afraid to ask him what she wanted to know? But how could she inquire about the nature of his relationship with Lady Something or with any other lady? Surely, this was the most irrational thing ever!

Putting any thoughts aside, Elizabeth draped her robe over her shoulders and knocked on the adjoining door. He opened it and met her with a surprised gaze. She stepped tentatively and looked around a moment. Then her eyes locked with his.

"I forgot to tell you that, tomorrow, Georgiana and I will go with Lady Maryanne to the modiste. Two other dresses are almost ready, and I need to try them on."

"Very well. May I help you with something?"

"No, not at all. I will ask for the carriage to be ready at noon. I wish you good night."

"Thank you." He smiled, and for a moment, there was silence again.

She wondered whether he would ask her to stay longer.

He was admiring her beauty, tempted to offer her a seat and a glass of wine, but he hesitated so long that she turned and exited the room in haste.

It took another hour before either of them finally fell asleep—one of them still struggling with wonderings and worries, the other blaming himself for his indecision. And both reached the conclusion that more steps should be taken after almost a week of marriage.

London, 2 January

After another agitated night, Elizabeth resolved not to allow anything to interfere with her marriage and to judge Mr. Darcy only by what she witnessed or could be certain of. Third parties she would not completely dismiss but would take to heart only if supported by solid proof. She was decided, though, to approach Mr. Wickham's situation at some point and to try to alleviate it if an injustice had been done.

Darcy was reading in the library when Elizabeth entered and greeted him.

"Forgive me. Am I disturbing you? I thought I would keep you company before breakfast."

"You never disturb me. I am happy to see you. May I offer you some tea or coffee?"

"I would like that very much. Do not interrupt your business. I shall order a tray," she said.

Very shortly, a maid brought the order then left. Elizabeth filled his cup with coffee and hers with tea. Darcy watched her with a smile, pleased to notice her increasing familiarity and easiness in accommodating to the house—and to him.

"So—are you working on something important?"

"I was just looking over the expenses of the Newcastle estate."

"You have an estate in Newcastle? Besides Pemberley?"

"There are several more. I shall tell you about them one day when you have time and desire to discuss boring business details," he said in jest.

"I should like to hear anything you would like to share with me. I feel it is part of my duty to know about your responsibilities and to help you with anything I can."

"It pleases me to hear that, Elizabeth. And I certainly feel I can share anything with you."

He turned his chair to face her and spoke with equal warmth and seriousness.

"Let me briefly describe the history of my family, as well as the estates I inherited. My mother had two siblings: Lady Catherine de Bourgh and Lord Matlock. Her father—my grandfather Fitzwilliam—was an earl, and my grandmother was an earl's daughter too. From my mother, I was left this house in London. My grandfather Darcy was the younger son of an earl, and he had two sons: my father and James's father. From my father, I was left Pemberley—the estate where we lived all my life—and three much smaller properties: one in Newcastle, one in Box Hill and another in Oxford."

"That is quite impressive," said Elizabeth, stunned. "And you manage all these by yourself? Now I understand why you are not inclined to either dance or speak much in large gatherings. I imagine you take any possible opportunity to rest peacefully."

He laughed loudly. "I appreciate that you find an excuse for my occasional rudeness. The properties are well organised and most of the tenants are excellent people, so my effort is not significant. There are also two estates which belong to James: one in Derbyshire and one in Newmarket that are also under my supervision for another year and a half until he turns twenty-five."

"You take care of six estates? For how long have you done that?"

"My excellent father passed away five years ago, but he mostly retired to Pemberley a year before. I took over James's estates four years ago when my uncle died."

"But you were almost James's age when this happened. How did you handle everything? Are you a sort guardian for James until he is twenty-five?"

"No quite. Robert and I are Georgiana's guardians by my father's will. When she turns one and twenty or at her marriage—if it occurs before—she will inherit 20,000 pounds from my father, 30,000 from my mother, and a house in Town. In James's case…" He hesitated again, watching her with a trace of discomfort. "James is my only relative from my father's side. He is younger than I am, and he was always a pleasant and happy child. His mother passed away from fever when he was twelve, and afterwards his father rarely refused him anything. Unfortunately, this made him take things very easily and persist in many errors during the last few years. That is why my uncle named me to manage his estates until he grows wise enough to be his own master."

"Will you decide whether he is wise enough to take over his estates?"

He did not miss the meaning of her words, and his expression tensed while his eyes locked with hers. "No, it will simply happen when he turns twenty-five. I can only hope that he will not waste his family legacy."

A paused followed, and she began to feel uncomfortable under his scrutiny. Both were well aware that they were also considering Mr. Wickham's situation.

"Elizabeth, I am not an unfair or cruel man; at least I try not to be. I do not take easily decisions which affect other peoples' lives. You accused me of always wanting to have my way. It might be so, but I never did an injustice to anyone only to have my way. And I know there are things I need to change in myself, but I trust justice is not one of them."

Without much thought, her right palm caressed his cheek and lingered on it a moment.

"I do not accuse you of anything; I only try to sketch your character. I know you are not unfair or cruel, and I know you are honest in your estimation of other people or situations. However, sometimes your judgment is too harsh, and your expectations might be too high for others to reach; therefore, they consider you to be cold and inconsiderate or even unjust. If there are things you should change, it would be to soften your manners a little."

He covered the back of her hand with his own then placed a warm, lingering kiss on her palm. She shivered, her eyes fixed on him. His lips departed from her skin a heartbeat then opened slightly and pressed again, tenderly.

"If you truly believe that I only need to soften my manners, I feel happy and relieved. I expected you to see more faults in me."

"Oh, there are certainly more, but we must preserve a few. It would be impossible for me to live with a husband at whom I could not criticise or laugh."

She teased him to conceal the shivers that his brief kiss sent from her palm along her body. He was still holding her hand, and his thumb stroked inside her palm, arousing the strangest feelings within her.

She startled, and he withdrew from her when knocks on the door interrupted them.

Mrs. Thomason entered, and Darcy resumed his seat at the desk. With the corner of her eyes, Elizabeth observed her husband and noticed the smile twisting his lips. She thought that, if Mrs. Thomason had been a few minutes later, he might have…

"Mrs. Thomason, good morning. Please tell me whether you have news about Janey and her daughter." Elizabeth struggled to sound casual.

"Dr. Philips was here very early in the morning. The child is reasonably well. Janey is trying to give her some tea and a little soup."

"I planned to visit them, but I thought they might still be asleep."

"They have been awake for some time, ma'am. That is why I dared to trouble you so early in the morning. The elder children asked me to give them something to do in the house to repay your kindness. I would like to ask you what tasks you suggest for them."

"What a lovely idea! But there is truly no need for them to do anything. They are eight and nine, are they not? Children should not work at such a young age."

Mrs. Thomason hesitated a moment and attempted to exit then returned hesitantly.

"I beg your forgiveness, madam. I do not wish to disobey your request, but the children seem very mature for their age. I believe they would feel better if they were given some duties… some things to accomplish around the house. Forgive me; it is just my suggestion."

Elizabeth was somehow disconcerted by the unexpected contradiction and was ready to insist on her previous resolution when she was interrupted by her husband.

"Mrs. Thomason, Mrs. Darcy and I will discuss what the best solution is. Please be so kind as to bring the children here in a quarter of an hour."

The housekeeper curtseyed and left. Elizabeth looked at her husband, puzzled.

"I agree that such young children should not work, Elizabeth. However, their request is a proof of the fair education Janey gave them. They are accustomed to working for what they get and might feel uncomfortable being offered something out of pity."

"I understand your point. But what kind of duties could they perform at their age, William?"

"I am not certain yet. Let us speak to them and decide afterwards."

Shortly, Georgiana entered with Lucky and Titan, who ran towards them, demanding attention. Georgiana was offered a cup of tea and the invitation to keep them company.

A gentle knock on the door announced the return of Mrs. Thomason. Near her, a girl and a boy with shabby yet clean clothes, their eyes mostly to the ground, stepped in hesitantly. Darcy asked them to approach. The girl curtseyed clumsily, and the boy bowed gravely. They were thin and pale, and it was difficult to say which of them was older.

"What is your name?" Darcy inquired, and Elizabeth smiled at them, encouragingly.

"My name is Peter, sir. She is my sister Libby."

"I am pleased to meet you, Peter and Libby. I am Mr. Darcy. You already met Mrs. and Miss Darcy last night." The children bowed to him but seemed to find it difficult to reply.

"So, Mrs. Thomason told me that you asked to be given something to do in the house. Do you think you are old and strong enough to bear responsibilities?"

"I am very strong, sir, and I am already nine. I will be ten soon! My sister is younger, but she can work, too. And I will help her if she can't," the boy replied in an instant.

"I like your determination, young man. Now we must decide what duties suit you best." Darcy rose from his seat and moved closer. His height and severe countenance immobilised the children. "Have you been to school? Do you know how to read and calculate?"

"Yes, master—a little. We went to school one year, but now we stay home to help Mama."

"I see…" Darcy finally resumed his seat. Titan and Lucky approached the children, sniffing and licking their hands. They made efforts to keep a serious posture, but their eyes lit as they gazed at the animals. Darcy looked at Elizabeth, and they smiled at each other.

"So, Peter, could I trust you with something that is very important to Mrs. Darcy and me?"

The boy's back straightened instantly. "Anything, master!"

"Very well then—look carefully at these dogs. They are very dear to us, and we would like to have someone in charge of them: to feed them, walk them in the back lawn, play with them, and so on. Do you think you could do that? It is a very difficult task, I warn you."

The boy watched the master with the utmost attention. "I can do it, master. You must not worry. I will take very good care of them!"

"Excellent. Stevens will instruct you on every detail, and you must pay close attention. He might also need you to assist him in some other activities. But there is another important thing that I absolutely demand from you both."

The children looked at him in complete silence, eyes and mouths wide open.

"You must improve your reading and calculating skills. Part of your daily responsibilities will be to spend at least two hours studying. We shall check your progress weekly. Do you think it would be too difficult?" His tone was severe and challenging. The girl only shook her head in silence while the boy responded in earnest.

"It's not difficult, master. I can do anything you ask me."

"Good! Now, Libby"—he moved towards the girl, who turned pale—"Mrs. and Miss Darcy will explain to you what task they require of you."

"Libby, there are a many things with which you might help us," Elizabeth intervened in a friendly voice. "You can start tomorrow by helping Molly to arrange some of my gowns.

"Yes, I would need that too," said Georgiana. "And sometimes I will need help when I practice at the piano. Someone must turn the pages for me."

"Can I start with the dogs today?" Peter asked anxiously, and Darcy smiled to his wife.

"You may. Stevens will explain your duties as soon as we all have breakfast."

The children left, holding hands and whispering to each other, followed by Mrs. Thomason. Elizabeth laughed to her husband. "Indeed, sir, I am astonished at how creative you can be in defining tasks and responsibilities."

"Children who are born in poor families have no other chance to surpass their situation except by gaining knowledge. I am not certain whether these children will show any inclination for learning, but I like to know that I provided them the opportunity. Peter seemed to discover his passion with Titan and Lucky. I am sure the dogs will love him."

"I still have some books in my apartment—from when I was studying. I may supervise Peter and Libby and perhaps help them learn," Georgiana said animatedly.

"Excellent, my dear. Now, shall we all go to breakfast? Mrs. Annesley surely waits for us."

Breakfast was spent in warm conversation. Elizabeth felt her husband's gaze on her and held it a few times. Warmth and shivers tantalised her skin, and the icy hole in her stomach seemed not to trouble her quite as much as in the previous days. The sense of peace and joy dissipated a small part of the longing for her family and for her childhood household. And once again, she told herself that, for the time being, she was happy to be Mrs. Darcy.

Around noon, Elizabeth, together with Georgiana and Mrs. Annesley, left in the direction of the modiste.

Darcy glanced through the window, pleased to see his wife on such close terms with his sister. Then he returned to a more unpleasant yet necessary task: the response to Lady Catherine's letter, which he had received the day before. He was relieved that Elizabeth had not read this letter, as she had been the recipient of Lady Catherine's unreasonable rage.

Keeping his feelings under control, he started with his regret for his aunt's distress. Then he underlined that the marriage was entirely his choice—and an excellent one as Elizabeth already proved herself worthy of her present position. He expressed his hope that Lady Catherine would soon come to accept his decision since he had often indicated no intention of binding himself to Anne, despite his genuine affection for his cousin. He ended by assuring Lady Catherine of his consideration and wished them both all the best.

Darcy was reasonably content with the letter, so he asked that it be delivered immediately. A stressful task was done. One more remained, but it had to wait a little longer.

He heard voices in the back yard and glanced outside. There was Peter, playing with Lucky and Titan under the strict supervision of Stevens. That seemed a good match, indeed. And even more, Elizabeth had been very pleased with his way of solving the problem.

Chapter 15

The ride from their house to Madame Claudette—the famous modiste—was rather short. They were met by a doorman, and inside, a young woman named Mabel—whom Elizabeth recognised as the one who brought her the first dresses a few days ago—invited them into a private room and offered tea and refreshments. Very soon, Lady Maryanne joined them.

Elizabeth looked around with curiosity. It was her first time in such an exclusive shop, and the attention bestowed upon them was beyond anything she expected. Lady Maryanne and Georgiana seemed to be well known by the staff. The shop owner, Madame Claudette, was introduced to Elizabeth.

"Mrs. Darcy, what an honour to meet you! We were all surprised to hear of Mr. Darcy's marriage. Allow me to congratulate you! We hope to see you as often as we see Lady Maryanne. Were the first two gowns to your liking? Was Mr. Darcy pleased with them?"

"Thank you, yes. The dresses were truly beautiful."

"Excellent! I hope you will approve these too. Oh, the gown for the Twelfth Night ball is a princess dress. The colour is exquisite! It was the only piece of fabric of that kind, and Mr. Darcy selected it himself. He possesses such flawless taste!"

Elizabeth barely concealed her grin as she was reminded of Miss Bingley praising his beautiful writing and offering to mend his pen. Madame Claudette seemed to be another admirer of her husband.

Two young maids, together with Mabel, brought the gowns, showing them to adjoining rooms to try them on. Lady Maryanne, however, intervened severely.

"There must be a mistake. This is not Mrs. Darcy's dress! The fabric is certainly different!"

Madame Claudette stared at the dress and paled then looked at the maids angrily.

"You are correct, of course, Lady Maryanne! I cannot imagine how this happened. I deeply apologise. I will bring Mrs. Darcy the correct dress in no time. Again, we deeply apologise."

"Since the error will be easily remedied, everything is fine," Elizabeth answered, amused by the modiste's panic and Lady Maryanne's frown. What a tragedy, indeed!

She waited in the small room lined with mirrors. In only a minute, the modiste herself came with the right dress, apologising again, and Elizabeth gasped in delight when she saw it, thinking that, in truth, her husband's taste seemed to be flawless in that area.

The dress fit her perfectly, and so did the second one. She invited Georgiana and Mrs. Annesley to give their opinion, and she was rewarded with heartfelt approval. Half an hour later, all the gowns were carefully checked and tried. While everyone else left the room, Elizabeth remained to adjust the locks of hair that refused to fit under her bonnet.

She turned with a smile when she heard someone entering, presuming it was Mabel. She froze when she saw Lady Annabelle Stafford, looking at her with a large smile.

"Mrs. Darcy, what a surprise! It must be fate that crosses our paths so often!"

"It is truly a surprise although I doubt fate has anything to do with it." Elizabeth attempted to conceal her nervousness.

"Are you ordering your dresses from Madame Claudette? Another lovely coincidence, I might say. But then again, since Lady Matlock and Lady Maryanne are old customers here, it was natural that they brought you too. It is unlikely that you had a choice in the matter."

"Lady Stafford, may I be of some use to you? If not, I must return to my relatives."

"Such a pity that you are in a hurry again. Your relatives are not very fond of me, and I have no desire to see them either. But yesterday would have been an excellent opportunity to improve our acquaintance. Although I can understand why Darcy was uncomfortable with the situation, I am sure we could all be civil under the circumstances."

"And what 'circumstances' are you precisely referring to?"

"The circumstance of your marriage, of course. All of London talks about it. I mean—the union is very advantageous for your family, of course. But why Darcy would accept it, why he chose you beyond any other woman, made everyone wonder."

"I fear this conversation has lasted long enough. For any wonder you may have, please apply to my husband for clarification."

"I do not need to ask anything. I know that Darcy was pressured to marry and to provide an heir to shelter his wealth. And what better choice than a country girl, shy and submissive, with no wealth, no connections, and no choice to oppose him in anything or to refuse any of his demands. Not that many women would refuse Darcy's demands. But an innocent, naïve young woman must be very appealing to him—at least until he becomes bored and looks around for more excitement. And then, his wife will remain at home, taking care of his sister and his children in the comfort of an elegant home without giving him any trouble. A perfect arrangement, indeed, for both of you. There is nothing to wonder about in this marriage after all. And I am sure the Matlocks supported his choice. They would have done anything to keep him away from other temptations."

"I am pleased that you have nothing to wonder about in my marriage. That gives me great hopes that we have no further subjects for conversation," Elizabeth replied, her hands trembling from anger, trying to end the conversation without starting an argument.

The heavy curtains were pulled away, and Mabel entered, then stopped and apologised, staring at both of them with obvious distress.

"Mrs. Darcy, is everything fine? Lady Stafford, did you miss your room? May I help you?"

"No, Mrs. Darcy and I had a little chat. Has Mr. Darcy arrived? I am speaking of the other Mr. Darcy this time," she said with a contented smile while Elizabeth stepped out.

In the hall, Georgiana smiled at her, but Elizabeth could not bring herself to smile back. She exited to the street, breathing the chilled air to regain her composure. Lady Maryanne asked Elizabeth whether she was well, and at her positive reply, she insisted no longer. They separated with the promise of meeting again at the opera the next evening.

Elizabeth kept her eyes fixed outside, avoiding any conversation, as she could not control her rage. She felt humiliated twice by that woman, and she was so silly that she found little to reply. *How dare that woman say those shameless things to me? What a ridiculous, pompous fool she is to consider me shy and submissive! If we should meet again, I will prove that I can give enough trouble and reason to worry to anyone who bothers me!*

She tightened her fists and bit her lips to calm herself. Georgiana's worried gaze and the girl's genuine care and distress melted her heart. Georgiana seemed to recognise Lady Stafford and to be concerned about their interaction. Had that woman been in their house and actually met Georgiana before? Was it possible that *he* brought *her* there?

They arrived home, and she went directly to her apartment. *The effrontery of that woman! Such impertinence! If she has some sort of relationship with William, why does she try so hard to prove it to the world? Only to humiliate me? Or just out of a mischievous character?* If only Elizabeth had the liberty to respond as she desired, Lady Stafford would not dare approach her again! She forced herself to behave with respect for her position as Mrs. Darcy, but Lizzy *Bennet* would have fought back with no restraint or consideration for that woman!

A knock on the door startled her, and she turned to the window to regain her calmness while she invited the caller to enter. It was Georgiana, apologising for the intrusion.

"Elizabeth, please forgive my boldness, but I did not fail to notice your distress. Did that woman say anything to hurt you? Please do not be upset. We should tell William…"

"NO!" Elizabeth said then softened her voice. "There is nothing to tell William and nothing for you to worry about. I had a rather unpleasant conversation with

Lady Stafford but nothing worse than the one with Miss Bingley. We should put all of it aside."

"As you wish...Lady Stafford spoke to us when we were at the theatre one evening, and she was also very rude to Maryanne. She tried to press for William's attention. I saw this many times with other ladies, but I never met anybody so uncivil. William was very upset and..."

"Georgiana, if he was upset, he would have done something to prevent this happening again. I thank you for supporting me, but enough of this for now. I look forward to the opera. Do you know Lady Isabella?"

"Yes. She is beautiful and very outspoken. I like her, but she frightens me a little."

"Such joy—another frightening lady. Do you think she hates me too?"

Georgiana panicked again, and Elizabeth laughed out loud. "Oh, come now—this cannot be true. Surely not all the ladies in London wished to marry your brother!"

"May I ask why you are gossiping about me?" A grave voice interrupted them from the doorway. Elizabeth avoided Darcy's large smile. She felt angry and blamed him for Lady Stafford's impertinence.

"Was your visit to Madame Claudette pleasing?"

"Yes. We were talking about Lady Isabella," Elizabeth said rather abruptly. "I want to be prepared in case *she* hates me, too."

He laughed. "You have no reason to worry. And to answer your question: not all, but many ladies wished to marry me and any other gentleman possessed of a similar fortune. It is not a personal matter but rather a business one, and there is no room for hate or love."

"Thank you for putting me at ease," Elizabeth said with sharp mockery. "Now, if you do not mind, I would like to rest a little."

She was allowed the required privacy, but as soon as the Darcy siblings left, Elizabeth felt ill for being so bitter. Her reason told her that she allowed herself to be tricked into that distress, but she failed to do otherwise.

She first felt offended that the Matlocks might pretend to favour her only to assure Darcy an honourable marriage, an heir, and a guard against *other distractions.* That would explain their strangely warm behaviour. Then, the more she thought, the clearer she understood that, even if Lady Stafford were correct, she had little to reproach anyone. It was, after all, logical for the Matlocks to be on friendly terms with her for reasons of their own as they had not come to know her well enough to appreciate her merits. And if Darcy wished to marry and have an heir, that was a natural desire too. His behaviour towards her was beyond reproach. He did everything to persuade her but nothing to force her will. If he were in hurry for an heir, he would have been...more insistent in consummating their marriage, yet he continued to be patient and caring.

Slowly, she managed to see things with less emotion. If Lady Stafford was still close to her husband, she would not put him in such a scandalous situation, nor would she keep approaching him, even when he was with his sister.

That Lady Stafford was very well informed of many details from his life was beyond doubt. And that she seemed very confident while she implied how well she knew him, his desires, and his inclination proved that there must be some truth beyond her words. And Elizabeth could not deny that she felt troubled and disturbed by that revelation.

Sometime later, Elizabeth's reason won over her emotions, and she felt guilty for rejecting Georgiana's attempt at comfort. The girl was so kind and caring—and in her case, Elizabeth could not suspect any hidden motives. She knocked on her sister's apartment. When she was invited in, she saw Mrs. Annesley sitting at the edge of the bed as Georgiana leant against the pillows, having a cup of tea.

"I came to speak to you, but I see you are resting. I shall return later."

"Oh no, I am happy to see you. Please take a seat. Would you like a cup of tea?"

"I am afraid Miss Darcy is a little…indisposed," Mrs. Annesley said, and Georgiana blushed.

"I see—may I help you with anything, dearest? Are you unwell?"

"Oh, nothing, thank you. I shall stay in bed for a couple of days and read. But I am afraid I will not join you at dinner tonight nor at the Opera tomorrow—would you mind?"

"Not at all, my dear. But are you sure you are well? I can stay home and keep you company."

"Thank you, it will not be necessary. Mrs. Annesley is here. But are *you* well, Elizabeth?"

"Yes, very well, I assure you."

They talked a few minutes until Mrs. Annesley excused herself, and then Georgiana spoke freely. "Elizabeth, please do not be upset with William. I saw you tried to evade his company earlier, but he was worried for you. It pains me to see you angry with him."

Elizabeth smiled at how much Georgiana reminded her of Jane. She took her hand gently. "I was a little upset but not at William. It is just that… I shall try to control my temper better."

"Oh, you should do that because William has a very bad temper, too," the girl whispered.

"It is then fortunate that you are the sweetest and most gentle person and will compensate for us. If my sister Jane comes to visit, there will be a perfect balance as she is just like you."

Georgiana blushed in embarrassment at such praise and averted her eyes for a moment.

"Elizabeth, there is something I must confess to you. When William told me about your marriage, I had decided to be cautious and to keep a distance from someone who seemed to marry my brother without valuing his qualities and having no affection for him. Forgive my indiscretion, but my brother told me the particulars of your wedding. And yet, only a few days have passed since then, and I am so happy to have you here. I could not wish for a better sister. And I hope you and William will overcome any obstacles and be very happy."

"Nor could I hope for more affection than you offered me, Georgiana. And please do not believe that I do not value William's qualities—quite the contrary. It is just that… it was rather difficult for me—for both of us, I believe—to have no choice in the matter."

"Yes, I imagined as much. But I feel that William *had* a choice. Do you know that he wrote me about you when you stayed at Netherfield? He seemed to admire you even then." The girl smiled, pleased with herself while Elizabeth looked at her in disbelief.

"Surely, you are joking…"

"I am not. Is it true that one evening you were invited to play cards but you preferred to read? And that you said a sonnet can kill a weak love? William was so amused by that! Do you need more proofs?"

Elizabeth's astonishment delighted Georgiana exceedingly, so when Mrs. Annesley returned to the room, Miss Darcy was laughing while Mrs. Darcy seemed strangely silent.

Eventually, Elizabeth returned to her apartment to prepare for dinner, disturbed by this new knowledge. Her husband confessed that he admired her while they were in Hertfordshire, but the fact that he wrote about her to his sister was nearly shocking.

Overwhelming warmth spread from her stomach to her entire body while she found herself smiling for no reason. What an extraordinary thing to be told by her new, caring sister! Did she need more proofs—as Georgiana asked in jest—to be convinced that he had a choice, that he did not propose just because he was forced to, and that he would not have proposed to any other woman in her place? Surely not. Despite the heat that coloured her cheeks, she started shivering, wondering whether she was pleased or disturbed by the discovery. She heard Darcy's strong voice censuring the dogs, and she suddenly had the answer to that delicate question: she was deeply disturbed—but also very pleased.

She was tempted to see what the dogs were doing—what *he* was doing—but she remained still, her eyes closed, her mind suddenly freed from any unpleasant thoughts.

After a few minutes, she noticed a sealed letter on the table with a handwriting she did not recognise. Curious, she opened it and glanced at the end, then smiled as she discovered the author: Lady Catherine de Bourgh. She sat comfortably in the chair, prepared to enjoy the criticism and the burst of disapproval of Mr. Darcy's aunt and Mr. Collins's benefactor.

Miss Elizabeth Bennet,

Be assured that I shall never address you in any other way than that, as I shall never recognise the outrageous alliance in which you trapped my nephew, nor shall I willingly ever mention your name.

As the weather and your horrible manipulations did not allow me to intervene before this vile act of deception took place, it is with the greatest contempt that I address you with this letter, letting you know my true feelings about you.

What kind of woman are you since you have no feeling of propriety and delicacy and no trace of honour or decorum? You trapped my nephew into an outrageous scheme that made him forget that he has been engaged to my daughter since they were in the cradle and forced him to enter into a family of the lowest kind, who will pollute the shades of Pemberley!

You have no regard for the honour or credit of my nephew and you have disgraced him in the eyes of everybody, throwing upon him a shame that only death could wash away!

Be not content and happy with your unexpected fortune, Miss Bennet, nor imagine that your ambition of greatness and climbing society's ranks will ever be gratified. You must know that my nephew only accepted the alliance with you for his conviction that you would be stronger than my daughter to bear the heirs he expects. But I suspect you already knew that, as not even you can be so self-deceiving as to imagine that you are worth anything more. And surely you must imagine what will happen should you not provide him with a male heir. If such a very probable outcome occurs, I wonder what you and your family will do since I strongly advised Mr. Collins that, in the event of your father's death, he should separate from all of you as quickly as possible.

I did not have the chance of meeting you, and I hope I never will! I am praying that you will not stay long at my nephew's side and that the Lord will soon rectify my nephew's reckless error! If you happen to provide a child by then, it will at least be raised in an honourable family with proper education and with a mother a Darcy and Fitzwilliam heir deserves!

Lady Catherine de Bourgh

Elizabeth ended the letter breathless, and her heart almost burst from her chest. Her hands were trembling so badly that she dropped the paper. She could feel tears falling down her face until she felt their saltiness on her lips.

She wiped her face furiously, clenching her teeth together. She tried to rise, but her feet would not support her. She gazed at the piece of paper, still unable to believe what she read. Such a malicious attack, such a humiliating insult, such an abominable abuse could not possibly belong to someone with such wealth, education, and status in society! And a relative of her husband!

That Lady Catherine would hate her for interrupting the imaginary engagement between her daughter and Darcy—Elizabeth expected and understood. To have that hate loudly expressed—she was not surprised. But to read those curses, that unconcealed desire for her to die, the revenge against her family—Elizabeth never could have imagined, and she found herself unable to endure.

Her mind reeled with the words: she was worth nothing more than to provide an heir for him, and the entire family considered her just that. After all, did not Lady Stafford say the same thing? It seemed the most rational explanation for his insisting on marrying her—only she had been a fool to not see it.

For a moment, her reason shyly recollected Georgiana's words, but she abruptly banished such favourable thoughts, angry with herself for being so easily deceived. She lay on the bed, staring at the fire, frozen and pale, while tears fell freely down her face, painfully missing someone to really care for her, to hold her hands, and to comfort her turmoil.

Darcy had spent the entire afternoon in his library, attempting to read though he could not put away the feeling that something troubled Elizabeth greatly. He questioned Georgiana, but she pretended ignorance of his meaning. He was not deceived by his young sister but decided not to insist further as he was content to see her protecting Elizabeth's privacy.

As the afternoon progressed, Mrs. Annesley informed him that his sister would stay in her room and read for a few days, and that Mrs. Darcy was keeping her company—and he had inquired no further.

Mrs. Annesley also announced that she would have dinner with Georgiana in her room, and he felt a strange sense of excitement at the idea of being for the first time alone with Elizabeth for dinner one week since they wed. He wondered whether he should ask for a special arrangement, but he discarded the idea immediately. Surely, she would be made uncomfortable by such a spectacle in front of the servants. However, he could invite her to have a glass of wine and talk a little more, only the two of them, after dinner.

He knocked at her door and stopped as he received no answer. Lucky was barking, and he knocked again—then slowly opened the door. The room was dark, and he first believed that Elizabeth was sleeping, so he attempted to withdraw, closing the door in silence. But Lucky ran to the bed and licked her hand, receiving a caress on his head from his mistress.

Darcy was impelled to step closer. "Elizabeth, forgive me for disturbing you. I was wondering whether you are ready for dinner. Are you well?"

"I am well," she replied with a weak yet sharp voice. "I am resting a moment longer, and I shall prepare for dinner soon." He looked at her through the darkness, lit only by the fire. She did not move from the bed as she continued to pet the dog.

Darcy froze, recognising the distress she tried so hard to conceal and wondering what could have happened to put her in such a state. He knew she had been in a poor mood when she returned home, but she seemed to be much worse now. She turned her back to him. He sat on the edge of the bed, close enough to see her face, hidden against the pillow.

"Elizabeth, what happened? You are not well. Please tell me what is wrong."

"Nothing happened; everything is as it is. I am just… I shall ring for Molly."

She rose from the bed, avoiding his gaze. He was ready to leave, giving her the privacy she seemed to desire, when his eyes dropped to a piece of paper fallen on the carpet.

"Here—you dropped something. I think it is a letter." He took it, handed it to Elizabeth, and startled when she cried, "Give it to me. Do not read it!"

Elizabeth's reaction disturbed Darcy greatly, and the reason for her distress was obvious. He was uncertain how to proceed. He did not see well, but he thought the writing seemed familiar. His heart nearly stopped beating, imagining the letter might have been from Wickham, and he tried to dismiss that troubling thought while speaking further.

"You are so troubled by that letter that you can barely hold your tears. I shall not invade your privacy if the letter is of a personal nature and completely unrelated to me. Is it?"

She remained silent then moved to the window, hiding the letter in her fist.

"So it *is* related to me. You cannot expect me to ignore it since it affected you so."

She finally faced him, and the effort of fighting her tears was painful to watch.

"It is from Lady Catherine de Bourgh, but I do not want you read it. It is so..."

Elizabeth saw him pale, his eyes and lips narrowing in an anger that twisted his features. He took her hand gently. Her grip was tight, and he slowly opened her hand. She resisted a moment longer but soon gave up and allowed him to take the paper, then sat on the bed, turning away from him. After a time that seemed like hours, she heard him whispering.

"Oh, Lord, I am so deeply sorry. Please forgive me. I am so very sorry..."

Her tearful eyes turned to him, and with disbelief, she saw him kneel to the floor near the bed. "I do not even know what to say. This is... I never imagined that..."

"I did not expect such a thing," she murmured. "That is why I was so shocked. I imagine what she said is true. Even you told me that your wish in this marriage is to have an heir. But I do not understand. People keep telling me that you married me to have an heir as if it were something horrible. I do not understand, and I almost fear to meet people as I am not sure what they will say. I am at a loss to know how I should react. I do not want to expose myself to criticism by improper behaviour in public, but I cannot accept being attacked."

He stared at her, then kissed her hands, as pale and disturbed as before. His eyes were telling her he wished to say more, but he seemed unable to speak.

"Everything is my fault. I failed to protect you as I should. But I did not marry you only to provide me with an heir, Elizabeth. I hope you know that."

She tried to swallow the sudden lump in her throat while he kissed her hands again.

"Lady Catherine sent me a very angry letter, and I replied to her in the deserved manner. I should have imagined that she might write to you directly. I shall solve this immediately. You will not be bothered again, I promise you. I will write her back this instant."

He attempted to rise, but she held his hands. "William, wait—please sit."

Darcy immediately obeyed, their hands still entwined.

"It is of no use to respond to Lady Catherine. Fighting with her would bring nothing but more anger. You may best protect me by telling me the entire truth. I can bear anything if I know where the danger might come from. You told me about your family and about your properties… Is there anything further you have kept from me?"

He slowly cupped her face with warm hands and with small kisses wiped the remaining tears from her lashes.

"I did not intend to keep them from you, but there are details I have not told you yet as I thought they would make you uncomfortable. But it seems that, again, I misjudged the best way of handling things." He invited her to sit in the armchair, and he took the seat opposite her near the small table by the window.

"First, I will tell you a few more things about my aunt. She is my mother's sister, and my cousin Anne bears my mother's name. Anne is very amiable but shy and lonely. She spends most of her time at Rosings, and she is rarely in company. Her health seems precarious, but we are not sure whether this is so or just my aunt's imagination."

"I am truly sorry for her…"

"Yes, I too. Robert and I have visited her every Easter for the last five years. Since we were infants, my aunt insisted that I should marry Anne, and she pretended that my mother had the same desire, but I never heard such expectations. I never intended to marry Anne, and I made myself clear without hurting their feelings. It is my fault that I was not more vigorous in expressing my opinion."

"I understand… I can imagine her anger when she heard the news."

"Going further to the other subject, I already told you about my properties. Pemberley was left to my father by his mother. All the other estates came from my grandfather Darcy's line, and they are entailed on heirs male. If either James or I do not provide such heirs, the other will inherit all the properties. The only exception is Pemberley and our town houses, which both of us received from our mothers."

"But surely neither you nor James needs to worry about that, at this young age! It is quite ridiculous, really! And even if that were so, neither of you is in danger of poverty. You both have impressive means for a carefree life for you and your future families—even if you should have no heirs or only daughters. Why do people make this sound so dramatic?"

"I have no worry that I might be reduced to poverty. Pemberley is more than enough for my family. Both Lord Matlock and I are preoccupied by this because—it pains me to say it—my cousin James makes no effort to develop responsibility or wisdom. Taking care of so many properties is a daunting task. They need hard work, time, and engagement, as they are the source of income not only for the master but also for the tenants, their families, and many others. And James… A few months ago he lost a very important sum of money on cards and dice games, and he put up his present estate as a guaranty. I purchased his debts to save his property, but I expect it to happen again."

"I imagine this is not an easy subject for you to speak of. I thank you for sharing it with me."

"It is not easy, but I am relieved that I spoke with you. I did not tell you all these details sooner because we had been married for just a few days, and I did not want you to feel forced or rushed in taking the next step. I trust everything will be fine at the right moment. I did not marry you to provide me an heir but because I knew you were the perfect choice for me. I only hope that someday you will consider me the perfect choice for you too and not regret your decision to accept my proposal."

"I do not regret it," she replied, emotion thrilling her voice and colouring her face. He took her hands in his on the table, while he responded with only a small smile.

Chapter 16

Silence fell upon the chamber, then his fingers caressed hers, betraying his nervousness. Elizabeth saw he was struggling with something, but before she inquired, he continued.

"There is more I should tell, as you asked me to not keep anything from you. I am afraid I will upset you, but it must be said. I do not want any other misunderstandings between us."

"From your expression, it seems rather grave..."

"It is about Wickham. I know you favoured his company, and it is not easy for me to hurt you with this, but it must be done. Despite his pleasant manners, he is not a good man. He is two years older than James, and they have been good friends since they were children. I am afraid many of James's bad habits are the result of his alliance with Wickham."

"I see. Would you please tell me why you judge Mr. Wickham as not being a good man? I am not debating your saying it. I just wish to understand. I know he was a favourite of your father, but you seem to disapprove of him completely."

"I will—and for everything I tell you, you may approach Robert for confirmation."

"Surely, you cannot imagine that I will doubt your words. I just need to know your side of the story as Mr. Wickham trusted me with his part. My opinion about what he told me has already changed during the last weeks as I noticed several details I had missed before."

"I imagined he told you something. Our conversation during the Netherfield ball revealed to me your reproaches about the way I treated him, and I was tempted to speak to you then, but I wonder whether you would have believed me. Besides, at that time I had decided never to return to Hertfordshire, so I selfishly decided to keep silent."

"I fear I would have doubted your words back then," she admitted with embarrassment.

"Many would have, considering my behaviour at that time. George Wickham is the son of a most honourable man who had the management of Pemberley estates for many years. My father valued him, and as a favour, he became the godfather of Mr. Wickham's son. He was fond of young Wickham—who knew very well how to gain his affection—and had a high opinion of him. He supported George at Cambridge and hoped the church would be his profession. I started to see George in a different manner many years ago, in unguarded moments, which my father could not have. He was lacking principles and honour, and his manners were superficial and not worth trusting. I am sorry if I pain you, and I can offer you many examples to illustrate my assessment."

"Please do not presume that you pain me with that disclosure and that I need additional proof. So Mr. Darcy left him a living?"

"In his will, my father recommended to me to promote his advancement in the best manner that his profession might allow and, if he took orders, desired that a valuable family living might be his. There was also a legacy of one thousand pounds. His own father did not long survive mine, and within half a year, Wickham informed me that he did not wish to take orders but had decided to study the law. He said he expected some immediate pecuniary advantage in lieu of the preferment by which he could not be benefited. He resigned all claim to assistance in the church and accepted in return three thousand pounds."

"Three thousand pounds? That is a very important sum!"

"A total of four thousand pounds was hardly enough for Wickham as his life was one of idleness and dissipation. For about three years, I heard little of him until he applied to me again, telling me that his situation was very poor—which I could believe—and asking me to grant him the living my father left him. You will hardly blame me for refusing to comply with this entreaty or for resisting every repetition of it, which made his resentment grow. He was doubtless as violent in his abuse of me to others as in his reproaches to myself."

Elizabeth listened to his confession with revulsion and self-reproach. She remembered how hastily she had believed Wickham and blamed Darcy, as well as Charlotte's words about her wrong judgment of both gentlemen. She could do little else but confess her failure.

"I am so sorry, William. What a fool I have been! When we all met in Meryton, he noticed that I observed your exchange. I was not very fond of you then, and I mentioned to him something about hoping he would not leave town because of you—and that was enough for him to understand that I was an easy recipient for his malicious stories."

"Please do not blame yourself. Many people have been deceived by George Wickham. So, he was left without resources until James's father passed away too. Three years ago, James became the master of a house in London and a very important sum, which was lost in a most dishonourable way. Starting last year, despite the debts I purchased to save him, James kept asking me for money in advance of his inheritance, which he will get when he turns twenty-five. I refused him, and our relationship began to worsen day by day. Of Wickham I heard little, but I was certain he was somewhere close to James."

"What a disturbing situation..."

"Indeed. I still hope James will prove that he is the worthy son of his excellent father and make us proud of him. And I give you my word: I would have supported Wickham too if I had the smallest sign that he intended to change his behaviour."

She held his gaze for a long while, hoping her eyes would tell him more clearly what her words kept repeating. She hesitated for a while, but she could not refrain from inquiring—carefully so as not to betray her new sister's confidence.

"But William—does Georgiana know about Mr. Wickham's true character? She must remember him as being the family friend, and she might be easily deceived—as I was."

He frowned and paced impatiently. His turmoil increased, arousing Elizabeth's worry.

"Georgiana is the reason I am so enraged with Wickham. Last summer, Georgiana was settled in Ramsgate with her companion from that time, a Mrs. Younge. Somehow, Mr. Wickham found out and joined them there, undoubtedly by design. There was proved to have been a prior acquaintance between him and Mrs. Younge, in whose character we were most unhappily deceived. In short, he visited Georgiana a few times, reminded her of the happy years at Pemberley and gave her special attention. Her kindness made her an easy victim, and she was persuaded to believe herself in love and to consent to an elopement."

"Dear Lord," cried Elizabeth, biting her lips in distress. "Is it possible?"

"It is... Fortunately, I joined them unexpectedly a day or two before the elopement, and Georgiana, unable to support the idea of grieving and offending me, acknowledged the whole to me. You may imagine what I felt and how I acted. Regard for my sister's feelings prevented any public disclosure. I also tried to protect her by not exposing the whole ugliness of Wickham's character to her. I convinced her that it was unwise to make such a gesture at a young age. I assured her that I should never stay in the way of her happiness once she is mature enough to know what is right for her. How could I have told her that Wickham only used her as a way to gain money for his gaming debts? That he would have done the same with any daughter of a shop owner who had a reasonable dowry?"

Elizabeth's eyes turned tearful, and cold shivers of panic travelled down her spine. The brief talks with Georgiana suddenly took on a dramatic meaning, and the perspective that she still had tender feelings for Wickham made Elizabeth dizzy. She understood her husband's reasoning and his desire to protect Georgiana, but she sensed the danger behind the story.

"With Wickham and with Mrs. Younge, though, I had a very angry meeting. I demanded they both leave and never cross paths with me, or I would take drastic measures against them. Wickham's chief object was unquestionably my sister's fortune, but I suppose that the hope of revenging himself on me was a strong inducement."

"Oh, dear Lord—I never imagined. I am so sorry. Poor, dearest Georgiana..."

She glanced at Darcy—who stood near the window, his back to her, his head slightly lowered. She slowly moved near him and gently took his arm, making him turn to her.

"I am so sorry," she whispered, and he smiled sadly then put his arms around her. She leant towards him, her hands circling his waist while her head rested against his chest.

"I am happy that Georgiana has a wise and affectionate sister, who will take care of her."

"Thank you for trusting me, William. Now that I know the gravity of the history, I can understand your reluctance to speak of it."

"There is still something more. I am afraid Wickham is responsible for spreading the gossip about us. He told James—and very likely, some other officers from London—and the words flew around until the damage was complete. I do not think he imagined the consequences of the gesture. He only searched for another way to harm my name. Unfortunately, this affected your life too."

He watched her closely, but her expression remained surprisingly calm. "I suspected as much after I talked to your cousin at the ball and he told me about his close friendship with Mr. Wickham. Both our lives have been affected, and neither of us is at fault."

In front of the window lit by the moonlight, their faces slowly regained their usual warmth. A sense of relief and alleviation from sharing their secrets and pain enveloped them. He gently caressed her hair, then his fingers brushed her face, and her smile widened.

A brief knock and Molly's impromptu entrance startled them, and they separated while the maid quickly closed the door behind her.

"We should establish some strict rules about the servant's entrance," he said.

"I doubt Molly will repeat the error." Elizabeth smiled, attempting to arrange her hair.

"Elizabeth, I am sorry to bring back an unpleasant subject but you said earlier—several times—that people kept telling you about my marrying you to have an heir. What people? Did anyone say that to you besides Lady Catherine?"

Surprise made her pale, and she held her husband's intent look. "Lady Stafford. We met at the modiste today. She came to speak to me while I was changing my dress."

He frowned and actually wobbled on his feet. The blood seemed to drain from his face, and he blinked rapidly a few times.

"Why did you not tell me sooner?"

"What was there to tell? We met with her yesterday, and you seem to know each other quite well. And since Madame Claudette is preferred by the ladies of the *ton*, it was somehow predictable that we should eventually meet there or some other place."

"It is true. I should have been more careful."

"More careful? What do you mean? Is there anything that I should know for my safety?"

"Nothing of consequence—only a private matter which I did not handle properly. Do not let it bother you. We have had enough tormenting and painful conversation for one night. Let us go to dinner, please. I promise you will not be disturbed anymore."

"I see… I will be ready for dinner shortly if that is what you want. I do not want to insist on something that seems painful and private to you…"

Her voice became weaker, and she turned her back to him as cold shivers of distress froze her feet. She heard him close the door to his rooms, and she leant against the pillows a little while. Perhaps he was right. That day was so full of sadness, regrets, and self-reproaches that she wondered whether she could bear more.

Her head was spinning, and her fingers turned cold. She recollected him warming her hands a few days earlier in the park, and she wondered how many times he had done that before. The way he touched her, his lips tantalising hers, the soft caress…

He surely was not ignorant of these things. No gentleman of eight and twenty was! And what he had done before their marriage was surely not her business. What about the things he was doing *after* their marriage? Could she dare question that since his behaviour towards her was beyond reproach? Should she even allow herself to think of that?

She heard a slight knock and remembered that Molly was waiting in the hall. But it was her husband who came in and sat on the bed, watching her.

"Elizabeth, I have seen that you were troubled by my refusal to speak about Annabelle Stafford. Am I correct in my observation? Do you wish to talk about it?"

"I do… I imagine it is uncomfortable and painful for you, and I know it is not my right to question you, but I feel… It troubles me not to know what is happening..."

"Very well then—if that is your wish, let us make this a night of full disclosure." He opened the door to the hall, where the maid was waiting in deep embarrassment. "Molly, please ask for dinner to be sent up and arranged in my suite. We shall not go downstairs tonight."

Darcy resumed his place, glancing at Elizabeth with obvious anxiety.

"I am glad you trust me enough to change your decision, William. I know it is your right to keep your business private, and I should not bother you by inquiring. But things have progressed in such a way that—"

"It was never my lack of trust in you but my concern that you might be troubled hearing such a story. It is not something that one would want to share with his young, innocent wife. That is why I delayed this conversation although I knew the time for it would come."

"Surely, it cannot be something so bad. I am not quite so innocent, you know. I am aware of how things go with gentlemen," she said daringly. He smiled and briefly kissed her hand.

"I will struggle to find the proper words to start, as I do not want to completely ruin your opinion of me. We both know that it has never been too high, anyway."

"Well, it is good that you are in a disposition to tease, sir. As for my opinion of you—surely, you can see how much it has changed, starting even before our wedding."

"I am glad to have your reassurance. It is truly helpful in such a moment."

He began to pace the room, his agitation obvious. Elizabeth sat in the armchair.

"I met Annabelle in Ramsgate when I was about twenty years old. It was the year after my mother passed away. Her death left me completely lost, and my father simply collapsed like a huge tree that was weakening day by day. Georgiana was about eight years old. She had a governess and a teacher, but she was shy and restrained. She rarely laughed, and she was afraid of almost everything. It was during that time that I taught her to ride, and she started to play on the piano. Then, as my father had lost all interest, I was sent from one estate to another to supervise their management. Everyone inquired after my mother and conveyed their condolences—which was even harder to bear. While I was away, George Wickham was at Pemberley, keeping my father company, and he had already gained a taste for gambling and compromising the daughters of shopkeepers or tenants."

Elizabeth's heart cramped, overwhelmed by the sadness and pain on his face.

"In the summer, between two trips around the country, Robert asked me to spend some time in Ramsgate with him and Thomas—only the three of us. They were attempting to cheer my spirits and to have me rest and relax. I reluctantly accepted. I was in no mood for parties, but I remember being too tired to argue with them. One evening at a ball, I met Annabelle Weston; that was her name at the time. She was a woman of exceptional beauty, two years my senior, but that I discovered later."

He glanced at her, then breathed deeply and continued.

"In the following days, I met her everywhere. She was neither insistent nor obvious in her attentions, but she was always there. I happened to meet her when I went to walk on the beach. We started to talk, and I found she had a fascinating story: she was French and married a British colonel in his majesty's army, who had died the previous year."

"Oh..." Elizabeth said.

"In Ramsgate, she was visiting some friends who were kind enough to host as she had not much family in England. She seemed a strong woman, fighting a difficult fate. She was so attentive, so gentle, so understanding, so undemanding without ever pressing her presence but always being present. She was admired by many gentlemen, but she showed a special interest in me. It is not difficult to guess that our acquaintance soon became very close."

"I imagine..."

"I do not attempt to excuse myself, but from the very beginning I told her that my future intentions could never involve her. She replied with much easiness, insisting that she was well aware of that. Also, she mentioned that she could not enter into a commitment herself as it was very likely she would be invited to live overseas with an older relative who had a great fortune. She said her only wish was to enjoy my company for a time, to comfort each other, and to be sure that we should always be friends."

He paused again, and his face darkened.

"In less than a week, our relationship assumed a private nature. I had generous funds at my disposal, so I rented a house to be separate from my cousins, and I spent the next fortnight with Annabelle. I felt free: no obligation, no responsibilities, only a beautiful woman whose goal seemed to be my well-being. I even wrote my father that I was delaying my return."

Elizabeth's eyes followed him as he paced the room.

"Robert went back to his regiment. He warned me about the possible outcome of that relationship, but I told him she was about to leave the country. So I was on my own with Annabelle's company all the time. I felt pleased and flattered. Now that I think back, there were things that should have told me about her duplicity—but then, at that age, I was oblivious to everything except how I felt with her. She was truly…her skills in seduction were impossible to resist even for a wiser man."

"It is understandable… You were young and innocent yet burdened with so many duties. It is easy to become enamoured with a beautiful woman. There is nothing to be ashamed of."

"I do have reasons to feel ashamed. I was not so innocent. I was twenty with two older cousins and. I had had my share of *knowledge of the world* by that age."

He avoided her eyes, and she felt her cheeks burning. He continued.

"I cannot excuse myself because of love, as not even then did I fancy myself being so. Perhaps I was smitten with her, but I was more flattered by the attentions of a beautiful woman—who seemed desired by many others—and content with the feeling of freedom and easiness she was giving me by her full attention. It was still my pride and vanity that put me in that situation—the faults for which even you reproach me now."

"William, I am not—"

"After a month, my state of comfort changed. I was preoccupied with my abandoned duties, I was missing my sister, and I was worried for my father. I told Annabelle that I must return to Pemberley. I asked her when she was due to leave for America. Through tears, she confessed she had not received any news from her relatives. She said she did not want to trouble me with her problems, but she did not know what to do. Her friends could not support her for long, and she had no means to leave by herself."

Darcy poured himself a glass of wine to moisten his lips.

"The situation suddenly took a worrisome turn for me. She insisted I should not be concerned for her. But of course I was—I believed her to feel real affection for me, and I was grateful for her company when I most needed it. So I told her that I was willing to rent her a house with all the expenses paid for the next few months in Ramsgate or wherever else she wished until she solved her situation. She at first refused, then she expressed her gratitude in a most *overwhelming* way and again, my vanity was rewarded."

His embarrassment increased and Elizabeth blushed again.

"A day before my departure, she said she had decided to remain in Ramsgate, close to her friends. She asked me to lend her the necessary funds for six months of rent. She promised she would repay me as soon as she found a way, but of course, I declared that was not necessary. I felt I owed her that help, so of course I gave her the money with no hesitation."

"It is understandable..."

"Perhaps... My separation from Annabelle went reasonably well. She cried, and I told her to let me know whether she needed any help, anytime. I left, and I confess I felt no regret but rather a sort of relief. I returned to Pemberley—guilty about my long absence and anxious to see my father and my little sister. She was so happy that she barely left my side. Wickham was there of course, and he seemed to provide companionship to my father and my little sister—and I was grateful to him for that. He was not inclined to learn anything or to work, but he was an affectionate friend, I thought back then. What would you now say about my foolishness? Could anyone have been more wrong in so many particulars?"

"Surely, you cannot blame yourself for trusting your friend! And Annabelle?"

"In my next journey, as I was in the vicinity, I stopped in Ramsgate to see her. I planned to stay only a few minutes to make sure she was well and that she had found a proper house. I arrived in the afternoon, and I called on her friends—who were obviously panicked. They told me she was out on a walk. They did not invite me to enter, and I did not request it. While departing, I noticed Annabelle on the arm of a gentleman, very affectionate to each other. She was shocked when she saw me, but I found the situation quite pleasing. She seemed well, and she had found another recipient for her affection. I left with an easy heart. When I returned to London, I found three letters in which she explained to me that the gentleman was a friend from her childhood. I wrote back, assuring her that she did not need to offer me any explanations and that I wished her all the best."

"So everything seemed settled," Elizabeth said, puzzled.

"I believed that too until two months later when I visited Robert at his regiment. There was a full encampment of officers, and one evening at a party, I met a Colonel Weston—a gentlemen in his early fifties. He spoke of his wife with much admiration, declaring her beauty was astonishing and he missed her very much. He said she was staying with some friends at the seaside, as the weather in the North and life in the encampment did not suit her too well. I was left in no doubt that he was Annabelle's husband."

"How is it possible?"

"I wondered the same! I was so furious at Annabelle's deception that for a moment

I was tempted to make full disclosure to Colonel Weston. My cousin scolded me. He reasonably said I had no reason to hurt the man. It became now obvious even to me that Annabelle's attachment to me was only her usual behaviour—most likely for monetary gain."

"How horrible!"

"I sent her a short message: 'I met your husband!' Of course, she wrote me back with a long and silly explanation about being so rapturously in love with me that she would have done anything for my company. I ripped up the letter. Two years later, Robert told me that her husband had died, and that was my last information about her for a while."

Elizabeth was breathless with anticipation. Darcy's distress was obviously growing with each moment and so was her anxiety.

"A year later, my father passed away. One day I was shocked to receive Annabelle at my door in London. I asked the servant to show her out, but she insisted she wished to tell me something of great importance. With much pathos, she said that, two and half years earlier, she had given birth to a child who was mine—a boy. I was so shocked that I could not breathe for a time."

Elizabeth was astonished. He avoided her eyes, his voice lowered by the lump in his throat.

"I asked whether she was certain the child was mine—such a stupid question as the answer she gave me was the obvious one. She said she decided to leave for America as she was in a difficult situation. She had debts she could not pay and she would take the child with her. She said she had only enough money to travel third class. I asked her where she lived, and she named a very questionable inn. I took Stevens and helped her move into a respectable hotel. The child struck me the moment I saw him—dark and curly hair, dark eyes. He looked so similar to me that I had few doubts remaining."

"Dear Lord, is it possible?"

"I felt lost, and went to speak to my aunt and uncle. Robert and Thomas were there too. I struggled with what to do; my feelings were so deeply torn. The idea of having a son warmed my heart, but I knew I needed to find an arrangement to keep Annabelle at a distance. However, I could not be so cruel as to separate a child from his mother."

"What a situation, William…

"I did not sleep a few nights from worry, and I spent each day visiting Annabelle and the boy. There were some details that drew my attention from the beginning: the child seemed frightened, and he did not want to interact with me or with Annabelle. He cried a lot, and I wanted to bring Dr. Taylor, but she said it was his usual way. He seemed to have no affection for her, and she barely gave him any notice. At first I thought I discovered another aspect of her ugliness—her lack of love for her own child."

"And…?"

"One day, Lady and Lord Matlock visited them with me and, while they admitted that the boy seemed to resemble me, Lady Matlock noticed no interaction between the child and his mother, which she found unbelievable. Having my suspicions doubled, I hired someone to investigate Annabelle's last years. A week passed before I had all the answers, and during this time, I became close to the boy."

"What did you discover?"

"Everything Annabelle told me was untrue. She was not French but from the North, from a family that was in trade. She married when she was nineteen and had spent most of her time in Ramsgate where she indeed had some friends. Nobody remembered her being with child, and on deeper investigation, we found that the child belonged to a shop girl, married to a young gardener. Annabelle used to purchase her gowns from that shop, and she put together a horrible scheme: she simply took the boy from his parents without anyone knowing where the poor child was! The man who discovered that outrageous truth brought the parents with him, and I found them at my door."

Elizabeth's shock made her stop breathing. He responded with a bitter smile.

"The boy's parents were desperate, but I could not pay much attention to them. Anger had taken control of me, and I could not think of anything except how to punish Annabelle. I still had enough reason to send for Robert, but he was away, and Lord Matlock came instead. He tried to calm me, but I saw he was in no better condition. We finally went to confront Annabelle, taking the child's parents with us. When she saw us all, her reaction was one of complete shock, and then she fainted. I confess I was not at all impressed. The mother took the child in her arms—if you could only see their happiness and the boy's joyous laughter!"

Another pause followed so he could gather himself enough to speak further. Elizabeth was silent and tearful, struggling to comprehend everything she heard.

"The discussion that followed still makes me furious. Annabelle kept insisting that she had done everything to get my attention, that she loved me and would do anything for me. I was equally angry, disconcerted and disgusted—with both of us. I could not believe that I had been such a weak fool, so easily deceived by a shameless woman. I could not bring myself to charge her. I thought of the scandal that would arise and its affect on the family, especially Georgiana. Besides, the child's parents begged us to let them return to their home. They were simple people who did not want any scandal either. I told Annabelle that I would pay for the room for another two days, and I did not wish ever to see her again. That was four years ago, and I never saw her again until this December."

"Dear Lord…what a story…How can anyone do such horrible things?"

He stood at the window, staring outside. "I hope you now understand my reluctance to share it with you and why I blame myself for allowing it to happen. But however ashamed I feel, it is better for you to know the truth and to be warned about it…and to discover more faults in the man you were forced to marry."

"Oh, stop such nonsense, William. Any man could have been in your place."

"You are too kind and too generous," he said, still avoiding her eyes.

"I am only being reasonable, I believe. Does Georgiana know anything of this?"

"No—how could I tell her such a story? But she knows the child—his name is Tommy—as he and his parents are now in Lambton. His mother works in a shop, making dresses for the women in the neighbourhood. The father is the fourth gardener at Pemberley."

A trace of a smile appeared on her lips. "Does Pemberley need a fourth gardener?"

He replied with diffidence. "Pemberley is a large estate and always needs strong men who work hard. Besides, I needed to know Tommy was safe. He is almost seven now."

"So there is yet another family that is under your protection…"

"And under yours, Mrs. Darcy," he replied then turned and embraced her.

"What a story…"Elizabeth kept whispering.

"I am so sorry that you had to hear all this…and I am so grateful and astonished that you found the generosity to not be more upset with me. I was afraid that—"

"William, I am glad you trusted me enough to reveal such truths to me. I know very well that a wife has no right to inquire, not even about her husband's present and even less about his past, just as I know very well that most men have a past—as well as a present—outside their marriage! You could have silenced me on this subject, and there was nothing I could have reproached you for."

Her voice was trembling with distress and embarrassment, and her cheeks were burning. He slowly turned her to face him. They gazed at each other—both of them dark, worried, wondering, and hoping. He tenderly cupped her face with his hands.

"Elizabeth, I wish nothing more than to make this marriage a happy one. I do have a past—like most men of my age—but I do not have a *present* outside of our marriage. I have a beautiful, bright, and most amazing wife—and that is the only thing I am interested in."

"Besides your thousand duties," she teased him with no little emotion. She laid her head on his chest, and his arms tightened around her.

"And now Annabelle is Lady Stafford. Does she chase after all the men with whom she has been closely acquainted, or does she only favour you with this special treatment?"

"Two and half years ago, she married Lord Stafford—who was in his seventies and had no close family. He passed away, and Annabelle returned to Town. She has a name, significant means, and a house—and she became friendly with James. I suspect she loaned him money for his gaming. What she wants I could not say, but she is impertinent and seemed vindictive to my aunt and uncle. And she keeps sending me notes to call on her. The first ones I did not read, but one evening—about three weeks ago I think—she came here."

"She came here? How can that be?"

"My shock was no less than yours. She said she now has everything she needs except for my company. She insisted she loved nobody but me."

His embarrassment was apparent, and Elizabeth blushed.

"I asked her to stop making a fool of herself and to take care of her own life. I assured her that any connection between us was impossible. She balanced between impertinence, threats, and begging, and finally I had to insist that she leave."

"That was before you proposed to me."

"Yes, a few weeks before. One evening I found her in front of the house. I had to enter her carriage for a moment and to promise I would call on her one of these days. I am sure she intentionally met us in the park yesterday with that fool James, and today she approached you at the modiste and—"

"I remember the evening with the carriage; I saw you from the window. And I heard you talking with the colonel in the library about Annabelle."

"I am sorry—that was a silly and improper discussion. I shall take care of you, Elizabeth."

This time she rose and moved near him, then daringly took hold of his hands.

"I know you will take care of me, but I am certainly not afraid of Lady Stafford. I confess I was distressed about the *subject,* and even more so when I saw your reluctance to speak of her. But now I understand why. Since I know the truth, I am well capable of bearing it."

"Had she been offensive to you earlier today? Perhaps we should change modiste, or I shall arrange that, for the time being, someone will come to our home when you need to order new gowns. And I will make sure to be always with you when you go out. I still hope to see a little reason in Annabelle and that she finally finds a life of her own. Besides, we will go to Pemberley soon. I truly wish to have some peaceful time...with you alone."

"I look forward to going to Pemberley but not because someone wishes to bother us. And yes, she attempted to offend and upset me. She implied that she was still intimate with you. She said you married me because I was shy and submissive, and you would always have your way with me—and that the Matlocks accepted me because they wished to separate you from her. I am not certain about the Matlocks' motivation, but calling me shy and submissive was rather ridiculous, and it made me angry more than anything. If not..."

She took a break to breathe.

"Yes...?" he encouraged her to continue.

"William, I try very hard to be a good Mrs. Darcy. I am careful and concerned for your name—our name—for our sister Georgiana, and for everything that is under my care. That is why I struggle not to behave as *Elizabeth Bennet* would sometimes be tempted to do. However, if either Mr. Bingley's sisters or Lady *Anybody* ever attempts to offend me or take me for a fool, I am afraid my patience and my good manners will evade me. After all, I have been *Elizabeth Bennet* for one and twenty years and *Mrs. Darcy* for only a week."

"There is nothing you must change, nor must you allow anyone to put you in uncomfortable situations. I wish to see all of Miss Elizabeth Bennet's traits together with Mrs. Elizabeth Darcy's excellent qualities."

He wrapped her in an admiring gaze and removed a lock from her temple. "You are such an amazing woman, Elizabeth. I do not believe any other man married for a week could share such terrible stories with his young wife and be rewarded with so much strength, warmth, and understanding. I know you are troubled by all these things—anyone would be—and that you could not forget so easily the horrible offenses brought by my aunt. And your wisdom in stepping through it amazes me."

"I am troubled and upset, but it is easy to be strong now that you have shared the truth with me. I feel much better that, besides your promise to protect me, you gave me the strength of the truth and proved to me that I have your trust and your respect."

"I am very proud and grateful to be your husband, Mrs. Darcy." His dark gaze and solemnity made her shiver.

"Now—after tormenting you for so many hours and discovering once again how much I have to improve to be worthy of you, would you do me the honour of joining me in a dinner to celebrate our seventh day of marriage?"

Chapter 17

Darcy directed her to his apartment. A round table near the window showed a generous display of inviting dishes. He helped her to sit and took the place opposite. For a while, they were preoccupied with their plates, but the tension was easily felt.

It was a day that seemed as long as a month and as hard to bear as a year. She watched her husband with growing attention and interest. So many new traits had been disclosed that even his features seemed somehow different in the light of the candles.

"Elizabeth, is something wrong? You seem preoccupied."

"I was thinking of you… Most of us believe that a great fortune is the guarantee of an easy and carefree life. We rarely consider the duties and responsibilities attached to these. But perhaps that happens because we mostly see wealthy people enjoying their benefits rather than accomplishing any work at all—more like your cousin James than like yourself."

"I am sure many other gentlemen are accountable to their obligations. I fear James is a painful exception—and I cannot understand why he became that way."

"Do you think he was aware of Mr. Wickham's plan to elope with Georgiana?"

"I asked Wickham, and he denied it. I did not inquire of James directly, but I know he was in London then, so he might have been innocent."

"Do you not think that Georgiana would be safer if she knew the degree of Mr. Wickham's deception? I am speaking for myself: although I began to doubt his words some time ago, I was reluctant to admit my error in judging him before you told me the entire truth."

"Elizabeth, are you pained to find out these things? I know you and Wickham were close friends, and I imagine you had some tender feelings for him…"

"Please, rest assured that I had no tender feelings for Mr. Wickham at all. I am only pained by my hurt pride in realising how easily I had been deceived."

"I am glad to hear it," he said, and she noticed he emptied his glass in one gulp. She smiled and felt herself blushing. Was it possible that he was jealous?

"You are probably correct about Georgiana. But I see no possibility of opening the subject now, after so many months. I am afraid it would only pain her more."

"If the subject does arise someday, would you mind if I speak to her about it? You may trust that I shall be careful not to hurt her."

He stretched to touch her hand and gently caressed it.

"Thank you, I would be very grateful to you for doing it…and I do trust in your care for her."

"And speaking of Georgiana—is there anything you can do to avoid future unpleasant encounters with Lady Stafford? I know Georgiana was quite distressed today too."

"I am still considering the best approach with Annabelle. It seems that ignoring her will not provide the desired result. Perhaps you should change your modiste. And I imagine she will be at the opera tomorrow too…"

"I have no intention of changing anything for the *named* lady. And I am no longer distressed about meeting her tomorrow at the opera. But it is all so strange. I cannot claim much experience is gaining a man's favour"—she blushed, lowering her eyes—"but does such behaviour ever meet with success? Could she imagine that you still have some regard for her? Does she imagine you would allow yourself to be seduced by her acting like a fool? Would *any* man allow himself to be captivated by such a shocking display of impropriety?"

"I am not certain about other men, but *I* had ceased having any interest in her when I left Ramsgate eight years ago."

"Could she hope that, if not for your marriage, there was a chance to renew your relationship? After all, it would not be a surprise for a man of your age to…"

He could discern her discomfort and looked straight into her eyes.

"Even if I had never seen you again after I left Hertfordshire, my feelings for Annabelle would be the same. Were I not married now and interested in a *close relationship* with a woman and somehow every other woman in London had suddenly disappeared, Annabelle would still not be a choice. I am sorry if I disturb you with my exaggeration. I only wish to make myself very clear."

"Well, you succeeded—everything is perfectly clear. But now, I am thinking of James. Does he know the extent of Annabelle's irrational behaviour? What if he becomes another oblivious victim? Are they…? Is it possible that she would become with child?"

"I cannot believe we are speaking of such things. I am not certain of the nature of James and Annabelle's relationship. I have avoided such an inquiry as I was afraid he would tell Annabelle and she would take it as a sign of my interest in her. Besides, I doubt he would listen to me. For the time being, she seems to be the one who supports his weaknesses."

"Perhaps you should speak to him anyway. He is your only relative from your father's side, and he is so different from you."

"He is… We shall see. Perhaps, I will speak to him."

"Did he ever travel with you for business?"

"No, never. He showed no interest in the management of his properties."

"How often do you visit the estates? Is your personal involvement there necessary? Would you take me with you on your next trip?"

"I would be very pleased if you could join me in my travels as soon as the weather is warmer and the roads are improved. I am delighted at *your* interest in this, Elizabeth. Most ladies are not concerned with that part of their husbands' lives."

"Surely, you cannot pretend to know what most ladies are concerned with," she teased him.

"True. I barely know what *one* lady is concerned with." He watched her closely, and she wondered whether he meant her or Annabelle. She had the answer a moment later.

"But it pleases me that tonight I begin to learn. Regarding the estates—I usually travel to each of them every three months. I struggled to hire a very proficient steward for each, and they keep me updated every fortnight. I also have my London solicitor, Mr. Aldridge, who is excellent in his profession and has been loyal to our family for more than fifteen years. He works with two sons—both attorneys—who sometimes visit the estates for me. "

"So when you came to Hertfordshire, you had recently dealt with Georgiana's elopement. And I imagine you were between your business journeys... How different things appear on closer examination! And how different *you* appear, Mr. Darcy. I am glad I listened to your advice and did not complete my sketch of your character back then."

She stepped close to him, rose on her toes and gently caressed his face. He captured her hand, then placed a lingering kiss inside her palm.

"Have you finished sketching my character?" he asked, his lips still caressing her hand.

"Not yet..." Her face was lifted to him, He embraced her while her hands shyly encircled his waist. Her head rested on his chest, and she could hear his heartbeat. One hand caressed her hair, rested on her nape a moment, then lowered along her spine. She shivered.

"Elizabeth, we should sleep now. It is long past midnight. Tomorrow we have a long day."

"Yes..." she whispered. "We should go to sleep. It is very late indeed."

He opened the door for her. At their entrance, Lucky rose from his place and sniffed them. He was rewarded with brief petting before he resumed his sleep. In the middle of the room, Darcy's arms captured her once again.

"I thank you again, Mrs. Darcy."

His close warmth ignited something inside while every inch of her skin became chilled. She prayed for the embrace to last longer, and he seemed reluctant to release her too.

"Will you call for Molly?"

"No...it is too late to disturb her. I will manage by myself."

"May I help you?" he asked, and she stared at him in shock. What could he possibly mean?

"I could just untie the back of your clothes, so you can remove them more easily."

She blinked repeatedly, licked her lips, and then bit them.

"Oh, I thank you but I do not know whether…" He smiled, and her anxiety increased. Her eyes followed him as he walked to her bed, took her night robe, then he slowly turned her back to him and put the robe in front of her, so she could cover herself.

"May I?" he inquired, and she silently nodded in agreement.

She spotted their image in the mirror, and she shivered again, covering herself in the robe. At her back, he gently brushed against her nape, then his hands rested on her shoulders. Cold shivers spread from his touch inside her body, and she closed her eyes as she felt his fingers unfastening the two laces of her dress. He gently pulled the dress down from her shoulders, and his fingers untied her corset. Through the thin fabric, his fingers burned her, and she could sense his stare caressing her back. The undergarment loosened around her. She tightened the grip of the robe at her chest as the dress fell from her shoulders, and she wondered how long her knees would support her. She knew she should be embarrassed by being almost undressed in front of him, but she felt nothing of the sort. His movements then stopped, and her eyes still closed, she felt his lips come to rest near her ear.

"Do you want me to help you with your hair pins, too?"

"No, thank you—I can manage," she replied in some haste, her voice slightly trembling.

"Then I shall leave you to rest and will see you in the morning. Good night… and thank you."

He briefly kissed her on the corner of her lips then closed the door behind him. She leant down on the chair near the mirror. For some time she just stared at her reflection, her mind filled with the storm of emotions aroused inside her by the stories she had learnt, by the distress they shared, by his closeness—both in spirit and in body. And while the fire burned strongly, cold shivers tormented her skin and her heart.

Some time passed before she remembered that she needed to loosen her hair. She pulled the pins out one by one, but her fingers seemed slower and clumsier than ever before—and she scolded herself for being so foolish as to refuse her husband's help.

More time passed until, wrapped in her blankets, Elizabeth put together everything she learnt, everything she felt, and everything she experienced that night. It was dawn before she finally surrendered to sleep, her mind still tormented as she struggled to put aside the past and imagine the future.

London, 3 January

DAWN CAME, AND DARCY HAD NOT SLEPT A MOMENT—YET HE WAS PERFECTLY rested. He could not believe what he had experienced the previous day and night. To have the burden of the past removed from his chest and to be blessed with Elizabeth's understanding was something he could not imagine even the day before. But it did happen, and his astonishment turned to joy. One week after a marriage that started under such unfavourable odds, he clearly saw the advantages he personally had gained from the alliance. And he suddenly realised that, although he believed himself in love with Elizabeth weeks before he proposed to her, he had never truly known her until the last few days. He had been bewitched by her beauty, her wit, and her spirit, but there were so many other things to admire in her, and she fully proved her worth the previous night.

The previous night—such a mix of pain, distress, worry and delight...

Her scent still made him dizzy, and his fingers still wore the feel of her skin. His mind vividly recollected her image as he untied her gown and touched her bare shoulders and she slightly leant towards him. His senses screamed in frustration that he had left and broken their intimacy then. He knew that, despite the distress she had to bear from his stories, Elizabeth also enjoyed his caresses, and she likely would have welcomed him staying longer. And yet, he had left like a fool—he scolded himself—a fool who cared more for her than for his own desires.

Had he not loved Elizabeth as he did, had he not hoped to have her love one day, the previous night would have been a good moment to stay longer and increase their intimacy. However, he could not allow the remembrance, years later, of their developing relationship to be so strongly bound to unpleasant histories and to shameless offenses that Elizabeth had to endure from his relatives or old acquaintances. His concern for her was stronger than his passion.

Breakfast was still far away, so he moved to his library and requested some coffee. He called for Stevens and instructed him in a hurry. Then he took a paper and wrote back to his aunt. He re-read the letter and ripped it up. It was too emotional, and it would only feed the conflict. He opened the window to feel the chilling wind then wrote another letter.

An hour later, Elizabeth entered. Her eyes were shining, and a smile brightened her face while her cheeks were slightly coloured. He went to her, taking her hand, and he noticed her pallor and the dark circles around her eyes. She clearly had not slept much either.

She accepted a cup of tea while assuring him that she had slept very well and was pleased to see him. A warm sense of peace enveloped him, and he could not restrain from hastily kissing her cheeks. She replied with a joyful smile and deeper blushes.

"Are you working on something special?"

"No, I was just..." He hesitated a moment, like a child caught doing something naughty. "I was writing to Lady Catherine."

She rolled her eyes in reproach.

"Elizabeth, I know you disapprove, but I cannot allow this to pass so easily. Here, this is my final version." He handed her the letter, and she took it with obvious surprise then read:

Lady Catherine,

With astonishment and great embarrassment, I read the letter you considered proper to send to my wife, and I am deeply ashamed to admit that such words were written by a person with education and genteel breeding, who happens to be my relative.

While Mrs. Elizabeth Darcy's generous heart induced her to try to forgive the undeserved offenses she had to endure, I cannot be equally forbearing. So until further actions are taken to remedy the present situation, I shall consider that Lady Matlock is my only aunt.

However, as your ladyship has always been preoccupied with helping others, you will surely be pleased to find that, due to your letter, I gained one more opportunity to come to a better understanding with my wife and to discover even more of her remarkable qualities.

Fitzwilliam Darcy

"Oh my—this is quite harsh, William."

"Perhaps, but well deserved, I would say. Please allow me to send it immediately."

His determination left her little chance to object. Besides, despite her wish to not increase familial conflict, she felt rather content with his desire to protect her.

"I also spoke with Mrs. Thomason earlier as I want to know how my aunt's letter reached you without my knowing about it. I cannot allow any suspicion of distrust regarding my staff. If I discover any betrayal, measures must be taken immediately."

"Let us hope it was only an innocent mistake. I will ask Molly about it too."

Stevens entered and took the letter, bowing to his master. Everything is taken care of, sir."

"Excellent. Keep me informed." Darcy poured himself another cup of coffee while meeting Elizabeth's puzzled expression.

"After our discussion last night, I realised that my decisions not to expose either Annabelle or Wickham's true characters, only to avoid a scandal, were selfish and could be dangerous for the people around them. I never thought of it in that way until you mentioned it to me. We should write to your father about Wickham too—not *everything* but enough for him to understand the man's true character and to be guarded against his pleasant manners."

"I wanted to speak to you about that too. I am happy to see we are of the same mind. Now please excuse me. I shall go and see how Georgiana is."

"Please wait a moment. There is something more I wish to tell you." He met her curious expression and suddenly felt uneasy again, wondering what she was thinking.

"Last night I realised that, while I kept thanking you for your commitment to this marriage, I have hardly done my share. I have spent very little time with you since we married."

"Oh, it is easy to understand. You are very busy and—"

"The main concern of a married man should be his wife—and only the remaining time should be split among his duties. It depends on whether the wife *wished* to spend time with the man—and how much."

She blushed and laughed nervously. "A married woman's main concern should be her husband, and if the husband possesses a strong character, education, intelligence and pleasant manners, the wife will surely want to spend as much time with him as possible."

Her eyes shone as a blush spread lower on her neck. He kissed her hand.

"I hope I meet at least some of those requirements. Because it is my intention, Mrs. Darcy, to start doing what is already long overdue." His voice sounded light, but Elizabeth felt that even her ears were burning as she tried to guess what he meant.

"It is my intention to court you properly, as I should have done before we married. You cannot sketch my character in an advantageous way—nor can I gain your affection—if I do nothing to deserve it. I convinced you to accept my marriage proposal, then I took you from your family and friends, and I expected you to adapt to your new life. Not to mention that I have exposed you to some terrible stories that would disturb even the strongest of men. You deserve much more, yet you did not receive the smallest amount of attention that a woman—a wife—deserves. That will change this instant. I hope you do not disapprove."

"No, not at all. Any woman would be flattered and pleased to be courted. Of course, it depends on the gentleman who is courting her. In that, a woman has little choice," she attempted to joke, and he smiled.

"Unfortunately, you have even less choice since you are rather stuck with me already. But I shall struggle to make you feel at least a little pleased and flattered by my effort."

He took her hand with great solemnity, and she laughed nervously.

"I am sure your efforts will be appreciated, sir."

"Sadly, you may be disappointed as my courting skills are rather poor. I did not…I have never *courted* anyone before, so in this you may be more experienced than I am. I count on your kindness to help me correct my clumsiness and improve myself. Lady Catherine always says that one cannot be truly proficient if one does not practice constantly. Just another of her pieces of advice that is helpful to me."

Despite his light tone, her emotions grew, and she felt uneasy in a delightful way. Of all the women who attempted to draw his attention, did he find none tempting enough to show her any attention? And what did he mean by courting her properly? Other than conversation, dancing, walking together, some small gestures of affection, what else can there be? He already did all those things—and even more: he had kissed her, caressed her, and even untied her gowns—things that surely did not usually happen during a courtship.

"I cannot claim much experience either, but I see the wisdom in Lady Catherine's advice. I am no longer surprised that my cousin Mr. Collins holds her ladyship in such high esteem."

He let out a small laugh then gently caressed her hair. His hands cupped her face, and she closed her eyes, waiting to feel the warmth of his lips. His fingers touched her chin, and his thumb tenderly stroked her face, slowly brushing against her lips. Her lips parted slightly, and his finally pressed over them with small, interrupted kisses that travelled to her cheek then along her jaw while his fingers played with her hair. Barely aware, her lips moved to search his until they met and tantalised each other for a long time—more a search and discovery than a real kiss.

Her warm body leant against his as she stood on her toes. His delight combined with joy as he felt her responsiveness and sensed her shy attempt to return his caresses. With each moment and each heartbeat, she felt a little closer to him—a little more his. He finally withdrew a bit, and his lips came to rest on her hair.

"I believe breakfast is ready," he said, and she raised her eyes in surprise. She obviously did not expect the interruption.

"Yes—I shall go to see Georgiana afterwards." She felt embarrassed, both for their closeness and for the regret she felt that it was over so soon.

As Mrs. Annesley chose to have breakfast with Miss Darcy in her apartment, Elizabeth was again alone with her husband at the table. Breakfast proceeded calmly with more glances and fewer words. Elizabeth found herself looking pointedly at her husband's lips and his long fingers as he enjoyed his meal. The recollection of caresses eliminated most of her appetite while she forced to keep her eyes on her plate. What was happening to her?

Was she a silly girl, with wanton manners, to think of such outrageous things? And why was he staring at her—again? Surely, he could not possibly guess her thoughts! Or could he?

Elizabeth was rather relieved when the meal ended. Darcy returned to the library while she finally went to visit her sister-in-law, her heart a little steadier as she left his presence.

After all she discovered the previous night, Elizabeth's affection for Georgiana was doubled by a particular care and deep concern. She promised herself to watch her carefully and to understand the nature of Georgiana's present feelings for a certain unworthy man.

They spent an hour together. When she left, Elizabeth briefly wondered whether she should spend time with her husband or retire to her room. She did not feel composed enough to be alone with him again, so she returned to her apartment. She froze as she entered, then her heart raced while she stopped breathing.

On the small table, a bouquet of pink and cream roses brightened the room. She gasped in disbelief: How could there possibly be roses in the middle of winter?

She convinced herself that the flowers were quite real as she caught their fragrance. Then she spotted a note resting near the ceramic vase.

With emotion and curiosity, she took the paper and read:

Elizabeth, I thank you for a week in which I have started to understand the meaning of happiness.

FD

She read the words again and again then gently touched the roses with trembling fingers. Their petals were silky and soft, just as the caresses she still remembered. She took the bouquet in her arms and leant in the chair, closing her eyes for a few moments, enjoying the sense of overwhelming delight. Then she put the flowers back on the table and left the room in a hurry.

Early in the morning, together with his awareness that he had not offered enough attention to his wife since they married, Darcy considered how he might show his admiration and gratitude. He had nearly wasted the first seven days of his marriage by selfishly admiring his wife's efforts to adapt to her new life yet not providing the attention she deserved. He dismissed the thought of purchasing any more jewels, as she had been rather overwhelmed with what he had already given her.

The idea of a lively bouquet came to him the next instant, and he asked Stevens to locate a hothouse that could provide the flowers. He had never before thought of offering flowers in the middle of winter. When Stevens returned with an unexpectedly positive answer, he hurried to choose the flowers himself. He was tempted to buy a very large, impressive bouquet, but he kept his impulse under control and selected twenty roses, pink and cream, that seemed to express liveliness, elegance, delicacy and passion—to express *her*.

He returned home, keeping the flowers hidden until he determined Elizabeth's whereabouts, then went to place them in her chamber together with the note. He found himself as happy as a child and tried to imagine her joy after receiving the flowers.

Yes, the roses were lovely, but her sparkling eyes must be lovelier. He wondered what she would say and what she thought of the note, which he wrote in the blink of an eye—the first honest words that crossed his mind.

More than an hour passed before Elizabeth finally appeared. A large, bright smile rewarded him, and she stopped a few inches away, looking deeply into his eyes.

"Where did you find the flowers?" She smiled with emotion. "They are astonishing."

"It is surprising how easily one can find anything if one is interested and willing to put a little effort into it."

"Did you choose them yourself?" she asked, stepping a little forward.

"I did..."

There was silence for a moment, and her eyes gazed into his as both attempted to read each other's thoughts. Finally, she leant to whisper into his ear, her lips briefly touching his skin.

"I thank you, husband. We have started to learn the meaning of happiness together."

Then she turned and left him with a single glance.

His heart rushed as his lips became dry, and he closed his eyes to keep her fragrance. She did not even touch him, and her low voice, closeness, and intimate gesture of leaning towards him were enough to make him warm inside. He shook his head in disbelief: Did she know how much power she had over him? Did she know that her playfulness was more appealing to him than any seduction? Probably not—she was only being herself. And she was obviously pleased—even delighted with his gesture. And was she honest? Had she started to feel happiness at his side? Even a little would raise his hopes—and why did he doubt? She would surely not deceive him nor conceal her true feelings. And yes, her eyes sparkling with joy wore a trace of happiness.

How could he possibly have wasted the first days of his marriage? Such a fool he was!

Elizabeth turned to her room pleased, cheerful, and flustered.

He searched the Town to find flowers for me. Did I thank him properly? Does he understand my intention? Does he realise that I meant more than the mere words? Does he know how much I appreciated his effort? Such beautiful flowers in the middle of winter! And such an overwhelming note—only a few words that make my head spin.

Elizabeth recollected everything that had happened in the last day and night. The more she thought of the amazing events, the more she felt the need to think of them again, to balance the meaning of each word and each gesture. It was a turning point in her marriage, and she wished to be certain that she understood it correctly.

She heard a gentle knock and invited her husband to enter. He approached and glanced at the flowers then brushed his fingers over them.

"I am glad you like them."

"How could I not? They are beautiful—and so is the note. I have never received flowers before—from a gentleman, I mean. They are such a wonderful surprise."

"And I have never sent flowers to a lady before—outside my family."

She looked at him in disbelief, doubting his words. Yet, his slightly embarrassed expression was enough proof, and she did not inquire further. Another long moment followed, both staring into each other's eyes, tension building between them, neither daring to make a gesture yet hoping the other would.

Darcy fought a difficult battle between his desire to touch her, caress her, taste her half parted lips and the soft skin of her throat, which was moving with her every breath, and his fear and concern that any attempt at closeness, the smallest gesture of intimacy might appear as if he expected a reward for the flowers he offered her—and that was what he loathed more. So he stood as steel, recognising her emotions, hoping he saw an invitation in her eyes—even a desire for more intimacy between them—and wishing for her to make the smallest gesture towards him. She did not, and neither did he.

"We should start preparing. I would like to arrive there by the second comedy. Robert specifically insisted we not be late," he said, and she was obviously surprised.

"Oh… You are right, or course. I shall prepare myself carefully. I imagine we will be in the midst of gossip again." She tried to sound teasing but did not completely succeed.

"I will stay by your side. Please do not worry about anything."

"I do not…" She playfully stretched towards him then daringly placed a kiss on his cheek.

An hour later, Elizabeth glanced at her image in the mirror. She was wearing one of the new gowns, very light green with discreet darker shades. She looked at the boxes of jewels, wondering which would suit better. Although she struggled to put the thought away, she wondered whether they would meet Lady Stafford again at the opera.

She noticed the entrance of her husband. She smiled, thinking that he was impatient.

"I am ready, but I cannot decide which set I should wear."

He moved closer, his eyes travelling from her eyes down to her shoes, then up again.

"You look beautiful. Truly, you do not need any jewels, but since you must choose, I would suggest the citrine set. The stones will shine on your skin."

She felt flustered, held his gaze for a moment, and then laughed nervously. "And here we are again: I am staring at them for half an hour and you only need a moment to decide."

"Not really," he replied humorously. "I could have said the same about any set. They would all look beautiful on you. Please allow me," he said, and she had no time to reply before he moved to her back and slowly guided the necklace around her neck, locking it.

She felt her knees suddenly weakening, and she cast a quick look at their image in the mirror. He was so close to her that she could feel his breath on her neck but also the warmth of his body. His fingers ended the task rather quickly then brushed gently along the necklace and around her neck, slightly touching her skin. He then handed her the box, and she put on her earrings with trembling fingers, Darcy not moving an inch from her. Finally, he gently turned her to him, took her hand, and put the bracelet and then a kiss on her wrist. She gulped to remove the lump in her throat and said, "We should leave."

Yet, neither of them moved for a long moment, holding gazes and tentative smiles until Stevens announced that the carriage was ready.

Chapter 18

The night was freezing, and the sky was covered with stars. A bright moon lit the white streets. When they arrived in front of Covent Garden, the entrance as well as the street was more crowded than Elizabeth had ever seen before.

They entered the hall, his hand covered hers, and she looked around, attempting to discern a familiar face, but with little success. Her husband, though, seemed to be known by everyone, and greetings flew in from all directions.

The hall was full of people, voices, hurried steps, and laughter, and Elizabeth wondered whether there was anyone among the London *ton* who was not there that evening. A smile twisted her lips when she spotted Miss Bingley and the Hursts, staring at her.

A short distance away but heading towards them, Elizabeth saw James Darcy with Lady Stafford on his arm and in the close company of Lord Clayton, a gentleman whose excellent dancing skills and conversation Elizabeth remembered from the ball. Lady Stafford wore a large smile while her eyes seemed fixed upon the elder Darcy.

In an excellent mood, Elizabeth's reaction to this potentially distressing situation was unexpected even to herself. The first thing that crossed her mind was that such persistence, such unbreakable hope for persuasion she had only seen once: in her cousin Mr. Collins.

The comparison between Lady Stafford and Mr. Collins became so clear in her mind that, by the time the couple stopped in front of them, she had to bite her lips to restrain her laughter. She glanced at Darcy and met his worried expression, which she could not clearly interpret, but her amusement did not diminish in the slightest.

Lord Clayton greeted Darcy, then bowed elegantly to Elizabeth with a friendly smile while he expressed his delight in seeing her again and complimented her appearance.

Elizabeth curtseyed and thanked him, while a glance at her husband showed her how displeased he was.

"What an extraordinary surprise to meet you twice in two days," James Darcy exclaimed.

"Even more extraordinary," Lady Stafford said, "since Mrs. Darcy and I meet for the second time today! As I said earlier at Madame Claudette's, it must be fate that we keep happening upon each other."

"Three times in two days seems a rather *ordinary* happenstance," Elizabeth replied, trying to soften her sharpness with a proper smile. "And, considering that all of London seems to be here tonight, it is unfair to blame fate for an encounter that was likely to occur."

She knew Lady Stafford was disconcerted by her answer and felt her husband glancing at her. Her amusement increased.

"True," said James. "All London is here! Have you come alone? Where is Georgiana?"

"She is at home. We are supposed to meet the Fitzwilliams," Darcy answered, and Elizabeth noticed his attempt to remain calm. She well remembered his attitude at the Netherfield ball when Mr. Collins introduced himself to him. And there was Mr. Collins again in comparison, and she could not hold back the smile that spread across her face.

"Mrs. Darcy, you seem in excellent spirits, which only adds more charm to your beauty," Lord Clayton said.

"I thank you, sir. I am in excellent spirits indeed." She tightened her grip on Darcy's arm.

"Then I shall take advantage of this favourable moment and beg you to favour me with at least one set at the Twelfth Night ball," Lord Clayton continued, Elizabeth sensed her husband's arm tensing. Amused, she wondered whether he might be jealous, but that seemed to be an irrational presumption, so she replied with a proper smile.

"Your request flatters me, but there are still three days until the ball."

"True—but I could not take the risk of not enjoying the pleasure of dancing with you."

"Sir, I shall discuss it with my husband, and I can promise that I shall reserve one set for you—that is, if you do not find other ways to better amuse yourself at the ball. It is well known that *unmarried* young ladies should be taken care of first at such events."

"Well, I hope your husband will not see anything unfavourable in my request."

"I shall decide what is favourable for *my wife*, I assure you," Darcy intervened seriously.

"I ask for a set too. And I should be upset that you always make family plans that exclude me," James continued with equal seriousness and mockery. "Well, since I imagine you will not invite us to join you, I shall come later to say hello to the Fitzwilliam family."

"Now please excuse us, we are expected." Darcy took Elizabeth's arm and directed her towards another side of the hall. She could feel three pairs of eyes on her back.

Ever since he received the invitation to the opera, Darcy was aware of the likelihood of meeting Annabelle Stafford again and was resigned to that event. However, after the night of confession and Elizabeth's repeated assurance that she was comfortable, he expected things to go well. When they spotted Annabelle in the main hall, he had glanced at his wife, and he became puzzled by Elizabeth's obvious yet strange amusement. Her reply to Annabelle was so spirited and well aimed that his heart filled with pride in her. And then—his distress increased and turned to another object, as Lord Clayton's insistence and his impertinent attempt to secure at least a set from his wife irritated him. The effrontery of that man—to compliment his wife in such an obvious and improper manner and with such familiarity! Suddenly Annabelle became less of a problem than Clayton, and he considered whether he should approve Elizabeth's dancing with him or not. Would Elizabeth be displeased if he did not agree to the set? She seems at ease with that man's compliments. Oh, that was truly ridiculous—*he* was truly ridiculous to think such things!

"Lord Clayton is right—you seem in excellent spirits," he whispered to her.

"I am indeed, and—unlike Lord Clayton—you should know the reason." She smiled meaningfully. "And speaking of Lord Clayton—you seem not very pleased to meet him."

"I was not. He is not a man to be trusted. He is five years James's senior, but he is not wiser or more accountable in the slightest. And he is much too easy with the ladies."

He is jealous, she suddenly realised, and her smile widened.

"I can see that you are rather amused. Which one of the three is the reason?"

"Lady Stafford. Her insistence, her lack of reason, and her persistence in hearing only what pleases her reminded me of my cousin and his marriage proposal. I have rarely seen such a resemblance, I assure you. My father would enjoy this exceedingly."

Darcy stared at her in shock: such an explanation he would never have guessed. He glanced at Annabelle—who was still staring at them—then back to his wife.

"I must beg you to share with me more details about that event and help me see your point. However, the comparison of Annabelle and Mr. Collins is deeply disturbing from a certain point of view," he said, and she pressed her hand over her lips to suppress her laugh.

Darcy looked at his wife, bewitched. "You are never as beautiful as when your eyes are laughing, Mrs. Darcy. I would be a fool if I do not give you reasons for happiness every day."

They continued to walk, Darcy searching for their party and Elizabeth glancing around.

A moment later, they were unceremoniously stopped by Miss Bingley and the Hursts. While Elizabeth's amusement remained, Darcy's vexation increased dangerously as he recollected his fight with Elizabeth, caused by those women.

"Mr. Darcy, Miss Eliza, what a surprise to see you here!" Miss Bingley exclaimed.

"Of what 'Miss Eliza' are you speaking, Miss Bingley? I would surely be offended if you refer to my wife as 'Miss' *anything.*" Darcy's response left the sisters speechless.

"We apologise. I believe the surprise of seeing you distressed my sister." Mrs. Hurst recovered first.

"And pray tell me, why would you be so surprised? Is attending the opera an activity you believe to be unsuited for me or Mrs. Darcy?"

His harsh inquiry surprised not only the sisters but also Elizabeth. The former two needed another moment of silence to recover, and Elizabeth intervened with a polite smile.

"It is nice to see you again, although not quite a surprise. I am only sorry to see Mr. Bingley is still not with you. I would guess he has not returned to Town yet."

"No, he has not, and we do not expect him anytime soon. And what about dear Georgiana? Did she rather stay home and miss such an important spectacle?"

"Yes," Darcy said. "She decided to allow us an evening alone. Very thoughtful of her—I am proud to see how wise she is at such a young age."

Although she sympathised with Darcy and was amused by his subtle offences towards his *old and intimate friends*, Elizabeth chose to end the discussion properly.

"When Mr. Bingley returns, we will be pleased to have dinner together one evening."

"We do not expect my brother soon. However, I will come to see *dear Georgiana* one of these days."

Caroline Bingley's rudeness and conceited voice instantly repealed Elizabeth's good intention of a truce.

"That would be lovely, Miss Bingley, but please remember to send a card first. As I am in charge of everything regarding the household, it is my decision which visits I allow or not. I would not want you to come to the door and be forced to return with not even a cup of tea."

Miss Bingley's expression of repressed rage and her mouth gaping in disbelief were enough compensation for Elizabeth, and her gratification enhanced when her husband continued.

"And please choose the time of your future visits carefully. Mrs. Darcy and I are fond of our privacy, and we only share our time with close friends. Oh, and I almost forgot to mention: I wrote Charles a few days ago to apologise for my involvement in his leaving Hertfordshire. I recently realised my error, and I am now convinced that one must follow one's own heart when it comes to personal matters. Now please excuse us. My cousin is approaching."

Neither Miss Bingley nor Mrs. Hurst recovered enough to speak, despite the colonel's greeting, and they remained in dumbfounded silence until the Darcys departed.

A mere glance was enough for Elizabeth to share her deep satisfaction with her husband. Her cheeks were still coloured at his remark about their privacy.

They stopped near the group consisting of Thomas and Lady Maryanne, another couple—Mr. George Hasting and his wife, Lady Mary—and her sister, Lady Isabella Simmons.

Introductions were performed, and Elizabeth felt less uncomfortable than she expected.

"I met Mrs. Darcy at the ball two days ago, but I imagine she does not remember my name as she was introduced to fifty people that night," said Lady Isabella with friendly politeness.

"I do remember meeting you, Lady Isabella. I am pleased to make your acquaintance again as I am happy to meet Mr. Hasting and Lady Mary."

The gentlemen offered their arms to the ladies. In friendly conversation, they walked towards the Matlocks' box, which—Elizabeth was told—was right beside Darcy's. The party stopped as, at a small distance, there were Lady Stafford, James, a few other ladies and gentlemen, and Lord Clayton—who greeted with much friendliness the new addition to their group. Elizabeth found that Lord Clayton was first cousin to Lady Isabella and Lady Mary Hasting, and his manners proved their familiarity.

Darcy's arms tensed, and she looked at him. His countenance was dark.

"Cousin, you seem to choose your company very poorly lately," Lady Isabella said.

"Do not be rude, Isabella. I know you hate Lady Stafford, but it is not her fault that your uncle married her and left her his entire fortune. Well, at least not entirely her fault."

"I am glad we are all in such cheerful moods. Now let us enter," the colonel said impatiently.

A moment before they finally entered their box, Elizabeth was stunned to see Lady Stafford greet the group with a conceited and defiant smile.

"Mr. Darcy," she said, to everyone's disbelief, "I wish to remind you about your promise to call on me soon. Your help is invaluable in a matter of great importance to me."

Darcy's astonishment at Annabelle's impertinent words made him so furious that he could not breathe. Had the woman completely lost her mind? What was to be done with her? Was she unaware that she appeared ridiculous? Did she have no shame?

The struggle to control himself was so strenuous that his head seemed cut by a thousand knives. He felt Elizabeth's hand entwining his fingers then looked at the people around them. There was no longer a chance to ensure privacy.

He tightened the grip of his fingers against Elizabeth's as he addressed Annabelle calmly.

"Lady Stafford, I am sorry to hear that you have problems that need my assistance. I was just talking with my wife last night about *your past and future problems*. If they are of a difficult nature, you should detail them in a letter, and I will write back, recommending to you the best persons to help you solve them. Otherwise, I shall not have time to respond to any requests in the future, even *should* one *wait for me at my door in the middle of the night.* As a newly wedded man, all my free time is dedicated to my wife."

He glanced at Elizabeth while, from the corner of his eye, he could spot Annabelle's face—red with shock—and the astonishment of the rest of the party. He then saw Elizabeth's smile widen and her eyes narrow in preparation while she added:

"And Lady Stafford, if you do decide to write a letter, please direct it to me. That way you may be certain of receiving a proper reply. I am aware of all the *particularities* of this story, and I shall help Mr. Darcy to decide the best way of proceeding further. Indeed—as you said several times—it seems fortunate that fate had us meet again today and settle all aspects of the situation."

Shock twisted Annabelle Stafford's features, and Elizabeth could not avoid rejoicing in her success. Lord Clayton took Annabelle's arm and decidedly directed her to their party while James followed them, looking nothing but amused.

The size of the Fitzwilliam box, united with the Darcy's next to it, could easily accommodate 20 people, and Elizabeth's first thought was how happy she would be to invite Jane and her uncle and aunt to join them on another evening. The ladies were invited to sit in the front row of chairs to have a better view of the stage, while each gentleman sat behind his wife.

In the general din of the theatre—loud laughter, blatant voices and noisy conversations—there was a strange silence in their box as none seemed to find a proper subject for discussion. A couple of minutes later, Lady Isabella broke the tension.

"Mrs. Darcy, please allow me to tell you that you are my hero! If I had any puzzlement regarding why Darcy married you, it has long gone. You have my complete admiration."

Elizabeth laughed and thanked her. Her husband responded in a low voice, "I assure you, Lady Isabella, that you should rather be puzzled that I was fortunate enough to be accepted by Elizabeth. I do approve of your words, though."

"Well, I do, too," the colonel intervened, exceedingly lively. "I say, this night has already proved to be more entertaining than I expected. I feel quite well so far."

"You mean you are surprised to feel well, since you expected this night to be unpleasant and not entertaining? That is surely not a compliment to any of us," Lady Isabella said with a sharpness that confused the colonel and made Elizabeth let out a small laugh.

"I believe the colonel chose his words in a rather unfortunate manner. I must share a secret, Lady Isabella: this appears to be a family trait," Elizabeth whispered, and all three ladies chuckled while she wondered what the gentlemen were thinking behind them.

She felt her husband's gentle hand on her shoulder as he spoke so close to her ear that she was certain he had touched her skin.

"You are my hero too, Mrs. Darcy. Now please take the opera glasses. You may need them."

She shivered, and her heart raced. She looked around to conceal her nervousness and vaguely listened to the discussions of the ladies beside her and the gentlemen in the back row. She noticed Lady Stafford about six boxes away in a large group including James Darcy and Lord Clayton—watching her with insistent curiosity—and on the other side of the theatre, Miss Bingley and the Hursts with some companions.

Elizabeth smiled to herself as a daring, shocking and abominable thought—at which Jane would surely be appalled—crossed her mind. With a smile, she turned to her husband and spoke, leaning back towards him. "I am grateful for your care."

He seemed surprised but quickly took her hand and briefly kissed it. "It is my pleasure to take care of you. Although I know you rarely need it—as you just proved."

Elizabeth more felt than saw Lady Stafford and Miss Bingley staring perplexedly at their barely proper exchange. She knew she was behaving horribly, but somehow she felt deeply satisfied to exhibit the closeness that existed between her and her husband if only to harass the women who had stressed her. She blushed with embarrassment for her own childish behaviour, but she did not withdraw her hand from his until he eventually released it.

"So the main opera is about to start, and it seems it will be a long evening," the colonel said. "I need something to drink. How about you, Darcy? I noticed you already had your share of excitement. Miss Bingley seemed not fully recovered from the shock of your marriage, and she was not the only one." Darcy's severe look did not diminish his amusement.

"Oh, many people have not recovered from the shock of your marriage, Mr. Darcy—actually all unmarried ladies and perhaps some of the married ones, too," Lady Isabella added. "You should not be bothered by this reality. And I hope Mrs. Darcy knows how many people are watching her right now only to find something to criticise."

Elizabeth laughed. "I have been hearing that for the last few days, and I keep hoping it is a joke. I cannot believe that London society has nothing more interesting to speak about, and although I do recognise my husband's remarkable qualities," she said teasingly, glancing at him, "it is hard for me to believe that all the ladies in Town entertained the hope of marrying him and now are all heartbroken. This cannot be anything but a joke."

"Of course it is a joke," Darcy intervened severely. "I am fortunate to have a bright wife who does not take this nonsense seriously."

"Well, although I can heartily testify about Elizabeth's intelligence, regarding the other part I have a different opinion," Colonel Fitzwilliam continued.

"We should go and look for something to drink, and perhaps the ladies will find a more proper subject to discuss in our absence," Darcy suggested, disapproval clear in his voice.

The gentlemen left the box, and the ladies remained by themselves.

"I look forward to seeing the opera." Elizabeth began a different conversation.

"I confess I am not quite so fond of it, but it is an excellent way to spend time and meet people when there is no ball to attend," Lady Isabella replied.

"I do enjoy opera very much," Lady Maryanne intervened. "Elizabeth, but are you well? I am sorry you had to bear a most uncomfortable conversation."

"I am fine, I assure you," she said, smiling.

"Indeed, Mrs. Darcy, your elegant sharpness in dealing with *that certain* person was astonishing and quite singular. We all have to face such particular behaviours from some women regarding our husbands, I believe, but I could never be so courageous and composed," Lady Mary Hasting added.

"I find it astonishing that a woman can trick an old man like my uncle to marry her, and after she inherits his entire fortune, she now dares to chase Darcy around Town."

"However," Lady Maryanne said, leaning towards Elizabeth, "did Darcy really tell you about her? How extraordinary. Most men never speak to their wives about such matters. I know Thomas would never do so—even if I dared ask him. And I am no fool. I noticed he is sometimes very late coming home, But I do not care since his behaviour towards me is beyond reproach. One can hardly find as perfect a husband as Thomas."

"A woman should never ask her husband about such things unless she wants to face an upsetting answer," Lady Mary added.

"Forgive my boldness, but I also noticed that Mr. Darcy is very affectionate with you," Lady Isabella said. "I confess we always believed him to be a rather cold man. I was astounded to see him dancing with his own wife at Lady Matlock's ball. We never expected a breach of propriety from him."

Elizabeth blushed. "Mr. Darcy is an excellent man, though not very easy to read from afar."

"We all presume he possesses many qualities. It seems we in fact know very little of him."

Elizabeth became uncomfortable with the subject yet not at all displeased. Joy warmed her as she found that others also observed his solicitous behaviour towards her.

Just in time to interrupt the conversation, the heavy curtains that covered the entryway to the box were pulled aside, and the smiling faces of Lord Clayton and James Darcy appeared. They greeted the ladies then took seats, expressing their pleasure in continuing their previous conversation.

"Well, it was your friend that interrupted us. But that is no surprise. She is always ill-mannered."

"Isabella, you are rather ill-mannered too. What will Mrs. Darcy think of you and of us?"

"Well, she surely cannot think well of a man in your position who is in the close company of a woman with questionable manners."

"Oh come now, Annabelle Stafford is a lady—just like you." Lord Clayton laughed.

Lady Isabella cut him off with severity. "Do not even joke like that. Being a lady is not a matter of title or means but of breeding, education and character!"

"Based on your standards, half of the peers' titles should be withdrawn."

Elizabeth could not decide whether she was amused or annoyed by the conversation but she noticed that she missed her husband and glanced around in the hope of spotting him. Instead, her eyes saw Lady Stafford and Bingley's sisters once more, and she was content to feel no worry about either.

She startled when Lady Isabella called her name. "You must join us at Madame Claudette's the day after tomorrow, Mrs. Darcy. We are going to fetch our dresses for the ball and to chat a little. You cannot refuse us; it will be a very enchanting day!"

"I would like very much to keep you company," Elizabeth replied, considering it would be a good move for Mrs. Darcy to strengthen the acquaintance with three illustrious members of the *ton* who were near her age. They seemed pleasant enough and not at all standoffish.

"I look forward to the ball," Lady Mary Hasting declared.

"I too, especially that I shall have the pleasure of dancing with some exceptional ladies," Lord Clayton said, looking pointedly at Elizabeth.

Shortly afterwards, Darcy and the others returned, and Elizabeth immediately observed his displeasure at her talking to Lord Clayton. He resumed his seat near her.

"Clayton, James, what are doing here? Do you chase after our ladies? Were you infected with the bug from your female friend?" the colonel asked with sharp mockery.

"The interlude will end soon," Darcy said coldly, and the gentlemen finally left.

The opera started, yet Elizabeth felt restless as she could still sense her husband's tension. She turned her head over her shoulder. He noticed and leant towards her.

"Are you well?" he inquired.

"I am… I wished to know whether you are well…and to tell you your company was missed."

There was a little pause, then she felt his touch on her shoulder. "Thank you. Enjoy the performance."

The rest of the evening passed uneventfully. When the spectacle came to an end, Elizabeth was enchanted yet relieved.

In front of the theatre, waiting for their carriage, it had begun to snow again slowly, and while the other ladies remained inside protected from the cold, Elizabeth and Darcy moved out, taking a friendly farewell from their party with the promise of seeing them again soon.

"Did you have a pleasant evening?" he inquired, arranging her bonnet already coated with snow.

She was flustered by the cold air and his caring gesture and wondered whether *the others* could see them.

"Very pleasant. But I never felt an evening at the theatre to be so tiresome although I have attended many performances with my relatives."

To their surprise, James approached them with a slightly uneasy countenance.

"Cousin, may I call on you tomorrow? There is something I would like to discuss."

Darcy glanced at Elizabeth. "Yes, of course. I shall wait on you around noon."

"Excellent! Good night, Mrs. Darcy. It was lovely to see you again."

After they entered their carriage, Elizabeth breathed in relief, looking at Darcy.

"I would say we made an excellent team tonight. I think neither of the ladies who seek your attention is fully recovered yet."

"We did—and that was to your merit. I was afraid you would disapprove my replying to Annabelle in public, but I believe it was the best approach. She certainly took it more seriously than any harsh private discussion. It might be the right way to treat her." He gazed at her and laughed. "Lady Isabella said you are her hero. That was true yet amusing."

"More amusing than true. I am glad we confronted Lady Stafford rather than avoided her. As for Miss Bingley and Mrs. Hurst—I so sorry to say that I have rarely felt so deeply satisfied. They are just…so different from Mr. Bingley."

"Your feelings are legitimate. What of the ladies who were in our party?"

"I truly enjoyed their company. Lady Isabella seemed to favour Robert."

"You are very perceptive. She would be a very good match for him."

"When we were alone, the ladies expressed their astonishment that I took the situation with Lady Stafford so calmly…and that you had told me about it…and that you broke the rules by dancing with me…and that you were not as cold in manners as they believed you to be." With each word, her eyes became brighter and his smile widened.

"I enjoy breaking the rules for you," he replied hoarsely, and she shivered.

Both became more aware that they would soon be home, alone in their suite. Elizabeth looked at her husband, struggling to bear his intense gaze. She felt her lips suddenly dry, and she licked them, blushing as she noticed his eyes lowering to them. She could almost feel his touch on her lips and averted her eyes, shivering again.

Opposite his wife, Darcy could not keep his eyes from her. The carriage seemed too small. He only needed to stretch his hand to reach her, to embrace her, to taste her moist lips.

The entire evening he had been proud of how easily she adapted to that din, admiring the elegance with which she dealt with Annabelle and Bingley's sisters, establishing her position, and overthrowing the attacks of those who dared to defy her while showing her impeccable manners and the strength of her character.

It was obvious that several others admired Elizabeth too, especially Lord Clayton, who annoyed Darcy exceedingly. *The effrontery of the man! Returning to our box and taking advantage of the ladies being alone! Surely, he was there to insinuate himself in Elizabeth's company. What did he imagine he could gain? He could not possibly hope for any special attention from her!*

He immediately realised his own absurdity. He had no reason for concern. She was there in front of him, smiling and slightly nervous. During the evening, she told him he was missed, and she obviously welcomed his attentions. And now they would soon be home—alone.

He followed her eyes out of the window: it was snowing beautifully, and she seemed enchanted. On a whim, he knocked for the coachman to stop and smiled at her.

"We are a few minutes from home. Would you like to walk back?"

Her eyes brightened, and her face lit with delight. He opened the carriage and helped her out then signed to the dumbstruck coachman to drive towards the house.

The street was empty, covered in soft whiteness, a few lamps glowing through the heavy curtain.

Elizabeth clung tightly to her husband's arm, laughing each time her shoes slipped. Snowflakes rested on her face, her eyelashes, and her hair. Her face was red from the cold and bright with joy. When they were almost home, she claimed she was not cold at all and begged him to go through Hyde Park a little longer. He was reluctant, as it was very late and cold, but incapable of refusing her, so they walked through the frozen streets for another half hour, staying in view of their house.

Elizabeth found great pleasure in touching the fresh snow, walking through it and brushing her husband's coat at times. Darcy found great pleasure in admiring her and sharing her liveliness. With each moment, their intimacy was enhanced in the midst of the large park.

Finally, her shoes heavy with snow, her petticoat frozen and stiff around her feet, and her bonnet and gloves wet and cold, Elizabeth declared it was time to return home, laughing at his obvious relief. She took his arm again as he removed her gloves and covered her hands in his. This time, his gesture was expected and welcomed, and she entwined her fingers warming in his palm, thanking him with a brief look. Holding her hands and watching her flushed face, Darcy wondered how long he would be able to contain the desire to kiss her frozen cheeks and red lips.

It took only a few minutes for them to enter the house, and he immediately took off his coat then removed hers and the bonnet, hurrying upstairs. He ordered that hot tea be sent to their room while he fetched his valet and her maid.

"The servants will believe we have lost our minds." She laughed as she took his arm again and her shoes and dress, beginning to thaw, became heavy to wear.

Inside Elizabeth's chamber, Lucky ran to them but, as he felt their cold, wet clothes, moved back.

"You should change your clothes immediately, and Molly will bring you hot water. We do not want this evening to end badly," he said, brushing drops of water from her hair.

"I promise I will change immediately." She wanted to ask whether they would speak again later, but Molly knocked and was invited in. Darcy left the room and closed the door.

Inside his own apartment, his valet helped him change then poured him a glass of brandy. Within a few minutes, Darcy was settled in nightshirt and robe, comfortable in his armchair, wondering what Elizabeth was doing.

He waited a few minutes then knocked. Elizabeth, in nightgown and robe, was in the middle of the bed. Her hair fell loose on her shoulders, and her knees, wrapped in her arms, were held to her chest. Her face coloured from warmth, her eyes laughing at him.

He sat at the edge of the bed, and Molly left immediately.

"You are still frozen," he said reproachfully.

"A little. Molly will return soon with hot tea and something to eat. I hope you will join me. And she promised to bring me some hot water, too," she said while rubbing her red and wrinkled feet. Her hair was slightly wet on her temple, and he brushed his fingers over it.

After knocking on the door, Molly brought a tray, put it on the table, and retired quickly.

"Wrap the blankets around you," he said, preparing her a cup of hot tea. He took one himself, staying on the bed facing her. She sipped the tea as they gazed at each other.

"That is much better! William, this evening was so wonderful! Thank you."

The joy was easy to hear in her voice and to see in her smile and in her eyes. On the small table, the bouquet of roses was smiling at them.

"This was a happy day—and a wonderful evening—and I hope it will be only the beginning. Please remember: I just started courting you."

She laughed, and he leant to briefly kiss her cheeks then poured her another cup of tea.

"Now, Mrs. Darcy, how are your feet?"

"Much better, thank you." A moment later, she frowned and almost dropped the cup as he slowly removed the blankets, brushing his fingers over her feet.

"They are still very cold and red. I shall order thick winter boots and coats for you," he said in earnest, and she laughed nervously, trembling but not from cold. "Now, please let me."

Without waiting for her acceptance, his fingers gently touched her toes, her ankles, her heels, and then held her feet in his palms, rubbing them gently.

She put down the cup and pressed her hands together, her heart racing. His fingers burned her skin, and each of his touches seemed to run from her feet and spread cold shivers inside her body while she was suddenly too warm. His palms cupped her heels as his fingers brushed along her foot. A moan escaped her lips, and his movements stopped, his eyes searching her face. She closed her eyes and leant against the pillows, and he smiled with contentment then resumed his caresses. It did not take long before his fingers felt differently, and Elizabeth bit her lips, not daring to move. His caresses shifted to her ankles, and then his palms covered her feet.

"Is it better now?" he asked in a low voice, and she needed a moment to realise he was talking to her. She opened her eyes and nodded, and his gaze held hers.

Slowly, he moved closer, his hands a little higher along her legs. Then he cupped her face, caressing her cheeks. He carefully searched her eyes for a sign of her wishes, then his lips brushed over hers. He withdrew a bit and searched her eyes again.

Elizabeth hesitated a moment, then her hands shyly encircled his neck.

He felt her lips tentatively touching his. One hand glided up her back while the other gently removed the blanket from her then entwined in her hair. He could feel her warm body close to his, and without thinking much, he climbed into the bed, leaning near her and looking at her once again. Her eyes were sparkling in a way he did not fail to recognise. He lowered his head and greedily captured her half-opened mouth, allowing himself to enjoy the flavour for which he longed.

The kiss started as sweetly as Elizabeth expected, and her heart skipped a beat when he lay near her. His lips were soft, warm and moist, and her own lips parted to welcome his growing passion. This kiss, though gentle and tender, was nothing like yesterday's, but it became bolder, even demanding. The shock of his tongue testing, parting, and conquering her lips shattered her body, and she let out a moan that seemed to increase his eagerness. She gasped and froze momentarily when she felt his tongue slipping inside, taking possession of her mouth. She tensed, almost frightened by such an intimate gesture and by the novelty of sensations engulfing her, trying to respond but not knowing how. His mouth left hers for a moment, and his lips traced countless small kisses over her face before returning to her mouth, resuming the sweet assault that found her breathless.

She lay against the pillows, and his body slowly moved closer, pressing against hers until he almost covered her, while his weight took her breath away completely. She struggled for air with no success, and she attempted to turn her head a little, but his eager lips refused to abandon hers. She moaned again when his right hand travelled lower, caressing her through the soft fabric.

Her head was spinning, and she shivered violently, unable to think. She gathered strength enough to push him a little and to whisper, "William, stop… Please, stop!" she said louder, and the next moment, Lucky was by the bed, barking loudly as a warning.

Darcy frowned as though awakened from a dream and rolled away, attempting to regain his control as he withdrew his hands from her. Lucky continued to bark at him and did not cease at Darcy's request until Elizabeth, finally able to breathe, sent him to his place.

She dared a glance at her husband who, pale and troubled, departed from the bed in haste.

"William, please do not leave," she managed to say.

"I am sorry. I completely lost myself. I apologise for behaving like a savage…"

"There is no need to go or to apologise. I just..."

It was too late, though, as the door had already closed behind him.

Elizabeth stared ahead, trying to regain her breathing and clear her mind. How much time had passed since he entered her room? A few minutes—an hour? She had completely lost track of time and of her own thoughts. Her lips still carried his taste while her feet were still burning from his touches. How could he leave that way? She did not want him to leave, but he did not even give her time to explain! She brushed her fingers over her lips and closed her eyes, recollecting the sensations which already seemed unreal. How could he just leave her there, with not a single glance?

And what was he doing now? She glanced at Lucky, who sat near the bed, watching her carefully. "Do not worry. All is fine, my friend. I am not in danger," she said, caressing his head. Lucky almost bit him. Was he upset? What was she to do now? Her mind was still troubled and her skin quivered while a hole of ice tightened her stomach. Only her feet were warm.

Molly returned with another servant, bringing a kettle of boiling water. She impatiently washed in haste and changed her nightgown. She became restless and irritated and kept asking herself what he was doing. While Molly settled things for the night, Elizabeth pulled the robe around her and knocked on his door, entering without an invitation.

Darcy had just washed too and was changing his clothes. He was wearing only his trousers, and she stopped in the deepest embarrassment at the image of his bare torso. His surprise was no less, and he hurriedly put a robe on.

She gathered her courage and stepped forward, addressing the valet.

"Stevens, please be so kind as to leave us a moment. I need to speak to Mr. Darcy privately."

The servant immediately obeyed, and silence fell upon the room. He tied the robe closed, and she could not help staring at him.

"Elizabeth, is anything wrong? I hope you can forgive me for that—"

"Oh, please stop. I came to speak not to listen." Her voice was so sharp that it surprised both of them. He looked at her wordlessly, and she needed time to pull her thoughts together.

"You are always in hurry to leave before I have time to speak my mind. I find this to be a very unpleasant habit, if I may be so bold as to say so. It was not my intention to push you away. I only wished you to stop for a moment. I never expected a kiss to be so... I could not breathe, and I did not know what to do. And then you left. You behave very strangely when we are alone. I do not know what *you* want, and that confuses me about what *I* want! You are a very annoying man sometimes, truly! This is so infuriating. I hope you are pleased that I just made a fool of myself!" She was tearful from distress and annoyed to see him staring at her so stupidly.

She left his room and slammed the door behind her, and both Molly and Lucky looked at her with curiosity and concern. She then sat in front of her mirror and started to brush her hair. *Hateful man, indeed!*

Darcy remained motionless in the middle of his room. He had left her chamber half an hour earlier, ashamed and angry with himself for allowing his weakness to control his reason. He had been so intoxicated by her beauty, so enchanted by everything that happened that day and evening that the moment his hands touched her skin, warming her feet, he could think of little else except wanting more. He saw and felt her acceptance, heard her soft moans, noted her beautiful eyes darkening, felt her lips opening for him, and her body slightly moving beneath his… He did not intend to go further than kisses and caresses that evening, but he did that with such savage haste that he frightened her—so she cried and begged him to stop. Instead of her enjoying the delight of their new intimacy, she was surprised by what seemed to be more an attack than a passionate mutual discovery.

The moment he left her room, he struggled to return and to apologise again, but what was to be said? How could he explain the feelings he struggled to overcome for more than three months, the passion he tried to control, or the desire and urges he worked to suppress?

As the fool he was, he waited too long, and she came to him with a most astonishing reproach, angry and embarrassed, more beautiful than ever—and again he stood like a dolt, struggling to comprehend the meaning of her words. When he finally understood, he opened the door without knocking. Elizabeth avoided his gaze, brushing her hair with increased diligence.

"Molly, will you please leave now. You may retire for the night. Mrs. Darcy will not need your services," he said, his eyes still on his wife.

Darcy stepped closer and stopped at the back of her chair. He put his hands on her shoulders then slowly urged her to stand. He cupped her face with strong, warm palms so she would meet his eyes. He was worried because she was still irritated.

"Elizabeth, I do not remember a task more daunting than keeping my promise to you. And I have never been so tempted to break the promise I made. That is why I left while I still have a shred of reason. I did not trust myself to stay a moment longer because my desire for you almost overcomes my self-control. Yet I do not want to force your decision in any way. I may behave foolishly, and my only excuse might be that it is the first time in my life that I have faced such a struggle. Please believe me that your well-being, your comfort, and your feelings are more important to me than my own, and that makes my struggle even more difficult. And that is why I keep apologising like a fool."

"Oh…" she whispered, astounded. Such a profession she did not expect, and while her face, neck and ears were burning from embarrassment, she daringly held his troubled gaze. She sat on the bed, as her knees suddenly weakened, and stretched her hand to him in a silent invitation. He stood by her, and she spoke hesitantly.

"William…I am not certain of my feelings or my desires, as this is the first time in my life that I must face such a struggle." She smiled with distress as she mirrored his words. "And I am not ready to release you from your promise just now, this moment…but this entire day—from early morning until now in the middle of the night—has brought me such joy and happiness as I have never felt before. I enjoy your company…very much…and when you left, I felt cold and lonely."

"I hoped for a long time that one day you would feel cold and lonely without me," he said hoarsely. Their lips almost met once more when Lucky jumped on the bed, attempting to slink near Elizabeth, uncertain what was happening. Elizabeth sent him to his place, but the dog sniffed and moved even closer to her. Instead of sharing a passionate kiss, Elizabeth burst out in laughter, and Darcy soon joined her.

Their foreheads touched and their arms entwined in an embrace as their laughter continued.

Finally, Elizabeth found a compromise solution: she pulled the sheets apart and commanded Lucky to sleep at her feet, which he reluctantly accepted. She then slowly leant back against the pillows, and her eyes spoke clearly to her husband. He stretched near her and remained still, and they were so close that their faces almost touched.

"I shall stay until you ask me to leave, and I shall not leave until I am certain it is what you wish."

"As always, your plan seems excellent," she replied, her voice slightly trembling.

They gazed at each other, and his hand tentatively caressed her hair. Her hand reached for his, and their fingers entwined.

"We should teach Lucky to sleep in the next room," he said, and she laughed again.

"He only attempted to protect me since he did not know what happened either. But he will become accustomed to what is happening… He is calm when I am."

"I am glad to hear you are calm now…"

"I did not say that—not at all. I am trying to become accustomed to what is happening too."

His fingers traced a gentle caress on her temple, her cheeks, the delicate line of her jaw, and her chin and then brushed lightly over her lips.

"I am not calm either—quite the contrary. Your closeness makes me happy—and nervous. You are so very beautiful," he whispered.

Tentatively, she started to mirror his moves, caressing his face just as he did. When her fingers reached his mouth, he held and kissed each of them. She shivered and closed her eyes, waiting. But the kiss she expected did not come. Instead, she felt his caresses move down to her throat and her shoulders, burning each spot that was not covered by her nightgown. His fingers were brushing her bare skin so gently that she wondered whether he was touching her or she was merely dreaming it. She opened her eyes and met his dark gaze then closed them again. She felt his fingers returning to her hair while his lips finally claimed hers—soft and gentle. Her hands lowered from his face to his neck, and his fingers slid the length of her bare arms up to her shoulders, her neck, and then back to her hair. His kiss grew more insistent, but his caresses remained gentle and patient.

With tender movements, barely touching the soft fabric of her gown, his hand moved along her body, exploring every spot of uncovered skin—and encircled her waist for a moment. She moaned as her lips parted, welcoming the kiss that became more passionate, eager, and demanding. Her heart nearly stopped when his fingers, gliding up along her ribs, touched the sides of her breasts. She tensed, and he could feel it, so he broke the kiss, looking at her, yet his hand remained on the same spot. She slightly opened her eyes and met his, then she moaned again when his fingers moved gently, tentatively, brushing against the spot where her heart was beating and burning her through the thin silk. She called his name, and he stilled his hand, but her mouth turned to seek his. Before he claimed her lips again, he whispered hoarsely.

"We will also learn the meaning of passion and desire together, *my love.*"

His words troubled her in a way she could not comprehend as her mind was unable to reach anything but the overwhelming feeling of his caresses. She intended to ask more, but her mouth was trapped, and she completely surrendered to the new kiss, wondering how it was possible to be so different each time. Her hands found their way into his hair while her heart raced so wildly that she was certain his fingers could feel it. Even she could hear the beats of her heart more powerfully than ever before. She needed a few long moments and her husband withdrawing to realise it was not her heart but a strong, determined knock on the door followed by Stevens' voice calling for his master.

Chapter 19

London, 3 January, night

Darcy pulled slightly away from Elizabeth and looked at her beautiful, flushed face, her long eyelashes trembling on her still closed lids, and her lips half parted, red and swollen from his kisses. The nightgown was slightly lowered from her shoulders, now covered only by her long, heavy locks, spread over the pillow.

He placed small kisses on her face while he rested near her a moment longer. "If something really dramatic has not occurred, it will now, as I shall kill Stevens. I will return shortly," he whispered against her temple, and she released a laugh while trying to breathe steadily.

She heard Stevens speaking with distress through the half open door.

"Everything is in the letter, sir. The messenger is waiting for your answer. It seems the fire destroyed the houses of two families of tenants and—"

"Stevens, I shall read it for myself. Go and give the man some warm food."

Shortly after, Darcy returned to sit near Elizabeth while he started reading the letter.

"A fire started on the Box Hill estate last night. Nobody was badly injured, but two households are entirely ruined, and two families are without shelter in the middle of the winter. Mr. Gordon, my steward, informs me the families have been hosted in the manor and he asks for my instructions."

He glanced at her then stood and walked about the room. "Thank the Lord nobody was hurt… I wonder what caused it. Could there be a problem with the houses—with the chimneys? Could other families be in danger?"

"William, calm yourself. There is not much you can do from here."

"True, I cannot do much from here. I shall write Mr. Gordon and instruct him. I am rather displeased that I do not have enough details. There are still so many questions and—"

"Has anything like this happened before? Is there something that can be done?"

"It happened two years ago in Newcastle, in October. Many of the crops of three families were ruined. It seemed it was the fault of some workers who made a fire in an open field. We managed to rebuild the damaged houses before winter came. It was easier to handle as I was there."

His agitation was obvious, and Elizabeth could do little but touch his arm in comfort. He smiled and kissed her hand. "I am sorry for this upheaval. You should go and rest now."

"Please do not say that, William. I could not sleep when you must face such a distressing situation."

"Forgive me—I shall go change and then speak with the messenger. I shall return shortly."

Elizabeth arranged her appearance, still wearing a trace of their shared passion. It was long past midnight, yet her concern kept her alert until he finally returned half an hour later.

Before she had time to ask anything, he took her hands in his. "Elizabeth, I must go to Box Hill to see the situation for myself. I know I have promised to spend more time with you, but I need to go. I hope you are not upset…"

"I am not upset, but do you have to leave in the middle of the night in such weather?"

"If the messenger managed to reach London and return, I can do the same. You must not worry. But I am reluctant to leave you and Georgiana alone. I shall send word to Robert…"

"You have no reason for concern for us. We shall be together in a house filled with servants, and Mrs. Annesley is here too. Everything will be fine. You should worry only about what you have to accomplish and the long road ahead of you. I will take care of Georgiana."

"Please, promise you will not leave the house unchaperoned. If you need anything, you should send a servant. I must take Stevens with me, but the rest will be at your disposal."

"I will not leave the house alone, I promise." She caressed his distressed face. "Why are you so troubled about this? Is it not true that you have been on journeys many times before and left Georgiana only with Mrs. Annesley? Now we shall be together."

"It is true," he admitted, wondering why indeed he was more concerned and heavyhearted at this departure than any others.

Within half an hour, one large valise was packed, together with some food and drink, and Stevens took them to the carriage.

Elizabeth walked after her husband, feeling as useless as Lucky and Titan, who ran between his legs, sensing the distressful situation.

"I will not stay a moment longer than is necessary. Once I evaluate the situation and take proper measures, I shall return without delay."

"Travel as safely as you can."

He kissed her hands, and with a long gaze, he left the room. Elizabeth ran to the window, watching the snow falling heavily, the carriage waiting…

Then the door opened again, and he hurried to embrace her painfully tightly while he kissed her with an urgency that seemed desperate. There was neither tenderness nor passion in his kiss, only shared worry that left her cold and lonely in the middle of the room when he left.

The night passed unbearably slowly while Elizabeth remained at the window, suddenly angry with the snow that continued to fall. Only a few hours earlier, she loved it, and she thought that walking in the park on the arm of her husband was the loveliest thing. Now it was just another reason to worry for his safety—among many other dangerous threats on the roads in the middle of the night.

It was unbelievable that a man in his situation in life should abandon his comfort and safety to attend the well-being of others. And that man was her husband!

Unsettled, a cold hole in her stomach, she looked at the roses on the table. It seemed such a long time since he offered them to her, yet it was only that early morning.

The revelation that struck her was that he had been gone for so little time and she missed him already. She was more concerned for his departure than she remembered being for the members of her own family. The second revelation came in the blink of an eye: he *was* her family now!

Her thoughts followed him along the road, and she took her diary and wrote down all that was in her mind and in her heart until she finally fell asleep. It was just as the household awoke at dawn.

London, 4 January

First thing next morning, Elizabeth visited Janey and her little girl—whose improvement was significant. She spent half an hour with them while Lucky and Titan—who had kept after Elizabeth—anxiously invited Peter to play.

As Georgiana was still in her room, Elizabeth decided to have breakfast with her and Mrs. Annesley. The news of the tragic incident and her brother having to leave worried Georgiana exceedingly. They shared concerns and hopes for a positive outcome, and Elizabeth wondered whether she should take the opportunity to raise the subject of Mr. Wickham. However, with Mrs. Annesley there and Georgiana already distressed, she decided to postpone the conversation.

On a happier note, Elizabeth told them about the opera, not speaking of Lady Stafford and briefly mentioning their meeting with Miss Bingley and Mrs. Hurst.

Breakfast was long finished, and the conversation had turned lighter when Miss Darcy's maid announced that Mr. James Darcy had arrived to meet the master.

Elizabeth was tempted to dismiss him with an apology and an invitation to return in a few days—then she suddenly changed her mind and asked that the guest be shown to the drawing room.

"Mrs. Darcy—I thank you for receiving me. I was told my cousin is not at home."

"Good day, sir. Indeed, Mr. Darcy was summoned away urgently. There was a fire at Box Hill, and he had to leave in the middle of the night."

"I see…then I do not want to disturb you. I shall come another time."

"If you are in no hurry, it would be my pleasure for us to have a drink together."

He seemed uncertain of how to respond then accepted and asked for a glass of brandy.

"So, Darcy left for Box Hill… It surely will be a difficult journey in the middle of this winter."

"Most certainly. But he thought his presence was needed, and he put others' problems before his comfort. I see he tends to do that."

"Yes, he was always very diligent with his duties," James said.

"One must be very diligent if one has to manage so many estates. I know only a few details about my husband's business, and I can imagine how difficult it must be for him. It is my goal to support and help him in any way I can. He will surely be more at peace once you take the management of your properties. I am sure you look forward to it."

"Yes…I look forward to not depending on anyone for my decisions—who would not be?"

"Indeed. It must be a matter of pride for a gentleman to use his mind and education to influence the life of many others and to prove himself worthy of his family inheritance."

She smiled charmingly while enjoying her tea. Her companion finished his brandy in one gulp.

"Some of us are not very skilful in managing business. We can only try to do our best."

"Perhaps. But where there is not enough skill, one can compensate with harder work and a willingness to learn, especially if one has an interest in the subject. I am hardly as talented at the piano as Georgiana, and until now, I had not given it much consideration. However, in my present position, I understand I have new responsibilities, and I must practice more. I am sure my husband would be happy to support you. He seems very fond of you."

"I am sure he would," James replied, growing uneasy. "I am very fond of him too, and I have admired Darcy since we were children. He always had the highest expectations of himself and of others, but sometimes people around him cannot meet his goals."

"That must be true, but I wonder: Is he allowed the luxury of not rising to those expectations? Can he afford to abandon his duties? If tomorrow he decides things are too hard to accomplish and retires to Pemberley, enjoying the benefits of his fortune and cutting off any distressing connections, is there anyone to take over his responsibilities?"

"I am not certain how to answer. We have always counted on his industry."

"We all do, it seems. However, perhaps things will change in time. I have only been near him a few days, and I find his knowledge quite fascinating. I can imagine how exciting it must be for a young gentleman, smart and educated like you, to learn the secrets of success from an older cousin."

"Indeed, Mrs. Darcy. I shall not detain you any longer. I thank you for this delightful conversation and hope to meet again very soon—perhaps at the ball in two days' time?"

"It was a pleasure to speak to you, sir. You are always welcome in your cousin's home."

"Mrs. Darcy... do you know whether my cousin is upset with me? We are very different and always will be, and we have had some differences, and—"

"I know that my husband is fond of you. Any other subject you should discuss with him."

"You are right, of course. I will." He took a few steps and stopped again. "I apologise for my improper behaviour when we first met. Now that I come to know you better, I can see how inappropriate my jokes have been."

"It is fine, sir. If one learns from one's own errors, that is always a praiseworthy trait."

He mumbled something and left, bowing again, while Elizabeth promised she would inform Mr. Darcy of his visit. Once alone, she felt lighthearted and rather satisfied. She did not break her husband's confidence nor actually tell James anything, but she implied more than enough to make him feel the scolding and understand her reproaches.

The rest of the day, Elizabeth read in the library—joined by Libby, Peter and both dogs. The children read diligently though Elizabeth noticed they were more preoccupied with the dogs that lay at their feet. A note from Lady Maryanne reminded her of their visit to the modiste the next day. Under the present circumstances, her interest in the event was lost, but spending time with ladies of her age would surely make the time pass easier.

During the afternoon, Elizabeth spent another half hour looking at the paintings, recollecting the first time she entered the house nine days earlier. So many things had happened since then, so many things she had discovered about the man whom she reluctantly married and about whose character she knew so little. She still had much to learn before sketching him completely—the man who had left the day before and whose absence she felt most vividly.

The night was no better. She rested less and more poorly than the previous one. Lucky seemed unsettled and distressed, and so was Titan—who barked at the adjoined door until Elizabeth opened it and invited him in. Some time was needed before the dogs fell asleep, and Elizabeth remained alert much longer.

She again went through each moment she and her husband spent together since they first met, the day he came to propose, then the time they shared after the wedding, and then last night when they were closer to each other than she could ever have imagined.

If he had not been forced to leave, that night might have ended differently. She blushed as she dared to wonder how it would have been if there had been *more*… and what would happen when he returned. Would he still keep his promise? Did she wish for him to keep his promise? Was she willing to deny him something that he confessed he desired and longed for so much?

Was it truly the first time that he was so passionate about a woman? About her? Or perhaps it was only the strong temptation of something that he wished for and could not have. Surely, other women with whom he had shared intimate moments had not refused him anything. Would he lose interest in her after *things* happened, as they should have more than a week ago? And was she able to offer him what he seemed to fantasise about?

She was not ignorant of what a woman and a man shared within a marriage. Her aunt had approached the subject with both her and Jane delicately and seriously. She trusted her aunt that a wife could enjoy the marriage bed as much as her husband did.

Regardless of what she knew, those small interludes with her husband, his embraces, his touches, his kisses, and the moments from last night—of which her mind was so full that it still made her quiver—were different from what she imagined. She had been told and shown in pictures what was supposed to happen, but she had not been warned of what she was supposed to *feel*. By morning, she realised she would by no means oppose becoming his wife as soon as he returned.

London, 5 January

A strong, bright sun was lightening the day, and the snow had finally stopped.

Georgiana and Mrs. Annesley joined Elizabeth for breakfast and declared they would keep her company to Madame Claudette's.

"To be honest, I would rather take a short stroll in the park. I have not much interest in getting the dresses today as we will likely not attend the ball. I doubt William will return by tomorrow, and if he does, he must be very tired from the road."

"But the dresses will be useful anyway. There will be other balls soon," Georgiana said.

"You are correct, of course," Elizabeth agreed with a large smile.

"Mrs. Darcy, I meant to ask you: Did you receive your letter a couple of days ago? I found it when I searched for Miss Darcy's correspondence, and I put it in your apartment."

Elizabeth looked at Mrs. Annesley with no little surprise.

"Yes… I was wondering who brought the letter; Molly knew nothing of it."

"I hope I did not do wrong. You were with Mr. Darcy in the library and—"

"It is fine," Elizabeth said. Mrs. Annesley little knew how her genuine error unleashed a succession of dramatic confessions, which most likely had changed the life of both her and her husband. How easily the mystery of the letter was solved!

The morning passed away, and around two in the afternoon, they left for the modiste.

Lady Mary, Lady Isabella and Lady Maryanne were already there, having tea and sweets and chatting animatedly. With a slight pettishness, Elizabeth observed that the ladies were accompanied by Mr. Hasting and Lord Clayton. The presence of the gentlemen on such a private visit made her uneasy, and Georgiana must have felt the same as she kept glancing out the window.

"How long will this last?" Mr. Hasting asked. "I must have been deranged to be persuaded to come here. I'd rather see ladies' gowns in their proper environment."

"Well, I know my husband would not have come," Lady Maryanne said with a smile.

"Neither has Darcy, as I see," Lord Clayton said, and Elizabeth frowned.

"My husband had to leave for Box Hill two days ago. There were some important problems there that needed his immediate attention," she answered.

"What problems could force him to travel in such weather?" Lord Clayton asked.

"How was it possible for Mr. Darcy to leave just before the ball," Lady Isabella continued. "What if he does not return in time? Surely, you cannot miss the Twelfth Night ball. Everyone who means anything in London will be there."

"I do not believe Mr. Darcy considered the ball when he decided to leave—nor the bad weather. I am very proud that he put comfort and enjoyment below his duties," Elizabeth replied rather sharply, realising that a stroll in the park would have been more pleasant than this gathering.

"Perhaps, but still—what if problems occur at each of his estates? He cannot be on the road all the time!" Mr. Hasting said, puzzled.

"Let us hope and pray that will not happen." Elizabeth smiled politely, considering again that her husband had a different sense of responsibility than people from his own circle.

"Well, since you gentlemen are here, you must give us your opinions about the dresses. We will show them to you as we try them on," Lady Mary said, and Lord Clayton approved energetically.

Elizabeth's patience slowly evaporated. Fortunately, a shop girl invited each of them into separate rooms. She tried on two gowns—the dress for the ball and another for frequent use—and she felt happy with her own image in the mirror. She wondered what her husband would say when he saw her and which set of jewels he would recommend. Perhaps he would again put the necklace around her neck and—

"Mrs. Darcy, is everything all right?"

Elizabeth startled and smiled at the shop girl. "Yes, perfect, thank you."

The girl changed her back into her morning gown, and Elizabeth returned to the others.

"Mrs. Darcy, is there any problem with the dresses?" Lady Isabella asked, proudly wearing a beautiful new gown.

"Not at all—everything is perfect." She smiled.

"Then why did you not show them to us?" Lady Mary continued, and Elizabeth could feel Lord Clayton's stare. She breathed deeply, forcing herself to keep her countenance.

"I believe Mr. Darcy should be the first person to see me in the new dresses," she said with complete seriousness, then attempted a smile to warm her sharp tone. "Besides, I am keeping the surprise for the ball. But your ladyship looks stunning."

About an hour passed before Elizabeth decided to leave. Even Georgiana had become uncomfortable with the long visit. Her intention to depart was met with regrets by the others, and friendly farewells were made with the promise of meeting again at the ball. Lord Clayton hurried to escort the ladies to their carriage, a proper gesture that Elizabeth could not refuse.

It took a moment for the carriage to arrive, and Lord Clayton helped Mrs. Annesley to enter. Elizabeth was stunned and left speechless by a well-known voice calling to them.

"Mrs. Darcy, Miss Darcy—what an astonishing surprise to see you both. I hardly remember when I was last so delighted!"

After a moment of complete shock, Elizabeth found the strength to speak calmly.

"Mr. Wickham! This is a surprise, indeed. I did not expect to see you in Town. I wonder why it is that I am faced lately with several surprises a day."

While Wickham politely greeted Lord Clayton—with whom he seemed slightly acquainted—Elizabeth's anger grew overwhelming, her head spinning from the questions that arose. How was it possible for him to be there at that precise time?

"We are in quite a hurry. I am afraid we should leave." She desired to end the encounter.

"Miss Darcy, you are well, I hope? If I were to consider your exceptional appearance, you must be very well indeed. I am truly happy to see you."

"I am very well, thank you," Georgiana replied, and Elizabeth frowned when she noticed the expression on the girl's face. "I am happy to see you too, sir. I hope you are well."

"Yes. I have been in town for a few days with some business for the regiment, and I will return to Meryton shortly. I intended to visit Mrs. Darcy and ask whether she has any note to send to her family, but I feared my endeavour would not be appreciated by *all* the members of your family. How fortunate that we happened to meet!"

Elizabeth interrupted. "You are very kind, but it will not be necessary to trouble yourself. I wish you a safe trip back to your regiment."

"Indeed, you must be careful. The weather might turn bad at any time," whispered Miss Darcy.

"Now that I have had the chance to see you ladies, no bad weather could ruin my disposition."

"I am rather happy that you leave, Wickham," Lord Clayton said in jest. "The fewer gentlemen and the more ladies at the ball is a merry situation for me. Now, Mrs. Darcy, I hope you did not forget your promise for at least one set tomorrow night."

"Let us wait for the ball to begin, Lord Clayton."

The earl's insistence had become tiresome and boring. She wondered how she possibly could have considered Mr. Wickham's manner to be charming, as he seemed so shallow and insincere in his compliments—and Lord Clayton was no different.

She tried to find a means of escaping from the company of the two troublesome men without making a spectacle in the street. She could not expose Georgiana to such torment, precisely in front of Lord Clayton and Mrs. Annesley, who was clearly oblivious of Mr. Wickham's identity.

"We truly must leave. I am afraid we are already late," Elizabeth said decidedly.

In front of those empty, flirtatious smiles, she recollected the conversations she conducted with her husband—his steady voice as he explained to her the nature of his business, his gravity in describing his duties, his deep gaze watching her—and she realised how keenly she missed him.

A moment later, a carriage halted a little distance from theirs and a well-known silhouette hastened towards them. *My mind must be deceiving me!* However, Georgiana's pallor and Mr. Wickham's backward step left her in no doubt. A strong voice spoke: "Good day. What a strange surprise to find you all here."

"William, I am so happy you have returned. We were just leaving," Elizabeth said, smiling at him with an open heart and watching with worry the dark shadows around his eyes, his less than proper appearance, and the trace of fatigue on his face. He looked at them coldly.

"I must leave too," Wickham said. "We shall return to Meryton immediately. I was asking Mrs. Darcy whether she wished to send a letter to her family." Darcy did not favour him with a glance.

The new arrival drew the attention of the others in the party, who joined them cheerfully.

"You must forgive me. I have not slept at all in more than three days. We must leave now." Darcy helped both Elizabeth and Georgiana into the carriage with a proper but hasty farewell. The carriage finally moved, the other one following.

"I am glad you are home," Elizabeth repeated gently. "Are things settled? Is everyone well?"

"Yes."

"You look very tired, Brother..." Georgiana dared to whisper.

"I am very tired. I have not slept a moment in two days and nights as I tried to finish my business and return home as quickly as I could. However, it seems you managed to entertain yourselves rather well without me. That is good to know for the next occasion."

His voice was cold, and he stared out the window, barely looking at either of them. Georgiana kept her eyes down while Mrs. Annesley watched him with obvious puzzlement.

"I went to fetch my dresses—for the ball," Elizabeth replied, struggling to keep her smile. She easily understood his disapproval of the company in which he found them, and it was clear that he was not only upset but really angry. She knew she had to wait to arrive home to speak to him properly.

"Yes, the ball… It is truly an extraordinary event." His sharpness cut her temples, and she ceased speaking further. She imagined he was too tired to think fairly.

Fortunately, they arrived home within minutes. Stevens waited for them in the main hall, and Darcy instructed that he was not to be disturbed by anyone under any circumstances.

"Brother, I need to speak to you… Please, if you do not mind, it is very urgent…"

"Not now, Georgiana. I just said under no circumstances. Does anyone listen to me?"

His voice was so cold that Miss Darcy stared at him tearfully while Mrs. Annesley's eyes widened in disbelief. Georgiana hurried upstairs, followed by her companion, and Darcy went to his room with Elizabeth a few steps behind, struggling to be patient and to find the proper words.

"William, I know you are upset, but please let us sit and speak calmly. And you should not censure Georgiana in such a way. It is not her fault. In truth—"

"Of course it is not her fault, Elizabeth! Please do not ask me to sit and have a calm conversation. I believe I deserve at least that much respect."

"I do not understand your meaning. Please tell me why you are so angry. I know you disapproved seeing us in the company of Mr. Wickham, but he had just arrived a few minutes before. We met by chance in the street, and he asked whether I wanted to write a letter to my family—"

"Do not take me for a fool, madam! Do you truly expect me to believe that it was a mere coincidence? Of all the places in London and all the times of the day, Wickham happened to be there out of the blue? And was your conversation with Lord Clayton cordial? How came he also to be there on the precise day that your husband happened to be out of town?"

"Lord Clayton might have been there on purpose," Elizabeth responded, holding his furious gaze. "At the opera, Lady Isabella invited me to go with her to the modiste—when you were away and Lord Clayton was there. It never occurred to me that he intended to be present."

"How is it possible that your husband did not know about the visit, yet another man did?"

"I forgot to tell you. We returned home that evening, and…then you left in a hurry and…"

"How convenient! The truth as I see it is that you took advantage of my absence to seek the company of the people I specifically told you to avoid. Did I not insist that you not leave the house alone? I completely trusted you, and you disregarded my wish and put my sister in danger by placing her in a harmful situation!"

"You are being unfair! I was not alone but with your sister and her companion. And I am more concerned for Georgiana's well-being than for my own! I have done nothing wrong, and if you were reasonable, you would see that for yourself! I met with several ladies whose company you seem to approve! I did not know that anyone else would be there."

"So it must have been fate again, was it not? And yet, I did not see you being uncomfortable and leaving. You seemed to have spent at least an hour and a half there—or at other places! Trying on dresses in the company of other men! While I have been such a fool to not even enter your room for days without your consent! I was afraid to even touch you, and I was frightened that any step might displease you. I am your husband, and I never asked you to try on dresses in front of me! I promised you I would be patient, to allow you time to adjust to your situation and—"

Elizabeth's anger almost suffocated her. With each word, she became furious and appalled by what he dared to imply. He might have been tired, but he was being outrageous, and she could not allow it. She moved closer, confronting him face to face.

"I could have ignored your unfair accusation had your manners been more gentlemanlike, Mr. Darcy! There is nothing more wretched than for a man to make a promise to a woman and then hold it against her! How dare you reproach me that I needed time and that I was uneasy and restrained with you after you offered your patience to me?"

His countenance darkened, and his eyes seemed to burn her as he took a step back.

"I am not reproaching your uneasiness and restraint towards me but your easiness and lack of restraint in bonding with others, madam! Especially with men whose only qualities are nice words and pleasant manners. It seems it is more important to you to enjoy flattery than to respect your husband's wishes, and as soon as you were alone, you sought the company you preferred most! "

She was breathless with fury.

"How dare you say such a thing? What exactly are you implying? That I purposely arranged that meeting? Can you not hear how ridiculous you sound? So *I* convinced Lady Isabella and Lady Maryanne to meet at the modiste, and *I* asked Lord Clayton and Mr. Wickham to come there too, so *I* could enjoy their flattery? That is so ridiculous that you clearly need to rest, sir. I shall end this conversation now before one of us says something we shall later regret."

She turned her back, but his icy voice stopped her.

"I already regret many of the things I have said and done, madam! I trusted in you as in no one else. I opened my heart to you, and you made a fool of me. I agree with you: we should end this conversation and any other. There is nothing to be said."

"I am more disappointed in you than I have ever been before, sir. How dare you offend me? Is this the way a gentleman treats his wife? Is this the behaviour of a husband? Can you expect me to nurture my affection for you with such manners?"

"The behaviour of a husband would be to offer little and demand more! A wife's due is to show affection to her husband, not to give it as a favour! As the fool I have been, I did otherwise, and now I receive the proper repayment."

"You should rest now, Mr. Darcy, as your reasoning is painfully wrong. And please rest assured that, had I wanted to secretly meet someone, I could do it without anyone finding out about it. I am smart enough for that, and you would never know."

The effect of her words was immediate, and she could see him turning completely pale. He stared at her, speechless, obviously fighting to keep his control. The pain she felt for saying such things put a sharp claw in her chest, but she felt he had deserved it, so she continued:

"If you were more reasonable and kept the promise you made me three days ago—of allowing me to speak without jumping to conclusions—I would have said that I have not slept much since you left, either, as I was worried for you, and I was happy to see you safely home. Now, because of your senseless behaviour, I will leave you alone, and for the first time since we married, I shall lock the door between us!"

She returned to her rooms, and he followed her, as he had trouble fully understanding her meaning. Only the last words coloured his face.

"You cannot possibly believe that locking your door will keep me away if I wish to enter! You are my wife and I can enter your room whenever I please. There are no boundaries you may put between us and force me to keep them if I want it otherwise!"

She stood still, pale, her back strengthening, her eyes narrowing while casting daggers at him. She took a step closer, then spoke rawly, her voice determined and apparently calm.

"I do not believe a locked door could keep you from entering, but I hoped that, finding the door locked, a gentleman would not wish to enter by force—just as I always believed that a gentleman would not use his right to his wife as a threat or for revenge. Indeed, you are the master of the house and my husband. You may enter my chamber and my bed this very moment if that is your desire. Shall I undress first, or will that not be necessary?"

Darcy paled, looking at her in shock, his mouth half open, his eyes widening in disbelief. He seemed unable to breathe and attempted to respond but his lips moved without sound. Then he suddenly turned and left, slamming the door forcefully behind him.

ELIZABETH LAY ON THE SETTEE IN HER ROOM, HER TEMPLES AND EYES IN SHARP pain from her distress. What had just happened, and how was such a horrible discussion possible? How could he accuse her and threaten her that he could do whatever he pleased? Had he completely lost his mind?

It was indeed a strange coincidence that he found her speaking to Lord Clayton and Mr. Wickham—whose appearance was a most unpleasant mystery even to her—and she could understand that he was displeased. But how was it possible for him to doubt her, to accuse her of bonding easier with other men? Had her manners been so careless that he would suspect her of being disloyal?

And does he truly believe that I do not care for Georgiana's well-being?

Of course, she cared—and she was deeply worried for her younger sister! The girl's behaviour was a sign of restlessness but not of the kind Elizabeth expected. Georgiana seemed nervous, yet not very surprised and not at all displeased to see Mr. Wickham! And then, in the main hall, she asked her brother to speak with her urgently—but of course he harshly refused her! Well, it was his right as the master of the house to decide with whom he wanted to speak and when!

What lovely manners for an educated, faultless man! If only she had been capable of better controlling herself, things would have gone better. *Why did I lose my temper so easily?*

He had unfairly insulted her in a most ungentlemanlike manner. But what was she thinking to reply in such a preposterous way? To suggest she could plan to meet other men without his even knowing? Had she lost her mind, too? She responded to offence with offence, and what should have been a joyful reunion turned into a heartbreaking fight!

She vividly recollected the moments before he left, and she still felt chills along her skin. He had called her "my love"—even if perhaps he did not mean it in such a way. He promised he would return soon—and he did. He confessed he did not sleep at all, hurrying to return home! And now he had left again—tired, dirty, angry and as unreasonable as ever!

Hateful, irritating, unpleasant, haughty man!

Angry, pained, disappointed, and feeling useless and restless, Elizabeth moved from the bed to the door.

The room was too warm, and she could barely breathe, so she opened the window wide—in time to see her husband enter his carriage and depart in haste.

Hateful man with very poor courting skills! She angrily glanced at the roses that already had started to fade. She then left the room, slamming the door behind her.

Chapter 20

Darcy yelled at Stevens to have the carriage prepared. He was not certain where he wished to go—as far away as possible so as not to be tempted to return and continue their fight.

He exited the front door, waiting for the carriage in full cold, hoping the chill would sharpen his exhausted mind.

He could not believe what had just happened and wondered whether it were not a nightmare, as he had not slept for so long. A sharp pain bound his temples. The headache had started halfway home from Box Hill. He counted three sleepless nights, starting with the one spent in conversation with Elizabeth, two on the road and several others before, when he could find little rest for thinking of her. *All* his restless nights were because of her since he was a complete fool and allowed himself to be defeated by those childish, unreasonable feelings for a woman who cared so little!

He had travelled back with his eyes mostly closed, imagining how she would receive him, how he would have a warm bath and lie in bed—and perhaps she would wish to stay by his side—just to keep him company, to allow his sleeping body to sense her presence, to feel her warmth. What a ridiculous fool, to beg a few shreds of attention from a woman who—in the end—was obliged to give him anything he might ask. Anything—except the feelings and affection he waited and hoped for. Such a fool he had been to hope that would change!

Yes, she had been kind, gentle, and even tender with him lately—and he sensed that she enjoyed his attentions. Of course, she did—those sorts of activities were pleasant for any woman. But that was not much—not more than any other woman would feel with any man under similar circumstances. And surely not what he expected from her!

She held no special feelings for him, nor was she offering him anything special! She had become more at ease in his company, but she was even more at ease in the company of other men whom she barely knew!

It was very likely that she believed what he told her about both Wickham and Clayton, and perhaps she did not trust any of them, but she still seemed to be delighted by their company! And of course that was not surprising—many other women did! Handsome cads with no honour but with charming manners seemed to be the great favourites of ladies!

She dared to insist that it was a mere coincidence. How much of a fool did she think he was?

That Clayton found out about the planned visit during the opera was not impossible. Was it possible that her open manners had induced him to believe she was favouring him? It was not unlikely: the same thing happened with him in Hertfordshire. Still—the effrontery of that man! Did he have no boundaries? Surely, he would not be allowed to dance with Elizabeth ever again—if they even attended a ball in the future.

He briefly remembered the dress he ordered for her and wondered how it would fit. Then he grew angry with himself for such shallow thoughts. A moment later, he wondered whether Clayton had already seen her wearing the dress, and his anger grew stronger.

The carriage was finally ready, and Darcy entered, suddenly realising that it was very cold and asking the coachman to just drive around the Town. From the corner of his eye, he spotted the window to Elizabeth's room opening, and he wondered whether she was looking after him—but he did not see her.

She seemed so offended by his words, but what other explanation could there have been? To meet both Clayton and Wickham by chance? It was stupid to even imagine such a coincidence!

She accused him of not allowing her to speak her mind, but what was there to be said? Perhaps he was unfair to accuse her of not caring for Georgiana, but at least she surely had been neglectful when she went to meet that man. Even if she did not have harmful intentions, just speaking to him was bad enough! It was hard to imagine that Wickham happened to be in Town precisely during those days when he was away. Was it possible that Elizabeth intentionally wrote to him in Hertfordshire?

No, that would not do. This was already madness. She never gave him any reason to doubt her loyalty. Her behaviour was always beyond reproach—until that day! And yet, she was the one who said that, had she wanted to meet someone behind his back, she could do it, and he would never know.

How could she say such outrageous things? Would an honourable wife say that? And she dared accuse him of not being a good husband! If she were a proper wife, she would have apologised and remained silent. She would not have dared answer in such a way.

Instead, she put the blame on him and twisted his words, suggesting he was dishonourable and implying he might impose himself on her just because he was the master! Had a woman ever been more unfair?

He closed his eyes as the sun seemed too strong. In silence and darkness, he recollected, moment by moment, what had happened since he saw her in front of the shop.

A cold pit opened inside his stomach—either from hunger, as he had not eaten much in the last two days, or from the disturbing revelation that the words he threw in her face were indeed ungentlemanlike. Even if she were to blame and even if his anger was justified, he did say things that should have not have been said. She did too, but he was the one who started it.

He briefly considered returning home, sleeping, and starting the entire conversation again. And perhaps he should see what Georgiana wanted from him, but he did not feel composed enough to speak to his sister—nor with his wife. And no, he could not return home. He could not picture himself finding sleep and rest a few steps away from her.

He suddenly opened his eyes, knocked on the wall, and gave the coachman a new direction.

Elizabeth entered Georgiana's apartment and was astounded to see the girl crying on the bed and Mrs. Annesley unsuccessfully attempting to comfort her.

"Mrs. Annesley, I thank you for your care. You may go and rest now. It has been a difficult day for us all. I will stay with Georgiana."

Mrs. Annesley seemed reluctant to leave, but at Elizabeth's encouraging smile, she did.

"Oh, Elizabeth, I am so sorry! Please forgive me…"

"What is wrong, dearest? Why are you apologising? It is I who feel sorry for the way William spoke to you. He is completely irrational."

"Oh no, he is not to be blamed. I knew he would be upset if he saw Mr. Wickham. It was entirely my fault… Now what will happen? William will blame Mr. Wickham, I am sure, but he did nothing wrong. And I am so sorry that William yelled at you because of me! I wanted to talk to him when we got home, but he dismissed me and…"

The girl's voice was trembling, and Elizabeth barely understood her meaning. She embraced Georgiana then, finally, revelation struck her! Was it really possible?

"My dear, let us speak calmly from the beginning. Tell me why you think it was your fault."

"My brother is upset with me, but I am certain you can understand me better. I have known George all my life and— Do you notice that our names are similar? I grew up with him at Pemberley. He was always so nice to me… He is so handsome and he is the most pleasant and amiable man I have ever met. And last year, George proposed to me, and he knew William would not approve, and George asked me to elope and marry anyway… It was so romantic… But I could not upset my brother, so and I told him, and I hoped he would understand, but William opposed it… He said I was too young to marry and I should wait a few more years to be certain of my feelings… He was right, I know that, but it was so hard to bear… And George left before I had any chance to speak to him. I suffered so much from not seeing him again… My brother said George has done nothing worthy and is not responsible enough to have a wife, but I know he can change…"

"Dearest… And have you keep in touch all this time?"

"No…I have known nothing about him for almost six months, and after Christmas, I received a note from him. He sent it by a servant of James, and I was so happy and wrote him back. He wrote me again a few times and… Two days ago, he informed me he was in town and would like to see me, and I did not know how to arrange it. He was staying with James. When I found out about your visit to Madame Claudette's, I wrote that we would be there at two o'clock… I meant no harm, only to see him a few moments since William was away and… Did I do anything so horrible? I hope William will not harm George for that."

Tears silenced Georgiana again, and Elizabeth embraced her tightly. What was to be said? Everything she was afraid of when she first heard the story proved to be true. Georgiana was truly in love with that man and still suffering for him.

Her correspondence with a man behind her brother's back was equally outrageous and dangerous. But how could she blame a girl of sixteen with the most generous heart for holding such tender feelings for a man related to her childhood, who possessed such an appearance of goodness and such well-developed skills in deceiving and fooling people?

And since her brother did not disclose to her the full extent of Wickham's character—how could she even doubt him? Would she wipe her affection from her heart if she were told the entire truth? Likely not. Would she be more careful in trusting him? Hopefully yes, in time.

"I do not think you did anything *horrible*, considering Mr. Wickham was a friend of your family for a lifetime. I understand your affection for him. But carrying on a correspondence with anyone behind your brother's back when he disapproved of that person could do more harm than you think, even if your intentions were admirable. And things are much worse since we speak of a man who proposed that you elope with him when you were fifteen. I do not wish to pain you, but I agree with William in this. If a man of twenty-seven proposed an illicit elopement to my sister of fifteen, I would surely break his legs!"

"I know it sounds bad when you say it, so…I shall stop any contact with George, but I cannot stop caring for him. I cannot command my heart even if I wish to. And I cannot forget that he was willing to put himself in danger to marry me."

Elizabeth embraced her more forcibly with the same love and worry she used to embrace Jane. Could Jane command her heart not to care for Mr. Bingley who—although by far more honourable than Mr. Wickham—was still not worthy of her love and loyalty?

Georgiana was genuinely in love with all her innocent heart, falling for the powerful charms of a man who almost enchanted Elizabeth too, even if she was much older.

"Elizabeth, I will speak to William immediately. He has no reason to be upset with you."

"William left a little earlier. I thank you for your trust in sharing this painful story with me. But there is nothing you should say to William tonight. Let us delay until we are all more calm and rested. I do not want him to misplace his anger from me to you. Besides, he is more upset with me, anyway. He already told me as much."

"But why would he be upset with *you* because he saw *me* speaking to Mr. Wickham?"

"I do not want to discuss it further. It is a subject that might distress you even more."

"If it is related to George, please tell me. Nothing could be more distressing than not knowing the truth."

"Very well, if you insist. Perhaps it is for the best. I met Mr. Wickham in Hertfordshire about two months ago, and from the beginning, I was pleasantly surprised by his amiable behaviour. On the other hand, I confess that I was rather displeased with the way your brother used to treat me and all our acquaintances in Meryton."

"Oh..."

"One day I was with my sisters in Meryton, and I noticed the cold greeting between Mr. Darcy and Mr. Wickham."

"Yes, I can imagine. That was because of me...because of my attempt to elope and..."

"Mr. Wickham noticed that I observed the incident and masterfully asked for my opinion about Mr. Darcy. I did not hesitate to declare him a cold, unfriendly man and to criticise his haughty manners. And that was enough for Mr. Wickham to inform me in detail that Mr. Darcy refused to give him the inheritance bequeathed by your father and left him in poverty with no compensation at all. Which now we both know to be untrue, but back then it led me to think very poorly of Mr. Darcy."

"But he was the one who asked William to give him the compensation to study the law!"

"Now I know that! But back then, I considered Mr. Wickham my friend, and I trusted him. And I was wrong! Mr. Wickham is a handsome, pleasant gentleman, but his words and intentions cannot be trusted. I am sorry to pain you, but that is the plain truth! He has done many bad things and little good. He has all the *appearance* of goodness but nothing more! He would do anything to gain monetary advantages for himself."

As Elizabeth spoke, Georgiana's eyes darkened and tears shadowed their clear blue.

"But my father loved George..."

"And what did George do with that love? Just think: William finished his studies, and then he was left with all the burden of such a fortune on his shoulders. He had to take care of everything by himself. If George Wickham were a man with honourable intentions, even if he had no inclination to study, he would have gone to William and said, 'Let me work and prove to you what kind of man I am. I shall learn to improve myself and show that I am worthy of your trust.' Instead, he chose an easy life, spent the money, and indulged himself in activities that are not likely to bring success to a gentleman."

Georgiana narrowed her eyes to fight the tears. Elizabeth sensed her suffering, and her heart ached for the girl, but it was too late to stop.

"I believe you feel I am right, my dear. There is no excuse for a man of twenty-seven to ask a girl of fifteen to elope with him! If you were both very young and fell in love, that would be understandable. But a mature, experienced man cannot do such a thing with good intentions. Am I wrong in this?"

"So you believe George never loved me…that I allowed myself to be fooled by him and exposed my family to public censure for nothing…"

Elizabeth struggled for the proper words to answer gently but truthfully. "I am sure he loved you. You are beautiful and bright and so talented—any man would be happy and proud to marry you! But not when you were fifteen! Such haste can only be explained by his intention to benefit from your dowry as soon as possible. And no, you did not expose your family to public censure because you were wise enough to avoid that."

Georgiana wiped her tears then said she wished to rest. Elizabeth gently caressed her hair.

"My dearest, it is hard for me to imagine the pain you feel now, but I promise it will all go away soon. As Papa said"—Elizabeth spoke with a voice that attempted to imitate her father—"'next to being married, a girl likes to be crossed in love a little now and then. It is something to think of, and gives her a sort of distinction among her companions.'"

Miss Darcy forced a tearful smile. "I thank you for your patience, Elizabeth. I know how troubled you must be, and yet you spent more than an hour with me. Is there anything I can do for you?"

"There is nothing that anyone can do to solve the present situation besides William and me. I shall leave now and send Mrs. Annesley to you. I will return to see you later."

Outside the girl's room, Elizabeth leant against the wall, exhausted, her eyes burning and a heavy weight pressing her chest, thinking of the difficult discussion with Georgiana and the pain she had caused her—although it was necessary.

Her own turmoil was put aside, but now she felt the urge to continue the discussion with her husband. She planned not to tell him about Georgiana's involvement until their argument was resolved and he saw how unfairly he had treated her. No matter who had called Mr. Wickham there and what gentleman might meet with her at the modiste, he had no right to accuse her in such a way or to treat her so disrespectfully. No matter what the rules might say about a wife and a husband, she would not tolerate such behaviour.

With every thought, her anger increased again, and she knocked on the door of his apartment then entered. There was only Stevens, arranging his master's clothes.

"Stevens. I need to speak to Mr. Darcy immediately."

"The master is not at home."

"I am aware of that, which is why I need your help, otherwise I would speak to him myself. Are you toying with me?"

"Indeed I am not, Mrs. Darcy. I beg your forgiveness if I upset you… Mr. Darcy is not home, and I am not aware when he will return."

"But you know where he is?"

"I do," the servant said after a brief hesitation.

"Then you shall take me there."

"I cannot do that, ma'am. The master gave me specific orders, and I cannot disobey."

After a short pause, Stevens spoke hesitantly. "However, if there is something urgent, I can provide him a note."

"Very well, I shall give you a note directly."

It took her more than half an hour to write two full pages, fold them, and hand them to Stevens, mentioning that she awaited a prompt answer. Then she returned to her room and threw herself into the armchair in frustration.

That was truly ridiculous! Hateful man, indeed!

Darcy entered the main hall without invitation.

"Martin, I would like to speak to James at once."

"Of course, sir. The master is sleeping. Shall I wake him up?"

"I don't know. Can I speak to him in his sleep?" he inquired sharply. "I am sorry. I am very tired. Please tell James I will wait for him in the library."

He poured himself a glass of brandy and began pacing the room. James's library was in perfect order as only rarely was anyone there. A few minutes later, his younger cousin arrived, dressed only in his robe, his surprise obvious.

"You returned so soon? Is anything wrong?"

"I need to know where Wickham stays in London. I need to speak to him without delay."

"Wickham? He stayed here for three days, but he left for Hertfordshire this morning."

"He did not. I saw him earlier, and I am tired of seeing Wickham so often. I do not want to see him anywhere near my family ever again. In fact, I do not want to see *any* of your friends near my family. Do I make myself clear?"

"I do not know why you are addressing me in such a way in my own house. And I am not certain which of my friends you speak of and what you consider to be your 'family.'"

"James, I have had enough of this. You befriended people like Wickham, Annabelle, Clayton—and refuse to see the harm you suffer from them. I have told you for five years now what you are doing wrong. I tried to sustain your requests, but I am no longer willing to do that. Please do not lie to me. If I discover that Wickham is still in Town, I shall—"

"I went to visit you two days ago as we had arranged, and I had an interesting conversation with Mrs. Darcy—uncomfortable and rather unpleasant but quite enlightening—a much more interesting half hour than your scolding me for five years. I am sorry you dislike my friends, but I cannot keep them away from your family. It is your duty to do that. Perhaps you do not like Wickham staying at my house, but he is great at entertaining large parties. And yes, I enjoy playing cards, and I might lose some money, but am I the only one in London doing this? If so, then how is it I always play with a large group of men? I am not certain what Wickham has done, but I am not to be blamed for it."

Darcy stared at his younger cousin, unable to decide whether to continue or to leave, and since he did not trust his judgment enough for the former, he opted for the latter.

He exited the library and almost collided with Annabelle Stafford in the main hall.

"Mr. Darcy—what a surprise! I thought I saw your carriage, and I was not wrong. What a pleasure to finally see you without company!"

She was wearing a charming smile, a satisfied expression, and an elegant dress.

Red-faced, Darcy turned to James—as to show him another proof of imagined guilt—but the latter only shrugged.

"Surely, you see that I could not have called Annabelle. I had no idea you were here. She lives a few houses away and must have spotted your carriage herself."

"Indeed—and I am glad," said the lady. "Since you are alone, you have no reason to refuse to speak to me. Surely, you cannot deny me a few minutes of—"

"Annabelle, I am in a great hurry."

"Oh, you do seem in a poor mood…and your appearance is poor too. Do not tell me that you already have problems at home after less than a fortnight?" she said officiously.

Darcy's head was spinning. Passing from the cold outside to the warmth of the house, together with a glass of brandy, broke the last trace of his resistance.

He turned to the woman in front of him and took a step forward.

"Annabelle, how little wit do you have that you fail to understand, even after eight years, that I do not wish to speak to you? How is it possible that my dog learnt in a week when to stay away from me, and you cannot stop chasing me around town? I have nothing to say to you! I have no patience, no interest, nor the slightest desire to spend a single moment with you! How can I be clearer? Why is it that you refuse to understand? You now have the means to do anything you want. Take advantage of it, and go do something, but stop annoying me! Good day to you both."

The door closed forcefully behind him, but neither Annabelle Stafford nor

James Darcy—or the doorman and servants gathered behind the doors—moved.

Inside his carriage, Darcy felt relieved. He had not learnt much about Wickham, but he had found the perfect moment to tell Annabelle what was on his mind and, likely, would not have said had he been less tired and angry.

He also told James a thing or two and now was pondering their exchange. So Elizabeth had talked to James. He wondered what it might have been about and why Elizabeth had not told him about it—then he realised she barely had time to speak before his outcry. Did he truly do that? Well, perhaps he did, but rightfully so, considering the situation in which he found her and Georgiana. James kept saying it must have been a coincidence that Wickham happened to be there, but James was always oblivious to the truth and easily deceived by his unworthy friends.

He needed to sleep and then return to speak to Elizabeth. She must have been very upset too. She looked pale, and her eyes were a little shadowed—the same eyes that seemed to smile at Clayton and Wickham—and he suddenly remembered why he became so angry in the first place. And Wickham, standing only a few inches from Georgiana, when he specifically demanded that he never speak to his sister again!

Was it possible that Wickham intentionally planned to see not Elizabeth but Georgiana? But how could he have known she would be there? And why did Elizabeth not leave immediately? What would have happened if he had not appeared at that moment?

The carriage stopped at his destination. He went directly to his room and found Stevens.

"Good to see you here. Give me something to change into. I am all dirt from the road. And I need to sleep a little. And a glass of brandy would be much appreciated."

The servant obeyed and helped him change then handed him a glass.

"Sir, I have a note from Mrs. Darcy. She inquired after you several times, and she was very displeased that I did not tell her your whereabouts."

"Give me the note," he said, taking it rather abruptly.

"Sir, the mistress is very upset and she seemed unwell…"

"Yes, well, I am glad you informed me of the facts," Darcy replied sharply, gazing at the paper—a two-page letter with tight writing that made him frown as he started to read.

William,

I choose this way of addressing you because you thought it proper to leave the house, avoiding a reasonable conversation on a subject that had become grave and harmful.

I was very tempted to open this letter by addressing you as 'Mr. Darcy' because I could hardly feel that I was talking to my husband. However, I believe that at least one of us should <u>think</u> more than <u>feel</u> and finally take proper steps in the right direction.

You gave me no information about your present location, and I find this to show a lack of respect that painfully matches your lack of trust. You have treated me undeservedly harshly for something that was out of my control, and you needed less than a moment to consider me guilty of betrayal although I have done nothing but prove my commitment to you and to this marriage.

I was surprised to see Lord Clayton at the modiste, but I did not consider it proper to leave in haste because of the unexpected presence of a man, even one who seemed to show a certain preference for me and bothered you greatly. I expect I will meet many other men in the future, and running away from them would be equally stupid and ridiculous—as I would never expect you to flee the presence of any lady in public, even if she openly expressed her admiration for you. I cannot believe that we even come to discuss such a subject, which I thought to be mutually understood by both of us. It seems I was wrong—at least in your estimation—as I consider my behaviour to have been beyond reproach. And, in case you might be interested, I did not show my new gown to anyone in the party, not even to Georgiana, as I believed my husband should be the first to see it. Little did I know that my husband would be much more preoccupied with offending and accusing me than admiring my gown.

Regarding Mr. Wickham's appearance, I can understand your concern at seeing him in the close presence of Georgiana, and his appearance shocked me to the point of immobility for a few moments. Had you came a minute before or a minute later, you would have not even found us in his company. My care and affection for Georgiana I shall not even discuss, as I would not debate my affection for my own sisters.

To know that you imagined I could have deliberately sought out the company of those gentlemen is so absurd that it is laughable to deny it. Would I accuse you of taking me to the opera for the purpose of meeting Miss Bingley and Lady Stafford? The difference is that I trust my husband and respect his intelligence enough to dismiss such thoughts.

Since we have married, you have continued to tell me how much you admire me and how grateful you were for my involvement in this marriage, and I cannot argue with your declarations, but I have seen little of these sentiments in your recent behaviour.

Three days ago, I had great hopes for our union—and I have spent all the time since then worrying about and regretting your departure—but this is not how I imagined your return and not how I imagined things would progress between us. We promised to speak honestly and not rush to hasty conclusions—yet it happened again, and our arguments seem to have become stronger and more painful.

I shall not deny my share of guilt in our fight. My own reaction was not faultless. Perhaps I should have behaved differently, but you left me little choice to think of what was best.

All these unreasonable arguments are more difficult to bear as I felt we were growing closer and I am now proved wrong. I am not certain what can be done, but

I know things are not progressing as they should. I am more pained and exhausted than I was two weeks ago, and I do not believe I shall be able to go through this over and over again.

I strongly believe that decisions should be made and respected for the benefit of us both.

Elizabeth

Darcy held the paper tightly in his fist as he stared at the fire. He was unable to move, and an enormous weight burned his chest. He attempted to stand, but he fell back into the armchair and opened the letter again.

His fingers trembled, and he could hardly keep the paper straight while he read it again and again—until it was too dark to see. Then his understanding was finally clear and complete. With hesitant steps, he moved to the drawer and took out a sheet of white paper then moistened the pen in ink several times before he finally started to write. Be it as she wished.

More than an hour and a half had passed since Stevens left, and Elizabeth could find no rest. She checked on Georgiana who was already sleeping. Then she took the children and the dogs to play in the back garden for a while, hoping the cold would refresh her and time would pass easier—and she might spot any carriage coming down the street.

They finally returned inside, and the dogs hurried to rest while the children went to their mother.

Elizabeth retired to her room, and her struggle continued. She wondered whether he had read her letter, whether he had found it too harsh, and whether he admitted his wrongs or was offended and another fight would follow—and wondered where he could possibly have been all that time.

When she finally heard movement in Darcy's apartment, she almost jumped to the adjoining door but was startled by strong knocks from the hall.

She opened, and Stevens bowed low to her, avoiding her eyes, and handed her a letter. She hurried towards the candles and lit two more.

Elizabeth

I shall not attempt to apologise for my behaviour, as I know it cannot be forgiven. I am aware that, as much as I did not like the earlier events, it cannot justify my outrageous outburst.

I cannot deny that I was disappointed to see you in the company of those whom I so despise, but I now understand that you had little chance to avoid it.

You are right: I cannot keep you away from people, even those I dislike, and it is unfair of me to accuse you for your natural inclination of enjoying amiable company, as it is unfair to put the burden of protecting my sister on your shoulders.

There are few things that I can say at the moment, and I am at a loss of how to proceed further. What I do know is that I wish everything that is best for you.

Therefore, I allow you the full liberty of choosing the path you take from this day forward.

Anything you decide I shall accept, and if you decide to return to Longbourn, have no worry for your comfort, as the settlement I offered you will not be diminished in the slightest.

Also, no matter what decision you make, I trust you will inform Georgiana in a gentle way, as she has already become fond of you.

I am willing to take full blame for any further developments.

In the meantime, I shall spare you my undesired presence. I will take a long trip to the North, as I have neglected my business lately, and I plan to be absent for at least three weeks.

I scheduled my departure for the day after tomorrow. Until then I shall stay in Georgiana's house, where I have been until now. I only returned for a short while to fetch some things and papers that I will need on my journey, but do not worry, as I shall not disturb you.

I deeply apologise, and please be assured that anything I have done wrong to pain you was done most unwillingly and pained me even more.

I know this is of little relief, but I beg you to be sure that I have never been more honest in my life than when I declared my long-lasting admiration for you.

F. Darcy.

Elizabeth stared at the letter, refusing to believe that she understood it properly. She read the letter again and then once more. With each word, her state changed as well as the colour of her face, and the turmoil soon became impossible to bear. She felt tears burning her eyes, and she wiped them furiously. Then she burst into the next apartment and stopped a few steps away from her husband, who was looking through some papers.

He was so pale, his countenance unreadable with dark circles around his eyes, that Elizabeth hesitated a moment, worrying for him. Then she straightened her back and gazed at Stevens—who was packing a valise—and the man left the room silently.

Elizabeth turned to her husband, the paper crumpled in her hand.

"I read the letter you sent me, sir. Do I understand correctly that you wish me to leave?"

"It does not matter what I wish, Elizabeth—not any longer," he replied with a voice so low that she barely heard it. "I am certain that you wish to distance yourself from me, and I think this would be the best resolution and the easiest way to protect yourself from this unfortunate situation into which I forced you to enter. I vividly remember when you told me that we might come to hate each other and that our lives would be ruined forever, and I am sure this is how you feel about me now. I can bear anything except knowing that you stay with me and hate me."

"Please do not presume to know my feelings. You can hardly claim a proficiency in that area. And you do not know me at all if you imagine you could have forced me to enter into any situation without my agreement or that I would choose the easiest way out of it."

"I want everything that is best for you, and that is certainly not to stay around a man who is incapable of controlling his anger and offends you so horribly. I know you will try to keep your promise to make this marriage work. But it just does not, and your qualities cannot compensate for my faults. I am tormented by the image of your face being appalled at my horrible threats and your eyes losing their brightness. You are worth more than that."

He moved to the window, turning his back to her. Elizabeth's voice trembled as she replied.

"I shall not pretend that you did not offend me and that I was not harmed by your unfair accusations. I surely did not deserve your anger and distrust, as I am certain I gave you no reason for that. I was—I am—nothing but committed to this marriage and to you. While I will never accept abandoning my friends just because someone—you included—might demand it of me, I long ago ceased to consider Mr. Wickham a friend. And I would never attempt to conspire to meet someone behind your back. So yes, you hurt me when you threatened to use your power over me to enter my room whenever you want—and that made me angry. I know my worth, Mr. Darcy, and I also know yours. I am well aware of my qualities and my faults, as well as yours."

"You have been nothing but faultless since the day we married."

"We both know that is not true! My behaviour was often far from what it should have been and most likely will be so again many times as I have not the slightest intention of leaving. Besides the strange circumstances of our marriage, I made a promise to you and to myself, and I intend to keep it. I do not take my promises lightly, nor do I abandon a path when it is difficult to climb. I have learnt that reaching the heights can be so rewarding as to compensate for the effort."

She looked at her husband. He turned pale, then his face coloured while he stared at her, as he could not comprehend her words.

"You do not wish to leave?" he inquired as if afraid of her answer.

"I searched for you all afternoon, I wrote you the letter, and I came here with the hope that we could find a way to reconcile our relationship, to keep our mutual agreement, and to straighten out this marriage—and to argue with you for leaving in such haste instead of staying and giving us the chance to explain our positions. That was disappointing."

"So you do not want to leave? Is that true? You wish to stay?"

"Both of us have difficult tempers, but I would rather find a way to correct our faults than abandon the battle. We promised to be open and honest with each other—to ask questions and give answers instead of starting unnecessary fights. How could you forget that?"

"I did not forget that. I simply could not think rationally. I have never felt so overwhelmed by emotion, and I am so afraid it might happen again! That is why I do not even dare to beg your forgiveness. I cannot trust myself and dare not ask you to do it. All the things I told you—I am horrified when I remember my words and how you might have felt."

"It seems that I had more trust in you than you have in yourself...and yes, you should be ashamed of the things you said!"

"I never intended to force you to do anything...and if you ever lock your door, I would not dare to enter... Those were just words that I did not mean the moment I said them."

"Not for a moment was I scared that you might hurt me or force me to do anything. But I was indeed astonished by your reaction! I knew you would be upset to find us in such company, but I never imagined you would be so furious! I planned to tell you about the incident the moment we arrived home, even if you had not seen us. But you did not allow me to speak a single word. You must promise not to allow this to ever happen again! I felt like you intentionally wished to hurt me with the most harmful words!"

She was tearful, drained by emotions, and expected him to contradict her.

"And so it was... I was so pained—I felt so deeply betrayed—that I wished to make you feel the same pain. Can anything be more horrible than that? Can such outrageous behaviour be forgotten?"

Elizabeth was shocked and froze, her lips trembling. She gave up fighting and allowed herself to lean on the armchair. Her strength had left her.

"How could you believe that I intentionally deceived you? How could you think so poorly of me? Why do you have so little trust in me?"

He looked at her in silence for a moment, and she saw his eyes darkening as his face turned as pale as the wall. He seemed unable to speak.

"Because I was jealous—can you not see? I was so angry when I saw Wickham near my sister, but it was your speaking with him and with Clayton that made me lose control. And I cannot promise you it will never happen again because things are not improving, quite the contrary. The more you are near me, the more I love you. It has been torture for me to keep myself away from you all this time. My love for you made me weak and turned me into a savage earlier. I wish to protect you, to offer you everything that is best. I tried to be patient, I tried to court you—and to no avail."

She looked at him in shock.

"Please do not look at me like that, Elizabeth. How can you be so surprised? How could you not see how ardently I have loved and admired you all this time? You cannot pretend you have not seen how jealous I was at the theatre when you spoke to Clayton."

"I knew you were not indifferent to me—of course, I could feel that. But to *love* me? So much that you lost control because of it? How can that be?"

"I cannot answer how, but it happened, and this love has tormented me for months. I have never felt so helpless. I have ceased to find sleep and rest since I fell in love with you."

Elizabeth's eyes widened in astonishment, and her pallor matched his.

"So when we married… You loved me when you proposed to me? How is that possible? Your behaviour to me was always cold and distant, and you had left Hertfordshire. If not for the rumours, you never would have proposed—that is what you told me…"

"It is true: if not for the accident and the rumours, I would have been gone forever. At that time, I wished nothing but to put distance between us as my love for you frightened me, and I fought my own weakness. I loved and admired you, and I was certain you would have been the perfect wife for me, but it never crossed my mind to connect myself to your family. I already confessed that to you."

"But why did you not tell me when you proposed? Why did you tell me only half the truth?"

"When I left Herefordshire, I was certain that you knew my feelings and shared them! I behaved so coldly precisely because I thought you were not indifferent to me, and I did not want to raise expectations that could not be fulfilled. When I returned to propose, I was sure that marriage would make you as happy as it made me. And when you proved me wrong, I was at a loss of how to proceed. You refused me, and I had to persuade you to accept me by speaking of your family's future. Had I revealed to you the force of my love—had I told you that the nasty rumours that made you so unhappy had been my escape, my inducement to see the right path to a happy future—that would have only frightened you. Is that not so?"

"I…I do not know how I would feel had I known from the beginning… I do not know how I feel now, either… If you had told me earlier—at least after we married…"

"If I could not confess it at the beginning, I simply could not find the right time afterwards. I kept waiting for the proper moment, but so many things happened in such a short time. And when we finally spoke honestly to each other, I decided to court you, to make you enjoy my company, to convince you we can be happy together—and I hoped things would turn out for the best eventually. I know I have no excuse for either my deception or my behaviour. I am trying to explain clearly enough for you to understand why I did some strange things during these weeks."

"I understand—I think I do… Now I must…there are still things I must ask you, but I cannot do it now… I need to rest…and to gather my thoughts. I cannot think properly now…"

She left before he had time to respond as her legs became weaker. Her mind was spinning in torment from his profession of love tangled with his admission of his own weakness and the explanation of his wild behaviour.

A sudden headache forbade her from even keeping her eyes open, and her heart beat painfully. He said all this time had been a torture for him to stay away from her. Was he out of his mind? Could he not see that she did not want him to keep away from her?

How could he have asked her to leave? And he wished to leave London, too? *Yes, he is most surely out of his mind*, she thought as she grew angrier.

She pushed away the door to his room—he was near the window, staring out. She noticed his luggage and Stevens searching in the closet then exiting the moment he saw her.

Darcy turned to face her, and their eyes seemed to confront each other in complete silence. She finally spoke, and the determination in her voice surprised even herself.

"I am very tired, and you must be much more so! I shall ask for dinner to be prepared in two hours so you have a chance to rest. You will surely reconsider the foolish idea of moving or leaving town! I expect to find you here later when my mind is clearer and I can put in order all the questions I have for you!"

He moved closer and hesitantly stretched his hands towards her.

"I will do as you wish. I know that I am being very selfish again, but I am so relieved to finally tell you how much I love you, that I must say it again. I was ready to let you go, but my life would have been empty without you. I know you do not love me, but the chance of allowing me to prove my love to you, to struggle to gain your affection is all I need."

He tentatively took her hands, waiting for a sign of rejection, but none came. Elizabeth's turmoil only grew at such words while her entire body became weak and heavy. She was still upset, angry, incredulous, and fearful. But strangely, a warm burst of joy spread inside her as she watched her husband, wondering whether she should do something—and what.

She allowed her hands to linger in his a moment longer. He was mere inches away, and her eyes looked deeply into his. For a moment she admired his handsome features, now changed by pain and sorrow. His lips were narrowed in anxiety, waiting for her answer, and the remembrance of his soft, gentle, tender, and passionate kisses invaded her senses.

She closed her eyes and recollected his anger from a few hours before—yes, it was from jealousy, but that was not an excuse. Yes, he admitted his errors and declared he did not mean those threatening words, and she believed him, but the fact remained.

This was hardly the best way to show his love or expect to gain hers. Her weakness was instantly replaced by a strength that straightened her shoulders, and she slowly withdrew her hands from his while her eyebrow rose in sharp reproach.

"I cannot claim much experience in this, but I find your skills in courting and proving your love very poor, indeed. You greatly need to improve your techniques, Mr. Darcy! Now please excuse me. I shall see you later!"

She elegantly returned to her chamber, struggling to hide the large smile that lit her still tearful eyes as she watched the incredulous expression of her husband.

She lay on the bed, covered her face with a pillow, and started to cry, unable to discern the storm of feelings rushing through her mind and her heart.

Sometime later, she opened the door to his room and entered, alert to her surroundings lit only by the fire. He was sleeping soundly. His shirt was untied, and she could see his bare neck, his chest moving with his steady breathing. His hair was in great disorder, and she gently touched a lock near his ear. He did not even move, so deeply was he lost in sleep. She stood near the bed, careful not to disturb him, while images from the first time they met until the present moment ran through her mind.

His courting skills had not been poor *all* the time, she thought, blushing. And now that she allowed herself to recollect everything, she did suspect that his feelings for her were deeper and stronger than mere admiration, even since the first day of their marriage. But not for a moment did she suspect his partiality to her when they were in Hertfordshire.

He had singled her out when he danced with her at Netherfield, but how could she imagine his reason when he was so distant, so aloof all the time? He thought she returned his feelings? How could that be? She only argued with him and found ways to underline his faults, as he seemed to do with her.

A bad temper, lack of patience, arrogance, a strange mix of generosity and selfishness—and inconsistent courting skills, which ranged from being excellently persuasive to very poor and offensive—these were some of her husband's faults. And yes, his qualities were a hundred times more plentiful but that did not diminish his errors.

And yet she had become accustomed to them, and the mere thought of not seeing him daily was a stab to her heart. How could he even imagine she might want to leave him?

She remembered him saying that his life would have been forever empty without her. *That* she could easily believe, as now she could not imagine her life without him, either.

Chapter 21

Elizabeth left her husband's room as carefully as she entered and went to see Georgiana.

"William is home. He is sleeping," Elizabeth said. "He will join us for dinner later."

"Is everything well?" Georgiana inquired, hopeful.

"We clarified the misunderstanding. I did not say anything about your confession, but I believe it must be done tomorrow."

"Yes…perhaps… Would you mind speaking to him? It is just that…"

"I will tell him what happened. But afterward, you will have to talk to him too."

"Yes, I know… I am just afraid he will believe I am ungrateful and disrespectful."

"That will not happen. His affection for you is admirable, which is why he might be too protective sometimes. I expect many handsome young men to fight for your attention once you are out. You must be aware that your brother will find faults in each of them."

Georgiana smiled bitterly. "I shall never be in love again… It hurts so much. I am just happy that you are here, Elizabeth. And I hope you are happy with us too."

"I am happy," Elizabeth answered in a trembling voice. "Now let us prepare for dinner."

An hour later, the ladies were surprised at the appearance of Colonel Fitzwilliam. Elizabeth invited him to join them for dinner, and he accepted. Shortly, Darcy entered, pale and wearing traces of exhaustion. He glanced at his wife then greeted his cousin.

"I was away from Town two days," said the colonel. "I just came to see you a few minutes, and Mrs. Darcy invited me to stay for dinner."

"Then surely you cannot refuse Mrs. Darcy," he said smiling, glancing at his wife once again. "I am glad to see you, Robert."

Darcy offered his arm to his wife. She took it but did not meet his eyes as they walked to the dining room. Georgiana, Mrs. Annesley, and the colonel followed them.

The dinner was a mostly quiet affair. Darcy seemed preoccupied, glancing from his wife to his sister—and also very hungry as the Colonel observed.

They were on the third course when a footman announced a messenger asking for Mrs. Darcy. The master of the house asked the man in then took the letter from him.

"It is from Miss Bennet," he said, handing it to his wife. "It was sent express and might require an answer," Darcy said.

Elizabeth excused herself and hurried to the drawing room, opening the letter. With each word, her eyes shadowed with tears and her trembling hands barely held the paper. Gathering her strength, she ran back, her expression so devastated that Darcy panicked, helping her to sit as she started to cry.

"My father fell in the back garden early in the morning. They found him after some time, and they could not make him speak… Jane said he was alive but not conscious. My Aunt and Uncle Gardiner are there too, and they fetched Mr. Jones, but I cannot think of what might happen. Oh, dear Lord, he might not recover or he might already be…"Her cries broke Darcy's heart. He embraced her, allowing her tears to fall on his shirt while he gently kissed her hair. Then suddenly he withdrew from her, still caressing her hands.

"I will send for Dr. Taylor, and as soon as he arrives, we will leave for Longbourn. Hopefully, we will be there in the morning."

Elizabeth looked at him as though she could not understand his words. Then she wiped her tears, whispered a "thank you," and ran from the room. Georgiana hastily followed.

"Do you want me to go with you?" the colonel asked.

"No, I do not believe it will be needed. If anyone can truly help, it will be Dr. Taylor. I would rather have you here, taking care of Georgiana. I have not had time to speak to you, but an unpleasant event occurred today that I want to avoid."

"James told me. I will be in town a few more days, and if I have to leave, Maryanne and my mother will visit Georgiana daily. You must not worry. Go with your wife."

"Very well. I shall send you a note as soon as I have further news."

Doctor Taylor arrived in less than an hour, and their journey began without delay. It started to snow steadily, and the carriage was chilly, the blankets wrapped around them doing little against the sharp cold.

Elizabeth did not allow her mind to think, nor did she attempt to keep track of the time passing. They stopped at an inn to change horses and have a hot drink. Then the carriage resumed its slow progress. While she tried to peer through the darkness, Elizabeth recollected the journey she had taken ten days before. Back then, she felt worried, sad, and a little frightened of what she would find at the end of the road, but it could not compare to the worry and fear that gripped her now.

The mere thought that she might never see her father again was as sharp as a knife in her chest. She sensed her husband's arm circling her shoulders and gently pulling her to him. She resisted only an instant then leant her head on his chest and closed her eyes.

Darcy forced himself not to move when Elizabeth finally fell asleep. His own fatigue vanished, and his pain on seeing her distress was stronger than his own fatigue. The frozen roads were very poor, and the horses continued at a slow pace. They had to stop again at an inn to change horses.

It was a late, sunny, and cold morning when they arrived at Longbourn. Elizabeth jumped from the carriage and, without waiting for the gentlemen, hurried through the door.

A moment later, the mistress of the house appeared, greeting both gentlemen with great effusion.

"Mr. Darcy! What a happy moment to see you again so soon! You heard about Mr. Bennet? What a tragedy indeed! I could not sleep the entire night, my heart is beating wildly, and I cannot breathe well, nor eat nor sleep! What a relief that you brought Dr. Taylor too! Oh, please do come in. You must be hungry and tired..."

"I should see Mr. Bennet at once," Dr. Taylor said, and Jane showed him inside.

The house was more crowded than Darcy remembered: four Miss Bennets, the Gardiners, their four children, and a very troubled Mrs. Bennet. Mr. Gardiner offered him a drink, expressing their gratitude for bringing Elizabeth and Dr. Taylor. Darcy rejected any thanks and enjoyed the brandy.

Half an hour later, Dr. Taylor entered the drawing room and said the patient was resting.

"May I see him?" asked Elizabeth impatiently.

"He should sleep a little, Mrs. Darcy. He seems to be well at present, but I wish to observe him closely a few more days. He is feverish, which is expected since he fell on frozen ground. What worries me is that he seems not to remember what happened before and after his fall. I am not certain whether this occurred because he injured his head during the fall or suffered an apoplexy which caused his present state of confusion."

"Do you think his life might still be in danger? What do you mean 'an apoplexy'? He has been very healthy all his life. What might have caused such a thing?" Elizabeth asked anxiously.

"It might be caused either by heart failure or a great distress of some kind. I shall take care of his fever for now and give him some herbs to strengthen his mind and his body. I hope it will be helpful."

"But—does he remember me?"

"He certainly does—quite vividly. He scolded all three of us for coming from London for a 'mere fall,' as he called it. You may expect some harsh censure when you first visit him."

Elizabeth laughed through her tears and thanked the doctor. Then she excused herself and went to the other ladies. A few minutes later, Dr. Taylor was required by Mrs. Bennet, asking his advice about her nerves.

Elizabeth and her aunt approached Darcy and Mr. Gardiner. With obvious distress, her cheeks crimson, Elizabeth spoke in a low voice to prevent the others from hearing.

"William, we have a delicate problem." Darcy looked puzzled, and Elizabeth continued, choosing her words carefully.

"Longbourn has one large guest room—which is already occupied by Mr. Collins, who arrived yesterday—and one smaller one, which will be offered to Dr. Taylor. The only available room would be my old chamber, but it is quite small."

Elizabeth noticed a slight colour on Darcy's face as he averted his eyes for a moment.

"I sent John to the inn as soon as you arrived, but they only have two small rooms available, which will be suitable for your servants," Mrs. Gardiner added. "And I thought about asking Mr. Collins to move to Lucas Lodge, but I fear we will be unsuccessful."

Darcy nodded. "I suggest not even attempting to convince him. I do not want to give him the satisfaction of refusing us. I plan to speak to him as little as possible. I am very tired, and I fear I will not be able to bear Mr. Collins."

"I think it would be best for us all to return to London today. That way, two more rooms will become available," Mrs. Gardiner offered.

"Please stay. Your presence is valuable for the family. We will find a way to accommodate ourselves in Elizabeth's room for a few days." *And a few nights*, his mind cried in warning. "Could we please eat something? And a glass of brandy would be an excellent addition."

Mr. and Mrs. Gardiner hurried to comply with his wishes. When they were alone, Elizabeth, red-faced and distressed, whispered to her husband, "My room is quite small, considering what you are accustomed to…and there is only one bed…" Her embarrassment deepened as she spoke.

"I imagined that. Do not worry. I may sleep in the library on the couch."

"I am afraid it will not be possible. Our couch is very small, unlike the one in your library."

"You did not express yourself properly, Mrs. Darcy. You should have said 'my *father's* couch is very small, unlike the one in *our* library.'"

She smiled, pleased by his censure. "You are correct, of course. But the fact remains…"

"We shall find a way. I will spend most of the evening after dinner reading, and then I may sleep on the floor, on a blanket, or something. It is important that your father is better than we feared. I hope to speak to him soon, and I am quite pleased to see you smiling."

"William, I shall never forget how you put everything aside without hesitation just to travel with me to see my father. How can I possibly thank you or repay you enough?"

"Nothing is more important to me than you. I cannot claim that I have the same affection for your parents and sisters as you have for Georgiana, but I would do everything to help them because I know your love for them. I did only what

I thought right."

They stared at each other for a moment, and she whispered another "Thank you."

Mrs. Bennet's voice interrupted their brief interlude, inviting them to breakfast.

Elizabeth's stomach was tightened in an icy grip. The worry for her father, the relief that he was better than she feared, the joy of being reunited with her sisters, the sense of being home, the prospect of spending a few days and nights with her husband in her old room with only one bed—all those overwhelming feelings extinguished her hunger completely.

He had been so generous in taking her to Longbourn without delay and sharing her fear and distress. He was certainly still tired—he slept only a couple of hours last evening and not a single moment during the journey—and now he insisted he would sleep on the floor.

After their recent fight, the awkwardness of sharing a room and a bed with her husband was difficult to overcome. He was still very much a stranger to her in that respect. How would they change their clothes, how would they walk in front of each other in nightclothes, and how would they wash in the same room? They could perhaps take turns—one would come and prepare for the night while the other was still downstairs?

She did not even consider that such closeness might force the consummation of their marriage. They still had some unresolved problems, and such an event in her house, filled with all the family, seemed impossible even to consider.

He admitted that he had barely slept a single night since he fell in love with her and it was a torture for him to keep his promise because of his "ardent love and passion." She remembered his words, chills shivering her skin while her cheeks flushed again. What could he mean by "torture"?

Allowing him to sleep on the floor was out of the question. She thought she might sleep with Jane and Mary and let him sleep in her room—and suddenly that seemed the best option. At least it offered an alternative to their uncomfortable situation.

WHEN JOHN INFORMED ELIZABETH THAT HER FATHER WAS AWAKE, SHE ALMOST leapt from the chair. Her husband left his seat and followed her. They slowly entered the patient's room. Elizabeth hurried to the edge of the bed while Darcy stood a little behind her.

"Papa, I am so happy to see you." She placed a loving kiss on her father's forehead. "I was so frightened when I heard. How do you feel? Are you in any pain?"

"Lizzy, what are you doing here, child? All the way from London in such weather? And Mr. Darcy! I thought you had more wisdom than Lizzy, but it seems I was wrong. How could you let her convince you to travel such a distance in the middle of winter for a mere fall?"

"I am pleased to see you in such excellent spirits, sir." Darcy smiled warmly.

"Papa, please be serious! I could not bear to be away from you when I knew you were hurt! Oh, you have a bruise on your temple, and you are feverish," she exclaimed as she examined him more closely, her smiles mixed with worry.

"This is nonsense. I am perfectly well, as you see. And, sir—do you make it a habit to bring poor Dr. Taylor to Hertfordshire every time someone suffers a little accident? I wonder that you do not purchase a house for him in the neighbourhood—it would be cheaper. Please take a seat. That is the least I can offer you since you travelled such a long way. I hope someone in this house gave you something to eat."

"We have been very well taken care of, sir." Darcy sat near the bed.

"I am glad to hear it. Now help me with a glass of brandy, I beg you."

"I am afraid I cannot do that without Dr. Taylor's permission." Darcy answered in earnest.

"Surely, you cannot be serious, sir! First, you take away my favourite daughter, and now you refuse to indulge me with a glass of my brandy in my own house? For this, I shall tell Mr. Collins that you expressed a special desire to sit by him at the dinner table."

"As you like, sir. But I am afraid brandy is out of the question—until the doctor approves it."

Darcy was amused and content to see Mr. Bennet being his usual self. A few minutes later, he left, allowing his wife to spend time alone with her father.

In the hall, he asked a servant about the location of Elizabeth's room. He opened the door and looked around before he stepped inside. The chamber was pleasantly furnished but small—half that of Elizabeth's bedroom in London. Someone had thoughtfully placed a large jug of warm water by the wash bowl. The bed was a generous size for a single person but not large enough to sleep in with Elizabeth. He would have to either spend the night in a chair or sleep on the thickly carpeted floor near the fireplace. He could bear it for two or three nights.

He moved around the bed, measuring it once more. They would both fit well enough if they were close to each other. If he were to put his arms around her and pull her against him, they would be both warm and comfortable. No, that was not true: it would be torture. How could he hold her in his arms with only thin nightclothes separating them, her hair falling on his chest, sensing her skin, her scent, her warmth… That was surely unthinkable!

But he would manage it somehow. If he could only rest for a few moments… He had not slept for so many nights…

Darcy removed his coat and boots then put another log on the fire and lay down on the bed. He closed his eyes, enjoying the surrounding so familiar to Elizabeth.

Just before sleep defeated him, he wondered about his sister and the urgent problem she wished to discuss with him. However, she seemed well enough at dinner, and he felt content to know Robert was there to protect her as he fell into a peaceful sleep.

As soon as Darcy left the room, Mr. Bennet's gaze rested upon Elizabeth's smiling face, and he kissed her hand. "How are you, dearest? I was quite worried, you know."

"I am so sorry that you troubled yourself! I am fine—in fact, I am more than fine. Things are much better than I could have hoped when I agreed to marry."

"Truly? Are you not deceiving me, Lizzy? How are his relatives?"

"I was stunned by my warm reception from the entire family! Georgiana is already as dear to me as a sister, and Lady Matlock and her daughter-in-law are more than friendly. We even had a ball, and she introduced me into society and—"

"Pray have mercy on a sick man, child—no balls! Save that for your mother and sisters. Now tell me: How is your husband? He bore my teasing remarkably well, I grant him that."

"He is a good man. He is kind and generous with me. He encourages me to have my own opinions, to make decisions for the household, and to challenge him if I do not agree with something. And his wealth is much larger than we knew—quite frightening, I might say. Papa, do you know that Jane and I met Lady Anne Darcy ten years ago in Brighton?"

Elizabeth's discussion with her father lasted another hour with questions and answers, shared worries, promises, and hopes for the future. The moment Dr. Taylor said the reason for the apoplexy might have been a major distress, Elizabeth felt she was the cause of it. She imagined the torment through which her father must have gone after she left Longbourn.

Mr. Bennet's tendency for mockery and his apparent lack of interest were not sufficient shields to protect him from the torment of losing his daughter to a stranger, even one with "ten thousand a year." Apparently, her two letters were not enough to put his mind at ease; therefore, she did everything to assure him that he had no cause for further concern.

She left her father's room and hesitated about her direction. She needed to change the clothes in which she travelled all night long. She also wondered about her husband's situation. Was he able to bear the level of noise in the house?

She opened the door to her old room with a heavy heart. The first twenty years of her life were there. But more than her past was her present: her husband, very informally dressed, sleeping soundly in her bed.

She watched his serene face: he looked much younger than usual. He occupied most of the bed, but there was a little space beside him. She lay down, careful not to move or touch him. From a few inches away, she continued to look at him with great interest, her heart racing. It was past sunset, and the room was rather dark. His features were lit only by the fire.

She gently caressed his hair then tried to rise in silence.

"Elizabeth?" she heard him whispering. He held her arm, and she blushed violently.

"Forgive me for waking you—I do not know what came over me. I just want to change my gown and… It will only take a moment, and I will go to change in Jane's room…"

"I just wished to rest a little, and I guess I fell asleep. May I help you with anything?"

"No. Papa and Mama are resting and so is Dr. Taylor. We shall have dinner in more than two hours, so please rest a little more. You must be very tired. I shall spend some time with Jane and my aunt." She hesitated a moment then moved closer to him. "I cannot tell you how grateful I am that you are here with me."

"Please never speak of gratitude again…"

"We had no time to speak last night, and you deserve to hear my answer."

"We shall have plenty of time to talk in the next days…"

"We have plenty of time now too." He rose and sat, facing her as she reached for his hand. "William, I am not sure how to name my feelings for you, but I know that I have never felt the way I do when I am in your presence. It gives me joy when we spend time together. I like the small things we share as much as I like the important things with which you trust me. Despite the difficulties of our marriage, I am happy to be your wife."

"Thank you for telling me that. It makes me very happy too…"

"Even during your stay at Netherfield, I had reactions to your closeness that I never experienced before. I shivered when we danced and you touched my hand, which I never sensed with any other man. Back then, I took it as an unpleasant reaction, a result of what I thought was your critical and disapproving stare. Your presence troubled me every time in a way I did not recognise. I was always preoccupied with guessing what you thought of me. And since we married, your nearness makes my mind and my body respond in a strange way, which worries me because I do not recognise it."

They were facing each other, and she could see his expression softening. He gently caressed her face, and her fingers mirrored his movements, caressing his handsome features. He closed his eyes, rejoicing in her touch, then turned and placed a kiss inside her palm.

"These feelings fill my heart, and the more I am with you, the more I want to be. And, after being together ten days, I cannot imagine my life without you either."

"My dearest Elizabeth," he whispered, and she continued, obviously embarrassed.

"The first evening of our marriage, we drank wine and talked, and since then I have waited for you to invite me again. You kissed my hands and then my cheeks, and the trace of your lips burned me for days and made me wish for more. Your hands touched my skin when you put on my jewellery or took off my gloves, and I was certain there was nothing more pleasant. And then we shared a real kiss, and I wondered how it would be if there were more. I feel ashamed for telling you all these things, and I am frightened to imagine that you might consider me wanton, but I do not want to keep anything from you."

"My love—I did not dare hope for such a response, and I have never been more grateful for the revelation that I was a fool for so many days. I was so concerned for your feelings that I failed to recognise them, and I was afraid to admit what I thought I recognised. I noticed that you enjoyed my company, but I believed your occasional restraint and your uneasiness were a reflection of the doubts and distrust you still have in this marriage. I was afraid to read too much, so I read too little—but I do not regret anything since that slowness has taken us to this wonderful moment. And now, I can see very clearly in your eyes everything that you just told me."

"And perhaps, if you look closer, you could see even more. Then you would never imagine that I prefer another man's company to yours..."

"May I hope you will forgive me for my behaviour yesterday?"

"I am not sure. I might require further apologies. I need to ponder this."

He leant closer, his eyes holding hers until they closed. His lips tentatively caressed her face, brushing her soft skin, exploring her temples, her jaw, and her throat, then stopping over hers. She was overwhelmed by the feelings she had missed, and for a moment, she responded with no less passion. Then she withdrew, barely regaining her breath.

"Jane is expecting me. I must go, and you must rest." His face was still close to hers.

"Do you plan to torment me on purpose? That would be quite unfair, you know..."

"Since you already questioned my loyalty, you may well doubt my fairness, sir."

He stared in disbelief at her harsh teasing.

"That was not fair, either. Tell me my punishment directly; do not torture me."

"I do not want to torture you, but I cannot easily forget that you believed me capable of deceiving you in the most horrible way."

"I have nothing to say in my defence—except that I was losing my mind. A man who loved you less and was less jealous would have probably thought more clearly."

"That is hardly an excuse, sir."

"I shall not attempt to deny it. But declaring that you can meet other men behind my back without my knowing was hardly better."

"I am astonished that, though you were so tired and had lost your reason, you still remember those silly words I said in anger."

Their voices became lighter, and their harsh words were half-serious. They teased to diminish the pain of their fight. A moment later, his lips found hers again.

"William, I must leave," she whispered.

"Very well." When she was ready to leave, his hand captured her arm.

"Elizabeth, I have many faults and have made many errors. But my feelings for you grow with each day. Of that you should have no doubt."

"I know that—now I really do. Oh, and it seems we do fit both in the bed, after all—so you must not think of sleeping anywhere else. Rest now, husband."

She quickly picked a dress from the closet, and it crossed her mind that it was the gown she was wearing the evening at Netherfield that they had spoken about accomplished ladies.

From the doorway, she glanced once more at him: his eyes were closed, and a contented smile was frozen on his lips.

Chapter 22

Longbourn, 6 January, evening

Elizabeth spent time speaking to her aunt and her sisters about her new home, her new sister, her new relatives, Lady Matlock's private ball, her beautiful gowns, and the astonishing jewels she received.

"Lizzy, I will delay coming to Town," Jane said. "I feel I should stay a few more weeks to be sure Papa is recovered, and I shall come a little later. I hope you do not mind."

"I will be upset not to have you with me sooner, but I believe you are right, Jane. I shall ask William to send a carriage to bring you to town at the right time," Elizabeth said. Jane replied that it would not be necessary to go to so much trouble. Elizabeth and Mrs. Gardiner disagreed with her, and they quickly put an end to the debate.

Dinnertime finally arrived. Elizabeth returned to see her father and worried that the bruise on his temple grew darker. He asked them to blow out some of candles as the light hurt his eyes. The doctor assured her that everything was as expected, but she insisted on staying with her father during the night. Mr. Bennet—as well as the doctor—strongly objected. It was decided that John would sleep on the couch in Mr. Bennet's room.

Mr. Darcy soon joined them in the dining room, his countenance changing instantly when Mr. Collins greeted him with bows and theatrical condescension. "Mr. Darcy, I cannot tell you how blessed I feel to be able to welcome you into our family, an event that I never would have dared to even imagine in my wildest dreams. I am—"

"Mr. Collins, your words flatter me, but they are completely unnecessary, I assure you. Let us dine—the entire family is very tired and surely very hungry. I confess your presence is quite unexpected. I thought you were busy in Kent, preparing for your upcoming wedding."

"I was indeed—it is quite an unfortunate coincidence that Mr. Bennet fell precisely when I returned to Hertfordshire. I am the happiest of men, and I hope to be even happier when the day of my wedding to my beloved Charlotte finally comes. I have been blessed beyond imagination with Lady Catherine's approval of my choice of a wife. Her ladyship granted me an hour to hear my description of my dear Charlotte's accomplishments."

"Miss Lucas is a worthy lady. You were very fortunate to secure her acceptance. I was quite surprised." The ladies paled at that harsh remark, yet Mr. Collins continued unmoved.

"Indeed, I was, sir. I can only imagine my marital felicity once I bring my new wife to the vicinity of Rosings' beauties."

"I congratulate you, sir, and I hope you and Charlotte will have a happy life," Elizabeth said.

"I thank you, Cousin Elizabeth. As Lady Catherine said—"

"But if everything is settled, I was wondering why you did not stay at Lucas Lodge. It would be more agreeable to you, I imagine, to be close to your betrothed," Darcy inquired.

"I was tempted to do so, but I realised that a man in my position can never be too careful in avoiding improper situations. I still remember Cousin Elizabeth's situation from a few weeks ago when her misconduct and imprudent behaviour placed her in questionable circumstances, which raised speculation and rumours."

Elizabeth's cheeks coloured, but her amusement overcame any other feeling.

"Excuse me? I am afraid I did not hear you correctly." Darcy's voice turned cold and severe.

"I was referring to the day you found her in the wood," Mr. Collins replied with serenity. "By the way, I must congratulate you, Cousin Elizabeth, for your unexpected nuptial. It is a very advantageous and unimagined alliance for you all to connect with a most illustrious personage, blessed with splendid property, noble kindred, and extensive patronage." He spoke with a most flattering smile, bowing deeply to Darcy, who stared at him in disbelief, undecided how to proceed to stop such an outrageous speech.

Mr. Collins then continued with equal condescension: "Yet, my conscience demands I inform you that Lady Catherine de Bourgh condemns this alliance, which, unlike my marriage to dear Charlotte, her ladyship considers to be the worst that could ever be imagined. Her ladyship expressed what she felt on the occasion regarding both Cousin Elizabeth and the entire family—which she rightly appreciates to be far below hers. Lady Catherine did—from my knowledge—put all this into an eloquent letter to Mr. Darcy, which, sir, you should expect to receive soon. Although it is late for any remedy, she declared she would never give her consent to what she called 'so disgraceful a match.' I thought it my duty to give you the full intelligence of this."

Darcy's face was so shadowed by fury that even Lydia and Kitty noticed it, staring in silence from him to Mr. Collins. Elizabeth turned white from shame, and Jane gently squeezed her hand to comfort her. Darcy gulped his wine then turned to his interlocutor.

"Mr. Collins, I thank you for this complete intelligence of your amazement and of my aunt's opinion about my marriage. However, the only opinion that matters to me is my wife's, and I could not care less about any others, including my aunt's. I do not need anyone's consent or approval for my marriage, and I certainly did not decide whether to marry based on someone else's estimation of my future wife's' qualities and accomplishments."

"Sir, I assure you it was not my intention to upset you, but you must admit that—"

"Mr. Collins, I 'must' not do anything! You either offended my wife intentionally or because you were oblivious to the meaning of your own words. Pray enlighten me: Which was it?"

"Indeed, I believed it to be my duty as a clergyman to bring and spread the words about what is right and proper. Lady Catherine herself insisted that—"

"Mr. Collins!" Darcy's voice rose, icy and sharp. "I am not interested in your sermons about this subject—and I assume that nobody in the room is—even you must see that. I have heard enough about my aunt, and I am sure the others, who do not even know her, care even less about her words of wisdom that you so frequently repeat."

"I must heartily contradict you, sir, although it pains me deeply. I am not—"

"And please weigh your words very carefully when you speak of my wife. I shall not admit any rudeness. Let us apologise to our hosts for such improper conversation at dinner, eat peacefully, and discuss the weather. Or please leave."

There was complete silence, and the redness of many at the table became pale. Lydia whispered to Kitty, loud enough to be heard by the entire party.

"Mr. Collins is jealous that Lizzy married Mr. Darcy, who is twenty times wealthier and more handsome than him."

Mr. Collins's eyes and mouth widened in shock. Elizabeth became as white as the wall and glanced with despair at Mrs. Gardiner, who put an end to the debate.

"Gentlemen, please let us give proper attention to this beef steak and let me know what you think of it. I am especially curious to hear Mr. Darcy's opinion on *this* subject."

"I am eager to enjoy it. I was just talking to Elizabeth and to my sister about the exquisite dishes I had the pleasure to taste when I last dined here."

Mr. Collins declared the meal at Longbourn was almost as good as the dinners served at Rosings. No more than a few minutes after Darcy's severe scolding, he mentioned that Lady Catherine considered it fortunate he would marry someone from the proximity of the estate he would someday inherit.

Darcy's anger became frustration and then resignation. There was nothing to be done about Mr. Collins. The man had no sensibility, no shame, and not enough wit to be silenced by censure. Darcy easily recognized his remarkable resemblance to Annabelle Stafford, just as Elizabeth had said.

After dinner, the gentlemen retired to the library to enjoy their drinks. The ladies, however, all declared they were weary and retired for the night.

Elizabeth washed herself, changed into her nightgown, and climbed into bed, wrapping the bedclothes around her. A strange peace enveloped her, and she closed her eyes, trying to recollect the events of the day. In no more than a few minutes, sleep overcame her as she wondered how long her husband would tarry downstairs.

AROUND MIDNIGHT, DARCY QUIETLY STEPPED INSIDE ELIZABETH'S ROOM. THE first thing he saw was the dwindling fire, so he added one more log before dressing for bed. A moment later, his eyes were caught by the image of her left foot, escaped from under the blankets. The perfect line of her ankle was intriguingly exposed to his gaze, and he suddenly felt a lump in his throat.

Elizabeth was sleeping so profoundly that she occupied more than half the bed. He pulled the blanket over her bare foot then took a seat on the chair. In the corner was a tray with a carafe of wine, one of brandy, and a jug of drinking water, together with two glasses. He smiled, considering that the staff—although few in number—were quite efficient.

Though it was snowing and windy outside, the room was warm and pleasant—too warm. Elizabeth slowly moved in her sleep, and his gaze turned to her again. Her hair was spread over her back on the pillow and her shoulders, her dark, rebellious locks playing unrestrainedly. He wondered whether her hair was as soft as he remembered, and he rejoiced in the delight of touching it again soon. But how could he push her towards the edge of the bed and make room for himself? She was exhausted by worry, sleepless nights, and the fight he had so stupidly started. He thought he might allow her to rest in peace a little while, so he poured himself a glass of wine and remained in the chair, looking at her.

Elizabeth gasped when, through her sleep, she observed a shadow near the window and then smiled when she recognised it. She sat, wrapping the bedclothes around her.

"William, why are you sitting there?"

"I did not want to disturb you. You were sleeping so soundly."

"Please come here. It is very late, and we both must sleep."

He hesitated a moment, but her voice, although soft, was too determined to argue. He sat on the free side, removed his robe and lay down, careful to keep a distance between them. They were facing each other, sharing a nervous, awkward smile.

"Cover yourself. It will be cold during the night," she told him with genuine care.

"Do not worry. I will take care of the fire. Sleep well," he whispered and gently touched her hair, which was even softer then he recollected.

She wished him a good night, and then closed her eyes. Her steady breathing proved that she had fallen asleep again. He pulled the blankets closely around her, and inhaled the dizzying scent of her hair, which was now touching him. His senses were more alert than ever before, and he had to struggle to keep his eyes from her curves clearly revealed by the bedclothes. She turned again, and her hand reached his nightshirt. A smile appeared on her face as she slept peacefully, and he gently removed a lock of hair that was tickling her face.

Darcy breathed deeply and wrapped the bedclothes around himself. It would be a very, very long night!

ELIZABETH WOKE IN THE MIDDLE OF THE NIGHT BEING WARM AND COLD AT THE same time. She searched for the blankets, but she was trapped by a weight that first panicked her. Then she realised she was held by her husband's arms, tightly wrapped around her.

She was lying with her back to him, so she could not see him—nor could he see her face, and for that, she felt relieved. Her mind and body became aware of every inch of their closeness. One hand was near her waist, and she could feel his fingers through the thin fabric of her gown.

With despair, she noticed that her nightgown had shifted to expose her feet and her shoulders—most likely, as she had moved in her sleep. She shivered when she sensed his legs entwined with hers. He was wearing a thin pair of trousers but no stockings, and his feet touched hers.

She slowly pulled her feet away a little, but his feet moved closer. She smiled to herself and, for a moment, lay still—then very gently brushed her feet against his. She heard a slight moan and froze, worried that her gesture woke him. *Suppose he notices what I have done!*

He did not wake, but he moved even closer to her, and his face rested near her shoulder. His warm breath heated her ear, and her heart began to race so fiercely that she was certain he would hear it. Her back was almost crushed against his torso, and the sensation was frighteningly pleasant.

Apparently still asleep, his hands moved from her waist along her body, briefly caressed her thighs, then up again, and she barely suppressed a cry when his fingers brushed over her breasts. Such a strong shiver shattered her body that she bit her lips. Then his fingers lingered a little over her neck, touched her bare shoulder, and finally stopped to caress her face and hair. His steady, hot breathing tickled her ear and she abandoned herself to the wondrous sensations.

Those shivers, travelling along her body and turning her stomach into an icy hole, were caused by only a few tentative caresses. *Then how would it be if he…* She did not dare think further, her head spinning at the mere thought.

The room was dark and silent, only the fire burning and the wind blowing outside so powerfully that the windows shook—and so did Elizabeth! What was happening to her? Was she losing her mind? Her father was ill, they still had reason to be worried for him, and her husband was so generous, kind, patient, and gentlemanlike—and she suddenly had turned into a shameless, wanton simpleton.

She withdrew a few inches to put some distance between them, but his arms pulled her back. She lay still. His hand slowly glided up and down her thin, silky nightgown and this time stopped on her thigh. She bit her lips while a wave of warmth shattered her inner body. All her senses seemed to gather on that spot where his fingers were touching her.

Without thinking, her hand caught his, stopping its exploration, and his fingers immediately entwined with hers. Then he lifted their joined hands to the level of their hearts. Her body was still warm and shivering, inside and out, but she regained some peace, and her heart beat steadily again for a little while until his lips touched her ear and he whispered her name.

"ELIZABETH? FORGIVE ME FOR AWAKENING YOU. I AM SORRY. I WAS VERY TIRED, and I slept too soundly. I hope I did not trouble you…by staying so close to you…"

She freed her hand from his and attempted to turn. Both of them moved away from each other, allowing a safe distance between them.

"No, not at all," she whispered back, feeling her cheeks colouring. "I slept very soundly, too. All is well." They were now facing each other as they lay on the pillows.

"I am glad." He smiled. "Would you like to drink something?"

"Yes, please…"

He rose, first tended the fire, and then filled two glasses of water and returned to her.

Elizabeth watched him as he moved around the room, unable to take her eyes away. His neck was completely uncovered, and he walked barefoot on the cold floor. Through the thin fabric of his trousers and shirt, lit from behind by the light of the fire, she could see the shape of his legs and his torso and…

She covered her face with the blanket to hide her embarrassment and her improper curiosity. When she heard him calling her name again, she rose to sit in the middle of the bed, taking the glass of water from him. She was thirsty too—so very thirsty. She took the glass, avoiding his gaze. He finished his water then went to pour a glass of wine.

"Would you like some?" he asked, and she shook her head in an energetic refusal. Surely, wine was not what she needed in this enormously confusing circumstance.

They glanced at each other in awkward silence for some time. She could see his eyes lowering from her face and suddenly felt cold.

As if guessing her thoughts, he said, "You should put your robe on or move down to cover yourself in the blankets. It is getting cold despite the fire. It seems a freezing night."

"So should you," she replied and blushed. "You walked around barefoot. Your feet must have frozen already." She averted her eyes and put aside the glass.

"You are right. We should sleep."

He decidedly resumed his position against the pillows, covered her tightly with one blanket, and put another around himself. The separate blankets seemed a safe shield to keep them apart, Elizabeth thought, and briefly wondered whether she was pleased by his idea. They were both lying on their backs a few inches apart, staring at the ceiling.

He leant slowly towards her, and when his face was only a breath away from hers, he gently removed a lock of hair from over her eyebrow. His fingers lingered on her temple a moment, and he smiled while she felt her cheeks burning.

"You were very gracious in bearing my family," she said, hoping to dissipate her emotions.

"Not at all…except, perhaps, your father's sharp teasing and severe censuring. In that, I feel I was gracious indeed."

"I am happy that you and Papa seemed to get along so well. He admires you very much."

"I hope not more than Mr. Collins. I fear I could not bear that!"

They laughed again, and Elizabeth suddenly pressed her fingers over his mouth.

"We should keep silent. My sisters are sleeping in the next room, and the walls are very thin," she whispered, barely able to control her own peals of laughter.

She felt her fingers trapped by his, and his head slowly moved towards hers. She closed her eyes, shivers thrilling her skin, and waited. His lips brushed her cheeks and moved further, resting near her ear lobe and touching it at each whisper as in a soft, tentative kiss.

"It is good to know about the walls being very thin…" He gently kissed her fingers, then the inside of her palm, then her wrist.

"Have you made any plans regarding the length of our stay?"

"I want to be sure Papa is truly recovered. Jane said she would rather not come to London now as she feels her presence is needed here."

"Miss Bennet is very wise. When she decides to come to Town, I will send a carriage for her. And if she agrees, she might stay in our house. I am sure Georgiana would be delighted."

He placed soft kisses along her temple, her cheeks, her eyelashes, and then went down to the corner of her mouth.

"That is perfect… Jane staying with us would be perfect," she murmured.

His lips entrapped hers, gentle and tentative at first, then growing impatient as he felt her willing response—testing, conquering her moist, shy, half opened lips which soon learnt to share his eager passion. Her hands were still resting between them as a shield that soon fell when she encircled his waist.

His fingers entwined in her hair, and his thumb fondled her earlobe until the sensation made her tremble and moan, but the sound was suppressed as the kiss deepened. His caresses travelled down her neck, stopped on her bare shoulder for a few torturous moments, then brushed over her throat and lowered along the neckline of her gown as though attempting to invade it.

She frowned and moaned again, her body quivering when his lips followed his fingers, kissing and tasting her skin until they reached the line of the gown—then stopped and returned to her face for a short while. He finally rested with his forehead pressed against hers.

"We should sleep now," he said, and she silently approved.

He kissed her hand then her temple, and his mouth remained near her ear. She shivered and moved closer while he spoke breathlessly.

"Elizabeth, before we return to London, I shall speak to your father about Wickham."

A moment of silence. "Yes, it should be done. I shall speak with Jane too."

"And tomorrow I will have a word with Wickham if he has truly returned to Meryton. I know my suspicion of your informing him about the visit to the modiste was ridiculous, but I cannot believe it was a coincidence. "

Her heart skipped a beat. She glanced at him through the darkness. "William?"

"Yes?" His hand climbed along her arm. She shivered again and closed her eyes a moment, wondering how best to start.

"There is something of great importance I need to speak to you about before tomorrow."

He rose from the pillow, looking at her with obvious concern.

"What is it, Elizabeth?"

"Please listen to me to the end. I know you will be displeased, but I have great hopes that things will be better." She took hold of his hands and breathed deeply.

"Do you remember that Georgiana asked to speak to you, and you refused to see her? I spent a lot of time with her after you left, as she was even more devastated than I was by your reaction. It was hard to persuade her to trust me, but finally she confessed that she had informed Mr. Wickham about our plans."

Darcy looked at her with a tormented expression and slowly withdrew his hands.

"Georgiana? That cannot be… He wouldn't dare… She could not lie to me in such a way…"

"Georgiana's affection for you is as strong as her esteem. But please remember that you stopped the elopement and sent Wickham away without giving her any details. You told her that Wickham was not worthy of her affection and that she was too young to know her heart. Not knowing his true character, her affection was enhanced by the longing of not seeing him. She thought his gesture of eloping with her was romantic, and she was convinced he was a good man by the fact that your father loved him."

He seemed to make a tremendous effort to follow her words and understand them. "But …does this mean that they have been in touch all this time? How?"

"She said Wickham only sent her a short note after Christmas then another three days ago when he likely learnt from James that you were out of town. The letters were delivered through James's servant. I think Mrs. Annesley found nothing strange in the letters that came from your cousin, as she is unaware of Wickham's history. Georgiana confessed everything to me in such terrible distress that she broke my heart. She is truly in love with him, William. She said she could not fight her heart. You must know what that means…"

Darcy gazed at her a few long moments, so intently that she felt a pain in her chest. Then he rushed out of the bed and went to the window, pouring himself a glass of wine.

"You have every right to be upset that I did not tell you sooner, but…"

"I am not upset with you. I am ashamed that in a week you gain more of my sister's trust than I have in a lifetime. You understood her heart and bonded to her, and she grew so affectionate towards you that she shared the most painful story of her life with you. And I only managed to frighten her and push her away when she wanted to speak to me."

"Oh, that is nonsense," she said decidedly, stepping near him. "She is a marvellous young woman, and it is your merit for how you helped her grow. She wanted to confess her guilt to protect me from your anger. She heard you yelling at me and was devastated for me. She put my comfort above her own. And I find little fault in her behaviour—only innocence."

"I do not fault her, either. And yes, I understand how it is to be unable to fight against your heart. But I cannot allow this to continue. I will speak to Wickham tomorrow and warn him again. I shall kill him if he ever comes closer to either you or Georgiana."

"Killing Wickham is not the answer. And forbidding Georgiana to be in touch with him will not help much either. She must learn to know her heart and separate right from wrong. And that is not easy. I am much older, and even I have been at fault on this subject recently. And I still cannot pride myself on knowing my own heart as well as I would wish to—not even when it comes to my own husband." She attempted to smile.

"Then what should I do? I must do something; I cannot abandon my sister to danger."

"Do you remember when I told you that the truth would help me fight the danger? It will also be helpful to Georgiana. She promised she would speak to you in person. You must only listen to her and answer any questions she might have."

His gaze caressed her, and he held her hands in a long silence.

"Do you remember a week ago when you did not know what to do with Janey and you were amazed that I have the perfect solution for everything? I can say that about you now."

She laughed with no little emotion. "It must be contagious. Now let us return to bed."

He put another log on the fire then sat near her, astonished at how beautiful she looked in the light of the fire. He then kissed her hand and whispered with deepest emotion.

"You show so much affection to my sister while I hurt yours…"

"True—but you still have time to improve. Oh, and I also told Georgiana that, if Wickham had eloped with my sister of fifteen, I would have broken his legs."

He looked at her in disbelief. She pressed her lips together to suppress her laughter.

"If I meet Wickham tomorrow, I would be happy to do it for you," he replied seriously, and she put her hand over her mouth, laughing in silence.

"But then you must take similar measures with Lady Stafford," she teased in a low voice.

"Speaking of that: yesterday I went to James to inquire about Wickham. We had a short argument and when I was about to leave, Annabelle entered. She behaved like her usual self and insisted on talking to me, but I was exhausted and angry, so I answered her as I had wished to for years. I truly believe she understood the message properly that time."

"Oh, I am frightened to even ask what you said to her..."

"I do not remember much, but essentially, I told her that she has less wit than my dog."

At Elizabeth's astonished expression, he continued with perfect calm.

"In my defence, I repeatedly insisted on not being bothered by her but with no success. Titan understands the first time I tell him."

She started to laugh, and he leant closer, staring at her. The tiredness made her face pale, but her eyes were sparkling although her eyelids seemed heavy. Her laughter soon vanished as his lips imprisoned hers in another long kiss.

"James told me that he visited and you spoke when I was away," he eventually said.

"We did."

"Would you tell me about the subject of your discussion? He said it was rather difficult but not unpleasant and that you were more convincing than I had been in five years."

His lips now caressed her temple, her jaw, and back to her cheeks. Every inch of her skin quivered, and her feet felt very cold. She struggled to answer.

"We spoke of your involvement...and his lack of interest in his duties...and that you are burdened with everything he used to neglect. I did not mention what he does wrong but what you do faultlessly to maintain everything under good regulation."

"I am not faultless," he whispered, and his lips brushed hers.

"I know you are not," she murmured, and their lips found and relished each other.

"We must sleep now. It is very late, and tomorrow we will awaken early," he said some time later. "Good night, my beautiful wife. Rest now."

Elizabeth's face lifted to reach his. She felt her cheeks and neck burning with shame, but her eyes daringly held his.

"I am not your wife yet, but I would not be opposed if you wish to. I would not mind at all."

"You are very generous, but our first time together cannot happen in a house full of people and thin walls. And I hope you will come to feel more than just *not being opposed* and *not minding*. I hope that soon you will not just *accept* my wishes but return my love and passion. I want you to become my wife when you hold no doubts, no fears, and no restraint. I can wait a little longer..."

A long silence, filled with emotion and broken only by the blowing wind outside and the crackling wood of the fire, enveloped them.

Slowly, Elizabeth leant her head to rest on his chest. His arms embraced her, and she closed her eyes, listening to his beating heart—first quick, wild, restless, then turning calmer, more steady, more peaceful, as was Elizabeth's first time sleeping in her husband's embrace.

Chapter 23

Longbourn, 7 January

It was full daylight when Elizabeth awoke, and she was alone in the bed. She allowed herself a few long moments to recollect the previous night. She still felt her husband's warmth on her body and the trace of his kisses on her lips.

As she started to dress, Jane entered, smiling lovingly. Elizabeth embraced her, ashamed to admit that she was disappointed for it not being her husband.

"Lizzy dearest, I dared to disturb you because I saw Mr. Darcy downstairs with Uncle."

"I am happy to see you Jane; I shall be ready in a moment."

The sisters chatted happily for a few minutes then hurried to join the others.

The first thing Elizabeth noticed in the drawing room was her husband's gaze and the hidden smile on his lips. They had no time to talk, though, as the din of voices covered any attempt at reasonable conversation.

"I am going to see Papa," Elizabeth said after Dr. Taylor gave his permission. She glanced at Darcy and exited precisely when Mr. Collins entered, complaining that he was very hungry.

"Did you sleep well, Papa? Have you eaten? And did you take your herbal medicines?"

"Lizzy, you are annoying. Sit down and tell me how the evening was. I understand Mr. Collins got a severe scolding from your husband. And yet, Mr. Collins cannot be defeated."

"Well, Mr. Collins never ceases to entertain us."

"Indeed. If you see your mother with her nerves wretched, please note it was my doing. I reminded her that, two weeks ago, she insisted on your marrying my cousin. I asked her how she feels knowing she almost ruined the chance of having Mr. Darcy as a son-in-law."

"Papa! Surely, you did not do that?"

"I most certainly did," he said, a smirk on his face.

As they spoke, they were surprised by Mr. Darcy's entrance. He inquired after

Mr. Bennet, who invited him to join them.

"I am pleased to see that you survived one day in this house, sir. Did you manage to rest?"

Darcy glanced at his wife. "I did, thank you," he said, slightly uneasy.

"I am glad to hear it. Before someone interrupts us, there is something I wish to ask you, sir, and I know this sounds very selfish. If something happens to me, I beg you to allow Elizabeth to take care of her sisters and mother. I am certain Mr. Collins would claim his inheritance at once. My brother Gardiner said he will take full responsibility, but I know it would be a difficult task for him alone."

"Sir, of that you may be certain. Elizabeth will have—at any time—the complete liberty to attend her mother and sisters in any way she wishes. If it becomes necessary to remove from Longbourn, they will be offered a comfortable home anywhere they wish, including in Hertfordshire or in London. However, I strongly believe this is not the time for such a conversation and will not be for many years. You must rest now."

"And have some more tea," Elizabeth continued.

Although he did not look at Elizabeth, Darcy felt her grateful smile. He also noticed Mr. Bennet's tearful eyes and his attempt to wipe them. "Very well, send John with some medicinal tea. Upon my word, I have not drunk so much tea in the last five years together. Go and have breakfast. Mr. Darcy, while the ladies are busy chatting, come and keep me company. Let Dr. Taylor be entertained by my brother Gardiner. I liked the doctor more when I was not his patient."

"Gladly, sir," Darcy said before closing the door behind them.

In the main hall, Elizabeth turned to her husband. "Thank you. I keep thanking you, and you continue to give me reasons for doing it."

"You are very welcome. And you should stop doing it—thanking me, I mean."

"You have grown very proficient at teasing and mocking. Papa is right."

"As I said some time ago, one can change after one marries, especially if he marries wisely. So—did you sleep well?" he inquired just before they returned to the dining room.

She blushed. "Very well, thank you. And you?"

"Quite poorly—but I am not complaining," he whispered, and she blushed even more.

BREAKFAST WAS A NOISY AFFAIR. MR. COLLINS'S STORIES WERE MOSTLY IGNORED between the chaotic conversation of Mrs. Bennet and her younger daughters. Mr. Collins talked another quarter hour on how small the house was for large gatherings, comparing it to Rosings.

Despite his previous decision to remain calm, Darcy said coldly, "Well, Mr. Collins, considering your passion for large rooms, windows, and stairs, it is a shame you cannot see Pemberley, which is far beyond Rosings in all these respects. However, I hope Mrs. Bennet will describe everything to you in great detail after the family spends the summer with us."

Mr. Collins paled and Mrs. Bennet almost fainted with emotion.

"Oh, my dear Mr. Darcy, I cannot imagine anything more delightful. I am sure Pemberley is beyond any other estate. It must be as big as an earl's domain. I only hope Mr. Bennet does not die before then—that would surely ruin our journey!"

"Mama!" cried both Elizabeth and Jane, pale with anger. "Please be aware of what you are saying. That is not something to jest about." Mrs. Bennet chose to ignore her.

"Mr. Darcy, let me know what dishes you favour for today. I shall ask cook to prepare them at once. There is no other opinion that matters to me! Anything you may ask, we shall be more than happy to comply."

Elizabeth looked around for a hole where she could bury herself in shame. For the next hour, the only privacy she shared with her husband was brief glances and smiles. She felt continually embarrassed while Darcy made efforts to accommodate the endless and meaningless chatter. His discomfort was obvious while the doctor seemed to enjoy the din—which, Elizabeth thought, must have been a result of his hard days in the army.

"Lizzy, Jane, we go to Meryton! Will you come with us?" Lydia asked. "Please do come!"

"Oh yes, and you must take Mr. Darcy's carriage! You left in such haste after the wedding that people barely had time to admire it," added Mrs. Bennet.

"I am not certain, Lydia," Elizabeth replied, glancing at her husband. She suppressed a laugh when she noticed the hope of relief on his face.

"Very well, let us go. I am sure the gentlemen will benefit from some time spent by themselves," Elizabeth responded, and Darcy's smile was a sure sign of his approval.

"Lizzy, will you buy us something? Please? I need a new bonnet—at least one—and perhaps a reticule! I know you have so much pin money now, you can buy anything!"

"Lydia!" Jane cried, turning red while Elizabeth felt the blood drain from her face.

"Jane, let the girls ask. I am sure Mr. Darcy would not mind a few gifts," Mrs. Bennet intervened.

Elizabeth barely dared to glance at her husband then declared she would go to change. She rushed to her room, trembling from shame, and a minute later, her husband followed her.

"William, I deeply apologise—sometimes my family is so…"

His smiled largely, gently cupped her face, and then kissed her cheek.

"My aunt treated you in the most horrible way and you bore it graciously. Surely, nothing your family might do can compare to that. As for your younger sisters—I think they deserve to be a little spoiled. After all, you were taken from them, and soon you will leave again. Do anything you can to please them for a couple more days."

He briefly kissed her lips then handed her a velvet bag that obviously contained an important sum of money. Elizabeth gasped.

"William—I could not possibly spend all this. It is too much!"

"I am just being selfish. The more you purchase, the longer you will stay in Meryton."

When they arrived in the drawing room, the noise level had increased acutely.

The girls seemed anxious to leave, and Jane could hardly temper them. Mr. Collins declared he would join them to visit his dear Charlotte.

"I would suggest you go in your own carriage, Mr. Collins. As you said, a clergyman can never be too cautious when it comes to his reputation, and travelling in a carriage with five young ladies might be seen in the wrong light," Darcy said, and the effect of his words was immediate.

MRS. DARCY'S RECEPTION IN MERYTON WAS AS ENTHUSIASTIC AS MRS. BENNET hoped. After greeting their friends, the entire party went to the shop. Lydia and Kitty—also Mary at Elizabeth's insistence—chose bonnets and reticules. To their surprise, they were also allowed to order a new dress each. Jane kindly declined, and Elizabeth did not insist further.

While her younger sisters were caught in the delightful distress of selecting fabrics and lace, through the shop window Elizabeth spotted Mr. Wickham and Lieutenant Denny. It was obvious they saw her too, so she left the shop and met them outside.

The lieutenant spoke first. "What a wonderful surprise to see you again, Miss Bennet—I mean Mrs. Darcy. You look lovelier than ever. It almost seems as if this marriage suits you."

"I thank you, sir, you are very kind. I am delighted to see you too."

Wickham tipped his hat. "Mrs. Darcy—I am very happy to see you again. I imagine you had a very important reason to travel here in such weather."

"I came to see my family."

"Yes, I heard about Mr. Bennet's accident. I hope he is recovering well, and I am equally pleased with the chance to talk with you. We had no time in London, and I imagined Darcy would forbid you to speak to me here too. By the way, did he remain in Town?"

"My husband is at Longbourn with my uncle and Doctor Taylor."

"Really? He came too? That is an even greater surprise."

"Why would you be surprised that my husband travelled with me to visit my ill father?"

Elizabeth's calm left her sooner than she wished, and she struggled to keep her smile. Lieutenant Denny excused himself and went to greet another acquaintance. Wickham took a step closer to her.

"To be honest, I am shocked that Darcy allowed you to come from London at all. I did not mean to say that Mr. Bennet's state was not a serious one, but I know

Darcy did not hurry to see his own father when he fell ill, so you must understand my puzzlement. But it is also true that, at that time, he was…younger and *otherwise engaged*. My godfather was very upset back then by his son's absence."

A smile twisted his lips. Elizabeth paled, attempting to control her anger. He noticed her emotions.

"Mrs. Darcy, it was not my intention to upset you, I assure you. We have always been good friends, and there was a time when we shared the same opinions."

"True, but that changed as I had the opportunity to gather more information about the subjects of those 'shared' opinions. Pray tell me: I understood Mr. Darcy was very fond of his parents and very diligent in attending his duties. Should I now understand the opposite? Am I to believe that Mr. Darcy did not take care of his father?"

"I did not say that. I only mentioned that, when my godfather fell ill, Darcy returned to Pemberley after more than a fortnight. I can easily see that Darcy succeeded in improving your opinion of him. That is hardly surprising. I imagine any woman would improve her opinion of a man—no matter his manners or character—who turned her into the mistress of such an impressive fortune. Darcy can be quite pleasant when he desires. Several ladies, including Lady Stafford, might testify to that."

"Mr. Wickham! I am not surprised to see how often and easily you cross the borders of propriety, and it is entirely my fault as I was not careful in choosing my friends two months ago. Since you mentioned your godfather, I wonder what he would say about the way you treated both his children and especially about your intention to elope with his fifteen-year-old daughter. Compared with that, your failure to properly use the inheritance he left you and your attempt to malign his son's name seem of little importance."

Wickham turned livid and seemed unable to stand. His effort to regain his composure was obvious, and he said in the gentlest of accents:

"Mrs. Darcy—it pains me that I upset you. It was certainly not my intention."

Elizabeth stepped closer to make sure nobody heard their conversation. She felt the anger stiffening her shoulders while her eyes held Wickham's hesitant glance and she spoke in a low, sharp voice.

"And what precisely was your intention, sir? What did you hope to gain by telling me the untrue story of your past business with Mr. Darcy and to speak so unfavourably about Georgiana? What was your purpose in sharing the story with all of Meryton once Mr. Darcy left the neighbourhood? What do you intend in keeping a secret correspondence with a sweet, gentle girl whom you already tried to deceive and compromise, although her brother warned you to stay away?"

"And what did you hope to obtain by spreading false and malicious gossip about Elizabeth's accident?" Darcy coldly inquired from behind Elizabeth.

She startled at her husband's voice. She tried to turn and see whether he was upset to find her speaking alone with Wickham, but his hands rested on her shoulders tenderly.

"Elizabeth, would you please allow me a little privacy with Wickham? We will have a drink at the inn as we have some unfinished business to settle. I will return shortly."

"Of course." She smiled nervously, witnessing Wickham's panicked expression.

"We may as well speak here. I must return to the regiment. I am already late."

"As you wish, though I would think you would not want the people of Meryton to hear what I have to tell you," Darcy replied coldly, his expression dark and severe.

"I... Well... Perhaps I could spare a half an hour, after all. Denny will wait for me."

"One of your rare excellent choices," Darcy concluded, departing towards the Inn with his childhood companion.

Elizabeth entered the shop, wondering how it happened that her husband was in Meryton. He looked calm although he made it clear that he heard her conversation with Wickham.

As upset as her husband might be and as harsh a conversation as he had planned, Wickham deserved it all. *What nerve, what shameless manners the man has!* He showed a complete lack of remorse in his impudent attempts to slander Darcy's name when he knew himself to be at fault. Elizabeth's anger turned into alarm, imagining the life Georgiana would have had if the elopement had taken place. Then the alarm grew back into anger with herself when she admitted that, not long before, she had considered Wickham an excellent man who could make an excellent husband. Foolish girl she was!

"Lizzy, are you unwell?" Was that Mr. Darcy?" Jane inquired worriedly.

"Everything is fine, Jane. Well, not really, but nothing of concern. We must talk about a very important subject as soon as we return home."

A full hour passed before the younger Bennet sisters were content and noisily left the shop. On the street, Mr. Darcy was waiting for them. Elizabeth met her husband's look and breathed in relief as soon as he smiled to comfort her. Everything seemed fine.

"I feared you would be upset when you saw me talking to Wickham, but I simply could not restrain myself when I saw his impertinent manners. I am glad you did not mind."

"My dear, I once made a foolish mistake, which you generously forgave. If I were to repeat it a second time, it would not be a mistake but a choice. I pride myself in not persisting in obtuseness."

She smiled, her cheeks coloured by the freezing wind. "That is true. We should go home now. It is very cold."

"I shall see you there." He kissed her hand, and she returned to her sisters.

THE RIDE BACK TO LONGBOURN WAS VERY SHORT WITH A FOUR-HORSE CARRIAGE. Mrs. Bennet greeted them with eagerness and inquired not so much about the gowns her daughters described in detail but about the reaction of the villagers at seeing the Darcy carriage.

Fortunately, the master of the named object soon retired to the library, together with Mr. Gardiner and Dr. Taylor, and refreshments were sent to match their drinks. Elizabeth hastened to visit her father and found him enjoying a cup of tea.

"Lizzy, your husband told your uncle and me a rather astonishing story about the family's favourite, Mr. Wickham. I say, we should all be ashamed by how easily that man fooled us."

"It was entirely my fault. I never doubted his words. I am truly ashamed of myself."

"And you have reason to be. Fortunately, your husband seems to blame himself and not you. I told Darcy he should speak to Colonel Forster to watch the fellow carefully."

"You must take care too, Papa. Mr. Wickham should not be allowed around Lydia and Kitty."

"Oh, do not worry—they are both too poor to tempt such a man. And too foolish—I doubt he is stupid enough to tie himself to any of them."

"But they are now Mr. Darcy's sisters-in-law, and they might be a temptation for anyone."

"Upon my word, if any of your sisters decide to foolishly elope with anyone, I shall not allow them to receive any other compensation besides their rightful dowry. I will never allow Darcy to be involved in such schemes."

"Papa, William offered me a very generous settlement with a large amount of pin money. I shall save everything in case some from the family might need anything. All will be well."

"Your sisters have been very fortunate in your marriage. I only hope you did not make too big a sacrifice. Darcy's behaviour towards me was praiseworthy, and I have come to respect and admire him quite a lot. I am still not certain that you are suited for each other as your dispositions seemed to be so different. I cannot rest from the concern that I might have pushed you to unhappiness."

"I am not at all unhappy—quite the opposite. I entered this marriage with my eyes open, and I accepted it willingly. But my heart slowly opened to my husband too. He is a very good man, Papa. If you only knew... Please believe that Mr. Darcy has proved his generosity and his kindness to me in ways I dare not tell you." She blushed.

"Oh..." Mr. Bennet was puzzled and distressed by a confession he did not know how to handle. "Well then... If you are at peace with your life, I have nothing more to add."

The conversation lasted for a little while, and then Mr. Bennet returned to rest, accusing Dr. Taylor's teas of forcing him to sleep all the time.

Elizabeth entered the drawing room and saw the entire family gathered again in a lively yet tiresome noise. She glanced at her husband, who was looking around somewhat uneasily. She then turned to Jane and whispered that there was something she wished to speak of privately. The matter of Wickham had to be concluded that very day and be put away for good. The elder sisters held hands as they went to Jane's room.

"What happened, Lizzy? You seem quite serious. I hope Papa is well."

"Yes, do not worry. It does not have to do with Papa but with Mr. Wickham. It is just another occasion to admit how utterly wrong I was in my judgment and how wise and fair you were. But Jane, you must keep this in complete secrecy! William already told it to Papa, and I will tell Aunt Gardiner, but not a word to any other living soul!"

Elizabeth needed less than half an hour to share with her sister the most important parts of the story involving Mr. Wickham and the Darcy family.

"I do not know when I have been more shocked," said Jane. "Wickham so very bad! It is almost past belief. And poor Mr. Darcy—what he must have suffered! Losing his parents at such a young age, then having to bear such betrayal from his friend and cousin, and the pain of his sister! It is really too distressing. I am sure you must feel it so."

"I do, and more so since I witnessed even today Wickham's impertinence and lack of remorse. Jane, you must be strong and not allow either Lydia or Kitty near him. I am afraid he might wish to purposely compromise one of them, and they are silly enough to fall for such a trap. I am thinking if it would be best to take them to London with me."

"Lizzy, that seems too much. Let us not consider Mr. Wickham an ogre. Perhaps he is willing to change for the better. Lydia and Kitty will be fine. You should be concerned for your husband. We all put our hopes in his help, and he might be overwhelmed by our family. He seemed to search for shelter with Aunt and Uncle."

"I know." Elizabeth smiled. "He is a very good man, Jane."

"He must be, Lizzy dear, considering the way he looks at you. Your feelings for him I cannot clearly read, but his affection for you is so obvious."

"My feelings for him are growing stronger every day, Jane. But tell me: How have you been? I missed you, and I needed you so much these past two weeks."

They were interrupted by the surprising appearance of Mrs. Gardiner who had been worried by their long absence. Another emotional half hour was spent by all three together. Everything she told Jane, Elizabeth shared with Mrs. Gardiner, but her aunt was very little surprised, declaring she had long suspected something similar. When she told her aunt and sister about Wickham's being responsible for spreading the gossip that led to her marriage, Elizabeth expected them to be appalled and horrified. She was astounded to see her aunt perfectly calm, patting her hand.

"For that, dear Lizzy, you should thank him. Indeed, we must find a way of expressing our gratitude for his gesture. And if your mother knew this side of the truth, her love for Mr. Wickham would be surpassed only by her admiration for Mr. Darcy himself. Now let us return to the gentlemen. I can hardly wait for the summer to come. I rarely wanted anything as much as I want to spend three months at Pemberley and to visit the estate in a barouche with white horses."

When Elizabeth, together with Jane and Mrs. Gardiner, returned to the drawing room, it was about four in the afternoon. She felt her heart racing with joy when her eyes met her husband's, and a pleasant warmth invaded her. She suddenly realised she had missed him!

Mrs. Bennet was already in her room, as were the Gardiner children, Mary planned to study at the piano, and Lydia and Kitty had run upstairs. Dr. Taylor, the Gardiners, and Jane were still there when Elizabeth suddenly stepped to her husband and whispered.

"Would you like to go for a walk?"

He looked at her in surprise and nodded, so she ran to get her coat, bonnet and gloves. It was freezing, and the snow was creaking under their feet as they stepped carefully. They walked in silence, as close to each other as possible, alone in the wasted fields, the darkness conquering the daylight.

"I really enjoy this: the fresh air, the peace, your company alone…" he said.

"As do I. It is so cold yet so beautiful!

"This is the perfect time for a sleigh ride. The cold is easier to bear under blankets."

She blushed, imagining the sensation of them cuddled together under the blankets, riding along white paths lit by the stars and bright moon, and wondered whether they could find a sleigh in the neighbourhood.

"We have a sleigh in London and one at Pemberley. I cannot believe it did not cross my mind until now. Riding in a sleigh is the best opportunity for one to court a lady."

"And may I ask how you know that, sir, since you claim no experience in matters of courtship?"

"I am inexperienced, not a fool, madam. Any man with some wit knows that."

She laughed. "I cannot believe it has been almost six weeks since my accident and less than two weeks since we married. It seems a lifetime ago."

"True. I remember the day we left for London. You looked sad and frightened."

"I was. I knew not what to expect from you. You were almost a stranger to me."

She stopped and turned to him.

"William, earlier today I realised that something has changed for me—*I* have changed—in these ten days. I love my family dearly, but I look forward to returning *home*. Everything is the same here at Longbourn, yet it feels so different to me! And…it seems silly, but I missed you while I was away today. How strange is that?"

He slowly leant down to her, and his eyes gazed intently into hers, their faces inches apart.

"It is not strange. I miss you all the time. Your words make me very happy."

"Then we are both silly." She attempted to mock him, hoping to conceal the depth of her emotion. "Knowing that everything is well here, I worry about Georgiana. I left her alone, to bear a most difficult situation and to struggle with sorrow. If Papa is improving tomorrow and feels well enough, we should return to London the next day."

"I am worried about Georgiana too, but I trust Robert and Mrs. Annesley to keep her good company. I am grateful for your genuine care, though, and I am certain she misses you."

"You should take both of us on a sleigh ride when we get home," she said and he earnestly promised to do so. They took the path through the groves where Elizabeth used to walk.

"Elizabeth, do you remember when we were at Netherfield? Every evening I prayed that dinner would last longer so I could be in your company more. My heart had long been overwhelmed by your charms, and my body painfully desired your closeness. Only my mind opposed the idea and fought against my chance for happiness. It was the most painful struggle. "

"A struggle you won, it seems, as you did little when we were in company at Netherfield. I cannot but wonder what would have happened had my accident not occurred…"

"I wonder too. And I worry every day. But I wish this to change when we return home, Elizabeth. I do not want to pressure you to consummate our marriage, but I want to share the evenings, the rooms, the beds… I want things to be in London as they were last night."

She held his gaze, and her knees weakened as she tried to find her voice.

"I want things to be *more* than they were last night, William. I want to share *everything* as soon as we return home. It is not that I accept your wishes, but that I am considering my own," she whispered. "My mind has long admired your qualities, and my body began to enjoy your presence some time ago. Now my heart is slowly opening to you."

Her voice trembled and her eyes burned with tears. She knew she should be embarrassed by her unrestrained words, but her soul was so full of joy that there was no room left for other feelings.

The expression of heartfelt delight brightened his face. He seemed unable to speak, just as she was, and his gaze trapped hers with no desire to release it.

With no words to disturb their understanding, she took his arm, and his hands entwined with hers, then they continued their solitary walk. Half an hour passed before they finally returned home, their feet, hands, hair and clothes completely frozen, and their eyes sparkling from the warmth inside.

"Lizzy dear, where have you been? Keeping Mr. Darcy outside in such weather? Indeed child, I can hardly believe you are my daughter with such savage inclinations," Mrs. Bennet cried then paled instantly. "Oh, I mean it in the best, most charming way, Mr. Darcy!"

"I am sure of that, Mrs. Bennet. I find Elizabeth's liveliness truly enchanting, and her inclinations for outdoor activities are perfect for the mistress of Pemberley."

"Oh, I knew that. I already told as much to my sister and to Lady Lucas. Lizzy, you must change to your best gown. I invited the Lucases and the Philipses to dine with us tonight."

Elizabeth stared at her mother then glanced at her uncle and aunt in despair.

"But we are not in a situation suitable for entertaining guests. Papa is still unwell, and he needs rest. And we are still tired after the long ride from London. Can we not cancel it?"

"Oh, Lizzy, what are you talking about? Cancel it? How can I lose the opportunity to host a large dinner in the presence of Mr. Darcy? If we are to spend the summer at Pemberley—Lord help us!—it is likely that such opportunities will not arise again anytime soon!"

Elizabeth fought against her distress, and her head started to ache. Nothing could be worse than a dinner with such a large, noisy gathering. She sought help from her aunt and uncle but with no success. Glancing briefly at her husband, she abandoned the fight.

"Be it as you wish, Mama, since I cannot convince you otherwise. I am going to rest and change for dinner. I am cold and my feet are frozen."

Elizabeth's excellent spirits were ruined. She visited her father, who was in the company of Dr. Taylor, and was content to see him reasonably well, so she withdrew to her room.

She put two logs on the fire, as she felt cold, and then removed her shoes. She took off her stockings and sat on the rug by the fire, rubbing her bare feet with a thick towel while she held her knees to her chest. She did not hear the door open and startled when she saw Darcy entering. Their eyes met as he removed his coat and his boots then sat beside her.

"I apologise for my mother. She wishes to brag about you to our Meryton neighbours. I am so ashamed. It will be a very hard evening."

He embraced her and kissed the top of her head. "I know…Sir William and Mr. Collins are truly the most frightening tandem."

"True—and Lady Lucas and my aunt Philips—but I promise to protect you."

"Will you, Mrs. Darcy? I must thank you for that."

He slowly removed the towel from her feet and covered them with his palms, stroking the skin reddened by their passage from snow to fire. Only the wood crackling in the fireplace and her soft moans of delight broke the silence for a while. His fingers turned more daring, caressing from her feet along her ankles and upward again and again, and she bit her lips, closing her eyes.

"I must change for dinner," she finally whispered, and he ceased his attention to her feet and turned her with her back to him. She did not oppose him. His palms rested on her shoulders and glided down along her arms, then moved to her nape.

"I shall help you," he whispered from behind, his lips tantalising her ear. With a skilfulness she remembered from a few nights ago, he untied her dress and pushed it down from her shoulders.

His movements were neither restrained nor shy this time as his fingers knew their rights and her desires. Her skin shivered and she burned inside when his hands lowered over her ribs, over her hips and thighs, then removed the dress completely. She attempted to turn to him but his arms forbade it, pulling her back close against his torso. Her spine pressed against his chest, her hips resting between his open legs.

His head rested on her neck, his lips tantalising her cheek, her temple, her ear, then lowered to her neck and bare shoulders. He took a blanket from the bed, wrapping it around them. She entwined her hands with his and leant her head back towards him. His hand caressed her face, brushing her lips with his thumb.

"What are we to do now?" he whispered while her lips parted slowly.

"We can stay and warm up a little...and rest," she barely answered.

She turned in his arms until his mouth finally captured hers. She moaned at his passionate exploration of her body covered only in a chemise. He stroked along her ribs, hips, and thighs, then cupped the roundness of her breasts.

The feeling was so powerful that both froze and broke the kiss. Her erratic breathing pressed within his strong palms, fitting perfectly inside them. He shyly tasted the skin of her neck, allowing her lips the freedom to oppose him if she wished to. She did not and only leant back against his chest. His thumbs brushed and traced circles around her breast, burning her through the thin fabric. She breathed heavier and whispered his name until her lips were captured once again. The kiss deepened, and passion overwhelmed her. Her hands tried to caress, to touch, to explore without her knowing what she was doing, except she heard his moans matching hers.

She could not speak nor breathe although her lips were now free. His hand slowly lowered to her thighs and tentatively brushed along her legs.

Darcy could feel her body shivering, silently begging for more, he recognised the truth of her confession about her body enjoying his presence. She now had a small taste of what pleasure meant, and her desire was growing stronger, almost matching his. No, not almost, not by far. He madly yearned for her—and she had just started to know her wishes, but those were closely related to him.

They were sitting near the fire, covered by a blanket, and his touches were still delighting her body. The knock on the door was so powerful that Elizabeth almost jumped from her husband's arms, attempting to rise, when she realised she was half-naked. She pulled a sheet from the bed around her and the knocking became stronger.

"Lizzy!" she heard Jane's voice, and she relaxed a little, moving closer to the door. "Lizzy!"

Elizabeth opened the door a little. "Jane, we shall be ready shortly. Is something wrong?"

"No, nothing is wrong, but Mr. Bingley is downstairs! He just arrived from London and stopped here directly. He said he received a letter from Mr. Darcy, and then he learnt of Papa's accident, and he came immediately. He looks so pale and tired. He had travelled a full day and night. He is waiting for Mr. Darcy. Oh, perhaps he could stay for dinner. He must be starved…"

"Jane dearest, go and prepare for dinner. I shall join you immediately. Yes, I am sure Mr. Bingley will stay and eat with us. Please tell him Mr. Darcy will see him in a few minutes."

Elizabeth barely managed to close the door, staring at her husband who was a step behind her. At her inquiring gaze, he shrugged.

"I know nothing more than you do. I sent him that letter and received no answer until now. He must have called on me and learnt about Mr. Bennet. It is to his merit that he came in such haste. Oh…and I am not certain whether he knows we are married," Darcy responded with perfect calmness.

"We must hurry. Please change your clothes, and I will go to Jane to help each other do our hair," she said in great excitement. "Poor Jane, oh how tormented she was. Mr. Bingley…"

She was silenced by a most unexpected kiss, and for a moment, she attempted to oppose. Only for a moment! He slowly pushed her onto the bed and leant over her, claiming her lips again.

"We may delay a moment longer. Bingley is not waiting in the cold. I cannot separate from you so abruptly," he whispered, and after another brief attempt at rejection, she abandoned herself to the delight of his passionate kiss.

Her husband was right once again. After all, Mr. Bingley had been gone almost six weeks. Surely, he could wait a few more minutes.

Chapter 24

Longbourn, 7 January, evening

Elizabeth hurried to Jane's room, allowing her husband time to change for dinner.

"Oh Lizzy, what do you say about this? I hope I did not bother Mr. Darcy with my knocking at your door. I must say I almost fainted when he entered—Mr. Bingley, not Mr. Darcy!"

Elizabeth laughed. "Jane, we must breathe deeply and calm ourselves. It may be a very distressing evening. Such a strange coincidence to have Mr. Bingley return just now!"

"But Lizzy, do you think he will return to Netherfield—to stay? If not, why would he come in such haste? Did you know that Mr. Darcy wrote him?"

"I did know. Mr. Bingley must have some keen interest in Hertfordshire, and I doubt he will leave again soon. What dress do you want to wear?"

A reasonable time later, the elder sisters went downstairs, as the Lucases and the Philipses had already arrived. Elizabeth took a turn to her father's room while Jane politely greeted the visitors. Mr. Bennet was asleep, so Elizabeth headed towards the gathering.

She noticed her husband, obviously uncomfortable, surrounded by Sir William and Mr. Collins, silently supported by Mr. Gardiner and Dr. Taylor. A strange sense of shyness averted her eyes from his.

Less than an hour before, she was in his arms, quivering from his passionate kisses. The traces of his hands on her skin were still vivid as well as the taste of his lips on hers, which she unconsciously licked then brushed with her fingers.

Her face and neck coloured in shame when she realised her husband was staring at her as if guessing her thoughts. He slowly gulped his wine, his eyes travelling along her body. She shivered.

Mr. Bingley's happy voice brought her back from her improper musings. She gave a friendly smile as he hastened to greet her. Elizabeth responded warmly and asked the gentleman about his sisters and his plans to stay in the neighbourhood. Elizabeth Bennet would surely not dare to ask Mr. Bingley so directly, but Mrs.

Elizabeth Darcy did it with perfect self-confidence. The gentleman seemed troubled.

"Well, my sisters are still in Town. I only saw them briefly. I was just talking to Darcy about that...about my plans... I would like to remain in Hertfordshire. I cannot remember a happier time than the last months spent at Netherfield. I was just asking Darcy..."

"Mr. Bingley!" Elizabeth interrupted him rather sharply but kept her smile. "I believe it would be wise to decide not what you would *like* to do but what you *want* to do—what you think is best for you. I know Mr. Darcy's advice might be invaluable at times, but there are moments when a man must make his own decisions and take the risk of following them."

"Yes, well...it is true... I shall... Yes, my men have already opened Netherfield and..."

"I am very pleased to hear that. We are all delighted to enjoy your company, Mr. Bingley."

"Thank you, Miss Bennet—I mean Mrs. Darcy."

Elizabeth offered her hand, which he hastily lifted to his lips. Then she was stopped by her mother's voice.

"Lizzy! Tell Lady Lucas how many jewels and gowns you have. She doubts me because you are still wearing your old dress and that garnet cross! Tell her what you told me."

"Mama!" Elizabeth cried with shame. She paled when her husband stepped forward.

"I assure you, madam, that Mrs. Darcy was offered everything that is fit for her position. We left London in such a hurry when we heard about Mr. Bennet's illness that we only packed what was urgent. We certainly did not expect to attend any parties, so we are rather unprepared in that respect. Besides, I believe that no special jewellery or clothing could add more to her natural beauty." Elizabeth stared at him and blushed.

"Oh, that is so gentlemanlike of you, sir! Such perfect manners, indeed! How have I been so fortunate to find a man so happily gifted as my son-in-law?"

"I did not doubt you, Mrs. Bennet. I was just a little surprised that I did not see much change in Lizzy," Lady Lucas said.

"Indeed, " Mr. Collins intruded. "I see no difference and no improvement in my cousin."

Darcy's teeth clenched. "What difference did you expect to see, Mr. Collins? And what improvement could occur when there was nothing to improve in the first place?"

His voice addressed Mr. Collins sharply, but his gaze caressed Elizabeth's face with a warmth that made her shiver. A little smile twisted his lips.

"I have seen Mrs. Darcy at a private ball and at the opera," Dr. Taylor intervened. "She was the centre of attention, and her gowns and jewels were much admired, as were her manners and dancing skills."

"Thank you, Dr. Taylor, you are too kind, sir." Elizabeth smiled at him. "May we exchange this conversation for another?"

"Mrs. Darcy is a wonderful dancer—as is Miss Bennet." Mr. Bingley's warm eyes fixed on Elizabeth as he forced himself not to look at her elder sister.

Lydia spoke cheerfully. "Lizzy was always a great dancer. I don't know why Mr. Darcy did not want to dance with her at the Meryton assembly! He was quite rude back then, but he has improved very much lately. Charlotte, you must take care of Mr. Collins. I imagine as a clergymen he rarely dances—which one can easily tell by watching him."

Elizabeth stared at her sisters in shock, not daring to meet her husband's eyes. The announcement that dinner was served sounded like a breath of fresh air to Elizabeth.

"I am very sorry," she whispered to Darcy, and he briefly brought her hand to his lips.

"Do not worry. I am becoming accustomed to the clamour."

She smiled bitterly. "I am certain you will reconsider your kind invitation for my family to spend the summer at Pemberley."

"Not at all—Pemberley is a very large estate. Your family will have a private wing and staff to attend their needs." His voice was light and his expression amused. She smiled back.

"Then perhaps we could invite Mr. Collins too?"

"Madam, do not abuse my generosity," he replied in earnest.

Dinner was as distressing as Elizabeth expected. She managed to place Darcy between Mr. Gardiner and Mr. Bingley, who did nothing but smile sheepishly at Miss Bennet. He entertained them with the story of his journey back to Hertfordshire and listened to Mr. Collins's long considerations about travelling in winter, but he barely heard a word.

Elizabeth sat near Charlotte, enjoying her old friend's company but heavyhearted imagining the future life of Mrs. Collins.

At the other corner of the table, Mrs. Bennet, Mrs. Philips, and Lady Lucas entertained themselves cheerfully until dinner was over. Mr. Gardiner invited the gentlemen for a drink. However, it started to snow steadily again, so the guests took their farewells early with no little regret.

The remaining gentlemen—including Mr. Collins—moved towards the library while the ladies discussed the dinner. Elizabeth could breathe a little easier. The evening was almost ended.

She excused herself to visit her father, and in the hall, she met her husband.

"Are you well? Are you trying to escape Mr. Collins?" she attempted to joke.

"No, I was actually coming to you. There is something we need to discuss."

She frowned although his expression was light.

"Bingley insists that I join him at Netherfield. He pointed out that Longbourn is very crowded."

Her face and neck coloured instantly as she thought she guessed his meaning.

"Of course… Netherfield is much more private. I shall pack a few things, and I will tell the others." She was so distressed that she could hardly speak. *So it will finally happen!*

"Pack? I was thinking to go alone. Bingley is anxious to speak to me. He seemed equally excited and tormented. And you will also have time to spend with your family, not to mention that we will finally find a little sleep." He smiled.

She stared at him, realising her foolishness and paled, averting her eyes.

"Oh, I thought… Yes, you are right. Of course, you should go alone. I am so silly."

"Elizabeth, what is wrong?" he inquired with obvious concern. "You seem displeased."

"Not at all… You will certainly be more comfortable at Netherfield. I shall stay here with my family. Now, please excuse me. I will go to my father."

"Please tell me what upsets you. I shall not go to Netherfield if you do not agree."

"It is quite foolish, actually. I thought you wanted me to go with you and… last night we…"

"I see… My dear, do you *want* to come to Netherfield with me?"

"No… Yes… I mean—if you wish. Oh, do not ask me that. I cannot speak of it."

He tipped her chin with his warm fingers, caressing her face. "Please do not turn the consummation of our marriage into a reason for turmoil. All will be well and happen in its own time in *our* own home. At Netherfield, I can speak to Bingley and allow us to rest. I can easily count almost a week of sleepless nights and distress for both of us. Do you agree?"

"Yes, I do. Completely. As you know, I rarely disagree with your proposals."

Their eyes and smiles met and held. He took her hand, then his lips tantalised her fingers and the inside of her palm, lingering on her wrist. He captured her lips for what he wanted to last a moment, but her hands encircled his waist, and the kiss turned more passionate. Some hurried steps were heard, and then Lydia and Mrs. Bennet's voices startled them.

"Mama, Lizzy is kissing Mr. Darcy in the hall! I told you she cannot be far away!"

"Hush, silly child, come here and be quiet! Do not bother them. Mr. Darcy hates noisy girls!"

Elizabeth and her husband separated a few inches, smiling and breathing erratically.

"I shall come with you to wish Mr. Bennet a good night. Tomorrow, I plan to spend the morning with him as we still have several subjects to discuss."

"He will be happy with your company. And if everything goes well, we should return to London the day after tomorrow. I am sure Georgiana misses us. Jane will take care of Papa."

"And since Bingley has opened Netherfield again, we can trust him to offer any support your family might need. I am sure he will be more than willing to assume that task."

"William, do you intend to tell Mr. Bingley anything special?"

"Do you *want* me to tell him something special?"

"Quite the opposite. I already suggested to him that he should make his own decisions. He must learn his own heart and fight for what he wants. He must cease depending on your opinions and advice for everything in his life."

"Your reasoning is sound. Besides, after all the distress I had to endure in the last month, it would be a relief to see him suffering too—although I doubt Miss Bennet will torment him too much. And by the way, I thought Miss Bennet looked remarkably beautiful today."

"You are right. If Mr. Bingley does the right thing, his suffering won't be too long."

AFTER A SHORT, YET PLEASANT VISIT WITH MR. BENNET, DARCY AND ELIZABETH returned to the drawing room.

With deep sadness, Mr. Collins informed them that he would return to Kent the next morning, news cheerfully accepted by the others.

However, the information that Mr. Darcy would move to Netherfield distressed Mrs. Bennet as she wondered whether her daughter had somehow upset her husband. She was relieved only when Mr. Darcy asked permission to return for breakfast. Mrs. Bennet assured him that nobody would eat a single gobbet before their arrival in the morning.

Darcy's distress was painfully obvious to Elizabeth. He still carried the fatigue of the sleepless nights in Box Hill, another night on the road, and the previous one in which he had barely slept. Then the noise in the house, Mr. Collins's annoyance, her mother, and now a house full of guests watching him as if he were a spectacle. How much effort he must exert to deal with everything—and for what other reason than to please her?

Before midnight, within the privacy of their small room, Elizabeth and Darcy took a brief farewell. Darkness and silence eventually fell upon Longbourn after a day equally eventful and painfully long.

THE FORMER MISS ELIZABETH'S ROOM WAS ANIMATED WITH THE CHATTING OF the two sisters: one speaking cheerfully, smiling more beautifully than ever, wondering about the astonishing surprise of the day, and afraid to be too happy or too hopeful. The other listened absentmindedly, glanced out the window, and forced herself to be happy and attentive.

Very late at night, Jane retired, and Elizabeth lay in the bed, which now seemed strangely large and cold. She *knew* she was very tired, and her eyelids grew heavier, yet her restlessness only increased.

She realised how acutely she missed her husband, and sleep evaded her completely. She turned from one side to the other, felt cold, then too warm, and then finally forced herself to close her eyes. In an instant, her mind and body were invaded with memories of his caresses, his kisses, his scent, and the warmth and safety his arms gave her. She quivered with cold shivers while she wondered what he was doing. In less than a month, her feelings had changed from almost hating him to almost loving him! How was it possible?

"Almost"? If she only *almost* loved him, how was it possible that she felt so alone without him? And how was it possible that she regretted so painfully that he did not ask her to go to Netherfield with him and consummate their marriage?

Did she just admit that? Yes—that was the truth! She had been a little concerned about that possibility, but she was more eager than worried.

I want to be his wife! But how can I possibly dare tell him that?

When Elizabeth was finally overcome with exhaustion, the servants awoke and started their duties. Another day began at Longbourn.

Longbourn, 8 January

A BRIGHT LIGHT BREAKING THROUGH THE CURTAINS TOLD ELIZABETH HOW LATE it was. She dressed, did her hair in hurry, and then hastened to the dining room. Breakfast was surely ready.

First, she went to check on her father, and with no little surprise, she discovered him sitting in the armchair fully attired and talking with Darcy. Both gentlemen smiled in welcome.

"Good morning and forgive me for being so late. Papa, are you allowed to leave your bed?"

"I most certainly am. Sit with us Lizzy. I just told your husband that it is time for you to return to London. A couple married in such unusual circumstances needs privacy."

"I agree. But you must promise that you will send us word of anything you might need. I cannot be at peace unless I am sure that I know whether something bad happens at Longbourn."

"I promise, my child," Mr. Bennet said, squeezing her hand. "I confess I was very worried when you left two weeks ago, Lizzy, but I am not anymore. I am more confident now that I did not force you into unhappiness."

Elizabeth tearfully embracing her father. Darcy intended to leave, but she held his arm.

"Please stay, William. I have nothing to hide from you. Papa, let me tell one more thing: last night William was at Netherfield, and I could not sleep without him until dawn. Do you need more proof that I am not unhappy in this marriage?"

Her father stared at her with the same astonishment as her husband. She smiled, flushing.

"Indeed, child, I now understand your mother's complaint about your tormenting her nerves. Go and speak of these ladies' matters somewhere else. Mr. Darcy and I have some business to tend," he said, his amusement matching his disbelief. Elizabeth laughed and finally met Darcy's eyes.

"Mr. Bennet and I agreed upon several ways to improve Longbourn's income. As Bingley decided to remain in the neighbourhood, he offered to help Mr. Bennet."

"He did?" Elizabeth answered with little surprise. "How lovely of him."

"Yes, yes, Bingley is such a joyful fellow. Your mother and your sister Jane seemed very pleased by his return. I say, Darcy, somehow you succeeded in making three women from my family happy—even four if we are to count my sister Gardiner. If you have ideas for the youngest three, I am open to any suggestion," Mr. Bennet said with perfect seriousness.

Elizabeth laughed, but Darcy was at a loss as how to reply. Mr. Bennet laughed too. "I am pleased that I can still surprise you with some of my remarks, sir. I will miss you starting tomorrow, and my cousin is not here to comfort me. Sad day, indeed. Now, we had better eat and return to business later."

BREAKFAST AT LONGBOURN WAS AS NOISY AS USUAL, BUT MR. BENNET'S COMPANY and Mr. Collins's absence made it really pleasant. Mrs. Bennet split her admiration between Mr. Darcy and Mr. Bingley, but she obviously favoured the former.

Later in the afternoon, Mr. and Mrs. Bennet retired to rest, and so did the Gardiners and Dr. Taylor, while the younger gentlemen and the sisters remained in the living room.

"What would you say to a short walk? The weather is lovely," Elizabeth proposed.

"Oh, Lizzy, what a strange idea—to walk in such freezing weather! Can we not go to Meryton with the carriage? That would be fun!"

"No, Lydia. We have no time and no reason to go to Meryton."

"I believe a walk would be lovely," Jane answered, casting a charming smile. Mr. Bingley approved eagerly. Mr. Darcy only smiled and fetched his coat.

"As you wish, girls, we will go and return shortly," Elizabeth addressed her younger sisters.

Elizabeth took her husband's arm, followed by Jane shyly walking with Mr. Bingley.

"I am sorry you did not sleep much last night," Darcy said to his wife.

Her cheeks warmed despite the cold weather. "I slept enough. I spoke to Jane until late. It was lovely to spend time with her. Did *you* sleep well?"

"Yes. We talked a great deal and enjoyed several glasses of brandy, which were helpful."

"I am glad…that you slept, I mean. And that you spoke to Mr. Bingley. Is everything well? Did he decide his future plans? I imagine his sisters are not at all pleased with his return."

"He seemed very decided. He is a smart man but does not trust himself enough. And yes, his sisters are quite upset. They argued when they saw him in London. He went to visit me, but obviously, I was not home. Robert told him what had happened, so after a terrible fight with Caroline, he hurried to Hertfordshire to offer his help. He said he had no hopes of his reception here, so he made no plans until after last night's dinner. Now, apparently, his hopes have grown significantly. He is a good man. He deserves happiness."

"He might, but he also easily fell in love; you said that. Should we trust his feelings?"

"I said he was easily *charmed*, but many young men are. As for the strength of his feelings: I believe your sister is wise enough to decide whether she should trust them."

A short silence followed, and then Elizabeth asked hesitantly, keeping her eyes ahead.

"I agree. It is time for both of them to be left to themselves. Will you still go to Netherfield tonight?"

"That was my intention."

They were still walking at a relative distance from Jane and Bingley. His steps slowed, and he looked at her. "Do you want me *not* to go to Netherfield?" he inquired gently.

She hesitated a single moment. "Yes… Unless you prefer it that way…"

"Elizabeth, I want to be honest with you. I would rather sleep at Netherfield because I do not have the strength to share that bed with you again. Last night I needed brandy to keep my mind from you. And even while I slept, I dreamt of you. I think of little else but your skin, your scent, your warmth, your caresses, the taste of your lips… It was one thing in London as I could easily step away when you wanted me to. But here, I have nowhere to go. And the knowledge that you would allow me to take you as my wife makes the struggle more difficult. Please forgive me if my words make you uncomfortable. I never have had so little control over myself, and I am ashamed of my weakness."

Another long pause followed, filled with tension and shared embarrassment.

"I am glad you told me. There are many things about which I wish to speak to Jane, and tonight will be a good opportunity," she concluded. He just smiled and kissed her hand.

Not only the Darcys but also the Gardiners decided to return to Town, so the rest of the day was exceedingly agitated and tiresome with preparation.

Dr. Taylor gave strict advice to Mr. Bennet and to Jane—who took the responsibility for following it. Mrs. Bennet's nerves struggled with all the excitement but were somehow calmed by Mr. Bingley's presence and the prospect of being Mr. Darcy's guest very soon.

Elizabeth spent half an hour speaking with both Lydia and Kitty. She made them see their future prospects. She warned them about the danger of jeopardising their good names and insisted on more propriety and decorum on their part. Elizabeth also promised to reward their good behaviour with invitations to Town for the Season, with a proper coming out party in the next year and a private ball for them, hosted at the Meryton assembly, with the attendance of all of Meryton society. Lydia and Kitty could not breathe from excitement.

Dinner was equally rich but more silent than previous meals yet by no means less pleasant. Mr. Bennet found great joy in teasing his wife and daughters but also his gentlemen guests.

It was discussed that their departure would take place early in the morning. Soon after dinner, the ladies retired to their rooms. The gentlemen, however—except Mr. Bennet—remained in the library to enjoy a last glass of brandy and finish discussing some business.

Elizabeth spent a few more minutes with Jane then changed for the night. She felt cold, put a log on the fire, pulled the curtains open so she could see outside, and wrapped herself in the blankets, waiting to fall asleep. The night was lit by the moon and stars, and she was suddenly bothered by so much light, so she pulled the curtains closed again then returned to bed wondering what *he* was doing. His words from earlier in the garden were still vivid in her mind, and she was equally ashamed, overwhelmed, and delighted by his improper confession. He was right to go to Netherfield. He was much wiser than she was. And tomorrow they would be back home—*their home.*

Finally, she felt warm and safe, and both her mind and body relaxed, diving into a most charming dream. She turned to find a more comfortable position, and only then did she realise it was real: the safety, warmth, and peace came from the arms of her husband wrapped around her. She sighed and moved closer, her head resting near his shoulder.

"You did not go to Netherfield..."

"No," he replied, pulling her near his chest and kissing her hair.

Her heavy eyes glanced at him. "But you said you cannot bear another night..."

"I know what I said, but I always prided myself on the power of my self-control. Besides, it is a husband's duty to put his wife's wishes above his own weakness. You wanted me to be here—and I am."

She brushed over his torso while searching for the perfect position. One hand glided down his shirt towards his waist, and her head rested upon his heart. He caressed her hair and breathed deeply, already struggling with his vaunted self-control.

"Are you comfortable?" he asked gently.

"Yes, perfectly, Thank you, my love," she whispered as she was quickly overcome by sleep.

Darcy held his breath, bewitched by her scent and her warm softness, and not daring to believe the meaning of the words he just heard.

Longbourn, January 9, morning

WHEN DAYLIGHT CAME, THE ENTIRE HOUSE WAS FULLY AWAKE AND READY FOR breakfast. Mr. Bingley also arrived, offering his help if it were needed. The luggage was arranged, good-byes shared, light tears and regrets hidden, and promises exchanged.

Mr. Darcy generously proposed that Elizabeth, Mrs. Gardiner, and the children take his carriage—which was significantly larger—while the three gentlemen travelled in the Gardiners'.

The journey back to London began on an icy, serene day. The roads were fairly good, and the distance, which in summer took less than three hours, was covered in almost eight with three stops.

After some brief conversation in the gentlemen's carriage, the time was mostly passed in silence. Darcy found a well-deserved rest and even fell asleep at times.

The ladies and the children spent an animated and trying time. Elizabeth settled with her aunt an invitation to dinner in two days. Mrs. Gardiner confessed her delight and her nervousness at the thought of being in Lady Anne's home and meeting her daughter.

London, 9 January, afternoon

Dr. Taylor was taken first to his residence and then the Gardiners to theirs.

Finally, Elizabeth and Darcy were alone in their carriage, peaceful and strangely uneasy. They sat opposite each other, smiling, holding gazes as he took her hands. No words were said, no other gesture made—only thoughts, hopes, and promises silently shared.

At five in the afternoon, Mr. and Mrs. Darcy arrived home, and their reception was heartwarming. Mrs. Thomason welcomed them first, and immediately after, lively barking and the sound of scrambling paws preceded the impetuous entry of Titan and Lucky, jumping so happily that they almost pushed the Darcys down. Both dogs were rewarded with tender attention

Shortly after, Peter entered, bowing properly to the master and mistress, and a few minutes later, Georgiana ran to embrace her brother and sister.

With great difficulty, Elizabeth and Darcy managed to walk to the stairs, promising to return shortly. The dogs followed them, then stopped and looked at Peter. Both remained uncertain, glancing to each of their favourite humans.

Darcy turned to Peter. "I can see you took good care of the dogs. They seem fond of you."

"Yes, master. I love them."

"The dogs suffered when you left," Georgiana intervened. "They barked and whined at your doors so I decided to let Peter sleep in the small guest room in the family wing with both Titan and Lucky. It was the only way to keep them at peace."

"I shall move at once, master," Peter said hastily.

"It seems a perfect arrangement, and I would like to keep it that way. Both Mrs. Darcy and I will need to rest undisturbed at least a few more days, and I think the dogs will be perfectly fine with you. Is that acceptable to you, Peter?"

The boy stared in disbelief at the master asking his opinion instead of chasing him away from the family wing. "Yes, sir, yes… Thank you."

"Excellent," Darcy said, forcing the smirk from his face.

"Brother—Robert, Thomas, and Maryanne are to visit later. They do not know you have returned. And Aunt Matlock invited me for dinner tonight, but I will postpone that. And there is something I need to speak to you about later," she said shyly.

"Excellent," Darcy repeated, barely hearing his sister's words.

Molly and Stevens unpacked their belongings and ordered hot water for bathing later in the evening. The two dogs ran freely between their feet, and the only privacy Elizabeth and Darcy could share were smiles and short whispers of "I am happy to be home."

While Darcy checked his mail, Elizabeth briefly changed her clothes and hastened downstairs. She greeted Mrs. Annesley, embraced Georgiana again, and then paid a short visit to the staff area. Her presence was much appreciated, and Carlton, the cook, asked her preference for dinner and then daringly inquired after her father.

After that part of her duties was accomplished, Elizabeth planned to return to Georgiana. However, her steps took her to the front of the gallery once again, and after looking around to be certain nobody observed her foolish gesture, she curtseyed properly and said:

"Good day, Lady Anne, we just returned home. I am so happy to see you again." Then she smiled at her own foolishness and brushed her fingers over the painting.

Precisely two weeks earlier at the same time, she had arrived at Darcy's house, overwhelmed by worries, questions, fears, and self-reproaches. And then, in front of that painting, she had recollected Lady Anne and their meeting ten years before. Her heart was suddenly filled with emotion, and her eyes moistened with tears. She decidedly wiped them and smiled as she stepped closer.

"Lady Anne, my eyes are full of joy again," she whispered.

"Elizabeth? I was looking for you and I thought I might find you here."

"I know it is silly, but I came to greet Lady Anne," she answered her husband.

His arms embraced her from behind as his lips touched her hair. "It is not silly…"

"I was remembering when I first arrived two weeks ago precisely. Was it only a fortnight? I truly feel as if it were a year at least. I clearly recollect my feelings as the memories of my meeting with Lady Anne and Georgiana came back to me."

"I remember too. I remember every moment of every day since I first met you, Elizabeth."

There was silence again, and his tender embrace proved the truth of his words. She felt warm, safe, and happy, and she turned in his arms to face him.

She released a small cry when, to her complete surprise, Lucky jumped on her. She leant to pet him while the dog moved from her to Darcy.

"My sweet boy, I missed you. I hope you missed me too, but you seem to favour a certain person at least as much as you do me."

She laughed, caressing the dog, and then turned to her husband. "I am so surprised at how quickly Lucky has grown fond of you. He liked you almost from the first moment. It was as if you were an old friend he forgot about and just met again."

"He must have felt from the beginning how much *I* liked *you*," Darcy said, smiling.

The dog played around a couple more minutes then ran off.

Darcy put his arms back around her, and she leant against him. He kissed her temple.

"Elizabeth," he said hesitantly, caressing her hair. "There is something I have wanted to tell you for the last two weeks, but I never found the right moment. Since we are here again, it seems the perfect occasion."

She withdrew slightly to meet his eyes. "This sounds very serious. Should I worry?"

"No, not at all—quite the opposite." He smiled, gently touching her face. "I… Ten years ago, I was with my father and Robert in Brighton, visiting my mother. Unfortunately, things did not progress as well as we expected, and by the time we arrived, she was in bed, too weak to walk. Poor Georgiana was so frightened, never leaving her side. My father was lost, and I was helpless. I was not even nineteen. And one day—it was cloudy and windy, and I went for a walk just to escape the pain I was feeling…"

Elizabeth listened, curious as to what else remained unsaid while a heavy weight burdened her chest. He tightened his arms around her as if he were afraid she might leave.

"Robert followed me until I reached the beach. I walked in haste, with no purpose, while the wind blew stronger; I remember it started to rain. Suddenly I heard the cries of a woman and a girl, and I looked towards the water. There, a small head appeared in the waves, and I immediately ran to it. The sea was not deep—it barely passed my chest. I walked through the water, easily grabbed the child—it was a girl—and took her out. She was crying, and on the beach I noticed in her arms a small black and white puppy that seemed drowned. I remember stroking the puppy's belly and heart; he quickly recovered. The girl thanked me for saving her puppy while the woman and the other girl embraced her."

His eyes were watching her face as he spoke, and he could easily perceive the turmoil inside her: the sadness, curiosity, surprise, disbelief, and shock, and then the pallor, the slight tremble of her lips, the tears in her eyes, and the quiver of her entire body. Her hands fell from around his waist, and she withdrew slightly, attempting to evade his arms.

Darcy continued. "I completely forgot about the story until the day we wed when you told me how you met my mother and a strange hero saved you and Lucky. I wished to tell you back then, but things were so strange between us. I was so much in love with you and so disappointed that your feelings were quite the opposite. Since you spoke so warmly about that young man you considered your hero, it seemed inappropriate to say, 'Well, I am that hero.' I simply could not do it. And then…I know it might sound selfish and arrogant, but I wished so much for you to care for me, to feel something for me without being influenced by the past. I wanted to gain your good opinion, your affection… I remember the first evening of our marriage when we drank wine together and you fell asleep: I promised myself to become your hero again. Pretty silly and childish, I know."

He smiled nervously, his arms tightening around her as she still attempted to pull away.

Elizabeth had no strength for a single word. Her mind was spinning as her heart raced wildly and her knees grew weaker each moment. It could not be—could not be possible!

He saved my life ten years ago? He was the one whose face I struggled to remember for so many years? The man whom my relatives tried so hard to find and thank? The one I have admired since I was ten? And Lucky—is it possible that Lucky somehow remembered him? He *saved me?* He?!

Questions flew inside her mind as she stopped breathing, staring as if seeing him for the first time. She pulled back again, and this time his arms released her. She turned to run, but her feet betrayed her, and she fell on her knees in front of Lady Anne's portrait, tearful and drained of emotion.

She felt herself lifted and carried. She recognised her husband's arms then the softness of her bed. As she closed her eyes, she felt his kiss on her temple and heard the door closing.

Chapter 25

Elizabeth was uncertain how much time passed before she woke from something like sleep.

Her husband's revelation was so powerful that it took her breath away again. Unbelievably, he was the one who saved her ten years ago—the son of the woman she so admired and whose brief acquaintance marked her childhood!

He was her hero? He was indeed, and two weeks after the wedding she finally discovered it. And yes, he was right again: fate had such a strange way of toying with them and their lives!

Had he told her earlier, perhaps… But no! She felt he was right in delaying the confession; otherwise, she never would have come to discover his true character.

He would not have had the chance to become her hero again. That is what he said. "Silly and childish"? Not at all…

There was still so much to ponder with this new disclosure, so many things to discuss, to clarify—but she had no strength or will to do so for the time being. It was evening, it was dark, and they were at home. She wished to speak to him.

As she tried to arrange her appearance, her mind kept repeating how such a coincidence was possible. She rang for Molly, who appeared immediately, informing her that the master was downstairs with Miss Darcy and Mrs. Annesley, entertaining Colonel Fitzwilliam, the viscount, and Lady Maryanne.

Elizabeth joined the rest of the family, and they received her with much warmth. She felt Darcy's worried gaze, and she responded with a quick smile.

"Elizabeth, I am so pleased that your father is well! Such a nice surprise that you have returned. We are going to dine with Thomas's parents, but I imagine neither you nor Georgiana will come now."

"No, we are very tired. However, I would very much like to have dinner together one of these days. So, how was the ball? You must give me details."

"The ball was lovely, but…" When Lady Maryanne hesitated, Darcy continued, slightly embarrassed.

"They just told me that Annabelle appeared at the ball with a dress exactly like the one I ordered for you, only a different colour."

"I hope it was not a tragedy," Elizabeth smiled. "I imagine many dresses look alike."

"Lady Isabella said it was not alike at all, as it was not about the dress but the person who wears it. Lady Stafford had a nasty argument with her. If you had been present, things might have become somewhat awkward but as it was, I would rather call it ridiculous."

"I agree." Elizabeth marvelled at how little affected she was about Annabelle.

"And there is another bad news: Lady Catherine is in Town," Darcy added. "She came here yesterday, but Robert did not allow her to enter beyond the main hall."

"Could this be a problem?" Elizabeth noticed the others' worried glances.

"Well, she—"

"No!" Darcy intervened. "I shall speak to her tomorrow. You have nothing to worry about."

"Then let us change the subject. Pray tell me, are Lord and Lady Matlock well, I hope?" Elizabeth said charmingly, unable to dissipate her concern completely.

After their guests left, dinner was ordered. It passed quietly and ended early. Elizabeth and Darcy retired to their suites soon after. The day had been long and exhausting.

While the servants prepared their baths, Elizabeth's anxiety increased. She felt troubled and embarrassed without knowing why. She delayed speaking to her husband until she could not avoid it. As they had not talked since the confession in the gallery, he began by apologising again.

"William, let us not speak of this now, please! I am not upset—in truth, I am a little—but I am too distressed now, and I cannot bear anything more."

"I am sorry. We will only speak of what you wish. But why are you distressed? What a silly question—you have so many reasons to be upset and troubled."

"True, but I shall put them aside for now. I will have a bath and then… I remember what I promised." She averted her eyes, blushing slightly.

He seemed puzzled, and then his fingers tipped her chin.

"Elizabeth, you have no reason to be troubled and no promise to fulfil. It has been a long day, and you have had to endure so much. There is no need for haste. I will take a bath too and will be in my room. I would be delighted to have a glass of wine with you and to speak a little more. And I may keep you company until you fall asleep if you wish."

Darcy briefly kissed her lips and embraced her tightly before he left. She looked at the closed door and breathed deeply. Suddenly, she felt lighthearted and calm.

Elizabeth spent half an hour enjoying the bath, which released all her worries and made room for her thoughts and memories of the last few days. The warm water caressed her body, and she blushed as she admitted that her husband's touches were even softer.

What is he doing? Finished with his bath? Shaving his face? Thinking of me?

He told her so many times how much he desired her and how difficult it was to bear her closeness without consummating their marriage. And now that he could do it, he allowed her to decide again. He offered his company, his patience, and his care and allowed her to choose. And she already had!

Darcy stood near the armchair by the window, staring outside, dressed in nightshirt and robe. The bath had been welcome, but he impatiently finished it then asked Stevens to shave him. He thought Elizabeth might come to him and did not want to have her wait.

He felt relieved after confessing the last secret of their relationship, but he blamed himself for hurting her. However, he was certain he had made the right decision in not telling her earlier. At least now, they both knew that she had started to grow fond of him.

What is she doing? Should I knock and check? Certainly not—I said I would wait.

Did she think I would insist on her becoming my wife this very night? Yes, we were very close to that at Longbourn, but I could not insist…unless she wanted to. If she should come to me…

The door opened so slowly that he did not hear it. He sensed—before he saw—Elizabeth a few steps away looking at him.

The nightgown draped over her curves, leaving exposed her arms, her shoulders, her neck, and her bare feet, suggesting what was not fully revealed. Her hair flowed in heavy, silky, dark curls while her lips and eyes smiled at him. He hurried to her.

"I am so happy to see you, my beautiful wife. May I offer you something?"

"Only your love," she said, her face, neck, and arms colouring. "I have come to you, husband, with passion and desire, and complete trust…with no fear, no doubts, and no restraint."

"Elizabeth…" he whispered, incredulous.

"I have been Mrs. Darcy for some time now. I wish nothing more than to be *your wife.*"

Her voice trembled slightly, and her strength vanished while his gaze penetrated her soul.

His arms conquered and imprisoned her, carrying her towards the bed that had sheltered his dreams and hopes for such a long time.

He set her down against the pillows while his eyes never released hers.

"I wish nothing more than to be your husband, to show and prove my love for you. With passion and desire, and complete trust. With no fears, no doubts, and no restraints."

He murmured her own words a moment before his lips captured hers with adoring tenderness that soon turned into fervour and eagerness.

The moment to fulfil their union had finally arrived—and the night was just beginning.

Darcy looked at Elizabeth, afraid to believe the moment was real.

She was lying still, her eyes closed, her dark, heavy locks falling across the pillow and covering her shoulders, her arms, her neck, her breasts. He leant closer. Her hair smelled of jasmine and had the softness of silk. He lowered himself atop of her, kissing her eyelids.

"Elizabeth? Please look at me, my love."

She obeyed and smiled shyly, breathing irregularly.

The room was lit only by a candle near the window and the fire burning steadily, and she thought she had never seen that glint in his eyes.

"You must tell me what to do…what you wish me to do…" she whispered.

His lips brushed over hers then covered her face with small kisses, resting upon her ear and tantalising her earlobe as he said hoarsely:

"I want you to do just what *you want* to do…and to allow me to do the same…"

She shivered, her heart racing. As she tried to inquire further, her dry mouth failed her.

He leant closer, his body almost crushing her, so he supported his weight on his elbows, and she could breathe again. Their nightclothes could not prevent the heat of their bodies, which brushed against each other.

Their eyes held, their lips almost touching. She entwined her fingers in his hair, and he smiled, his fingers gliding through her hair as well.

"Elizabeth…" he said again, and his low voice spread shivers along her spine. How was it possible that her name on his lips built such astonishing reactions within her?

She struggled to breathe while his lips returned to caress her face, her jaw, her throat—then he stopped and looked at her again.

"For more than two days I have not kissed you as I wished," he said, his mouth capturing hers for only an instant. "No, that is not true… I have *never* kissed you before *as I wished…*"

The grip of his fingers tightened in her hair, and he leant closer. His weight was breathtaking and intoxicating. His face was so near, and she admired his handsome features just as he whispered: "You are so beautiful…"

His lips finally met hers, and she sighed in delight, abandoning herself to the pleasure that slowly grew while the kiss deepened, his tongue tasting her possessively. She released a small cry when his legs abruptly separated hers, resting between them. Her nightgown was too tight, and she felt his hands hastily pull it up along her thighs then return to caress her hair while the passion and eagerness of his kiss almost frightened her.

Then he suddenly withdrew and looked at her flushed face, caressing it gently.

"I will stop anytime if you want. I might die of despair, but I will stop if you ask me to."

She laughed, slightly nervous, and then caressed his face just as he did hers.

"I would not want you to die…and I do not want you to stop. I like it so much when you kiss me."

He rolled from atop her, then leant down and whispered. "So do I…but starting tonight, I hope you will like more than just kisses…"

He hastily removed his shirt. Her eyes stared at his bare torso, and she tentatively touched his shoulder. He took her hand and lifted it to his lips, kissing each finger, her palm, and her wrist, then slowly kissed along her arm to her shoulder, where he lingered a moment. Then he renewed the sweet exploration: along her neck, down to her throat, to the neckline of her gown.

There he stopped and looked at her again. She gulped for a little air and licked her lips. His eyes holding hers, his fingers slowly brushed over her breasts, gently as a barely felt caress. She groaned, and her back arched. He leant near her, and one hand trapped her hands over her head while he spread soft kisses over her face, tantalising her lips.

Soft moans betrayed her delight while his other hand slowly touched, felt, and caressed the softness of her breasts, closing upon each of them with possessive tenderness. There was no haste, no impatience in his moves, and the slowness of his gestures made her head spin. She called his name and freed her hands to encircle his neck, pulling him to her.

"Is there something you wish from me?" he whispered, and she formed a weak "no."

She knew she wished *something* but did not know what—and would never dare voice it aloud anyway. His hand travelled gently along her body through the silky gown, brushing over her skin and sliding down along her ribs. It lingered a moment on her belly then caressed her hips. Her body quivered, and her fingers tightened in his hair when his hand returned to her breasts, tracing slow circles around them. His lips found hers for a brief moment then stopped, and he released her arms from his neck, withdrawing slightly.

She struggled to breathe as his eyes locked with hers. Gently, he lowered the nightgown from her shoulders then a little down from her neckline. His eyes were dark, and she could not bear his stare any longer. However, his fingers caressed her face and brushed over her eyelids, and she opened them again. A smile she had not seen before twisted his lips while his fingers moved lower and slowly pulled the nightgown down, brushing over her breasts.

She shivered again and closed her eyes right before his fingers burned her skin with torturous caresses around her breasts, sending waves of warmth inside her. She was unexpectedly trapped into another kiss, passionate, eager, demanding, and she responded without hesitation, her lips and tongue joining his with growing boldness.

She heard her husband groaning, and for an instant, wondered about it, but her thoughts vanished as his hand lowered and pulled down her gown. She felt his caresses on her thighs, her legs, her feet. Then the fabric was gone—she briefly panicked, realising she was completely naked—and the caresses returned to her lower body. Instinctively, her thighs locked together. His touch ceased, and the kiss broke.

Elizabeth opened her eyes to see her husband watching her. She sensed the coolness on her bare skin as she burned inside. His eyes slowly travelled along her body, and she shivered as though she could feel the touch of his gaze.

"You are so beautiful," he whispered. "Would you let me see you, please?"

She only nodded, unable to speak or even think, and he leant closer.

"Thank you, my love," he said, gently kissing her face while his hand continued its provocative conquest. His strokes tantalised her legs then parted them daringly.

To her shock, his hand moved higher. She moaned and bit her lower lip, trying to clasp her thighs again. She heard him whispering her name, and then his lips tasted hers. His hand never left the place it had just conquered, and the other one glided and encircled her shoulders as if wishing to hold her closer. She opened her eyes, met his gaze, and breathed steadily a moment. Then her back arched, and her eyes closed again when his hand began to move, first gently then more daringly, burning her.

"I want to kiss you as I have so long desired to…" he said, and her mind vaguely wondered what he could mean. She had her answer a moment later when his mouth hungrily tasted every inch of her skin that his hand had already caressed.

A trail of warm kisses encircled her breast until they finally closed upon the soft hardness and captured it. Her fingers tightly entwined in his hair, pulling him closer to her, more painfully as pleasure overwhelmed her. Several moments later, his mouth released its captive only to conquer the soft hardness of the other.

Elizabeth bit her lips to stop a scream, her senses split between the sweet torture of his lips and that part where, shockingly, his fingers began an astonishing and intoxicating exploration, which she still doubted was really happening. Her legs gripped his hand but the caresses did not cease this time as he seemed to know her desires better than she did.

Amazed, she realised that every stroke left her wanting more, every demanding touch seemed to gratify the deepest need inside her, and every movement of his fingers sent waves of pleasure through her body. She heard herself begging him again and did not know for what until she heard nothing except the violent beating of her heart, fighting to overcome the storm of fire and ice that had trapped her body and her mind...

Some long moments passed before Elizabeth finally gathered herself together. She could not and wished not to open her eyes and meet his gaze. She was spent from emotion and mortified at her lack of shame for what had just happened and for how she felt—as well as how much she desired his touches again.

She tried to cover herself and to hide her nakedness from his gaze, which she could sense. His hands gently arranged the sheet around her, then he slid beneath it.

She frowned when she felt his leg brushing hers and realised he had also removed his trousers.

"Please look at me, my love," he whispered, and she could guess the smile in his voice.

It took some time before she dared open her eyes and distinguished the smile twisting his lips. *That* she did remember and recognise. In the dim firelight, he caressed her face.

"You are so beautiful," he whispered, bringing her hands to his lips.

She averted her eyes but met the shape of his naked body through the sheet and blushed violently.

"Oh, I cannot possibly believe that… I am afraid to even imagine how I look…"

"You look just as I dreamt so many times…only lovelier…"

She finally met his gaze with wonder. "Surely, you never dreamed of what just happened…"

"I did—so many times. Every night since I fell in love with you, I have dreamt of being the one who would teach you about passion and desire although I believed it would never happen. The mere thought of another man loving you was the most painful torture for such a long time. And after we decided to marry, not a single day passed without imagining the expression on your beautiful face when you reached your pleasure for the first time."

Her eyes widened with every word, and her entire body coloured self-consciously.

"Forgive me if my words embarrass you. They are nothing but the truth."

"Your words did not embarrass me, but your gestures…and what I sensed… I never imagined something like that… My feelings were… Now I fully understand what you meant when you said it could not have happened at Longbourn."

He smiled and kissed her hands again.

"Forgive me, my love, but I must prove you wrong: you do not *fully* understand what I meant…not by far. You are not mine yet, my love…and I did not even kiss you as I wished…"

"What do you mean?" she barely managed to inquire. Her skin shattered as if freezing while the fire grew inside her, astounding and frightening her as much as his hoarse voice and dark gaze. "I do know that I am not your wife *yet*, but… William…"

His fingers turned her head to meet her lips, which he tasted softly, gently, tenderly, and his hands possessively returned under the sheets. With a moan, she anticipated the pleasure he would give her again, and her body arched to him. His hands eagerly touched and caressed her softness, and she slightly moved under his touches.

He abandoned her mouth and travelled back to her breasts, savouring what his hands had already discovered and conquered. His hand climbed back down to the warmth of her thighs, and she moaned even before she felt his touch. His lips followed his hand, tasting every inch of her skin.

Every sensation she had experienced before paled as though a prelude to what he was offering her that moment. The kisses lingered on her breasts only torturous moments then lowered even more, closer to what she thought to be unthinkable.

The novelty of his lips and tongue tasting the skin of her thighs made her quiver, and her hands gripped the sheets around her. All her senses rushed to the place that still ached for his touch.

She thought she was aware of what would follow, but he proved her wrong. Nothing could have prepared her for the shock of feeling the softness of his lips or the unbearable pleasure that overwhelmed her.

She bit her lips painfully when she felt his tongue exploring her, tentatively at first then more and more daringly, tasting her with an intimacy that could not be imagined. Her mind was screaming that he must stop, but it was only a weak whisper compared to her body's demand and the sound of her crying his name. Her reason told her this was mortifyingly improper while her senses betrayed her delight and abandoned her to the blissful pleasure he was giving her.

He was gently conquering her and breaking down the resistance of her mind with an insatiable need that overcame her senses until she knew nothing else. A deep moan escaped her as she struggled for air while she shuddered violently under the countless chills that coursed throughout her burning skin.

When her senses finally returned, her entire body still trembled. She could scarcely breathe from the excitement and the weight of his strong, naked body covering hers.

Every inch of his skin was touching her. His strong palms cupped her face, kissing her tenderly. His gaze had darkened while she knew something more was to come.

Her breasts painfully brushed over his chest, and his hands caressed and parted her legs.

"You are my wife now," he groaned, and her heart nearly stopped as his body finally joined with hers, entering her with eager strength—powerful yet gentle—breaking the last barrier between them.

She screamed, and her body stiffened in pain while her nails dug into his back.

He remained still inside her and put a little distance between them so she could breathe. Then his lips kissed her face while his hands gently caressed her legs, helping her to calm and relax.

"You are my wife now," he repeated, and she nodded.

He slowly moved inside her, and her moans mixed with another cry.

"Does it hurt?"

"A little," she barely spoke, her body struggling to adjust to the sharp pain. Her lips were dry, and her voice trembled. "But I knew it would… You are my husband now…"

A gentle, loving kiss, sweet and tender, rewarded her words—only an instant before it turned passionate and eager again.

"Oh, God…please," she moaned while his hands glided between their united bodies, caressing the parts of her that already craved his touch. She felt him inside her, strong, warm, invading her body with his passion.

"This is so perfect…so perfect," he groaned while his thrusts shattered her body. It began gently, slowly, and then became more intense, stronger, harder, eager, faster.

The pain increased, but then it seemed to dissipate, mixed with a strange, unknown, and unrelieved pleasure that slowly enveloped her entire body.

His thrusts increased while his mouth trapped hers, his tongue moistening her swollen, dry lips while her moans mixed with his, her soft cries with his deep groans.

Unconsciously, her legs entwined on his back, and she felt him even deeper inside her.

She barely heard his tender whispers, released through the possessive kisses, then her hands tightened on his back while her body began to move beneath him.

The sounds of their united passion were crushed between hungry lips, and she completely lost herself to the renewed pleasure that filled her again for what seemed an eternity until he finally reached the long desired moment, shuddering in release and spreading warm waves inside her trembling body.

It was not him and her anymore, but them together—finally, husband and wife.

They lay on the pillows, exhausted from the turmoil of feelings, their bodies still joined.

Elizabeth thought of nothing but her need for air and the revelation of their fulfilled union.

Her mind refused to admit *how* it happened, to recollect the astonishing moments before and during the unbelievable, torturous, delightful journey through which her husband had led her. But her mind mattered little when her body and her heart were still joined with him and his hands were still holding her tight, stroking her back, her arms, her hair…

One thing she remembered vividly: the sensation of his hands touching hers had *always* aroused her since they first danced together at Netherfield. She might have thought that his hands could delight her—but how much more, she did not realise until that night. And no, not only his hands were responsible for her most exquisitely pleasant enjoyment, but also his lips and…every part of him—of her husband.

Darcy held his wife as close to his body as she was to his heart.

He felt her still shivering, barely regaining her breath, but not for a moment did she attempt to withdraw from him. Her head still rested near his shoulder, and her eyes were closed while one of her hands was placed over his heart.

Her skin was warm and soft, traces of redness betraying the spots where his hunger allowed him so little patience. The mere thought of her savour aroused his desire again, and he was angry with himself for this lack of control.

He knew he had not been patient enough, and likely, his pleasure must have been a painful time for her.

He was certain that she enjoyed their lovemaking—even more than he hoped for the first time. But he also knew he must have frightened her with his unbridled behaviour as he himself was amazed by some of his gestures. Everything he imagined had become true—every inch of her skin he had discovered, explored, and conquered.

He had showed her his love and his passion, he had taught her body the taste of pleasure, and he had learnt what she liked—perhaps much better than she knew. He remembered every moment of their union, from the exquisite feeling of being inside her, of releasing his long-caged desire, to the most gratifying sensation of seeing her beautiful face glow from the pleasure he was giving to her—to the beautiful woman who was finally his wife.

He had conquered her body, but what about her heart. And he learnt how to give her pleasure, but could he also give her happiness?

His fingers got lost in her hair, and her breathing became steadier. There was complete silence for some time, then she moved slightly, and her hand stretched to reach his. He gently kissed her palm, then his fingers entwined with hers.

"I thought you fell asleep. You must feel tired," he whispered.

She needed a moment to reply. "I do not feel tired, only exhausted…and astounded…"

"I am astounded, too…but I am not tired, nor exhausted. I am happy—happier than I can remember before…and not just because I had the joy of loving you as I did but because I feel I am your husband—truly and completely."

"And I feel I am your wife—truly and completely."

Darcy leant her on her back so that her beautiful face was exposed to his admiring gaze. He pulled the bedclothes over them, but her body was mostly covered by his. He touched her lips. They were red, swollen, and slightly bitten. She moaned, and he gently tasted them.

"Is it painful? I am so sorry. I cannot believe I was such a savage…"

"It is nothing; it is not so much your doing as mine. I bit my lips many times, when… Oh, William… I cannot believe that such feelings exist…that such caresses are real…"

"They are real. They must be as we shared them together…and I hope to do it again soon…"

His lips were kissed her face gently, barely touching her skin. She slowly relaxed under his caresses and spoke more freely.

"Is it always like that?" she suddenly asked, and he did not stop his attentions.

"It will always be like that…and even better once your discomfort and pain vanishes."

"No…I mean—was it always like that? I know you have done that many times and…"

He withdrew and stared at her. "What are you asking me, Elizabeth?"

"Forgive me—this is a silly question at the most improper time. I do not know what came over me. Shall we sleep now? It must be very late…" She turned to leave the bed, but he gently trapped her and set her back on the pillow while his eyes deepened into hers.

"I am being so silly, more silly than the wife of a gentleman like you should be," she whispered, her eyes moistened with tears of embarrassment.

"You are not—but you do ask strange questions at strange moments, questions which surely no wife of a gentleman like me would ever ask." He laughed then kissed her cheek.

"Elizabeth, I am happy that you dare to ask me anything that crosses your mind. As for your inquiry—I did have enough…intimate encounters with other women. I cannot deny that it was pleasant. I would say that, for a man, it always is. But I never felt this way before. I never experienced such joy, such complete delight, such deep pleasure."

"You are very considerate to tell me such lovely words," she answered, caressing his face. But he recognised her doubts, so he whispered, although there was nobody to hear:

"I have kissed you ten times more than I ever did before in my entire life. And I have never kissed anyone *the way* I kissed you. It never even crossed my mind to do such a thing…that is…until I fell in love with you and I could think of little else…"

His tone was low and serious, and she knew he was not speaking of complacency. She distinguished the truth in his voice, and the burden vanished from her heart while she shivered and coloured at the meaning of his words.

She gulped and licked her swollen lips while he gently brushed over them again.

"I shall teach you everything I know about sharing love, but there are still many things we will have to learn together, my dearest wife."

"I would love to learn everything you want to teach me." She repeated what she had told him before, although in a completely different context.

He recognised her words and embraced her tenderly. They remained embraced in silence for some time, and then he was the first to speak again.

"My dearest, we should rise and clean ourselves then change and go to sleep in your room. My bed is in a rather bad condition." He tried to joke, and she blushed again.

He gently put a blanket around her to protect her modesty.

"I shall join you shortly, and I will bring something to drink. I am very thirsty," he said while thinking that his thirst was not entirely for water, brandy, or wine. However, he would be content with some of those for the time being.

He was not tired—quite the contrary. He had longed for her for so long that his body was barely satiated by their lovemaking. His urge increased after tasting what he so much desired. He wanted nothing more than to love her again until he satisfied his hunger.

However, he struggled to temper his desire and to be patient for her sake—and for his. It was a less difficult task now that he knew for certain that his waiting would be rewarded soon, but it was not an easy one.

He dismissed his thoughts while he cleaned himself in haste then put on some new nightclothes, glancing at the bed, which was left in terrible disorder. He felt relieved that he could trust Stevens' discretion. The last thing he wanted was gossip in the household.

He knocked and entered. She was in the bed, wearing a nightgown and a robe, her hair slightly arranged on her shoulders. She smiled as he entered with the wine and two glasses.

"I am dizzy enough even without wine," she said.

"It will help you sleep better," he said as he filled each glass.

He took her hand and helped her to the chair near the window. Then he covered her with a blanket and sat near—just as he did on the first night of their marriage. Both remembered and shared a smile as bright as a promise while enjoying their wine, which was less intoxicating than each other's presence.

She sipped some more wine and hid her lips behind the glass, but she could not conceal the laughter in her eyes and the blush of her cheeks. He looked at her, inquiringly.

"May I ask of what you are thinking, Mrs. Darcy?"

"Of nothing…that I could possibly tell you."

He put his glass on the table and leant towards her. "In truth, you should know by now that there is nothing you can hide from me—in any aspect."

She almost choked. "Surely, this is not a proper way of speaking, sir."

"Nor are your thoughts more proper since they made your lips twist mischievously and your eyes sparkle in such a way."

She attempted to cover her laugh with her hand, glancing around.

"It is such a fortunate coincidence that Lucky sleeps with Peter. A perfect arrangement."

"True… but let us return to your thoughts, madam."

"Oh, you are truly annoying at times, sir. I was just thinking…" She held his gaze for a moment, stood and took a few steps, then resumed her place.

"I was thinking that… I know it sounds horribly wanton, and I might appear ungrateful, but I remembered the first night and…"

He took her hands and tried to search her eyes, lowered to the ground. He could not say whether she was amused or troubled. She finally met his gaze, which already had become worried, and said:

"I was thinking how it would have been if you had not kept your promise…if we shared the bed from the first night…"

He looked at her in disbelief then cupped her face and gently tasted her lips.

"I have thought of the same thing many times. I confess I knew from the first evening that I could convince you to allow me in your bed and that you would have enjoyed *my company.*"

He paused a moment, searching for the proper words his eyes holding hers.

"Probably your body and mine would have felt the same pleasure, but it certainly would have not been the same. We had not known each other well enough then, you did not trust me enough to open yourself to me, and I never would have dared to unleash my passion as I do now. Do you understand my meaning?"

"Of course, I do… And I feel you are right. Just as I feel you were right to delay the revelation of the story of ten years ago. It would have been difficult for me to see the man here now behind the shadow of my imagination. When you told me, the first thought that crossed my mind was how close I was to never discovering the truth—of never discovering you as you truly are. I felt as if I had fallen into a dark hole. I am silly after all, you must admit that..."

"I certainly must not. What I must do is to make use of the future to compensate for my past misjudgement as this is what almost made us never discover each other. But now you are here—we are here together—and enough of this talk for tonight. I was away from you for too long, my love," he said, then he suddenly lifted her in his arms and put her in the bed.

He slowly but decidedly removed her robe, then embraced her tightly and pulled the blankets over them both. She cuddled near his chest, sighing in contentment, while his fingers played in her hair. She felt so much joy, so much happiness, so much fulfilment—so much love—that she could hardly breathe.

Elizabeth turned to tell him of her feelings, but her lips met his, and his hands moved slowly along her spine then rested on her hips. She gasped in surprise when he lay back and pulled her atop of him, trapped by his arms and his strong legs.

She was lying perfectly along his body—her face only an inch away from his and her breasts pressed to his chest. His hands continued to tantalise her shoulders, her back, her hips, her thighs.

Elizabeth did not know what to expect and did not dare anticipate. His hands hastily removed her gown then opened his shirt, briefly caressing her breasts—already heavy from desire—and pulled her against him so tightly that it took her breath away. What she did not dare guess, now was beyond doubt, and she brushed slightly over him, trying to voice her barely coherent thoughts while every movement made him moan and aroused painful delights inside her.

His eyes searched hers, but his hands never ceased caressing her.

"Do you wish me to stop?"

"No... Yes... I do not know... I do not think I can bear it again, so soon..."

He frowned. "Are you in pain?"

"In pain? No... It is not the pain...but the pleasure... I cannot bear it again so soon..."

He stared at her in surprise, then his eyes darkened while his caresses became more demanding. "You must allow me to prove you wrong, Mrs. Darcy..."

Her resistance broke—as little as it was—and she completely abandoned herself to him. How could she argue when she already knew he was correct most of the time?

It was almost dawn when silence finally filled Mrs. Darcy's chamber, and she fell asleep, exhausted in her happiness, wrapped in her husband's love and tightly embraced by his strong arms.

The last thought that crossed her mind was that, in truth, he was right again!

Vigorous barking, a whispered voice, a breeze of fresh air, and a strong scent of summer awakened Elizabeth. She remained still, her eyes closed, enjoying the first moments of a new day, her mind, her body, and her heart still trapped in the recollections of the longest and most astonishing night.

Her hand brushed over the bedclothes then farther away, and she finally glanced around.

From her husband's rooms, a chilling breeze entered below the closed door, and she imagined the room was being cleaned. The mere thought coloured her cheeks, and she covered her face with the pillow, trying to hide what she thought to be a shameless smile.

A moment later, she glanced towards the window and gasped. On the small table was an enormous bouquet of red roses—all red and bright.

She hastily put a robe on then ran to touch and smell them. She quickly counted them: one and twenty. With eager fingers, she searched between the flowers and found his note, which she unfolded anxiously. It said:

My dearest wife,

Thank you for allowing me to love you.

Your husband,
F. Darcy.

Her fingers trembled, and she brought the note to her heart, her eyes tearful.

Then she rang for Molly, who arrived only minutes later and entered with Lucky squirming quickly past her leg. It was not difficult for Elizabeth to notice Molly's glance towards the ravished bed and her insistence in avoiding her mistress's eyes.

Elizabeth was completely mortified, imagining that both Stevens and Molly guessed what had happened. Yet, in her thoughts, there was little room for anything else except her husband, whose presence she already missed dearly.

Half an hour later, she was bathed and her hair beautifully arranged. Molly, who was sent to inquire about the master, informed her he was in the library.

While the maid searched for the proper dress, a daring thought surfaced in Elizabeth's mind. She pulled out the new ball gown and asked a shocked Molly to help dress her.

The maid obeyed silently, expressing her astonishment at the beauty of the gown without daring to inquire what the mistress was doing with it. Elizabeth took pity on the girl and laughed.

"I just received it before we left for Longbourn. I will show it to the master and ask his opinion of it. Then you will need to help me change into a regular dress."

"Ma'am, you are beautiful," the maid exclaimed, and Elizabeth blushed with contentment. She wished to be beautiful for him. Then she took a piece of paper and wrote briefly.

My dearest husband,

Thank you for teaching me the meaning of love.

Your wife,
E. Darcy

Elizabeth took a red rose, folded the paper over the stem and hurried to her husband, wondering how long it had been since she had seen him.

She slowly opened the door and found him at his desk, reading.

His eyes met hers, followed by surprise, astonishment, and tentative steps walking towards her. His soft gaze caressing her appearance and then the gentle kiss on her hands were her gratifying rewards.

"My beautiful wife," he whispered, and his voice thrilled her.

She then handed him the paper and the rose, saying, "How else could I repay you, my husband, but by wearing something that you already gave me?"

Chapter 26

London, 10 January

Elizabeth's visit with her husband in the library became a tender interlude. She was exceedingly pleased by his admiration of how the dress suited her, but even more, she was delighted by his emotional reaction when he read her note.

The previous night had united them in a way that still astonished her. Besides their union as husband and wife, something more had changed, grown, and deepened in their mutual understanding. At daylight, their tender holding of hands, enchanted smiles, and stolen glances turned into pure, complete, and powerful happiness.

"I missed you," Darcy said, embracing his wife tightly then inviting her to sit.

"I missed you too. I was wondering why you left, but then I saw the beautiful red roses."

"Red roses seemed more proper this time. But to be completely honest, I left because, otherwise, I would have been tempted to awaken you," he said hoarsely, and for a moment she was puzzled, then her face and neck coloured. "As I said, I *really* missed you," he added.

"Please do not hesitate to awaken me whenever you wish…"

"I shall remember that. Now should we have breakfast?"

"Yes… This dress is beautiful. Your choice was perfect, and I only need the proper occasion to wear it."

"You might have one soon. We received an invitation to Lady Isabella's ball in two days' time. Do you wish us to attend?"

"Well, it depends. Will I be allowed to dance with other gentlemen?" She was teasing him about his jealousy and ridiculous accusations from a week earlier, but he remained serious.

"It is not for me to *allow* you anything, but I cannot deny that it would *not* make me happy."

"I am certain you are only mocking me, but I find your jealousy rather appealing."

"I could not be more serious, but I will try to keep my distress under good regulation."

"And I am sure you will succeed—as always. Is there anything I may do to relieve your distress?"

"I shall think on it. In the meantime, you should remember to dismiss Molly for after the ball," he whispered, demanding her lips, which joined his with eager delight.

The kiss reluctantly broke a few minutes later when Darcy remembered the time and Elizabeth hurried to change her dress.

During breakfast, the ladies carried most of the conversation. Darcy's eyes were quite often on his wife, rarely paying attention to anything else and making her blush the whole time.

"I shall visit Aunt Catherine later. Or tomorrow," Darcy finally said. "It should not last long."

"Brother, you should be careful!" Georgiana exclaimed with distress.

"Come, dearest, I am not going to war. You cannot be frightened by your aunt." He laughed.

"She was very upset! Please trust me—I have never seen her in such a state."

"Let us not trouble too much about that. So tell me: how were your days alone?"

"I truly missed you and Elizabeth, but I had a lovely time with Mrs. Annesley. Robert and Maryanne visited me every day. Oh, and Peter and Libby! I am so happy that Elizabeth decided to bring them into the house! They are such lovely children!"

"Really?" Darcy smiled at his sister's genuine enthusiasm.

"Really! Peter is very good with animals—not only with Titan and Lucky but also with the horses! Maryanne's carriage waited in front of the house the day before yesterday, and Peter happened to be in the yard with the dogs. The horses were scared by something, and Peter just ran in front of them, grabbing the reins. We were so frightened, but he just stood there, perfectly calm."

"That is truly astonishing," Darcy admitted.

"Indeed! And Libby possesses uncommon intelligence! Anything she sees once, she never forgets! She stood by me at the piano, and I played a little song that I learnt as a child. She just touched the keys in the order she saw me play with no other practice. And she is amazing at calculating. I mean, she does not really know that she is calculating—she is just doing it. She multiplies, divides, and so on. Mrs. Annesley and I were shocked."

"So she learnt all these things in a few days?" inquired Elizabeth.

"Not at all! To be honest, neither of them is fond of study—I believe very few children are—and they are rather far behind their age in knowledge as they had barely gone to school. Peter seems fascinated by a book given him by Robert about army and war—but not much else, at least for the time being. And Libby—she learns if someone teaches her rather than by reading. These are just their natural qualities. Janey was unaware of all this too! She never had the chance to observe such talents in her children before now."

"This is very surprising. I shall speak to them myself after breakfast," Darcy declared.

"I cannot think of what would have happened to Cathy and even to the older children had they been left alone. It is so unfair… In the past, I have rarely considered the situation of the families unconnected to us—and now I can think of little else," Georgiana continued.

"Please do not be sad, dearest," Elizabeth said. "We should be grateful that we have the means to help as much we can. Peter, Libby, and Cathy were fortunate that their mother worked in the house of Mr. Darcy, who is a generous and kind master."

"Yes, the best master and the best landlord, as Mrs. Reynolds says," Georgiana concluded. She and Elizabeth shared a warm smile. Darcy felt suddenly uneasy.

"I do not deserve such praise. I am doing little more than any other man in my position would do. But if we are to speak of children, I was thinking…perhaps you could go further and accomplish our mother's long time desire—to build the school for girls in Lambton. It will be a demanding and perhaps daunting task, and I do not want to force your decision."

"I would love that," Elizabeth said. "Nothing would give me more joy."

"Oh, Brother, that would be wonderful! I would do anything I can to help."

"I am sorry I will not be able to participate," Mrs. Annesley said. "But I will come to visit when it is ready. I am certain Mrs. and Miss Darcy will accomplish a wonderful result."

"I thank you both," he said, gently bringing Elizabeth's hand to his lips.

"Please do not thank me. It is such an honour. So when shall we go to Pemberley?"

"Soon if you have no other reason to stay in Town. The Season starts in March."

"I would rather see Pemberley. The balls may wait."

AFTER BREAKFAST, THEY ASKED FOR PETER AND LIBBY TO BE FETCHED. THE FIRST to arrive was Janey, who could hardly contain her tears while she thanked them for the generosity they bestowed upon her children and assured them once again that they had saved their lives.

"Janey, let this be the last time we discuss it. We have done what we thought to be right," Elizabeth said. Just then, Mrs. Thomason entered with the children, who shyly greeted the master.

"I was informed of only good things about you two. You seem to have performed your duties in an excellent way. Mrs. Darcy and I are very pleased," Darcy said, and the children watched him, eyes widening, mumbling a "Thank you."

"As you have been working for a week now, it is time for the first payment. I expect you to help your mother increase your family income. Here is one shilling for each of you."

The children took the money with trembling fingers, forgetting to breathe.

"If you each gain a shilling every week, and there are fifty-two weeks in a year, it means you will be able to help your mother with…"

"A hundred and four shillings," Libby whispered. The others looked at her in astonishment.

"Precisely! Excellent answer, Libby, you are a very smart girl," Elizabeth spoke warmly.

Peter lowered his eyes in front of the master. "I knew that too," he said hesitantly.

Darcy put a hand on his shoulder. "No, you did not, Peter, and let this be the last time you tell a lie to impress others. Do I have your promise on this?"

"Yes, master," the boy of nine answered, his voice trembling.

"Very well. Even if you are not as sharp at calculating as your sister, I was told you have other qualities equally important. I expect you to continue to use them."

"Yes, master."

"Good. You may go now, and we shall meet to talk again in a week," Darcy dismissed them. The children bowed and curtseyed again, then held hands and hurried to their mother, whispering to her while they exited the library, followed by Mrs. Thomason.

Elizabeth spent the next hour in the music room, listening to Georgiana's exquisite performance at the pianoforte.

Earlier in the day, Georgiana had confessed to her brother the entire story of her correspondence with Wickham, and she received his understanding and forgiveness in exchange for her promise of complete honesty.

Later, Elizabeth told the girl about meeting Wickham and the demands she made of him to stop any illicit contact. Georgiana's frown whenever she spoke of him was a clear proof that her heart was not as ready as her mind to abolish his memory, and the music helped her fight against her weakness.

Mr. Darcy soon joined them. He sat by his wife and took her hand in his. The beautiful music enchanted them for another half an hour, and Elizabeth allowed herself to be slowly pervaded by a new kind of joy. Her husband brought her hand to his lips several times when he was certain nobody would notice, and his thumb gently caressed the inside of her palm, making her skin tingle. His small gesture was a sweet recollection of the past night and a daring promise for the night to come. It was a moment of perfect intimacy although they were in company. She was happy to be *home.* To be his wife. To be with him.

Their peace was disturbed by a servant who reluctantly entered to announce that there were two visitors waiting in the main hall for Mr. Darcy.

"Who is it?" he inquired, displeased to be interrupted.

"Mrs. Hurst and Miss Bingley. They said they wish to speak to the master urgently."

Elizabeth and Darcy glanced at each other. They kept their places, their hands still joined.

"William, do you know what might be the problem?" she asked.

"Bingley sent an express to inform them about his decision to remain at

Netherfield. I imagine they are not happy about it. Bingley will be in my debt for this conversation. I shall meet them in the drawing room; hopefully, it will not last long."

"No," Elizabeth said calmly. "This will not do! Hodge, please tell Miss Bingley and Mrs. Hurst that we cannot receive them at this time. I would be happy to establish an appointment as soon as possible if they will only send me a note with specific details. Thank you."

The servant glanced at his master, puzzled, then he returned to accomplish his duty.

Elizabeth looked at her husband, uncertain of his opinion. "I told them the rules that night at the opera. They chose to ignore them—I chose how to respond."

"It sounds perfect to me," he said as he took her hand again, resuming his caresses, and kindly asked Georgiana to continue playing.

Cries of disbelief and indignation could be heard from the main hall, louder than the piano.

"I am glad to see you commanding your wishes in the house," he whispered, his lips touching her ear.

IN THE LATE AFTERNOON, DARCY DECIDED TO TAKE THE PLUNGE AND VISIT LADY Catherine. He avoided the moment as long as possible as he dreaded the certain ruin of one of the loveliest days of his life with a terrible argument. His greatest concern was maintaining his composure whilst fighting with his mother's sister and also putting an end to the outrageous offences she continually threw at Elizabeth. He would have to be harsh—and he would be.

Elizabeth moved into the drawing room with Georgiana, allowing Mrs. Annesley some time to rest. She asked Mrs. Thomason to have tea with them and discuss some household issues—an invitation the housekeeper accepted with pleasure. A few minutes later, she called for Peter and Libby as she wished to talk a little more with them. In truth, she mostly wanted to fill the time until her husband's return and to dissipate her anxiety.

A tumult of loud voices from the main hall startled them. Both Mrs. Thomason and Elizabeth hurried to see what was happening, followed by Peter. Georgiana and Libby remained in the doorway. Elizabeth halted, staring at a woman of impressive stature, wearing a most fashionable hat and holding a walking stick.

The servant said humbly but decidedly: "I apologise but I cannot allow you in! Mrs. Darcy requires that you send a note, and she will set an appointment with you!"

The woman's face turned red, and she yelled in anger, "Away from my face, you creature." Then she furiously hit the servant with her stick and stepped forward. She stopped only when she laid eyes on Elizabeth.

Mrs. Thomason curtseyed hesitantly to the newly arrived, "Lady Catherine…"

"Good day, Lady Catherine. I am Elizabeth Darcy. We have not been introduced," Elizabeth said firmly.

"You are no Darcy but a country nobody, an impostor who deceived my nephew and usurped the place which belonged to my daughter! How dare you change the rules of this house? I can enter whenever I wish. This is my sister's house, and you are the one who should be thrown out of here!"

"Lady Catherine, I understand you came to express your disapproval, which had already come to our attention through your letters. I am sorry that you are upset, but you must remember that you are a *guest* in this house, and you are in no position to offend or hurt anyone!"

"I am no guest! I am Darcy's closest relative, and I shall not be prevented from saying what I want! My character has ever been celebrated for its sincerity and frankness, as well as for my loathing of chicanery! I shall not allow this scandalous charade of a marriage to go further!"

"Aunt Catherine, you cannot speak to Elizabeth in such a way," murmured Georgiana.

"Oh, shut your mouth, girl! You know nothing but playing the piano. I shall not speak to you. And your foolish brother is no better. He might be good at managing an estate but completely stupid and mindless when it comes to the important things of life!"

"Lady Catherine, you forget yourself! I am Mr. Darcy's wife and the mistress of this house, and I shall not allow this kind of behaviour! I suggest you return home. Mr. Darcy is on his way to visit you, and you will be able to speak properly. I have nothing further to add!" Elizabeth struggled to speak whilst anger and shame suffocated her. Drawn by the scandal, Stevens and Mrs. Annesley also appeared near Mrs. Thomason, staring without knowing how to intervene.

"I do not wish to speak to Darcy, but to you who made him neglect his mother's strongest desire and throw away his family's legacy and his own duty! He must have lost his mind, and you are the only one to be blamed for that! His parents would roll in their graves if they knew of how low their son had fallen because of the arts and allurements of a worthless woman!"

Elizabeth stepped closer to speak in a lower voice. "I wonder what Mr. and Mrs. Darcy would say on hearing the malicious offences you bestow on both their children! You pretend to be William's close relative, but not even a mere stranger would be so spiteful and venomous in their accusation. Your position might allow you to be frank, but then so does mine! You shall leave the house now!"

"I shall not! Not before I am certain you will disappear from our lives forever!" she yelled louder, which drew the attention of Lucky, who immediately barked and growled at his mistress's feet.

Lady Catherine, only a few steps away, raised her cane. In an instant, Peter placed himself between the two women, his eyes narrowing in angry determination, and he held the cane with all his strength.

"You cannot speak to the mistress like that! She said to leave—you leave!" the boy yelled back. For a moment, shock silenced everybody. Lady Catherine's rage distorted her face into a grimace, and she violently pulled back, but Peter resisted fiercely.

"Lady Catherine!" a strong voice thundered from the doorway, and Darcy's strong hands held the woman's arms. "You have completely lost yourself," he said, grabbing her cane.

"Darcy! I am so glad you are here. Do you see what is happening? Did you see how this woman treated me? Me—your only aunt and your beloved mother's sister!"

"Lady Catherine!" he repeated, staring at his aunt, his eyes dark, his face pale from anger. "A child of nine said it better than I could have: the mistress said to leave—you leave!"

"What? How dare you? Do you presume to cast me out of this house?" she yelled while Darcy held her arm tightly and pulled her through the front door, ignoring her curses. He entered the carriage with her and left while Elizabeth gazed at the closed door, her strength fled completely under the burden of shame and pain.

She wiped her tears and turned to the servant, asking how badly he was injured. The man assured her he was perfectly well, but she noticed he barely moved his arm, so she asked for Dr. Taylor to be fetched and sent Hodge to wait in his room. Then she took Georgiana's arm and returned to the drawing room, followed by Mrs. Annesley. Mrs. Thomason and Stevens silently returned to their duties, feeling they had failed their mistress.

Georgiana ceased fighting her tears and embraced her sister-in-law, apologising for the distress she was made to endure. Lucky came to comfort his mistress while Libby and Peter looked on from a few steps away, obviously shocked by the incident. Elizabeth tried to calm Georgiana, then she smiled at the children and stretched her hand to Peter.

"You both may return to your mother. She must be worried for you. Peter, I thank you for being so courageous and protecting me," Elizabeth said to the boy then gently kissed his cheeks while he looked at her, breathless.

On their way out, Libby said animatedly, "Peter, you are really brave—like a soldier!"

Elizabeth and Georgiana smiled at each other and could not agree more.

More than an hour passed before Darcy returned with an expression of deepest distress. His eyes met his wife's, and he sat near her as he did not know nor dare what to do next.

"I am so sorry," he whispered. "I feel so helpless and weak as I have failed again to protect you. The moment I was told she was not at home, I came here directly, but it was too late. I believe she must have stayed in the carriage, waiting for the moment I left the house, so she could enter and talk to you. Georgiana was correct: Lady Catherine is worse than ever. It is as if our marriage was a crossroad for her, and she lost all common sense. I sent for Robert, and we both spoke to Anne. We will make sure they return to Rosings tomorrow. I am so sorry. How are you feeling?"

"I am fine, do not worry. Dr. Taylor checked on Hodge. Lady Catherine hurt his arm quite badly. He will rest and perform no hard tasks until Dr. Taylor tells me he is fine. Dinner will be ready in two hours. And I ordered the dishes for tomorrow when my aunt and uncle dine with us. We should invite the Fitzwilliams too. It would be a lovely chance to introduce my uncle and aunt to Lady Matlock and Maryanne. Georgiana thinks it is a good idea."

She spoke more and more animatedly, barely meeting his eyes, until he gently cupped her face and asked gently. "Elizabeth, how are you *feeling*, my love?"

Georgiana and Mrs. Annesley left silently to allow them privacy. He embraced Elizabeth, pulling her head to his chest while kissing her hair.

"I am fine, truly," she whispered. "But I was so ashamed to see all the servants listening. The things she said about me and the way she offended Georgiana… I did not care much about her words, but to raise such a scandal… It was almost frightening. Something is very wrong with your aunt…"

"How could you be ashamed for my aunt's outrageous behaviour? Let me blame myself and feel the shame, as I deserve it. We have always considered Aunt Catherine to be too outspoken and too accustomed to having her own way, but we should have seen that it was more than that. How did she enter the house against my precise orders?"

"It was just a horrible coincidence, I believe. No servant is at fault. But I cannot understand what she wants. Our marriage is already accomplished. Does she really hope I will die so you can still marry Anne? So what should I do? Do I have to always live in fear?"

Elizabeth felt chills along her skin as she spoke. Darcy kissed her temple to comfort her.

"Elizabeth, can you believe that your life is more important to me than my own? And that I will take better care of you than of myself?"

His eyes were open for her to see inside his mind and his soul, and she had no doubts remaining.

"I believe you," she answered, the burden dissipating from her heart. He held her hands to his chest.

"Starting today, I will place two doormen, so nobody will enter unannounced. You will not be fetched to talk to anyone besides the Matlocks and your relatives. Mrs. Thomason and the butler will take care of any unexpected guests if I am not at home. And you will not go anywhere outside the house without me or two servants and the coachman at least."

"Very well—but it seems ridiculous to take so much trouble over an argument with your aunt. I hope things will calm down soon. She must see reason eventually. Poor Anne…"

"Yes, poor Anne. I shall speak to my uncle. Perhaps we should do something for her too. For now, my only care is for you. I will not allow anything or anyone to trouble you again!"

THE TIRESOME DAY ENDED WITH A PLEASANT DINNER, TO WHICH WAS ADDED Colonel Fitzwilliam's presence. He apologised to Elizabeth for his aunt's outrageous behaviour, but she turned the conversation to more pleasant subjects, asking whether he would be present at the ball.

"Of course! So, you will attend the ball too? I wish to dance two sets with Elizabeth, and before you hurry to oppose me, Darcy, you should consider that it is to your advantage that she dances with me and not with others," the colonel said, and Georgiana chuckled.

"I will not object, but I was wondering whether you will open the ball with Lady Isabella," Darcy replied.

"Well, yes, I might..." The colonel hesitated.

"I like Lady Isabella very much," said Elizabeth. "If her dowry is only half as great as her beauty and her wit, she surely must be a most desirable young lady."

"She truly is," Darcy concluded.

"And yet, as I said before, you did not marry *her*," the colonel said, and it was Darcy's turn to laugh.

"That is because I was fortunate to find the most perfect choice." Darcy smiled, glancing at his flustered wife. "But Lady Isabella is certainly one of the most worthy young ladies—if only a man feels confident enough to handle her wit and daring character."

"I am sure an honourable, brave officer would be a perfect choice for a witty, daring, and healthy lady," Elizabeth intervened and then added to relieve the colonel's uneasiness, "Speaking of brave officers, I am proud to say we have one in our home. Did William tell you about Peter?"

"He did! I say, that boy is really something! Did you know that he stopped the horses too? Oh well, horses and Lady Catherine—not much difference. At least horses can be kept outside."

"Robert, let us not speak of Lady Catherine again," Darcy said severely. "We have had enough for one day. We might debate the subject further over a glass of brandy without bothering the ladies."

After dinner, the gentlemen enjoyed their drinks while Georgiana amused them with her music.

As the hours progressed, Elizabeth became overwhelmed by a strange sense of fatigue and restlessness, of warmth and cold, of nervousness and eagerness while her mind was occupied by the revelation that very soon she would be alone with her husband in the solitude of their suite.

When Georgiana and Mrs. Annesley retired, Elizabeth did the same. With a "good night" to the colonel and a glance at her husband, she hurried to her room and called for Molly to prepare her bath. Yes, a warm bath would do perfectly well—and perhaps her husband would not delay too long.

Elizabeth realised that she needed to order some new outfits for nights too. Her old ones were quite inappropriate. She closed her eyes and sank into the water, her entire body burning as she remembered what happened the previous night with two of her gowns.

She heard steps and opened her eyes. "Molly, I would like to get out now, please"

"May *I* help you, Mrs. Darcy? I took the liberty of dismissing Molly for tonight."

Elizabeth startled and wrapped her arms over her chest while she watched her husband's approach. He was dressed only in trousers, his face freshly shaved, his hair slightly wet.

"Am I making you uncomfortable?" he inquired from only a few inches away.

"A little..." she barely spoke.

"I am very sorry to hear that," Darcy said, holding her gaze.

He knelt near her tub, his eyes still locked with hers, and without another word, he claimed her lips, tasting them eagerly. His hand caressed her face then glided to her wet nape.

He deepened the kiss while his hand lowered into the warm water, stroking her shoulders and arms, then cupped her breasts with tender possessiveness. She moaned, and her hands slid around his neck, allowing his caresses to spoil her. Their lips were crushed into an ardent kiss while his hands brought back the most astonishing sensations, which grew more powerful than she remembered. After some tormenting moments of tantalising passion, he lifted her from the tub, wrapped her in a large towel, and carried her to the bed. He lowered her towards the pillows, slowly wiped her warm, wet skin with the towel, and then gently tasted her with thirsty lips. He started with her face, then down to her throat, her neck, and her shoulders. He stopped and returned to her face, caressing her cheeks.

"I missed you so much, Mrs. Darcy," he murmured hoarsely. "I know it was a terrible day, but I hardly thought of anything else but this moment. I missed you painfully."

Elizabeth caressed his face, her heart and her body yearning for his touch.

"I missed you painfully too."

"My beautiful wife," he whispered, covering her face with loving kisses. "You have been the perfect mistress of the house the entire day. Now you are just *my* perfect mistress."

"As you are now only *my* master." Elizabeth smiled at him with her sparkling eyes and her dry lips, which happily joined his.

Her body, warmed by the hot water and burned from the kisses that covered, tasted, and pleasured every inch of her shivering skin, learnt new meanings of passion and delight.

His eager, tender, powerful love banished any other feelings except happiness and gratifying fulfilment—which he generously offered her again and again—until she felt herself nothing but the mistress of her master.

Chapter 27

London, 11 January

Daylight and the sound of the wind blowing in the windows awakened Elizabeth from a dream she could not remember. She felt her husband's gaze and smiled at him. He was sitting in the armchair, a book beside him. He moved to the bed.

"It seems I am late again," she said.

"Much earlier than yesterday."

"How long have you been sitting there?"

"Not very long. The time passed while I admired your sleeping beauty."

"Oh, surely you did not watch me sleep?"

"I did." He caressed her hair. "It gives me such joy to know I can admire you without restraint, that there is no obstacle between us."

She gently touched his face, and he placed a lingering kiss within her palm. "You should have wakened me. I would like to spend the morning in bed with you," she said then blushed at the meaning of her words.

He smiled at her embarrassment then leant on the pillows and pulled her to him. She was still wrapped in the sheet and sighed while he put his arms around her and her head found the perfect place upon his heart. "This is perfect," she whispered, spoiled by his finger playing with her hair.

"Did you sleep well, Elizabeth?"

"I did."

"Are you… Do you feel any pain? I know it was only the second night and…"

"No, I…" She wished to put him at ease then chose complete honesty. "It is somehow painful when we…when you…but I believe it should be."

"I have not been patient enough, I fear. I should not have bothered you for a few days."

"Surely not," she said, nestling in his arms then lifting her face to him. "The slight pain means nothing compared to the joy I feel with you, William. And you have been very patient indeed."

"I am glad to hear that…and relieved… Just please always let me know if my insistence makes you uncomfortable in any way, and I will stop."

"I will." She rested her head on the hollow of his shoulder then suddenly chuckled. He tipped her chin to watch her face inquiringly. She laughed.

"Last night when I was in the bathtub and you entered, I did tell you that your appearance made me uncomfortable, but that did not stop you."

He slightly frowned, but she laughed and daringly brushed her lips on his.

"Everything that happened these two nights has made me uncomfortable, but not for a moment did I want you to stop," she whispered, her long hair tantalising him while the scent of her naked body, barely covered by the sheet, intoxicated him. His hands trapped her back, gliding along her spine.

"You make me lose my control and my mind, Elizabeth. My heart has long been lost to you."

He kissed her forehead then slowly separated from her while his entire body craved her. His lack of control had almost betrayed him once again, but he owed it to her to fight against it. They had made love twice the previous night, and while he could easily see how much she enjoyed their intimacy, he also noticed—and she had just confirmed it—that she was still in pain at times. He could and would wait at least until evening.

Elizabeth tried to conceal her disappointment—as well as her shame at admitting that she regretted the interruption of their interlude. She knew she should be embarrassed by having her husband be more reasonable than she was, and she promised herself to censor her gestures in the future. But in truth, she felt cold as soon as he left to his room.

Breakfast ended rather quickly, and then each returned to their scheduled activities.

Darcy went to meet his cousin and arrange for Lady Catherine to return to Kent, a task that was expected to be highly distressing.

Elizabeth was concerned about Darcy's success in his endeavour but also preoccupied with the first dinner she was hosting for her relatives—and his. She knew she had little reason to worry, yet she felt nervous about how his noble family would treat hers: a tradesman from Cheapside and his wife. The fact that the Fitzwilliam gentlemen had already met them was an excellent start though.

With Darcy's approval, she sent a note to the Gardiners, inviting them an hour earlier. She wished to speak to her aunt privately as there were many new things about which she needed advice.

Around noon, Elizabeth had everything settled and the preparations handled by the efficient staff. Darcy returned with the news that Lady Catherine had left Town the previous evening with Anne and her companion. He was relieved but somehow troubled by the easy resolution. He needed a way to calm his suspicious mind, so he invited his wife to have a cup of tea with him.

The first thing that Elizabeth noticed was the frown on her husband's face.

"You look concerned."

"I am thinking of Anne. And it seems too easy a resolution, which worries me."

"Could you find a way for Anne to spend more time with her cousins? I am sure Maryanne would be pleased to have her as a guest. And I would love to welcome Anne to our home."

"You are very kind. We shall think of something."

They sat—she with a cup of tea, he with his brandy.

"I made an appointment with the modiste for the day after tomorrow for the last two dresses. And I should order some nightgowns, too. I did not think of that before, but my old ones are not fashionable enough." She flushed and his eyes narrowed in laughter.

"You may order what you like, but I would suggest not wasting the family income on too many things that you will rarely wear." His lips twisted mischievously, and her eyes widened in disbelief.

"I would never have imagined your speaking in such an improper manner, Mr. Darcy!"

"I am sorry if I disappoint you, but you must remember that a man is defined more by his actions than by his words."

Her eyebrow arched in challenge, and her cheeks coloured while her eyes laughed at him.

"If we are to consider the *same subject*, your actions are by no means more proper than your words."

"True," he admitted without hesitation then kissed her hand again and spoke seriously. "Forgive me if I cross the line with some things that I say or do. I barely recognise myself at times. I often wonder whether I have lost my mind since I met you, and I believe it to be so! But I am so happy that you seem to accept my madness."

She caressed his face with lingering touches. "William, each moment I feel more and more that your 'madness' is everything that I have ever wished for in a marriage. And the fact that you have lost your mind—as you said—since you met me, I believe to be the most wonderful compliment a woman could receive."

He gently captured her lips for only a heartbeat, then both withdrew.

"I believe I should go and change. My uncle and aunt should arrive shortly."

"I will do the same in a minute. I look forward to spending some time with Mr. Gardiner."

Molly arranged her appearance. Elizabeth heard her husband in his apartment, but wisely, neither of them opened the adjoining doors, so they managed to be ready on time.

While waiting for the guests in the drawing room, an unexpected call disturbed the serenity of the evening. James Darcy's appearance took both by surprise, but they invited him in, both remembering that they had last heard of him during their most tormenting fight.

"Mrs. Darcy, what a pleasure to see you again! Forgive me for intruding. I would like a few private moments with my cousin if possible."

"You are not intruding, sir—you are family. Would you like to stay for dinner?"

Both men looked at her with surprise, and she responded with the most charming smile.

"No, but I thank you. I am in a great hurry."

"I shall leave you alone then." She exited the library, noticing her husband's frown.

Darcy had no time to inquire about the nature of the urgency as James started. "I need an advance on my inheritance. I have to make an urgent payment of one thousand pounds."

"I am certain this must be a joke before dinner, James."

"It is not. And I do not understand why I have to plead for something that is my right!"

"How can it be your right since it is my duty to take care of it for two more years? How will you ever repay me for all the effort I put in managing your properties, for my sleepless nights, and for the time I wasted on the road while you did nothing but enjoy yourself? How can it be your right to waste what I struggle so hard to increase?"

Darcy grew angrier, and James stepped back. "I only want one thousand. The income is at least three times as much for each property."

"You threw away another two thousand two months ago. I have a nine-year-old boy in the house who worked more for one shilling than you have worked in the last five years!"

"This is scandalous, Darcy! You cannot compare me with the child of a servant!"

"Sadly, that is true." He paced the room, followed by James's worried gaze. "I must know why you need the money. If you have gaming debts, I will purchase them. I refuse to give you such a sum."

"But I need the money! If you do not give it to me, I shall ask Annabelle Stafford."

Darcy's face darkened, and his voice sharpened. "Surely, you do not intend to use that as a threat against me! Go ask Annabelle Stafford, and you may repay her in two years' time as soon as you take the estates under your full command."

"That is unfair! You behave like the master of us all! You cannot run everybody's life."

"I would gladly put all the paper in your hands and be rid of the burden of your two properties! I am upset with myself for accepting your excellent father's requests. I should have refused and allowed a stranger to guard your fortune. Or I should do nothing more to improve it—only wait two more years. But sadly I am an unreasonable fool who entertains silly hopes that you will change. Now go and do not ruin my evening further! As I said, I agree to purchase your debts from whoever owns them—but no other arrangement."

Darcy rang for the servant, his anger mixed with sadness and disappointment. While James turned to leave, furious and red faced, he almost knocked Elizabeth down in the hall. He apologised and kissed her hand, and she said, smiling and holding his arm:

"Mr. Darcy, have you come to establish a schedule with William to learn the business of your estates as we discussed? I hope you will start soon and we shall see each other often."

James Darcy stared at her, frozen, his redness slowly turning white.

"No… We had some business to discuss of a different nature. Good evening, Mrs. Darcy."

Elizabeth glanced after him—guessing the reason for his unexpected visit—then stepped to her husband who was staring out the window. She touched his arm, and he turned with a bitter smile then embraced her and kissed her hair.

"He will never change," Darcy said.

"I am sorry to see you so pained." She rested her head on his chest while her hands encircled his waist. For a long moment, there was nothing but silent tenderness and mutual comfort. Then he withdrew and caressed her forehead, his face somewhat lighter.

"I believe the Gardiners are here. I think I heard a carriage."

THE JOY OF RECEIVING HER RELATIVES IN HER NEW HOME WAS OVERWHELMING to Elizabeth. Tearfully, she noticed her uncle and aunt's shyness in walking along the main hall.

She kissed them lovingly, and Darcy invited the guests into the drawing room. However, Elizabeth declared she wished to speak a few minutes alone with her aunt, and without further explanation, she took Mrs. Gardiner's arm and showed her to her apartment.

Inside Elizabeth's suite, Mrs. Gardiner remained still with an expression of wonder on her face. "Oh, Lizzy, I cannot believe you stay in Mrs. Darcy's rooms. That you *are* Mrs. Darcy."

"I cannot believe it myself, yet, dear Aunt. Here, take a seat wherever you want."

Mrs. Gardiner chose a small chair as she was afraid to disturb anything. "Aunt, I am so happy you are finally here! I have so many things to tell you!"

"Lizzy dearest, red roses in the middle of winter?" Mrs. Gardiner's astonishment grew beyond words, and Elizabeth laughed, her eyes sparkling with tears.

"Yes! William brought them to me yesterday morning! And last week, I received another bouquet with pink and cream roses." She touched the petals and enjoyed the soft scent.

"You seem so happy, Lizzy—both you and Mr. Darcy. And you look different from when I saw you before."

Elizabeth's cheeks flamed. "We *are* different, Aunt—just like the roses."

"What do you mean? Oh, Lizzy, what beautiful furniture—such exquisite taste! Forgive me, dearest, I became distracted. What were you saying? What do you mean *different*?"

Elizabeth gathered her courage for a confession while the redness on her face matched the roses.

"Aunt, I have so many things to tell you, but one is the most extraordinary! I just learnt two nights ago myself. Do you remember ten years ago in Brighton when I nearly drowned with Lucky? It was William, Aunt! He was the one who saved me! He was there with his cousin, visiting Lady Anne! Could such a coincidence be possible?"

"I cannot believe it! How can this be? What a strange thing! But how did you find out? Lizzy, I really cannot believe it! Is it true?" Mrs. Gardiner was beyond astonishment.

"On our way to London after the wedding, I tried to make conversation, and I told William that I met Lady Anne and Georgiana ten years ago. And then, as a joke, I mentioned the accident. His reaction made me wonder even then, but he did not say anything. Only when we last returned from Longbourn did he confess. He said he avoided telling me before so as not to influence my opinion of him. He said he wanted me to know him as he is now, to grow fond of him without being impressed by the past."

"That is truly incredible, Lizzy. Just wait until your uncle finds out. He spent years searching for that young man, only to find ourselves in his own house tonight. How can this be?"

"I asked myself the same thing. At first, I was a little upset with William, but then I understood his reason. I think it was best that he waited before telling me because now I am certain of my feelings for him, and I know his true worthiness as he is now."

"What a story! So many coincidences, my dear! I am relieved that you seem so serene, so happy. When I remember the day when he proposed to you less than a month ago…"

"I had no tender feelings for him at that time. In truth, I barely knew him. It was so difficult to be alone in London and to adjust to everything. We fought a few times—very badly indeed. I do not even want to remember it. Those first two weeks passed as a year, but I have come to see him in such a different way. I have to thank you for insisting on my marrying him."

Mrs. Gardiner smiled. "So, am I to understand that all goes well now? Do you enjoy your husband's company? In every particular? Even when you are *alone*?"

Elizabeth felt her face burning with shame, and she averted her eyes. "Oh, Aunt, it is… I remember when you told Jane and me that the marriage bed is not something to fear…"

"I remember too. I hope you will not prove me wrong. Was your husband patient with you? Sometimes young men may show a certain eagerness."

"He was very patient and caring. I enjoy his company so much—all the time. We spoke of his business, and he shared his problems with me. And when we are alone, the things that happen… I know I should be ashamed of such feelings, but I am not. Is that wrong?"

"So I have no reason to worry that you do not enjoy your husband's attentions."

The lady laughed and, observing Elizabeth's agitation, caressed her hand.

"You must not be ashamed of what you feel when you are with your husband. If he is pleased and you are pleased with what happens between you, nothing else matters."

"It is true—when I am with him, nothing else matters. I must be losing my mind. Two weeks ago I was certain I hated him, and I despaired at marrying him, and now…"

"He seems to be a smart man who knew how to win you, I believe."

"It started so gradually that I cannot remember the moment I started to become attached to him. I think it is because he always seems more preoccupied with my happiness than with his own—in everything, even when we… You know what I mean…"

"I do know, my dear. If you ask me, I think your feelings were not as opposed to him as you believed, even at the beginning of your marriage. And by the time you returned to Longbourn, you both seemed quite affectionate with each other."

"Yes, I believe we were, although we had just had an enormous fight. But all is well now."

"Lizzy, you must consider yourself a very fortunate woman. If I understand your words correctly, Mr. Darcy is not only a worthy gentleman, but also a *generous* husband."

"Yes, he is," Elizabeth answered, disconcerted by the sudden change of subject. "The settlement he offered me was beyond what I could hope for, and the jewels—"

"My dear, I am not talking of that sort of generosity but of the care and attention he gives you in private. Do you understand what I mean?"

"Oh, I see… Yes… You are right—my husband is a generous man, and I am very fortunate." Elizabeth's face, neck and shoulders were covered in a rosy hue. "Now should we not return to the others? I do not wish to appear impolite to our hosts."

"Of course, how silly of me. I thank you so much, dear Aunt! Your advice is always so useful. There is nobody with whom I can talk as I do with you."

"Talk to your husband now, Lizzy. It seems you can safely do so. Let him know what and how deeply you feel. I dare say he will be very pleased to hear it."

"I will—and I already have. We have learnt to be very open with each other. I am truly a fortunate woman."

"I am so glad for you! Oh, I forgot to ask you: Was I correct when I said a handsome husband made everything easier to bear?"

"Indeed you were," Elizabeth said, laughing through the embarrassment that never left her while she showed her aunt back to the drawing room.

They were met by their husbands, who were caught in pleasant conversation and the enjoyment of fine brandy.

With no little emotion, Mrs. Gardiner approached the master of the house. "Mr. Darcy, I have just discovered something that has troubled our peace for years, and

I cannot keep the secret any longer. It seems we owe you not only for the present felicity of our niece but also for her life. Edward, let me introduce to you the man you have sought for so long."

Darcy attempted to stay the words of gratitude. "Mrs. Gardiner, it is not—"

"Madeline, what are you speaking of?" Mr. Gardiner inquired, embarrassed by his wife's behaviour. Elizabeth stepped closer and took hold of Darcy's arm.

"Uncle, William is the young man who saved my life ten years ago! I know he loathes having his merits acknowledged, but he has no choice. He must accept the fact that he is my hero."

The astonishment that followed that revelation struck Mr. Gardiner so forcefully that he needed to sit, staring in silence, and then asked rather impolitely to have his glass refilled. Only then did he find the strength to shake Darcy's hand. Nothing could prevent his expressions of gratitude for what Darcy felt was quite a long time.

Darcy's embarrassment made him silent. He felt slightly displeased with Elizabeth's confessing to her relatives something that he considered unworthy of such praise.

But her eyes sparkling with tears of emotion, her hands gripping his arm, and her tender smiles eliminated his discomfort. And he had no choice but to accept becoming what he had so much wished without even knowing what he had done to deserve the title: her hero!

The introduction of the Gardiners to Miss Georgiana Darcy was filled with emotion on both sides. Mrs. Annesley greeted the guests then chose to return to her room and not intrude on the family's first dinner together. Her absence increased Georgiana's reticence, but it only needed a few minutes before Mrs. Gardiner's gentleness and her genuine admiration of Lady Anne Darcy conquered Miss Darcy's shyness.

Darcy offered to give the guests a tour of the house before the others arrived. A long and heartfelt moment was spent in the large gallery in front of the beautiful paintings of the family, and Mrs. Gardiner recollected in great detail the day they had encountered Lady Anne and Georgiana on the beach in Brighton.

Soon enough, the Fitzwilliam family arrived. Elizabeth did not fail to notice her aunt's uneasiness before the illustrious company, and she was grateful for Lady Matlock and Lady Maryanne's warm politeness as well as for the gentlemen's amiability.

The dinner progressed much to Elizabeth's hopes and expectations. She gracefully received their compliments for the selection of courses and for the arrangements.

They discussed the next evening's ball, which the younger members of the family planned to attend, while Lord and Lady Matlock had declined the invitation. It was also agreed that the ladies would go together to the modiste the day after the ball. Mrs. Gardiner secretly confessed to Elizabeth that she had long wished to order a dress from Madame Claudette but had never been able to secure an appointment at that prestigious establishment. Elizabeth was pleased to be able to help her aunt with just another small thing.

The evening ended very late with admirable performances at the piano by Miss Darcy, Elizabeth, and Lady Maryanne.

While Miss Darcy returned to her room, Elizabeth and Darcy stood outside, taking a warm farewell and waiting for the carriages to depart. Even then, they remained a moment longer, admiring the frozen, white streets.

"Would you like to take a short walk? I would enjoy some fresh air," Elizabeth said. He looked puzzled and not without reason: it was the middle of an icy night.

"I would rather go upstairs and open the window wide instead of walking in the park at this hour. It would be strange and rather dangerous."

He was right, of course. London was not Longbourn, and she was still thoughtless about such details. She attempted to laugh.

"Well, at least I am not the only one with reckless ideas. Look, there is a carriage just across the street. I imagine it is expecting someone who enjoys a late night stroll."

Darcy glanced at the carriage strangely waiting on the deserted street, but it was unfamiliar to him, so he escorted his wife inside and closed the door behind them.

Molly and Stevens helped them prepare for the night then were quickly dismissed. While Elizabeth brushed her hair, Darcy entered, placed a chair behind her stool, and tenderly encircled her with his arms. She glanced at their image in the mirror and planned to talk to him about the evening, but she shivered as his lips whispered near her ear.

"I opened the windows in my room."

He gently freed her neck from their heavy curls and tasted her skin.

She moaned and attempted to turn to him, but he trapped her body in his arms, tantalising her neck, ears, and shoulders with warm kisses. Her back was pressed against his chest, and his hand slowly pulled the gown down from her shoulders then glided lower, caressing her thighs through the soft fabric and pressing until her skin began to burn.

With eager passion, his caresses overspread her body until his palms closed possessively on her breasts and his lips captured hers with a hunger that seemed to grow. Then he abandoned the sweet roundness and glided between her warm legs. Her hands attempted to touch him, but her movements only made her gown reveal more of her soft skin. Her eyes caught their scandalous reflection in the mirror, and she briefly remembered her aunt's words—that she should not be ashamed of anything when she was with her husband. She was not, as the feelings that built inside her were stronger than any shame. Chills shattered her, and she cried against their joined lips when his finger slowly glided inside her, stroking and caressing until she lost her senses and found the delight so well known and desired.

Darcy stared at their image in the mirror. They were both sitting—he on a chair, she on a stool in front of him, her back pressing against his chest and his hands still resting on the warmest parts of her beautiful body. Her face was flushed and her eyes closed while she had abandoned herself against him. This time he had not even asked if she wished him to stop, as he had come to know her body so well as to feel what she enjoyed most. His body could sense her pleasure, and he was aroused just from sharing hers. She was soft, warm, and ready for him. For a moment, he thought the bed was too far away, but he abandoned his little mischievous plan for a later night.

He carried her to his chamber and gently set her on the bed then hurried to close the windows. He noticed the carriage was in the same spot, but he ignored it.

The room was very cold, but he felt a burning inside, so he quickly removed his clothes and lay beside her. As her arms encircled his neck, he hastily removed her rumpled gown then pulled a cover over their united bodies. Her body opened for him, and he easily glided inside her warmth with a deep moan of contentment.

His fingers cradled her head, sliding into her rich hair. Their eyes met, and there were no words needed until he started to move slowly in her—with her.

Elizabeth's astonishment was aroused when her husband joined with her, and she felt only a little pain, which she barely noticed. Her relief was soon combined with the most delightful sense of being united with him, and soon a different sort of pleasure built and expanded inside her.

"William..." she whispered, breathless.

"Yes, my love. Is something wrong?" His movements ceased, and he looked at her with concern.

"No...it is wonderful..." Her legs wrapped around his waist, and his thrusts deepened, growing faster and stronger. Her body moved tentatively beneath his, against his, together with his until waves of delight spread inside her and her moans of fulfilment matched his.

Their kisses and caresses lasted long after their bodies rested in exhaustion as his hunger for her face, her eyes, her hair, and her soft lips was impossible to satiate.

Elizabeth struggled to breathe, but not for a moment did she attempt to withdraw from him. He suddenly turned over on his back and moved her perfectly atop him. While he kissed her, his hands rested on her hips, caressing her buttocks and pressing her against him. She gasped in surprise to realise that this sudden change of position did not separate them. He was still warm, strong and hard inside her. She withdrew from him slightly, and her hair as well as her beautiful breasts brushed his chest.

"Oh, God, Elizabeth...this is so good," he said hoarsely.

She leant a little lower, puzzled as to what precisely he meant. She felt the hair of his chest tantalising her skin, and she sighed. She now understood and slowly started to move against him, their bodies still joined. Her heavy locks tickled her skin and his, and her nipples became harder while stroking his torso. His hand tightly gripped her hips and pushed them against his.

She called his name again, and he pulled her lower to capture her dry lips.

"Slowly, my love," he whispered, testing her mouth. "Search for your pleasure... It is your turn to do whatever you like..."

"You must guide me... I do not know..." she barely answered.

"Your desire and your pleasure will be enough guidance..."

He smiled, his dark gaze locked with her clouded eyes, and his lips held hers captive a few moments longer. Then he slowly pushed her back until she was sitting astride him.

Her hair fell loose on her shoulders, sheltering her breasts from his greedy eyes. His hands found their way towards the heavy roundness that fit perfectly in his palms. She supported her hands on his chest and started to move shyly, her face showing her surprise and delight at the newly discovered sensations. Her movements increased more daringly—hastier and more eager until she fell on his chest, exhausted and breathless.

Then he turned over, leaning her against the pillows as he lay atop her, and finally reached his long awaited completion.

"I missed you so much, my beautiful wife," he whispered when he finally caught his breath.

Their faces almost touched, and Elizabeth caressed his face, watching him in long silence.

"I completely lost myself to you in every sense, my husband, and nothing could make me happier."

Nothing but silence was needed to seal another day of their marriage. They fell asleep, tightly embracing as the night met the dawn.

And only then did the carriage across the street finally depart.

Chapter 28

London, 12 January

Elizabeth listened to Georgiana's beautiful playing while Darcy was in the library with Mr. Aldridge, his solicitor, with whom Elizabeth had the pleasure of meeting earlier in the day.

That evening would be marked by Lady Isabella's ball, and Elizabeth expected it to be another opportunity for distress. Her preparation for the ball was more careful than ever before. She wished to receive her husband's admiration and to make sure he was proud of her appearance on his arm.

She chose the ball gown ordered by her husband and the set of emerald jewels. Georgiana and Mrs. Annesley—who were not to attend the ball—complimented her repeatedly, but no praise came close to her husband's dark stare that enveloped her from the door.

"Mrs. Darcy, you look absolutely beautiful."

With a warm farewell from their sister and her companion, the Darcys elegantly entered the carriage, and in less than a quarter hour, they arrived in front of Lady Isabella's house.

As Elizabeth anticipated, the number of guests surpassed that from Lady Matlock's ball on New Year's Eve.

It was with no surprise that Mr. James Darcy was among the guests. He briefly greeted them and attempted to speak to his cousin, but Darcy answered with little encouragement.

A chorus of gasps was heard as Lord Clayton entered with two other gentlemen and three ladies, one of them being Annabelle Stafford. Elizabeth noticed her husband's frown, and their eyes met briefly. She smiled, and the emeralds shining from her earrings and necklace reflected beautiful shades of green in her sparkling eyes.

Lady Isabella confronted her cousin Lord Clayton, whose serene expression dismissed any reproach with mockery and indifference. Elizabeth watched them speaking in low voices, apparently in contention for a little while, then Lady Isabella gave up while Lord Clayton's entire group—of which the other two pairs seemed to be French—sat on one side of the room, speaking by themselves.

Another thing that both Elizabeth and Darcy observed were Lord Clayton's repeated glances towards them. While Elizabeth was amused, Darcy became increasingly annoyed.

"Is there anything that bothers you?" she inquired, teasingly.

"I was wondering what Clayton was thinking by bringing Annabelle here. And how could she be such a fool as to insinuate herself at a ball hosted by a woman who despises her."

"This is scandalous!" Lady Maryanne said, outraged.

"Come dear, do not exaggerate," her husband answered patronisingly.

"It is a silly, awkward situation but not unexpected. Besides, half of London seems to be here, so what does it matter that one more annoying person is present? And by the way, Darcy, I spotted Bingley's sisters too," concluded the Colonel.

"And why not?" asked Mr. Hasting. "Hurst is a cousin of mine, and he is a rather pleasing fellow."

"Speaking of annoying persons," Darcy said sharply, as Lord Clayton approached them together with Lady Isabella, whose face was still red with anger.

Greetings were exchanged before Lord Clayton spoke. "Mrs. Darcy, what a pleasure to see you here! We were not aware that you returned to town! Such a lovely surprise you have given us all. I must say, you look exceptionally beautiful tonight."

"I thank you, sir." She smiled in reply. "I confess that I own my appearance to my husband, who has chosen both my dress and jewels."

"When one has such an exceptional wife, it is easy for one to choose such finery," the earl continued. Darcy's face proved he was at the edge of his patience.

"True, Clayton. What is truly difficult is for one to have the wisdom to choose the correct wife." Darcy placed Elizabeth's hand on his arm and covered it with his hand.

"Mr. and Mrs. Darcy gave us a lovely surprise by attending this evening, unlike you who gave the worst one! What effrontery of that woman," Lady Isabella commented.

"Annabelle is very fond of both marquises and their wives. They are quite lonely in London without any friends, and you agreed to invite them to the ball," Lord Clayton replied.

"You tricked me into this!" Lady Isabella struggled to keep her voice down.

"Mrs. Darcy, I hope *you* are not disturbed by Lady Stafford's presence," Lord Clayton asked.

"Why should I be? I am grateful to Lady Isabella for the lovely invitation. The others present are not for me to discuss. Besides," she said, her cheeks blushing, "I confess my husband's company is enough for me to forget everything else."

The others stared at her in disbelief and smiled, as they did not know what to do with such a confession. Both the gentlemen and the ladies experienced a sense of jealousy, although for different reasons.

With little propriety, Darcy brought her hand to his lips for a brief yet meaningful kiss.

"Please excuse us now, the first set is about to start, and I wish to dance with my wife."

"Mrs. Darcy, I hope you remember that you owe me a set from the Twelfth Night ball," Lord Clayton said. Elizabeth barely took her eyes from Darcy to glance at him.

"I do not remember owing your lordship any set, but I will be pleased to save one for you anyway. I have already received invitations from the colonel, from the viscount and from Mr. Hasting. Except for those, I will happily stand with you for any other."

She then followed her husband onto the dance floor as the music started. If there were any whispers of disapproval for Mr. Darcy's dancing with his own wife, neither of them noticed.

They moved gracefully, eyes locked, barely touching hands and speaking to each other wordlessly.

From time to time, Darcy glanced at Clayton, who continued to stare at them, and she could barely suppress her laughter. When the dance steps brought them close, she whispered, "I find your jealousy rather alluring, Mr. Darcy."

"Should I be worried that you can read my mind, Mrs. Darcy?"

"Come, sir, I am certain half the room can," she teased him.

"The idiot was right, though. You look exceptionally beautiful."

"And, as I told '*the idiot*,'" she whispered, careful not to be heard, "I owe my appearance to you. Not just because of the jewels and gown but because of *everything* you offered me."

Darcy had no reply to such a confession. His eyes remained on his wife as he struggled to hide his emotions and an urge to kiss her in the middle of the ballroom.

As soon as the set ended, Miss Bingley and Mrs. Hurst stepped towards Elizabeth and Darcy, still wearing grudging, cold expressions on their faces.

"What a surprise, Mr. Darcy. Are we allowed to speak to you here, or should we also ask Mrs. Darcy's permission?" Miss Bingley asked sharply while cold greetings were exchanged.

"For anything related to me, you should ask Mrs. Darcy's permission. As for anything regarding Mrs. Darcy, you should ask for mine. However, we are pleased to see you, Miss Bingley, Mrs. Hurst. Is there anything we might do for you? Anything you wish to discuss?"

"Surely you know what we want to discuss, sir. My brother has returned to Hertfordshire!"

"Miss Bingley, Mrs. Hurst, I shall allow you to speak to my husband privately," Elizabeth said graciously while she went to join Lady Maryanne. Darcy gazed after her.

"So, more precisely, what is the problem?"

"The problem is that he returned to the place from which we struggled to send him away! He said he wished to remain there, and I am afraid he will end up marrying Jane Bennet!"

"If so, that is entirely his business. He is capable of knowing his desires and behaving accordingly."

"But you agreed that such an unequal marriage would be disastrous for him! To join such a terrible family, to marry a woman so below him! You must advise him!"

"Miss Bingley!" Darcy's voice sharpened. "Since I married a Bennet daughter and congratulate myself every day for doing so, how could I advise Bingley against it? Miss Bennet is an admirable woman who would make a wonderful wife. Besides, let us be honest: since the Bennet family was not a problem for me, it certainly should not be for Bingley. I do not wish to be rude, but Miss Bennet is a gentleman's daughter while your fortune was made by your excellent father in trade. *That* seems unequal to me."

Both sisters turned pale in disbelief. Darcy showed a proper, polite smile. "May I be of assistance with anything else? If not, please excuse me. I shall seek my wife."

Elizabeth had decided to leave as she imagined there would be a discussion about her family and especially Jane, and she trusted him to settle things properly. She spotted Lady Maryanne and Lady Mary across a small foyer, and she moved towards them.

Half way, she was interrupted by Lady Stafford. Elizabeth was tempted to continue walking but decided otherwise. She turned to the lady and moved near a wall to assure them some privacy.

"Lady Stafford! May I help you with anything?"

"Mrs. Darcy—what a lovely surprise."

"I beg you—do not tell me again that it is fate or coincidence that brings us together. It has become quite boring and slightly ridiculous" Elizabeth attempted a light tone.

The lady appeared disconcerted. "And yet, it is. I did not know you were to be here tonight."

"Yes, Lord Clayton told us that. May I ask why you approach me? Is there anything you wish to discuss? Do you want me to settle that appointment with my husband to help you with your business? Do you have a letter for me about that?"

Her old self-confident impertinence seemed to elude Lady Stafford with each of Elizabeth's words, but she continued with a mischievous smile and a most insinuating tone.

"Not exactly. I was just wondering… It is strange that you wear that dress. I have one amazingly similar that I wore at the Twelfth Night ball. People might think you copied mine. And I wish to inquire how your marriage is going so far? Are you satisfied with your position? I understand Darcy is still attending his business often, which is quite strange for a newly wedded man. Might it be that he is already bored with his married life?"

A wide smile lit Elizabeth's face as her back straightened and she took a step closer.

"Lady Stafford, please allow me to clarify any remaining misunderstanding.

I know the entire past history between you and my husband. *Everything* in the smallest detail, starting with the private month you spent in Ramsgate and ending with little Tommy."

Lady Stafford paled and took a step backward.

"I also know that you ordered a dress similar to mine and intended to create some sort of a scandal at the Twelfth Night ball. You keep chasing my husband, and I do understand you. I imagine it must be difficult to have enjoyed even a short amount of time with him then to lose him forever. And *since I spend every night and most of the day in his arms,* I understand even more clearly your desire to win him back. But you must understand: this will not happen, ever. You have brought him such distress that he was forced to compare your wit to that of his dog! How does that make you feel? You cannot go on in this manner!"

"You have no right to speak to me like this!" Annabelle Stafford blurted. "I shall do whatever I please. Nobody can stop me or force me to do otherwise! You may hate me, you may be scared of me, you may wish to get rid of me, but it will never happen! And I know Darcy once loved me. If it were not for you, he would have returned to me."

"No, he would not." Elizabeth's voice softened, and she felt nothing but compassion for the spiteful woman in front of her.

"He told me that, even if he was not married and all the other women were to suddenly disappear, he still would not have been interested in you. I know this to be true, and I am sure you know it too, but you attempt to deceive yourself. And Lady Stafford—I do not hate you, and I am certainly not scared of you. I only pity you—deeply. I feel sorry for you, and I wonder that such a beautiful woman who now has means, position, and wealth, refuses to enjoy life and instead prefers to make a fool of herself and expose herself to ridicule and the censure of the world. People consider you an annoyance, Lady Stafford, not a menace!"

Lady Annabelle Stafford became as pale as the white silk damask-covered wall against which she searched for support. Though her mouth opened wide, no words came out. Elizabeth continued to look at Annabelle, her compassionate smile unchanged, while the lady made another attempt to speak.

Only then did both notice that their conversation had been witnessed by the unexpected approach of Lady Isabella, Lady Mary, Lady Maryanne—and Mr. Darcy!

Lady Stafford's pallor turned into a deep flush, and she almost ran away, seeking escape from the gazes that seemed to illustrate exactly what Elizabeth had told her. Elizabeth was troubled by the conversation and sought shelter on the arm of her husband.

The ladies smiled with certain embarrassment, and Lady Isabella apologised for any inconvenience Elizabeth had to bear. A minute later, a footman discreetly informed the host that Lady Annabelle Stafford was unwell and had left the ball unexpectedly.

The second set began, and all the ladies were claimed by their partners.

Darcy remained near the wall, employing his time in admiration of his wife as she danced with his cousin Robert. Exceptionally beautiful, indeed—in this, "the *idiot" Clayton* had been right. She was also keenly bright, generous, loving, and passionate—but all these things only he knew and was eager to enjoy again soon.

The way she spoke to Annabelle—her perfect calm and her elegant, yet harsh reasoning were truly admirable, and he noticed the same admiration in the ladies who unwillingly witnessed the scene.

When he had observed Elizabeth—and Annabelle approaching her—he hastened to them, being certain that the latter would do something to trouble Elizabeth. He intended to save her, but there was no need. Just as she told him a week ago—was it truly only a week ago?—as soon as she knew the whole truth, she was able to bear and handle anything.

Darcy startled when his thoughts were disturbed by his Cousin James's voice from nearby.

"I want to know whether you have considered what I asked you. Will you help me?"

"James, I would rescue you from yet another troublesome situation but only if you tell me the details. And I need a paper to testify to whom I am giving the money."

"I will sign any paper you want. I must insist on this—these are my funds, and I can give them to whomever I please."

"I see. James, I am rapidly losing my patience now. Have the wisdom to speak again tomorrow, although I can hardly see a reasonable resolution to this."

"Tomorrow afternoon, I will call on you."

"Such a joyful moment," Darcy concluded as he took a glass of brandy, allowing his eyes and his anger to calm under the lovely image of Elizabeth dancing.

The rest of the ball progressed reasonably well. Elizabeth danced every set, including with Lord Clayton and James Darcy, but she skilfully avoided any disturbing subjects.

Darcy danced once with Lady Isabella, once with his cousin Maryanne, and the last again with his wife. More than one disapproving opinion was shared about his poor manners—especially since several unmarried ladies were without partners. However, Mr. Darcy seemed oblivious to anything but his wife.

Later, the Darcys were among the first guests to leave.

A moment after the carriage moved, Elizabeth began to chat about the ball, but she was silenced as her husband's arms entrapped her and his lips captured hers.

Fortunately, the ride was brief. They entered the house quickly, and Darcy briefly spotted another carriage near the entrance to the park. It was certainly a different one than the previous evening, so he immediately took his mind from it, imagining it was a couple indulging in some illicit affair and seeking privacy.

Darcy dismissed Molly and Stevens, then the heavy doors closed, happily allowing Mr. and Mrs. Darcy full privacy in the silence and comfort of their apartment.

Elizabeth waited, somehow uneasy, as her husband did nothing but stare at her as they stood in the middle of the room. The fire burned steadily, and there were two candles on the table by the window and another two at the fireplace.

"Will you help me undress?" she asked, her lips and eyes smiling at him.

"Not yet…" His voice was hoarse, and his gaze dark. He took one more step then cupped her face and tasted her lips for an instant.

"Elizabeth, I want to do something that you might find disturbing… It has tormented me this entire night, and I could only think of the moment we would finally be alone…"

She struggled to gulp and to breathe, her heart beating wildly. "What is it?"

"I want to love you just as we are now—just as *you* are now—this very moment…"

Her eyes widened in miscomprehension. "You mean dressed like this?"

He started to kiss her face, his lips tantalising her skin and gently biting her earlobe.

"Dressed like this—just as I admired you and yearned for you every moment of the last hours." His lips brushed over hers. "Would you, my love?"

"Would I what?" She struggled to understand, breathless and already burning inside.

"Would you allow me to love you this way?"

He gently pushed her against the wall, and her arms encircled his neck. She still did not understand what he meant but soon ceased to wonder as she abandoned herself to him.

"I would *'allow' you* to love me any way you want." She daringly spoke her heart.

Astonished and overwhelmed by impatient kisses, she felt trapped between the cold wall and her husband's warm passion, and hers soon was aroused just as strongly. He caressed her, supported her, revealed her, and possessed her with such powerful desire, eagerness, and thirst that her remaining senses were only connected to him.

Sometime later, she felt herself lifted in haste and placed on the small dressing table. He pulled her legs around him as her beautiful dress was gathered around her thighs and pulled down from her shoulders. His kisses covered her face, her neck, and her shoulders while his hands explored the unrevealed parts of her burning body.

His thrusts inside her grew more intense, and she tried to stifle her cry of delight by biting the warm, sweaty skin of his neck. He turned his head so that his mouth captured hers at the precise moment of complete fulfilment of their bodies, which shuddered in relief.

When Elizabeth was eventually able to think properly, her eyes were still closed, and she refused to even imagine the position in which they were lying.

She heard her husband whisper something. His voice was tender, sweet, and gentle, but she could not understand the words. Her legs were still entwined around him, her hands around his neck.

His coat and vest had been removed, and his shirt was half-open. His arms closed around her, and she felt herself carried and laid on the bed.

She kept her eyes closed while he gently undressed her completely, his lips tasting her uncovered skin. Then his fingers removed the pins, freeing her heavy, dark tresses. Only when there was no fabric between them did he lie beside her—their warm bodies touching and embracing in silence—and put the bed sheets over them.

"I should take off the jewels, too," she whispered.

"No. I love the green reflection of the stones on your skin."

"This dress must be completely ruined. Such a pity, I liked it so much. It fit me perfectly."

"You should ask for it to be cleaned and keep it. But I would like you never to wear it again in public."

His lips brushed over her ear while he spoke the wonder that was troubling her too.

"Elizabeth, how is it possible that I feel I just cannot have enough of you?"

"I do not know... When you have the answer, please help me understand too..."

"I promise..." His gentle yet daring caresses increased, and he spoke through repeated kisses. "Mrs. Darcy, since you so kindly allowed my outrageous earlier request, is there some way to repay you?"

She moaned when their lips finally met.

"You seem quite proficient at guessing my mind lately, sir...so I would just trust your well known generosity."

"A very wise decision, I would say," he answered, and those were the last coherent words as he did everything in his power to prove himself worthy of her trust.

Chapter 29

London, 13 January

Just before noon, Mr. Bingley barged in, unexpected, unannounced, and tired from the road. The first thing that crossed Elizabeth's mind was that something tragic happened at Longbourn, but Bingley's smile was so wide and he so hastily embraced her that Elizabeth's heart melted with joy. The guest then bowed to Georgiana and Mrs. Annesley and took a seat. Food and drinks were ordered as he began to speak enthusiastically.

"I apologise for arriving so unexpectedly, but I need Darcy's assistance in an urgent matter. Jane—I mean Miss Bennet… I asked her to be my wife, and she accepted last evening. So after having Mr. Bennet's consent, I hurried to London as I need to know how to procure a special licence. I want to marry as soon as possible… perhaps in a month or so? Oh, and Miss Bennet—Jane—sent this letter to you, Mrs. Darcy. And Mr. Bennet sent one to you, Darcy," he said, barely catching his breath as he handed them the papers.

Elizabeth and Georgiana smiled at his obvious agitation while Elizabeth embraced him once again, expressing her delight at having him as a brother. Darcy filled a glass for him.

"Bingley, you express yourself as poorly in speech as in writing. You do not need a special license to marry in a month! I congratulate you, and I will be happy to be your brother. But not so much your sister's brother," Darcy concluded while Georgiana and Elizabeth laughed and Bingley began to mumble worse than before. Eventually, he returned to his old self, and he could hardly cease sharing his happiness with them.

"Oh, I forgot to mention something important! Wickham left his regiment two nights ago. Such effrontery—I was very close to calling him out!"

"Bingley, what on earth are you saying? Perhaps we should speak of this later," Darcy interrupted him, glancing with panic at his sister. Georgiana paled but asked courageously.

"Brother, if you do not mind, I would like to hear Mr. Bingley's story. What happened, sir?"

"That is the second reason for my arrival in Town. Mr. Bennet said I should talk to Darcy. You have everything in the letter. Wickham was involved in some sort of a scandal a few nights ago regarding some card debts and—you will not believe this—he secretly planned to leave the regiment and to convince Miss Lydia—your sister—to elope with him!"

"What?" Elizabeth cried in disbelief, turning white. Mr. Bingley continued unruffled.

"Even before you visited Longbourn, he was conducting a secret correspondence with Miss Lydia, declaring his admiration and intention to marry her. So two nights ago—one evening after you left—he convinced her. She was ready to leave her family without telling anyone but Miss Kitty. Fortunately, she changed her mind just a few hours before. He came to wait for her, and she left the house to speak to him. I found them in the middle of the night. You may easily imagine how strong my reaction was! I tried to avoid a scandal, but I pushed Wickham away, and I went to awaken Colonel Forster despite the late hour. By morning, Wickham had not appeared with the regiment, leaving behind a large number of creditors."

Georgiana's hands trembled. Darcy struggled to express his astonishment without disturbing the ladies further.

"Thank God that Lydia made a wise decision," Elizabeth finally said. "Although God knows that I wonder how it happened. I love my sister, but her decisions are rarely wise." Elizabeth spoke mostly to herself, but Mr. Bingley seemed happy to know the answer.

"Well, Miss Bennet—Jane—explained it in the letter. Miss Elizabeth—I mean Mrs. Darcy—promised to take Miss Lydia and Miss Kitty to Town for the Season and to offer them a private coming out ball in Meryton next year. Miss Lydia said she could not abide that only Miss Kitty would have the private ball and the chance of staying in London for the Season, so she decided she would rather not marry than miss such opportunities. She said—I believe I can quote—that she loved Mr. Wickham dearly, but she could easily find another gentleman officer, while a private coming out ball was once in a lifetime."

Darcy, Elizabeth, and Georgiana stared in disbelief, struggling to understand Mr. Bingley's tangled explanation.

"So...Miss Lydia refused to elope in order to not miss any balls?" Darcy attempted to conclude. This time Bingley seemed puzzled himself.

"I believe so..."

"This must be a first for Wickham," Darcy said as he filled Bingley's glass—and his own.

Miss Georgiana Darcy—pale and tearful from the emotion and her own embarrassment—started to laugh, unable to stop despite the others' astonished faces. She covered her mouth with trembling hands, excusing herself and hurrying to her room. Elizabeth followed her while a grave Darcy remained still, his half-empty glass in his hand, as he stared, confounded, at the closed door. Then he emptied the glass and turned to his friend.

"Bingley, I thank you for your invaluable help in handling this situation, but I must ask: What on earth were you doing near the Bennet's house in the middle of the night?"

Mr. Bingley choked on his brandy, turned pale then crimson and put some meat into his mouth while he mumbled an incoherent response. Darcy did not inquire further.

Inside Georgiana's room, the girl continued to laugh for a little while, tears rolling from her eyes. Elizabeth put her arms around her. Slowly, Georgiana's laughter became sobs, and she embraced Elizabeth. They sat together, holding hands.

"I have been such a ridiculous fool, Elizabeth. He tricked me as easily as if I were a child."

"I am sorry you suffer so much, dearest, but I believe it is for the best. Now you can easily see how little Mr. Wickham deserved your affection and how right William was about him."

"It is true. Forgive me for laughing so foolishly, but it is all so ridiculous and painful. I hope your sister does not suffer. It seems she was very wise in her decision—wiser than me."

"This is not true, my dear. Your behaviour was admirable too. Although I never would have imagined it, I admit that Lydia surprised me pleasantly this time."

"Oh, I am sorry—I did not even congratulate you for the news. I know how fond you are of your sister, and I am sure she will be very happy with Mr. Bingley."

Elizabeth chuckled. "I am beyond joy for my dear Jane, but I am even happier imagining the faces of Miss Bingley and Mrs. Hurst when they learn the news. Does that make me a bad person?"

"A little," Miss Darcy answered in jest. "But I can surely sympathise with you."

The light conversation and Elizabeth's warm care eventually calmed Georgiana. And despite her troubled countenance, Elizabeth was certain that the wound inflicted on the girl by Mr. Wickham had begun to heal. Oddly enough—with Lydia's help!

It took a full hour before the three ladies were ready to visit the modiste.

Since Mrs. Gardiner was expected to join them too, Darcy found no cause for him to accompany four ladies to try on dresses. He had planned a meeting with Mr. Aldridge, but he assigned three servants and the coachman to chaperone them.

They fetched Mrs. Gardiner from Gracechurch Street and spent the long ride to Madame Claudette's discussing the wonderful news of the anticipated wedding.

In her letter, Jane had repeatedly told Elizabeth how grateful she was for Mr. Darcy's help in achieving the happy resolution. Jane insisted that, without Mr.

Darcy, Mr. Bingley would likely not have returned to Netherfield and they would have probably not met again.

Elizabeth fully agreed with her sister: without Mr. Darcy's letter and encouragement, Mr. Bingley would not have returned to Hertfordshire. What Jane did not know—and Elizabeth still remembered with shivers—was his involvement in Mr. Bingley's leaving in the first place. That, however, was a fact she would not recollect again. For the time being, there were plans to make, perhaps new dresses to order, and joy to share.

The visit at the modiste lasted an hour, and another half hour was needed to take Mrs. Gardiner to her house and finally return home.

When the carriage entered their street, the nearly setting sun was painting the sky with spectacular colours. The weather was pleasant and rather soft for a January day. Elizabeth considered asking her husband for a walk when her attention was drawn by activity, voices, and barks on the paths of Hyde Park across the street from their house. She easily recognised from afar the familiar forms of Peter, Libby, the dogs, and one of the footmen. She turned to her companions.

"Would you like a stroll before returning home? It will surely benefit our appetites. I think the children and dogs will all be happy to see us," Elizabeth said with a laugh.

Her companions agreed somewhat reluctantly, Mrs. Annesley expressing her concern about walking in cold weather and insisting the outing be short. Elizabeth dismissed the carriage and asked the footmen to inform Mr. Darcy of their whereabouts.

There were very few visitors in the park. A few carriages rode by them at a slow pace, and Elizabeth remembered her husband's promise about the sleigh ride.

In a little while, the children noticed and loudly greeted them. The ground was slippery, and the ladies' steps small and careful.

Their progress was abruptly interrupted by a carriage stopping near them and three men hurrying down from it. Elizabeth was certain they must be some new acquaintances she could not recall, so she smiled at them.

"Mrs. Darcy ma'am, you must come with us. If you make no noise, nobody will be hurt," one of them said in a low, cold voice.

Elizabeth looked in disbelief. They wore regular winter clothes and appeared as any other visitor to the park. A moment later, she observed the shape of pistols in their coats and looked closely at their faces. She was too bewildered to react. Mrs. Annesley spoke first.

"Have you lost your minds? How dare you! Mr. Darcy lives just across the street and I am sure he can see you this very moment! He would kill you for simply speaking to his wife!"

"Shut your mouth, woman," one of the men said threateningly. "Ma'am, we have a job to do, and we will do it. You will come with us no matter what. We mean no harm, but we will do what we need to do. It is best you not resist us if you do not want somebody to be hurt."

The men's expressions were stern, and their determination obvious. Elizabeth's head was spinning, and her heart chilled with dread.

She still could not credit what was happening, but she knew it was entirely her fault. She should not have stopped in the park and dismissed the servants. She should not have walked without escort and recklessly disobeyed her husband again!

But she did, and her thoughtlessness put innocent people in danger: Georgiana, Mrs. Annesley, the children who were happily approaching, and the poor servant who certainly had no chance against three armed men.

Only God knew what they wanted from her. She squeezed Georgiana's hand.

"Gentlemen, could we please settle this without any harm? I understand you have a duty to accomplish for which you have been paid. Mr. Darcy will offer you double the sum, without asking any questions, if we could just find a resolution to the advantage of us all."

"Ma'am, of this we cannot speak, and we cannot make such a decision. We must keep you company to a certain address. For the rest, we are not responsible."

"Of course you are, you wretched scamps! You shall be hung for this!" Mrs. Annesley cried.

"Mrs. Annesley!" Elizabeth intervened as calmly as possible. "Please take Georgiana and leave. I will be fine. Tell Mr. Darcy. He will find a way to solve this," she ordered decidedly, praying those men would not find that the girl was Mr. Darcy's sister. Mrs. Annesley seemed to understand her reasoning. She stepped closer to Elizabeth, speaking decidedly.

"I will do no such thing! They may well shoot me, but I will not leave! Georgiana, you should go away at once!"

"Mrs. Annesley!" Elizabeth shouted, but the lady clenched her arm with no intention of letting her go. Georgiana was frozen, lost, and frightened.

One of the men yelled angrily. "Are you out of your mind, woman? Do you want to die?"

The second man stepped closer, looked around to see whether anybody was approaching, then took out his pistol and hit Mrs. Annesley on the side of her head so powerfully that she fell to the ground. Georgiana cried out and went to her aid while one of the men took the reins of the horses and the other two pulled Elizabeth into the carriage, which began to move only a moment before Lucky and Titan jumped on the carriage, barking wildly.

"Damn, whose are these crazy animals?" one of them cursed furiously while shouting at the coachman to whip the horses.

Elizabeth felt the small carriage enclosing her. She knew she should be frightened, but fear raised her spirits rather than paralysing her. Within a minute, she came to her senses and grew angry with anyone who was doing such harm to their family, and her mind kept asking who that might be while her attention and strength sharpened.

She was grateful that neither the dogs, nor the children, nor the servant arrived a moment earlier, or they would have been in deadly danger. But she found it ridiculous to be kidnapped in the afternoon in the middle of London!

The two horses pulled the carriage at a low speed along the narrow Hyde Park path. The intention was to exit on the main street so they could gallop freely, which would certainly happen within minutes.

Elizabeth watched the man opposite her who had hit Mrs. Annesley. She could easily remember his face any time and would make sure he was punished. Then suddenly she understood the horrible truth: they did not cover their faces because they did not plan to allow her to ever identify them. They had no intention of leaving her alive.

Her body stiffened as if trapped in a block of ice. One man attempted to cover her mouth with a cloth. A strange smell made her dizzy and burned her eyes. Through a dirty peep-hole, she noticed Peter and the dogs chasing them along the left side of the carriage.

"That bloody lad is hanging on the back. Get rid of him!" The man sitting on her left took the pistol and leant out the window to reach for Peter.

"Please, he is just a boy," Elizabeth cried, fighting with him.

He pushed her away and she fell on the floor, near the right door of the carriage.

Her body shuddered with countless chills of fear, panic, and hopelessness. She tried to kneel, and glanced outside. The sky was still beautifully coloured just as it was a few minutes before the nightmare began. Her heart nearly stopped then beat wildly, and her eyes shadowed with tears when she saw her husband running desperately along the path on the right side of the carriage.

The man on her right took out his pistol, and suddenly her own life meant nothing compared to her unbearable desperation that something might happen to him.

And there, in that tremendous, horrific moment, she realised that she had never told him she loved him! She had never told him those three words that he so wanted to hear.

Her only remaining thought was that she would gladly exchange her entire future for the chance to spend only a moment longer with him.

Then she lost consciousness as her mind was a tumult of sounds: strange noises, cries, barking, and neighing. A terrible jolt knocked her against the bench—and all was darkness and silence.

DARCY HAD SPENT THE AFTERNOON AT HOME, MEETING WITH MR. ALDRIDGE while Bingley accepted his invitation to rest in a guest room. He seemed reluctant to go to his own house—and considering his sisters' likely hostile reaction to his news, Darcy could easily sympathise.

In the afternoon, Stevens had asked his permission for the dogs to run in the park with the children and a footman, which Darcy easily approved.

As time passed, he eagerly checked his pocket watch, wondering when Elizabeth would return. When he heard the carriage in front of the house, he hurried outside and was displeased to see only the servants, who informed him that the ladies were across the street in the park.

Darcy hastily grabbed a coat and hurried to the park without even putting it on.

A sharp claw pierced his chest when he saw three men speaking with his wife. He did not need to hear the words to know that something was terribly wrong. He threw down the coat and increased his pace. He was frozen in shock when he saw from afar Mrs. Annesley thrown to the ground and Elizabeth pushed inside a carriage that started to move off. His mind ran faster than his feet, and he immediately understood that he only had a chance to stop them while the carriage was still in the park. Once it reached the main street, it would be easily lost.

Not for a moment did he consider the danger. He knew he had no time to call for help and was ready to trade his life for hers in a heartbeat.

While he gathered the last drop of his strength in his attempt to chase the carriage, he thought he spotted Elizabeth falling down inside and Peter gripping the back of the carriage. He was getting closer as the dogs barked and ran through the feet of the horses, which suddenly stopped and reared, then straightened and attempted to run to the right to escape them. Darcy threw himself ahead and grabbed the reins while the horses dragged him down, trying to get free. The carriage hit a tree, then another one, and crashed while the horses pulled free and escaped, throwing Darcy to the ground so forcefully that he remained motionless, his head aching sharply and his body refusing to obey him.

As if in a dream as he lay there, Darcy saw another carriage stop nearby. A man helped the three villains out of the damaged carriage and into a second one, which sped out of the park.

He cared little for that, though, as he tried to ignore the pain enveloping his body. His mind and his heart wailed from only one sorrow, and he called Elizabeth's name—then once again, louder. He heard nothing but Georgiana's cries, Libby's call for her brother, the servant's worried voice, and the whine of the dogs as they circled around.

And then, his blurred mind caught the sound that he had yearned and prayed for—weaker than a whisper but strong enough to allow him to breathe again.

"William, I am well..."

Darcy slowly rose from the ground, carefully seeing whether he was hurt. The servant who was with the children in the park came to help him. He was finally on his feet, looking at the carriage. It was broken but not in small pieces due to the low speed at which it had travelled.

He saw Elizabeth on the frozen ground a few steps away from him on the right side of the carriage, calling his name. He breathed in relief, and a sharp pain struck his torso. He was certainly hurt, but it mattered little. Elizabeth narrowed her eyes, as she could not see him well although he was near her then, carefully searching her face, her arms, and her legs for any injury.

"My love, how are you? Can you speak to me? Are you in pain?" He gently kissed her hands, incredulous that she seemed unharmed. Her eyes, however, were blurred and her eyelids tightened as she tentatively returned the caresses, trying to be certain he was not hurt.

"I am fine… My head hurts and my eyes are burning so… How are you, my love?" She held his hands, tried to stand, but fell against him and then forced herself to stand again. Georgiana ran to them, crying in apprehension and gratitude as she saw them both walking.

"Where is Peter?" all three of them asked together, moving to the back of the carriage where the dogs and Libby were crying steadily.

They bent down, their own pain vanishing instantly as they saw Peter's weak body among the pieces of wood and iron. The back wheel seemed to have fallen over him. They called to him, but there was no response, and they slowly removed the pieces of wreckage from him.

Only a few minutes had passed since the accident, but Stevens and four male servants from Darcy's house had already arrived in haste.

"Stevens, send for Dr. Taylor!" Darcy shouted.

"It has been done already, sir! We also sent a note to Lord Matlock," Stevens said while taking off his coat and putting it around Peter. "Sir, is the boy alive? Let me carry him inside. We brought chairs and a blanket in case any of you needed to be carried inside."

"Good thinking—make sure Mrs. Darcy and Mrs. Annesley are carried inside. Peter needs to be moved carefully. Dr. Taylor always said that more damage can happen after an accident by disturbing wounds if the patient is moved carelessly."

Darcy briefly glanced at his wife to be certain she was safe then moved around, helpless and angry, watching the boy's still body, unsure how to better attend him. Cries of despair from Janey and the grieved mother throwing herself down on her son made Darcy almost lose control. He clenched his fists and pounded them against the broken carriage.

"Stevens, give me the blanket," he demanded. "We will put Peter in it slowly and carry him gently, moving him as little as possible. Janey, please step aside—we must hurry."

"Let me do it, Darcy," Bingley said, bending to the child, and only then did Darcy notice his friend. With care, the boy was transferred to the blanket, which was lifted slowly by Bingley and Stevens.

The dogs, Janey, and Darcy—who held the maid's arm in a poor attempt at comfort—followed them. Darcy slowly regained his reason and called Hodge—who stood by, trying to help in some way as his hurt arm did not allow much exertion.

"Hodge, please remain here. I will send someone to keep you company in a minute. I need you to watch the remains of the carriage. Someone might come to fetch it, and I need to know who. I need to find those responsible—and make them pay."

In less than half an hour after the accident, everyone involved was safely inside and being cared for. Dr. Taylor arrived shortly, together with his partner, Dr. Philips. While they examined the patients, Darcy sent two male servants to search with Hodge for any indication of the carriage's owner.

A few minutes later, the Fitzwilliams came, except the colonel who was still with his regiment. They speculated about who could possibly have done such a horrible thing, impressed and astonished by Mrs. Annesley's loyalty to Elizabeth and by young Peter's extraordinary sacrifice on behalf of his mistress.

Dr. Taylor returned with a full report and his dark countenance spoke clearly of his concern.

"Peter is badly injured, but thank God, he is alive. His left leg is wounded, and I believe his ribs were harmed. I cannot be certain as he is barely conscious, and I am not sure of how much pain he feels when I touch him. Also, he has deep bruises all over his body. His right shoulder was dislocated. He apparently held tightly to the carriage."

"Oh, dear Lord," cried Lady Matlock.

"That is the least concern, your ladyship. Dr. Philips helped me put his shoulder back in place. From that, he will surely heal. I have treated many such situations on the battlefield but never on such a young boy. Quite astonishing. He is now kept in tight bandages as he must not move at all. We will give him herbs to strengthen him and to diminish his pain."

"What else can we do?" Darcy asked, pale and unable to control his growing anger.

"Dr. Philips and I will take turns in the house, day and night. There is nothing more you can do—only pray. His mother is with him now. He must be watched continuously."

"Of course..." Darcy said, pacing the room. "He will have the same care as anyone in the family. Is Mrs. Annesley recovering?"

"She is. She has a very bad bruise, and I expect her temple and eye will turn black, but she will be fine soon enough"

"She was so anxious to be reunited with her daughter... Thank God she is well."

"I also examined Mrs. Darcy. She was only slightly harmed when the carriage crashed. Her headache and dizziness as well as her blurred sight are due to the opium-infused cloth they used to try to subdue her. She must rest a few days. She needs silence, darkness, and sleep—and quite a lot of my herbal tea. Molly is taking care of her now."

"To subdue her? How can that be?" Lady Matlock cried as Darcy's pacing increased.

"Aunt, it is quite clear," Darcy said harshly, gulping a full glass of brandy. "Someone hired three men to kidnap Elizabeth, and Mrs. Annesley and Peter almost died trying to save her! Who did it and why? Only the Devil knows! But I shall find out very soon—and not even the Devil will save them from my punishment!"

"Darcy!" cried both ladies, trembling in astonishment at such language.

"Don't you even attempt to censure me! If you disapprove my coarse words, you had better leave! My mind is set. As soon as I am certain beyond a doubt who is responsible for this, I shall pay to have them killed! And even that will not be enough if Peter dies!"

"Darcy, let us calm ourselves, son," said Lord Matlock while the viscount and Bingley looked at each other, bewildered and helpless.

"Mr. Darcy, before anything else, I insist on examining you too—immediately."

"I am perfectly fine, Dr. Taylor. Take care of those who need help. Do not waste your time on me. I must go. I have to talk to someone who might know—"

"I did not miss that frown of pain when you moved, sir. I insist on your letting me see how badly you are injured. That way, you will know for certain what you can or cannot do."

Darcy continued to object until all his relatives insisted with such determination that he acquiesced only to put an end to the argument. They moved to the library, and Dr. Taylor's examination was brief. Some of Darcy's ribs were affected—not broken but badly bruised, the doctor presumed.

"Sir, you should lie still in bed. You need rest to heal, you must avoid any exertion, and—"

"Dr. Taylor, I shall do what you advise, but do not ask me to lie still while I can stand. Do not ask me to rest as long as my family is in danger!"

"But sir… I am sorry you are so unreasonable. You have fifty people who could take care of this," the doctor said then he gave up, impressed by Darcy's troubled countenance. "Be it as you will, but you must wear a very tight bandage around yourself to protect your chest from any dangerous movement. And you need to drink some herbal tea and—"

"Very well." Darcy hastily interrupted the doctor, ringing for Stevens. "Doctor, tell my man what you need and put any bandages you want around me and be done with it. Then please see to Elizabeth, Peter, and Mrs. Annesley. Let us both do our duties."

His words sounded harsh even to himself, but Darcy could not control his anger. He knew he should be grateful for the doctor's care, but he had no strength for politeness.

Darcy returned to his relatives in less than fifteen minutes although he felt he had wasted hours. The bindings limited his movements, but he felt better as the pain diminished. He quickly told his worried relatives that he was fine and put an end to any further inquiries.

Georgiana entered, holding Libby's hand tightly, both still pale and wearing the traces of fear. She was embraced by her aunt and cousin. Libby hid behind Georgiana at the sight of so many new people—but she never let go of her hand.

"Mrs. Thomason fetched Sarah to take care of little Cathy, but Libby preferred to stay with me," Georgiana whispered. "Mrs. Annesley sleeps and Elizabeth too… and Peter… I do not know what to do. How are you, Brother?"

"I am fine, dearest. Do not worry about me."

His uncle shook his head. "We tried to force him to rest and let others do what is needed. He is not well at all."

"Rest?" Darcy burst out furiously. "Uncle, do you hear yourself? My wife was viciously attacked in the middle of the day a few steps from our home, and I was not even there to protect her! I was occupied with business, and I let an elder lady and a child of nine fight for my wife's life, risking their own! And those responsible for this are still free out there! And you want me to rest? Can you not see that everything happened today because of me? Nobody would have had anything against Elizabeth had she not been married to me! And you say I should rest?"

"Darcy, I did not mean to upset you. I am only worried for you, and you cannot make me feel bad for that. Your anger with me does not help much."

"Brother, please," Georgians said, gently holding his arm. "Would you not go upstairs and stay with Elizabeth a little? I am sure she would welcome your company."

"And what should I tell her? I have promised her so many times that I will protect her, and I failed horribly. She is better resting. You should go to her if you want. Tell her I shall solve this situation."

"Brother…"

Darcy had already shifted his attention from Georgiana, pacing the room as he spoke. "It must be someone with means and connections. Surely, it was planned a few days ago. We saw a carriage lingering near the house for the last two nights, but I did nothing—fool that I was. And a second carriage collected the three men after the first one crashed. I wonder if they planned to demand a reward for Elizabeth."

"That must very likely have been the reason," the earl answered.

"I do not think so," Georgiana intervened. "Elizabeth tried to speak to them, and she promised you would pay them double the sum if they would just leave us alone. They said they had already been paid to take her somewhere and could not make such a decision."

"Could Annabelle Stafford be behind this?" Lady Matlock inquired with obvious restraint.

"I thought of her at first, or James might have something to do with it. I thought of Wickham too, but that idiot does not have enough money to plan something like this. It could be anyone, and I do not want to decide on a culprit before I have proof. But once I am sure…"

"Yes, it could be anyone," the earl said. "And I am afraid you are right: the cause must be related to you. Elizabeth was only a means to force your hand in some way."

"Let us waste no more time with talk. Bingley, take Stevens and hire some men—at least twenty. Send them to every place where such people might gather. Any piece of information will be rewarded. I will wait for Robert and… No, I had better come with you. I cannot sit and wait. I wonder whether anyone showed any interest in the broken carriage. I shall ask Elizabeth whether she heard any name—anything that might help us find them."

Darcy's agitation increased as well as the tension within the room. All of them shared his concern and feeling of helplessness.

"I saw the carriages too—both of them," Georgiana whispered, burdened by guilt, while Lady Matlock attempted to comfort her. "And the three men, but I did not notice anything special, and I heard no names. I cannot help much… I am very sorry."

"I heard the names." Libby stepped forward, and all eyes turned to her. "When they got out of the carriage, I heard them. One was Pierce, one was Wayland, and one was Baines. The man from the second carriage called them—very angry with them."

"Libby, are you sure? Absolutely sure? Think hard—you cannot lie or jest about this!" Darcy said, severe and incredulous.

"I do not lie," Libby answered tearfully.

"She is only trying to help you!" Georgiana intervened. "I am sure she is right."

Darcy apologised to the frightened girl and gently embraced her.

"I believe you. You said Pierce, Wayland and Baines? Thank you, my dear."

He called for Stevens and asked for his coat and a carriage. He had a clue, and he could do something to put an end to the feeling of being a useless disappointment to his family.

Darcy almost collided with Colonel Fitzwilliam, who entered hastily and discomposed, still in his uniform. The colonel greeted everyone, and little Libby stared at him, her eyes widened as she held Georgiana's hand tightly.

The colonel embraced Georgiana, relieved to see her unharmed, and he was briefly informed of the latest news regarding the others' state of health and also their speculations.

"Robert, I have no time to lose. Bingley and I were about to hire some men and send them to every corner of London. I want to know the identity of the three men, and I want to know who was in the second carriage. And once I find out—I want them all dead."

Darcy's sharp voice and his threatening words made the ladies gasp and the gentlemen gape in disbelief. The colonel stepped forward.

"Darcy, let us be calm. You seem quite unwell yourself. You will only slow things down and might cause other problems if you go by yourself. Besides, you are known, and you will be easily recognised by precisely those people you are looking for. We must take another approach. Ladies, please excuse us. We have some business to settle."

The ladies left the room without delay, but Libby broke loose from Georgiana's hand and approached Darcy.

"Master, I…" The men, however, stepped into a corner to continue the discussion. Georgiana took the girl's hand decidedly.

"Come, dearest, let us go with the other ladies."

Once the men were alone, the colonel took the lead again. "Stevens will fetch

Mr. Adam Bourne. He is our man for this job. He is even acquainted with Sir John Blades, the Sheriff of London. We will tell him what we need and will provide the money to accomplish it. I expect to have news within hours, especially since you have some names."

That was done, and as soon as Stevens left, Darcy began to count the minutes to his return. Then he suddenly turned to his friend.

"Bingley, you should go speak to the Gardiners in Cheapside. It would be terrible if they learnt this from someone else. Tell them everything is fine now, and kindly ask them not to come here tonight. Elizabeth must rest, but we will happily welcome them tomorrow."

The second task was accomplished easily, and Darcy and his male relatives moved to the library. The others chose to let him release his turmoil by pacing until Stevens returned with Mr. Bourne. Information was exchanged, two bags of money were handed to him and specific requirements made, then Mr. Bourne left in the same haste as he arrived.

The third task was complete, and again Darcy had little to do but wait.

The announcement of Mr. James Darcy calling startled Darcy, and he struggled to keep calm as his cousin entered in obvious distress.

"I just heard what happened—this is terrible! Thank God nobody was badly hurt."

"Peter was hurt in the worst way. We fear for his life," Darcy replied coldly.

"Yes, yes—but I mean someone from the family. I am so relieved that everybody is fine."

"One can hardly be closer to the family than a boy younger than ten who risked his own life to save Elizabeth's."

"Well, yes, you are right, of course… I just wanted to—"

"James, did you have anything to do with this? Do not answer in a hurry, but think seriously and tell me the truth. Once you lie to me, you shall not be allowed to remedy it. Did you have any involvement in this?"

"No, of course not! You cannot imagine that I would do anything to harm Mrs. Darcy!"

"You may well have! It would be to your advantage if my marriage were broken. It would be to your convenience if I had no heir. You might want my wife to disappear—and perhaps me too. Then the entire fortune would be yours, and you would be free to waste it any way you please."

"Darcy, you forget yourself," the colonel intervened. "Let us speak calmly."

"Cousin, you cannot seriously believe that I planned to harm your wife—or you! This is madness. I do not want you to disappear—and I do not want your fortune! Hell—I do not even want mine! I want you to take care of all the properties and only give me the bloody thousand when I need it!"

Both Darcys glared at each other, their faces red and ominous. After long moments of burgeoning silence, the elder took a step back.

"But do you know anything of this? Do you suspect any of your friends are involved—Annabelle Stafford, Wickham, those to whom you owe money?"

"I know nothing. My debtors could have attempted this, but I doubt it. From Wickham I have no news since he returned to Hertfordshire, and Annabelle—I last saw her when she left the ball last night."

"I hope you are not deceiving me, James. I would never forgive you if you did. And I hope you are not involved in any way, as I shall have no mercy for those responsible."

"I am not, but I will ask around and let you know if I have any news."

"James, do not do anything stupid," Darcy said, but his younger cousin had already left.

No news arrived for the next two hours. The Fitzwilliams made their farewells, asking to be fetched if they were needed. Bingley finally determined to stop by his house and talk to his sisters while the colonel returned to his regiment, both planning to return and spend the night at the Darcys' in case their urgent help might be needed.

When he was finally alone, Darcy's restlessness and torment again increased. He also became aware of the pain he chose to neglect before, so he decided to rest a little.

He moved to his apartment, changed his clothes with Stevens' help, then entered Elizabeth's room silently. To his surprise, she was sitting in the middle of the bed, her back supported by pillows, watched by Molly and Lucky, the latter on the carpet.

Darcy petted the worried animal that had spent the last hours moving between Elizabeth and Peter. Elizabeth gazed at the fire, still and silent, her expression deeply distressed and her hands clasped to stop their trembling. Darcy sat by her and took her hands in his while he dismissed Molly with a sign. He gently caressed Elizabeth's face and kissed her eyes.

"What is it, my love? Are you in pain? Should I call Dr. Taylor?"

"Oh no… Do not call him… I am not in pain. I am just…"

"I know you are troubled and sad, but you are safe now. Nobody will harm you."

"Please do not worry. I am fine. Georgiana is resting with Libby and Cathy. She has such a sweet, generous heart and is such a comfort to the children! I should not lie here from mere dizziness and be so useless to everyone around me. I know you were hurt much worse, and you have not rested a single moment today," she whispered, stroking his pale face. He kissed her hands several times.

"I do not need rest, but I would be happy to stay with you a few minutes. I still have some urgent business to finish, but there is nothing better than your warm presence, my love."

He brushed his lips over her eyelids and felt the salty tears. She noticed his worry.

"I am troubled because I saw Peter. I stood beside him a few minutes. He seems so small, so pale… I would give anything to see him recovered. What a boy he is, William! And what a woman Janey is to have raised such a boy!"

"I would do anything to see him recovered too. That boy fought for you with a courage that few men possess. And I am angry that I cannot help him now. Dr. Taylor will take care of him day and night. We must pray that the Lord will allow him to receive our gratitude for many, many years. I cannot imagine what Janey feels now, and I cannot help her, either."

"William, she kept thanking us for the care we showed to her son! Can you imagine that? I shall never forgive myself for my thoughtless disobedience and stupid stubbornness. I almost killed Peter, and you, and Mrs. Annesley, and poor Georgiana… Things could have been much worse, horribly worse. I am so sorry, my love, so very sorry…"

"Elizabeth, what are you saying?" Darcy kissed her hands repeatedly and then her forehead, then he gently caressed her face, almost afraid to touch her. "What are you speaking of, my dearest? Surely you cannot blame yourself for what happened?"

"How could I not? It is entirely my fault! You told me so many times not to go out alone, and when I listened to your advice, everything was fine! We went to Cheapside and back twice, and nobody bothered us. And then I foolishly decided to disobey you and take a walk! Can anybody be more stupid than I am? How could a responsible woman behave in such a way?" She cried erratically, and Darcy fought his emotions while attempting to calm her.

"And Mrs. Annesley stood by me so bravely! She has only known me for two weeks, and she jeopardised her life for me. And poor Peter—when I saw him running for the carriage, I wanted to shout at him to go away, but I could not. My mouth was covered, and I tried to fight with the man who wanted to shoot Peter—a boy of nine, and he wanted to shoot him. And then I saw you, and I was so frightened for you! Oh, William, I would have readily given my life to save yours… I prayed to God to allow me one more moment with you…"

"My love…" he whispered, kissing her hands again. "You should never think of this. Giving your life for me would do no good as my own life would mean nothing without you. And how can you blame yourself? If anyone is to be blamed it is me. It was my duty to protect you, and I failed…"

"William, no…"

"Yes! It is true that I gave orders for you to always have protection, but this was beyond imagining from the beginning—to not be safe to go wherever you want, whenever you want because of some of my relatives or acquaintances. Everything happened because of me. Your life has been so deeply disturbed since you married me. You have given me happiness, and I have given you distress and torment, and you almost lost your life…" He could hardly speak from distress—words were difficult because of the lump in his throat—and even harder to understand.

"No, please do not say that, please…"

They struggled to comfort each other: hands were caressed and kissed, loving gazes shared, and eyes moistened with tears of guilt, relief, and fear for what might have been.

She cupped his face with trembling hands, smiling through her tears.

"When I saw you running towards the carriage, when I realised that I might never see you again, that we might lose each other… I remembered that I never told you I love you!"

He looked at her, holding his breath. Her smile turned even warmer and—to his utter shock—she kissed his hand, just as he had done with her so many times.

"I love you, my husband! I love you so much that my heart ached and yearned for you! I love you so much that I prayed the Lord should take my future if He wished for just one more moment with you."

He stared at her, on the edge of tears and overwhelmed by the power of the words he hoped to hear. He had started to feel them—the expression in her eyes spoke more than the words themselves—but still longed to hear them. Her smile widened through her tears.

"I know you believe I might say it because of the accident, but I do not. I know now that what I felt for you in the last two weeks was love—slowly building in my heart. When you were away, I missed your presence, your smiles, and your warmth. The gratitude and admiration I felt for you, the fears and longing, the tenderness, the passion, the joy—everything means love! I love you, my beloved husband, with all my mind, my body, and my heart—with all my being. I love you, I love you." She continued to repeat the words as if they had waited for so long to be said that she could hold them back no longer.

Darcy finally found the strength to speak, stroking her face. "A week ago, I told you that you taught me the meaning of happiness, but you also taught me the meaning of love! I thought I was in love with you when we were in Hertfordshire, but what I felt then pales next to what I feel now. My soul is so full of you, Elizabeth…"

"We learnt the meaning of happiness together—as well as the meaning of love, my husband. I love you," she said then laughed tearfully at her childish desire to repeat the words. He laughed too, covering her face with countless kisses, and she did not know whether she should laugh or cry.

They spoke and shared worries, hopes, and caresses with tenderness and pure joy. No other gesture was needed to settle what they now both knew: that there was no longer her and him, only them together with no one and nothing able to break their tight bond.

They were tired, pained, dizzy, and exhausted—and there was still much to clarify, discover, and settle from that day's terrible experience—but neither wished to allow ugliness to shadow their moment or to have that moment end.

A soft knock was enough for Darcy to hasten out of bed in such a hurry that the pain cut his chest. He opened the door slowly and saw Stevens waiting in the hall.

"Sir, forgive me for disturbing you. Mr. Adam Bourne is waiting downstairs."

Chapter 30

"Forgive my intrusion, but you asked me to deliver news as soon as I had any," Mr. Bourne said.

"Thank you, please come with me." Darcy invited the gentleman into the privacy of the library and nodded to Stevens to join them.

"Mr. Darcy, the three men have been discovered. The names were correct: Wayland was a second lieutenant in the army until three years ago, Pierce was a private soldier, and Baines is nothing but a thief, well known for scandals and illicit activity."

"Where are they now? I want to speak to them."

"My men hold them captive in a tavern on Aldersgate Street. We shall put them in gaol tomorrow morning if there is evidence against them."

"Of course, there is. Three ladies can identify them, and most likely my dogs could too if I put them together in a locked room," Darcy said sharply. "I want to talk to them now."

"Sir, should I fetch Colonel Fitzwilliam and Mr. Bingley?" asked Stevens.

"What on earth for? I shall go with Mr. Bourne. Please get my coat."

"But, sir..."

"Stevens, my coat! And please inform Mrs. Darcy that I will be late and I insist that the ladies have dinner without me.

Within minutes, he left the house with Mr. Bourne, followed by the worried gaze of Stevens.

Darcy returned around ten o'clock and was not surprised to find his cousin Robert and Bingley waiting. They scolded him severely for leaving without them, and he responded with only a dismissive gesture of his hand.

"It was not worth bothering you. Those three were already captured—Mr. Bourne is truly efficient. They pretended they had been hired yesterday morning by a man whom they did not know to take Elizabeth to the Bull and Mouth Inn, leave the carriage there, and leave. They received three hundred pounds for that. They were given a carriage and asked to follow another one. They said they had been shown Elizabeth when she left the house earlier today. They pretended they did not know her or me before and had no personal involvement in this! Can you believe it? They hit Mrs. Annesley, they were about to shoot Peter, and almost took Elizabeth's life, but they continued to say nothing against anyone personally. I was so tempted to strike the shameless smirks from their faces! But they seem not to know more, and believe me, I tried to convince them in every possible way."

"I would imagine as much. Will Bourne continue searching?"

"Of course. The men we hired will continue to search for any indication of the one responsible for planning all this. Those three will go before the magistrate this morning. It seems they have committed many other crimes."

"Will you have them killed? If you wish it, this would be a good time before they are actually tried," the colonel inquired coolly with perfect detachment.

"What nonsense is this?" Darcy replied, meeting the colonel's challenging look. "Yes, I know I said that, and I would have strangled them with my bare hands if I had caught them when they kidnapped Elizabeth. But I cannot just pay someone to murder them in cold blood. And if their crimes are as Mr. Bourne says, I doubt their punishment will be any different."

"So what should we do now?" asked Bingley.

"I will check on Peter and then speak to Elizabeth. Have you dined? We can only wait for news. Or you could return home, and I can send for you if needed."

"I would rather stay...in case you need me," Bingley answered, and Darcy laughed bitterly.

"How was it with your sisters? Wait, best not to tell me—your expression is more than eloquent. I say, man, you must do something with them, especially if you intend to marry. You cannot allow your sisters to be so disrespectful to you and your future wife."

"I know. They are unreasonably angry with the Bennets. They seemed very close friends with Jane and now are completely opposed to her."

"Come now, even you must have observed that they were never truly friends with Jane."

"Of course they are angry since they hoped you would marry Georgiana and your sister would marry Darcy," said the colonel laughingly, and Bingley turned white then red.

"Your sister Caroline would be a good catch. She is a handsome woman and has a nice dowry. But her bitterness and her tendency to criticise everybody is very unbecoming and would easily end any man's temptation to court her," the colonel continued.

"Yes, well... May I have a brandy?" Bingley could barely hide his embarrassment.

"Please suit yourself. I shall see you again shortly," Darcy said.

He walked to the door, still heavyhearted. He could not evade the feeling that he was failing Elizabeth's trust. Every movement gave him pain, but his distress was even more agonising.

He entered Peter's room. Janey was sleeping in a chair, her head lying on the bed. In the armchair, Dr. Philips watched them. Darcy gently touched the boy's forehead. He looked pale and thin, breathing regularly, his small body covered in bandages, and Darcy thought that perhaps the idea of murdering those poor excuses for men was not such a bad one.

Eventually, Darcy returned to Elizabeth's apartment, closing the door with infinite care to not disturb her. With no little surprise, he found her by the window, pacing nervously.

"Thank God!" She ran to him, embracing him tightly, and he moaned from the sharp pain that struck his chest. "I was so worried! What happened?"

He tenderly kissed her face, attempting to calm her.

"You are frozen. Let us go to bed. I would carry you, but I am afraid I cannot do so at the moment," he teased, kissing her hair and her hands. They lay on the bed, and Darcy told her everything that occurred, struggling to conceal his concern and frustration.

"I was tempted to conduct the search myself, but Mr. Bourne and Robert said I would do more harm than good as I would be easily recognised by precisely the men I sought."

"I agree—besides, you are not well, my love."

A shy knock on the door broke the silence, and Georgiana stepped in, her hand held tight by Libby. "Forgive me for disturbing you. I just want to ask William if he has news."

"Please take a seat, dearest. Yes, I do have news, unfortunately very little." Darcy offered her the same information he gave to Elizabeth.

"So we will continue the quest, but do not worry. I shall discover the man in the second carriage. Then we will find out who is behind this scheme."

"I am so sorry I did not pay more attention," Georgiana said. "I only saw a silhouette, but I was so preoccupied with Mrs. Annesley, and I just could not think… Silly me, I am useless."

"Please do not say that," Elizabeth intervened. "We were all shocked and frightened, and none of us remembered much. You cannot blame yourself."

"Master, I saw the man in the second carriage," Libby said. Three pairs of eyes stared at her.

"You did? Why did you not tell me sooner? Did you hear his name? What did you see?" Darcy's questions were overwhelming, and the girl took a step back.

"Because you did not ask me," she whispered. "And I tried to say, but Miss Georgiana said I should go with the ladies."

Again, their amazement was beyond expression. "So I did," Georgiana admitted.

"Dear girl, please forgive us. Adults are so silly sometimes! Can you please tell us what you saw?" The girl nodded and again took hold of Georgiana's hand.

"I did not hear his name. He kept a cloth over his mouth, and I only saw his eyes, and he had a golden watch in his pocket and a golden ring on his pinkie."

"A ring? Do you remember the colour?"

"Only gold. And his coat opened a little, and I saw that he looked just like the colonel."

"Like the colonel? You mean he was as tall as the colonel? Did he have brown eyes too?"

The girl shook her head. "Yes, he had brown eyes and hair and he was not as tall as the colonel. But he looked just like the colonel looked today."

"Libby, what do you mean 'like the colonel today'? Did the colonel not look the same yesterday?"

"No—he wore special clothes today, and the man was the same. Only the trousers were different. He had some dark ones and the colonel had white."

"You mean he was an officer? And he wore a golden watch and a gold ring?"

"Yes, master."

"Thank you, my dear!" Darcy caressed the girl's hair and hurried to the door.

Libby took hold of his coat. "Master, do you want me to tell you about the lady too?"

He turned in disbelief, all the blood draining from his face.

"There was a woman in the carriage? Can you describe her?"

"I can, but you know her too. She was here a few days ago, and she hurt Hodge."

Elizabeth and Georgiana gasped in surprise. Darcy sat on the bed as his knees weakened.

"Libby, are you certain? Is it not possible that you confused her with someone else? I would have recognised my aunt's carriage. I know you dislike her. She behaved very badly, so—"

"No, master. The carriage was different from the one she came in last time. She sat back in a corner, but I saw her. She had a brown coat and a brown bonnet with many folds, and I think she had a dark green scarf around her neck, but I am not quite sure of this. And she had evil eyes."

Darcy looked at the girl a long moment. His wife and sister were equally pale. His head was spinning and his thoughts chaotic. He supported his head with trembling hands to gather himself then turned to his sister.

"Georgiana, was Wickham wearing a golden ring when you last saw him?"

"Oh, William, I do not think that… He could not…"

"Georgiana!"

"Yes, he was, but most of the officers do. That cannot mean…"

"Thank you, Libby," Darcy said. With a last glance, he met Elizabeth's troubled eyes, but he hurried from the room before she had time to say a word. In the dining room, Bingley and the colonel were eating, but Darcy's expression made them stop and rise immediately.

"We are a bunch of idiots saved by a girl of eight," Darcy shouted. "It was Lady Catherine and Wickham. She must have planned everything and he executed the plan. Let us go now!"

"But Darcy…" the colonel mumbled in complete shock.

"Robert, send Stevens to fetch your father. He should be there when I find his sister. And your offer to kill Wickham is most welcome. I should have taken your advice years ago."

"But where are you heading?"

"To Mrs. Younge's house—how stupid I have been not to think of this before!"

It was midnight when Darcy, his cousin, and his friend arrived at the house kept by Mrs. Younge. They had first gone to Lady Catherine's house but—as expected—with no success.

Mrs. Younge appeared frightened the moment she laid eyes on them. The conversation was harsh and lasted longer than Darcy would have wished before the lure of a hundred pounds induced her to confess.

She declared that Wickham had stayed at her house several times in the last month, but she had only seen him briefly in the last days. She admitted that she had loaned him a carriage, for which she had been paid entirely, and she did not expect to retrieve it. She insisted she knew nothing more except that he had left earlier that day after generously paying all his expenses. And yes, she confirmed he was dressed in his uniform. After more coercion, threats—and another fifty pounds—Mrs. Younge remembered she heard Wickham say something about the Bull and Mouth Inn, and Darcy recollected that the three thieves mentioned it as the place where they were supposed to take Elizabeth.

Darcy's carriage arrived at the new destination rather quickly, and just as they were about to enter, a man approach them and declared he and two others were hired by Mr. Bourne to watch the inn but had found nothing suspicious so far.

A short conversation with the owner was enough for Darcy, and a few minutes later, he entered the room where Wickham was enjoying the favours of a young girl. At their entrance, he cursed and the girl cried and left the room in a great hurry while Wickham tried to put his clothes on. His uniform lay on the floor in a corner of the room.

"I have long wondered how stupid you can be, Wickham, but today I have the answer."

Darcy sat in a chair, struggling against his anger and the pain along his ribs. The colonel and Bingley remained at the door.

"Look, Darcy, I know you are angry, but I did nothing wrong. Surely, you know that your aunt asked me to bring Miss Bennet—I mean Mrs. Darcy—to speak to her. You cannot hold me culpable for that."

Darcy moved forward, his jaw clenched in anger. "You planned to kidnap my wife! You put her life in danger, as well as the lives of other innocent people! I warned you to stay away from my family, and you planned to kidnap my wife! I should kill you right now!"

Wickham stepped back. "Let us talk calmly. As I said, your aunt asked me to bring Mrs. Darcy to her. Nobody would consider that a crime. It was only an unfortunate accident that the carriage crashed—and honestly, it was mostly your fault. Come now—I am certain you would not want to cause a scandal. Just imagine what people would say if they knew your aunt found such a questionable way to talk to your wife. Not to mention my close connection to your family—"

"Wickham, your stupidity amazes me. Surely, you cannot think to force my hand by threatening scandal!"

Darcy yelled, red-faced, moving closer to Wickham, who stepped back until he reached the wall. "I would exchange your life and my aunt's life in a heartbeat for a single bruise on my wife! You try to threaten me? You think I care about scandal? I will strangle you with my bare hands! You deserve to die like the rat you are!"

Darcy was so close that his body almost touched Wickham's, and he clenched his fists to control his fury as he continued to shout.

"You almost murdered a child of nine who is ten times better than you! If I do not kill you this moment, I will surely do so if Peter does not recover! You may take that as a promise!"

"Surely, you cannot hold me responsible," Wickham said impertinently. "He should have stayed away. Who asked him to run after the carriage like a fool?"

"Wickham—shut your mouth! Shut—your—mouth!" Darcy shouted again. "Stupid idiot!" Darcy breathed deeply and withdrew a few steps.

The colonel left and returned a minute later with the two men hired to watch the inn and also Mr. Bourne himself, whose unexpected appearance did not surprise Darcy.

"Sir, we will guard Mr. Wickham and lock him in gaol for now. He will have the chance to defend himself later. Come," Mr. Bourne said, his men holding Wickham's arms.

"What should I do to him? He is either a complete fool or the most shameless of men. He deserves to rot in a prison hulk and even worse! How did he fall so low? He is my father's godson! What is to be done with him? And Lady Catherine—I must find her at once!"

He descended the stairs of the inn, drawing the attention of a number of curious people. He entered the carriage, followed by the colonel and Bingley.

"So, Cousin, what do you plan to do now? And what if you find Lady Catherine? What will you do? Surely, you will not have her held for trial—"

"Why does she deserve less? She is responsible for all that happened!"

"Come, Darcy, let us speak calmly…"

"Robert, don't you dare repeat Wickham's words!" Darcy's anger turned on his cousin.

"I will not, but this needs to be discussed calmly. And, surely, you do not intend to go after Lady Catherine now! You should let Bourne's men discover her whereabouts first."

"She is likely on her way back to Rosings. It is to her advantage to be found at home in case anyone questions her. Let us fetch the earl if you want, but I am going tonight. I want to be done with this. I want to return home to my wife and tell her she is safe."

"You should go home, rest, and speak to your wife then decide tomorrow."

"I am going to Kent," Darcy concluded. "Bingley, please remain at my house and tell Elizabeth what happened. Tell her not to worry. We will settle this entire situation tonight. There is no need for you to waste time with us on the road. We three are enough."

"Admit that you do not want to enter your house because you do not want to see Elizabeth. You are afraid she will make you see reason and stay home," the colonel insisted.

"Of course, I admit that. Once I see Elizabeth, I will not want to leave her."

It was past midnight when the carriage stopped at Darcy House to drop off Bingley then moved on in haste. At the Matlocks', however, they had to wait half an hour, increasing Darcy's agitation. Lord Matlock was deeply disturbed by the latest news, demanding to be informed how they could suspect his sister of such an outrageous plan.

"I am afraid you are making a big mistake, and I cannot allow you to accuse my sister out of hand. How can you even consider believing a child of eight without further proof?"

"Uncle, we are leaving in a few minutes. Please decide whether you will come with us or not. It is not just that Libby was correct so far—and I have every reason to trust her—but Wickham confirmed it."

"Wickham—bloody scoundrel!"

The earl's opposition diminished as Darcy's impatience increased. The colonel—more clear-headed—brought along drinks and food as it was expected they would travel the entire night. When they were about to leave, they were surprised by Mr. Bourne's arrival.

"I searched for you at home, and Mr. Bingley informed me I might find you here. We continued our search based on what Wickham told us. My men discovered that Lady Catherine de Bourgh—or a lady of her description—was seen exiting London in the direction of Kent four hours ago. Should we follow her? I may go in person."

"We already suspected that—in fact, we are ready to travel to Kent as we speak. You may join us. Your presence might be needed."

Two carriages moved at a quick pace along the frozen city streets and beyond. They stopped at each tavern and inn along their route, inquiring for more information. Darcy grew increasingly anxious. He never pondered what he would do once he met his aunt. He only wished to be done with it.

"I believe Lady Catherine should be kept under continuous care. We can all see that she is not well," Darcy heard himself saying.

"What do you mean 'continuous care'?" The earl's expression was incredulous.

"She must not be allowed to live where she wants! She is out of her mind and dangerous! I have heard that Bedlam is rebuilding at St. George's Fields in Southwark. It should be ready in a couple of years. We should make a donation and assure her a comfortable residence. Until then, we will hire additional servants to keep her supervised."

"Darcy, have you lost your mind too? You cannot be serious. This is outrageous!" The earl paled in distress, but Darcy—cold and calm—continued.

"Either that or I shall ask Mr. Bourne to confine her and put her before a judge. I will leave the decision to you, Uncle, once we find her. But those are your only choices."

Lord Matlock continued to provide Darcy with reasons against his intentions, but all met little success as Darcy's gaze was fixed outside, counting the horses' steps.

They stopped at another inn to change horses, and again, Mr. Bourne gathered information. He confirmed that Lady Catherine had left her own carriage at the inn several days ago and purchased a simpler one that she had taken and returned a few hours earlier.

"This is really a plan born of madness!" said the colonel. "Can you imagine how much she plotted? Father, I believe Darcy's suggestion of Bedlam is the only acceptable one.

"But…is it certain beyond a doubt that it was Lady Catherine de Bourgh?" the earl asked.

"Her identity is certain, milord: first, because of the carriage and, second, because she entered into a very unpleasant argument with some drunk men who were singing loudly. Lady Catherine—I was told—expressed her disapproval in a very harsh manner and demanded silence. She even attempted to pay them to 'not hear or see their faces for as long as she was in the inn.' At the men's vulgar response, she disclosed her identity and threatened that they would be properly punished."

Lord Matlock arranged his gloves nervously. All his attempts to disbelieve her culpability proved to be misplaced.

They resumed the journey at a slow pace due to the bad weather, and an hour and a half later, they reached another inn—just as they entered Kent. There, however, nobody had seen anyone remotely resembling Lady Catherine de Bourgh, who—the owner declared—he knew quite well.

Mr. Bourne proposed they rest while he sent his three men and two other servants from the inn to inquire about the houses and taverns in the area. Inside, they ordered food and drinks, waiting impatiently.

"Mr. Darcy, forgive my impropriety, but may ask how you discovered the identity of the persons behind this situation? I mean Wickham and Lady Catherine de Bourgh. When we first spoke, you had no clues about who it was, and you did not even mention the presence of a lady. I am just curious. I want to know why my efficiency was not at its best this time."

"Do not worry, your efficiency was impressive, and you will be paid the entire sum for all the men involved in the search. How did we discover their identity? With the help of an eight-year-old girl. Is that not strange? The children of a servant, whom we brought into the house to offer them shelter, helped us discover the vicious plan against my family—made by someone from inside my family."

"Darcy..." The earl attempted to censure his words.

"It is the simple truth, Uncle. Let us not discuss it further as I am already very angry."

One by one, the men sent in quest returned without any news. The last one, however, entered impatiently, clearly distressed.

"Sir, I— You had better come with me this moment. Take your carriage and follow me."

A quarter of an hour later on the road back towards London on a hidden path, split from the main road and covered by the night and a small hill with trees full of snow, they found a broken carriage that none of them failed to recognise.

They hurried to it. A little further away was the coachman, shot dead.

On the ground near the carriage was Lady Catherine de Bourgh—lifeless, silenced in stillness, her face and body in great disorder, revealing signs of violent abuse.

She wore a brown coat, a brown bonnet with many folds, and a dark green scarf around her neck. Just as Libby had said.

The shock stunned them. Lord Matlock knelt by his sister and gently arranged her clothes. The colonel helped his father put the body in their carriage. Darcy stood back, watching.

Mr. Bourne searched the ground carefully, declaring there were footsteps from at least four men. He asked the Earl whether he had found Lady Catherine's reticule or any other bag, but he received no answer.

"Mr. Darcy, we will continue our quest. I trust we will shortly find who has done this. It appears to be a robbery. I wonder how it was possible that her ladyship travelled in the middle of the night with only the coachman as chaperone—even more so that she supposedly carried a large sum of money."

"Yes...yes...you do that, Mr. Bourne," Darcy said absentmindedly.

Lord Matlock and the colonel laid Lady Catherine on the bench. The earl turned to Darcy. "All has ended now. We must take her home to Rosings, Nephew. There is nothing more you can do. We must take care of her funeral—and of her name. We cannot allow any details to slip out to the world. She was your mother's sister. She is your family."

Darcy was frozen in a silence he could not overcome. He stared at his uncle—whom he heard but barely understood—at his cousin, at the men searching the ground outside, then glanced back at his late aunt, transfigured by death, lying only a few inches away.

"Do what is needed, Uncle. This is truly the end. But I will go home to my wife this very moment. She is my closest family now. She is my life now, and she was almost taken from me. I am going back to her, and I will try to put everything else aside. But I cannot forget nor forgive, at least not for now... Maybe in time... God help us all... I am going home."

"But Darcy, how? We need your carriage to go to Rosings..."

"Of course you do—use my carriage. Mr. Bourne, can you take me back to the inn? I shall find a means of transportation to London."

Chapter 31

London, 14 January

Elizabeth's heart was in a storm of feelings that brought her to the edge of tears. Her husband had left in the middle of the night. Now it was full daylight, and still he had not returned. Travelling from London to Kent and back was a long journey even in the middle of the summer—even worse in bad winter weather. Her tormented mind measured and counted each minute, and the turmoil of waiting was hard to bear.

She struggled to keep her temper and show confidence to all the others who depended on her. She spoke to the staff, explaining what happened to calm them and prevent gossip—if possible.

Mr. Bingley had remained in the guest room in case his help was required. Mrs. Annesley was resting peacefully. Her eye and temple were dark—just as Dr. Taylor predicted—but she was reasonably well, just overwhelmed by the thanks and gratitude bestowed on her, as she could not understand what she had done that was so praiseworthy.

Cathy and Libby slept in Georgiana's bed, watched by both Miss Darcy and her maid.

Peter had not recovered during the night. He was lost in a deep sleep but not feverish. Elizabeth's worry as well as Janey's despair increased with every passing hour. Dr. Taylor and Dr. Philips took turns, one of them always present at the boy's side.

Elizabeth was burdened by her distress for her husband. Aside from the natural concern of his travelling so far in the middle of the night, Elizabeth knew he was hurt and in pain—and he had barely rested at all after the accident. Her only relief was that the colonel and Lord Matlock were there with him—as well as that strange Mr. Bourne.

Georgiana also woke while it was still dark outside. Elizabeth spent an hour with her, sharing their worries and their astonishment about Lady Catherine's actions, as well as their guilt for the trust they had once placed in the most unworthy man with pleasant manners. They also discussed—most astounding!—Libby's extraordinary keenness of mind and Peter's remarkable courage.

Food and drink were sent to every room, as nobody was inclined to a formal breakfast. Georgiana and Elizabeth, though, had to keep company with Mr. Bingley, who ate most eagerly, wondering whether he should stay another day in London or return to Netherfield. Elizabeth wrote a detailed letter for Jane as Mr. Bingley's attention was not to be trusted.

As soon as the hour was reasonable, Mr. and Mrs. Gardiner arrived. Soon, the gathering was completed by the arrival of the three Fitzwilliams not involved in the search. And around noon, James Darcy made his appearance, asking to speak to his cousin then to Elizabeth.

"Mrs. Darcy, I cannot express how sorry I am for everything that happened. I am so happy to see you recovered! And please let me assure you that I had no involvement in this—and neither did Annabelle Stafford. I investigated this and I am very sure of it."

"We know that, Mr. Darcy. I am sorry if my husband's suspicions offended you or Lady Stafford. It is certainly not our intention to quarrel with either of you. William is not home, and we do not know when he will return. But you are welcome to keep us company."

To Elizabeth's surprise, James accepted, and he was introduced to her relatives. With disbelief, James heard the last details and seemed incredulous to learn of his friend's involvement.

"Well, to complete your astonishment, just let me tell you how he planned to elope with the youngest Miss Bennet, who is only fifteen," Mr. Bingley said severely. "I say, I believe this man is deranged. He will not end well—I can tell you that."

In the early afternoon, a carriage stopped in front of the house, and Elizabeth hurried to the window then to the main door. She was disappointed when she did not recognise it, and she unconsciously took a step back into the house, slightly scared of the strange vehicle.

She breathed in relief when she saw her husband step down, and she ran to him, ignoring the chilly air and slippery ground.

"William—I am so happy to see you home! What happened? Are you well?"

"Let us go inside, my dear. There is much to tell."

Darcy was surprised to see his family and hers together—such a strange gathering, he might have said a month ago. He sat on the settee, carefully leaning back. Elizabeth ordered fresh food and drink then sat beside him. He took her hand in his.

"Darcy, where are my husband and my son?" asked Lady Matlock in distress.

"They are taking Lady Catherine back to Rosings. I lent them my carriage. They will likely be there for two or three more days."

With a strangely composed voice, Darcy told them all the aspects of the terrible events.

James emptied two glasses in only a few minutes while the Fitzwilliams could scarce believe what they heard. Georgiana listened in silence, her hands and lips trembling, and Elizabeth stared at her husband's pale face.

"Dear Lord! So Catherine is dead? " inquired Lady Matlock. "And she planned this whole scheme? But to what purpose? Are you absolutely certain?"

"Yes. Lady Catherine chose to put aside any prudence or wisdom because the only solution for her was the one she wanted. She devised a plan to kidnap Elizabeth—with what final purpose I can only speculate. I believe she wished to simply make Elizabeth disappear by any means. She wished to force me to marry Anne under any circumstances. It had to be her will or no will at all. And she found that idiot Wickham to join her game."

"And what will happen to Wickham now? Is he still in gaol?" the viscount asked.

"He is, but we do not have much against him. He just did what he was asked to do, took his payment, and left. He is nothing but the worst sort of scoundrel," Darcy said with sharp anger. The ladies gasped, and Georgiana was tearful.

"I understand why you are upset with Catherine," Lady Matlock said. "It was an insane plan. God have mercy on her soul."

"It was as equally insane as it was purely evil, and she thought she could have it done because she was Lady Catherine de Bourgh, and anyone who was not her equal did not matter. And the most terrible thing is that we all—we, the Fitzwilliams and the Darcys—were used to thinking that way too. I had this revelation very clearly today, and I said as much to Uncle and to Robert. And that makes me even angrier."

"Darcy, I understand you are pained, but such words are neither kind nor fair, and they do no good. I strongly believe our families have always done their share of generous works. We are honest and moral people, and our worth is much valued by everyone who knows us," Lady Matlock said, trying to conceal her anger and offence.

"Forgive me for not searching for more proper words, but we both know them to be true, Aunt. I shall only speak of myself then. I have been a selfish being all my life, in practice, though not in principle. As a child, I was taught what was right, but I was not taught to correct my temper. I was given good principles but left to follow them in pride and conceit. I was spoilt by my excellent parents, who allowed, encouraged, almost taught me to be selfish and overbearing—to care for none beyond my own family circle, to think meanly of the rest of the world. Such I was from eight to eight and twenty, and such I might still have been but for the woman who changed my life for the better. And to this woman I am today married by accident! If not for Elizabeth's fall and for the rumours spread about Town by this idiot here"—he pointed to James—"and by the other idiot who is in prison, I probably never would have met Elizabeth again and would have lost my chance for happiness."

Darcy glanced at his wife—who was watching him tearfully—and briefly kissed her hand.

"I fell in love with Elizabeth almost at the beginning of our acquaintance. I loved her wit, her spirit, her confidence after so many years of being surrounded by women who were always speaking for *my* approbation alone. I knew very soon that she would be the perfect wife for me, but for weeks, I struggled to put distance between us because I considered her unworthy of me. Her situation in life, her lack of connections, I assessed to be so much below ours that I could not see beyond those things."

He paused again, looking at his astonished audience.

"I severely criticised her family's behaviour. I loathed Mrs. Bennet's attempts to find good matches for her daughters without realising that all the mothers in Town were doing the same thing! I made fun, together with your sisters, Bingley, of their relatives in Cheapside—forgive me, Mrs. and Mr. Gardiner. I was so preoccupied in finding faults in Elizabeth's family that I failed to recognise the faults in mine. And here I am now, admiring the worthiness of Elizabeth's uncle and aunt, the nobility of my sister's companion, the courage and genuine affection of the children of a servant whom I have barely noticed before."

His words aroused a palpable tension in the room, and everyone's embarrassment was apparent. His aunt was about to interrupt again, but Darcy stopped her with a gesture.

"Yes, I know I have helped every time I was asked to because I was raised to be generous whenever it was needed. Every time I heard about a problem, I tried to solve it, but I never gave a second thought to either the persons or the situation. I helped because I could, and I knew it was just. But Mrs. Annesley and Peter and Libby acted with generous affection without thinking of anything else but the person whom they helped! Dear Aunt, I love you deeply, but you are wrong. We—and others like us—do not value the *true* value, but the price, income, property, connection, and situation in life! We believe ourselves to be better and worth more than others around us—you cannot deny that! This is why Lady Catherine could conceive her horrible plan without thinking of the consequences. She demanded her will be obeyed because of who she was, and anybody who was in her way should disappear. Her wrong has cost her dearly—just as my wrong could have cost me my own happiness. And I cannot easily forgive myself as I cannot easily forgive her—God have mercy of her soul."

Even the air had become heavy in the room, and a deep, burdening silence fell upon them. Finally, Darcy glanced at each of them and said, his voice low from exhaustion:

"I shall leave you now. I must rest. Hopefully, we shall see each other again soon. Bingley—have a good journey back to Netherfield if you must leave. James, Mr. Aldridge will come tomorrow morning to discuss your request. I shall give you the amount you asked for, but you must stand in front of Mr. Aldridge and explain to him that you wish to waste another thousand from your inheritance. And we will discuss a plan for you to visit your estates by the end of the month to see how things are going on and to think of how you can improve your income. I cannot and will not travel in the near future. And I shall certainly not steal from the time I could be spending with my wife just to take care of other people's business."

James's face darkened from shock. "Travel? What do you mean? But it is winter, roads are frozen, it is cold and… I cannot travel in such weather! Why do I need to do it?"

"You seem surprised that it is cold and roads are frozen in the winter. You might be pleased to find that travelling in the summer in hot, dry weather can be even worse, so cheer your spirits, Cousin. We shall speak again tomorrow. Now excuse me, I need to lie down."

He stepped to the stairs hesitantly, helped by Stevens, while the others stared after him, unable to completely recover from the dreadful news and Darcy's severe tirade.

Elizabeth glanced from her husband to her guests, uncertain how to proceed, torn between her heart and her duty. She met her relatives' restrained smiles, Bingley's large grin, the Fitzwilliams' puzzled expressions, James's incredulous gaze, and Georgiana's shy look.

She breathed deeply and searched for a proper smile.

"I am grateful to you all for your generous care and for calling to support us today. However, I must leave you now. I am sure Georgiana will attend you properly. Please forgive my poor manners, but my husband needs me, and I have not an instant to lose."

She curtseyed then hurried upstairs. Her heart had won.

Elizabeth entered her apartment and knocked on the adjoining door. Darcy's voice invited her in, but she stopped in the doorframe and gasped: her husband was being examined by Dr. Taylor, watched by Stevens. He was naked from his waist up, and his entire torso—ribs, arms, and shoulders—were darkly bruised.

"Do not worry. It looks much worse than it is," Darcy said as Elizabeth stepped closer, her eyes on his injured body. She glanced at the doctor, who shook his head in disapproval.

"That is not quite true, Mrs. Darcy. I told your husband even yesterday that he needed to rest, to wear a tight bandage, and to stay still in bed. Fortunately, I believe he has no ribs broken, or else his life would have been in great danger by now. No effort is allowed for a few days! If he obeys my recommendation, he will improve in that time. "

"Do not worry. I shall take care that your request is strictly followed," Elizabeth answered.

She went to visit Peter and Mrs. Annesley and returned to find her husband lying in his bed, cleaned, shaved, bandaged, and arguing with Stevens. She smiled to the loyal servant.

"Thank you, Stevens. I shall continue your argument with the master now. You may retire."

As Stevens left, Elizabeth stepped to his bed, removed her shoes and lay beside him. He took her hand and kissed it briefly, then tried to pull her to his chest, but he moaned in pain. She withdrew a few inches and sat, wrapping the blanket around him.

"You are forbidden to move unless it is absolutely necessary. You will have no other choice but to obey my orders," she said in earnest, and he brought her hand to his lips.

"I could by no means oppose your wish, Mrs. Darcy."

"I am glad to hear it!" She lay beside him, turned on her side to watch him. He was resting, unmoving, on his back. Only his head turned to her, and his fingers gently brushed her hair.

Elizabeth lightly stroked his cheeks, and her eyes tenderly caressed his handsome face.

"The things you said earlier to your family—I never imagined how much it affected you."

"I felt the burden more painfully this last day since I realised how close I came to losing you—twice. I know I am correct in everything I said. I owe my present happiness to fate, which wisely corrected my foolish, arrogant error and brought you back into my life against my will, dearest, loveliest Elizabeth. How can I apologise for everything that you suffered from my family?"

Her eyes moistened and sparkled with tears. "Perhaps you are right about your faults and errors and fate, but all is over now. You must learn some of my philosophy: think only of the past as its remembrance gives you pleasure. This is my first order that you must obey."

"Then I have no choice but to agree. I shall think more of the present and the future."

Elizabeth wiped a few stubborn tears from her eyes then placed a soft kiss on his lips.

"If Peter recovers and you feel better, let us go to Pemberley—just the two of us. I am sure Georgiana would not mind. I want you to show me your home. I want to learn together about the present and prepare for the future—only you and I."

"I would wish nothing more! As soon as we are certain that Peter is well, we will leave. Do not worry about my wounds. I am well enough to go with you to the end of the world."

She laughed in a burst of joy then rose and kissed him soundly—passionate, daring, and careful not to touch his body. His hands readily reached for her, but she pulled back.

"You shall sleep now, husband, and I will stay here to watch you. No disturbance will interfere until you are well again."

"You are the most wonderful disturbance of my life, Elizabeth, and a moment with you is more powerful than any rest or medicine. I will sleep if you stay by my side. Your love is everything I need to heal."

"I will never leave your side, William," she whispered tearfully, kissing his closed eyes. "And if my love is all you need, you should be fine when you wake up."

London, January, 1812

The next days were peaceful and quiet in Darcy's house at Elizabeth's request.

Mr. Bingley returned to Netherfield, eager to start the preparations for his wedding.

The four men responsible for murdering Lady Catherine were discovered and imprisoned by Mr. Bourne the next morning as they woke from their drunkenness. They remembered little except their anger at the annoying woman who carried lots of money with her—and a desire to punish her for humiliating them.

Lord Matlock and the colonel returned two days later, burdened by their connection to the person who was inadvertently killed through her own violent plan. They brought Miss de Bourgh with them, and she found residence with the Matlocks. Anne sent Elizabeth a touching letter, apologising for her mother's actions, and Elizabeth responded warmly, assuring Miss de Bourgh that she would always welcome her in their home.

Due to Lord Matlock's insistence on keeping his sister's name unsullied, justice was handled with discretion. The men who attacked Elizabeth were charged with other crimes they had committed previously while Wickham remained in debtors' prison, being dismissed from his regiment.

James met with his elder cousin and Mr. Aldridge. He received a thousand pounds, signed a receipt for it, and also agreed to join Mr. Aldridge's sons on business trips to his estates.

Darcy delayed any other activities. He spent most of his time in bed, joined by Elizabeth—or a book when she had to attend to other duties.

On the morning of the third day, Peter spoke animatedly. Elizabeth and Darcy hurried to his side. Surrounded by his mother, his sisters, a few maids, and Dr. Taylor, the boy seemed torn between the pain of his injuries and the joy at everyone's praise.

"Peter, how are you feeling?" Darcy asked gently, hardly controlling his emotion.

The boy's face lit. "I am very well, master! I caught the carriage—did you see? I am not as smart as Libby, but I do have some good qualities you said—don't I?"

"You have been braver, faster, and more agile than many men. You are an impressive boy, and we are all grateful to you. We could not thank you enough for your courage."

"Thank me? Oh no, master—I had to protect the mistress. You must not thank me."

"We shall speak of it later when you are recovered. Peter, you made us all very proud. I hope one day to have a son who resembles you," Darcy continued. Janey looked at him tearfully while Peter stared in wonder.

"As soon as you are well, we must also speak about prudence and safety, young man. I would not have you ever put yourself in such danger again as I expect you all to come to Pemberley and help me with my duties there," Darcy concluded, caressing the boy's hair.

Before leaving, Elizabeth bent down and placed an affectionate kiss on Peter's forehead.

"I thank you for fighting for me, dear boy. And thank you, Janey, for raising such a worthy young man." The maid had no strength to reply to such an extraordinary compliment.

Elizabeth hurried out of the room with her husband, fighting her tears and praying to the Lord that the boy would recover completely.

In the next few days, Peter's state improved steadily under Dr. Taylor's constant care.

Four days later, though he still kept to his bed—fed only by his mother and wrapped in tight bandages—Peter could enjoy his sisters playing in his room and Titan and Lucky spending most of the time near his bed. And he could laugh and tell everyone of his struggle to catch the carriage and thieves, and his delight that the master said he was proud of him!

The days that kept Darcy mostly in his room were a time for Elizabeth to grow in her role as mistress of the house as well as mistress of her husband.

She struggled to keep a good balance between spending time with Georgiana and Mrs. Annesley, speaking to Mrs. Thomason, and enjoying Darcy's company.

Their bond strengthened along with their perfect understanding of each other.

Elizabeth's enhanced self-confidence led her to discover new ways to share passion with the man who captured her mind, her heart, and her body and was now barely moving from pain.

She found great enjoyment in teasing him with soft kisses, touches, and caresses, and she soon understood that she had the same power over him that he had over her. It was her time to give, and she was delighted to do so.

Day by day, as the doctor approved Darcy's progress, Elizabeth's gestures became more daring. After a week, she tentatively reached the next step and allowed herself to join with her husband just as he had taught her the night before the accident, bringing fulfilment to their yearning bodies.

In two weeks, Darcy's recovery was complete, and Dr. Taylor declared that there was no longer any reason for concern. The first one who learnt the news—and felt it in a most powerful and tormenting way—was Mrs. Darcy, who was generously rewarded for her care during the master's illness.

Chapter 32

The dreadful story of Elizabeth's kidnapping was slowly put aside. George Wickham remained in prison for two weeks, and Darcy—through his cousin Robert and with James's assistance—purchased his debts. As soon as Darcy felt well enough, he spoke to Wickham in person and convinced him to leave England as his name had been tarnished enough to jeopardise his career.

Wickham opted for America, admitting he had some money from Lady Catherine, enough for a modest start in the former colonies. Darcy agreed to purchase him a comfortable cabin on the first ship but pointed out once again that, were he ever to be seen near any member of the Darcy family, he would be thrown into debtors' prison and left there.

Wickham was accompanied to the ship by Mr. Bourne and his men and left in the care of the captain to ensure he reached his destination. The news of his departure was received with relief by everyone, including Miss Darcy.

Equally reassuring for some of the Darcys was that Lady Annabelle Stafford, together with Lord Clayton and the two French families, had left England for Italy at the end of January, and not even Lady Isabella or James Darcy had details about either of them—nor were they missed by many.

At the beginning of February, Elizabeth, Darcy and Georgiana travelled to Hertfordshire to attend Jane's wedding to Mr. Bingley. They decided to depart for Pemberley—only the two of them—soon afterwards, which made them both anxious for the days to pass.

The reunion with the Bennets was lighthearted and joyful. The Gardiners were already there, which diminished somewhat Miss Darcy's nervousness at meeting so many new people.

The Darcys' stay was planned for two nights. To everyone's surprise, Darcy declined the invitation to stay at Netherfield, choosing to remain at Longbourn instead. Mr. and Mrs. Gardiner already occupied the large guest room, and Miss Darcy was offered the smaller one.

Mr. Darcy declared he and Elizabeth would be content to take her old room again. His words made Elizabeth turn crimson as she hurried to support her husband's idea. Mrs. Bennet was beyond herself in delight, being certain that this was further proof of her son-in-law's affection for their family.

For Darcy and Elizabeth, the small room and narrow bed, which brought them so much distress only a month ago, proved to be larger and more comfortable than any elegant room at Netherfield. The only serious problem was the thin walls, which forced them to struggle to keep silent through two entire nights in which neither of them slept much.

On the morning of her wedding, Miss Bennet was more beautiful than ever, her happiness clearly displayed on her perfect features. Mr. Bingley, whose smile was larger and more handsome than anyone could remember, could not take his eyes from his bride, whom he compared to an angel, and kept marvelling that she had finally accepted him.

The ceremony was as lovely and emotional as expected. Mrs. Bennet could hardly bear the joy of having a second daughter married before Charlotte Lucas, whose wedding had been postponed to March due to Mr. Collins's deep mourning for his noble patroness, Lady Catherine de Bourgh.

Elizabeth and Darcy prepared to leave the day after the wedding.

To everyone's surprise, Georgiana asked her brother's permission to invite Mary to keep her company in London. Her idea was most welcomed by Darcy and accepted by Mr. and Mrs. Bennet to Mary's great felicity. Elizabeth calmed her younger sisters, reminding them that there was little to do in London at that time besides reading and playing the piano—which both Kitty and Lydia found not worth the effort of travelling.

MR. AND MRS. DARCY'S JOURNEY TO PEMBERLEY FROM LONDON BEGAN VERY early on a frozen day, and it appeared it would be a long and difficult one, but they both were eager to accomplish it.

They took a warm farewell from Georgiana and Mary, as well as from Libby and Peter. Mrs. Annesley received a warm half an hour of thanks and mutual gratitude as it was uncertain whether they would find her in the house on their return. Together with his appreciation, Darcy offered Mrs. Annesley a generous and unexpected reward: to assure her comfort for at least two years and his promise to always help her in any way she might need.

At dawn, Molly, Stevens—together with three other footmen and the coachman—loaded the luggage and the carriage moved slowly, soon leaving London behind.

The journey to Pemberley lasted three nights and three full days with frequent stops and changes of horses at inns and taverns. The roads were difficult, and it snowed steadily almost the entire time. The first two nights they slept at inns, but on the last one, Elizabeth preferred to continue travelling, eager to reach their destination. For a few hours, fatigue overcame her, and she fell asleep on her husband's shoulder while Stevens and Molly rested on the seat across from them.

She woke up under a soft touch caressing her face and a warm whisper.

"Elizabeth, we have entered the Pemberley estate."

She responded with a quick smile, and then her hand grasped his as she looked through the window with perturbation for the first appearance of Pemberley. The carriage rode through a wood then through a vast park. Her heart beat stronger and more rapidly, and anticipation overwhelmed her. They ascended for half a mile, and the carriage stopped on a high hill where the wood ceased, and her eager gaze was instantly caught by Pemberley House, situated in the valley, surrounded by frozen, white lanes and guarded by a large lake.

Elizabeth gasped in wonder, and her eyes moistened with tears. She impatiently opened the door and stepped out to fully enjoy the view while she pressed her hands over her chest to quiet her excitement, marvelling at her future home.

The stone building was handsome and imposing, impressive in its beauty, without any artificial appearance. It was simply perfect in its natural splendour, lit by the winter sun just rising.

"Oh, mistress, this is so wonderful," Molly said from inside the carriage.

"I have never seen a place more beautiful," Elizabeth whispered when she felt her husband's warmth behind her and his arms embracing her. "It is so much more than I imagined!"

"It is beautiful indeed. I feel proud and happy to call it my home. And I am even happier that you will bring the only things that Pemberley previously lacked: joy, liveliness, warmth, and love."

They stood in silence a few minutes, taking deep pleasure from the image of their future.

"We must go now, my darling, but I promise I will show you every spot of the estate during the next days. You will come to know it and love it as much as I do."

"I love it already. I believe it was love at first sight!" she said, laughing with emotion.

"Unlike its master," he teased her, and she answered with a meaningful smile.

The carriage stopped before the front door, and Elizabeth looked around, her eyes wide and her heart racing. While she heard Molly's gasps of admiration, Elizabeth's feet were too weak to move. She took Darcy's arm, and he gently put his hand over hers.

"Let us enter, Mrs. Darcy. We are finally home." They were welcomed by Mrs. Reynolds, who seemed overwhelmed with excitement.

"Oh, dear Lord! Master, what joy to see you back home. You have been missed! Mrs. Darcy, we are honoured to receive you. Welcome! I hope you approve of Pemberley—I hope very much. Oh, I am such a fool—please enter. I am standing in the way. I heartily apologise…"

"Mrs. Reynolds, please calm yourself. In four and twenty years, I have never seen you so agitated! We are very happy to be home at last. I am certain that Mrs. Darcy approves of Pemberley and will come to love it as much as we do," Darcy said light-heartedly.

"It is a pleasure to meet you, Mrs. Reynolds," Elizabeth said warmly. "As for Pemberley, I feel it is already part of my heart."

"Oh, what a wonderful thing to hear! The staff are very eager to meet Mrs. Darcy. Shall I fetch them to the main hall? Oh, you must be Molly—welcome to Pemberley!"

"I would like very much to meet them. Mr. Darcy speaks so highly of you and his entire staff! Would half an hour be acceptable? I would like to arrange my appearance a little. It would not do to make a poor first impression," Elizabeth said, smiling.

"Perfect, ma'am, although, if I may be so bold to say, your appearance is quite charming."

"Mrs. Reynolds, we very much appreciate your boldness," Darcy said, laughing, and the housekeeper lowered her eyes a moment before a hidden smile twisted her lips.

"Then I shall take the chance and say that you, sir, look more dashing than ever before. It seems marriage suits you very well, indeed. Mrs. Thomason was right in this."

"I am quite disconcerted that my housekeepers seem to talk about me behind my back," Darcy replied with mock severity.

"As long as the talking is honest and true, I find it acceptable," Elizabeth intervened, and Mrs. Reynolds' face lit with joy while she hurried on.

The first day at Pemberley was equally wonderful and nerve-racking for Elizabeth.

The introduction to the staff went as well as in London due to her and her natural friendliness. She asked some additional questions to be sure that she learnt everyone's names and duties. Her open manners and warm smile brought relief to the servants' faces, and she smiled nervously when Mrs. Reynolds confessed that they knew about Mrs. Darcy's generous help for Janey and her children.

After meeting the staff, Darcy took her on a short tour of the main rooms in the house, many others being left for the following days. Elizabeth asked about the family gallery, and there Darcy revealed every painting, every history, and every memory he had of his loved ones.

The beauty of Pemberley's interiors charmed and bewitched Elizabeth as it was much more than she had imagined from what she had been told. But most overwhelming was the realisation that she now owned everything that had belonged to Lady Anne—that she was now the mistress of all those beauties. It was not the richness, nor the greatness of her status, but the importance of her new position and the power of the legacy she needed to carry.

The day ended with a dinner prepared with much ceremony, which they enjoyed and praised though they did not eat much. Shortly after, they retired to their glamorous apartments.

Molly and Stevens helped them with their baths and preparations for the night, and then both were dismissed, allowing the couple the long awaited and needed privacy.

After a month spent as husband and wife—sharing so much distress, joy, fear, and happiness—and after getting to know each other so deeply and completely in every possible way, the feeling of finally being in the place that would be their home added the last piece to complete their bond and their union.

The exhaustion of the journey and the excitement of the day quickly turned into a passion that burnt them like a flame. Their lovemaking was meant to tell, to show, and to prove the force of their love and the complete union of Mr. and Mrs. Darcy. There was no restraint, no doubt, and no fear to burden their minds, their bodies, or their hearts.

During their stay at Pemberley, the master and mistress rarely left the house, however both of them complied diligently with their duties.

Mrs. Darcy spent a much time with Mrs. Reynolds, acquainting herself with everything related to Pemberley's household, and the master met with his steward to discuss the progress of the last months since he had left Pemberley. He also introduced all his tenants—who came to greet and congratulate him—to his wife as well as young Tommy and his parents, whose genuine happiness on seeing Darcy melted Elizabeth's heart.

The new mistress was much admired by the staff for her warmth and kindness, as well as for her interest in everything related to the house. She also took a keen interest in the food preparation for the master, and the revelation that she had relatives who once resided in Lambton and was remotely connected to *Aunt Teresa* gained everyone's genuine approval.

Whenever they had the opportunity, the couple spent time together in the library, for which Mrs. Darcy seemed to have the same fondness as the master. Stevens sternly asked that nobody disturb the master, except himself if needed, and his request was obeyed. A footman once went to announce a call for the master, but the library door was locked, and Mr. Darcy had received the visitor only half an hour later, looking rather displeased. After that, everybody concluded that Stevens was always right where the master was concerned.

For Elizabeth, the days at Pemberley were as a fairy tale, and she dreaded the moment she would have to return to Town. She was curious and eager to be involved in everything that surrounded her. She felt herself blooming at her husband's side, and each moment meant something new to find, to learn, to experience, to feel.

She finally had the long-desired sleigh ride—twice in one week—and the joy of riding in the snow, covered in blankets along the Pemberley paths, followed her even in her dreams. That was when she finally managed to sleep, which had rarely happened since they arrived at Pemberley, as their desire and need for each other seemed to increase every day—and night.

On the tenth day of their visit, after breakfast, Mrs. Reynolds asked for a private moment with them both. With their approval, she returned with a locked box the size of a large book. Hesitantly, her eyes to the floor, she addressed Elizabeth.

"Mrs. Darcy, this box was given to me by Lady Anne two days before she passed away. She asked me to give it to the future Mrs. Darcy *if* I was certain she was the proper match for the master. If not, I was supposed to give it to Miss Georgiana when she turned one and twenty. I have no doubt of what I must do," Mrs. Reynolds said, tearfully handing the box to Elizabeth.

She took it with trembling hands, thanking the housekeeper and glancing at her husband.

"Mrs. Reynolds, I did not know of this box," Darcy said with no little wonder.

"Lady Anne wished it this way. She put inside everything she noted in the last weeks of her illness. I am sorry for not telling you sooner, but I could not betray her trust. I prayed the Lord not to take me to Him before I could accomplish Lady Anne's request."

"I understand, and I am grateful for your wisdom and loyalty," he said warmly as Mrs. Reynolds excused herself, leaving the library in haste.

Elizabeth sat on the settee and opened the box nervously. On the top was a brief note on which Darcy recognised from afar his mother's writing.

My dear daughter,

I take the liberty of addressing you in such a way because, if my son chose to share his life with you and Mrs. Reynolds decided to give you this box, I am sure you would be as dear to me as my beloved Georgiana.

You will find here everything that I thought and wished and struggled to accomplish. I beg you not to take it as a burden but as a kind and gentle request to try to bring to completion some of the things that might bring relief and joy to the people around you. Which and when you will do them, is entirely your decision. I shall be happy only knowing you took the time to acknowledge them.

I am proud to say without a doubt that you found yourself a most worthy husband, as very few are. I pray to the Lord to bring you all health and a long, happy life. As you will see, Pemberley can give you everything you need for that, if only you will bring love, warmth, and joy to live within its cold and often too silent walls.

Most sincerely,
Your loving Lady Anne

Elizabeth did not attempt to stem the tears that flowed down her cheeks, and she carefully wiped the drops from the paper, while Darcy watched her at the edge of his own feelings. She spent the next two hours reading every piece of paper that Lady Anne had generously struggled to write down as a legacy with her last strength.

At the end of it, Elizabeth just nestled in Darcy's arms. She was silent for such a long while that he thought she had fallen asleep, except he heard her sigh from time to time. He placed a trace of warm kisses along her temples, jaw, on the tip of her nose, and on her closed eyelids then whispered:

"Would you like a ride before dinner? It could be by carriage or by sleigh, as you prefer."

"Could we walk? I would like that very much."

He briefly kissed her lips. "Of course. It is good that you reminded me—I will send Stevens to order you two pairs of heavy winter boots right away."

She laughed, her heart still heavy, prisoner of the powerful emotions she just experienced and content to be in his safe embrace.

Under the surprised looks of the staff, they left the house arm in arm, walking with no direction or time constraints, enjoying the winter chill, the snow falling slowly, and their solitude.

Their stroll lasted a full hour although they did not leave the vast back garden. When they returned, their clothes were half frozen, their hair wet with melted snow, their faces red, and their hands entwined. It was no surprise that they hurried to their rooms, asking not to be disturbed.

Just before dinner, they lay tightly embraced in Darcy's bed, warmed by the strong fire and their united bodies, and hot from passionate lovemaking. Elizabeth's head was resting upon Darcy's heart when she suddenly rose and looked into his eyes.

"William, I would rather not return to London. Could we please remain at Pemberley?"

He was not as surprised as she expected.

"We can do whatever you wish. Will you not regret losing the enjoyment of the Season?"

"I care little about the Season. There will be time for it in the future. I want to see Pemberley during an entire year—spring, summer, and autumn. I want to find ways to finish the school Lady Anne planned for so long. I want to feel useful. I want to be with you throughout the year. And do not worry—I shall not be a burden if you need to travel for business. I have had enough of London lately and so little of Pemberley."

"Your decision makes me happy. We will stay here for as long as want. I would like nothing better."

"Can you arrange for Georgiana and Mary to join us since Mrs. Annesley will be leaving?"

"Of course. And I am thinking to invite your younger sisters too, sooner than we arranged with your parents. Their company will be a nice—although a little overwhelming—diversion for Georgiana, and they might help you with the school project."

"That would be wonderful if Georgiana approves."

"As for my business travel—I will find a way to reduce it. I will take James with me several times and slowly pass the task to him. He might hate me even more, but as you once said, he will not have the luxury of refusing it two years from now. Then we shall see."

"An excellent plan, I might say." Elizabeth smiled as his arms tightened around her.

"I will also bring Janey and the children when the Gardiners come. Hopefully, Peter will be healthy enough to travel by then. They will like Pemberley, and I like to have them around."

"Yes, I too. They will always be part of the family to me." She then laughed, caressing his face and placing soft kisses on his jaw. "Indeed sir, you think of everything."

Darcy gently pulled her on her back then leant closer until she could feel his breath. Just before his lips captured hers, he whispered hoarsely, "I shall always take care of everything for you, my beautiful wife."

"And I shall always take care of you and our happiness, my beloved husband."

Epilogue

Georgiana and Mary travelled to Pemberley in the middle of February, together with Georgiana's personal maid, four male servants to chaperone, and Titan and Lucky.

By Easter with Darcy's help, Elizabeth had chosen and rented a building suitable for the school in Lambton and hired help for transforming one wing for girls and another for boys.

Having to travel often from Pemberley to Lambton—and eager to fully enjoy the blossoming lanes of their estate—Elizabeth Darcy learnt to ride under the strict protection of her husband. She was given a beautiful white horse called Faith, whose good nature induced Elizabeth to become proficient in a short time.

In March, Elizabeth's younger sisters joined them. Surprisingly, Kitty and Lydia got along with Miss Darcy better than expected. Georgiana borrowed from the girls' energy while she lent them talent, wisdom, gravity, impeccable manners, and the beauty of Pemberley. All were involved in Elizabeth's excitement with the school project, and Mary declared that, were she to stay at Pemberley longer, she would love to spend a few hours a week sharing her knowledge with the girls.

Darcy carried on a regular correspondence with Mr Aldridge as well as with Lord Matlock and his cousin James. He only travelled once in February, March, and April, taking James with him and explaining in detail everything he needed to know—just as he should have done years ago. Then, starting in May, he transferred the responsibility to James's shoulders, giving him only the support of Mr. Aldridge and his son. James expressed his frustration and displeasure in every letter and face-to-face meeting—with little success as Darcy remained unmoved.

James Darcy gave up neither his friends nor his habits, and he found Darcy's insistence on managing the business disagreeable, boring, and useless as none of his peers did such things. However, he felt guilty enough for Darcy's past efforts and for what his cousin had to bear because of his friend Wickham that he accomplished his duty regardless. His travelling—even if once a month—made him so tired that, when he returned to London, he slept several days to recover. That reduced significantly the time he spent with his card-playing friends and consequently the debts he accrued in such activity. Moreover, having felt first-hand the effort needed in making the money, he became more reluctant to throw it away.

At the end of May, the party grew larger again with more additions from the family.

The invitation from the master, passed to Janey, made the children cheer with joy and Janey cry with gratitude many days. They travelled with Mr. and Mrs. Bingley and the Gardiners in two carriages filled with the voices and laughter of happy children. Mr. Bingley's sisters refused to attend in the presence of a servant and her children; somehow, their refusal distressed no one.

Once she arrived at Pemberley, Janey's modesty made it difficult for her to adapt to being part of such illustrious company. She asked Mrs. Reynolds to give her some duties in the house to make herself useful. But the children, with their innocence and genuine affection for the Darcys, soon became friends with the young Gardiners—and all with Lucky and Titan, who were the masters of Pemberley's gardens. The story of Libby and Peter's bravery was much told and praised, and soon they became the small heroes of Pemberley and Lambton's residences.

In June, all Pemberley's guests—including Janey and the three children—went for three weeks to Brighton, where Mr. Darcy rented three large cottages.

It was to his merit that he found perfect accommodations for his guests and still saved some private time for his wife. Their favourite moments were walking along the seashore, early in the morning or late at night, recollecting memories of their distant or recent past, and sharing the beauty of the sea with no one else.

Mr. and Mrs. Bennet arrived at Pemberley at the beginning of July and stayed for two months. Mrs. Bennet was happier than ever before, having an apartment with beautiful views and two maids at her disposal, and she expressed her thanks and admiration for her son-in-law several times a day. She kept as the deepest secret the nightmares in which she had forced Elizabeth to marry Mr. Collins that November day, and the blame and guilt for her own foolishness almost eliminated her appetite for the exquisite Pemberley fare.

Mr. Bennet spent most of his time in the library, enjoying the generous collection of books and brandy. His health seemed to be excellent, as well as his spirit every time he observed his beloved daughter and her husband displaying such true, complete understanding and affection.

In the last days of August, Lady Anne's greatest wish came to life through the constant effort of the new Mrs. Darcy. The school—new and clean, with a teacher hired for the boys and another for the girls—was ready to open its doors to the children.

Both Elizabeth and Darcy knew that the work was just beginning—that much effort was needed for the school to be properly valued by the children and their parents—but the biggest step had been made. The first children to attend the school were Libby and Peter, whose residence—together with their mother and younger sister—had been established at Pemberley, so they could not refuse the master's special request.

The Bennets and the Bingleys returned to Hertfordshire in September but received another invitation to spend Christmas at Pemberley, which they readily accepted. Mrs. Bennet carefully shared with Meryton society all the details of Mrs. Darcy's splendid estate and her situation beyond imagination, and she did not forget to mention—repeatedly—how wise Elizabeth had been to accept the right marriage proposal at the precise moment when Charlotte and Mr. Collins happened to visit. Mr. Collins, though, was too devastated by the irrevocable loss of his noble patroness and barely heard anyone around him. However, Mrs. Bennet was content with the glances of jealousy from Sir William and Lady Lucas as well as several other families of the four and twenty she had been visiting.

Pemberley, 27 December, 1812

DAYS, WEEKS, AND MONTHS FLEW BY, AND CHRISTMAS TIME CAME TO THE DARCYS with the celebration of their first year of marriage and the most wonderful gift they had received: their son, Alexander William Darcy, born six weeks earlier and about to be christened that day.

Pemberley was more animated than in many years, full of people, joy, and Christmas decorations, and Mrs. Reynolds could hardly express her joy amidst the stress of ensuring all the arrangements would be perfect.

Both Elizabeth and Darcy's families and some friends were gathered together, including James Darcy, Miss Anne de Bourgh, Lady Mary and Mr. Hasting, Lady Isabella—smiling on Colonel Fitzwilliam's arm—and Mr. Bingley's sisters.

Elizabeth's present felicity was enhanced by the news that Jane expected a child herself and Mr Bingley had purchased an estate only thirty miles away from Pemberley, which would bring her beloved sister close to her again.

In the splendour of her apartment, Elizabeth Darcy glanced at her image in the mirror. The dress fitted her well enough, as well as the set of garnet and diamond jewels that she had worn one year ago during their first appearance as husband and wife at Lady Matlock's ball.

She was ready to leave the room when her eyes fell upon the diary started eleven years earlier and filled with her fears, hopes, wonderings, questions, sadness, and joy. She opened the first page, and her eyes smiled with tears as she read the notes written such a long time ago. She spotted the clumsy sketch she had made of the man she thought had appeared from nowhere to save her life—and her puppy's—and whose features none of them could remember back then.

That man had returned to her life ten years later to save it once more and to change it forever.

The drawing was complete now—she had long ago sketched his face and his character—and every feature was clearly drawn in her mind and soul.

That man was her destiny, her pride, her happiness—her husband.

She closed the diary, brushed her fingers over it, and put it in the drawer. She had given it to her husband to read on their six-month anniversary, and now she did not need it except as a sweet memory. There was nothing she thought or felt that she could not reveal to her husband.

She sensed Darcy entering and spotted him in the mirror behind her. Her heart, her lips, and her eyes smiled at him, and he came closer, wrapping his arms around her and placing a soft kiss on her neck. She met the depths of his dark eyes, so full of love, passion, generosity, and tenderness—all the traces that finally completed the sketch she started eleven years before.

"You look beautiful, my darling. Truly beautiful."

"Are we expected?" she asked, turning in his arms to face him.

"Perhaps, but you are worth waiting for, no matter how late—although our son might feel your loss soon."

She smiled and gently caressed his face.

"Did you see how dashing he looks? Mrs. Reynolds said he is even more handsome than you were at his age."

"It must be true, since he mostly resembles you."

She laughed and briefly brushed her lips to his.

"I have the love of the present and the future masters of Pemberley—what else could I wish for? I still wonder what I did to deserve all this."

"You deserve everything, Elizabeth, as you generously give everything. You are my love and my joy. You have brought so much happiness to my life—to our lives, my dearest, loveliest Elizabeth."

"And you, dearest Mr. Darcy, are just as I wrote in my journal eleven years ago: the hero of my heart," Elizabeth whispered as she took her husband's arm and elegantly descended the main staircase of Pemberley to the ballroom and their waiting guests.

The End

Printed in Great Britain
by Amazon.co.uk, Ltd.,
Marston Gate.